SONS OF ENCOURAGEMENT

SONS *of*

Five stories of faithful men who changed eternity

ENCOURAGEMENT

FRANCINE
RIVERS

TYNDALE HOUSE PUBLISHERS, INC., CAROL STREAM, ILLINOIS

Visit Tyndale's exciting Web site at www.tyndale.com.

Check out the latest about Francine Rivers at www.francinerivers.com.

TYNDALE and Tyndale's quill logo are registered trademarks of Tyndale House Publishers, Inc.

Sons of Encouragement

Designed by Jessie McGrath

Edited by Kathryn S. Olson

Published in association with Browne and Miller Literary Associates, LLC, 410 Michigan Avenue, Suite 460, Chicago, IL 60605.

Scripture quotations are taken from the *Holy Bible*, New Living Translation, copyright © 1996, 2004, 2007 by Tyndale House Foundation. Used by permission of Tyndale House Publishers, Inc., Carol Stream, Illinois 60188. All rights reserved.

ISBN 978-1-4143-4816-2

Printed in the United States of America

17   16   15   14   13   12   11
7   6   5   4   3   2   1

To men of faith who serve

in the shadow of others.

✦ ✦ ✦

contents

acknowledgments

From the beginning of my writing career, my husband, Rick, has blessed me continually with his encouragement. Without him, I might not have had the courage to send in the first manuscript that began my journey as a writer. He listens to my ideas, makes space for me in his office at Rivers Aviation, brews great coffee, and edits the final draft. He even builds me a fire on cool mornings. I delight in his company!

The Lord has also blessed me with encouraging friends. I want to mention two in particular: Peggy Lynch and Pastor Rick Hahn. I can't even count the number of times I've called Peggy or Pastor Rick to ask where a Scripture passage is and/or to check my understanding of God's Word. Both of these friends have loved Jesus since childhood, have a passion for God's Word, and are gifted teachers. Each played an important part in bringing my husband and me to Jesus, and each continues to teach and encourage us in our walk with the Lord today. May the Lord bless you for your kindness!

I also want to thank Scott Mendel for sending me materials on the Jewish perspective. And Danielle Egan-Miller, who calmed the turbulent waters of sorrow when my friend and agent of many years, Jane Jordan Browne, passed away. Jane taught her well, and I know I'm in good hands. I offer special thanks to Peter Parsons for his great love of Amos. He was the first to encourage me to write this prophet's story. May my rendering of Amos's story be all you hoped it would be, Peter.

I want to thank my editor, Kathy Olson, and Ron Beers for their continued support and encouragement. I greatly appreciate their willingness to work with me to strengthen each story. There are so many people at Tyndale who have encouraged and prayed for me over the years. From the beginning of our relationship, I have felt part of the team.

To all of you who have prayed for me over the years and through the course of this particular project, thank you. When I'm assailed by doubts, which often happens, I remember you are praying. May the Lord use these stories to draw people closer to Jesus, our beloved Lord and Savior.

introduction

Dear Reader,

The five novellas in this volume are about biblical men of faith who served in the shadows of others. These were Eastern men who lived in ancient times, and yet their stories apply to our lives and the difficult issues we face in our world today. They were on the edge. They had courage. They took risks. They did the unexpected. They lived daring lives, and sometimes they made mistakes—big mistakes. These men were not perfect, and yet God in His infinite mercy used them in His perfect plan to reveal Himself to the world.

We live in desperate, troubled times when millions seek answers. These men point the way. The lessons we can learn from them are as applicable today as when they lived thousands of years ago.

These are historical men who actually lived. Their stories, as I have told them, are based on biblical accounts.

For a more thorough reading of the life of Aaron, see the books of Exodus, Leviticus, and Numbers. Also compare Christ, our High Priest, as found in the book of Hebrews.

For the facts we know about the life of Caleb, see the books of Numbers, Joshua, and the beginning of Judges. Caleb lived God's commandment in Deuteronomy 6:5: "You must love the Lord your God with all your heart, all your soul, and all your strength." May we show his passion and surrender in following our Lord and Savior, Jesus Christ.

For the facts we know about the life of Jonathan, see the books of 1 and 2 Samuel.

For the facts we know about the life of Amos, see the biblical book that bears his name.

For the facts we know about the life of Silas, see Acts 15:22–19:10; 2 Corinthians 1:19; 1 Thessalonians 1:1; 2 Thessalonians 1:1; and 1 Peter 5:12.

These novellas are also works of historical fiction. The outline of each story is provided by the Bible, and I have started with the information provided for us there. Building on that foundation, I have created action, dialogue, internal motivations, and in some cases, additional characters that I feel are consistent with the biblical record. I have attempted to remain true to the scriptural message in all points, adding only what is necessary to aid in our understanding of that message.

At the end of each novella, we have included a brief study section. The ultimate authority on people of the Bible is the Bible itself. I encourage you to read it for greater understanding. And I pray that as you read the Bible, you will become aware of the continuity, the consistency, and the confirmation of God's plan for the ages—a plan that includes you.

Francine Rivers

BOOK ONE

THE PRIEST

ONE

Aaron sensed someone standing close as he broke loose a mold and put the dried brick aside. Skin prickling with fear, he glanced up. No one was near. The Hebrew foreman closest to him was overseeing the loading of bricks onto a cart to add on to some phase of Pharaoh's storage cities. Wiping the moisture from his upper lip, he bent again to his work.

Through the area, sunburned, work-weary children carried straw to women who shook it out like a blanket over the mud pit and then stomped it in. Sweat-drenched men filled buckets and bent beneath the weight as they poured the mud into brick molds. From dawn to dusk, the work went on unceasingly, leaving only a few twilight hours to tend small garden plots and flocks in order to sustain life.

Where are You, God? Why won't You help us?

"You there! Get to work!"

Ducking his head, Aaron hid his hatred and moved to the next mold. His knees ached from squatting, his back from lifting bricks, his neck from bowing. He set the bricks in stacks for others to load. The pits and plains were a hive of workers, the air so close and heavy he could hardly breathe for the stench of human misery. Sometimes death seemed preferable to this unbearable existence. What hope had he or any of his people? God had forsaken them. Aaron wiped the sweat from his eyes and removed another mold from a dried brick.

Someone spoke to him again. It was less than a whisper, but it made his blood rush and the hair on the back of his neck stand on end. He paused and strained forward, listening. He looked around. No one paid him any notice.

Maybe he was suffering from the heat. That must be it. Each year became harder, more insufferable. He was eighty-three years old, a long life blessed with nothing but wretchedness.

Shaking, Aaron raised his hand. A boy hurried over with a skin of water. Aaron drank deeply, but the warm fluid did nothing to stop the inner quaking, the feeling of someone watching him so closely that he could feel that gaze into the marrow of his bones. It was a strange sensation, terrifying in its intensity. He leaned forward on his knees, longing to hide from the light, longing to rest. He heard the overseer shout again and knew if he didn't get back to work he would feel the bite of the lash. Even old men like him were expected to fulfill a heavy quota of bricks each day. And if they didn't, they suffered for it. His father, Amram, had died with his face in the mud, an Egyptian foot on the back of his neck.

Where were You then, Lord? Where were You?

He hated the Hebrew taskmasters as much as he hated the Egyptians. But he gave thanks anyway—hatred gave a man strength. The sooner his quota was filled, the sooner he could tend his flock of sheep and goats, the sooner his sons could work the plot of Goshen land that yielded food for their table. *The Egyptians try to kill us, but we go on and on. We multiply. But what good does it do us? We suffer and suffer some more.*

Aaron loosened another mold. Beads of sweat dripped from his brow onto the hardened clay, staining the brick. Hebrew sweat and blood were poured into everything being built in Egypt! Raamses' statues, Raamses' palaces, Raamses' storage buildings, Raamses' city—everything was stained. Egypt's ruler liked naming everything after himself. Pride reigned on the throne of Egypt! The old pharaoh had tried to drown Hebrew sons in the Nile, and now Raamses was attempting to grind them into dust! Aaron hoisted the brick and stacked it with a dozen others.

When will You deliver us, Lord? When will You break the yoke of slavery from our backs? Was it not our ancestor Joseph who saved this foul country from starvation? And look at how we're treated now! Pharaoh uses us like beasts of burden, building his cities and palaces! God, why have You abandoned us? How long, oh, Lord, how long before You deliver us from those who would kill us with labor?

Aaron.

The Voice came without and within, clear this time, silencing Aaron's turbulent thoughts. He felt the Presence so acutely that all else receded and he was cupped silent and still by invisible hands. The Voice was unmistakable. His very blood and bone recognized it.

Go out into the wilderness to meet Moses!

The Presence lifted. Everything went back to the way it had been. Sound surrounded him again—the suck of mud from stomping feet, the groan of men lifting buckets, the call of women for more hay, the crunch of sand as someone approached, a curse, a shouted order, the hiss of the lash. Aaron cried out as pain laced his back. He hunched over and covered his head, fearing the overseer less than the One who had called him by name. The whip tore his flesh, but the Word of the Lord ripped wide his heart.

"Get up, old man!"

If he was lucky, he would die.

He felt more pain. He heard voices and drifted into blackness. And he remembered . . .

How many years since Aaron had thought of his brother? He had assumed he was dead, his dry bones forgotten somewhere in the wilderness. Aaron's first memory was of his mother's angry, anguished weeping as she covered a woven basket she had made with tar and pitch. "Pharaoh said we have to give our sons to the Nile, Amram, and so I will. May the Lord preserve him! May the Lord be merciful!"

And God had been merciful, letting the basket drift into the hands of Pharaoh's daughter. Miriam, at eight, had followed to see what became of her baby brother, and then had had enough boldness to suggest to the Egyptian that she would have need of a wet nurse. When Miriam was sent for one, she ran to her mother.

Aaron had been only three years old, but he still remembered that day. His mother pried his fingers loose. "Stop holding on to me. I have to go!" Gripping his wrists tightly, she had held him away from her. "Take him, Miriam."

Aaron screamed when his mother went out the door. She was leaving him. "Hush, Aaron." Miriam held him tight. "Crying will do no good. You know Moses needs Mama more than you do. You're a big boy. You can help me tend the garden and the sheep. . . ."

Though his mother returned with Moses each night, her attention was clearly on the infant. Every morning, she obeyed the princess's command that she take the baby to the palace and stay nearby in case he needed anything.

Day after day passed, and only Aaron's sister was there to comfort him. "I miss her, too, you know." She dashed tears from her cheeks. "Moses needs her more than we do. He hasn't been weaned yet."

"I want Mama."

"Well, wanting and having are two separate things. Stop whining about it."

"Where does Mama go every day?"

"Upriver."

"Upriver?"

She pointed. "To the palace, where Pharaoh's daughter lives."

One day Aaron snuck away when Miriam went out to see about their few sheep. Though he had been warned against it, he went along to the Nile and followed the river away from the village. Dangerous things lived in the waters. Evil things. The reeds were tall and sharp, making small cuts on his arms and legs as he pressed through. He heard rustling sounds and low roars, high-pitched keens and frantic flapping. Crocodiles lived in the Nile. His mother had told him.

He heard a woman laughing. Pushing his way through the reeds, he crept closer until he could see through the veiling green stalks to the stone patio where an Egyptian sat with a baby in her lap. She bounced him on her knees and talked low to him. She kissed his neck and held him up toward the sun like an offering. When the baby began to cry, the woman called out for "Jochebed." Aaron saw his mother rise from a place in the shadows and come down the steps. Smiling, she took the baby Aaron now knew was his brother. The two women talked briefly, and the Egyptian went inside.

Aaron stood up so that Mama could see him if she looked his way. She didn't. She had eyes only for the baby she held. As his mother nursed Moses, she sang to him. Aaron stood alone, watching her tenderly stroke Moses' head. He wanted to call out to her, but his throat was sealed tight and hot. When Mama finished nursing his brother, she rose and turned her back to the river. She held Moses against her shoulder. And then she went back up the steps into the palace.

Aaron sat down in the mud, hidden among the reeds. Mosquitoes buzzed around him. Frogs croaked. Other sounds, more ominous, rippled in deeper water. If a snake got him or a crocodile, Mama wouldn't care. She had Moses. He was the only one she loved now. She had forgotten all about her older son.

Aaron ached with loneliness, and his young heart burned with hatred for the brother who had taken his mother away. He wished the basket had sunk. He wished a crocodile had eaten him the way crocodiles had eaten all the other baby boys. He heard something coming through the reeds and tried to hide.

"Aaron?" Miriam appeared. "I've been looking all over for you! How did you find your way here?" When he raised his head, her eyes filled with tears. "Oh, Aaron . . ." She looked toward the palace, yearning. "Did you see Mama?"

He hung his head and sobbed. His sister's thin arms went around him, pulling him to her. "I miss her, too, Aaron," she whispered, her voice breaking. He rested his head against her. "But we have to go. We don't want to cause her trouble."

He was six when his mother came home alone one night, grieving. All she could do was cry and talk about Moses and Pharaoh's daughter. "She loves your brother. She'll be a kind mother to him. I must take comfort in that and forget she's a heathen. She'll educate him. He will grow up to be a great man someday." She balled up her shawl and pressed it to her mouth to stifle her sobs as she rocked back and forth. "He will come back to us someday." She was fond of saying that.

Aaron hoped Moses would never come back. He hoped never to see his brother again. *I hate him,* he wanted to scream. *I hate him for taking you away from me!*

"My son will be our deliverer." All she could talk about was her precious Moses, Israel's deliverer.

The seed of bitterness grew in Aaron until he couldn't stand to hear his brother's name. "Why did you come back at all?" he sobbed in rage one afternoon. "Why didn't you just stay with him if you love him so much?"

Miriam cuffed him. "Hold your tongue or Mama will think I've let you run wild while she was gone."

"She doesn't care about you any more than she cares about me!" he yelled at his sister. He faced his mother again. "I bet you didn't even cry when Papa died with his face in the mud. Did you?" Then, seeing the look on his mother's face, he ran. He ran all the way to the mud pits, where his job was to scatter straw for the workers to stomp into the mud in the making of bricks.

At least, she had spoken less of Moses after that. She had hardly spoken at all.

Now Aaron roused from the painful memories. He could see the heat through his eyelids, a shadow falling over him. Someone put a few drops of precious water to his lips as the past echoed around him. He was still confused, the past and present mingling.

"Even if the river spares him, Jochebed, whoever sees he's circumcised will know he is condemned to die."

"I will not drown my own son! I will not raise my hand against my own son, nor can you!" His mother wept as she placed his sleeping brother in the basket.

Surely God had mocked the Egyptian gods that day, for the Nile itself, the life's blood of Egypt, had carried his brother into the hands and heart of the daughter of Pharaoh, the very man who commanded all Hebrew boy babies be drowned. And furthermore the other Egyptian gods lurking along the shores of the Nile in the form of crocodiles and hippopotamuses had also failed to carry out Pharaoh's edict. But no one laughed. Far too many had died already and continued to die every day. Aaron sometimes thought the only reason the edict had eventually been lifted was to make sure Pharaoh had enough slaves to make his bricks, chisel his stone, and build his cities!

Why had his brother been the only one to survive? Was Moses to be Israel's deliverer?

Miriam had ruled Aaron's life, even after their mother had returned home. His sister had been as protective of him as a lioness over her cub. Even then, and despite the extraordinary events regarding Moses, the circumstances of Aaron's life didn't change. He learned to tend sheep. He carried straw to the mud pits. At six, he was scooping mud into buckets.

And while Aaron lived the life of a slave, Moses grew up in a palace. While Aaron was tutored by hard labor and abuse at the hands of taskmasters, Moses was taught to read and write and speak and live like an Egyptian. Aaron wore rags. Moses got to wear fine linen clothes. Aaron ate flat bread and whatever his mother and sister could grow in their small plot of hard, dry ground. Moses filled his belly with food served by slaves. Aaron worked in the heat of the sun, up to his knees in mud. Moses sat in cool stone corridors and was treated like an Egyptian prince despite his Hebrew blood. Moses led a life of ease instead of toil, freedom instead of slavery, abundance instead of want. Born a slave, Aaron knew he would die a slave.

Unless God delivered them.

Is Moses the one, Lord?

Envy and resentment had tormented Aaron almost all his life. But was it Moses' fault he had been taken from his family and raised by idol-worshiping foreigners?

Aaron didn't see Moses until years later when Moses stood in the doorway of their house. Their mother had come to her feet with a cry and rushed to embrace him. Aaron hadn't known what to think or feel, nor what to expect from a brother who looked like an Egyptian and knew no Hebrew at all. Aaron had resented him, and then been confused by Moses' desire to align himself with slaves. Moses could come and go as he pleased. Why had he chosen to come and live in Goshen? He could have been riding a chariot and hunting lions with other young men from Pharaoh's household. What did he hope to gain by working alongside slaves?

"You hate me, don't you, Aaron?"

Aaron understood Egyptian even though Moses didn't understand Hebrew. The question had given him pause. "No. Not hate." He hadn't felt anything but distrust. "What are you doing here?"

"I belong here."

Aaron had found himself furious at Moses' answer. "Did we all risk our lives so you could end up in a mud pit?"

"If I'm to try to free my people, shouldn't I get to know them?"

"Ah, so magnanimous."

"You need a leader."

Their mother defended Moses with every breath. "Didn't I tell you my son would choose his own people over our enemies?"

Wouldn't Moses be of more use in the palace speaking on behalf of the Hebrews? Did he think he would gain Pharaoh's respect by working alongside slaves? Aaron didn't understand Moses, and after years of disparity in the way they lived, he wasn't sure he liked him.

But why would he? What was Moses really after? Was he Pharaoh's spy sent to learn whether these wretched Israelites had plans to align themselves with Egypt's enemies? The thought may have occurred to them, but they knew they would fare no better at Philistine hands.

Where is God when we need Him? Far off, blind and deaf to our cries for deliverance!

Moses might have walked the great halls as the adopted son of Pharaoh's daughter, but he had inherited the Levite blood and the Levite temper. When he saw an Egyptian beating a Levite slave, he became a law unto himself. Aaron and several others watched in horror as Moses struck the Egyptian down. The others fled while Moses buried the body in the sand.

"Someone has to defend you!" Moses said as Aaron helped him hide the evidence of his crime. "Think of it. Thousands of slaves rising up against their masters. That's what the Egyptians fear, Aaron. That's why they load you down and try to kill you with work."

"Is this the kind of leader you want to be? Kill them as they kill us?" Was that the way to deliverance? Was their deliverer to be a warrior leading them into battle? Would he put a sword in their hands? The rage that had built over the years under slavery filled Aaron. Oh, how easy it would be to give in to it!

Word spread like fine sand blown before a desert wind, eventually reaching the ears of Pharaoh himself. When Hebrews fought among themselves the next day, Moses tried to intercede and found himself under attack. "Who appointed you to be our prince and judge? Do you plan to kill me as you killed that Egyptian yesterday?" The people didn't want Moses as their deliverer. In their eyes, he was an enigma, not to be trusted.

Pharaoh's daughter couldn't save Moses this time. How long could a man survive when he was hated and hunted by Pharaoh, and envied and despised by his brethren?

Moses disappeared into the wilderness and was never heard from again.

He didn't even have time to say good-bye to the mother who'd believed he had been born to deliver Israel from slavery. And Moses took their mother's hopes and dreams with him into the wilderness. She died within the year. The fate of Moses' Egyptian mother was unknown, but Pharaoh lived on and on, continuing to build his storage cities, monuments, and grandest of all, his tomb. It was scarcely finished when the sarcophagus containing Pharaoh's embalmed body was carried to the Valley of the Kings, followed by an entourage of thousands bearing golden idols, possessions, and provisions for an afterlife thought to be even grander than the one he had lived on earth.

Now Raamses wore the serpent crown and held a sword over their heads. Cruel and arrogant, he preferred grinding his heel into their backs instead. When Amram could not rise from the pit, he was smothered in the mud.

Aaron was eighty-three, a thin reed of a man. He knew he would die soon, and his sons after him, and their sons down through the generations.

Unless God delivered them.

Lord, Lord, why have You abandoned Your people?

Aaron prayed out of desperation and despair. It was the only freedom he had left, to cry out to God for help. Hadn't God made a covenant with Abraham and Isaac and Jacob? *Lord, Lord, hear my prayer! Help us!* If God existed, where was He? Did He see the bloody stripes on their backs, the worn-down, worn-out look in their eyes? Did he hear the cries of Abraham's children? Aaron's father and mother had clung to their faith in the unseen God. *Where else can we find hope, Lord? How long, O God, how long before You deliver us? Help us. God, why won't You help us?*

Aaron's father and mother had long since been buried beneath the sand. Aaron had obeyed his father's last wishes and married Elisheba, a daughter from among the tribe of Judah. She had given him four fine sons before she died. There were days when Aaron envied the dead. At least they were at rest. At least their unceasing prayers had finally stopped and God's silence no longer hurt.

Someone lifted his head and gave him water. "Father?"

Aaron opened his eyes and saw his son Eleazar above him. "God spoke to me." His voice was scarcely a whisper.

Eleazar leaned down. "I couldn't hear you, Father. What did you say?"

Aaron wept, unable to say more.

God had finally spoken, and Aaron knew his life would never be the same.

✦   ✦   ✦

Aaron gathered his four sons—Nadab, Abihu, Eleazar, and Ithamar—and his sister, Miriam, and told them God had commanded him to go to meet Moses in the wilderness.

"Our uncle is dead," Nadab said. "It was the sun speaking to you."

"It's been forty years, Father, without a word."

Aaron held up his hand. "Moses is alive."

"How do you know it was God who spoke to you, Father?" Abihu leaned forward. "You were out in the sun all day. It wouldn't be the first time the heat got to you."

"Are you sure, Aaron?" Miriam cupped her cheeks. "We have been hoping for so long."

"Yes. I'm certain. No one can imagine a voice like that. I cannot explain, nor do I have the time to try. You must all believe me!"

They all spoke at once.

"There are Philistines beyond the borders of Egypt."

"You can't survive in the wilderness, Father."

"What will we tell the other elders when they ask after you? They will want to know why we didn't stop our father from such folly."

"You won't make it to the trade route before you're stopped."

"And if you do, how will you survive?"

"Who will go with you?"

"Father, you're eighty-three years old!"

Eleazar put his hand on Aaron's arm. "I'll go with you, Father."

Miriam stamped her foot. "Enough! Let your father speak."

"No one will go with me. I go alone, and God will provide."

"How will you find Moses? The wilderness is a vast place. How will you find water?"

"And food. You can't carry enough for that kind of journey."

Miriam rose. "Would you try to talk your father out of what God instructed?"

"Sit, Miriam." His sister merely added to the confusion, and Aaron could speak for himself. "God called me to this journey; surely God will show me the way." Hadn't he prayed for years? Maybe Moses would know something. Maybe God was finally going to help His people. "I must trust in the God of Abraham, Isaac, and Jacob to lead me." He spoke with more confidence than he felt, for their questions troubled him. Why should they doubt his word? He must do as God said and go. Quickly, before courage failed him.

+ + +

Carrying a skin of water, seven small loaves of unleavened barley bread, and his staff, Aaron left before the sun came up. He walked all day. He saw Egyptians, but they paid him no attention. Nor did he allow his steps to falter at the sight of them. God had given him purpose and hope. Weariness and desolation no longer oppressed him. He felt renewed as he walked. *God exists. God spoke.* God had told him where to go and whom he was to meet: Moses!

What would his brother be like? Had he spent all forty years in the wilderness? Did he have a family? Did Moses know Aaron was coming? Had God spoken to him as well? If not, what was he to say to Moses when he found him? Surely God would not send him so far without purpose at the end. But what purpose?

His questions made him think of other things. He slowed his steps, troubled. It had been easy to walk away. No one had stopped him. He had taken up his staff, shouldered a skin of water and a pouch of bread, and headed out into the desert. Maybe he should have brought Miriam and his sons with him.

No. No. He must do exactly as God said.

Aaron walked all day, day after day, and slept in the open at night, eyes on the stars overhead, alone in silence. Never had he been so alone, or felt so lonely. Thirsty, he sucked on a small flat stone to keep his mouth from going dry. How he wished he could raise his hand and have a boy run to him with a skin of water. His bread was almost gone. His stomach growled, but he was afraid to eat until later in the afternoon. He didn't know how far he had to go and whether his supply of bread would hold out. He didn't know what to eat out here in the desert. He didn't have the skills to hunt and kill animals. He was tired and hungry and beginning to wonder if he really had heard God's voice or just imagined it. How many more days? How far? The sun beat down relentlessly until he looked for escape in a cleft of rocks, miserable and exhausted. He couldn't remember the sound of God's voice.

Was it all his imagination, birthed by years of misery and a dying hope that a Savior would come and deliver him from slavery? Maybe his sons were right and he'd been suffering from the heat. He was certainly suffering now.

No. He had heard God's voice. He had been on the point of exhaustion and heatstroke many times in his life, but he had never heard a voice like that one:

Go out into the wilderness to meet Moses. Go. Go.

He set off again, walking until nightfall and finding a place to rest. The inexorable heat gave way to a chill that gnawed at his bones and made him shiver. When he slept, he dreamed of his sons sitting with him at the table, laughing and enjoying one another while Miriam served bread and meat, dried dates and wine. He awakened in despair. At least in Egypt, he had known what to expect; every day had been the same with overseers to regulate his life. He had been thirsty and hungry many times, but not as he was now, with no respite, no encouraging companion.

God, did You bring me out into the wilderness to kill me? There is no water, just this endless sea of rocks.

Aaron lost count of the days, but he took hope in that every day there seemed to be just enough water and food to keep him going. He headed north and then east into Midian, sustained by infrequent oases, and leaning more heavily on his staff with each day. He didn't know how far he had come, or how far he had to go. He only knew he would rather die in the wilderness than turn back now. What hope remained was fixed on finding his brother. He longed to see Moses as intently as he had longed for a long draught of water and hunk of bread.

When his water was down to a few drops and his bread was gone, he came to a wide plain before a jagged mountain. Was that a donkey and a small shelter? Aaron rubbed the sweat from his eyes and squinted. A man sat in the doorway. He stood, staff in hand, and came out into the open, his head turned toward Aaron. Hope made Aaron forgot his hunger and thirst. "Moses!" *Oh, Lord, Lord, let it be my brother!* "Moses!"

The man came toward him at a run, arms outstretched. "Aaron!"

It was like hearing the voice of God. Laughing, Aaron came down the rocky slope, his strength renewed like an eagle's. He was almost running when he reached his brother. They fell into one another's arms. "God sent me, Moses!" Laughing and sobbing, he kissed his brother. "God sent me to you!"

"Aaron, my brother!" Moses held tight, weeping. "God said you would come."

"Forty years, Moses. Forty years! We all thought you were dead."

"You were glad to see me go."

"Forgive me. I am glad to see you now." Aaron drank in the sight of his younger brother.

Moses had changed. He was no longer dressed like an Egyptian, but wore the long dark robes and head covering of a nomad. Swarthy, face lined with age, his dark beard streaked with white, he looked foreign and humbled by years of desert life.

Aaron had never been so glad to see anyone. "Oh, Moses, you are my brother. I am glad to see you alive and well." Aaron wept for the lost years.

Moses' eyes grew moist and tender. "The Lord God said you would be. Come." He took Aaron by the arm. "You must rest and have something to eat and drink. You must meet my sons."

Moses' dark and foreign wife, Zipporah, served them. Moses' son Gershom sat with them, while Eliezer lay pale and sweating on a pallet at the back of the tent.

"Your son is ill."

"Zipporah circumcised him two days ago."

Aaron winced. *Eliezer* meant "my God is help." But in which God did Moses place his hope? Zipporah sat beside her son, dark eyes downcast, and dabbed his forehead with a damp cloth. Aaron asked why Moses had not done it himself when his son was eight days old as the Jews had done since the days of Abraham.

Moses bowed his head. "It is easier to remember the ways of your people when you dwell among them, Aaron. As I learned when I circumcised Gershom, Midianites consider the rite repugnant, and Jethro, Zipporah's father, is a priest of Midian." He looked at Aaron. "In deference to him, I did not circumcise Eliezer. When God spoke to me, Jethro gave me his blessing, and we left the tents of Midian. I knew my son must be circumcised. Zipporah argued against it and I delayed, not wanting to press my ways on her. I didn't see it as rebellion until the Lord Himself sought to take my life. I told Zipporah that unless my sons both bore the mark of the Covenant on their flesh, I would die and Eliezer would be cut off from God and His people. Only then did she herself take the flint to our son's flesh."

Troubled, Moses looked at the feverish boy. "My son would not even remember how the mark came to be on his flesh had I obeyed the Lord instead of bending to others. He suffers now because of my disobedience."

"He will heal soon, Moses."

"Yes, but I will remember the cost to others of my disobedience." Moses looked out the doorway to the mountain and then at Aaron. "I have much to tell you when you are not too tired to listen."

"My strength returned the moment I saw you."

Moses took up his staff and rose, and Aaron followed. When they stood in the open, Moses stopped. "The God of Abraham, Isaac, and Jacob appeared to me in a burning bush on that mountain," Moses said. "He has seen the affliction of Israel and is come to deliver them from the power of the Egyptians, to bring them into a land flowing with milk and honey. He is sending me to Pharaoh so that I may bring His people out of Egypt to worship Him at this mountain." Moses gripped his staff and rested his forehead against his hands as he spoke all the words the Lord had spoken to him on the mountain. Aaron felt the truth of them in his soul, drinking them in like water. *The Lord is sending Moses to deliver us!*

"I pleaded with the Lord to send someone else, Aaron. I said who am I to go to Pharaoh? I said my own people will not believe me. I told him I have never been eloquent, that I'm slow of speech and tongue." He let out his breath slowly and faced Aaron. "And the Lord whose name is I AM THE ONE WHO ALWAYS IS said you will be my spokesman."

Aaron felt a sudden rush of fear, but it subsided in the answer of a lifetime prayer. The Lord had heard the cry of His people. Deliverance was at hand. The Lord had seen their misery and was about to put an end to it. Aaron was too filled with emotion to speak.

"Do you understand what I'm saying to you, Aaron? I'm afraid of Pharaoh. I'm afraid of my own people. So the Lord has sent you to stand with me and be my spokesman."

The question hung unspoken between them. Was he willing to stand with Moses?

"I am your older brother. Who better to speak for you than I?"

"Are you not afraid, Brother?"

"What does a slave's life matter in Egypt, Moses? What has my life ever mattered? Yes, I'm afraid. I have been afraid all my life. I've bent my back to taskmasters, and felt the lash when I dared look up. I speak boldly enough in the privacy of my own house and among my brethren, but it comes to naught. Nothing changes. My words are but wind, and I thought my prayers were, too. Now, I know better. This time will be different. It won't be the words of a slave that are heard from my lips, but the Word of the Lord, the God of Abraham, Isaac, and Jacob!"

"If they don't believe us, the Lord has given me signs to show them." Moses told him how his staff had become a snake and his hand had become leprous. "And if that is not enough, when I pour water from the Nile, it will become blood."

Aaron didn't ask for a demonstration. "They will believe, just as I believe."

"You believe me because you are my brother, and because God sent you to me. You believe because God has changed your heart toward me. You have not always looked at me as you do now, Aaron."

"Yes, because I thought you were free when I wasn't."

"I never felt at home in Pharaoh's house. I wanted to be among my own people."

"And we scorned and rejected you." Perhaps it was living among two separate peoples and being accepted by neither that made Moses so humble. But he must do as God commanded, or the Hebrews would go on as before, toiling in the mud pits and dying with their faces in the dust. "God has chosen you to deliver us, Moses. And so you shall. Whatever God tells you, I will speak. If I have to shout, I will make the people hear."

Moses looked up at the mountain of God. "We will start for Egypt in the morning. We will gather the elders of Israel and tell them what the Lord has said. Then we will all go before Pharaoh and tell him to let God's people go into the wilderness to sacrifice to the Lord our God." He shut his eyes as though in pain.

"What is it, Moses? What's wrong?"

"The Lord will harden Pharaoh's heart and strike Egypt with signs and wonders so that when we leave, we will not go empty-handed, but with many gifts of silver, gold, and clothing."

Aaron laughed bitterly. "And so God will plunder Egypt as Egypt plundered us! I never thought to see justice prevail in my lifetime. It will be a joyous sight!"

"Do not be eager to see their destruction, Aaron. They are people like us."

"Not like us."

"Pharaoh will not relent until his own firstborn son is dead. Then he will let us go."

Aaron had been beneath the heel of Egyptian slave drivers too long and had felt the lash too many times to feel pity for any Egyptian, but he saw Moses did.

They set off at daylight, Zipporah taking charge of the donkey carrying provisions and pulling a litter. Eliezer was improved, but not well enough to walk with his mother and his brother. Aaron and Moses walked ahead, each with a shepherd's staff in hand.

+ + +

Heading north, they took the trade route between Egypt and southern Canaan, traveling by way of Shur. It was more direct than traveling south and west and then north through the desert. Aaron wanted to hear everything the Lord had said to Moses. "Tell me everything again. From the beginning." How he wished he had been with Moses and seen the burning bush for himself! He knew what it was to hear the sound of God's voice, but to stand in His presence was beyond imagining.

When they reached Egypt, Aaron took Moses, Zipporah, Gershom, and Eliezer into his house. Moses was overcome with emotion when Miriam threw her arms around him and Aaron's sons surrounded him. Aaron almost pitied Moses, for he saw that Hebrew words still did not come easily to his brother, so he spoke for him. "God has called Moses to deliver our people from slavery. The Lord Himself will perform great signs and wonders so that Pharaoh will let us go."

"Our mother prayed you were the promised one of God." Miriam embraced Moses again. "She was certain when Pharaoh's daughter saved you that God was protecting you for some great purpose."

Zipporah sat with her sons, watching from the corner of the room, dark-eyed and troubled.

Aaron's sons went back and forth through Goshen, the region of Egypt that had been given to the Hebrews centuries earlier and in which they now lived in captivity. The men carried the message to the elders of Israel that God had sent them a deliverer and the elders were to gather and hear his message from God.

Meanwhile, Aaron talked and prayed with his brother. He could see him struggling against fear of Pharaoh and the people and the call of God on him. Moses had little appetite. And he looked more tired when he rose in the morning than when he had retired to bed the evening before. Aaron did his best to encourage him. Surely that was why God had sent him to find Moses. He loved his brother. He was strengthened at his presence and eager to serve.

"You give me the words God speaks to you, Moses, and I will speak them. You will not go alone before Pharaoh. We go together. And surely the Lord Himself will be with us."

"How is it you have no fear?"

No fear? Less perhaps. Moses had not grown up suffering physical oppression. He hadn't lived longing for the promise of God's intervention. Nor had he been surrounded by fellow slaves and family members who relied on each other for strength just to survive each day. Had Moses ever known love other than those first few years at his mother's breast? Had Pharaoh's daughter regretted adopting him? In what position had her rebellion against Pharaoh placed her, and what repercussions had it caused Moses?

It occurred to Aaron that he had never thought of these things before, too caught up in his own feelings, petty resentments, and childish jealousies. Unlike Moses, he hadn't grown up as the adopted son of Pharaoh's daughter among people who despised him. Had Moses learned to keep out of sight and say little in order to survive? Aaron hadn't been caught between two worlds and accepted in neither. He hadn't sought to align himself with his people, only to find they hated him as well. Nor had he needed to run away from Egyptian and Hebrew alike and seek refuge among foreigners in order to stay alive. Nor had he spent years alone in the desert tending sheep.

Why had he never thought of these things before? Was it only now that his mind and heart were open to consider what Moses' life must have been like? Aaron was filled with compassion for his brother. He ached to help him, to press him forward to the task God had given him. For the Lord Himself said Moses was to be Israel's deliverer, and Aaron knew God had sent him to stand beside his brother and do whatever Moses could not do.

Lord, You have heard our cry!

"Ah, Moses, I've spent my life in fear, bowing and scraping before overseers and taskmasters, and still getting the lash when I failed to work fast enough for them. And now, for the first time in my life, I have hope." Tears came in a flood. "Hope casts out fear, Brother. We have God's promise that the day of our salvation is at hand! The people will rejoice when they hear, and Pharaoh will cower before the Lord."

Moses' eyes were filled with sorrow. "He won't listen."

"How can he not listen when he sees the signs and wonders?"

"I grew up with Raamses. He is arrogant and cruel. And now that he sits on the throne, he believes he is god. He won't listen, Aaron, and many will suffer because of him. Our people will suffer and so will his."

"Pharaoh will see the truth, Moses. Pharaoh will come to know that the Lord is God. And that truth will set us free."

Moses wept.

✦   ✦   ✦

Israel gathered, and Aaron spoke all the words the Lord gave to Moses. The crowd was dubious, some outspoken and some derisive. "This is your brother who murdered the Egyptian and ran away, and he is to deliver us from Egypt? Are you out of your mind? God would not use a man such as he!"

"What's he doing back here? He's more Egyptian than Hebrew!"

"He's a Midianite now!"

Some laughed.

Aaron felt the rush of hot blood. "Show them, Moses. Give them a sign!"

Moses threw his staff on the ground and it became a huge cobra. The people cried out and scattered. Moses reached down and took the snake by the tail and it became his staff again. The people closed in around him. "There are other signs! Show them, Moses." Moses put his hand inside his cloak and drew it out, leprous. The people gasped and recoiled from him. When he tucked his hand inside his cloak and drew it out as clean as a newborn child's, they cried out in jubilation.

There was no need for Moses to touch his staff to the Nile and turn it to blood, for the people were already shouting with joy. "Moses! Moses!"

Aaron raised his arms, his staff in one hand and shouted, "Praise be to God who has heard our prayers for deliverance! All praise be to the God of Abraham, Isaac, and Jacob!"

The people cried out with him and fell to their knees, bowing low and worshiping the Lord.

But when asked, the elders of Israel refused to go before Pharaoh. It was left to Aaron and Moses to go alone.

✦   ✦   ✦

Aaron felt smaller and weaker with each step inside Thebes, Pharaoh's city. He had never had reason to come here amid the bustle of markets and crowded streets that stood in the shadow of the immense stone buildings that housed Pharaoh, his counselors, and the gods of Egypt. He had spent his life in Goshen, toiling beneath overseers and toiling to eke out his own existence through crops and a small flock of sheep and goats. Who was he to think he could stand before mighty Pharaoh and speak for Moses? Everyone said that even as a small boy, Raamses had shown the arrogance and cruelty of his predecessors. Who dared thwart the ruling god of all Egypt? Especially an old man of eighty-three, as he was, and his younger brother of eighty!

I am sending you to Pharaoh. You will lead my people, the Israelites, out of Egypt.

Lord, give me courage, Aaron prayed silently. *You have said that I am to be Moses' spokesman, but all I can see are the enemies around me, the wealth and power everywhere I look. Oh, God, Moses and I are like two old grasshoppers come to the court of a king. Pharaoh has the power to crush us beneath his heel. How can I give Moses courage when my own fails me?*

He could smell the rankness of Moses' sweat. It was the smell of terror. His brother had hardly slept for fear of standing before his own people.

Now he was inside the city with its thousands of inhabitants, its enormous buildings and magnificent statues of Pharaoh and the gods of Egypt. He had come to speak to Pharaoh!

"Do you know where to go?"

"We are almost there." Moses said nothing more.

Aaron wanted to encourage him, but how, when he was fighting the fear threatening to overwhelm him? *Oh, God, will I be able to speak when my brother, who knows so much more than I do, is shaking like a bruised reed beside me? Don't let any man crush him, Lord. Whatever comes, please give me breath to speak and the spine to stand firm.*

He smelled smoke laden with incense and remembered Moses talking about the fire that burned without consuming the bush, and the Voice that had spoken to him from the fire. Aaron remembered the Voice. He thought of it now and his fear lessened. Had not Moses' staff turned to a snake before his eyes and his hand shriveled with leprosy, only to be healed as well? Such was God's power! He thought of the cries of the people, cries of thanksgiving and jubilation that the Lord had seen their affliction and had sent Moses to deliver them from slavery.

Still . . .

Aaron looked up at the enormous buildings with their massive pillars and wondered at the power of those who had designed and built them.

Moses paused before a huge stone gate. On each side were carved beasts—twenty times the size of Aaron—standing guard.

Oh, Lord, I am but a man. I believe. I do! Rid me of my doubts!

Aaron tried not to stare around him as he walked beside Moses to the entrance of the great building where Pharaoh held court. Aaron spoke to one of the guards and they were brought inside. The hum of many voices rose like bees amid the huge columns. The walls and ceilings were resplendent with colorful scenes of the gods of Egypt. Men stared at him and Moses, frowning in distaste and drawing back, whispering.

Aaron's palm sweated as he held tight to his staff. He felt conspicuous in his long robe and woven sash, the woven shawl that covered his head dusty from their journey. He and his brother looked strange among these other men in their short fitted tunics and elaborate wigs. Some wore long tunics, ornate robes, and gold amulets. Such wealth! Such beauty! Aaron had never imagined anything like this.

When Aaron saw Pharaoh sitting on a throne flanked by two huge statues of Osiris and Isis, he could only stare at the man's magnificence. Everything about him announced his power and wealth. He glanced disdainfully at Aaron and Moses and said something to his guard. The guard straightened and spoke. "Why have you come before mighty Pharaoh?"

Moses lowered his eyes, trembling, and said nothing.

Aaron heard someone whisper, "What are these stinking old Hebrew slaves doing here?" Heat filled him at their contempt. Uncovering his head, he stepped forward. "This is what the Lord, the God of Israel, says: 'Let My people go, for they must go out into the wilderness to hold a religious festival in My honor.'"

Pharaoh laughed. "Is that so?" Others joined in. "Look at these two old slaves standing before me, demanding that their people be released." The officials laughed. Pharaoh waved his hand as though brushing aside a minor irritation. "And who is the Lord that I should listen to Him and let Israel go? Let you go? Why would I do that? Who would do the work you were born to do?" He smiled coldly. "I don't know the Lord, and I will not let Israel go."

Aaron felt the anger rise in him. "The God of the Hebrews has met with us," he declared. "Let us take a three-day trip into the wilderness so we can offer sacrifices to the Lord our God. If we don't, we will surely die by disease or the sword."

"What does it matter to me if a few slaves die? Hebrews reproduce like rabbits. There will be more to replace those who die of pestilence." Counselors and visitors laughed as Pharaoh continued to mock them.

Aaron's face burned, his heart thundered.

Pharaoh's eyes narrowed as Aaron stared up at him. "I have heard about you, Aaron and Moses." The ruler of Egypt spoke quietly, his tone filled with threat.

Aaron felt chilled that Pharaoh knew him by name.

"Who do you think you are," Pharaoh shouted, "distracting the people from their tasks? Get back to work! Look, there are many people here in Egypt, and you are stopping them from doing their work."

As the guards moved closer, Aaron's hand clenched his shepherd's staff. If any man tried to take hold of Moses, he would receive a clubbing.

"We must go, Aaron," Moses said under his breath. Aaron obeyed.

Standing in the hot Egyptian sun once again, Aaron shook his head. "I thought he would listen."

"I told you he wouldn't." Moses let out his breath slowly and bowed his head. "This is only the beginning of our tribulation."

✦   ✦   ✦

An order came quickly from the taskmasters that straw would no longer be given them to make bricks, but that they would have to scrounge for their own. And the quota of bricks would not be lessened! They were told Pharaoh's reason. The ruler of Egypt thought them lazy because Moses and Aaron had cried out to let them go and sacrifice to their god.

"We thought you were going to deliver us, and all you asked was that we be allowed to go for a few days and sacrifice!"

"Away with you!"

"You have made our lives even more unbearable!"

When the foremen among the sons of Israel were beaten for not completing their required number of bricks, they went to Pharaoh to beg for justice and mercy. Moses and Aaron went to meet them. When they came out, the foremen were bloodied and worse off than before.

"Because of you Pharaoh believes we are lazy! You have caused us nothing but trouble! May the Lord judge you for getting us into this terrible situation with Pharaoh and his officials. You have given them an excuse to kill us!"

Aaron was appalled at their accusations. "The Lord will deliver us!"

"Oh, yes, He will deliver us. Right into Pharaoh's hands!"

Some spit at Moses as they walked away.

Aaron despaired. He believed the Lord had spoken to Moses and promised to deliver the people. "What do we do now?" He had thought it would be easy. One word from the Lord and the chains of slavery would fall away. Why was God punishing them again? Hadn't they been punished enough all these long years in Egypt?

"I must pray." Moses spoke quietly. He looked so old and confused, Aaron was afraid. "I must ask the Lord why He ever sent me to Pharaoh to speak in His name, for He has only done harm to this people and not delivered them at all."

✦ ✦ ✦

The people Aaron had known all his life glared at him and whispered as he walked by. "You should have kept your mouth shut, Aaron. Your brother was out in the desert too long."

"Speaking to God! Who does he think he is?"

"He's mad. You should've known better, Aaron!"

God had spoken to him as well. Aaron knew he had heard the voice of God. He knew. No one would make him doubt that!

But why hadn't Moses thrown down his staff and shown Pharaoh the signs and wonders the moment they were in the ruler's presence? He asked Moses about it. "The Lord will tell us what to say and what to do, and when we are not to do anything less or more than that."

Satisfied, Aaron waited, ignoring the taunts and watching over Moses while he prayed. Aaron was too tired to pray, but he found himself distracted by concerns about the people. How could he convince them that God had sent Moses? What could he say to make them listen?

Moses came to him. "The Lord has spoken again: 'Now you will see what I will do to Pharaoh. When he feels my powerful hand upon him, he will let the people go. In fact, he will be so anxious to get rid of them that he will force them to leave his land!'"

Aaron gathered the people, but they wouldn't listen. Moses tried to speak to them, but stammered and then fell silent when they shouted at him. Aaron shouted back. "The Lord will deliver us! He will establish a covenant with us, to give us the land of Canaan, the land we came from. Isn't this what we have waited for all our lives? Have we not prayed for a deliverer to come? The Lord has heard our groaning. He has remembered us! He is the Lord and He will bring us out from under the burdens the Egyptians have put on us. He will deliver us from slavery and redeem us with great judgments with an outstretched arm!"

"Where is his outstretched arm? I don't see it!"

Someone shoved Aaron. "If you say anything more to Pharaoh, he will kill us all. But not before we kill you."

Aaron saw the rage in their eyes and tasted fear.

"Send Moses back where he came from!" another shouted.

"Your brother has caused us nothing but trouble since he came here!"

Despondent, Aaron gave up arguing with them and followed Moses out into the land of Goshen. He stayed close, but not too close, listening intently for God's voice and hearing only Moses speaking low, beseeching God for answers. Aaron covered his head and squatted, his staff held across his knees. However long it took, he would wait for his brother.

Moses stood, face to the heavens. "Aaron."

Aaron raised his head and blinked. It was near twilight. He sat up, gripped his staff, and rose. "The Lord has spoken to you."

"We are to speak to Pharaoh again."

Aaron smiled grimly. "This time—" he instilled confidence into his voice—"this time, Pharaoh will listen to the Word of the Lord."

"He will not listen, Aaron. Not until the Lord has multiplied His signs and wonders. God will lay His hand on Egypt and bring out His people by great judgments."

Aaron was troubled, but tried not to show it. "I will say whatever words you give me, Moses, and do whatever you command. I know the Lord speaks through you."

Aaron knew, but would Pharaoh ever realize it?

✦   ✦   ✦

When they returned to the house, Aaron told their families they were going to stand before Pharaoh again.

"The people will stone us!" Nadab and Abihu argued. "You haven't been to the brick fields lately, Father. You haven't seen how they treat us. You're only going to make things worse for us."

"Pharaoh didn't listen the last time. What makes you think he'll listen now? All he cares about is bricks for his cities. Do you think he'll let his laborers go?"

"Where is your faith?" Miriam was angry with all of them. "We have been waiting for this day since Jacob set foot in this country. We don't belong in Egypt!"

As the arguments swirled around him, Aaron saw Moses drawn away by his wife. Zipporah was as upset as the rest of them and speaking low. She shook her head, drawing her sons close.

Miriam reminded Aaron's sons again of how the Lord had protected Moses when he was put into the Nile, how it had been a miracle that the old pharaoh's own daughter had found him and adopted him. "I was there. I saw how the Lord's hand has been on him since he was born."

Abihu was unconvinced. "And if Pharaoh doesn't listen this time, how do you suppose we'll all be treated?"

Nadab stood, impatient. "Half of my friends won't even speak to me now."

Aaron blushed at his sons' lack of faith. "The Lord has spoken to Moses."

"Did the Lord speak to *you?*"

"The Lord told Moses we are to go to Pharaoh, and to Pharaoh we must go!" He waved his hand. "All of you, out! Go tend the sheep and goats."

Zipporah went out quietly behind them, her sons close at her side.

Moses sat at the table with Aaron and folded his hands. "Zipporah is returning to her father, and taking my sons with her."

"Why?"

"She says she has no place here."

Aaron felt the rush of blood to his face. He had noticed how Miriam treated Zipporah. He had talked with her about it already.

"Let her share your work, Miriam."

"I don't need her help."

"She needs something to do."

"She can do as she wishes and go where she likes."

"She is Moses' wife and the mother of his sons. She is our sister now."

"She is not our sister. She is a foreigner!" Miriam said in hushed tones. "She is a Midianite."

"And what are we but slaves? Moses had to flee Egypt and Goshen. Did you expect him not to marry or have children of his own? She is the daughter of a priest."

"And that makes her suitable? Priest of what god? Not the God of Abraham, Isaac, and Jacob."

"It is the Lord God of Abraham, Isaac, and Jacob who has called Moses here."

"A pity Moses didn't leave his wife and sons where they belong." She rose and turned her back.

Angry, Aaron stood. "And where do you belong, Miriam—you without a husband and sons to take care of you?"

She faced him, eyes hot and moist. "*I* was the one who watched over Moses while he drifted on the Nile. *I* was the one who spoke to Pharaoh's daughter so our brother was given back to Mother until he was weaned. And if that is not enough, who became mother to your sons when Elisheba died? Lest you forget, Aaron, I am your *older* sister, firstborn of Amram and Jochebed. I had much to do with taking care of you as well."

Sometimes there was no reasoning with his sister. It was better to let her think things through for herself and keep peace in the family. Given time, Miriam would accept Moses' sons, if not his wife.

"I will speak with Miriam again, Moses. Zipporah is your wife. Her place is here with you."

"It is not only Miriam, Brother. Zipporah is afraid of our people. She says they blow hot and change direction like the wind. She has already seen that the people won't listen to me. Nor are they willing to listen to you. She understands that I must do as God tells me, but she is afraid for our sons and says she will be safer living in her father's tents than in the houses of Israel."

Were their women destined to make trouble? "Is she asking you to return with her?"

"No. She only asks that I give my blessing. And I have. She will take my sons, Gershom and Eliezer, back to Midian. She has spent her life in the desert. They will be safe with Jethro." His eyes filled with tears. "If God is willing, they will be returned to me when Israel has been delivered from Egypt."

Aaron knew from his brother's words that worse times were ahead. Moses was sending Zipporah home to her people, home to safety. Aaron would not have that luxury. Miriam and his own sons would have to remain and endure whatever hardships came. Hebrews had no alternative but to hope and pray that the day of deliverance would come swiftly.

TWO

❖❖❖❖❖

"Show me a miracle!" Pharaoh raised his hand and smirked. The laughter rippling in the great chamber left a hollow echo in Aaron's chest. The ruler's smug pride was evidence he felt no threat from an unseen God. After all, Raamses was the divine child of Osiris and Isis, wasn't he? And, indeed, Raamses looked godlike in all his finery as he rested his hands on the arms of his throne. "Impress us with the power of your invisible god of slaves. Show me what your god can do."

"Aaron." Moses' voice quavered. "Th-throw . . ."

"Speak up, Moses!" Raamses mocked him. "We can't hear you."

"Throw d-down your shepherd's staff."

The laughter grew louder. Those closest imitated Moses' stammer.

Aaron's face went hot. Furious, he stepped forward. *Lord, show these mockers that You alone are God and there is no other! Let Israel's oppressor see Your power!*

Aaron moved in front of Moses to shield his brother from the sneering crowd and looked straight at Pharaoh. He would not cower before this despicable tyrant who laughed at God's anointed prophet and ground his heel into Hebrew backs!

Pharaoh's eyes narrowed coldly, for who dared look Pharaoh in the face? Aaron did not look away as he held his staff up in challenge, and then tossed it to the stone floor in front of the ruler of all Egypt. The moment it hit, it transformed into a cobra, the very symbol of power Pharaoh wore on his crown.

Gasping, servants and officials drew back. The snake moved with ominous grace, head rising as the cape of skin spread and revealed a mark on the back of its head, a mark unlike any other. The snake hissed and the sound filled the chamber. Aaron's skin prickled from head to foot.

"Are you all afraid of this sorcerer's trick?" Pharaoh looked around the room in disgust. "Where are my magicians?" The cobra moved toward Pharaoh. At a flick of his hand, four guards moved in front of their ruler, spears down and ready to jab if the snake came any closer. "Enough of this!

Send for my magicians!" Running footsteps echoed off the stone as several men entered from each side, bowing low to Pharaoh. He waved his hand imperiously. "Deal with this farce. Show these cowards it is a trick!"

Uttering incantations, the sorcerers came toward the snake. They tossed their staffs on the floor, and their staffs also transformed into snakes. The floor teemed with serpents! But as each raised its evil head, the Lord's struck hard and fast, swallowing one after another.

"It's a trick!" Pharaoh paled when the great cobra seemed to fix its dark, unblinking eyes on him. "A trick, I say!" It moved toward him.

Moses gripped Aaron's arm. "Take hold of it."

Aaron longed to see that cobra strike Pharaoh, but he did as his brother said. Heart thumping, sweat trickling down the back of his neck, he stepped forward, leaned down, and grasped the snake in the middle. The cool scaly skin and muscle of the cobra hardened into wood, straightening into his staff. Aaron stood tall before Pharaoh, staff raised, his fear gone in the rush of awe. "The Lord God says, *'Let My people go!'*"

"Escort them out." Pharaoh waved them away like flies. "We've had enough entertainment for today."

Guards flanked them. Moses bowed his head and turned away. Aaron followed, teeth clenched. He heard the whispered insults as the Egyptians blasphemed God.

"Whoever heard of an invisible god?"

"Only slaves would think of anything so ridiculous."

"One god? Should we fear one god? We have *hundreds* of gods!"

Resentment and bitterness over the years of slavery and abuse filled Aaron. *It's not over!* He wanted to shout back at them. *"Many signs and wonders,"* Moses had told him. This was only the beginning of the war God was waging on Egypt. His father, Amram, had waited for this day, and his father before him and his father before him. The day of deliverance!

The guard left them at the entrance. Aaron put his hand on Moses' shoulder. His brother was trembling! "I know fear, too, Moses. I've lived with it all my life." How many times had he cowered before a taskmaster's whip or looked at the ground rather than allow those above him to see his true feelings? Aaron squeezed tightly, wanting to give comfort. "They will mourn the day they treated God's anointed with such contempt."

"It is God they reject, Aaron. I am nothing."

"You are God's prophet!"

"They do not understand, any more than our own people understand."

Aaron knew the Hebrews treated Moses with as much contempt as Pharaoh had. He bowed his head and let his hand hang at his side. "God speaks through you. I *know* He does. And God *will* deliver us." He was as certain of that as he was that the sun would go down tonight and come up again in the morning. The Lord would deliver Israel by signs and wonders. He didn't know how or when, but he knew it would happen just as the Lord had said it would.

Aaron shuddered at the power that had turned his staff into a cobra. He ran his thumb over the carved wood. Had he imagined what had just happened? Everyone in that great chamber had seen the Lord's cobra swallow those brought forth by Pharaoh's sorcerers, and *still* they dismissed God's power as nothing.

Moses stopped along the road to Goshen. The hair prickled on the back of Aaron's neck. "The Lord has spoken to you."

Moses looked at him. "We are to go to the Nile and wait near Pharaoh's house. We will speak with him again tomorrow morning. This is what you are to say. . . ."

Aaron listened to Moses' instructions as they walked along the riverbank. He did not question his brother or press him for more information once the command was given. When they came near Pharaoh's house, Moses rested. Weary, Aaron squatted and covered his head. The heat was intense this time of day, making him lethargic. He watched as shimmering light danced on the surface of the river. Across the way, men were cutting reeds that would be woven into mats and pounded and soaked into papyrus. On this side of the river, near Pharaoh's house, the reeds were left untouched.

Frogs croaked. An ibis stood motionless, feet spread, head down, waiting for prey. Aaron remembered his mother weeping as she placed Moses in the basket. Eighty years had passed since that morning, and yet Aaron remembered it now as clearly as if it had happened this morning. He could almost hear the echo of other weeping mothers as they obeyed the old pharaoh's law and gave up their infant sons to the river. The Nile, Egypt's river of life, controlled by the god Hapi, had run with Hebrew blood as crocodiles grew fat during those years. His eyes filled with tears as he looked out over the Nile. He doubted Pharaoh would feel any remorse over what had happened to the Hebrew babies eighty years ago on the banks of this river. But perhaps his historians would remember and explain after tomorrow. If they dared.

God, where were You when the old pharaoh was making us cast our children into the brown, silt-rich waters of the Nile? I was born two years before the edict or I, too, would be dead. Surely, it was You who watched over Moses and allowed him to drift into the hands of one of the few who held sway over Pharaoh. Lord, I don't understand why You let us suffer so much. I never will. But I will do whatever You say. Whatever You tell Moses to do and he tells me, that will I do.

Moses walked along the shore. Aaron rose to follow. He did not want to think of those days of death, but they often came to him, filling him with helpless wrath and endless despair. But now, the Lord God of Abraham, Isaac, and Jacob had spoken to a man again. God had sent Aaron into the wilderness to find Moses, and He had told Moses to lead His people from Egypt. Finally, after centuries of silence, the Lord had promised an end to Israel's misery.

And revenge would come with freedom!

Help me stand tall beside my brother tomorrow, Lord. Help me not to give in to my fear before Pharaoh. You have said Moses is the one to deliver our people. So be it. But please, Lord, don't let him stammer like a fool before Pharaoh. Moses speaks Your words. Give him courage, Lord. Don't let him tremble for all to see. Please give him strength and courage to show everyone that he is Your prophet, that he is the one You have chosen to bring Your people out of bondage.

Aaron covered his face. Would the Lord hear his prayer?

Moses turned to him. "We will sleep here tonight." They were only a short distance from Pharaoh's house on the river, only calling distance from the platform where the barge would dock and board Egypt's ruler for a journey up the Nile to visit temples of lesser gods. "When Pharaoh comes out at first light to make his offerings to the Nile, you will speak to him again." Moses repeated the words the Lord had given him for Aaron to say.

Torn between fear and eagerness for morning, Aaron slept little that night. He listened to the crickets and frogs and the rustle of reeds. When he did finally sleep, he heard the dark voices of the river gods whispering threats.

Moses shook him awake. "It will be sunrise soon."

Bones aching, Aaron stretched and stood. "Have you been up all night?"

"I could not sleep."

They looked at one another and then went down to the river and drank their fill. Aaron walked shoulder to shoulder with his brother to the stone landing at the river's edge. The moon and stars shone overhead, but the horizon was turning lapis. Before the first golden beams emerged, Pharaoh emerged from his house, his priests and servants in attendance, all in readiness to welcome Ra, father of the kings of Egypt, whose chariot ride across the sky brought the sunlight.

Pharaoh paused when he saw them. "Why do you trouble your people, Aaron and Moses?" Pharaoh stood arms akimbo. "Why do you give them false hope? You must tell them all to go back to work."

Without his cape of gold and jewels and the double crown of Egypt, Pharaoh looked smaller, more like a man. Perhaps it was because he stood in the open rather than inside that huge chamber with its massive columns and vibrant paintings, surrounded by his finely dressed servants and sycophants.

Aaron's fear evaporated. "The Lord, the God of the Hebrews, has sent me to say, 'Let My people go, so they can worship Me in the wilderness.' Until now, you have refused to listen to Him. Now the Lord says, 'You are going to find out that I am the Lord.' Look! I will hit the water of the Nile with this staff, and the river will turn to blood. The fish in it will die, and the river will stink. The Egyptians will not be able to drink any water from the Nile."

Aaron struck the water with his staff, and the Nile ran red and smelled of blood.

"It is another trick, great Pharaoh!" A magician pressed his way forward. "I will show you." He called for his assistant to bring a bowl of water. Uttering incantations, the magician sprinkled granules and turned water to blood. Aaron shook his head. A bowl of water was not the Nile River! But Pharaoh had already made up his mind. Turning his back on them, he walked up the steps and went into his house, leaving his magicians and sorcerers to deal with the problem.

"We will return to Goshen." Moses turned away.

Aaron heard the priests making supplications to Hapi, calling on the god of the Nile to change the river back to water again. But the river continued to run blood and dead fish floated on the surface.

Every water vessel of stone or wood was filled with blood! All Egypt suffered. Even the Hebrews had to dig pits around the Nile to find water fit to drink. Day after day, Pharaoh's priests called to Hapi and then to Khnum, the giver of the Nile, to help them. They called to Sothis, god of the Nile floodwaters, to wash away the blood and fight against the invisible god of the Hebrews who challenged their authority. The priests made offerings and sacrifices, but still the land reeked of blood and rotting fish.

Aaron had not expected to suffer along with the Egyptians. He had been thirsty before, but never like this. *Why, God? Why must we suffer along with our oppressors?*

"The Egyptians shall know that the Lord is God," Moses said.

"But we know already!" Miriam paced in distress. "Why must we suffer more than we have already?"

Only Moses was calm. "We must examine ourselves. Are there any among us who have embraced other gods? We must cast out their idols and make ready for the Lord our God."

Aaron felt the heat flood his face. Idols! There were idols everywhere. After four centuries of living in Egypt, they had made their way inside Hebrew households!

The stench of blood turned Aaron's stomach. His tongue clove to the roof of his mouth as he stood at the edge of the pit his sons had helped dig. Moisture slowly seeped into cups. The water tasted of silt and sand, leaving grit between his teeth. His only solace was knowing that Egyptian taskmasters and overseers were now suffering the same thirst he had every day he had worked in the mud pits and brick fields.

The Israelites wailed in despair. "How long, Moses? How long will this plague last?"

"Until the Lord lifts His hand."

On the seventh day, the Nile ran clean.

But even Aaron's neighbors talked about which god or gods might have made the waters drinkable again. If not Hapi, then maybe Sothis, god of the Nile floodwaters, or perhaps the gods of each village had joined together!

"We are to return to Pharaoh."

"Signs and wonders," Moses had said. How many signs? How many wonders? And would Hebrews have to suffer everything the Egyptians suffered? Where was the justice in that?

A plague of frogs this time, dozens, then hundreds, then thousands.

Pharaoh was unimpressed. So were his sorcerers, who were quick to point out, "It is a small matter to make frogs come from the river."

Aaron longed to call out, "Yes, but can you stop them?" As the barge was poled out from the shore, the magicians and sorcerers remained beside the Nile, casting spells and calling on Heket, the frog goddess, to stop the plague of frogs. The frogs kept coming until they were a hopping, writhing mass along the shores of the Nile. They hopped into courts and houses and fields. They hopped up from streams. They hopped out of pools where no frogs had been. They hopped into kneading bowls and ovens.

Even in the land of Goshen.

Aaron could not stretch out on his mat without sweeping frogs away! The croak and rustle were maddening. He prayed as fervently as any Egyptian for respite from this plague, but the frogs kept coming.

Miriam flung another frog out the door. "Why did God see fit to send these frogs into our house?"

"I wonder." Aaron looked pointedly toward their neighbor, shrieking as she beat frogs to death with her statue of Heket.

+ + +

Flanked by soldiers, Aaron and Moses were escorted respectfully to the palace this time. Aaron heard Pharaoh before he saw him. Shouting curses, he kicked a frog away from the throne. Croaking and ribbeting echoed in the great chamber. Aaron smiled faintly. Clearly, Heket had failed to recall her frogs to the waters of the Nile.

Pharaoh glared. "Plead with the Lord to take the frogs away from me and my people. I will let the people go, so they can offer sacrifices to the Lord."

Triumphant, Aaron looked at Moses for the words to speak, but Moses spoke this time, quietly and with great dignity. "You set the time!" Moses replied. "Tell me when you want me to pray for you, your officials, and your people. I will pray that you and your houses will be rid of the frogs."

"Do it tomorrow!" Pharaoh leaned back in his throne and then jerked forward, snatched a frog from behind him and heaved it against the wall.

Perhaps the ruler still held out hope that his priests would prevail, though it was clear to all present that the number of frogs was increasing exponentially.

"All right," Moses replied, "it will be as you have said. Then you will know that no one is as powerful as the Lord our God."

The Lord answered Moses' prayer. The frogs stopped coming. But they didn't return to the waters from which they came. They died in the fields, streets, houses, and kneading bowls of Egyptian and Hebrew alike. The people gathered the carcasses and piled them in heaps. The stench of rotting frogs lay like a cloud over the land.

The smell didn't bother Aaron. In a few days, he figured they would be out in the desert, breathing fresh air and worshiping the Lord.

Moses sat in silence, his prayer shawl over his head.

Miriam sewed sacks in which to carry grain. "Why are you so downcast, Moses? Pharaoh agreed to let us go."

The next morning, Pharaoh's soldiers arrived. When they left, the Hebrew taskmasters ordered the people back to work.

Joy quickly turned to rage and despair. The people blamed Moses and Aaron for giving Pharaoh an excuse to make their lives even more unbearable.

Go back . . .

Aaron and Moses obeyed the Lord.

Pharaoh sat smug. "Why should I let you go? It was Heket who stopped the plague of frogs, not your god. Who is your god that I should let the slaves go free? There is work to be done, and the Hebrew slaves will do it!"

Aaron saw his brother's calm ripple. "Stretch out your staff, Aaron, and strike the dust of the earth!"

Aaron obeyed, and swarms of gnats came up as numerous as the particles of dust he'd stirred, invading the flesh and clothing of those watching, including Pharaoh himself.

Aaron and Moses departed.

People poured into the shrines of Geb and Aker, gods over the earth, and gave offerings to pay for relief.

No relief came.

Aaron sat waiting with Moses near Pharaoh's palace. How long before the wretched man relented?

A pleading Egyptian official approached one afternoon. "Great Pharaoh's magicians tried to bring forth gnats and couldn't. Pharaoh's sorcerers say this is the finger of your god who has brought this upon us." Shuddering, he scratched the hair beneath his wig. His neck showed angry welts and scabs. "Pharaoh won't listen to them. He has told them to keep offering to the gods." He uttered a frustrated groan and scratched at his chest.

Aaron cocked his head. "If this is but God's finger, consider what God's hand can do."

The man fled.

"We are to rise early in the morning," Moses said, "and present ourselves before Pharaoh as he goes down to the river."

Aaron was torn between dread and excitement. "Pharaoh will let us go this time, Moses. Pharaoh and his counselors will see that they and all the gods of Egypt cannot prevail against the God of our people."

"Raamses will not let us go, Aaron. Not yet! But only Egypt will suffer this time. The Lord will make a distinction between Egypt and Israel."

"Thanks be to God, Moses. Our people will listen now. They will see that the Lord has sent you to deliver us. They will listen to us and do as you say, for you will be as God to them."

"I do not want to be as God to them! It was never in my mind to lead anyone. I begged the Lord to choose someone else, to let another speak. You have seen how I tremble before Raamses. I am more afraid of speaking before men than I am of facing a lion or a bear in the wilderness. That's why the Lord brought you to stand beside me. When I saw you standing on the hill, I knew there would be no turning back. But the people must put their trust in the Lord, not in me. The Lord is our deliverer!"

Aaron knew why God had sent him to his brother. To encourage him, not just be his spokesman. "Yes, Moses, but you are the one to whom the Lord speaks. The Lord told me to go to you in the wilderness, and I did. When He speaks to me now, it is to affirm the word He has given you. You *are* the one who will lead us from this land of misery to the place God promised Jacob. Jacob is buried in Canaan, the land God gave him. And when we go from this place, we will carry his son Joseph's bones with us, because he knew the Lord would not leave us here forever. He knew the day would come when our people would return to Canaan."

Aaron laughed, exultant. "I thought never to see it happen in my lifetime, Brother, but I believe. However many plagues it takes, God will deliver us from bondage and take us home." Tears ran down his cheeks. "We're going home, Moses. Our real home, the home God will make for us!"

✦   ✦   ✦

Aaron stood with Moses before Pharaoh again. He felt the silence around them, the uneasiness of some, and the fear of others. More unnerving was the hatred in Pharaoh's dark glistening eyes as he listened, hands taut on his scepter.

"This is what the Lord says: 'Let My people go, so they can worship Me.

If you refuse, I will send swarms of flies throughout Egypt. Your homes will be filled with them, and the ground will be covered with them.' "

Alarmed whispers surged around Aaron, echoing faintly in the massive chamber. Aaron did not stop. He looked straight at Pharaoh. " 'But it will be very different in the land of Goshen, where the Israelites live. No flies will be found there. Then you will know that I am the Lord and that I have power even in the heart of your land!' "

Pharaoh did not listen, and the land was infested with armies of flies. They filled the air and scurried over the land. They swarmed up from the Nile, seeking warm human blood; they blanketed dung and infested the marketplace and houses. Bugs swarmed into sleeping mats. The Egyptians could not escape the torment.

Aaron felt little pity for the Egyptians. After all, when had the Egyptians ever shown pity to the Hebrews? While thousands cried out to Geb, god of the earth, or to their village gods for rescue, a few came to plead with him and Moses. Flies continued to swarm, sting, bite, and draw blood.

And then the Egyptian guards came again to usher Aaron and Moses to Pharaoh's house.

Counselors, magicians, and sorcerers thronged the great hall while Pharaoh, grim-faced and glowering, paced the dais. He stopped and glared at Moses and then at Aaron. "All right! Go ahead and offer sacrifices to your God," he said. "But do it here in this land. Don't go out into the wilderness."

"No," Moses said. Aaron felt his heart swelling with pride as his brother stood firm before the man who had once made him tremble. "That won't do! The Egyptians would detest the sacrifices that we offer to the Lord our God. If we offer them here where they can see us, they will be sure to stone us. We must take a three-day trip into the wilderness to offer sacrifices to the Lord our God, just as He has commanded us."

Pharaoh's face darkened. His jaw clenched. "All right, go ahead. I will let you go to offer sacrifices to the Lord your God in the wilderness. But don't go too far away." He lifted his hand. "Now hurry, and pray for me."

Aaron saw the armed guards move closer and knew death was close. If Moses prayed now, they would die the instant he finished. Clearly, Pharaoh thought killing two old men would stop the God of the universe from carrying out His will for His people. But Aaron had no wish to die. "Moses . . ."

Moses did not turn to him, but addressed Pharaoh again. "As soon as I go, I will ask the Lord to cause the swarms of flies to disappear from you and all your people. *Tomorrow.*"

Aaron breathed again. His brother had not been fooled.

Mouth tight, Pharaoh feigned confusion.

Moses looked from the guards to Pharaoh. "But I am warning you, don't change your mind again and refuse to let the people go to sacrifice to the Lord."

When they were safely outside, Aaron slapped Moses on the back. "They were closing in around us." He felt hope again. The prospect of freedom rising. "Once we are three days into the wilderness, we can keep going."

"You have not listened, Aaron. Remember what I told you when you met me at the mountain of God?"

Confused by his brother's frustration with him, Aaron bristled. "I listened. There would be signs and wonders. And so there have been. I remember."

"Raamses' heart is hard, Aaron."

"Then don't pray for him. Let the plague go on."

"And be like Pharaoh, who makes promises only to break them?" Moses shook his head. "The Lord is not like man, Aaron. He keeps His word. As I must keep mine."

Stung and ashamed, Aaron watched Moses go off by himself to pray. He followed Moses at a distance. Why should they keep their word to someone who broke his at every turn? It galled him that his brother was praying for relief for the Egyptians. Generations of them had abused and persecuted the Hebrews! Shouldn't they suffer? Shouldn't they learn what Israel had endured at their hands?

A group of Hebrew elders approached. Aaron rose to greet them. "We want to speak to Moses."

"Not now. He is praying."

"Praying for us or for Pharaoh?"

Aaron heard his own thoughts spoken back to him. He blushed. Who was he to question the Lord's anointed? Moses had not accepted the Lord's commission eagerly, and leadership still did not rest easily on his shoulders. As Moses' encourager, he must listen and learn rather than chafe at God's command.

"Aaron!" The elders demanded his attention.

He raised his head and faced them. "It is not for any of us to question the one God has sent to deliver us."

"We are still slaves, Aaron! And you say Moses will deliver us! When?"

"Am I God? Not even Moses knows the hour or the day! Let him pray! Perhaps God will speak and we will know more in the morning! Go back to your houses! When the Lord speaks to Moses, he will tell us what the Lord says."

"And what are we to do while we wait?"

"Pack for a long journey."

"What does a slave have to pack?" Grumbling, they went away.

Sighing, Aaron sat and watched his brother lying arms outstretched on the ground.

+ + +

As soon as God removed the flies, Pharaoh sent soldiers to Goshen and ordered the Hebrews back to work. The Egyptians knew Pharaoh's edict would bring more trouble upon them. Dread of the God of the Hebrews had filled them. They bowed their heads in respect when Aaron and Moses passed by. And no one dared abuse the slaves. People from the villages brought gifts to Goshen and asked the Hebrews to pray for mercy on them.

And still, Pharaoh did not let the Hebrews go.

Aaron no longer yearned to see the Egyptians suffer because of Pharaoh's stubbornness. He just wanted to be free! He stood beside his brother. "What next?"

"God is sending a plague on their livestock."

Aaron knew fear ran rampant among his people. Some said he should have left his brother in Midian. Frustrated and frightened, they wanted answers when none were to be had. Moses was in constant prayer, so it was left to Aaron to try to calm the elders and send them back to calm the people. "What will we sacrifice when we go into the desert to worship the Lord?" Would the plague fall on them? Was their lack of faith in God any less sinful than bowing down to idols?

But Moses continued to reassure him. "Nothing that belongs to the sons of Israel shall die, Aaron. The Lord set a time for the plague to start. Pharaoh and all his counselors will know the plague is of the Lord God."

+ + +

Buzzards circled the villages and came down to tear at the bloated flesh of dead sheep, cattle, camels, and goats rotting in the hot sun. In Goshen, the herds of cattle, flocks of sheep and goats, and the many camels, donkeys, and mules remained healthy.

Aaron heard the Voice again and bowed his face to the ground. When the Lord stopped speaking, he rose and ran to Moses. Moses confirmed the words and they went into the city, took handfuls of soot from a furnace, and tossed it into the air within sight of Pharaoh's seat of power. The dust cloud grew and spread like gray fingers over the land. Everywhere it touched, Egyptians suffered an outbreak of boils. Even their animals were afflicted. Within a few days, the city streets were empty of merchants and buyers. All were afflicted, from the lowly servant to the highest official.

No word came from Pharaoh. No soldiers came to order the Hebrews back to work.

The Lord spoke to Moses again. "Tomorrow morning, we stand again before Pharaoh."

+ + +

Dressed in splendor, Pharaoh appeared, two servants supporting him. Only a few counselors and magicians were present, all pale, their faces taut with pain. When Raamses tried to sit, he groaned and cursed. Two servants came forward quickly with cushions. Raamses clutched the arms of his chair and eased himself down. "What do you want now, Moses?"

"The Lord, the God of the Hebrews, says: 'Let My people go, so they can worship Me. If you don't, I will send a plague that will really speak to you and your officials and all the Egyptian people. I will prove to you that there is no other God like Me in all the earth. I could have killed you all by now. I could have attacked you with a plague that would have wiped you from the face of the earth. But I have let you live for this reason—that you might see My power and that My fame might spread throughout the earth. But you are still lording it over My people, and you refuse to let them go. So tomorrow at this time I will send a hailstorm worse than any in all of Egypt's history. Quick! Order your livestock and servants to come in from the fields. Every person or animal left outside will die beneath the hail.'"

Those in attendance whispered in alarm.

Pharaoh gave a bitter laugh. "Hail? What is hail? You have lost your mind, Moses. You speak nonsense."

When Moses turned away, Aaron followed. He saw the anxiety in men's faces. Pharaoh might not be afraid of the God of the Hebrews, but clearly others knew better. Several backed quickly between the pillars and headed for the doors, eager to see to their animals and protect their wealth.

Moses held his staff toward the sky. Dark, angry clouds swirled, moving across the land away from Goshen. A cold wind blew. Aaron felt a strange heaviness building in his chest. The darkening skies rumbled. Streaks of fire came from heaven, striking the land west of Goshen. Shu, the Egyptian god of the air, separator of earth and sky, was powerless against the Lord God of Israel.

Aaron sat outside all day and night listening and watching the hail and fire in the distance, awestruck by the power of God. He had never seen anything like it. Surely Pharaoh would relent now!

Guards came again. Aaron saw the flattened and scorched fields of flax and barley. The land was in ruins.

Pharaoh, thought to be descended from the union of Osiris and Isis, Horus himself in man's form, looked cowed and cornered. Silence rang in the chamber, while the question pulsed: If Pharaoh was the supreme god of Egypt, why couldn't he protect his realm from the invisible god of Hebrew *slaves*? How could it be that all the great and glorious gods of Egypt were no match against the unseen hand of one unseen god?

"I finally admit my fault." Pharaoh cast a sallow look at his advisors clustered near the dais. "The Lord is right, and my people and I are wrong. Please beg the Lord to end this terrifying thunder and hail. I will let you go at once."

Aaron felt no triumph. Pharaoh's heart was not in his words. No doubt he had succumbed to pressure from his advisors. They still did not understand that it was God who was at war with them.

Moses spoke boldly. "As soon as I leave the city, I will lift my hands and pray to the Lord. Then the thunder and hail will stop. This will prove to you that the earth belongs to the Lord. But as for you and your officials, I know that you still do not fear the Lord God as you should."

Pharaoh's eyes gleamed. "Moses, my friend, how can you speak so to one you once called little cousin? How can you bring such heartache to the woman who lifted you from the river and reared you as a son of Egypt?"

"God knows you better than I, Raamses." Moses' voice was quiet but steady. "And it is the Lord who has told me how you harden your heart against Him. It is *you* who brings judgment on Egypt. It is *you* who makes your people suffer!"

Bold words that could bring a death edict. Aaron stepped closer to Moses, ready to protect him if any man should come close. Everyone moved back. Some lowered their heads just enough to show their respect to Moses, much to Pharaoh's ire.

Moses prayed, and the Lord lifted His hand. The thunder, hail, and fire stopped, but the quiet after the storm was even more frightening than the roaring winds. Nothing changed. Pharaoh wanted his bricks, and the Hebrew slaves were to make them.

The people wailed, "Pharaoh's sword is over our heads!"

"Have you no eyes?" Aaron shouted. "Have you no ears? Look around you. Can you not all see how the Egyptians fear what the Lord will do next? More come to our people every day bringing gifts. They hold Moses in great respect."

"And what good does that do us if we are still slaves?"

"The Lord will deliver us!" Moses said. "You must have faith!"

"Faith? That's all we've had for years. *Faith!* We want our *freedom!*"

Aaron tried to keep people away from Moses. "Leave him alone. He must pray."

"We are worse off now than we were before he came!"

"Cleanse your hearts! Pray with us!"

"What good have you done us when we are called back to the mud pits?"

Incensed, Aaron wanted to use his staff on them. They were like sheep, bleating in panic. "Have your gardens turned to ash? Are your animals sick? The Lord has made a distinction between us and Egypt!"

"When will God get us out of here?"

"When we know *the Lord is God and there is no other!*" Hadn't they bowed down to Egyptian gods? They still turned this way and that! Aaron tried to pray. He tried to hear God's voice again, but the jumble of his own thoughts crowded in like a council of discordant voices. When he saw a scarab amulet around his son Abihu's neck, his blood ran cold. "Where did you get that thing?"

"An Egyptian gave it to me. It's valuable, Father. It's made of lapis and gold."

"It's an abomination! Take it off! And make certain there are no other idols in my house. Do you understand, Abihu? Not a scarab, nor a wooden Heket or the eye of Ra! If an Egyptian gives you something made of gold, melt it down!"

God was sending another plague, and it would only be by His grace and mercy that He didn't send it on Israel as well. Israel, so aptly named, "contender against God"!

God was sending locusts this time. Still, Pharaoh would not listen. Even as Aaron walked with Moses from the great hall, he could hear the counselors crying out to Pharaoh, pleading, begging.

"How long will you let these disasters go on?"

"Please let the Israelites go to serve the Lord their God!"

"Don't you realize that Egypt lies in ruins?"

Aaron turned sharply when he heard running footsteps behind them. No one would take Moses! Planting his feet, he gripped his staff in both hands. The servant bowed low. "Please. Great Pharaoh wishes you to return."

"*Great* Pharaoh can take a flying leap into the Nile!"

"Aaron." Moses headed back.

Tense with frustration, Aaron followed. Would Raamses ever listen? Should they go back and listen to another promise, knowing it would be broken before they stepped foot in Goshen? Hadn't God already said He was hardening Pharaoh's heart and the hearts of his servants?

"All right, go and serve the Lord your God!"

Moses turned away; Aaron fell into step beside him. They had not reached the door when Pharaoh shouted again. "But tell me, just whom do you want to take along?"

Moses looked at Aaron, and Aaron turned. "Young and old, all of us will go. We will take our sons and daughters and our flocks and herds. We must all join together in a festival to the Lord."

Pharaoh's face darkened. He pointed at Moses. "Thus *I* say to you, Moses: The Lord will certainly need to be with you if you try to take your little ones along! I can see through your wicked intentions. Never! Only the *men* may go and serve the Lord, for that is what you requested!" He motioned the guards. "Get them out of my palace!"

Pharaoh's servants came at them, shoving and pushing at them, shouting curses from their false gods. Aaron tried to swing his staff, but Moses held his arm back. They were both flung outside into the dust.

+ + +

All that day and night, the wind blew, and in the morning, locusts came with it. While Egyptians cried out to Wadjet, the cobra goddess, to protect her realm, locusts swarmed over all the land of Egypt, thousands upon thousands in ranks like an army devouring everything in its path. The ground was dark with creeping, leaping grasshoppers eating every plant, tree, and bush that the hail had left. The crops of wheat and spelt were consumed. The date palms were stripped bare. The reeds along the Nile were eaten down to the water.

By the time Pharaoh's soldiers summoned Moses and Aaron, it was too late. Every crop and source of food outside Goshen was gone.

Shaken, Pharaoh greeted them. "I confess my sin against the Lord your God and against you. Forgive my sin only this once, and plead with the Lord your God to take away this terrible plague."

Moses prayed for God's mercy, and the wind changed direction, blowing westward and driving the locusts away toward the Red Sea.

The land and all upon it was still and silent. The Egyptians huddled in their houses, afraid of what new catastrophe would come next if Pharaoh did not let the slaves go. Gifts appeared at Hebrew doorways. Gold amulets, jewelry, precious stones, incense, beautiful cloth, silver and bronze vessels were given to honor God's people. "Pray for us in the hour of our need. Intercede for us."

"They still don't understand!" Moses gripped his head covered by the prayer shawl. "They bow down to us, Aaron, while *it is God who holds the power."*

Even Miriam was afire with frustration. "Why doesn't God kill Pharaoh and be done with it? The Lord has the power to reach inside that palace and crush Raamses!"

Moses raised his head. "The Lord wants the entire world to know He is God and there is no other. All the gods of Egypt are false. They have no power to stand against the Lord our God."

"We know that!"

"Miriam!" Aaron spoke sharply. Wasn't Moses plagued enough? "Be patient. Wait on the Lord. He will deliver us."

When Moses stretched out his hand again, darkness came over Egypt. The sun was blotted out by an inky darkness heavier than night. Sitting outside Pharaoh's palace, Aaron drew his robe around himself. Moses was silent beside him. They could both hear the priests crying out for Ra, the sun god, the father of the kings of Egypt, to drive his golden chariot across the sky and bring light again. Aaron gave a contemptuous laugh. Let these stubborn fools cry out to their false god. The sun would appear when God willed it—and not before.

Moses rose abruptly. "We must gather the elders, Aaron. *Quickly!*" They hastened to Goshen, where Aaron sent out messengers. The elders came, asking questions, grumbling.

"Be silent!" Aaron said. "Listen to Moses. He has the Word of the Lord!"

"Prepare to leave Egypt. All of us, men and women alike, are to ask their neighbors for articles of silver and gold. The Egyptians will give you whatever you ask of them, for the Lord has given us favor in their sight. The Lord says that this month will be the first month of the year for you. On the tenth day of this month, each family must choose a lamb or a young goat for a sacrifice. Take special care of these lambs until the evening of the fourteenth day of this first month. Then each family in the community must slaughter its lamb. . . ."

Moses told them of the plague to come and what they must do to survive. They all left in silence, the fear of the Lord upon them.

+ + +

For three days, Aaron waited with Moses near the palace entrance, before they heard Pharaoh's cry of fear and rage echo in the columned chambers. *"Moses!"*

Moses put his hand on Aaron and they rose together and entered. Aaron did not falter in the darkness. He could see his way as though the Lord had given him the eyes of an owl. He could see Moses' face, solemn and filled with compassion, and Pharaoh's eyes darting this way and that, searching, blind.

"I am here, Raamses," Moses said.

Pharaoh faced forward, leaning his head as though to hear what he could not see in the darkness that enfolded him. "Go and worship the Lord," he said. "But let your flocks and herds stay here. You can even take your children with you."

"No," Moses said, "we must take our flocks and herds for sacrifices and burnt offerings to the Lord our God. All our property must go with us; not a hoof can be left behind. We will have to choose our sacrifices for the Lord our God from among these animals. And we won't know which sacrifices He will require until we get there."

Pharaoh cursed them. "Get out of here!" he shouted. "Don't ever let me see you again! The day you do, you will die!"

"Very well!" Moses shouted back. "I will never see you again!" His voice changed, deepened, resonated, and filled the chamber. "This is what the Lord says: 'About midnight I will pass through Egypt. All the firstborn sons will die in every family in Egypt, from the oldest son of Pharaoh, who sits on the throne, to the oldest son of his lowliest slave. Even the firstborn of the animals will die.'"

Aaron's skin prickled and sweat broke out.

"Moses!" Pharaoh roared as he spread his arms and swept his hands back and forth, trying to find his own way out of the darkness. "Do you think Osiris will not defend me? The gods will not let you touch my son!"

Moses went on speaking. " 'Then a loud wail will be heard throughout the land of Egypt; there has never been such wailing before, and there never will be again. But among the Israelites it will be so peaceful that not even a dog will bark. Then you will know that the Lord makes a distinction between the Egyptians and the Israelites. All the officials of Egypt will come running to me, bowing low. "Please leave!" they will beg. "Hurry! And take all your followers with you." Only then will I go!'" Face flushed with anger, Moses turned and strode from the great hall.

Aaron caught up and walked beside him. He had never seen his brother so angry. God had spoken through him. It had been *God's* voice Aaron heard in that immense hall.

Moses prayed fervently under his breath, eyes blazing as he strode through the streets of the city heading toward Goshen. People drew back and ducked into their houses or shops.

When they reached the edge of the city, Moses cried out. *"Oh, Lord! Lord!!"*

Aaron's eyes welled at the anguished cry. "Moses." His throat closed.

"Oh, Aaron, now we shall all see the destruction one man can bring upon a nation." Tears ran down his face. "We shall all see!"

Moses went down on his knees and wept.

THREE

❖❖❖❖❖

The lamb struggled when Aaron held it firmly between his knees. He slit
its throat and felt the small animal go limp as the bowl filled with its blood.
The smell turned Aaron's stomach. The lamb had been perfect, without a
blemish, and only a year old. He skinned the lamb. "Pierce it through and
roast its head, legs, and inner parts."

Nadab took the carcass. "Yes, Father."

Taking up the bowl, Aaron dipped sprigs of hyssop into the blood and
painted the door lintel of his house. He dipped again and again until the top
of the doorway was stained red, and then he began to do the same on the
doorposts on either side of the entrance into his home. All over Goshen and
into the city, each Hebrew family was doing the same. Egyptian neighbors
watched, confused and disgusted, whispering.

"They threw away all the yeast in their houses yesterday."

"And now they're painting their doorframes with blood!"

"What does it all mean?"

Some had come to Aaron and asked what they could do to be grafted in
among the Hebrews. "Circumcise every male in your household, and then
you may be like one born among us."

Only a few took his words seriously and went through with it. Afraid for
their lives, they moved their families in among the dwellings of the Hebrews,
and listened to whatever Aaron and Moses had to say to the people.

Aaron thought of what this night would hold for the rest of Egypt.
In the beginning, he had wanted revenge. He had savored the thought of
Egyptians suffering. Now he was filled with pity for those who still foolishly
clung to their idols and bowed down before their empty gods. He longed
to be away from this land of desolation. Finishing his task, he entered the
house and closed the door securely. Piled in one corner were objects and
jewelry of silver and gold that Miriam and his sons had collected from their
Egyptian neighbors. All his life, Aaron had scratched out a meager living
from the soil and his small flock of sheep and goats, and now his family had

silver and gold to fill sacks! God had made the Egyptians look on Aaron and Moses and all the Hebrews with favor, and they had given whatever was asked for, even unto their wealth. Without question, the Egyptians had given up things they had prized only days before, hoping they could buy mercy from the Hebrew God.

God's mercy was not for sale. Nor could it be earned.

On such a night as this, gold and silver did not matter, even to Aaron, who had once thought wealth could bring him solace and salvation from taskmasters and tyrants. Whatever he had done in the name of the Lord in the past did not count on this night. Had the Egyptians offered everything they owned to their gods tonight, they could not buy the lives of their first-born sons. Had they smashed their idols, it would not have been enough. Pharaoh had brought this night upon Egypt, his pride the people's bane.

God, who established the heavens, set the price for life, and it was the blood of the lamb. The Angel of the Lord was coming, and he would pass over every house that had its lintels and doorposts painted with the lamb's blood. The blood was a sign that those inside the house believed in the God of Abraham, Isaac, and Jacob, believed enough to obey His command and trust His word. Only faith in the one true God would save them.

Aaron looked at his firstborn son, Nadab, as he sat at the table with his brothers. Abihu sat alone, deep in thought, while Ithamar and Eleazar sat with their wives and small children. Little Phinehas turned the spitted lamb over the fire. When he tired, another took his place.

"Grandfather—" Phinehas slipped onto the bench beside Aaron— "what does this night mean?"

Aaron put his arm around the boy and looked at his sons, their wives, and the small children. "It is the Passover sacrifice to the Lord. The Lord will come tonight at midnight and see the blood of the lamb on our door and pass over us. We will be spared, but the Lord will strike down the firstborn sons of the Egyptians. From the firstborn of Pharaoh who sits on the throne, to the firstborn of the prisoner who is in the dungeon, to the firstborn of all the livestock as well."

The only sound in the house was the crackling fire and the pop and hiss of fat as it dropped onto the hot coals. Miriam ground wheat and barley to make bread without yeast. The hours wore by. No one spoke. Moses rose and closed the window openings, securing them as though for a sandstorm. Then he sat with the family and covered his head with his shawl.

The smell of roasting lamb filled the house, along with the bitter herbs Miriam had cut and put on the table. Aaron cut into the lamb. "It is finished." Miriam added oil to the ground flour and patted out thin cakes of bread that she laid over a round pan and set over some coals she had raked to one side.

Night was heavy upon them. Death was coming.

The men rose, girding their loins and tucking their cloaks into their belts. They put their sandals on again and stood at the table, staffs in hand, and the family ate of the lamb, the bitter herbs, and unleavened bread.

A scream rent the air. Aaron's skin crawled. Miriam stared at Moses, her dark eyes wide. No one spoke as they ate. Another scream was heard, closer this time, and then wailing in the distance. Outside someone cried out in anguish to Osiris. Aaron shut his eyes tightly, for he knew Osiris was nothing but an idol made by men's hands, his myth crafted by men's imaginings. Osiris had no substance, no power, other than the fictitious power men and women had given him over the centuries. Tonight, they would learn what men design cannot bring salvation. Salvation is in the Lord, the God of all creation.

The screams and wailing increased. Aaron knew by the sounds when the Angel of Death had passed over the house. He felt a rising joy, a thanksgiving that swelled his heart to bursting. The Lord was trustworthy! The Lord had spared His people Israel! The Lord was destroying His enemies.

Someone pounded on the door. "In the name of Pharaoh, open the door!"

Aaron looked to Moses and at his nod rose to open the door. Soldiers stood outside, and they bowed low when Aaron and Moses came through the door. "Pharaoh has sent us to bring you to him." As they went out, the soldiers fell in around them.

"Pharaoh's son is dead." The soldier to Moses' right spoke softly.

Another spoke to Aaron. "He was the first in the palace to die, and then others fell, many others."

"My son." A soldier wept behind them. "My son . . ."

All of Thebes was wailing, for every house suffered loss.

"Hurry! We must hurry before all Egypt dies."

They had barely crossed the threshold when Aaron heard Pharaoh's anguished cry. "Leave us! Go away, all of you!" He hunched on his throne. "Go and serve the Lord as you have requested. Take your flocks and herds, and be gone. Go, but give me a blessing as you leave."

Aaron stood in the flickering torchlight, hardly able to believe he had heard Pharaoh relent. Was it over? Was it really over? Or would they get no farther than the streets of Thebes and find out Pharaoh had changed his mind again?

Moses turned away without a word. "Go!" one of the guards urged Aaron. "Go quickly, or we will all die!"

As they hurried through the streets, Aaron shouted, "Israel! Israel! Your day of deliverance is at hand!"

+   +   +

Egyptians rushed from their houses, crying out to the Hebrews. "Hurry! Hurry! Go before Great Pharaoh changes his mind and we all die!" Some gave them donkeys and added gifts of goodwill as they helped to strap possessions to the animals' backs. Others gave portions of what little they had left from the plagues. "Take whatever you want and get out of Egypt! Hurry! Hurry before another plague falls upon us and we are no more!"

Aaron laughed in exultation, so full of emotion he couldn't think of anything but rushing, rushing. Miriam and his sons and their families caught up to him and Moses at the front of the congregation. The noise was deafening. People called out praises to the Lord and Moses and Aaron. Large flocks of bleating sheep and goats swirled alongside the mass of population. Herds of cattle followed so that the people would not choke in their dust. Six hundred thousand men left on foot as the sun came up, and headed for Succoth, accompanied by their wives and children.

Women carried their kneading bowls on their shoulders, while balancing a child on their hips and calling out to other children to stay close and keep up with the family. They had had no time to prepare food for the journey.

Aaron heard the cacophony of voices and tasted the dust stirred by over a million slaves hurrying away from Pharaoh's city. More joined them along the way. The tribes of Reuben, Simeon, Judah, Zebulon, Issachar, Dan, Gad, Asher, Nephtali, and Benjamin followed Moses and Aaron's tribe of Levi. Representatives of the half tribes of Ephraim and Manasseh traveled close to Moses, carrying with them the bones of their ancestor Joseph, who had once saved Egypt from famine. The elders of each tribe had made standards so that their relatives might gather together and march in divisions out of Egypt, every man armed for battle. And behind them and alongside came Egyptians who fled the desolation of their homeland and sought the provision and protection of the Lord God of Israel, the true God over all creation.

As the sun rose, Aaron watched the rising of a pillar of cloud. The Lord Himself was shielding them from the burning heat and leading them out of bondage, away from suffering and despair. Oh, life was going to be good! In a week, they would reach the Promised Land of milk and honey. In a week, they could pitch their tents and stretch out on their mats and revel in their freedom.

Men and women wept with joyful abandon. "Praise the Lord! We are free—free at last!"

"No son of mine will ever make another brick for Pharaoh!"

"Let him make his own bricks!"

People laughed. Women warbled in joy. Men shouted.

"I should have made more unleavened cakes! We have so little grain!"

"How far are we going today? The children are already tired."

Aaron turned, face hot at the sound of his own relatives grumbling. Would they rather have stayed behind? "This is the end of your captivity! Rejoice! We have been redeemed by the blood of the lamb! Praise the Lord!"

"We do, Father! We do, but the children are exhausted. . . ."

Moses raised his staff. "Remember this day! Tell your sons and daughters of what the Lord did for you when He brought you out of Egypt! Remember that you consecrated to the Lord every firstborn male, the offspring of every womb among Israel, whether man or beast, for the Lord made death pass over us! Commemorate this day! Never forget it was the Lord who with a mighty hand brought you out of Egypt!"

Because Pharaoh stubbornly refused to let God's people go, the Lord killed every firstborn in Egypt, both man and beast. Therefore, every first male offspring of every womb belonged to the Lord, and every firstborn son would be redeemed by the blood of a lamb.

"Praise the Lord!" Aaron raised his staff. He would not listen to the few grumblers among his people. He would not let them spoil this moment, this day. He would not listen to those who looked back over their shoulders like Lot's wife. He had dreamed all his life of what it would be like to live as a free man. And now he would know freedom firsthand. He wept in thanksgiving. *Praise the Lord!* A resounding shout came from men and women around him, spreading back until the praise rose thunderous to the heavens. The women sang.

Moses did not stop as the sun began its descent, for a pillar of fire appeared, leading them to Succoth, where they rested before moving on. They camped at Etham on the edge of the desert.

Korah and a delegation of other Levite elders came to Moses. "Why are you leading us south when there are two other routes to Canaan that are shorter? We could go by way of the sea."

Moses shook his head. "That would take the people through Philistine country."

"We are many and armed for battle. What about the way of Shur to southern Canaan?"

Moses stood firm. "We are armed, but untrained and untried. We go where the Angel of the Lord leads us. The Lord has said if the people face war, they might change their minds and return to Egypt."

"We will never return to Egypt!" Korah lifted his chin. "You should have more confidence in us, Moses. We have craved freedom as much as you. More so."

Aaron's head came up. He knew Korah was alluding to Moses having lived forty years in the corridors of palaces and another forty among the free men of Midian. Others came, asking for Moses' attention. He rose to see what the problem was. Problems were already mounting.

"Aaron." Korah turned to him. "You understand us better than Moses. You should have some say about which road we travel."

Aaron saw through their flattery. "It is God's choice, Korah. God made

Moses our leader. He is above us. He walks before us." Did they not see the Man who walked ahead of Moses, leading the way? Close enough to follow, but not close enough to see His face. Or could the people see Him?

"Yes." Korah was quick to agree. "We accept Moses as God's prophet. But Aaron, so are you. Think of the children. Think of our wives. Speak to your brother. Why should we go the long way rather than the short? The Philistines will have heard about the plagues. They will be in fear of us just as the Egyptians are now."

Aaron shook his head. "The Lord leads. Moses does not take one step without the Lord directing him. If you do not understand that, you have only to raise your eyes to see the cloud by day and the pillar of fire by night."

"Yes, but I'm sure if you asked the Lord, He would listen to you. Didn't He call you into the wilderness to meet Moses at Mount Sinai? The Lord spoke to you before He spoke to your brother."

Korah's words troubled Aaron. Did the man mean to divide brothers? Aaron thought of what jealousy had wrought between Cain and Abel, Ishmael and Isaac, Esau and Jacob, Joseph and his eleven brothers. No! He would not give in to such thinking. The Lord had called him to stand beside Moses, to walk with him, to uphold him. And so he would! "The Lord speaks through Moses, not me, and we will follow the Lord whatever way He leads us."

"You are Amram's firstborn son. The Lord continues to speak to you."

"Only to confirm what He has already said to Moses!"

"Is it wrong to ask why we must go the more difficult way?"

Aaron rose, staff in hand. Most of these men were his relatives. "Should Moses or I tell the Lord which way we are to go? It is for the Lord to say where we go and how long and how far we travel. If you set yourself against Moses, you set yourself against God."

Korah's eyes darkened, but he raised his hands in capitulation. "I do not doubt Moses' authority, or yours, Aaron. We have seen the signs and wonders. I was just asking . . ."

But even then, as the men turned away, Aaron knew there would be no end to the asking.

+ + +

Aaron joined Moses on a rocky hill overlooking the stretch of land to the east. Others were nearby, just down the hill, watching, but respecting Moses' need for solitude, waiting for Aaron to speak for him. Aaron realized Moses was becoming more accustomed to speaking Hebrew. "Soon you will have no need of me, my brother. Your words are clear and easily understood."

"The Lord called *both* of us to this task, Aaron. Could I have crossed the desert and stood before Pharaoh had the Lord not sent you to me?"

Aaron put his hand on Moses' arm. "You think too much of me."

"The enemies of God will do all they can to divide us, Aaron."

Perhaps the Lord had opened Moses' eyes to the temptations Aaron faced. "I don't want to follow in the ways of those who came before us."

"What is worrying you?"

"That one day, you will have no need of me, that I will be useless."

Moses was silent for so long, Aaron thought he did not intend to respond. Should he add to Moses' burdens? Hadn't the Lord called him to assist Moses, not to plague him with petty worries? How he longed to speak with Moses as they had when they were alone and crossed the wilderness together! The years of separation had fallen away. The imagined grievances dissolved. They were more than brothers. They were friends joined in one calling, servants of the Most High God. "I'm sorry, Moses. I will leave you alone. We can talk another time."

"Stay with me, Brother." He continued to look out over the people. "There are so many."

Relieved to be needed, Aaron stepped closer and leaned on his staff. He had never been comfortable with long silences. "All these descended from Jacob's sons. Sixty-six came into Egypt with Jacob, and Joseph's family made seventy in all. And from those few came this great multitude. God has blessed us."

Thousands upon thousands of men, women, and children traveled like a slow-moving sea into the desert. Clouds of dust rose from their feet and the hooves of their flocks and herds. Overhead was the heavy gray cloud canopy of protection, a shield from the burning heat of the sun. No wonder Pharaoh had feared the Hebrews! Look at them all! Had they joined with Egypt's enemies, they could have become a great military threat within the borders of Egypt. But rather than rebel, they had bent their necks to the pharaohs' will and served as slaves. They had not tried to break the chains of bondage, but had cried out to the Lord God of Abraham, Isaac, and Jacob to rescue them.

Egyptians traveled among the people. Most stayed on the outer edges of the mass of travelers. Aaron wished they had stayed behind in the Nile Delta or Etham. He didn't trust them. Had they cast aside their idols and chosen to follow the Lord, or had they come along because Egypt was in ruins?

People waved. "Moses! Aaron!" Like children, they called. There was still jubilation. Maybe it was only Korah and his friends who questioned the route they traveled.

Moses began walking again. Aaron raised his staff and pointed in the direction he led. He did not ask why Moses headed south and then east into the heart of the Sinai. The gray cloud transformed into a swirling pillar of fire to light their way and keep them warm through the desert night. Aaron saw the Angel of the Lord walking ahead, leading Moses and the people deeper into the wilderness.

Why?

Was it right that he should even think such a question?

Moses did not make camp again, but continued traveling, resting for brief periods. Miriam and Aaron's sons' wives made enough flat bread to eat on the way while children slept using a stone for a pillow. Aaron sensed Moses' urgency—an urgency he also felt, but did not understand. Canaan was north, not east. Where was the Lord leading them?

The mouth of a great wadi opened ahead. Aaron thought Moses might turn north or send men ahead to see where the canyon led. But Moses did not hesitate or turn to the right or the left. He walked straight into the canyon. Aaron stayed at his side, looking back only to make certain Miriam, his sons, and their wives and children followed.

High cliffs rose on either side, the cloud remaining overhead. The wadi narrowed. The people flowed like water into a river basin cut for them. The canyon twisted and turned like a snake through the jagged terrain, the floor flat and easily traveled.

After a long day, the canyon opened wide. Aaron saw rippling water and smelled the salt-sea air. Whatever waters had come through the wadi during the times of Noah's flood had spilled a sandy pebbled beach wide enough for the multitude to encamp. But there was nowhere to go from here. "What do we do now, Moses?"

"We wait on the Lord."

"But there is no place to go!"

Moses stood in the wind facing the sea. "We are to encamp here opposite Baal-zephon as the Lord said. And Pharaoh will pursue us, and the Lord will gain glory for Himself through Pharaoh and his army, and the Egyptians will know that the Lord is God and there is no other."

Fear gripped Aaron. "Should we tell the others?"

"They will know soon enough."

"Should we make battle lines? Should we have our weapons ready to defend ourselves?"

"I don't know, Aaron. I only know that the Lord has led us here for His purpose."

A cry rose from among the Israelites. Several men on camelback rode out onto the beach. Pharaoh's horses and chariots, horsemen and troops were coming up the canyon. Horns sounded in the distance. Aaron felt the rumble beneath his feet. An army that had never known defeat. Thousands of Hebrews wailed so loudly they drowned out the sound of the sea at their backs. People ran toward the sea and huddled in the wind.

Moses turned toward the deep waters and raised his arm, crying out to the Lord. The battle horns sounded again. Aaron shouted. "Come here to Moses!" His sons and their families and Miriam ran to them. "Stay close to us no matter what happens!" Aaron beckoned. "Do not be separated from us!" He took his grandson Phinehas up into his arms. "The Lord will come to our rescue!"

"Lord, help us!" Moses cried out.

Aaron closed his eyes and prayed for the Lord to hear.

"Moses!" the people cried out. "What have you done to us?"

Aaron handed Phinehas to Eleazar and stood between his brother and the people, staff in hand.

"Why did you bring us out here to die in the wilderness? Weren't there enough graves for us in Egypt?"

"We should've stayed in Egypt!"

"Didn't we tell you to leave us alone while we were still in Egypt?"

"You should've let us go on serving the Egyptians."

"Why did you make us leave?"

"Our Egyptian slavery was far better than dying out here in the wilderness!"

Moses turned to them. "Don't be afraid!"

"Don't be afraid? Pharaoh's army is coming! They're going to slaughter us like sheep!"

Aaron chose to believe Moses. "Have you forgotten what the Lord did for us already? He smote Egypt with His mighty hand! Egypt is in ruins!"

"All the more reason for Pharaoh to want to destroy us!"

"Where can we go now with our backs to the sea?"

"They're coming! They're coming!"

Moses raised his staff. "Just stand where you are and watch the Lord rescue you. The Egyptians that you see today will never be seen again. The Lord Himself will fight for you. You won't have to lift a finger in your defense!"

Aaron saw by Moses' expression that the Lord had spoken to him. Moses turned and looked up. The shining Angel of the Lord, who had been leading them, rose and moved behind the multitude, blocking the entrance of the great wadi that opened out upon Pi-hahiroth. Raising his staff, Moses stretched out his arm over the sea. The wind roared from on high and came down from the east, slicing the water in two, rolling it back and up so that walls of water rose like the sheer cliffs of the wadi from which the Israelites had come. A pathway of dry land sloped down where the depths of the sea had been and straight across and up to land on the other side of *yam suph*, the Red Sea.

"Move on!" Moses called out.

Heart leaping, Aaron took up the cry. "Move on!" Raising his staff, he pointed it forward as he followed Moses into the great, deep walls of water on either side.

The strong east wind blew all night as thousands upon thousands of Israelites raced for the other side. When Aaron and his family reached the eastern shore, they stood on the bluff with Moses, watching the multitude come through the sea. Laughing and crying, Aaron watched the people come out of Egypt. Impenetrable darkness was over the rocky terrain of the canyon through which they had come, but on this side, the Lord provided light so the Israelites and those traveling with them could see their way through the Red Sea.

When the last few hundred Israelites were hurrying up the slope, the fiery barrier holding the Egyptians back lifted and spread like a shimmering cloud over land and sea. The way opened for Pharaoh to pursue. Battle horns blasted in the distance. Chariots spread across the beach, then narrowed into ranks. Drivers whipped their horses down into the pathway into the sea.

Aaron continued standing on the bluff, leaning into the wind. Below him, Israelites struggled against exhaustion, hunched beneath the weight of their possessions. "They must hurry! They must . . ." He felt Moses' hand on his shoulder and drew back, submitting to the silent command to be calm. *"Don't be afraid,"* Moses had said. *"Just stand where you are!"* But it was so hard when he could see the charioteers coming, and the horsemen and troops behind. There were thousands of them, armed and trained, in a race to kill those who belonged to the God who had destroyed Egypt, the God who had killed their firstborn sons. Hatred drove them.

As the Egyptians neared the slope upward from the sea, a horse went down, overturning the chariot behind him, crushing the driver beneath. The chariots behind veered off. Horses screamed and reared. Some shook their riders loose and galloped back. The troops broke ranks in confusion. Some were trampled beneath the hooves of riderless horses.

The last few Israelites scrambled onto the eastern shore. The people screamed in terror of the Egyptians. "Israel!" Moses' voice boomed. He raised his hands. "Be still and know that the Lord is God!" He stretched out his hand and held his staff over the Red Sea. The east wind lifted. The waters spilled into the pathway, covering the panic-stricken Egyptians, the tumbling current drowning out their screams. A mighty flume of water rose skyward and then descended with a mighty splash.

The Red Sea rippled. All fell silent.

Aaron sank to the ground, staring at the azure water—tumultuous just seconds before, now tranquil. The waves lapped against the rocky shore and soft wind whispered.

Did they all feel as he did? Terror at seeing the power of the Lord visited upon the Egyptians, and exultation, for the enemy was no more! Egyptian soldiers washed up on the shore below him, hundreds facedown in the sand, their limbs gently lifting with the waves and resting again in the sand.

Aaron looked at his sons and daughters-in-law, his grandchildren gathered close around him. "Egypt boasted of its army and weapons, its many gods. But we will boast in the Lord our God." All the nations would hear what the Lord had done. Who would dare come against the people God had chosen to be His own? Look to the heavens! The God who laid the foundations of the earth and scattered the stars across the heavens was protecting them! The God who could call forth plagues and part the sea was overshadowing them! "Who will dare stand against a God like ours? We will live in security! We will thrive in the land God is giving us! No one will stand against our God! We are free and no one will ever enslave us again!"

"I will sing to the Lord, for He has triumphed gloriously!" Moses' voice carried on the wind. "He has thrown both horse and rider into the sea."

Miriam took her tambourine and hit it, shaking it and singing out. "I will sing to the Lord, for He has triumphed gloriously!" She hit the tambourine again, dancing and shaking the instrument. "He has thrown both horse and rider into the sea!" Aaron's daughters-in-law joined her, laughing and crying out in abandon, "Sing praises to the Lord! Sing praises . . ."

Aaron laughed with them, for it was a wonderful sight to see his aged sister dancing!

Moses strode down the rise. The people parted for him as the sea had parted for all of them. Aaron walked with him, tears streaming down his cheeks, his heart bursting. He had to sing out with his brother. "The Lord is my strength and my song; He has become my victory!" He felt young again, full of hope and adulation. The Lord had fought for them! Aaron looked up at the cloud spread over them. Light streamed shimmering colors as though God was pleased with their praise. Aaron raised his hands and shouted his thanks and praise.

Thousands cried out in jubilation, hands reaching toward the heavens. Some knelt, weeping, overcome with emotion. Women joined in Miriam's dance until there were ten, a hundred, a thousand women spinning and dipping.

"He is my God!" Moses sang out.

"He is my God!" Aaron sang out. He strode alongside his brother. His family members fell in behind them. Others gathered around, raising their hands and singing out.

Miriam and the women danced and sang. "He is our God!"

Aaron's sons sang out, faces flushed, eyes bright, hands raised. Filled with triumph, Aaron laughed. Who could doubt the power of the Lord now? With His mighty hand, He had broken the chains of their captivity. The Lord had mocked the gods of Egypt and swallowed up in the depths of the sea the army of the most powerful nation on earth! All those who had boasted that they would draw their swords and destroy Israel were now dead along the shores. Man planned, but God prevailed.

Who among the gods is like You, Lord? There is no other so awesome in glory who can work wonders! The nations will hear and tremble. Philistia, Edom, Moab, Canaan will melt away before us because we have the Lord, the God of Abraham, Isaac, and Jacob on our side! By the power of Your arm, they will be as still as a stone until we pass by. When we reach the land God has promised our ancestors, we will have rest on all sides!

"The Lord will reign forever and ever!" Moses raised his staff as he led the people away from the Red Sea.

"Forever and ever." *Our God reigns!*

As the jubilation subsided, the people rejoined their divisions. Families clustered together and followed Moses inland. Aaron called his sons and daughters-in-law close. "Keep within the ranks of the Levites." The tribal leaders held up their standards, and family members fell in behind them.

Aaron walked beside Moses. "It will be easier now that the worst is behind us. Pharaoh has no one to send after us. His gods have proven weak. We are safe now."

"We are far from safe."

"We are beyond the borders of Egypt. Even if Pharaoh could muster another army, who would heed his commands and follow when they hear what has happened here today! Word will spread through the nations of what the Lord has done for us, Moses. No one will dare come against us."

"Yes, we are outside the boundaries of Egypt, Aaron, but we will see in the days ahead whether we have left Egypt behind."

✦ ✦ ✦

It was not long before Aaron understood what his brother meant. As the people followed Moses into the Desert of Shur and headed north through the arid land toward the mountain of God, their songs of deliverance ceased. There was no water. What they had brought out of Egypt was nearly gone, and there had been no springs at which to relieve their growing thirst or replenish their water bags. The people mumbled when they rested. They muttered on the second day when no water was found. By the third day, anger brewed.

"We need water, Aaron."

Aaron's tongue began to cleave to the roof of his mouth, but he tried to calm those who complained. "The Lord is leading Moses."

"Into the desert?"

"Have you forgotten the Lord opened the sea?"

"That was three days ago, and we are without water now. Would that it had been a body of freshwater so that we could have filled our bags! Why is Moses leading us into the desert?"

"We are going back to the mountain of God."

"We'll be dead of thirst long before we get there!"

Aaron tried to restrain his anger. "Should Moses' own kin grumble against him?" Perhaps it was thirst that lessened his patience. "The Lord will provide what we need."

"From your mouth to God's ears!"

They were like tired, cranky children, whining and complaining. "When will we get there?!" Aaron felt compassion for those who were sick. Some of the Egyptians traveling with them had boils; others still suffered from rashes and infections caused by insect bites. They were weary with hunger and thirst, sweating doubt and fear of what added miseries lay ahead. "We need water!"

Did they think he and Moses were God that they could produce water from the rocks? "We have no water to give you." Their bags were just as flat as everyone else's. They were just as thirsty. Moses had given the last of his water to one of Aaron's grandsons this morning. Aaron had a few drops left, but hoarded them in case his brother became weak from dehydration. What would they do without Moses to lead them?

When they came to a rise, Moses pointed. "There!" Like thirsty animals, they stampeded toward the growing pond, falling on their knees to drink. But they reared back and spit it out, wailing, "It is bitter!"

"Don't drink it! It's poison!"

"Moses! What have you done? Brought us out here into the desert to die of thirst?"

Children wept. Women wailed. Men shouted, faces twisted in wrath. Soon they would pick up stones to hurl at Moses. Aaron called for them to remember what the Lord had done for them. Had they forgotten so quickly? "Only three days ago we were singing His praises! Only three days ago, you were saying you would never forget the good things the Lord had done for you! The Lord will provide what we need."

"When? We need water *now!*"

Moses headed for the hills, and the people cried out louder. Aaron stood between them and his brother. "Leave him alone! Let Moses seek the Lord! Be still. Be quiet so he can hear the voice of the Lord."

Lord, we do need water. You know how weak we are. We are not like You! We are dust. The wind blows and we are gone! Have mercy on us! God, have mercy! "The Lord will hear Moses and tell him what to do. The Lord sent my brother to deliver us, and he has."

"Delivered us unto death!"

Angry, Aaron pointed to the sky. "The Lord is with us. You have only to look up and see the cloud over us."

"Would that the cloud would give us rain!"

Aaron's face went hot. "Do you think the Lord does not hear how you speak against Him? Surely the Lord has not delivered us from Egypt only to die of thirst in the desert! Have faith!" Aaron prayed fervently even as he spoke. *Lord, Lord, tell us where to find water. Tell us what to do! Help us!*

"What are we going to drink?"

"We will die without water to drink!"

Moses returned within minutes, a gnarled piece of wood in his hands. He tossed it into the water. "Drink!"

The people scoffed.

Aaron knelt quickly, cupped his hands, and drank. Smiling, he ran his wet hands over his face. "The water is sweet!" His sons and their families knelt and drank deeply.

People ran for the water, crowding around the edges, pushing, shoving, and clamoring to get their share. They drank until they could drink no more and then filled their water bags.

"Listen carefully," Moses called out to them. "If you will listen carefully to the voice of the Lord your God and do what is right in His sight, obeying His commands and laws, then He will not make you suffer the diseases He sent on the Egyptians; for He is the Lord who heals you."

Had anyone heard him? Was anyone listening? They all seemed so intent on taking care of their immediate needs that they scarcely looked up. Aaron shouted, "Listen to Moses! He has words of life to give us."

But the people weren't listening, let alone listening carefully. They were too busy drinking the water God had provided to stop and thank God for providing it.

✦ ✦ ✦

When they left the sweetened waters of Marah, the people followed Moses and Aaron to Elim and camped. They ate dates from the palm trees and drank from the twelve springs. When they were rested, Moses led them into the Sin Desert.

Aaron heard the complaints daily until he was worn down by them. They had come out of Egypt only one month and fifteen days ago, and it seemed years. They walked through the arid land, hungry and thirsty, vacillating between the dream of the Promised Land and the reality of hardship in getting there.

The Egyptians traveling among the people stirred up more complaints. "Oh, that we were back in Egypt!" a woman cried. "It would have been better if the Lord had killed us there! At least there we had plenty to eat."

"Do you remember how we sat around pots of meat and ate all the food we wanted?" Her companion tore off a bit of unleavened bread and chewed it with distaste. "This stuff is awful!"

The men were more direct in their rebellion. Aaron could not go anywhere without hearing someone say, "You and your brother have brought us into this desert to starve us to death!"

When the Lord spoke to Moses again, Aaron rejoiced. With Moses, he carried the message to the people, speaking before gatherings of the tribes. "The Lord is about to rain down food from heaven for you! You are to go out each day and gather enough for that day. In this way, the Lord will test us to see if we will follow His instructions. On the sixth day, you are to pick up twice as much as usual. In the evening you will realize that it was the Lord who brought you out of the land of Egypt. In the morning you will see the glorious presence of the Lord. He has heard your complaints, which are against the Lord and not against us!"

When Aaron looked out toward the desert, the glory of the Lord shone in the cloud. The people huddled together in fear, silent as Moses raised his hands. "The Lord will give you meat to eat in the evening and bread in the morning, for He has heard all your complaints against Him. Yes, your complaints are against the Lord, not against us!"

And so it was. When the sun began to set, quail flew into the camp, thousands upon thousands of them. Aaron laughed as he watched his grandchildren run and catch birds and bring them to their mothers. Before the stars shone, the camp smelled of roasting meat.

Stomach full, Aaron slept well that night. He did not have dreams of the people stoning him or his bag spilling out sand instead of water. He awakened to people's voices. "What is it?" When he went outside his tent, he saw the ground covered with flakes like frost, white like coriander seed. He put a few pieces to his mouth. "It tastes like wafers with honey."

"*Manna*? What is it?"

"It is the bread God promised you. It is the bread of heaven." Had they expected loaves to rain down on them? "Remember! Collect only what you need for the day. No more than that. The Lord is testing us." Aaron took a jar and went out with his sons, daughters-in-law, and grandchildren. Miriam shooed the family along.

Moses squatted beside Aaron. "Fill another jar and place it before the Lord to be kept for the generations to come."

When they set out again, they traveled from place to place in the desert, and the people complained again because they were thirsty. Each time their wants were not immediately met, they grew louder and more angry. When they camped at Rephidim, their frustration overflowed.

"Why are we camped here in this forsaken place?"

"There is no water here!"

"Where is the land of milk and honey you promised us!?"

"Why do we listen to these men? We have done nothing but suffer since we left Egypt!"

"At least in Egypt we had food to eat and water to drink."

"And we lived in houses rather than tents!"

Aaron could not silence their fears with words, nor cool their anger. He was afraid for Moses' life, and his own, for the people grew more demanding with each miracle the Lord performed.

"Why are you arguing with me?" Moses pointed to the cloud. "And why are you testing the Lord?"

"Why did you bring us up out of Egypt? To make us and our livestock die of thirst?"

Aaron hated their ingratitude. "The Lord is providing bread for you every morning!"

"Bread with maggots in it!"

Moses held out his staff. "Because you collected more than you need!"

"What good is bread without water?"

"Is the Lord among us or not?"

How could they ask such questions when the cloud was over them by day and the pillar of fire by night? Each day brought renewed complaints and doubts. Moses spent every day in prayer. And so did Aaron when he wasn't forced to quiet the people's fears and encourage them with what the Lord had already done. They stopped their ears. Didn't they have eyes to see? What more did these people expect of Moses? Several picked up stones. Aaron called out to his sons and they stood around Moses. Had these people no fear of the Lord and what God would do to them if they killed His messenger?

"Aaron, gather some of the elders and follow me."

Aaron obeyed Moses and called for representatives he trusted from each of the tribes. The cloud descended on the side of the mountain where the people were camped. Aaron's skin prickled, for he saw a Man standing within the rock. How could this be? He closed his eyes tightly and opened them again, staring. The Man, if man he be, was still there. *Lord, Lord, am I losing my mind? Or is this a vision? Who is it who stands at the rock by the mountain of God when You overshadow us in the cloud?*

The people saw nothing.

"This place shall be called Testing and Arguing!" Moses struck the rock with his staff. "For the Israelites argued here and tested the Lord!" Water gushed forth, as though from a broken dam.

The elders ran back. "Moses has given us water from a rock!"

"Moses! Moses!" The people rushed toward the stream.

Exhausted, Moses sat. "God, forgive them. They don't know what they are saying."

Aaron could see how the responsibility of these people weighed on his brother. Moses heard their complaints and beseeched God for provision and guidance. "We will tell them again, Moses. It is the Lord who has rescued them. It is the Lord who provides. He is the one who has given them bread and meat and water."

Moses raised his head, his eyes full of tears. "They are a stubborn people, Aaron."

"And so shall we be! Stubborn in faith!"

"They still think like slaves. They want their food rations on time. They have forgotten the whips and the heavy labor, the unrelenting misery of their existence in Egypt, their cries to the Lord to save them."

"We will remind them of the plagues, the parting of the Red Sea."

"The sweetened waters of Marah and the streams of water from the rock at Mount Sinai."

"Whatever you tell me to say, I will say, Moses. I will shout the words God gives you from the hilltops."

"Moses!" It was a cry of alarm this time. "Moses!"

Aaron pushed himself to his feet. Would trouble never depart from them? He recognized the voice. "It's Joshua. What is it, my friend? What's happened now?"

The young man sank to his knees before Moses, panting, red-faced, sweat pouring down his cheeks, his tunic soaked through. "The Amalekites—" he gasped for breath—"they're attacking at Rephidim! They've killed those who haven't been able to keep up. Old men. Women. The sick . . ."

"Choose some of our men and go out to fight them!" Moses swayed as he stood.

Aaron caught hold of him. "You must rest. You haven't eaten all day, nor have you had so much as a cup of water." What would he do if Moses collapsed? Guide the people himself? Fear gripped him. "The Lord has called you to lead His people to the Promised Land, Moses. A man cannot do that without food, water, and rest. You can do nothing more today!"

"You are three years older than I, Aaron."

"But you are the one God has called to deliver us. You are the one bearing the weight of responsibility for God's people."

"God will deliver us." Moses sank down again. "Go out and fight them, Joshua. Call the Israelites to arms, and fight the army of Amalek." He sighed, exhausted. "Tomorrow, I will stand at the top of the hill with the staff of God in my hand."

+ + +

In the morning, Aaron and Moses went to the top of the hill overlooking the battlefield. Hur came with them. Moses held up his hands and Joshua and the Israelites gave battle cries and launched attack. Aaron saw how they cut through the Amalekites advancing on them. But after a while, the tide of the battle turned. Aaron looked to his brother to call on the Lord and saw Moses' hands at his side. He rested for a few moments and raised his hands again, and immediately the Israelites seemed to gain strength and advantage.

"I cannot keep this up long enough for the battle to be won." Exhausted, Moses' hands dropped to his sides.

"Here!" Aaron called to Hur. "Help me move this rock." They rolled and shoved the rock until it was at the crest of the hill overlooking the battle. "Sit, my brother, and we'll hold your hands up!" Aaron took his right arm and Hur his left and they held them up. As the hours wore on, Aaron's muscles trembled and burned from the effort, but his heart remained strong as he watched the battle below. The Israelites were prevailing against their enemies. By sunset, Joshua had overcome the Amalekites and put them to the sword.

Moses rallied long enough to pile up rocks for an altar. "It will be called 'The Lord Is My Banner.' Hands were lifted up to the throne of the Lord today. They have dared to raise their fist against the Lord's throne, so now the Lord will be at war with Amalek generation after generation. We must never forget what the Lord has done for us!"

When they returned to camp, Moses went into his tent to write the events meticulously on a scroll to be kept and read to Joshua and future generations.

✦ ✦ ✦

When they set out from Rephidim and headed into the Desert of Sinai, a messenger came from Midian. Moses' father-in-law, Jethro, was on his way to meet him and was bringing Moses' wife, Zipporah, and his sons, Gershom and Eliezer.

Miriam came into Aaron's tent. "Where was Moses going in such a hurry?"

"His father-in-law is here with Zipporah and the boys."

She hung the water bag. "She would've been better off staying in Midian."

"A wife belongs with her husband, and sons belong with their father."

"Does Moses have time for a wife when the people are always clamoring for his judgments? What time do you have for your own sons?"

Aaron broke bread with his family members each evening. He prayed with them. They talked about the events of the day and the blessings of the Lord. He rose, in no mood to listen to more of Miriam's complaints about what might happen in the days ahead. She liked managing his household. All well and good. He would leave her to her duties. But there was room enough for everyone beneath God's canopy.

Miriam made a sound of disgust. "The woman cannot even speak our language."

Aaron did not point out that Miriam had not helped Zipporah while they lived beneath the same roof in Egypt. Zipporah would learn Aramaic just as Moses had, and so would Moses' sons, Gershom and Eliezer.

Joshua came to Aaron's tent. "Moses' father-in-law has brought offerings and sacrifices to God. Moses said to come with all the elders of Israel to eat bread with them in the presence of God."

So, was Joshua now acting as Moses' spokesman?

When Aaron arrived at Jethro's camp, he was gratified to see Moses' smile. It had been a long time since his brother had been so happy. Zipporah did not take her eyes from Moses, but she looked thinner than Aaron remembered. Gershom and Eliezer were speaking rapidly in their mother's tongue as they vied for their father's attention. They looked more Midianite than Hebrew. That would change, given new circumstances. He watched his brother hug his sons against him, speaking tenderly to them.

For all the familiarity and affection between the brothers, there was an element of foreignness about Moses. Forty years with Egyptians and another forty years with Midianites set him apart from his people. Aaron sat among these people and felt uncomfortable. Yet, his brother was at ease now, speaking Midian and then Aramaic without faltering. Everyone understood him.

Aaron felt the difference between them. He still thought like a slave and looked to Moses as his master, waiting on his instructions. And he was glad for Moses who spoke to God before speaking to others. Sometimes Aaron wondered if Moses realized how God had been preparing him to lead from the day of his birth. Moses wasn't born to die in the Nile, but was saved by God and given into the hands of Pharaoh's own daughter so the son of Hebrew slaves would grow up a freeman in palace corridors, learning the ways of the enemy. Moses moved between worlds, from palaces to poor brick houses to a nomad's tent. He lived beneath the canopy of God Himself, hearing the Voice, talking with the Lord as Adam must have in the Garden of Eden.

Aaron was in awe of Moses, proud to be of his flesh and blood. Aaron, too, heard God's voice, but for Moses, it would always be different. His brother spoke to the Lord and God listened as a father would listen to his child. God was Moses' friend.

As night came and the pillar of fire glowed, the scent of Jethro's burnt offering filled the air. While they all partook of Jethro's feast of roasted lamb, dates, and raisin cakes, Moses spoke of all the things the Lord had done in bringing His people out of Egypt. There were bread and olive oil in which to dip it. Wine flowed freely. Nadab and Abihu held up their cups for more each time a servant passed near.

Surely, this is what life would be like when they reached the Promised Land. Ah, but Canaan would be even better, for the Lord Himself had said it would be a land of milk and honey. To have milk, there must be herds of cattle and flocks of goats. To have honey, there must be fruit trees and grapevines with blossoms where the bees could gather their nectar.

After centuries of slavery, Israel was *free*.

Aaron took another piece of lamb and some dates. This was the life to which he wanted to become accustomed.

+   +   +

Aaron's head ached from too much wine, and he had to force himself to rise the next morning. Moses would need his help soon. People would be clamoring for his judgment over whatever difficulties had arisen in the last twenty-four hours. Mediating and arbitrating went on from dawn to dusk. The people scarcely gave Moses time to eat. With so many thousands living so close to one another, clashes were inevitable. Each day had new challenges, more problems. A minor infraction could lead to heated arguments and fighting. The people didn't seem to know what to do with their freedom other than fight with one another and complain to Moses about everything! Aaron was torn between wanting them to think for themselves, and seeing the consequences when they did—trouble, out of which Moses had to judge fairly between opposing parties.

More people stood waiting for Moses' attention than had yesterday. Squabbles between tribes, arguments between tribal brothers. Maybe it was the heat that kept them from getting along. Maybe it was the long days and deferred hope. Aaron didn't have much patience today. He longed for his tent and a rolled-up blanket under his head.

"Is it like this every day?"

Aaron hadn't noticed Jethro's approach. "Every day gets worse."

"This is not good."

Who is he to talk? "Moses is our leader. He must judge the people."

"No wonder he has aged since the last time I saw him. The people are wearing him out!"

Two men shouted at one another while waiting in the line. Soon they were shoving each other, involving others. Aaron left Jethro quickly, hoping to curb the disturbance, calling on the assistance of several of his relatives to help break up the fight and restore order to those waiting.

The men were separated, but not before one was injured.

"Go and have someone see to the cut over your eye."

"And lose my place in line? *No!* I was here yesterday waiting, and the day before that! I'm not leaving. This man took the bride-price for his sister and now won't let me have her as my wife!"

"You want a wife? Here! Take mine!"

While some laughed, another lost his temper. "Maybe the rest of you can stand around making jokes, but I've got serious business. I can't stand here until the next full moon waiting for Moses to hack off this man's hand for stealing my sheep and making it a feast for his friends!"

"I found that mangy animal caught in a bramble! That makes it my sheep."

"Your son drove it away from my flock!"

"Are you calling me a liar?"

"A liar and a thief!"

Aaron's relatives helped separate the men. Angry, Aaron called for everyone to listen. "It would be easier for everyone if you all tried to get along with one another!" He gripped his staff. Sometimes they acted like sheep, Moses as their shepherd, and other times, they were more like wolves intent on tearing each other apart. "Anyone else who causes trouble in the line will be sent back to their tents. They can go to the end of the line tomorrow!"

The silence was anything but peaceful.

Jethro shook his head, expression grim. "This is not good. These people are worn-out from waiting."

For all the pleasurable memories of the feast the night before, Aaron was annoyed that the Midianite felt free to criticize. "It may not be good, but it is the way things must be. Moses is the one with the ear of God."

"It is almost evening, and there are more people here now than there were when the day began."

Aaron could see no good reason for stating the obvious. "You are a guest. It is not your problem."

"Moses is my son-in-law. I would like to see him live long enough to see his grandsons." He went into the tent. "Moses, why are you trying to do all this alone? The people have been standing here all day to get your help."

Aaron wanted to hook Jethro with his shepherd's staff and haul him from the tent. Who did this uncircumcised pagan think he was to question God's anointed?

But Moses answered with grave respect. "Well, the people come to me to seek God's guidance. When an argument arises, I am the one who settles the case. I inform the people of God's decisions and teach them His laws and instructions."

"This is not good, my son! You're going to wear yourself out—and the people, too. This job is too heavy a burden for you to handle all by yourself. Now let me give you a word of advice, and may God be with you."

Moses rose and asked those present to leave. Aaron didn't listen to the arguments, but upheld Moses' decision, urging those inside the tent to leave. They would not lose their places, but would have the first hearing when Moses sat as judge again. He signaled his relatives to send the rest to their tents, and tried to ignore the rumble of discontent. Aaron drew the tent flap down and rejoined his brother and Jethro.

"You should continue to be the people's representative before God, bringing Him their questions to be decided." Jethro sat, hands spread in appeal. "You should tell them God's decisions, teach them God's laws and instructions, and show them how to conduct their lives. But find some capable, honest men who fear God and hate bribes. Appoint them as judges over groups of one thousand, one hundred, fifty, and ten. These men can serve the people, resolving all the ordinary cases. Anything that is too important or too complicated can be brought to you. But they can take care of the smaller matters themselves. They will help you carry the load, making the task easier for you. If you follow this advice, and if God directs you to do so, then you will be able to endure the pressures, and all these people will go home in peace."

Aaron saw that Moses was listening intently and weighing, measuring the merit of Jethro's words. Had Moses always been this way or had circumstances made him so? The Midianite's suggestion did seem a reasonable one, but was this a plan the Lord would approve?

Aaron did not need Jethro to point out the lines deepening in Moses' face, or how his hair had turned white. His brother was thinner, not for lack of food but for lack of time to eat it. Moses did not like to leave important matters to another day, but with the increasing number of cases coming before him, he could not manage them all before sundown. And unless the Lord instructed him to do so, Aaron had no intention of sitting in Moses' judgment seat. But something had to be done. The dust and heat frayed the most patient among them, and every time Aaron heard arguing, he was in fear of what the Lord would do to these belligerent people.

Over the next few days, Aaron, Moses, and the elders met together to discuss men best suited to serve as judges. Seventy were chosen, able men of faith, trustworthy and dedicated to obeying the precepts and statutes God gave through His servant Moses. And there was some rest for Moses and for Aaron as well because of Jethro's suggestion.

Still, Aaron was glad to see the Midianite depart and take his servants with him. Jethro was a priest of Midian, and had acknowledged the Lord as greater than all other gods, but when the invitation to stay had been given by Moses, Jethro chose to go his own way. He had rejected being part of Israel, and therefore, rejected the Lord God as well. For all the love and respect Moses and Jethro shared for one another, their people were on different paths.

Sometimes Aaron found himself longing for the simplicity of slavery. All he had to do then was make his quota of bricks for the day and not draw the attention of the taskmaster. Now, he had all these thousands and thousands watching his every move, making demands, vying for his attention and the attention of Moses. Were there enough hours in a day to do all the work required? No! Was there any escape from this kind of servitude?

Worn down and burned out, lying sleepless on his pallet, Aaron couldn't keep the betraying thought from entering his mind and taunting him: *Is this the freedom I wanted? Is this the life I longed to live?* Granted, he no longer worked in a mud pit. He no longer had to fear the taskmaster's whip. But the joy and relief he had felt when death passed over him were gone. He had marched out into the desert, jubilant and filled with hope, secure in the future God had promised. Now, the constant carping, complaints, and pleas of the people weighed him down. One day they were praising the Lord and the next whining and wailing.

And he had no right to condemn them when he heard his own words echoing back from the days he had traveled this land in search of his brother. He, too, had complained.

When God brought the people into the Promised Land, then he would have rest. He would sit beneath the shade of a tree and sip nectar made from his own vines. He would have time to talk with his sons and surround himself with his grandchildren. He would sleep through the heat of the day, untroubled by worry.

The cloud was his solace. He would look up during the day and know that the Lord was near. The Lord was protecting them from the scorching heat of the sun. At night, the fire kept the darkness away. It was only when he was inside his tent, eyes closed, trapped in his own thoughts, assessing his own abilities, that his faith wavered.

In the third month after leaving Egypt, the cloud settled over Sinai and the people camped in the desert in front of the mountain where Aaron had found his brother, the mountain where the Lord had first spoken to Moses from the burning bush. The people were at the place where Moses had received the call. Holy ground!

As the Israelites rested, Aaron went up with Moses to the foot of the mountain. "Tend the flock, Aaron." From there, Moses went on alone.

Aaron hesitated, not wanting to go back. He watched Moses climb, feeling more bereft as the distance grew between them. Moses was the one who heard the Lord's voice most often and most clearly. Moses was the one who told Aaron what to say, what to do.

If only all men heard the Voice. And obeyed.

As I must obey. Aaron dug his staff into the rocky ground. "Come back soon, my brother. Lord, we need him. I need him." Turning away, Aaron went down to the camp to wait.

FOUR

❧❧❧❧❧❧❧

"You're to come with me this time, Aaron." Moses' words filled Aaron with joy. He had wanted . . . "When I go up before the Lord, you will stand so that the people will not come up the mountain. They must not force their way through or the Lord will break out against them."

The people. Moses always worried about the people, as Aaron knew he must.

Moses had already climbed the mountain twice, and Aaron longed to go and see the Lord for himself. But he was afraid to ask.

Moses and Aaron gathered the people and gave them instructions. "Wash your clothes and get ready for an important event two days from now. The Lord will descend on the mountain. Until the shofar sounds with a long blast, you must not approach the mountain, on penalty of death."

Miriam greeted him with tears. "Think of how many generations have longed for this day, Aaron. Just think of it." She clung to him, weeping.

His sons and their wives and children washed their clothing. Aaron was too excited to eat or sleep. He had yearned for the Voice to come upon him again, to hear the Lord, to feel God's presence over, around, in, and through him as he had before. He had tried to make his sons understand, his daughters-in-law, his grandchildren, even Miriam. But he could not explain the sensation of hearing God's voice when all around were deaf to it. He had felt the Word of the Lord from within.

Only Moses understood—Moses, whose experience of God must be far more profound than Aaron could even imagine. He saw it in his brother's face each time he returned from the mountain of God; he saw the change in Moses' eyes. For a time, on that mountain with God, Moses lived in the midst of eternity.

Now, all Israel would understand what neither man could explain. All Israel would hear the Lord!

Awakening before dawn, Aaron sat outside his tent, watching and waiting. Who could sleep on a day like this? But few were outside their tents. Moses came out of his tent and walked toward him. Aaron rose and embraced him.

"You're shaking."

"You are the friend of God, Moses. I am only your spokesman."

"You were called to deliver Israel, too, my brother." They went out into the open to wait.

The air changed. Lightning flashed and was followed by a low, heavy roll of sound. People peered out of their tents, tentative, frightened. Aaron called out to them. "Come! It is time." Miriam, his sons, and their wives and children came outside, washed and ready. Smiling, Aaron followed Moses and beckoned the people to follow.

Smoke billowed as from a giant furnace. The whole mountain shook, making the ground beneath Aaron's feet shake. His heart trembled. The air grew dense. Aaron's blood raced as his skin prickled with sensation. The cloud overhead swirled like great waves of dark gray moving around the mountaintop. A spear of light flashed and was answered by a deep roar Aaron could feel inside his chest. Another spear of light flashed and another, the sound so deep it rolled over and through him. From within the cloud came the sound of the ram's horn—long, loud, recognizable and yet alien. Aaron wanted to cover his ears and hide from the power of it, but stood straight, praying. *Have mercy on me. Have mercy on me.* All the great winds of the earth were coming through the shofar, for the Creator of all was blowing it.

Moses walked toward the mountain. Aaron stayed close to him, as eager as he was terrified. He couldn't take his eyes from the swelling smoke, the streaks of fire, the brilliance amidst the gray churning cloud. The Lord was coming! Aaron saw the red, orange, and gold flickering light descending, smoke billowing up from the mountain. *The Lord is a consuming fire!* The ground shook beneath Aaron's feet. There was no hint of ash in the air despite the fire and smoke from the mountaintop.

The deep blast of the shofar continued until Aaron's heart ached with the sound. He stopped when he came to the boundary God had set and watched as Moses went up the mountain alone to meet with the Lord face-to-face. Aaron waited, breath shallow, arms outstretched so that the people would know to stay back. The mountain was holy ground. When he looked over his shoulder, he saw Joshua and Miriam, Eleazar and little Phinehas, and others. They all stood looking up, faces rapt with awe.

And then Aaron heard the Lord again.

I am the Lord your God, who rescued you from slavery in Egypt.

The Word of the Lord rushed in, through, and out of Aaron.

Do not worship any other gods besides Me. Do not make idols of any kind, whether in the shape of birds or animals or fish. . . . Do not misuse the name of the Lord your God. . . . Remember to observe the Sabbath day by keeping it holy. . . . Honor your father and mother. Then you will live a long, full life in the land the Lord your God will give you. . . . Do not murder. . . . Do not commit adultery. . . . Do not steal. . . . Do not testify falsely against your neighbor. . . . Do not covet your neighbor's house. Do not covet your neighbor's wife, male or female servant, ox or donkey, or anything else your neighbor owns.

The Voice overshadowed and shone through, and drew up from the depths inside him and spilled out with unbridled joy. Aaron's heart sang even as the fear of the Lord filled him. His blood raced like a cleansing stream washing away everything in a flood of sensation. He felt the old life ebb and true *life* rush in. The Word of the Lord was there inside him, stirring, swelling, blazing bright in his mind, burning in his heart, pouring from his mouth. Pure ecstasy filled him as he felt the Presence, the Voice within, heard without, all around him. *Amen! And amen! Let it be! Let it be!* He wanted to stay immersed. *Reign in me, Lord. Reign! Reign!*

But the people were screaming, "Moses! Moses!"

Aaron didn't want to turn away from what he was experiencing. He wanted to scream back at them not to refuse the gift offered! *Embrace it. Embrace Him. Don't bring an end to the relationship we were born to have.* But it was already too late.

Moses came back. "Don't be afraid, for God has come in this way to show you His awesome power. From now on, let your fear of Him keep you from sinning!"

The people ran. "Come back!" Aaron called, but they had already fled in terror and remained at a distance. Even his own sons and their children! Tears of disappointment burned his eyes. What choice had he now but to go to them?

"You tell us what God says, Moses, and we will listen," the leaders called out. "But don't let God speak directly to us. If He does, we will die!"

"Come and hear for yourself what the Lord says to you."

They cowered from the sound and wind. They would not raise their heads and look up at the smoke and fire.

The thunder ceased and the wind died down. The shofar no longer sounded from the mountaintop. The earth grew still.

Aaron was in anguish over the silence. The moment was over, the opportunity lost forever. Did these people fail to understand what had been offered, what they had rejected? His throat was tight and hot as he held in his grief and disappointment.

Will I ever hear His voice again? Miriam said something to him, then to his sons. Aaron could not speak for the choking sorrow holding him where he was. He kept looking up at the glow of glory on Sinai. He had felt that fire burning within him, igniting his life with what it would mean to be like Moses. Oh, to hear the Lord daily, to have a personal relationship with God, the Creator of all things. And if all had heard, the heavy burden of responsibility for this multitude would be lifted from his back and from Moses'. Each person would have heard God's voice. Each person would know God's Word. Each would be made to understand and could then choose to obey the will of God.

The dream of it gripped him. Freedom from the responsibility of so many lives. And the people! No more complaining! No more grumbling! Every man in Israel would be equally yoked!

But the dream was already slipping away and the weight of God's call was on him again. Aaron remembered the days of his youth when he had no one to worry about but himself, no responsibility but to survive the slave masters and the Egyptian sun.

The fire on Sinai was a red-gold haze through his tears. *Oh, Lord, Lord, how I long to . . . to what?* He had no words, no explanation for what he felt. Just this pain at the center of his being, the ache of loss and longing. And he knew it would never really go away. God had called them to the mountain to hear His voice. God had called them to be His people. But they had rejected the proffered gift and cried out instead for a man to lead them: Moses.

✦   ✦   ✦

"Do not be downcast, Aaron." Miriam sat with him and put her hand on his head. "We could not help but be afraid. Such sound. Such fury."

Did she think he was a little boy to be comforted? He stood and moved away from her. "He is the Lord! You have seen the cloud and the pillar of fire. My own family fled like frightened sheep!" His sons and their wives and children had cried out for Moses like the rest. Did his words to them mean nothing? Was he still a slave? All these months he had tried to tell them what it was like to hear the voice of the Lord, to know it was God speaking and not some voice in his own imaginings. And when their chance came, what did they do? They ran from God. They shook inside their newly washed robes. They wept in terror and cried out for Moses to listen to God's voice and speak the Word to them.

"You're acting like a child, Aaron."

He turned on his sister. "You're not my mother, Miriam. Nor my wife."

Blushing, she opened her mouth to retort, but he walked past her out of the tent. There was no silencing her. She was like the wind, ever blowing, and he was in no mood to listen to her counsel, or her complaining.

Moses approached. "Gather the people and have them assemble at the foot of the mountain."

They all came, Aaron leading them. Joshua was already at the foot of the mountain, standing beside Moses. Aaron was annoyed that Eliezer and Gershom were not there to serve their father. Why should it be this young man of the tribe of Judah who stood near Moses rather than one of their own relations? From the beginning of the journey out of Egypt, Joshua had stationed himself as near Moses as possible, serving him with every opportunity given. And Moses had embraced the young man as his servant. Even when Jethro had brought Eliezer and Gershom with Zipporah, Joshua remained at Moses' side. Where were Moses' sons this morning? Aaron spotted them among the people, standing on either side of their ailing mother.

"Hear the Word of the Lord!" The throng fell silent and listened as Moses told them all the words the Lord had given him, laws to keep the people from sinning against one another, laws to protect foreigners who lived among them and followed the way of the Lord, laws concerning property when it would be given to them, laws of justice and mercy. The Lord proclaimed three festivals to be celebrated each year: the Festival of Unleavened Bread to remind them of their deliverance from Egypt, the Festival of Harvest, and the Festival of the Final Harvest to give thanks for the Lord's provision. Wherever they lived in the Promised Land, all the men of Israel were to appear before the Lord at a place the Lord set during these three celebrations.

No longer would they be able to do whatever was right in their own eyes.

"The Lord is sending His angel before us to lead us safely to the land He has prepared for us. We must pay attention to Him, and obey all of His instructions. Do not rebel against Him, for He will not forgive your sins. He is the Lord's representative—He bears His name."

Aaron's heart raced as he remembered the Man he had seen walking in front of his brother. He had not been a figment of his imagination! Nor was the Man who had stood within the rock at Mount Sinai and from whom the water had flowed. They were one and the same, the Angel of the Lord. Leaning in, he drank in his brother's words.

"If you are careful to obey Him, following all of the Lord's instructions, then He will be an enemy to our enemies, and He will oppose those who oppose us." Moses spread his arms, palms up. "We must serve only the Lord our God. If we do, He will bless us with food and water, and He will keep us healthy. There will be no miscarriages or infertility among our people, and He will give us long, full lives. When we get to the Promised Land, we must drive out the people who live there or they will cause us to sin against the Lord because their gods are a snare." He lowered his hands. "And what do you say to the Lord?"

Aaron called out, "Everything the Lord says, we will do!" And the people repeated his words until over a million voices rang out before the Lord God of Israel.

Early the next morning, Moses built an altar of earth before the mountain of God. Twelve uncut stone pillars stood, one for each of the tribes of Israel. Young Israelite men were chosen to bring forward sacrificed young bulls as fellowship offerings to the Lord. Moses took half the blood of the bulls and put it into bowls. The other half he sprinkled on the altar. He read the Word of the Lord that he had written into the Book of the Covenant, and the people said again that they would obey the Word of the Lord. The air was filled with the scent of burnt offerings.

Moses turned to him. "Aaron, you and your two sons, Nadab and Abihu, and the seventy leaders are to come with me up the mountain." Aaron savored the command. He had waited for this moment, a time when he would not only hear the Word of the Lord, but stand in His presence. Joy mingled with fear as he followed his brother up Mount Sinai, the elders behind him.

The climb was not easy. Surely, it was the Lord Himself who had given Moses the strength to make this climb four times before! Aaron felt every day of his eighty-three years as he followed in his brother's footsteps, weaving his way upward along the rough path. His muscles ached. He had to pause for breath and start again. Above was the swirling cloud of the Lord, the fire on the mountaintop. When Aaron, his sons, and the elders reached a level space, Moses stood waiting. "We will worship the Lord here."

Aaron saw the God of Israel. Under His feet there seemed to be a pavement of brilliant sapphire, as clear as the heavens. Surely now, Aaron would die. He trembled at the sight before him and fell on his knees, bowing his head to the ground.

Arise and eat. Drink the water I give you.

Never before had Aaron felt such exultation and thanksgiving. He never wanted to leave this place. He forgot all those around him and those who waited on the plains below. He lived in the moment, filled up and fulfilled with the sight of God's power and majesty. He felt small but not insignificant, one among many, but cherished. The manna tasted of heaven; the water restored his strength.

Moses put his hand on Aaron's shoulder. "The Lord has called me up the mountain to give me the Law for His people. Stay here and wait for us until we come back."

"We?"

"Joshua is going up the mountain with me."

Aaron felt a cold wave of anger. He looked past Moses to the younger man. "He is an Ephraimite, not a Levite."

"Aaron." Moses spoke quietly. "Are we not to obey the Lord in all things?"

His stomach clenched tight. His mouth trembled. "Yes." *I want to go,* he longed to say. *I want be the one at your side! Why do you set me aside now?*

All the feelings he had as a lonely boy sitting in the reeds came rushing back. Someone else was being chosen.

Moses spoke to them all. "If there are any problems while I am gone, consult with Aaron and Hur, who are here with you."

Bereft, Aaron watched Moses turn away and take the high path farther up the mountain, Joshua close behind. Tears burned in Aaron's eyes. He blinked them away, fighting against the emotions warring inside him. *Why Joshua? Why not me?* Hadn't he been the one to find Moses in the desert? Hadn't he been the one God had chosen as Moses' spokesman? Aaron's throat closed, hot, tight, choking him. *It's not fair!*

As Moses and Joshua ascended, Aaron remained with the others, and the weight of people was heavier now than it had ever been before.

✦   ✦   ✦

For six days, Aaron and the others remained on the mountain, the cloud shrouding its top, Moses and Joshua within sight, but separated from them. And then on the seventh day, the Lord called to Moses from within the cloud. Aaron and the others heard the Voice, like low, rolling thunder. Moses rose and continued up the mountain, Joshua following for a ways and then remaining like a sentry on guard as Aaron's brother entered the cloud. A rush of sound came, and a blaze of fire flashed brilliant from the mountain peak. From below, they could hear people screaming.

"Aaron!" Hur cried out. "The people need us to reassure them."

Aaron kept his back to the others. "Moses said to wait here."

"The elders are going down."

"We were to wait!"

"Aaron!" Hur called out. "They need you!"

Aaron wept bitterly. *Why? God, why must I be left behind?*

"Moses said they were to come to us for counsel. If they cross the boundaries, the Lord will strike out against them!"

Aaron shut his eyes tightly. "All right!" His shoulders sagged as he turned away. He started back down the mountain pathway, fully intending to do what the Lord required of him.

Glancing back one last time, Aaron looked up. Joshua stood in the haze at the edge of the cloud that shrouded the mountain.

✦ ✦ ✦

The elders surrounded Aaron, frightened, confused. "It's been ten days, Aaron! And the fire has burned constantly."

"The people believe Moses is dead."

"Would the Lord God kill His anointed?" Aaron said, angry.

"No man could live in the midst of that fire!"

"Nor has Joshua returned."

"Someone should go up and see if——"

Aaron rose, glaring at his sons. "No one is to go near the mountain! Have you forgotten the boundaries God set? It is holy ground! Any who come near will be struck dead by the Lord!"

"Then surely Moses and Joshua are dead already."

"My brother is alive! The Lord Himself called him to the top of the mountain to receive the Word. He will come back to us!"

Korah shook his head. "You are a dreamer, Aaron! Look up! What man can survive such a fire?"

"That fire will consume *you* if you rebel against the Lord!"

They all spoke at once.

Aaron shouted, "Go back to your tents. Gather the manna each morning as you have been instructed. Drink the water the Lord has supplied. And wait as I wait!" He went back inside his tent and yanked the flap closed. He sat on a cushion and covered his face. He didn't want to listen to their doubts. He had enough doubts of his own. Moses said, "wait." *I have to wait. God, help me wait!*

He thought of Joshua standing up there beside Moses. Joshua, the one his brother had chosen . . .

"Don't you think you should . . ."

He glared at his sister.

She sighed loudly. "I was just thinking . . ." She held his gaze for a moment and then lowered her head and went back to carding wool.

Even Aaron's sons plagued him with questions. "I don't know why he remains so long on the mountain! I don't know if he is well! Yes! He is an old man, and I am older still. If you keep on besieging me, you will wear me down to the grave with your demands!"

Only after a long, exhausting day of counseling and judging did Aaron stand alone. While the people slept, he looked up at the mountain and watched the consuming fire. How had Moses born such pressure? How had he listened to case after case and kept himself clear of sides?

I can't do this, Moses. You've got to come down off that mountain. You've got to come back!

Was Moses dead? He shut his eyes tightly at the thought, fear welling up inside him. Was that why there was no sign of him after so many days?

And where was Joshua? Was he still waiting on that rocky slope? His provisions must be gone by now.

The people were like sheep without a shepherd. Their questions had become like bleats and *baaa*s. Aaron knew he was going to have to do something to keep the people from wandering off. Some wanted to go back to Egypt. Others wanted to take their flocks to Midian pastures. No one was content.

He couldn't sleep. He gathered the manna with everyone else, but could barely eat. Everywhere he went, he was met with the same questions:

"Where is Moses?" *On the mountain with God.*

"Is he alive?" *I am certain he is.*

"When is he coming back?" *I don't know. I don't know!*

✦   ✦   ✦

Thirty-five days went by, then thirty-six, thirty-seven. With each day that passed, Aaron's fear and anger grew.

It was hot inside the tent, but he didn't go outside. He knew the moment he did, people would clamor for answers he didn't have. He was sick of their grumbling and whining. How should he know what was happening on the mountain?

Moses! Why do you linger?

Did his brother have any idea what Aaron was going through with these complainers down here on the dusty plains? Or was Moses just basking in the presence of the Lord? Aaron knew if he didn't do something soon, these people would stone him to death and then scatter across the wilderness like wild donkeys!

Miriam looked at him gravely. "They're calling for you."

"I can hear."

"They sound angry, Father."

They sound ready to stone someone.

"You have to do something, Aaron."

He turned on Miriam. "What would you suggest?"

"I don't know, but they are past patience. Give them something to occupy them!"

"Have them make bricks again? Build a city here at the foot of the mountain?"

"Aaron!" The elders were outside his tent. *"Aaron!"* Korah was with them. Even Hur was losing faith. "Aaron, we must talk with you!"

He fought tears. His heart trembled. "God has abandoned us." Maybe the only one God cared about was Moses. For the fire still burned on the mountain. Moses was still up there alone with God. Maybe God and Moses had forgotten about him and the people. His breath shook as he exhaled.

If Moses was still alive. Forty days had passed. An eighty-year-old man couldn't last . . .

The elders and people surrounded him when he came outside. He felt oppressed by their impatience. They were no longer worried about his brother. The tribes were ready to split off and go in a dozen directions rather than remain at the foot of the mountain. They were no longer willing to hear the words, "Wait here until Moses returns."

"This man Moses, who brought us here from Egypt, has disappeared. We don't know what has happened to him."

This man Moses? They saw the miracle God performed in Egypt! They saw Moses hold out his staff while God opened the Red Sea so they could cross over on dry land! And they could speak about Moses' disappearance with such indifference? Fear gripped Aaron. If they cared so little about his brother who had delivered them from Pharaoh, how long before they despised him too?

"You must lead us, Aaron."

"Tell us what to do."

"We can't stay here forever waiting for an old man who is dead."

"Make us some gods who can lead us!"

Aaron turned away, but there were more people behind him. He looked into their eyes. Everyone was talking at once, crying out, pushing. Some raised fists. He felt the heat of their fetid breath, the pull of their fear, the shove of their anger.

"Give them something to do," Miriam had said. *"Give them something to occupy them!"*

"All right!" Aaron shoved back, wanting distance between himself and the people. How he longed to be up on that mountain. Better dead in the flames of God than alive down here on the plain, with the dust and the rabble. He hated being pushed and shoved. He hated their demands and complaints. He hated their constant whining. "All right!"

When they fell silent, he felt relief and then pride. They were listening to him, leaning toward him, looking to him to lead.

To give them something to do.

Yes, I'll give them something to do. "Take off the gold earrings that your wives, your sons, and your daughters are wearing." He would not ask these men to give up their own ornaments. "Bring them to me."

They scattered quickly to do his will. Exhaling, he went back into his tent. Miriam stood, shaking in confusion. "What are you doing, Aaron?"

"I'm giving them something to do!"

"What are you giving them to do?"

Ignoring her, Aaron emptied baskets and set them out. People came with gifts and offerings. The baskets were soon overflowing. Every man and woman, boy and girl gave a pair of gold earrings. Everyone in the camp participated, even Miriam and his sons and their wives.

Now what?

Aaron built a fire and melted the earrings, taking the gold God had given them from the vanquished Egyptians. *How do you make something that represents the God of the universe? What would He look like?* Aaron looked up at the mountain. Moses was up there looking at God. And Joshua was with him.

Aaron made a mold and poured the molten gold into it. Weeping angrily, he fashioned a golden calf. It was ugly and roughly hewn. Surely, when the people looked on his effort—and then up at the mountain still ablaze with the glory of the Lord—they would see the difference between the false statues of Egypt and the living God who could not be shown by human hands. How could they not see?

"These are your gods, O Israel!" the elders called out. "These are the gods who brought you out of Egypt!"

Aaron shuddered as he looked up at the consuming fire still ablaze on Mount Sinai. Was God watching, or was He too busy talking to Moses? Did God understand what was happening down here? *Do not worship any other gods besides Me.*

Fear gripped Aaron. He tried to justify himself. He tried to rationalize why he had made the idol. Hadn't God always given the people exactly what they asked for and then disciplined them? Wasn't Aaron doing the same thing? They demanded water. God gave it. They demanded food. God gave it. And each time, discipline had followed.

Discipline.

Aaron's body went cold.

The people bowed down to the golden calf, oblivious of the cloud and the fire above them. Had they become so accustomed to the sight that they no longer noticed them? They chanted and moaned their reverence for the golden calf that could not hear, see, or think. No one looked up as he did.

Nothing happened. The cloud remained cool; the fire above, warm.

Aaron took his eyes from the mountain and watched the people.

An hour passed, then another. They grew tired of bowing down to the ground. One by one, they stood and looked at Aaron. He could feel the gathering storm, the low hum.

He built an altar of stones in front of the calf as it stood before the mountain, uncut stones as God required. "Tomorrow there will be a festival to the Lord!" He would remind them of the manna God provided. They would have rested by then. Things always looked better in the morning.

Laughing and clapping their hands, they scattered like children eager to make preparations. Even his own sons and their wives were eager for the next day to come as they laid out the finery of Egypt.

The elders presented the burnt offerings and fellowship offerings to the golden calf as the sun's glow lit the eastern horizon. With that formality completed, the people sat down to feast. Scorning the manna that rained softly, they slaughtered lambs and goats to roast. Nor did they drink the water that still flowed unceasingly from the rock near Mount Sinai. They drank deeply of fermented milk. Those with harp and lyre played the music of Egypt.

Sated and drunk, the people rose to indulge themselves in dancing. They became louder and more raucous as the day wore on. Fights broke out. People stood around, laughing as blood was shed. Young women eager to be caught ran laughing from the young men pursuing them.

Face red with shame, Aaron went inside his tent. His younger sons, Eleazar and Ithamar, sat in grim silence while Miriam huddled in the back with their wives and children, hands over her ears. "This isn't what I intended. You know it isn't!" Aaron sat grimly, head down as he listened to the shouting outside his tent.

"You have to do something to stop it, Aaron."

"It was your idea in the first place."

"My idea?! This isn't what I—" She clamped her mouth shut.

He covered his face. Everything was out of control. The people were running wild. If he tried to stop them now, they'd kill him, and nothing would change.

The people took pleasure anywhere and any way they wanted. They had not made this much noise when they left Egypt on the day after the Angel of Death had passed over them! It was up to the Lord now to deal with them. If the Lord remembered them at all. . . .

He heard a low rumble and felt cold. He held his breath until his lungs hurt and breathed slowly, quietly. His hands were shaking.

Nadab and Abihu entered the tent, swaying, skin containers limp in their hands. "Why are you in here? There's a celebration outside."

A man's voice wailed in the distance, and the sound echoed and grew louder in rage and anguish.

Aaron felt the hair on the back of his neck rise. "Moses!" He threw the tent flap back and ran out, relief filling him. His brother was alive! *Moses!* Pushing his way through the revelers, he ran toward the boundary at the foot of the mountain, eager to welcome his brother home. Everything would be all right now. Moses would know what to do.

When Aaron came near the mountain, he saw his brother high on the pathway, head thrown back as he wailed. Aaron stopped running. He looked back and saw the debauchery, the shameless parading of sin. When he looked up again, he wanted to back away, to run and hide in his tent. He wanted to cover his head with ashes. He knew what Moses saw from his high place.

And God could see too.

With a scream of rage, Moses raised two stone tablets above his head and hurled them. Aaron drew back, terrified the Lord would give Moses strength to bring the weight of those two slabs down on his head. But the tablets shattered on the ground, merely pelting Aaron with bits of stone and a cloud of dust. The loss hit him, and he covered his face.

Pandemonium prevailed around him as people scattered. Others paused in confusion, all talking at once. Some were too drunk and caught up in their debauchery to hear or care that the prophet of God had returned. Some had the audacity to call out greetings to Moses and invite him to join the celebration!

Aaron drew back into the crowd, hoping to hide his shame among the others, hoping Moses would forget about him for the moment and not make his disgrace public.

His brother went straight through the throng and stood before the golden calf. "Burn it!" At Moses' command, Joshua tumbled the idol. "Melt it down and grind the gold into dust and scatter it over the water. Let them drink it!"

The crowd parted like the Red Sea as Moses walked toward Aaron. It took every ounce of Aaron's courage not to run from his own brother. Moses had once murdered an Egyptian in anger and buried him beneath the Egyptian sand. Would Moses now raise his hand against his own brother and strike him down? Moses' knuckles whitened around his shepherd's staff.

Aaron closed his eyes. *If he kills me, so be it. It's no less than I deserve.*

"What did the people do to you?" Moses demanded. "How did they ever make you bring such terrible sin upon them?"

"Don't get upset," Aaron replied. "You yourself know these people and what a wicked bunch they are. They said to me, 'Make us some gods to lead us, for something has happened to this man Moses, who led us out of Egypt.' No one knew what happened to you. It's been over forty days, Moses! I didn't know if you were alive or dead! What did you expect me to do?"

His brother's eyes flashed. "You accuse me?"

Mortified, Aaron whined, "No. I didn't know what to do, Moses. So I told them, 'Bring me your gold earrings.' When they brought them to me, I threw them into the fire—and out came this calf!" He felt the heat flood his cheeks, and he could only hope his beard covered the telltale color of his lie.

It didn't. The fury died in Moses' eyes, but the look that came in its place filled Aaron with shame far deeper than any fear he had felt. He would have felt better if Moses had beaten him with his staff. Eyes filling with tears, Aaron bowed his head, unable to look at Moses. The people were running wild, and Aaron knew it was his fault! He had not had the strength to shepherd this wayward flock. As soon as Moses was out of sight, he had begun to weaken. Was Israel now a laughingstock to the nations watching them? The people wouldn't even listen to Moses! They were out of control!

Moses turned his back on Aaron and went back to stand at the entrance of the camp. Facing in, he shouted. "All of you who are on the Lord's side, come over here and join me."

Aaron ran to his brother. "What are you going to do, Moses?"

"Take your place at my side."

Moses did not look at him, but surveyed the riotous Israelites. Aaron knew that look and shuddered. Aaron saw his sons and relatives among the throng. Fear filled him for their sake. "Come on! Hurry! Stand with Moses!" His sons came running and so did his uncles and cousins and their wives and children. "Hurry!" Would fire come from the mountain?

Eliezer and Gershom raced to their father, taking their places behind Moses. Even Korah the troublemaker came. The Levites stood as one with Moses. Joshua, an Ephraimite, stood firm beside his mentor, grim-faced when Moses' and Aaron's relatives continued to ignore Moses' command.

Moses raised his staff and spoke to the Levites. "This is what the Lord, the God of Israel, says: 'Strap on your swords! Go back and forth from one end of the camp to the other, killing even your brothers, friends, and neighbors.'"

Joshua drew his sword. Standing in horrified silence, Aaron watched as he cleaved the head of a man mocking Moses. Blood sprayed as the body sank lifeless to the ground.

The hair rose on the back of Aaron's neck. "Moses! I am more guilty than these wretched people! It's my fault they behave like sheep without a shepherd."

"You're standing with me."

"Let the blame fall on me."

"It is for the Lord to decide!"

"Perhaps they didn't hear over the din." The screams of the dying tore at Aaron's heart. "Have mercy! How can I kill them when it's my own weakness that has brought this upon them?"

"They've shunned their opportunity for salvation!"

"Speak to them again, Moses. Shout louder!"

Moses' face darkened. "Be silent! They will learn—*as you will learn*—to heed the Word of the Lord when it is spoken."

Obey or die.

Joshua and the others waded into the throng. A man red-faced with rage, shouting blasphemies, ran at Moses. "No!" Aaron drew his sword and hacked the man down. Rage such as he had never before experienced flooded his body.

The sheep he had been left to tend had become attacking wolves barking obscenities. A drunken man shouted curses at the mountain of God, and Aaron silenced him forever. The smell of blood and death filled his nostrils. His heart pounded. Another man laughed hysterically. Aaron swung his sword and took off the man's head.

Sounds of terror filled the camp. Women and children scattered. Men turned this way and that. Those who rose up were cut down. Aaron went through the camp with the Levites, killing any who stood against the Lord. Those who cried out for the Lord's mercy and prostrated themselves, he left alive in the dust.

The battle ended swiftly.

Silence fell.

All Aaron could hear were moans and the rushing blood in his ears. He stood among the dead, his shepherd's robes stained with blood. Dazed, he looked around, his pulse slowing. Anguish filled him . . . and guilt too heavy to bear.

Oh, Lord, why am I yet alive? I am as guilty as any of them. More so.

His arm lost strength as he surveyed the carnage.

These people needed a strong shepherd, and I failed them. I've sinned against You. I don't deserve Your mercy. I don't deserve anything!

His bloodied sword hung at his side. His chest heaved.

Why have You spared me?

Sobbing, Aaron sank to his knees.

All the rest of the day, the tribes carried their dead outside the camp and burned them.

No one came near Aaron as he sat, and wept, and threw dust on his head.

+   +   +

When Aaron entered his tent, Miriam was kneeling beside Nadab, wiping his ashen face. Abihu was vomiting into a bowl. His sister looked up at him. "How many?"

He saw no accusation in her eyes. "More than three thousand." The trembling had started, and his knees would no longer hold him. He sat heavily, his sword dropping beside him. Moses had praised the Levites and said they had been set apart to the Lord for what they had done today. They had fought and killed some of their own sons and brothers, and been blessed for it because they had chosen the Lord God of Israel over their erring fellowmen.

Aaron looked at his two elder sons and wanted to weep. If Eleazar and Ithamar had not found them and brought them inside the tent before Moses had returned to camp, they would be dead. But they had been found in time. Nadab and Abihu had come out and fought beside him, drink firing their courage. Sober now, they were aware of where they might have been had their younger brothers not dragged them away from their revelry. Aaron stared at them. How were they any different from those who had been killed? How was he any different? At least, they shared his shame. They couldn't look him in the face.

The next morning, Moses assembled his people. "You have committed a terrible sin, but I will return to the Lord on the mountain. Perhaps I will be able to obtain forgiveness for you."

Heartsick, Aaron stood in front, sons behind him, elders around them. His brother would not even look at him. Turning away, Moses headed back up the mountain. With Joshua.

Moses had only been gone a few hours when the plague hit, and more died from sickness than had died by the sword.

✦   ✦   ✦

Aaron stood in front of the repentant multitude, watching Moses make his way down the mountain path. It had been his sin that had brought death on so many, his weakness that allowed them to stray. He fought tears, overwhelmed with relief that his brother had come back so soon. Moses came toward him, staff in hand, his face filled with compassion. Aaron's throat closed and he hung his head.

Moses put his hand on Aaron's shoulder. "We are to leave this place, Aaron." He stepped away and addressed the people. "We are to leave this place!"

Aaron realized then that Moses no longer needed him. Where once he had been helpful, now he had proven himself unworthy to act as spokesman. Was this the cost of his sins? To be cut off from fellowship from the one he loved most in the world? How could he bear it?

Moses stood alone before the people, Joshua at a distance, watching. "We are to go up to the land the Lord solemnly promised Abraham, Isaac, and Jacob. He told them long ago that He would give this land to their descendants. And He will send an angel before us to drive out the Canaanites, Amorites, Hittites, Perizzites, Hivites, and Jebusites. Theirs is a land flowing with milk and honey. But the Lord will not travel along with us. . . ."

Tearing his robes, Aaron fell to his knees, weeping in anguish. This, then, was the cost of his weakness. All the people would be cut off from the Lord who had delivered them from Egypt!

"The Lord will not travel along with us, for we are a stubborn, unruly people. If He did, He would be tempted to destroy us along the way."

The people wailed and threw dust on their heads.

Moses did not weaken. "Remove your jewelry and ornaments until the Lord decides what to do with us!"

Aaron was first to strip off his earrings and gold bracelets. He rose and left them at the boundary near the foot of the mountain. The people followed his example.

Remaining in camp, Aaron grieved as he watched Moses go to the tent he had pitched at a distance. If Moses ever spoke to him again, it would be more than he deserved. Aaron watched as the cloud moved from the mountaintop and came down before the entrance of Moses' Tent of Meeting. He stood at the entrance of his own tent with his sons and daughters-in-law, his grandchildren and Miriam, and bowed low, worshiping the Lord and giving thanks for his brother, God's messenger and the people's mediator. Aaron and all those who belonged to him did not leave the front of their tents until the pillar of cloud returned to the mountaintop.

And the people followed his example.

✦   ✦   ✦

When Moses did not return to camp, Aaron gathered his courage and went out. He found his brother on his knees chiseling rock. Aaron went down on one knee beside him. "Can I help you?"

"No."

Nor did it appear could Joshua, who stood at the entrance of the tent where Moses met with God. Even when Moses came into the camp, Joshua remained at the Tent of Meeting, as it had come to be called.

"I'm sorry, Moses." His throat was so tight and hot he had to swallow hard before he could say more. "I'm sorry I failed you." He had not been strong enough to serve the Lord faithfully. He had let his brother down.

Moses' face was gaunt from days of fasting and praying on the mountaintop, but his eyes glowed with an inner fire. "We have all failed, my brother."

My brother. Forgiven, Aaron's knees buckled. He knelt, head down, tears streaming. He felt Moses' hands on his head and then his kiss.

"And could I condemn you when the tablets I threw at the people from the mountain were God's workmanship? It is not the first time I have allowed anger to rule me, Aaron. But the Lord is merciful and gracious. He is slow to anger and rich in unfailing love and faithfulness. He shows this unfailing love to many thousands by forgiving every kind of sin and rebellion." The weight of Moses' hands lifted. "But even so, He does not leave sin unpunished. If He did, the people would scatter wild across the desert and do whatever was right in their own eyes." Moses gripped Aaron's shoulder. "Now, go back to camp and watch over the people. I must finish chiseling out these tablets by morning and carry them back up the mountain."

Aaron wished the Lord had given him some act of penance for his sins. A whipping might make him feel better. Leaving him in charge brought the full weight of his failure down on his shoulders. Joshua was looking at him, but Aaron saw no condemnation in the younger man's eyes.

Aaron rose and left his brother alone. He prayed that the Lord God of Israel would give Moses strength to do as the Lord commanded. For the sake of them all.

Without the Lord, the Promised Land would be an empty dream.

+ + +

Eleazar ran inside the tent. "Father, Moses is coming down the mountain."

Aaron hurried outside with his sons and hastened toward the boundary line, but when he saw Moses' white hair and glowing face, he drew back in fear. Moses did not look like the same man who had gone up the pathway days ago. It was as though the Lord Himself was coming down that pathway, the Law He had written on two stone slabs tucked beneath His arm.

The people ran.

"Come and hear the Word of the Lord!" Moses' voice carried across the plain.

Stomach clenched with fear, Aaron obeyed. Others followed, tentative, ready to flee at the first sign of threat.

This is my brother, Moses, Aaron told himself in order to have the courage to stand before the mountain. *My brother, the chosen prophet of God.* Was the Shekinah glory of God inhabiting Moses? Or was this merely a reflection of the Lord? Sweat beaded and ran down the back of his neck. Aaron didn't move. He opened his heart and mind to listen to every word Moses said, promising himself he would live by it, no matter how hard it was.

"On these tablets I have written the Word the Lord gave me, for He has made a covenant with me and with Israel." Moses read for all to hear the Law God had handed down from Mount Sinai. He had spoken the words once, but now they were written in stone and could be kept as a perpetual reminder of God's call on their lives.

When Moses finished speaking, he surveyed the multitude. No one spoke. Aaron knew Moses was waiting for him to come near, but he did not dare. Joshua remained at Moses' side—a silent, solemn sentry. Moses spoke to him quietly. Joshua said something in response. Taking the thin shawl from around his shoulders, Moses veiled his face.

Aaron approached him cautiously. "Is all well now between us, Moses?"

"Don't be afraid of me."

"You are not the same man you were."

"As you are changing, Aaron. When you receive and obey the Word of the Lord, you cannot help but change when you stand in His presence."

"My face does not glow with holy fire, Moses. I will never be as you are."

"Do you wish for my place?"

Aaron's heart drummed. He decided on truth. "I did. And I led like a rabbit rather than a lion." Perhaps it was because he couldn't see his brother's face that he felt free to confess. "I have envied Joshua."

"Joshua has never heard the voice of God as you have, Aaron. He is close to me because he longs to be close to God and do whatever God asks of him."

Aaron felt the envy rise. Here it was again. Another choice. He let his breath out slowly. "There is no other like him in all Israel." Strange that in the wake of that confession, he felt affection for the younger man, and hope that he would stand firmer than his elders had.

"Joshua is wholeheartedly for God. Even I wavered."

"Not you, Moses."

"Even I."

"Not as greatly as I did."

Moses smiled faintly. "Will we compete over whose sin is greatest?" He spoke gently. "We all sin, Aaron. Did I not plead with God to send someone else? The Lord called you, too. I needed a spokesman. Don't ever forget that."

"You don't need me anymore."

"You are needed, Aaron, more than you realize. God will use you yet to serve Him and lead His people Israel."

Before Aaron could ask how, others interrupted. He was not the only one who yearned for personal contact with the only man in the world who spoke to God like he would to a friend. To be close to Moses made them feel closer to God. Veiled, Moses moved among them, touching a shoulder here, stroking the head of a child there, speaking to everyone tenderly, and always of the Lord. "We are called to be a holy nation, set apart by God. The other nations will see and know that the Lord, He is God and there is no other."

God's promise to Abraham would be fulfilled. Israel would be a blessing to all nations, a light to the world so that all men might see there was one true God, the Lord God of heaven and earth.

Aaron walked with his brother whenever he came into camp, relishing what time they had together, listening to Moses' every word as though the Lord Himself were speaking to him. When Moses spoke, Aaron heard the Voice come through his brother's words.

Moses pleaded with the Lord for the people's sake, and God stayed with them. Everyone knew it was for the sake of Moses that God changed His mind, for had the Lord left them, Moses' gray head would have gone down to the grave in grief. God knew Moses loved the people more than he loved his own life.

Each time Moses spoke, Aaron saw the gap between the ways of God and the ways of men. *Be holy because I am holy*. Every law was aimed at removing sin from their lives. God was the potter, working them like clay and reshaping them into something new. All the things they had learned and practiced in Egypt, and still practiced in the hidden recesses of their tents and hearts, would not go unpunished. God would not allow compromise.

Every time Moses came out of the Tent of Meeting, he came with more laws: laws against the abominations of Egypt and the nations around them; rules for holy gifts, holy convocations; crimes that required death; Sabbath days and Sabbath years; Jubilee and the end of slavery; prices and tithes. Every part of their lives would be governed by God. How would they ever remember it all? The laws of God were in complete opposition to everything they had ever known and practiced in Egypt.

Through the Law, Aaron realized how deeply immersed his own family had become in practicing the ways of the people around them. He and his brother and sister were children of incest, for their father had married his aunt, sister to his own father. The Lord said Israelite men were to marry outside their immediate families, but within their own tribes to keep the inheritance He would give them from being cut apart. And never were they to take women from other nations as their wives. Aaron wondered how Moses had felt when he heard the Lord say this, for he had taken a Midianite to be his wife. Even their ancestor Joseph had broken this law, marrying an Egyptian, and Joseph's father, Israel, had given his favorite son, Joseph, a double blessing, acknowledging Manasseh and Ephraim.

All those years, the Israelites had not known how to please the Lord other than to believe He existed, that His promise to Abraham, Isaac, and Jacob remained, and that one day He would deliver them from Egypt. Even during the years of living under the shadow of Pharaoh, and following too many of the ways of their oppressors, the Lord blessed them by multiplying their numbers.

The seventy elders once again mediated cases, referring only the most difficult to Moses to resolve. Aaron longed for more time with his brother, but when Moses was not hearing cases, he was hard at work writing down all the words the Lord gave him so that the people would have a permanent record.

"Surely, the Lord will let you rest for a little while." Aaron worried about his brother's health. Moses hardly ate and he slept little. "We can't survive without you, Moses. You must take care of yourself."

"My life is in God's hands, Aaron, as is every life in Israel, and all the earth for that matter. It is the Lord who has told me to write His words down. And write them I will, for words spoken are quickly forgotten, and ignorance will not be accepted as an excuse by the Lord. Sin brings death. And what does God consider sin? These things the people must know. Especially you."

"Especially me?" Living with the magnitude of the sin he had committed in allowing the people to have their way, and the number of lives that sin had cost, Aaron did not dare hope the Lord might use him again.

Moses finished the brush strokes of the last few letters on the papyrus scroll. He set the writing tools aside and turned. "Once the Law is written, it can be read many times and studied. The Lord has set the Levites aside as His, Aaron. Remember the prophecy of Jacob: 'I will scatter their descendants throughout the nation of Israel.' The Lord will scatter our brothers among the tribes and use them to teach the Law so the people can do what is right and walk humbly before our God. The Lord has called you to be His high priest. You will bring the atonement offering before Him, and one of your sons—I don't know which one yet—will begin the line for the high priests to follow in the generations to come. But all this must be explained to everyone."

High priest? "Are you certain you heard right?"

Moses smiled gently. "You confessed and repented. Were you not the first to run to me when I called for those who were for the Lord? Once we have confessed them, the Lord forgets our faults and failures, Aaron, but not our faith. It is always His faithfulness that lifts us to our feet again."

As they went outside, Aaron remembered the entire blessing Jacob had given, if blessing it could be called:

"Simeon and Levi are two of a kind—men of violence. O my soul, stay away from them. May I never be a party to their wicked plans. For in their anger they murdered men, and they crippled oxen just for sport. Cursed be their anger, for it is fierce; cursed be their wrath, for it is cruel. Therefore, I will scatter their descendants throughout the nation of Israel."

Did not Aaron's family suffer from hot tempers, Moses included? Hadn't it been his temper that brought about the murder of an Egyptian? And lest he cast stones at Moses, what about his own sins? He suffered bouts of fury as well. How easily his sword had been raised against his people, slaughtering sheep he had been left to lead!

In his heart, Aaron was in fear for what the future could hold when the priesthood rested in the hands of a tribe so bent on violence and self-service. "Oh, Moses, if I am to teach and lead the people, God must change me! Plead with Him for my sake. Ask Him to create in me a pure heart and upright spirit!"

"I have prayed for you. I will never stop. Now gather the people, Aaron. The Lord has work for them. We will see if their hearts are up to it."

FIVE

✦✦✦✦✦

Moses received instructions from the Lord to build a tabernacle, a sacred residence where God could dwell among His people.

The instructions were specific: Curtains were to be made, and poles to hang them. A bronze basin for washing and an altar for burnt offerings would stand in the court of the Tabernacle. Inside the Tabernacle would be another smaller chamber, the Most Holy Place, where a table, a lampstand, and an ark would be placed.

Details on how everything was to be made were given to Moses and handed over to two men the Lord named to oversee the work: Bezalel son of Uri, grandson of Hur; and Oholiab son of Ahisamach, of the tribe of Dan. When they came forward, eager to do God's will, the Lord filled them with His Spirit, so that they had the skill, ability, and knowledge in all kinds of crafts. God even gave them the ability to teach others how to do the work required! All skilled in any craft came to help.

The people rejoiced to hear that their prayers and Moses' pleading had been answered. The Lord would remain with them! They returned to their tents and laid out all the gifts the Egyptians had given them, gifts that had come from hearts stirred by fear of the Lord God of Israel, and they gave the best of what they had to the Lord.

Aaron felt shame for having used gifts God had given the people to fashion the golden calf. God had lavished wealth on them before they left Egypt, and he had wasted a portion in worshiping a hollow idol. That gold had ended up burned, ground, and cast on the water that ended up as refuse in the latrines outside of camp.

Aaron took all the gold he had and gave it back to the One who had given it to him in the first place. His sons and their wives and Miriam gave the best of what they had. They spread ram skins dyed red and piled up gold jewelry, silver, and bronze. Miriam filled a basket with blue, purple, and scarlet yarn and another with fine linen, excited that what she had to give might end up as part of the Tabernacle curtain.

Others in camp came with the hides of dugongs, jugs of olive oil, spices for the anointing oil, and fragrant incense. Some had onyx stones and other gems. The people brought their gifts before the Lord, waving them in offering, and placing them in baskets set out. Soon the baskets were filled with brooches, earrings, rings, and ornaments.

Groups of men went out into the desert and cut down acacia trees. The best pieces were set aside for the ark, the table, posts, and crossbeams. The bronze was melted down for the basin with its stand, the bronze grating for the altar and utensils. Everyone brought something, and everyone who was able worked.

Fires were kept burning so the bronze, silver, and gold could be melted down, impurities strained off, and then be poured into molds made under Bezalel's watchful eye. Women wove fine cloth and made garments for Aaron and his sons to wear when they began ministering in the sanctuary.

As the work progressed, more gifts poured forth. Every day, more piled up near the work sites until Bezalel and Oholiab left their work and went to Moses and Aaron. "We have more than enough materials on hand now to complete the job the Lord has given us to do!"

Aaron rejoiced, for surely the Lord would see how the people loved Him. He and his sons and their wives and Miriam brought offerings each day, eager to see God's plan accomplished, eager to have part in it.

Moses looked at Aaron, his eyes awash with tears. "Gather the elders. Tell them no more offerings must be brought. We have all we need."

✦   ✦   ✦

By Moses' command, Aaron's son Ithamar recorded everything that was given and used for the main Tabernacle and the Tabernacle of the Testimony. Almost everyone in camp was busy on some aspect of building the Tabernacle. Aaron was happy. He looked forward to each sunrise, for the people were content in the service of the Lord. Their hands were busy and their hearts and minds set on carrying out the work God had given them.

Nine months after reaching Mount Sinai and two weeks before the second celebration of Passover, the Tabernacle was completed. Bezalel and Oholiab and the people brought everything that was made to Moses. Moses inspected the tent and all its furnishings, the articles to be placed in the Most Holy Place, and the clothing for the priests. Everything had been done exactly as the Lord had commanded.

Smiling, Moses blessed them.

Under Moses' watchful eye, the Tabernacle was set up on the first day of the month. The Ark of the Covenant was placed inside and a heavy curtain hung to veil it from sight. To the right was the table of the Bread of the Presence and to the left the golden lampstand of pure gold, six branches coming out from the center, three on the left and three on the right with flowerlike cups at the top. In front of the curtain, Moses placed the gold altar of incense. Heavy curtains were drawn around and over the Most Holy Place.

The altar of burnt offerings was placed in front of the entrance to the Tabernacle. The basin was placed between the Tent of Meeting and the altar and filled with water. Curtains were hung around the Tabernacle, the altar, and basin; and another more elaborate curtain hung at the entrance for the courtyard.

When everything was set up according to the Lord's instructions, Moses anointed the Tabernacle and everything in it with oil and pronounced it holy to the Lord. He then anointed the altar of burnt offerings and the basin and consecrated them to the Lord.

Aaron and his sons were called forward. Aaron felt the eyes of all on him as he entered the courtyard. Men, women, and children stood by the thousands behind him, just beyond the curtain. Moses removed Aaron's clothing and washed him from head to foot, then helped him slip on a fine woven white tunic and a blue robe with pomegranates of blue, purple, and scarlet yarn around the hem and gold bells between them. "When you enter the Most Holy Place, the Lord will hear the bells, and you will not die." Moses straightened Aaron's garment.

Stomach quivering, arms outstretched, Aaron stood still while Moses secured the ephod with the shoulder pieces, two onyx stones engraved with the names of the sons of Israel and mounted in gold filigree. "You will bear the names of the sons of Israel as a memorial before the Lord."

Upon the ephod rested the square chestpiece with four rows of precious stones mounted and set in gold filigree: a ruby, topaz, beryl, turquoise, sapphire, emerald, jacinth, agate, amethyst, chrysolite, onyx, and jasper, each engraved for a son of Israel. "Whenever you enter the Holy Place, you will bear the names of the sons of Israel over your heart." Moses tucked the Urim and the Thummim in the chestpiece over Aaron's heart. "These will reveal the will of the Lord."

Aaron shut his eyes as Moses placed the turban on his head. He had seen the plate of engraved gold: *Holy to the Lord*. It now rested snuggly against his forehead. Moses left him standing alone and went to prepare Aaron's sons.

Standing in the shadow of the cloud, Aaron trembled. His heart pounded. From this day forth, he would be high priest of Israel. He looked at the basin, the altar of burnt offerings, and the curtain that enclosed the holy pieces inside the Lord's Tabernacle, afraid he would faint. Never again would he be an ordinary man. The Lord had elevated him, and at the same time made him a servant. Every time he entered the courtyard, he would carry responsibility for the people. He felt the weight of them on his shoulders and over his heart.

When Nadab, Abihu, Ithamar, and Eleazar were dressed in their priestly garments, Moses stood before them and anointed them with oil, consecrating them to the Lord. Then he brought forward a young bull for the sin offering. Aaron remembered his sin in making the golden calf. Blushing, he laid his hand on the head of the animal whose blood would be shed for his sin. His sons placed their hands on the animal's head as well. Moses slit the throat of the bull and took some of the blood in a bowl and put it on all the horns of the altar. He poured out the rest at the base. He slaughtered the bull and placed the fat around the inner parts, the covering of the liver, and both kidneys as a burnt offering on the altar. The rest of the bull would be burned outside the camp.

The second offering for Aaron and his sons was the ram for the burnt offering. Again, Aaron and his sons laid their hands on the animal. Moses sprinkled the ram's blood on the altar and then cut the animal into pieces, washed the inner parts and legs, and burned the whole ram on the altar. The smell of roasting meat made Aaron's stomach clench with hunger. It was a pleasing aroma made to the Lord.

The third offering was another ram, this one for Aaron and his sons' ordination. Aaron placed his hand on the animal's head. At his nod, his sons followed his example. Moses cut the animal's jugular and collected the blood in a bowl. He came to Aaron and, dipping his finger into the blood, put it on Aaron's right ear. Moses dipped his finger again and anointed Aaron's right thumb. Kneeling, he dipped his finger one last time and put the blood on the big toe of Aaron's right foot. He did the same for Aaron's four sons, and then sprinkled blood against the altar on all sides.

The rams for Aaron and his sons were slaughtered, the pieces stacked with the washed inner parts, and a cake of bread made with oil and one wafer were placed on top. Moses placed the first in Aaron's hands. Aaron raised the sacrifice before the Lord and then gave it back to his brother, who placed it on the altar. Flames leaped up. Aaron's sons waved their offerings and gave them to Moses to place on the altar, and each time, the flames exploded around the slaughtered animal, taking it in the place of the sinful men who gave it as offering.

Aaron stood solemn and humbled as Moses sprinkled him first with the fragrant anointing oil and the blood of the sacrifice. Finally, his sons were anointed, from the eldest to the youngest.

Aaron felt the change in the air. The cloud swirled slowly, glowing strangely. His heart raced as the cloud compressed and moved down from the mountain. He heard the people behind him, drawing in their breath, holding it, releasing it in trembling fear. The cloud covered the Tabernacle.

A thousand shimmering colors flashed and glowed from within the cloud, and then it poured into the chamber of the Most Holy Place, and the glory of the Lord filled the Tabernacle.

Even Moses could not enter.

The people moaned in awe and reverence and bowed low.

"Cook the meat remaining at the entrance of the Tabernacle and eat it there with the bread from the basket of ordination offerings. Then burn the rest of the meat and bread. Do not leave the entrance of the Tabernacle. You must stay here, day and night for seven days or you will die."

Aaron watched his brother walk away. When Moses reached the entrance to the courtyard, he looked back solemnly; then he drew the curtains closed.

Aaron faced the Tabernacle. He knew all had been done to cleanse this place and make it sacred. Even he had been washed and dressed in new garments so he could stand before the Lord. But he could not stop the trembling inside, the quiver of fear that the Lord was within feet of him, hidden only by curtains. And Aaron knew he wasn't worthy to be in this place. He wasn't clean, not inside. As soon as Moses was out of sight, he turned weak. Hadn't he allowed his jealousy of Joshua to taint him? Hadn't he let the people's fears rule over the commands given to him. Why would God appoint a man like him to be high priest?

Lord, I'm unworthy. You alone are faithful. I am only a man. I failed to lead Your people. Three thousand lost their lives because I was weak. And You spared my life. You appointed me Your high priest. Lord, such mercy is beyond me. Help me to know Your ways and follow them! Help me to be the priest You want me to be! Instruct me in Your ways so that I can serve Your people and keep them strong in faith. Oh, Lord, Lord, help me. . . .

When he was too tired to stand, Aaron knelt, praying that the Lord would give him the strength and wisdom to remember the Law and do everything the Lord commanded. When he became weak from hunger, he and his sons gave thanks, cooked the meat and ate the bread left for them. When he couldn't keep his eyes open any longer, he prostrated himself before the Lord and slept with his forehead on his hands.

Eleazar and Ithamar stood before the Tabernacle, arms outstretched, palms up as they prayed. Nadab and Abihu knelt, sitting back against their heels when they tired.

Each day that passed softened Aaron's heart until he thought he heard the Lord's voice whispering to him.

I am the Lord your God, and there is no other.

Aaron lifted his head, listening intently, content.

Nadab stretched and yawned. "So begins the fourth morning."

Abihu sat cross-legged, forearms resting on his knees. "Three more to go." Aaron felt a coldness in the pit of his belly.

✦ ✦ ✦

On the eighth day, Moses summoned Aaron, his sons, and the elders of Israel. Moses gave them the instructions of the Lord.

Aaron took a bull calf without defect and offered it as sacrifice to atone for his sins. He knew every time he did this, he would remember how he had sinned against the Lord by making a calf idol. Would his sons remember? Would their sons after them? Did the blood of this living calf really ransom him from the sin of making an idol?

More sacrifices followed. When he had made atonement for himself, he would be ready to stand and make the sin offering, burnt offering, and fellowship offerings for the people. The ox fought against the rope, kicking Aaron. He thought he would pass out from the pain, but kept his feet. His sons held the animal more firmly as Aaron used the knife. Next he killed the ram. The sight and smell of blood and the sound of the dying animals filled him with loathing for the sins that brought death. And he thanked God that the Lord allowed these poor beasts to substitute for each man, woman, and child. For all sinned. None could stand before the Lord with a pure heart.

Aaron's hands were covered with blood, and the corners and sides of the altar dripped with it. Arms aching, he lifted the breasts and right thigh of the sacrifices before the Lord as a wave offering. When all the sacrifices were made, Aaron lifted hands shaking with exhaustion toward the people and blessed them. Then he stepped down.

Moses went with him into the Tabernacle. Aaron's heart thundered in his ears. His stomach clenched. He was thankful for the heavy curtain that hid the Lord from his sight, for he knew he would die if he ever saw God. If he washed himself in the blood of calves and lambs, it still wouldn't wash all the sin away. He prayed for himself. He prayed for the people. And then he went outside with Moses and blessed the people.

The air around them changed. He held his breath at the movement—silent, powerful. The glorious presence of the Lord appeared for all to see. He gasped and the people cried out in awe when fire blazed forth from the Lord's presence and consumed the burnt offering and the fat on the altar.

As sinful as he was, as sinful as these people were who stood trembling in fear, the Lord had accepted their offerings!

Aaron shouted joyfully, tears of relief streaming down his cheeks as he fell facedown before the Lord.

And the people followed his example.

✦ ✦ ✦

Aaron's service fell into a routine. Every day, offerings were given at dawn and dusk. The burnt offering remained on the altar hearth throughout the night till morning. Aaron wore his fine linen clothes when performing sacrifices, but changed into others when carrying the ashes of the offerings outside camp. The Lord had said, "The fire must never go out." And Aaron saw to it that it did not.

Still he worried about it. He dreamed about fire and blood. Even when he was clean, Aaron could smell smoke and blood. He dreamed of people screaming like animals because he had failed to perform his duties properly and appease the Lord's wrath. Even more disturbing, he knew people went on sinning. Hundreds waited in line to take grievances to the elders, and Moses was always busy with one case or another. The people could not seem to live at peace with one another. It was in their nature to argue, contend, and fight anything that curtailed them in any way. They did not dare question God, but they questioned His representatives without end. They were no different from Adam and Eve, wanting what was denied them, no matter what harm would come in the having.

Aaron tried to encourage his sons. "We must be living examples of righteousness before the people."

"No one is more righteous than you are, Father."

Aaron fought the pleasure of Nadab's flattery, knowing how quickly pride destroyed men. Hadn't it destroyed Pharaoh and Egypt with him? "Moses is more righteous. And no one is more humble."

Abihu bristled. "Moses is always in the Tent of Meeting, and where are you? Out there serving the people."

"It seems to me we have the heavier workload." Nadab leaned back on a cushion. "When was the last time you saw one of our cousins lift a finger to help?"

Eleazar looked up from a scroll. "Eliezer and Gershom are tending their mother." He spoke quietly, frowning.

Nadab sneered, pouring himself more wine. "Woman's work."

Miriam stood over them. "Don't you think you've had enough to drink?"

Nadab glanced at her before holding out his goblet. Abihu refilled it before hanging the wineskin on its hook.

Aaron did not like the tension in their tent. "We are each called to be where we are called to be. Moses is the one who hears the voice of the Lord and brings us God's instructions. We carry them out. We have been given a great honor by the Lord to serve—"

"Yes, yes." Nadab nodded. "We know all that, Father. But it is boring to do the same thing day in and day out, knowing we will be doing it for the rest of our lives."

Aaron felt a wave of heat come up inside him and then sink into a cold lump in his stomach. "Remember whom you serve." He looked from Nadab to Abihu and then to his two younger sons, who sat silent, heads down. Did they feel as their brothers did? Aaron felt an urgency to warn them. "You will do exactly as the Lord commands. Do you understand?"

Nadab's eyes changed. "We understand you, Father." His fingers tightened on his wine goblet. "We will honor the Lord in everything we do. Just as you always have." He finished his wine and rose. Abihu followed his brother from the tent.

"You shouldn't let them talk to you that way, Aaron."

Irritated, he glared at Miriam. "What do you suggest?"

"Take them by the ear! Give them a whipping! Do something! They both think they're more righteous than you!"

He could think of a dozen men who were more righteous than he was, starting with his brother and his assistant, Joshua. "They will come to their senses when they think about it."

"And if they don't?"

"Let it be, woman! I have enough on my mind without your constant nagging!"

"Nagging? As if I haven't always had your best interest in mind!" Miriam yanked the curtain aside to the women's chamber. She pulled the curtain down behind her.

The silence was anything but peaceful. Aaron rose. "We have work to do." He was thankful it was time to return to the Tabernacle. He had no peace in his own tent.

Eleazar sat up. "We'll be along shortly, Father." He reached out a hand to help Ithamar.

Aaron let Eleazar and Ithamar precede him. "See that you are." He snapped the tent flap down behind him.

Eleazar walked beside Aaron. "You're going to have to do something about them, Father."

"Is it your place to speak against your brothers?"

"It's for their sake I speak."

As Aaron performed his duties, Eleazar and Ithamar worked with him. Disturbed, Aaron thought about what Eleazar had said. Where were Nadab and Abihu? Aaron could not understand his elder sons. There was nowhere Aaron wanted to be so much as in the courtyard of the Lord. To stand in God's presence was Moses' calling, but to be this close to the Lord filled Aaron with joy. Why could his elder sons not feel the same way?

Laughter startled Aaron. Who dared laugh inside the courtyard of God? Turning, he saw Nadab and Abihu at the entrance. Dressed in their priestly garments, they held censers in their hands. What did they think they were doing? Aaron started toward them, ready to take them to task when Nadab took a small bag from his sash. He sprinkled dust over the burning coals. Yellow, blue, and red smoke rose, the same kind that Egyptian priests had used in their pagan temples.

"*No!*" Aaron cried out.

"Relax, Father. We are only paying homage to our God." Abihu held his censer out and Nadab sprinkled particles into the coals.

"Would you desecrate God's holy—"

"Desecrate?" Nadab stood defiant. "Are we not priests? We can show honor to God as we want!" He and Abihu stepped forward.

"Stop!"

A stream of fire shot past Aaron and struck his two elder sons in the chest. The force knocked Aaron and his two younger sons off their feet. Aaron heard Nadab and Abihu screaming and clambered to his feet. The shrieks of their unbearable agony lasted only seconds before they were consumed by flames. They had fallen where they stood in defiance, burned beyond recognition.

With a cry, Aaron's hands went to his robe. A heavy hand grabbed his shoulder and jerked him back. "No." Moses spoke heavily. "Do not mourn by letting your hair hang loose or by tearing your clothes. If you do, you will die, and the Lord will be angry with the whole community of Israel."

Lungs aching, Aaron swayed.

Moses gripped his arm, steadying him. "Aaron, listen to me. The rest of the Israelites, your relatives, may mourn for Nadab and Abihu, whom the Lord has destroyed by fire. But you are not to leave the entrance of the Tabernacle, under penalty of death, for the anointing oil of the Lord is upon you."

Aaron remembered the law: No priest was to touch a dead body.

"This is what the Lord meant when He said, 'I will show Myself holy among those who are near Me. I will be glorified before all the people.'"

Aaron fought back tears, fought down the anguished cry that threatened to choke him. *The Lord is holy. The Lord is holy!* He fixed his mind on the Lord's holiness, bending to it. Eleazar and Ithamar lay prostrate before the Tabernacle, faces in the dust, worshiping the Lord.

Moses summoned Aaron's cousins Mishael and Elzaphan. "Come and carry the bodies of your relatives away from the sanctuary to a place outside the camp."

Aaron watched them lift the charred bodies of his two elder sons and carry them away from the front of the Tabernacle. He faced the Tabernacle and didn't look back. His chest ached, his throat burned. Would Nadab and Abihu be cast into the refuse for their sin?

The Voice spoke, still and quiet.

You and your descendants must never drink wine or any other alcoholic drink before going into the Tabernacle.

"Aaron." Moses was speaking to him, and Aaron tried to absorb his instructions. "Aaron." Aaron and his younger sons were to remain where they were and complete their duties. They were to eat the leftovers from the offerings of grain and the goat of the sin offering. Aaron did all Moses instructed, but neither he nor his two sons could eat. The smell of burning meat made Aaron's gorge rise, and he had to clench his teeth to keep from vomiting.

Moses' face was red with anger. "Why didn't you eat the sin offering in the sanctuary area?" he demanded. "It is a holy offering! It was given to you for removing the guilt of the community and for making atonement for the people before the Lord. Since the animal's blood was not taken into the Holy Place, you should have eaten the meat in the sanctuary area as I ordered you."

Aaron groaned. "Today my sons presented both their sin offering and their burnt offering to the Lord." He swallowed convulsively. "This kind of thing has also happened to me." He fought his rising emotions, trembling under the strain. "Would the Lord have approved if I had eaten the sin offering today?" When sin lurked so close at hand, waiting to prey on his shattered family and sink its teeth into his weakened heart? *My sons,* he wanted to cry out. *My sons! Have you forgotten my sons died today?* He would have choked on the meat of the sin offering and defiled the sanctuary.

Nadab's words had come back over and over to haunt him all day: *"We will honor the Lord in our own way, Father. Just as you have."*

With a golden calf and a feast day of pagan celebration.

Even after the atoning sacrifices, Aaron still felt his sins heavy upon him. *If only the Lord would erase them forever. If only . . .*

Moses looked on Aaron with compassion and said no more.

✦   ✦   ✦

Aaron was with Moses when Moses invited Hobab, Jethro's son, to go with them to the Promised Land. "Stay with us, Hobab. Make your life with God's chosen people, Israel."

When Hobab left the camp, Aaron had a sick feeling in his stomach that they would meet Hobab again, under less than friendly circumstances. All the while the Midianite remained camped close by, Aaron had wondered if Hobab was merely watching for their weaknesses and how to make use of them.

"I hope we do not see him again."

Moses looked at him and Aaron said no more. His brother had spent many years with the Midianites and had deep affection and respect for his father-in-law. Aaron could only hope Moses knew these people as well as he thought he did and no threat would come from them. For what would Moses do if he ever found himself torn between the Israelites and his wife's family? For forty years, the Midianites had treated Moses with love and respect, even making him a member of their family. The Israelites had given Moses grief, rebellion, constant complaints, and work; then they made him a slave to them.

Worry seemed a constant companion these days. Aaron worried about Moses' health, his stamina, his family. Zipporah was near death. The only good that had come of her illness was the softening in Miriam, who often tended her now. Aaron also worried about getting things right. So far, he had made one mistake after another. He studied the laws Moses wrote down, knowing they were straight from God. But sometimes, when he was tired, he would think of his dead sons and the tears would come up, quick and hot. He had loved them, even knowing their sins. And he could not help feeling he had failed them more than they had failed him.

The people were complaining again. They couldn't seem to remember from one day to the next what the Lord had already done for them. They were like children, whining with every discomfort. It was the Egyptian rabble who traveled with them that caused the most trouble now.

"We're sick of nothing at all to eat except this manna!"

"Oh, for some meat!"

"We remember all the fish we used to eat for free in Egypt."

"And we had all the cucumbers and melons we wanted. They were so good."

"And the leeks and onions and garlics."

"But now our appetites are gone, and day after day we have nothing to eat but this manna!"

Aaron said nothing as he gathered his portion of manna for the day. He squatted and picked up the flakes, putting them into his container. Eleazar was scowling. Ithamar moved a little farther off.

Miriam was red-faced. "Maybe you should have stayed in Egypt!"

A woman glared. "Maybe we should have!"

"Fish and cucumbers," Miriam muttered under her breath. "We were lucky to have enough to eat at all. Just enough to keep us *working*."

"I am sick of eating the same thing every day."

Miriam straightened. "You should be thankful. You don't have to work for your food!"

"You don't call this work? We're down on our knees every morning, grubbing around for flakes of this stuff."

"If only we had meat to eat!" An Israelite joined in the complaining.

"Oh, Mama, do we have to eat manna again?"

"Yes, poor baby, you do."

The child began to whine and cry.

"Surely we were better off in Egypt!" The man spoke in a loud voice, knowing Aaron would hear.

Miriam glowered. "Aren't you going to say something, Aaron? What are you going to do with these people?"

What did she want him to do? Call down fire from the mountain? He thought of his sons again, and his throat closed hot and dry. He knew Moses heard the people complaining. He saw what it was doing to his brother. "Don't make more trouble than we already have, Miriam." He was weary of all of them.

"*I* make trouble! If you'd listened to me about . . ."

He rose, staring at her. Did she realize how cruel and thoughtless she could be at times? The fire went out of her eyes. "I'm sorry." She lowered her head. He loved his sister, but sometimes he could not abide her. He took his container and walked away.

Moses came outside the Tabernacle. Aaron went to him. "You look tired."

"I am tired." Moses shook his head. "So tired of trouble I asked the Lord to kill me and have done with it."

"Do not speak so." Did Moses think Aaron would do any better? God forbid Moses should die. Aaron never wanted to be left in charge again.

"You need not worry, my brother. God said no. The Lord has given instructions that seventy men be chosen, men known to us as leaders and officials among the people. They are to come here before the Tabernacle, and the Spirit of the Lord will fall on them and they will help lead God's people. We need help." He smiled. "You are older than I, my brother, and showing every day of your eighty-four years."

Aaron laughed bleakly, and savored the relief. Two men could not bear the burden of six hundred thousand men on foot, not counting their wives and sons and daughters!

"And the Lord will send meat."

"Meat?" *How? From where?*

"Meat for a whole month, until we gag and are sick of it, because the people have rejected the Lord."

Sixty-eight men came to the Tabernacle. As Moses laid hands on each man, the Spirit of the Lord came on each new leader and he spoke the Word of the Lord as Moses did.

Joshua came running. "Eldad and Medad are prophesying in the camp! Moses, my master, *make them stop!*"

"Are you jealous for my sake? I wish that all the Lord's people were prophets, and that the Lord would put His spirit upon them all!"

Aaron heard the sound of wind coming out from the cloud over the Tabernacle. He felt the warmth of it lift his beard and press his priestly robes close to his body. And then it moved above and away. Aaron returned to his duties in the Tabernacle, but kept apprehensive watch on the sky.

Quail flew in from the sea, thousands of them. The wind drove them in a flurry of feathers straight down into the camp until they were piled up three feet deep on the ground. All that day and night, the people gathered birds, ringing their necks and stripping them of feathers in their haste for meat. Some didn't even wait to roast the quail before sinking their teeth into the flesh they craved.

Aaron heard the groans and feared he knew what was coming. Groans turned to wails as men and women sickened before the meat was even consumed. They fell to their knees, bent over, vomiting. Some died quickly. Others, as they suffered, cursed God for giving them the very thing they had demanded. Thousands repented, crying out to the Lord to forgive them. But the quail kept coming as the Lord had promised. Day after day, until the people were silent and filled with dread of the Lord.

✦   ✦   ✦

After a month, the cloud lifted from the Tabernacle. Aaron entered the Most Holy Place and covered and packed the lampstand, table of the Bread of the Presence, and the incense altar. The Tent of Meeting and the Tabernacle were dismantled, packed, and the clans of Levites carried what the Lord had assigned to them. At Moses' signal, two men blew trumpets. The people gathered.

"Rise up, O Lord!" Moses' voice boomed. "May Your enemies be scattered; may Your foes flee before You!"

The Ark of the Covenant was lifted by four men. Moses walked ahead, his eyes on the Angel of the Lord who led him. The people left the place that had come to be called Graves of Craving. They traveled day and night until the cloud stopped at Hazeroth.

Moses held his arms up in praise. "Return, O Lord! To the countless thousands of Israel."

The Ark of the Covenant was set down. The Tabernacle was set up around it. Aaron placed the holy items in their proper places, as his sons and the heads of the Gershon, Kohath, and Merari clans of Levites finished putting up the poles and curtains, the altar for the burnt offerings, and the bronze basin.

And the people rested.

✦   ✦   ✦

Aaron wanted to close his eyes and not think about anything for a little while, but Miriam was upset and would not allow him any peace. "I've come to accept Zipporah." She paced, agitated, cheeks flushed. "I've been the one taking care of her all this time. I've been the one seeing to her needs. Not that she has shown any particular appreciation. She has never tried to learn our language. She still relies on Eliezer to translate."

Aaron knew why she was upset. He, too, had been surprised when Moses told him he was taking another wife, but he had not seen fit to comment on it. Miriam had never had such inhibitions, though Aaron doubted she had spoken to Moses yet.

"He needs a wife, Miriam, someone who can see to the needs of his household."

"A wife? Why does Moses need a wife other than Zipporah when he has me? I saw to everything before that Cushite entered his tent. He welcomed my help in the beginning. So that I could take care of his wife! Zipporah couldn't do anything without help. And now that she's dying, he's taken another wife! Why does he need a wife at his age? You should've talked him out of this marriage before he took that foreigner into his tent. You should've said something to keep him from sinning against the Lord!"

Had Moses sinned? "I too was surprised when Moses told me."

"Just surprised?"

"He's not so old he doesn't need the comfort of a woman." Aaron sometimes wished he could take another wife, but after mediating between the mother of his sons and Miriam for years, he decided it was wiser to remain chaste!

"Moses seldom spent time with Zipporah, and now he has this woman." Miriam threw her hands in the air. "I wonder if he listens to what the Lord says. If he must have a wife—and I don't see why he must at his age—he should have chosen a wife from among the women of the tribe of Levi. Hasn't the Lord told us not to marry outside our tribes? Have you seen how foreign that Cushite is? She is black, Aaron, blacker than any Egyptian I ever saw."

Aaron had been troubled about Moses' marriage, but not for Miriam's reasons. The woman had been a slave to one of the Egyptians who had come with the people out of Egypt. Her mistress had died during the festival of the golden calf, and the Cushite had continued to travel among the people. As far as Aaron knew, she bowed down before the Lord. But still . . .

"Why do you just sit and say nothing, Aaron? You are a servant of the Lord, aren't you? You are His high priest. Has the Lord spoken only through Moses? Didn't the Lord direct me when I spoke to Pharaoh's daughter? Did the Lord not give me the words? And the Lord called you, Aaron. You have heard His voice and spoken His word to the people more often than Moses! I have never known Moses to show so little wisdom."

Aaron hated when his sister was like this. He felt like a little boy again, ruled by his older sister, overpowered by her personality. She had a will of iron. "You should be pleased that you will have less work to do."

"Pleased? Maybe I would be if he hadn't married a *Cushite!* Don't you care that Moses brings sin on all of us by this unwholesome marriage?"

"What is unwholesome about it?"

"You have to ask?" She pointed angrily. "Just go out to his tent and look at her! She should go back to her own people. She does not belong among us, let alone have the honor of being the wife of Israel's deliverer!"

Aaron wondered if he should talk to Moses. Truly, he had been taken aback when Moses took a Cushite slave woman into his tent. Perhaps he should speak with some of the elders before he approached his brother. What did the people think of Moses' marriage? Miriam would not keep her thoughts to herself for long.

Doubts filled Aaron. Miriam had tried to warn him about Nadab and Abihu, and he hadn't listened to her. Was he making another mistake now by not listening to his sister and standing against Moses' decision to marry again?

Go out to the Tabernacle, all three of you!

The hair rose on the back of Aaron's neck. He raised his head, in fear of that Voice.

Miriam straightened and tilted her chin. Her eyes glowed. "The Lord has called *me* to the Tabernacle. And you as well, if I can tell by the look on your face." She walked out of the tent. Standing in the sunlight, she looked back at him. "Well? Are you coming or not?"

Moses was waiting for them, perplexed. The cloud swirled overhead and compressed, descending.

Miriam looked up, her face flushed and tense with excitement. "You'll see now, Aaron."

He shook as the pillar of cloud stood at the entrance of the Tabernacle, and the Voice came from within the cloud.

Now listen to Me! Even with prophets, I the Lord communicate by visions and dreams. But that is not how I communicate with My servant Moses. He is entrusted with My entire house. I speak to him face to face, directly and not in riddles! He sees the Lord as He is. Should you not be afraid to criticize him?

The pillar of thick mist rose, and Aaron felt the deep anguish of his sin once more. He hung his head, ashamed.

Miriam drew in her breath in a soft shriek. Her face and hands were streaked white like a stillborn baby coming from its mother's womb, her flesh half eaten away. She fell to her knees, screaming and throwing dirt over her head.

"Ohhhh!" Aaron wailed in terror. He turned to Moses, hands outstretched, shaking. "Oh, my lord! Please don't punish us for this sin we have so foolishly committed." Fear ran cold in his veins.

Horrified, Moses was already crying out to the Lord, begging for mercy on behalf of his older sister.

And the Voice came for all three to hear:

If her father had spit in her face, wouldn't she have been defiled for seven days? Banish her from the camp for seven days, and after that she may return.

Sobbing, Miriam fell to her knees and prostrated herself before the Lord. Her outstretched sickly white hands became strong and brown again, worn from years of hard work. She put her hands near Moses' feet, but did not touch him. Aaron bent toward her, but Miriam drew back sharply. "You mustn't touch me!" She rose clumsily and backed away. The leprosy was gone, but her dark eyes were awash with tears and her cheeks red with humiliation. She drew her veil across her face and bent toward Moses. "Forgive me, Brother. Please forgive me."

"Oh, Miriam, my sister . . ."

Aaron felt her shame like a mantle on his own back. He should have told her to be silent, to stop gossiping about anyone, especially Moses, whom God had chosen to deliver Israel. Instead, he had allowed himself to be swayed by her words and had joined in her rebellion.

People had come out of their tents and stood staring. Some came closer to see what was going on. "Unclean!" Miriam cried out as she hurried toward the edge of the camp. "I'm unclean!" The people drew back from her as though she carried plague. Some wailed. Children fled for their mother's tent. "Unclean!" Miriam ran, stumbling in her shame, but did not fall.

Aaron's throat tightened. Was he destined to fail the Lord, to fail Moses in everything he did? When he didn't listen, Abihu and Nadab died. When he did listen, his sister bore the leprosy of his lack of perception. He should be the one living outside the camp! He had known better than to heed her jealousy. Instead, he had given in to her. He had allowed her to fan his own unanswered dreams of leadership. Every time he tried to step out ahead, disaster fell not only on him, but on those he loved.

"Aaron."

The tenderness in his brother's voice made Aaron's heart ache even more. "Why did God spare me when it was as much my sin as hers?"

"Would you have grieved as deeply if the discipline had fallen on you? Your heart is soft, Aaron."

"And so is my head." He looked at his brother. "I wanted her to sway me, Moses. I have struggled with my role as the older brother who must stand aside for his younger. I have not wanted to feel these things, Moses, but I'm just a man. Pride is my enemy."

"I know."

"I do love you, Moses."

"I know."

Aaron shut his eyes tightly. "And now, Miriam suffers while I go about my priestly duties."

"We will all wait until her time of quarantine is over."

Before the pillar of fire warmed the chill desert air, all the nation of Israel would know how he and Miriam had sinned.

It would soon be time for the evening sacrifice.

Lord, Lord, have mercy. My sins are heavy upon me.

✦   ✦   ✦

When the seven days had passed and Miriam returned to camp, the pillar of cloud rose and led the people away from Hazeroth. The cloud stopped over the wilderness of Paran and the people camped there at Kadesh. Aaron and his sons and the clans of Levites set up the Tent and the Tabernacle, and the tribes set up their camps in their designated areas around the Tent. Everyone knew their place and responsibility, and the people were quickly settled.

Moses received instructions from the Lord and gave Aaron a list of twelve men, one from each of the tribes of Israel, excluding Levi, whose duties centered around the worship of the Lord. Aaron sent for the tribal representatives and stood before Moses when the Lord's instructions were given.

"You are to go into Canaan and explore the land the Lord is giving us."

Aaron saw excitement flood Joshua's face, for he was the man chosen to represent the half tribe of Ephraim, son of Joseph. Some of the others looked frightened by their assignment. They had no provisions, no maps, no experience for spying out the strengths and weaknesses of their enemies. Most were young men like Joshua, but there was one other, older than the rest, and unshaken by the task before him: Caleb.

Moses walked among them, putting his hand on each man's shoulder as he passed by, his voice filled with confidence. "Go northward through the Negev into the hill country. See what the land is like and find out whether the people living there are strong or weak, few or many. What kind of land do they live in? Is it good or bad? Do their towns have walls or are they unprotected? How is the soil? Is it fertile or poor? Are there many trees?"

Moses paused when he reached Joshua. He clasped his hand, looked into the younger man's face. Releasing Joshua's hand, he turned to the others. "Enter the land boldly, and bring back samples of the crops you see."

Each man was given a water bag. They would not have manna during the time they were away from the camp. They would have to eat whatever the land of Canaan had to offer.

And the people waited.

✦ ✦ ✦

A week passed, then another and another. A new moon came, and still the spies did not return. How far had they gone? Had they met with resistance? Had some been killed? And if they had all been taken captive and executed, what then?

Aaron encouraged the people to be patient, to trust in the Lord to fulfill His promise. He prayed unceasingly for the twelve spies, Joshua often foremost in his mind.

He knew the younger man mattered greatly to Moses, for his brother often spoke of him with affection. "I know of no other like him, Aaron. He is dedicated to the Lord. Nothing will sway him."

How sad that Moses' own sons and brother should fall so short. Aaron no longer resented Joshua. He knew his own weaknesses and felt his age. Younger men would have to step into leadership if the people were to be hedged in and guided into their inheritance.

"They're coming! I see them! The men are returning!"

Excited cries filled the camp as family members surrounded the returning spies overladen with samples of what Canaan had to offer. Laughing, Joshua and Caleb had a pole stretched between their shoulders and on it was one cluster of grapes! Blankets were opened, spilling out bright red pomegranates and purple figs.

Joshua spoke first, directing his words to Moses. "We arrived in the land you sent us to see, and it is indeed a magnificent country."

Caleb raised his hands, jubilant. "It is a land flowing with milk and honey. Here is some of its fruit as proof."

Milk and honey, Aaron thought. That meant there were herds of cattle and goats, and fruit trees that flowered in the spring. There would be fields of wildflowers and plenty of water.

But the other spies focused on other things.

"The people living there are powerful."

"Their cities and towns are fortified and very large."

"We also saw the descendants of Anak who are living there!"

A low rumble of fear went through the listeners. The Anaks were giants, warriors who knew no fear and showed no mercy.

"The Amalekites live in the Negev."

Caleb turned. "They are cowards who attack from behind and kill those who are too weak to defend themselves."

"What about the Hittites? They are fierce warriors."

"The Hittites, Jebusites, and Amorites live in the hill country."

"The Canaanites live along the coast of the Mediterranean Sea and along the Jordan Valley."

"They are too strong for us."

Caleb's eyes blazed. "Is anyone too strong for the Lord? Let's go at once to take the land! We can certainly conquer it!"

Aaron looked to Moses, but his brother said nothing. Aaron wanted to cry out that the Lord had promised the land, and therefore, the Lord would see that they conquered it. But he had not been among the spies to see everything. He was an old man, not a warrior. And Moses was God's chosen leader. So Aaron waited, edgy, for Moses to decide. But his brother turned away and went into his tent.

Several spies shouted. "We can't go up against them! They are stronger than we are!"

Caleb's face was flushed with anger. "Canaan is the land God promised us! It is ours for the taking!"

"How can you be so sure? Hasn't God been killing us one by one since we left Egypt? With thirst and hunger and plagues!" Ten of the spies left and the people followed after them.

Caleb faced Aaron. "Why didn't Moses speak for us? Why didn't you?"

"I . . . I am only his spokesman. Moses always seeks the will of the Lord and then instructs me in what I'm to say."

"The Lord has already told us what He wills." Caleb pointed angrily. "Go and take the land!" He stalked away, shaking his head.

Aaron looked at Joshua. The younger man's shoulders were slumped and his eyes were shut. "Rest, Joshua. Perhaps tomorrow the Lord will tell Moses what we are to do."

"There will be trouble." Joshua looked at him. "Caleb is right. The land is ours. God has said so."

By the next morning, Aaron was hearing the rumors. The land would swallow up any who went into it. All the people living there were huge! There were even giants among them! The spies had felt like grasshoppers next to them! The people would be squashed like bugs if they dared enter Canaan!

But the Lord said . . .

No one was listening to what the Lord had said. No one believed.

"We wish we'd died in Egypt, or even here in the wilderness!"

"Why is the Lord taking us to this country only to have us die in battle?"

"We are not warriors! Our wives and little ones will be carried off as slaves!"

"Let's get out of here and return to Egypt!"

"Egypt is destroyed. There is nothing for us there!"

"The people fear us. We will be their masters for a change!"

"Yes! Let's go back!"

"Then we need a new leader."

Aaron saw the rage in their faces, their clenched fists. He was afraid, but less of them than of what God would do at the sight of this open rebellion. Moses fell facedown before the people, and Aaron dropped down beside him, close enough that if it became necessary, he could use his body to shield Moses. He could hear Caleb and Joshua shouting to the people.

"The land we explored is a wonderful land!"

"If the Lord is pleased with us, He will bring us safely into that land and give it to us!"

"It is a rich land flowing with milk and honey, and He will give it to us!"

"Don't rebel against the Lord."

"Don't be afraid of the people of the land. They are only helpless prey to us! They have no protection, but the Lord is with us!"

"Don't be afraid of them!"

The people grew more enraged with their words and shouted against them. "Stone them!"

"Who are you to speak to us, Caleb? You would lead us to death, Joshua!"

"Kill them!"

Screams rent the air. Aaron felt the strange prickling down his back once again and looked up. The glorious Presence rose into the air above the Tabernacle. Moses stood, head thrown back, arms raised. The people scattered, running for their tents, as if goatskins could hide them. Joshua and Caleb remained where they were, their beards whipped by the wind.

Moses stepped forward. "But Lord, what will the Egyptians think when they hear about it? They know full well the power You displayed in rescuing these people from Egypt."

Oh, Lord, hear his prayer! Aaron went down on his face again, for the lives of the people were at stake. *Lord, Lord, hear my brother.*

"Oh, Lord, no!" Moses cried out in horror. "The inhabitants of this land know, Lord, that You have appeared in full view of Your people in the pillar of cloud that hovers over them. They know that You go before them in a pillar of cloud by day and the pillar of fire by night. Now if You slaughter all these people, the nations that have heard of Your fame will say, 'The Lord was not able to bring them into the land He swore to give them, so He killed them in the wilderness.' Please, Lord, prove that Your power is as great as You have claimed it to be. For You said, 'The Lord is slow to anger and rich in unfailing love, forgiving every kind of sin and rebellion. Even so He does not leave sin unpunished, but He punishes the children for the sins of their parents to the third and fourth generations.' Please pardon the sins of this people because of Your magnificent, unfailing love, just as You have forgiven them ever since they left Egypt."

Moses fell silent. Aaron raised his head enough to peer up at his brother standing, arms still outstretched, palms up. After a long while, Moses' arms lowered to his sides and he let out a long, deep sigh. The glorious Presence came down once again and rested within the Tabernacle.

Aaron stood, slowly. "What did the Lord say?"

The only two men standing near were Caleb and Joshua, silent, terrified.

"Have the people gather, Aaron. I can only bear to say it once."

The people came quietly, tense and afraid, for all had seen the glorious Presence standing above, and had felt the heat of wrath. They remembered too late how easily God could take the lives of those who rebelled against Him.

And the Lord's anger was in Moses' voice as he spoke God's Word to the people. "The Lord will do to you the very things you said against Him. You will all die here in this wilderness! Because you complained against Him, none of you who are twenty years old or older and were counted in the census will enter the land the Lord swore to give you. The only exceptions will be Caleb and Joshua.

"You said your children would be taken captive. And the Lord says He will bring *them* safely into the land, and *they* will enjoy what you have despised! But as for you, your dead bodies will fall in this wilderness! And your children will be like shepherds, wandering in the wilderness forty years. In this way, *they* will pay for your faithlessness, until the last one of you lies dead in the wilderness! Because the men who explored the land were there for forty days, you must wander in the wilderness for forty years! One year for each day, suffering the consequences of your sins. You will discover what it is like to have the Lord for your enemy! Tomorrow we are to set out for the wilderness."

The people wailed.

The twelve men who had gone into the land to explore it were standing in the front lines of people. Ten of them groaned in pain and fell to their knees. Rolling in agony, they died where all could see them, near the entrance to the great tent that held the Tabernacle of the Lord. Only Caleb and Joshua remained standing.

Aaron wept in his tent, feeling he had somehow failed again. Would things have been different if he had stood with Joshua and Caleb? Was the Lord saying even he and Moses would never see the land promised? When Miriam and his sons tried to console him, he left them and went out to sit with Moses.

"So close." Moses' voice was filled with sorrow. "They were so close to all they have ever dreamed of having."

"Fear is the enemy."

"Fear of the Lord would have been their greatest strength. In Him is the victory."

Eleazar ran into the tent early the next morning. "Father! Father, come quickly. Some of the men are leaving camp."

"Leaving?" Aaron went cold. Did these people never learn?

"They say they are going into Canaan. They say they're sorry they sinned, but now they're ready to take the land God promised them."

Aaron hurried out, but Moses was already there, crying out at them to stop. "It's too late! Why are you now disobeying the Lord's orders to return to the wilderness? It won't work. Do not go into the land now. You will only be crushed by your enemies because the Lord is not with you!" Joshua and Caleb and others faithful had joined them, trying to block their way.

"The Lord is with us! We are the sons of Abraham! The Lord said the land is ours!" Heads high, they turned their backs on Moses and headed for Canaan.

Moses cried out one last time in warning. "The Lord will abandon you because you have abandoned the Lord!" When none turned away from certain disaster, Moses sighed wearily. "Prepare the camp. Go about your duties as the Lord has assigned. We're leaving today."

The Lord was taking them back to the place where they thought they had left Egypt behind: the Red Sea.

SIX

The people had not traveled a day when they started grumbling. Aaron saw the scowls and resentful looks. Wherever he walked, cold silence fell around him. The people did not trust him. After all, he was Moses' brother and had taken part in the decision to turn back the way they had come. Back to the hardship. Back to fear and despair. The Lord had issued the order because of their disobedience, but now the people sought a scapegoat.

As they continued to rebel against the Lord, Aaron felt the mounting weight of their sins being loaded onto his back. Conquering his fear, Aaron walked among the people and tried to fulfill the thankless responsibilities the Lord had given him to perform for their sake.

Stragglers returned from Canaan. Most had been killed. Those who had survived were driven back as far as Hormah.

"Those ten spies were telling the truth! Those people are too strong for us!"

Aaron knew trouble was ahead, and did not know how to turn these people's hearts toward God. If only they could see that it was their stubborn refusal to believe what God said that brought continued disaster on them.

They headed back because of their sin, but God continued to extend His hand to His people through Moses. When Aaron sat with his brother and heard the Word of the Lord, it flowed over him clearly and was so full of purpose and love. Every law given was meant to protect, to uphold, to sustain, to guide, to fix the people's hope on the Lord.

Even the offerings were meant to serve a purpose and build a relationship with Him. The burnt offerings made payment for sins and showed devotion to God. The grain offerings gave honor and respect to the Lord who provided for them. The peace offerings were to be given in gratitude for the peace and fellowship the Lord offered. The sin offerings made payment for unintentional sins and restored the sinner to fellowship with God, and the guilt offerings made payment for sins against God and others, providing compensation for those injured.

Every festival was a reminder of God's intended place in their lives. Passover reminded the people of God's deliverance from Egypt. The seven-day Festival of Unleavened Bread reminded them of leaving slavery behind and beginning a new way of life. The Festival of Firstfruits reminded them how God provided for them with Pentecost at the end of the barley harvest and beginning of the wheat harvest to show their joy and thanksgiving over God's provision. The Festival of Trumpets was to release joy and thanksgiving to God and the beginning of a new year with Him as Lord over all. The Day of Atonement removed sin from the people and the nation and restored fellowship with God while the seven-day Festival of Shelters was intended to remind future generations of the protection and guidance God provided in the wilderness and instruct them to continue to trust in the Lord in the years ahead.

Sometimes Aaron despaired. There was so much to remember. So many laws. So many feast days. Every day was governed by the Lord. Aaron was glad of that, but afraid that he would fail again as he had failed thrice before. How could he ever forget the molten calf, the deaths of two of his sons, and Miriam's leprosy?

I am weak, Lord. Make me strong in faith like Moses. Give me the ears to hear and eyes to see Your will. You have made me Your high priest over these people. Give me the wisdom and strength to do what pleases You!

He was all too aware of the pattern of faith. He would witness a miracle and follow God in abject sorrow and repentance. God would seem to hide for a time and the doubts would begin. The people would start grumbling. Skepticism would spread. It seemed faith was strong when it suited the people's purposes, but waned quickly under the stress of hardship. God's divine presence was overhead in the cloud by day and pillar of fire by night, promising to carry them through defeat to victory, but the people grew angry because it wasn't soon enough to suit them.

Had any nation ever heard the voice of God speaking from fire as they had and survived? Had any other god taken one nation for Himself by rescuing it through means of trials, miraculous signs, wonders, war, awesome power, and terrifying acts? Yet that is what the Lord had done for them right before their eyes!

And still they complained!

It would take a bigger miracle than plagues and parting the Red Sea to change the hearts of these people. Not an outside miracle like raining manna from heaven or water from a rock, but something inside.

Oh, Lord, You've written the Law on stone tablets, and Moses has written Your Word on scrolls. Will it ever be written into our hearts so that we might not sin against You? Transform me, Lord. Change me because I'm hot and tired and irritated by everyone around me, by my circumstances. I hate the dust and the thirst and the hollow ache inside me because You seem so far away.

It was not the war ahead that threatened to defeat Aaron, but the daily step-by-step journey in the wilderness. Every day had its challenges. Every day had its tedium.

We've been this way before, Lord. Will we ever get it right?

+ + +

Aaron sat in Moses' tent, resting in the congenial company of his brother. There would be no work today. No reading scrolls and going over instructions. No traveling. No gathering of manna. Aaron had been waiting for six days to have this one day of peace.

And now there was a commotion in the camp. He heard his name shouted. "What now?" He groaned as he rose. It was the Sabbath. Everyone was to rest. Surely, the people could leave him and Moses alone for one day out of the week!

Moses rose with him, tight-lipped and tense.

A gathering of men stood outside. One man was held between two others. "I didn't do anything wrong!" He tried to jerk free, but was held firmly.

"This man was found gathering wood."

"How do you expect me to make a cook fire and feed my family without wood?"

"You should have gathered wood yesterday!"

"We were walking yesterday! Remember?"

"Today is the Sabbath! The Lord said not to work on the Sabbath!"

"I wasn't *working*. I was *gathering*."

Aaron knew the Law was clear, but he didn't want to be the one to pronounce judgment on the man. He looked to Moses, hoping he would have a ready and just answer that would also be merciful. Moses' eyes were shut, his face tight. His shoulders slumped and he looked at the man in custody.

"The Lord says the man must die. The whole community must stone him outside the camp."

The man tried to fight free. "How do you know what the Lord says? Does God speak to you when none of us can hear Him?" He looked at the three men pulling and pushing him. "I didn't do anything wrong! Are you going to listen to that old man? He'll kill all of you before he's through!"

Aaron walked beside Moses. He didn't question what the Lord had said. He knew the Ten Commandments. *Remember to observe the Sabbath day by keeping it holy. Six days a week are set apart for your daily duties and regular work, but the seventh day is a day of rest dedicated to the Lord your God.*

The people gathered around the man. "Help me, brothers! Mama, don't let them do this to me! I didn't do anything wrong, I tell you!"

Moses took up a stone. Aaron bent to take up another. He felt sick. He knew he had committed greater sins than this man. "Now!" Moses commanded. The man tried to block the stones, but they came hard and fast from all directions. One hit him in the side of the head, another squarely between the eyes. He fell to his knees, blood streaming down his face as he screamed for mercy. Another stone silenced him. He fell face first into the dust and lay still.

The people surrounded him, crying out and weeping as they threw harder. It was his defiance that had brought them to this, his sin, his insistence that he do as he wanted when he wanted. If anyone turned away, they would be siding with him, siding with doing whatever they pleased in the face of God. Everyone must participate in the judgment. Everyone must know the cost of sin.

The man was dead, and still the stones came, one from each member of the assembly—men, women, children—until the body was covered over with stones.

Moses sighed heavily. "We must stand on higher ground."

Aaron knew the Lord had given his brother words to say. He walked with him and stood beside him. Raising his hands, Aaron called out. "Come, everyone. Listen and hear the Word of the Lord." He stepped aside as the people came and stood before Moses, their faces bleak. Children wept and clung to their mothers. Men looked less sure of themselves. God would not compromise with sin. Living had become a hazard.

Moses spread his hands. "The Lord says, 'Throughout the generations to come you must make tassels for the hems of your clothing and attach the tassels at each corner with a blue cord. The tassels will remind you of the commands of the Lord, and that you are to obey His commands instead of following your own desires and going your own ways, as you are prone to do. The tassels will help you remember that you must obey all My commands and be holy to your God. I am the Lord your God who brought you out of the land of Egypt that I might be your God. I am the Lord your God!'"

The people moved off slowly, heads down.

Aaron saw the strain in Moses' face, the anger and the tears brimming as the people walked away in silence. Aaron wanted to comfort him. "The people hear the Word, Moses. They just don't yet understand it."

Moses shook his head. "No, Aaron. They understand and defy God anyway." He lifted his head and closed his eyes. "Are we not called Israel? We are people who contend with God!"

"And still, He chose us."

"Don't become proud on that account, my brother. God could have made these rocks into men and probably had better luck with them. Our hearts are hard as stone, and we're more stubborn than any mule. No, Aaron. God chose people beneath the heel of man's power to show the nations that God is all-powerful. It is by and through Him we live. He is taking a multitude of slaves and making them into a nation of freemen under God so that the nations around will know *He is God*. And when they know, they can choose."

Choose what? "Are you saying He is not just *our* God?"

"The Lord is the *only* God. Didn't He prove that to you in Egypt?"

"Yes, but . . . " Did that mean anyone could come to Him and become part of Israel?

"All who crossed the Red Sea with us are part of our community, Aaron. And the Lord has said that we are to have the same rules for Israelite and foreigner. One God. One covenant. One law that applies to all."

"But I thought He meant only to deliver us and give us a land that would belong to us. That's all we want—a place where we can work and live in peace."

"Yes, Aaron, and the land God has promised us is at the crossroads of every major trade route, surrounded by powerful nations, filled with people stronger than we are. Why do you suppose God would put us there?"

It was not a question that lightened Aaron's burdened heart. "To watch us."

"To see God at work in us."

And then to say God was not God would be to deny and defy the power that had created the heavens and the earth.

+ + +

Every day seemed to get worse, until Aaron found himself with Moses standing before an angry delegation formed by Korah, one of their own relatives! Korah wasn't content to stand against them by himself, but had brought Dathan and Abiram, leaders of the Reubenite tribe as his allies, together with two hundred and fifty leaders well-known to Aaron, men who had been appointed to the council to help Moses shoulder the load of leadership. And now, they wanted more power!

"You have gone too far!" Korah stood in front of his allies, speaking for all of them. "Everyone in Israel has been set apart by the Lord, and He is with all of us. What right do you have to act as though you are greater than anyone else among all these people of the Lord?"

Moses fell face to the ground before them, and Aaron threw himself flat on the ground beside him. He knew what these people wanted, and he was powerless against them. Even more terrifying was what the Lord might do in the face of their rebellion. Aaron did not intend to defend his position when he knew his faith was weak and his mistakes so many!

Korah shouted to the others, "Moses sets himself up to be king over us and makes his brother his high priest! Is that what we want?"

"No!" Moses rose from the dust, his eyes blazing. "Tomorrow morning the Lord will show us who belongs to Him and who is holy. The Lord will

allow those who are chosen to enter His holy presence. You, Korah, and all your followers must do this: Take incense burners, and burn incense in them tomorrow before the Lord. Then we will see whom the Lord chooses as His holy one. You Levites are the ones who have gone too far!"

Korah lifted his chin. "Why should we do what you say?"

"Now listen, you Levites! Does it seem a small thing to you that the God of Israel has chosen you from among all the people of Israel to be near Him as you serve in the Lord's Tabernacle and to stand before the people to minister to them? He has given this special ministry only to you and your fellow Levites, but now you are demanding the priesthood as well! The one you are really revolting against is the Lord! And who is Aaron that you are complaining about him?"

Who am I that I should be high priest? Aaron wondered. Any time he had tried to lead, he had brought disaster. No wonder they did not trust him. Why should they?

Lord, Lord, whatever You will, let it be done.

"Let Dathan and Abiram come forward so that I can speak to them."

"We refuse to come! Isn't it enough that you brought us out of Egypt, a land flowing with milk and honey, to kill us here in this wilderness, and that you now treat us like your subjects? What's more, you haven't brought us into the land flowing with milk and honey or given us an inheritance of fields and vineyards. Are you trying to fool us? We will not come."

Moses raised his arms and cried out to the Lord, "Do not accept their offerings! I have not taken so much as a donkey from them, and I have never hurt a single one of them."

"Nor have you given us what you promised!"

"It is not mine to give!"

Korah spit in the dust at Aaron's feet.

Moses shook with rage. "Come here tomorrow and present yourself before the Lord with all your followers. Aaron will also be here. Be sure that each of your two hundred and fifty followers brings an incense burner with incense on it, so you can present them before the Lord. Aaron will also bring his incense burner. Let the Lord decide!"

Crushed in spirit, Aaron made his preparations. Had all these men forgotten the fate of Nadab and Abihu? Did they think they could make their own fire and stir in their own incense and not face God's wrath? He couldn't sleep thinking about what might happen!

The next morning Aaron went out with his censer. Breathing in the sweet scent of frankincense, he stood with Moses at the entrance to the Tabernacle.

Korah came, head high. The number of his followers had multiplied.

The air became denser, warmer, humming with power. Aaron looked up and saw the glory of the Lord rise, Shekinah streaming light in all directions. Aaron heard the indrawn breath from the Israelites who had come to see whom God would choose. Aaron knew they were disappointed, as they had fixed their anger on God's prophet and spokesman. They stood en masse behind Korah.

Aaron heard the Voice.

Get away from these people so that I may instantly destroy them!

As God had put an end to Nadab and Abihu! Crying out, Aaron fell on his face before the Lord, not wanting to see the nation obliterated by fire. Moses fell down beside him praying frantically. "O God, the God and source of all life, must You be angry with all the people when only one man sins?"

The people talked nervously, looking this way and that, looking up, edging back.

Moses came to his feet clumsily and shouted, "Move away from the tents of Korah, Dathan, and Abiram!" He spread his hands and hurried toward the people. "Quick! Get away from the tents of these wicked men, and don't touch anything that belongs to them. If you do, you will be destroyed for their sins!"

"Do not listen to him!" Korah shouted. "Every man you see standing with a censer is holy!"

Aaron stayed on the ground. *God, forgive them. They don't know what they're doing!*

Nothing had changed within the people. They were the same as they had always been—hard-hearted, stubborn, defiant. Just like Pharaoh, who had forgotten the hardships of the plagues each time God lifted His hand, these people forgot God's kindness and provision when hardship came. Just as Pharaoh had clung to Egypt's ways and his pride, these people clung to their longing for a self-indulgent life. They longed to return to the idol-infested country that had enslaved them.

"Were we not ourselves chosen by God to lead as a council?" Someone else called out in rebellion.

"What has this old man done for you? We will show honor to God by leading you into the land God conquered for us. We will return to Egypt, and we will be the masters this time!"

Moses cried out, "By this you will know that the Lord has sent me to do all these things that I have done—for I have not done them on my own. If these men die a natural death, then the Lord has not sent me. But if the Lord performs a miracle and the ground opens up and swallows them and all their belongings, and they go down alive into the grave, then you will know that these men have despised the Lord!"

The earth rumbled. Aaron felt the ground roll violently beneath him as if the Lord were shaking dust from a blanket. Aaron rose, spreading his feet for balance, holding tight to his censer. Rocks cracked and a chasm opened. Korah pitched forward, screaming, and fell headfirst into the gaping hole, his men after him. Down went his tent with his wife and concubines, his servants. All of those whom the Lord found guilty went down into the earth alive. The horrific screams that rose from the crevice sent the people scattering in terror.

"Get back! Get away! The earth will swallow us, too!"

The chasm closed, deadening the horrific sounds of pain and terror that came up from the earth.

Fire blazed forth from the Lord and burned up the two hundred and fifty men offering incense, turning them into charred corpses like Nadab and Abihu. They dropped where they stood, their bodies smoldering, blackened fingers still gripping the censers that clattered to the ground spilling out homemade incense.

Aaron alone remained standing before the entrance of the Tabernacle, the censer of incense still clutched in his hand.

"Eleazar!" Moses beckoned Aaron's son. "Collect the censers and hammer them into sheets to cover the altar. The Lord has said this will remind the people now and in the future that no one except a descendant of Aaron should come to burn incense before Him, or he will become like Korah and his followers."

All through the night, Aaron heard the echo of hammer against bronze as his son obeyed the Word of the Lord. Far into the night, Aaron prayed with tears streaming into his beard. "According to Your will, Lord . . . as You will. . . ."

+   +   +

Aaron thought he was still dreaming when he heard angry cries. Exhausted, he rubbed his face. He wasn't dreaming. He groaned as he recognized Dathan's and Abiram's voices. "Moses and Aaron have killed the Lord's people!"

Would these people never change? Would they never learn?

He rose quickly, his sons Eleazar and Ithamar with him, and met Moses before the Tabernacle. "What do we do?" The people were heading toward them.

The mob came, shouting accusations. "You two have killed the Lord's people."

"Korah was a Levite just as you are and you killed him!"

"The Levites are servants of the Lord!"

"You killed them!"

"You two won't be satisfied until we're all dead!"

The cloud came down and covered the Tent of Meeting and the Shekinah glory glowed from within the cloud.

"Come with me, Aaron." Moses went to the front of the Tabernacle, and Aaron joined him there. Shaking, Aaron heard the Voice fill his mind. He fell on his face, arms outstretched.

Get away from these people so that I can instantly destroy them!

And what would the nations say then if the Lord could not bring His people into the land He promised?

People screamed, and then Moses spoke. "Quick, take an incense burner and place burning coals on it from the altar. Lay incense on it and carry it quickly among the people to make atonement for them. The Lord's anger is blazing among them—the plague has already begun."

Aaron clambered to his feet and ran as fast as his aging legs could carry him. Breathing hard, he took the censer and ran to the altar. He took the golden utensil and scooped burning coals into his censer. His hand shook. People were already dying!

Thousands fell on their faces, crying out to the Lord, crying out to Moses, crying out to him. "Lord, have mercy on us. Have mercy! Save us, Moses. Aaron, save us!"

He must hurry! Aaron sprinkled the incense onto the coals and turned back. Huffing and puffing, heart pounding and pain spreading across his chest, he headed straight into the midst of men and women falling to the right and left. He held the censer high. "Lord, have mercy on us. Lord, forgive them. Oh, God, we repent! Hear our prayer!"

Dathan and Abiram lay dead, their faces stiff in agony. Everywhere Aaron looked, men and women were dropping from the plague.

Aaron stood in the midst of them and cried out, "Those who are for the Lord, get behind me!" The people moved like the tide of a sea. Others who stood their ground screamed and fell, groaning in agony as they died. Aaron did not move from his post, the living on one side and the dying on the other. He stayed, arm trembling as he held the censer high and prayed.

The plague abated.

His breathing slowed. Bodies sprawled all over the camp, thousands of them. Some lay close to the burned places where the two hundred and fifty Levites had died only yesterday. Survivors clutched one another and wept, wondering if they would be struck down by fire or die in agony of plague. Each body would have to be lifted and carried for burial outside the camp.

Weary, Aaron walked back to Moses standing at the entrance of the Tabernacle. Aaron looked into the stricken faces of the people staring at him. Would another rebellion begin tomorrow? Why couldn't they see that he wasn't their leader? Even Moses did not lead them. When would they understand that *the Lord* directed their path! It was God's divine presence that would make them into a holy nation!

Lord, Lord, I am so tired. They look to me and Moses, and we are just men like they are. You are the one leading us into the wilderness. I don't want to go any more than they do, but I know You are training us for a purpose.

How long will we fight against You? How long will we bow down to our own pride? It seems such an easy thing to look up, to listen and live! What is it in our nature that makes us fight against You so hard? We go our own way and die, and still we don't learn. We are foolish, all of us! I, most of all. Every day I fight the battle within me.

Oh, Lord, You lifted me from a mud pit and opened up the Red Sea. You brought me through the desert. Not once did You abandon me. And still . . . still I doubt. Still I fight a battle within myself I can't seem to win!

These people wanted someone else to stand between the Lord and them, someone more worthy to offer atonement. He couldn't blame them. He wanted the same thing.

Moses spoke again, his voice calm and clear. "Each leader from each ancestral tribe will bring me his staff with his name written on it. The staff of Levi will bear Aaron's name. I will place them in the Tabernacle in front of the Ark of the Covenant, and the staff belonging to the man the Lord chooses will sprout. When you know the man whom God has chosen, you will not grumble against the Lord anymore."

The tribal leaders came forward and handed Moses their staffs, their names etched into the wood. Aaron stood to one side. In his hand, he held the staff that had become a snake before Pharaoh and swallowed the snakes created by the Egyptian sorcerers. This was the same staff he had held over the Nile when the Lord turned the waters to blood and then brought forth the frogs. The Lord had told him to strike the ground with this staff and then the Lord had sent a plague of gnats.

"Aaron." Moses held out his hand.

Tomorrow everyone would know if his staff was simply a gnarled piece of acacia wood that offered him support as he walked the desert road, or an emblem of authority. He gave it to Moses. If God willed it, let another more worthy be chosen to become high priest. As a matter-of-fact, Aaron hoped He would. These men didn't understand the burden that came with the position.

Next morning, Moses summoned the people again. He held each staff high and returned it to its rightful owner. Not one had sprouted so much as a nub. When he held Aaron's staff high, the people murmured in awe. Aaron stared, amazed. Not only had his staff sprouted leaves; it had budded, blossomed, and produced almonds!

"The Lord has said that Aaron's staff will remain in front of the Ark of the Covenant as a warning to rebels! This should put an end to your complaints against the Lord and prevent any further deaths!" Moses took Aaron's staff back into the Tabernacle and came out empty-handed.

"We are as good as dead!" The people huddled together and wept. "We are ruined!"

"Everyone who even comes close to the Tabernacle of the Lord dies."

"We are all doomed!"

Moses entered the Tabernacle.

Aaron followed. His heart ached with compassion. What could he say that would do any good? Only God knew what the days ahead would reveal. And Aaron doubted the way would be any smoother than it had been so far.

The people continued to cry in despair. "Pray for us, Aaron. Moses, plead for our lives."

Even in the shade of the Tabernacle, standing before the veil, he could hear their weeping. And he wept with them.

+   +   +

"Be ready." Aaron kept his sons close, watching over them. "We must wait on the Lord. The moment the cloud rises, we must move quickly."

As the sun rose, the cloud rose and spread out over the camp. He watched it and saw that it was moving. "Eleazar! Ithamar! Come!" They headed quickly for the Tabernacle. "Don't forget the cloth." His sons took up the heavy chest and followed him inside the inner chamber. Removing the shielding curtain, he covered the Ark of the Covenant with it, then covered it with heavy, protective hides and spread a solid blue cloth over it. He slid the acacia wood poles into the golden rings.

Feeling clumsy in his haste, Aaron tried to calm himself and remember the details of preparing for travel. At his instructions, Eleazar and Ithamar spread another blue cloth on the Table of the Presence and placed on it the plates, dishes, bowls, and jars for the drink offerings. The Bread of the Presence remained. Everything was covered by a scarlet cloth and then covered again with hides. The lampstand was covered in blue and wrapped, along with the wick trimmers, trays, and jars for the oil. A blue cloth was spread over the gold altar. As soon as the ashes were removed and properly deposited, the bronze altar was covered with a purple cloth, along with all the utensils. When each item was properly stowed for travel, Aaron nodded. "Summon the Kohathites." The Lord had assigned them to carry the holy things.

The Gershonites were responsible for the Tabernacle and tent, its coverings, and the curtains. The Merarite clans were responsible for the crossbars, posts, bases, and all the equipment.

The Lord moved out before them overhead. Moses followed, staff in hand. Those who carried the Ark followed Moses; Aaron and his sons came next. Behind them, the multitude gathered in ranks with their tribes and proceeded in order.

Eleazar watched the cloud. "Where do you think the Lord will take us, Father?"

"Wherever He wills."

They traveled until late in the afternoon and the cloud stopped. The Ark was set down. Aaron oversaw the rebuilding of the Tabernacle and the raising of the curtains around it. He and his sons unwrapped each item carefully and placed it where it belonged. Eleazar filled the seven-branched lampstand with oil, and prepared the fragrant incense. At twilight, Aaron made the offering before the Lord.

As night came, Aaron stood outside his tent and surveyed the arid land by moonlight. There was little pasturage here and no water. He knew they would be on the move again soon.

In the morning, the cloud rose again and Aaron and his sons set to work quickly. Day after day, they did this until Aaron and his sons moved with quick precision, and the people fell into order with a single blast of the shofar.

One day Aaron rose expecting to move, but the cloud remained. Another day passed and another.

When Aaron and his sons and the people settled easily, relaxing their vigil, the cloud rose again. As he walked, Aaron remembered the jubilance and celebration as they had left Egypt. Now, the people were silent, stoic as they began to realize the fullness of God's decree that they would wander in the wilderness until the rebellious generation had died.

They came to rest again.

After performing the evening sacrifice, Aaron joined Moses. They ate together in silence. Aaron had spent the entire day at the Tabernacle, performing his duties from dawn to dusk, and overseeing that the others did as the Lord bade them. He knew his brother had spent his day reviewing difficult cases and bringing them before the Lord. Moses looked tired. Neither felt like talking. They spent their days talking.

Miriam served manna cakes. "Perhaps we will stay here for a time. There's plenty of grass for the animals and water."

The cloud rose just as Aaron completed the morning sacrifice. Aaron swallowed his sorrow and called out to his sons. "Come! Quickly!" His sons hastened to him. The people rushed to their tents to make preparations for travel.

They only traveled half a day this time, and then remained camped in one place for a month.

"Does God tell you beforehand, Father?" Eleazar walked beside Aaron, his eyes on the Ark. "Does God give you any indication that we will be moving?"

"No. Not even Moses knows the day and the hour."

Ithamar hung his head. "Forty years, the Lord said."

"We deserve our punishment, Brother. If we had heeded Joshua and Caleb instead of the others, perhaps . . ."

Aaron felt such a heavy sorrow inside that he could hardly breathe past it. It came upon him so strongly he knew it must be from the Lord. *Oh, God, God, do we understand Your purposes? Will we ever understand?* "It is not merely punishment, my sons."

Ithamar looked at him. "What is it then, Father? This endless wandering?"

"Training."

His sons looked perplexed. Eleazar looked acquiescent, but Ithamar shook his head. "We move from one place to another, like nomads with no home."

"We look at the outer purposes and think we understand, but remember, my sons: God is merciful as well as just."

Ithamar shook his head. "I don't understand."

Aaron sighed deeply, keeping his pace steady, his gaze straight ahead on the Ark and Moses in the distance. "We came through the Red Sea, but we brought Egypt with us. We have to let go of who we were and become what God intends us to be."

"Free," Eleazar said.

"I don't call this freedom."

Aaron glanced at Ithamar. "Do not question the Lord. You are free, but you must learn obedience. We must all learn. We became a new nation when God brought us out of Egypt. And the nations around watch us. But what have we done with our freedom but drag all the old ways with us? We must learn to wait on the Lord. Where I have failed, you must succeed. You must learn to keep your eyes and ears open. You must learn to move when God tells you to move, and not before. One day, the Lord will bring you and your children to the Jordan. And when God says, 'Take the land,' you must be ready to go in and take and hold it."

Ithamar raised his head. "We'll be ready."

The arrogant impetuousness of youth. "I hope so, my son. I hope so."

✦   ✦   ✦

The years passed slowly as the Israelites wandered in the wilderness. The Lord always provided enough pasture for the animals. He gave the people manna and water to sustain them. Their shoes and clothing never wore out. Each day, Aaron arose from his pallet and saw the presence of the Lord in the cloud. Each night before he entered his tent to rest, he saw the presence of the Lord in the pillar of fire.

Year after year, the people traveled. Every morning and evening, Aaron offered sacrifices and fragrant offerings. He pored over the scrolls Moses wrote, reading them until he had memorized every word the Lord had spoken to Moses. As the high priest, Aaron knew he must know the Law better than anyone else.

The people God had delivered from Egypt began to die. Some died at an early age. Others lived into their seventies and eighties. But the generation that had come out of Egypt dwindled, and the children grew tall.

Aaron never let a day go by without instructing his children and grandchildren in the law of the Lord. Some of them had not been born when God brought the plagues upon Egypt. They never saw the Red Sea parted, or walked on the dry land to reach the other side. But they gave thanks for the manna they received every day. They praised the Lord for the water that quenched their thirst. And they grew strong as they walked the wilderness and relied on the Lord for everything they needed to live.

+   +   +

"He's asking for you, Aaron."

Aaron rose slowly, his joints stiff, his back aching. His grief deepened each time he sat with an old friend who was dying—deepened and remained. There were so few left now, a mere handful of those who had worked in the mud pits making bricks for Egypt.

And Hur had been a good friend, one of those Aaron could trust to strive to do right. He was the last of the first seventy men chosen to judge the people, the other sixty-nine now replaced by younger men, trained and chosen for their love of and adherence to the Law.

Hur lay on a pallet in his tent, his children and grandchildren gathered around him. Some wept softly. Others sat in silence, heads bowed. His eldest son sat close beside him, leaning down to hear his father's final instructions.

Hur saw Aaron standing in the doorway of the tent. "My friend." His voice was weak, his body emaciated by age and infirmity. He spoke softly to his son and the younger man withdrew, making a place for Aaron. Hur raised his hand weakly. "My friend . . ." He squeezed Aaron's hand weakly. "I am the last of those condemned to die in the wilderness. The forty years are almost over."

His hand felt so cold, the bones so fragile. Aaron put his hands around his as though he were holding a bird.

"Oh, Aaron. All these years of wandering and I still feel the weight of my sin. It's as though the years have not diminished it, but removed my strength to endure it." His eyes were moist. "But sometimes I dream I am standing on the shores of the Jordan, looking across at the Promised Land. My heart breaks at the loss of it. It is so beautiful, not at all like this wilderness in which we live. All I can do is dream of the fields of grain and the fruit trees, the flocks of sheep and cattle, and hope my sons and their sons will soon sit under an olive tree and hear the bees humming." Tears trickled into his white hair. "I am more alive when I sleep than when I wake."

Aaron fought the emotions gripping him. He understood what Hur was saying, understood with every fiber of his being. Regret for sins committed. Repentance. Forty years of walking with the consequences.

Hur let out his breath softly. "Our sons are not as we were. They have learned to move when God moves, and rest when He rests."

Aaron closed his eyes and said nothing.

"You doubt."

Aaron stroked his friend's hand. "I hope."

"Hope is all we have left, my friend."

And love.

It had been a long, long time since Aaron had heard the Voice, and he uttered a sob of gratitude, his heart yearning toward it, leaning in, drinking. "Love," he whispered hoarsely. "The Lord disciplines us as we discipline our sons, Hur. It may not feel like love when we're living in the midst of it, but love it is. Hard and true, lasting."

"Hard and true, lasting."

Aaron knew death was drawing near. It was time to withdraw. He had his duties to perform, the evening sacrifice to offer. He leaned close one last time. "May the Lord's face yet shine upon you and give you peace."

"And you. When you sit beneath your olive tree, Aaron, think of me. . . ."

Aaron paused outside the tent, and let his mind wander to the past. He would always remember Hur standing on the hilltop with him, holding Moses' left hand in the air while he held his brother's right, and below them Joshua defeating the Amalekites.

He knew the moment Hur breathed his last. Clothes ripped, men sobbed, and the women keened. It was a sound oft heard in camp over the years, but this time it brought with it a sense of completion.

Their wandering was about to come to an end. A new day was coming.

✦ ✦ ✦

Aaron stood in his priestly garb before the curtain that hid the Most Holy Place from sight. He shook as he always did when the Lord spoke to him. Even after forty years, he had not become accustomed to the sound within and without and all around him, the Voice that filled his senses with delight and terror.

You, your sons, and your relatives from the tribe of Levi will be held responsible for any offenses related to the sanctuary. But you and your sons alone will be held liable for violations

connected with the priesthood. Bring your relatives of the tribe of Levi to assist you and your sons as you perform the sacred duties in front of the Tabernacle of the Covenant. But as the Levites go about their duties under your supervision, they must be careful not to touch any of the sacred objects or the altar. If they do, both you and they will die.

Let it sink in and remain fresh in my mind, Lord. Don't let me forget anything.

I myself have chosen your fellow Levites from among the Israelites to be your special assistants.

Oh, Lord, let them be men whose hearts are fixed on pleasing You! From the time of Jacob, we have killed men in anger. Cursed is our anger. It is so fierce. And we tend to cruelty. Oh, Lord, and now You are scattering us throughout Israel just as Jacob prophesied. We are dispersed as priests among Your people. Make us a holy nation! Give us tender hearts!

I have put the priests in charge of all the holy gifts that are brought to Me by the people of Israel. I have given these offerings to you and your sons as your regular share.

Let my life be an offering!

You priests will receive no inheritance of land or share of property among the people of Israel. I am your inheritance and your share. As for the tribe of Levi, your relatives, I will pay them for their service in the Tabernacle with the tithes from the entire land of Israel.

Aaron surrendered to the Voice, listening, listening, drinking in the words like living water.

The Lord commanded that a red heifer without defect or blemish and that had never been under a yoke be given to Eleazar to be taken outside the camp and slaughtered. Aaron's son would take some of the blood on his finger and sprinkle it seven times toward the front of the Tent of Meeting. The heifer was to be burned, the ashes collected and put into a ceremonially clean place outside the camp for use in the water of cleansing, for purification from sin.

So much to remember: the festivals, the sacrifices, the laws.

Aaron sat with Moses and looked out over the tents and flickering lights of thousands of campfires. "We are all that is left of the generation that left Egypt." Thirty-eight years had passed from the time they left Kadesh-barnea until they crossed the Zered Valley. The entire generation of fighting men had perished from the camp, as the Lord had sworn would happen. "Just you and me and Miriam."

Surely now, the Lord would turn them toward the Promised Land.

+ + +

The cloud moved and the whole community traveled with the Lord until He stopped over the Desert of Zin. The people made camp at Kadesh.

While Aaron studied the scrolls, Miriam laid her hand on his shoulder. "I love you, Aaron. I have loved you like a son."

His sister had spoken very little since the Lord had afflicted her with leprosy, healed her, and commanded her to spend the seven days of cleansing outside the camp. She had returned a different woman—tenderly patient, quiet. She served the family with her customary devotion, but kept her thoughts to herself. He was perplexed by her sudden need to say she loved him.

She went outside the tent and sat at the entrance.

Troubled, Aaron rose and went out to her. "Miriam?"

"It is our own pride that slays us, Aaron."

Aaron searched her face. "Shall I send for Eleazar's wife to tend you?" She looked so old and worn down, her dark eyes soft and moist.

"Come closer, Aaron." She cupped his face and looked into his eyes. "I have made terrible mistakes."

"I know. So have I." Her hands were cool, her fingers trembling. He remembered when she was robust and full of fire. He had learned long ago not to argue with his sister. But she was different now. Humiliated before all Israel, humbled before God, she had become strangely content when God had stripped her of the one thing she could not conquer—her pride. "And the Lord forgave us both."

"Yes." She smiled and took her hands from him. She folded them in her lap. "We contend with God and He disciplines us. We repent and God forgives." She looked up at the cloud moving in slow undulating circles overhead. "Only His love endures forever."

Aaron felt a niggling fear grow inside him. Miriam was slipping away. Fear gripped him. She was dying. Surely the Lord would allow Miriam to enter Canaan. If she was not spared, would he also die before they reached the Jordan River? He could not imagine life without his sister. She had always been there for him, from the time he was a little boy. She had been like a second mother, scolding and disciplining him, guiding and teaching him. At eight, she had been bold enough to approach Pharaoh's daughter. Her quick thinking had brought Moses home for a few years before he was taken into the palace.

He beckoned Ithamar. "Bring Moses." Ithamar took one look at his aunt and ran. Aaron took Miriam's hand and tried to warm it between his. "Moses will come." She was just tired. She would be better soon. She would be refreshed after a rest and rise again.

"Moses cannot stop what God has ordained, Aaron. Have I not been just as disobedient as the others of our generation who have died? It is just that I go the way of all flesh here in the wilderness."

And what about me?

The cloud changed from gray to gold and from gold to fiery orange and red as day became night. The Lord stood guard, giving them light and warmth by night, just as the Lord gave them shade during the heat of the day.

"I'm not afraid, Aaron. It's time."

"Don't talk that way." He rubbed her hand. "The forty years are nearly up. We are about to go into the Promised Land."

"Oh, Aaron, don't you understand yet?"

Moses hurried toward them, staff in hand. Aaron rose. "Moses. Help her. Please. She can't die. We're so close."

"Miriam, my sister . . ." Moses knelt beside her. "Are you in pain?"

Her mouth curved. "Life is pain."

The family gathered: Eleazar and Ithamar and their wives and children; Eliezer and Gershom sat with her. Moses' Cushite wife approached. Smiling, Miriam lifted her hand. They had long since made their peace and become dear friends. Miriam spoke in a whisper, her strength ebbing. The Cushite woman wept and kissed Miriam's hand.

Aaron was frantic with fear. This couldn't be happening! Miriam couldn't die yet. Hadn't she been the one to lead the people with songs of deliverance, songs of praise to the Lord?

It was near dawn when Miriam sighed deeply. She died with her eyes still open and fixed on the pillar of fire that now became the swirling gray cloud. Spears of sunlight came from it, making spots of light on the desert ground.

With an anguished cry, Aaron reached toward her, only to be pulled back by Eleazar. "You can't touch her now, Father." A high priest could not allow himself to become unclean. He would be unfit to perform his duties for the people as their high priest! Sobbing, Aaron straightened with difficulty.

"Father?" Eleazar supported him.

"It is time for the morning sacrifices." Aaron heard the harshness in his own voice and did not regret it. Is this the kindness of God, to allow his sister to live so long and then have her die so close to the borders of the Promised Land?

You never forget our sins, do You, Lord? Never.

Grieving and angry, he walked away as his sons' wives and servants began the warbling scream of grief.

People nearby heard and came running. Soon the entire camp was wailing.

✦ ✦ ✦

No sooner was Miriam buried than the people complained again. A crowd stood before the Tabernacle and quarreled with Moses. "Why did you bring the Lord's community to this place?"

Aaron could not stop thinking about his sister. Every day he awakened with an aching heart. Every day he had to come here and serve the Lord, and every day these grown children turned out to be no better than their fathers and mothers!

"There's no water here!"

"Why did you make us leave Egypt and bring us here to this terrible place?"

Aaron stepped forward. "What do you know of Egypt? You were not even born when we left that place!"

"We've heard!"

"We have come close enough to look back and see the green along the Nile."

"What have we had in this desert?"

"There's no grain!"

"And no figs!"

"No grapes or pomegranates."

"And there is no water to drink!"

"We wish we had died in the Lord's presence with our brothers!"

Aaron turned away, so angry he knew if he remained, he would say or do something he would later regret. He looked at Moses, hoping to draw wisdom and patience from him, but his brother too was red with anger. Moses fell on his face at the entrance of the Tabernacle and Aaron went down beside him. He wanted to pound his fists on the ground. How long would the Lord expect them to lead these people? Did they think he and Moses had water to drink? How many times did these people have to witness a miracle before they believed that he and Moses were appointed by the Lord to lead them?

You are the one who brought us to this place! They always blame us! Is it Your plan that my brother and I die at their hands? They are ready to kill us! Lord, give them water to drink.

You and Aaron must take the staff and assemble the entire community. As the people watch, command the rock over there to pour out its water. You will get enough water from the rock to satisfy all the people and their livestock.

Moses rose and went inside the Tabernacle. He came out with Aaron's staff in his hand. "Gather those rebels!"

Aaron went out ahead of him and shouted at the people to gather together in front of the rock. "You want water? Come and see it pour from the rock!" They swarmed there, empty water bags in hand, still complaining.

Moses pushed Aaron to one side and stood in front of all of them, the staff in his hand. "Listen, you rebels! Must we bring you water from this rock?"

"Yes! Give us water!"

Moses took the staff with both hands and hit the rock.

"Water, Moses! Give us water, Moses!"

Face red, eyes blazing, Moses struck the rock again, harder this time. Water gushed forth. The people pressed forward, crying out, rejoicing, filling their cupped hands, filling their skin bags, laughing and cheering Moses and Aaron. Aaron laughed with them, exultant. See how water flowed when his staff was wielded.

"Blessings on you, Moses! May you be praised, Aaron!"

Moses stood apart from them, staff in hand, head high, watching.

Aaron cupped his hands and drank with the people. Aaron blushed with pleasure as people called out praise to him and Moses. The water continued to flow and the Israelites brought their flocks and herds to drink. And still the water came. Never had water tasted so good. He wiped the droplets from his beard and grinned at Moses. "They do not doubt us now, do they, my brother?"

Because you did not trust Me enough to demonstrate My holiness to the people of Israel, you will not lead them into the land I am giving them!

God spoke softly, but with a finality that made Aaron's blood go cold. The curse of the Levites was on him. He had lost his temper and given in to pride. He had forgotten the Lord's command. *Command the rock.* No, that wasn't true. He hadn't forgotten. He had wanted Moses to use his staff. He had cheered when water gushed from the rock. He had been proud and delighted when the people slapped him on the back.

How quickly he had fallen headlong into sin. And now, he would pay the consequences just like the rest of his generation, even Miriam who had repented and served others with gladness for almost forty years! He would not set foot in the land God had promised the Israelites either. Miriam had died, and now he would die, too.

Aaron sank down and sat on a boulder, shoulders slumped, hands limp between his knees. What hope had he of ever being any different than what he was: a sinner. Pride, Miriam had said. Pride slays men. Pride strips men of a future and a hope. He covered his face. "I have sinned against the Lord."

"As have I."

Aaron glanced up. His brother's face was ashen. He was bent like an old man, leaning heavily on the staff. "Not as I have sinned, Moses. You have always praised the Lord and credited Him with all righteousness."

"Not today. I allowed anger to rule me. Pride made me stumble. And now, I too will die on this side of the Jordan River. The Lord has told me that I will not enter the land He promised."

"No." Aaron wept. "I am more to blame than you, Moses. I cried out for you to give us water as loudly as any of them. It is right that I be denied a land of my own. I am a sinner."

"Sin is sin, Aaron. Let's not get into a quarrel over who has outdone the other in that regard. We are all sinners. It is but for the grace of God that we live and breathe at all."

"You are the one God chose to deliver Israel!"

"Do not let your love for me blind you, my brother. *God* is our deliverer."

Aaron held his head. "Let your one mistake be on my head. Wasn't I the one who fashioned the molten calf and let the people run wild? Did I not try to steal some of your praise just now?"

"We both stole glory from God, who gave the water. All I had to do was speak to the rock. And what did I do but make a show for their benefit? And why else but to gain their attention, rather than remind them God is their provider."

"You have been telling them that for years, Moses."

"It needed to be said again." Moses sat beside him on the boulder. "Aaron, are we not each responsible for our own sins? The Lord chastens me because I didn't trust Him. The people need to trust in Him, only in Him."

"I'm sorry."

"Why are you sorry?"

"The Lord called me to stand beside you, to help you. And what help have I been over the years? If I were a better man, a better priest, I would have realized the temptation. I would have warned you."

Moses sighed. "I lost my temper, Aaron. I didn't forget what the Lord commanded. I didn't think speaking would be . . . impressive enough." His fingers tightened on Aaron's knee. "We must not be discouraged, Aaron. Doesn't a father discipline a son in order to train him up in the way he should go?"

"And where will we go now, Moses? God has said we will never set foot in the Promised Land. What hope have we?"

"God is our hope."

Aaron could not stop his tears. His throat ached. His chest heaved. *Oh, God, I've failed You and my brother yet again. Was I destined to stumble through life? Oh, Lord, Lord, surely, of all men, Moses has been the most humble. Surely he deserves to cross the Jordan River and walk in the pastures of Canaan, even if only for a day.*

I understand why You are keeping me out. I deserve to remain in the desert.
I deserved death for making that detestable golden calf! Am I not reminded
of it every time I sacrifice a bullock? But, oh, Lord, my brother has been Your
faithful servant. He loves You. No man is more humble than my brother.

Let the blame fall on me for being such a fool and being so weak a priest
that I failed to see sin when it crouched ready to kill our hopes and dreams.

Be silent, and know that I am God!

Aaron swallowed hard, fear coursing through him. It would do no good
to beg or argue. And he knew the rest as though spoken into his heart. The
people had to know the cost of sin. In the eyes of God, all men and women
were equal. Aaron was without excuse. And so was Moses.

Only God is holy and to be praised.

They returned together to the Tabernacle. Moses went inside and Aaron
stood outside the veil, his heart heavy. He could hear Moses speaking softly,
his words indistinct, his anguish clear. Aaron bowed his head, the pain in
his chest suffocating.

My fault, Lord. My fault. What kind of high priest am I who fails at every
turn of life and cannot see sin when it stands before him? Forgive me, Lord.
My sins are ever before me. I have done what is evil in Your sight. You have
judged me justly. Oh, if only You would purify me so that I could be clean like a
newborn child. If only You would wash me clean of my sins and make me hear
with renewed joy the promise of Your salvation!

He wiped his tears away quickly lest they fall on the chestpiece of his
priestly garment. *I must be clean. I must be clean!*

Oh, God of Abraham, Isaac, and Jacob. God of all creation. How will I
ever be clean, Lord? I am clean on the outside, but inside I feel like a grave
of old bones. I am full of sin. And it poured over today, as from a fouled pot.
Even when I offer the atonement sacrifice, I feel the sin in me. I fight against
it, Lord, but it is still there.

Aaron heard Moses weeping. God had not changed His mind. The
Promised Land was lost to both of them. Aaron covered his face, heartbroken.

Moses! Poor Moses.

Oh, God, hear my prayer. If You see me weaken, don't let me succumb to
sin again or cause trouble for my brother. Don't let me stand up in pride and
lead the people astray. Oh, God, I would rather You took my life than I give
in to sin again!

✦   ✦   ✦

Moses sent messengers to the king of Edom requesting permission to cross
his land in order to lessen the distance to Canaan. Moses promised that the
Israelites would not go through any field or vineyard, or drink water from

any well. They would turn neither to the right nor to the left until they reached the trade route called the King's Highway.

The king of Edom answered that he would not give permission, and if the Israelites tried to cross his land, he would march out and attack them with the sword. Moses sent messengers again with assurances that they would only go along the main road and would pay for any water their animals might need. Again, the king of Edom denied them passage and came out with a large army to make sure no attempt was made to cross his land.

The cloud moved from Kadesh, and Moses followed the Angel of the Lord along the boundary of Edom toward Mount Hor. Aaron walked beside his brother, desolate. When they camped, he performed the evening sacrifice. Depressed, he returned to his tent and carefully removed his priestly garments. Then he sat in the doorway and stared out. All day, while walking, he had felt the barrenness of the land around him. And now, sitting here, he remembered the fields of wheat in Egypt, the barley, the green pasturelands of Goshen.

We were slaves, he reminded himself. He thought about the taskmasters. He tried to remember how many times he had felt the lash on his back, and the heat of the desert sun beating down on him.

And the green . . . the smell of water filled with silt washing along the banks of the Nile . . . the ibises tipping their beaks in and drawing out fish . . .

Raising his head weakly, he looked up at the pillar of fire. *God, help me. Help me.*

And he heard the Voice again, soft yet firm.

Aaron waited all night and then rose in the morning and put on his priestly garments. He went to the Tabernacle, washed, and performed the morning sacrifice as usual. And then Moses came to him, Eleazar at his side. Moses took a slow breath, but could not speak. Eleazar looked perplexed.

Aaron put his hand out and gripped his brother's arm. "I know, Moses. The Lord spoke to me, too. Yesterday, at sunset."

Eleazar looked between them. "What has happened?"

Aaron looked at his son. "We are to go up Mount Hor."

"When?"

"Now." Aaron was thankful his son did not ask why. Nor did he ask that they postpone the journey until the cool of the evening. Eleazar simply started out toward the foot of the mountain.

Maybe there was hope for Israel after all.

+   +   +

The climb was difficult, for there was only a narrow pathway between and around rugged rock outcroppings. Up, up Aaron climbed until he was exhausted and every muscle in his body ached. He kept putting one foot in front of the other, praying the Lord would give him strength. It would be the first time the Lord had called him to the top of a mountain. And the last.

After long hours of travail, he reached the top. His heart was pounding heavily, his lungs burning. He felt more alive than he ever had before as he stretched out trembling hands and gave thanks to God. The cloud pressed in and rose, turning from gray to orange-gold, then flashing red. Aaron felt warmth course through him and then dissipate, leaving him weak. He knew if he sat down, he would never rise again, and he needed to stand a little longer.

So he stood alone for the first time in years and looked at the plain below, speckled with thousands of tents. Each tribe had its position, and in the center was the Tabernacle. Flocks of sheep and herds of cattle grazed on the outer edges of the camp, and the vastness of the wilderness spread out before him.

Eleazar helped Moses up the last few feet, and then the three stood together, gazing out over Israel. "You need to rest, Father."

"I will." *Forever.*

Moses looked at him and still could not speak. Aaron went to him and embraced him. Moses' shoulders shook and Aaron held him tighter and spoke softly. "Oh, my brother, I wish I had been a better and stronger man to stand at your side."

Moses did not let go of him. "The Lord sees our faults, Aaron. He sees our failures and frailty. But what matters to Him is our faith. We have both stumbled, my brother. We have both fallen. And the Lord has lifted us back up with the strength of His mighty hand and remained with us." He drew back slowly.

Aaron smiled. Never had he loved and respected a man as much as he did his younger brother. "It is not our faith, Moses, but God's faithfulness."

"What's going on?"

Aaron turned to his son. "The Lord has said the time has come for me to join my ancestors in death."

Eleazar flinched, his eyes darting from Aaron to his uncle. "What does he mean?"

"Your father is to die here on Mount Hor."

"*No!*"

Aaron felt the hair stand on the back of his neck. "Yes, Eleazar." He could see already the seed of rebellion in his son's eyes.

"This can't be."

"Do not question the Lord—"

"You have to go with us into Canaan, Father!" His eyes filled with angry tears of confusion. "You have to come!"

"*Be silent!*" Aaron gripped his son's arms. "It is for the Lord to say when a man lives or dies." *Oh, God, forgive him. Please.* He gentled. "The Lord has shown me more kindness than I deserve. He has allowed you to come and attend me." He would not die surrounded by all the members of his family as so many did. But he would not die alone.

Sobbing, Eleazar bowed his head. Aaron ran his hand over his son's back. "You must be strong in the days ahead, Eleazar. You must walk the road the Lord gives you and never depart from it. Cling to the Lord. He is our father."

Moses let out his breath slowly. "Remove your clothing, Eleazar."

Eleazar's head came up. He stared at him. "What?"

"We must fulfill the Lord's command."

Aaron was as surprised as his son. When Eleazar looked at him, he couldn't answer the silent question. "Do as you're told." He only knew he was to die here on top of the mountain. Beyond that, Aaron knew nothing.

Moses shrugged off the water bag he had carried. When Eleazar was undressed, Moses washed him from head to foot. He anointed him with oil and took new linen undergarments from another pack. "Put these on."

And then Aaron understood. His heart swelled until he felt it would burst with joy. When Moses looked at him, Aaron knew to remove his priestly garments. He laid them out carefully on a flat boulder, one piece at a time, until he was standing in his linen undergarments.

Moses took the blue robe and helped Eleazar slip it over his head, the tiny woven pomegranates and gold bells tickling at the hem. Next, he put the embroidered tunic on his nephew, then tied the multicolored sash snugly around his waist. He attached the blue, purple, scarlet, and gold ephod at Eleazar's shoulders with the two onyx stones, six tribes of Israel engraved on each. Eleazar would carry the nation on his shoulders every day for the rest of his life. Moses hung the chestpiece on which were the twelve stones representing the tribes of Israel. He took the Urim and Thummim and tucked them into the pocket over Eleazar's heart.

Tears ran down Aaron's face as he looked at his son. Eleazar, God's chosen high priest. The Lord had once told Aaron that the line of high priests for generations to come would descend from him, but he had been convinced he had spoiled all possibility of that great honor happening. How many times he had sinned! He had been just like the people, complaining of hardships, lusting after things he didn't have, rebelling against Moses and God, greedy for more power and authority, blaming others for trouble he brought on himself by his own disobedience, afraid to trust in God for everything. Oh, that golden calf, that wretched golden idol of sin.

And yet, God kept His promise.

Oh, Lord, Lord, You are merciful to me. Oh, Lord, You alone are faithful!

Even as the joy spread through him, sorrow was in its wake, for he knew Eleazar would struggle as he had struggled. His son would spend the rest of his life trying to learn and obey the Law. The weight of it would press him down, for he too would come to realize how sin dwelt in the secret dark places of his heart. He would try to crush its head with his heel, but he too would fail.

All eyes would be on him, listening to what he said, watching how he lived. And the people would see that Eleazar was merely a man trying to live a godly life. Every morning and every evening, he would perform sacrifices. He would live with the smell of blood and incense. Once a year he would pass through the veil into the Most Holy Place and put the blood of the atonement sacrifice on the horns of the altar. And his son would know then, as Aaron knew now, that he would have to do it again and again and again. Eleazar would be burdened by his sin forever.

God, help us! Lord, have mercy on us! My son will try, as I have tried, and he will fail. You have given us the Law so that we can live holy lives. But Lord, You know we are not holy. We are dust. Will there ever come a day when we will be one people with one mind and heart, one spirit, one in striving to please You? Wash us with hyssop, Lord. Cleanse us from iniquity! Circumcise our hearts!

Trembling and too weak to stand any longer, Aaron sank to the ground and rested his back against a stone.

Is that the reason for the Law, Lord? To show us we can't live it out perfectly? When we break one law, no matter how small it seems, we are lawbreakers. Even if we returned to our mother's womb and started over, we would sin again. We would have to be born again, made into entirely new creations.

Oh, Lord, save us. Send us a Savior who can do all You ask, who can stand before the Most Holy Place without sin, someone who can be our high priest and present the perfect sacrifice, someone who has the power to change us from within so that we can stand without sinning. We need a high priest who can understand our weakness; a high priest who has faced all of the same temptations we face, and yet has not sinned; a high priest who can stand near the throne of God with confidence so that we may receive mercy and find grace to help us when we need it.

Moses sat beside him and spoke softly. Eleazar came near, but Aaron lifted his hand, staying him. "No. For the sake of the people . . ." Aaron could see him struggle.

His son wanted to embrace him, but death was too close to risk reaching out and embracing one another one last time. A high priest must remain clean. Eleazar must not be defiled. Hands clenching and unclenching, Eleazar remained at a distance.

Another stood on the mountain with them. A Man. Yet not a man. Aaron had seen Him walking beside Moses and leading the people out into the desert. He had seen Him again standing within the rock of Marah when water had poured forth for the people.

Moses' friend.

He was wearing a long white robe with a gold sash across His chest. His eyes were bright like the pillar of fire. His feet were as bright as bronze refined in a furnace. And His face was as bright as the sun in all its brilliance. The Man extended His hand.

Aaron.

With a long, deep sigh, Aaron breathed out softly in obedience, *Yes, Lord, yes.*

SEEK AND FIND

❦❦❦❦❦

Dear Reader,

We hope you enjoyed this fictional account of the life of Aaron, Israel's first high priest and brother of Moses. This finely woven tale by Francine Rivers is meant to whet your appetite. Francine's first and foremost desire is to take you back to God's Word to decide for yourself the truth about Aaron—his duties, dilemmas, and disappointments.

The following Bible study is designed to guide you through Scripture to *seek* the truth about Aaron and to *find* applications for your own life.

God called Aaron to encourage Moses. He got off to a great start, but stumbled along the way. Aaron was the middle child—caught between a bright, creative, gutsy older sister and a younger brother who from birth was considered "special." It's not hard to see how Aaron would be, by nature, a people pleaser. A peacekeeper—at all costs. His uncomplaining acceptance of God's timing for his death whispers of Aaron's desire to trust God as fervently in the end as when he started out on the journey.

May God encourage you as you seek Him for the answers to your life's challenges, dilemmas, and disappointments. And may He find you willing to walk with Him through it all.

Peggy Lynch

CALLED TO ENCOURAGE

SEEK GOD'S WORD FOR TRUTH

Read the following passage:

> Then the Lord said to Moses, "Go back to Pharaoh, and tell him to let the people of Israel leave Egypt."
>
> "But Lord!" Moses objected. "My own people won't listen to me anymore. How can I expect Pharaoh to listen? I'm no orator!"
>
> But the Lord ordered Moses and Aaron to return to Pharaoh, king of Egypt, and to demand that he let the people of Israel leave Egypt.
>
> These are the ancestors of clans from some of Israel's tribes:
>
> The descendants of Reuben, Israel's oldest son, included Hanoch, Pallu, Hezron, and Carmi. Their descendants became the clans of Reuben.
>
> The descendants of Simeon included Jemuel, Jamin, Ohad, Jakin, Zohar, and Shaul (whose mother was a Canaanite). Their descendants became the clans of Simeon.
>
> These are the descendants of Levi, listed according to their family groups. In the first generation were Gershon, Kohath, and Merari. (Levi, their father, lived to be 137 years old.)
>
> The descendants of Gershon included Libni and Shimei, each of whom is the ancestor of a clan.
>
> The descendants of Kohath included Amram, Izhar, Hebron, and Uzziel. (Kohath lived to be 133 years old.)
>
> The descendants of Merari included Mahli and Mushi.
>
> These are the clans of the Levites, listed according to their genealogies.
>
> Amram married his father's sister Jochebed, and she bore him Aaron and Moses. (Amram lived to be 137 years old.)
>
> The descendants of Izhar included Korah, Nepheg, and Zicri.
>
> The descendants of Uzziel included Mishael, Elzaphan, and Sithri.
>
> Aaron married Elisheba, the daughter of Amminadab and sister of Nahshon, and she bore him Nadab, Abihu, Eleazar, and Ithamar.
>
> The descendants of Korah included Assir, Elkanah, and Abiasaph. Their descendants became the clans of Korah.
>
> Eleazar son of Aaron married one of the daughters of Putiel, and she bore him Phinehas.   EXODUS 6:10-25

✦ List everything you learn about Aaron from this Levitical lineage.

Read the following passages:

> One day Moses was tending the flock of his father-in-law, Jethro, the priest of Midian, and he went deep into the wilderness near Sinai, the mountain of God. Suddenly, the angel of the Lord appeared to him as a blazing fire in a bush. Moses was amazed because the bush was engulfed in flames, but it didn't burn up. "Amazing!" Moses said to himself. "Why isn't that bush burning up? I must go over to see this."

When the Lord saw that he had caught Moses' attention, God called to him from the bush, "Moses! Moses!"

"Here I am!" Moses replied.   EXODUS 3:1-4

"Now go, for I am sending you to Pharaoh. You will lead my people, the Israelites, out of Egypt."

"But who am I to appear before Pharaoh?" Moses asked God. "How can you expect me to lead the Israelites out of Egypt?"   EXODUS 3:10-11

But Moses protested, "If I go to the people of Israel and tell them, 'The God of your ancestors has sent me to you,' they won't believe me. They will ask, 'Which god are you talking about? What is his name?' Then what should I tell them?"   EXODUS 3:13

But Moses protested again, "Look, they won't believe me! They won't do what I tell them. They'll just say, 'The Lord never appeared to you.'"   EXODUS 4:1

But Moses pleaded with the Lord, "O Lord, I'm just not a good speaker. I never have been, and I'm not now, even after you have spoken to me. I'm clumsy with words."   EXODUS 4:10

But Moses again pleaded, "Lord, please! Send someone else."

Then the Lord became angry with Moses. "All right," he said. "What about your brother, Aaron the Levite? He is a good speaker. And look! He is on his way to meet you now. And when he sees you, he will be very glad. You will talk to him, giving him the words to say. I will help both of you to speak clearly, and I will tell you what to do. Aaron will be your spokesman to the people, and you will be as God to him, telling him what to say. And be sure to take your shepherd's staff along so you can perform the miraculous signs I have shown you."   EXODUS 4:13-17

Now the Lord had said to Aaron, "Go out into the wilderness to meet Moses." So Aaron traveled to the mountain of God, where he found Moses and greeted him warmly. Moses then told Aaron everything the Lord had commanded them to do and say. And he told him about the miraculous signs they were to perform.

So Moses and Aaron returned to Egypt and called the leaders of Israel to a meeting. Aaron told them everything the Lord had told Moses, and Moses performed the miraculous signs as they watched. The leaders were soon convinced that the Lord had sent Moses and Aaron. And when they realized that the Lord had seen their misery and was deeply concerned for them, they all bowed their heads and worshiped.   EXODUS 4:27-31

+ Contrast Moses and Aaron from these passages.

+ Discuss God's role and response from the same passages.

+ What roles did Moses and Aaron take/accept?

+ How did the Israelite people respond? What did they conclude about the two men?

+ What impact, if any, do you think Aaron had on Moses at this juncture? Why?

FIND GOD'S WAYS FOR YOU

+ How do you respond when God impresses you to do something?

+ Which of the two leaders (Moses or Aaron) do you identify with and why?

> The Lord is for me, so I will not be afraid. What can mere mortals do to me? Yes, the Lord is for me; he will help me. I will look in triumph at those who hate me. It is better to trust the Lord than to put confidence in people.
>
> PSALM 118:6-8

+ What do you learn about God from these verses?

STOP AND PONDER

> Now glory be to God! By his mighty power at work within us, he is able to accomplish infinitely more than we would ever dare to ask or hope.
>
> EPHESIANS 3:20

CALLED TO EGYPT

SEEK GOD'S WORD FOR TRUTH

Moses and Aaron both chose to obey God and return to Egypt to help deliver their relatives out of bondage. Read the following passage:

> So Moses and Aaron returned to Egypt and called the leaders of Israel to a meeting. Aaron told them everything the Lord had told Moses, and Moses performed the miraculous signs as they watched. The leaders were soon convinced that the Lord had sent Moses and Aaron. And when they realized that the Lord had seen their misery and was deeply concerned for them, they all bowed their heads and worshiped.
>
> After this presentation to Israel's leaders, Moses and Aaron went to see Pharaoh. They told him, "This is what the Lord, the God of Israel, says: 'Let my people go, for they must go out into the wilderness to hold a religious festival in my honor.' "
>
> "Is that so?" retorted Pharaoh. "And who is the Lord that I should listen to him and let Israel go? I don't know the Lord, and I will not let Israel go."
>
> But Aaron and Moses persisted. "The God of the Hebrews has met with us," they declared. "Let us take a three-day trip into the wilderness so we can offer sacrifices to the Lord our God. If we don't, we will surely die by disease or the sword."
>
> EXODUS 4:29–5:3

+ What steps did Aaron and Moses take upon returning to Egypt?

+ What supporting evidence do you find that Aaron was an encouragement to Moses?

Read the following passage:

> After this presentation to Israel's leaders, Moses and Aaron went to see Pharaoh. They told him, "This is what the Lord, the God of Israel, says: 'Let my people go, for they must go out into the wilderness to hold a religious festival in my honor.'"
>
> "Is that so?" retorted Pharaoh. "And who is the Lord that I should listen to him and let Israel go? I don't know the Lord, and I will not let Israel go."
>
> But Aaron and Moses persisted. "The God of the Hebrews has met with us," they declared. "Let us take a three-day trip into the wilderness so we can offer sacrifices to the Lord our God. If we don't, we will surely die by disease or the sword."
>
> "Who do you think you are," Pharaoh shouted, "distracting the people from their tasks? Get back to work! Look, there are many people here in Egypt, and you are stopping them from doing their work."
>
> Since Pharaoh would not let up on his demands, the Israelite foremen could see that they were in serious trouble. As they left Pharaoh's court, they met Moses and Aaron, who were waiting outside for them. The foremen said to them, "May the Lord judge you for getting us into this terrible situation with Pharaoh and his officials. You have given them an excuse to kill us!"
>
> So Moses went back to the Lord and protested, "Why have you mistreated your own people like this, Lord? Why did you send me? Since I gave Pharaoh your message, he has been even more brutal to your people. You have not even begun to rescue them!"
>
> "Now you will see what I will do to Pharaoh," the Lord told Moses. "When he feels my powerful hand upon him, he will let the people go. In fact, he will be so anxious to get rid of them that he will force them to leave his land!"
>
> Then the Lord said to Moses, "Pay close attention to this. I will make you seem like God to Pharaoh. Your brother, Aaron, will be your prophet; he will speak for you. Tell Aaron everything I say to you and have him announce it to Pharaoh. He will demand that the people of Israel be allowed to leave Egypt."
>
> So Moses and Aaron did just as the Lord had commanded them. Moses was eighty years old, and Aaron was eighty-three at the time they made their demands to Pharaoh.
>
> Then the Lord said to Moses and Aaron, "Pharaoh will demand that you show him a miracle to prove that God has sent you. When he makes this demand, say to Aaron, 'Throw down your shepherd's staff,' and it will become a snake."
>
> So Moses and Aaron went to see Pharaoh, and they performed the miracle just as the Lord had told them.   EXODUS 5:1-5, 19–6:2; 7:1-2, 6-10A

+ How did Pharaoh react to the demands of Aaron and Moses? How did the Israelites react to Pharaoh's demands?

+ What does Moses do when he is confronted by the Israelite foremen?

+ Just as God laid out His plan to Moses, what role did He give Aaron? Why?

+ Notice Moses' and Aaron's response to God's plan (7:8). Discuss the possible reasons for the change in their attitudes.

FIND GOD'S WAYS FOR YOU

✦ Have you ever needed to "go back" in order to go forward? Explain.

Share a time when someone was willing to support you, stay by your side, through a difficult time.

> A person standing alone can be attacked and defeated, but two can stand back-to-back and conquer. Three are even better, for a triple-braided cord is not easily broken.   ECCLESIASTES 4:12

✦ Discuss this verse in light of Moses and Aaron. Who is always there to form the triple braid?

STOP AND PONDER

> God has said, "I will never fail you. I will never forsake you." That is why we can say with confidence, "The Lord is my helper, so I will not be afraid. What can mere mortals do to me?"   HEBREWS 13:5B-6

CALLED TO HIGHER GROUND

SEEK GOD'S WORD FOR TRUTH

Read the following passage:

> The Lord instructed Moses: "Come up here to me, and bring along Aaron, Nadab, Abihu, and seventy of Israel's leaders. All of them must worship at a distance. You alone, Moses, are allowed to come near to the Lord. The others must not come too close. And remember, none of the other people are allowed to climb on the mountain at all."
>
> When Moses had announced to the people all the teachings and regulations the Lord had given him, they answered in unison, "We will do everything the Lord has told us to do."
>
> Then Moses carefully wrote down all the Lord's instructions. Early the next morning he built an altar at the foot of the mountain. He also set up twelve pillars around the altar, one for each of the twelve tribes of Israel. Then he sent some of the young men to sacrifice young bulls as burnt offerings and peace offerings to the Lord. Moses took half the blood from these animals and drew it off into basins. The other half he splashed against the altar.
>
> Then he took the Book of the Covenant and read it to the people. They all responded again, "We will do everything the Lord has commanded. We will obey."
>
> Then Moses sprinkled the blood from the basins over the people and said, "This blood confirms the covenant the Lord has made with you in giving you these laws."

Then Moses, Aaron, Nadab, Abihu, and seventy of the leaders of Israel went up the mountain. There they saw the God of Israel. Under his feet there seemed to be a pavement of brilliant sapphire, as clear as the heavens. And though Israel's leaders saw God, he did not destroy them. In fact, they shared a meal together in God's presence!

And the Lord said to Moses, "Come up to me on the mountain. Stay there while I give you the tablets of stone that I have inscribed with my instructions and commands. Then you will teach the people from them." So Moses and his assistant Joshua climbed up the mountain of God.

Moses told the other leaders, "Stay here and wait for us until we come back. If there are any problems while I am gone, consult with Aaron and Hur, who are here with you."

Then Moses went up the mountain, and the cloud covered it.

EXODUS 24:1-15

+ Who was invited to the mountain? What took place among them while they were there?

+ When Moses went up the mountain with Joshua, what were his instructions to the other leaders?

With all this in mind, read the following passage:

When Moses failed to come back down the mountain right away, the people went to Aaron. "Look," they said, "make us some gods who can lead us. This man Moses, who brought us here from Egypt, has disappeared. We don't know what has happened to him."

So Aaron said, "Tell your wives and sons and daughters to take off their gold earrings, and then bring them to me."

All the people obeyed Aaron and brought him their gold earrings. Then Aaron took the gold, melted it down, and molded and tooled it into the shape of a calf. The people exclaimed, "O Israel, these are the gods who brought you out of Egypt!"

When Aaron saw how excited the people were about it, he built an altar in front of the calf and announced, "Tomorrow there will be a festival to the Lord!"

So the people got up early the next morning to sacrifice burnt offerings and peace offerings. After this, they celebrated with feasting and drinking, and indulged themselves in pagan revelry.

Then the Lord told Moses, "Quick! Go down the mountain! The people you brought from Egypt have defiled themselves. They have already turned from the way I commanded them to live. They have made an idol shaped like a calf, and they have worshiped and sacrificed to it. They are saying, 'These are your gods, O Israel, who brought you out of Egypt.'"

Then the Lord said, "I have seen how stubborn and rebellious these people are. Now leave me alone so my anger can blaze against them and destroy them all. Then I will make you, Moses, into a great nation instead of them."

But Moses pleaded with the Lord his God not to do it. "O Lord!" he exclaimed. "Why are you so angry with your own people whom you brought from the land of Egypt with such great power and mighty acts? The Egyptians will say, 'God tricked them into coming to the mountains so he could kill them and wipe them from the face of the earth.' Turn away from your fierce anger. Change your mind about this terrible disaster you are planning against your people! Remember your covenant with your servants—Abraham, Isaac, and Jacob. You swore by your own self, 'I will make your descendants as numerous as the stars of heaven. Yes, I will give them all of this land that I have promised to your descendants, and they will possess it forever.'"

So the Lord withdrew his threat and didn't bring against his people the disaster he had threatened.

Then Moses turned and went down the mountain. He held in his hands the two stone tablets inscribed with the terms of the covenant. They were inscribed on both sides, front and back. These stone tablets were God's work; the words on them were written by God himself.

When Joshua heard the noise of the people shouting below them, he exclaimed to Moses, "It sounds as if there is a war in the camp!"

But Moses replied, "No, it's neither a cry of victory nor a cry of defeat. It is the sound of a celebration."

When they came near the camp, Moses saw the calf and the dancing. In terrible anger, he threw the stone tablets to the ground, smashing them at the foot of the mountain. He took the calf they had made and melted it in the fire. And when the metal had cooled, he ground it into powder and mixed it with water. Then he made the people drink it.

After that, he turned to Aaron. "What did the people do to you?" he demanded. "How did they ever make you bring such terrible sin upon them?"

"Don't get upset, sir," Aaron replied. "You yourself know these people and what a wicked bunch they are. They said to me, 'Make us some gods to lead us, for something has happened to this man Moses, who led us out of Egypt.' So I told them, 'Bring me your gold earrings.' When they brought them to me, I threw them into the fire—and out came this calf!"

When Moses saw that Aaron had let the people get completely out of control—and much to the amusement of their enemies—he stood at the entrance to the camp and shouted, "All of you who are on the Lord's side, come over here and join me." And all the Levites came.

He told them, "This is what the Lord, the God of Israel, says: Strap on your swords! Go back and forth from one end of the camp to the other, killing even your brothers, friends, and neighbors." The Levites obeyed Moses, and about three thousand people died that day.

Then Moses told the Levites, "Today you have been ordained for the service of the Lord, for you obeyed him even though it meant killing your own sons and brothers. Because of this, he will now give you a great blessing."

The next day Moses said to the people, "You have committed a terrible sin, but I will return to the Lord on the mountain. Perhaps I will be able to obtain forgiveness for you."

So Moses returned to the Lord and said, "Alas, these people have committed a terrible sin. They have made gods of gold for themselves. But now, please forgive their sin—and if not, then blot me out of the record you are keeping."

The Lord replied to Moses, "I will blot out whoever has sinned against me. Now go, lead the people to the place I told you about. Look! My angel will lead the way before you! But when I call the people to account, I will certainly punish them for their sins."

And the Lord sent a great plague upon the people because they had worshiped the calf Aaron had made.   EXODUS 32

+ Discuss the circumstances surrounding the creation of the golden calf: Who? What? When? Where? Why? How?

+ What did Moses find when he returned? What was his response?

+ Compare Aaron's response to the people's request in verses 2-4 with his reply to Moses' questions in verses 22-24.

+ Moses took drastic measures within the camp of Israel when he discovered their sin. He drew a line in the sand. Who crossed that line to join him in obedience? What might this also imply about Aaron?

FIND GOD'S WAYS FOR YOU

+ Both Aaron and Moses were put on the spot, each revealing himself in his response. Share a time when you were put on the spot by other people. What did you learn about yourself by the way you handled it?

+ With whom do you identify now—Moses or Aaron? Why?

+ Discuss steps Aaron should have taken when the people came to him for leadership.

STOP AND PONDER

We can gather our thoughts, but the Lord gives the right answer. People may be pure in their own eyes, but the Lord examines their motives. Commit your work to the Lord, and then your plans will succeed.   PROVERBS 16:1-3

CALLED TO HOLINESS

SEEK GOD'S WORD FOR TRUTH

Read the following passages:

"Bring Aaron and his sons to the entrance of the Tabernacle, and wash them with water."   EXODUS 40:12

The Lord said to Moses, "Now bring Aaron and his sons, along with their special clothing, the anointing oil, the bull for the sin offering, the two rams, and the basket of unleavened bread to the entrance of the Tabernacle. Then call the entire community of Israel to meet you there."

So Moses followed the Lord's instructions, and all the people assembled at the Tabernacle entrance. Moses announced to them, "The Lord has commanded what I am now going to do!" Then he presented Aaron and his sons and washed them with water. He clothed Aaron with the embroidered tunic and tied the sash around his waist. He dressed him in the robe of the ephod, along with the ephod itself, and attached the ephod with its decorative sash. Then Moses placed the chestpiece on Aaron and put the Urim and the Thummim inside it. He placed on Aaron's head the turban with the gold medallion at its front, just as the Lord had commanded him.

Then Moses took the anointing oil and anointed the Tabernacle and everything in it, thus making them holy. He sprinkled the altar seven times, anointing it and all its utensils and the washbasin and its pedestal, making them holy. Then he poured some of the anointing oil on Aaron's head, thus anointing him and making him holy for his work. Next Moses presented Aaron's sons and clothed them in their embroidered tunics, their sashes, and their turbans, just as the Lord had commanded him.　　　LEVITICUS 8:1-13

✦ Discuss the anointing of Aaron. What stands out to you from this account?

✦ What do you learn about God from this passage, especially in light of the previous lesson?

After such a high point in Aaron's life, it is hard to conceive that he would ever vacillate again. Read the following passage:

While they were at Hazeroth, Miriam and Aaron criticized Moses because he had married a Cushite woman. They said, "Has the Lord spoken only through Moses? Hasn't he spoken through us, too?" But the Lord heard them.

Now Moses was more humble than any other person on earth. So immediately the Lord called to Moses, Aaron, and Miriam and said, "Go out to the Tabernacle, all three of you!" And the three of them went out. Then the Lord descended in the pillar of cloud and stood at the entrance of the Tabernacle. "Aaron and Miriam!" he called, and they stepped forward. And the Lord said to them, "Now listen to me! Even with prophets, I the Lord communicate by visions and dreams. But that is not how I communicate with my servant Moses. He is entrusted with my entire house. I speak to him face to face, directly and not in riddles! He sees the Lord as he is. Should you not be afraid to criticize him?"

The Lord was furious with them, and he departed. As the cloud moved from above the Tabernacle, Miriam suddenly became white as snow with leprosy. When Aaron saw what had happened, he cried out to Moses, "Oh, my lord! Please don't punish us for this sin we have so foolishly committed. Don't let her be like a stillborn baby, already decayed at birth."

So Moses cried out to the Lord, "Heal her, O God, I beg you!"

And the Lord said to Moses, "If her father had spit in her face, wouldn't she have been defiled for seven days? Banish her from the camp for seven days, and after that she may return."

So Miriam was excluded from the camp for seven days, and the people waited until she was brought back before they traveled again.

NUMBERS 12:1-15

+ What complaints did Aaron and Miriam have about Moses?

+ What did God have to say about these complaints?

+ Who do you think started the complaints and why?

+ What does this imply about Aaron? about his motives?

FIND GOD'S WAYS FOR YOU

+ What significance do you see for yourself that God continued to work with, work through, and use Aaron? Explain.

For our earthly fathers disciplined us for a few years, doing the best they knew how. But God's discipline is always right and good for us because it means we will share in his holiness. No discipline is enjoyable while it is happening—it is painful! But afterward there will be a quiet harvest of right living for those who are trained in this way.
So take a new grip with your tired hands and stand firm on your shaky legs. Mark out a straight path for your feet. Then those who follow you, though they are weak and lame, will not stumble and fall but will become strong.   HEBREWS 12:10-13

+ What is the difference between God's discipline and our earthly father's discipline?

+ What benefits are there from God's discipline? For you? For others in your sphere of influence?

STOP AND PONDER

If we confess our sins to him [Jesus], he is faithful and just to forgive us and cleanse us from every wrong.   I JOHN 1:9

CALLED TO LEAD

SEEK GOD'S WORD FOR TRUTH

Read the following passage:

One day Korah son of Izhar, a descendant of Kohath son of Levi, conspired with Dathan and Abiram, the sons of Eliab, and On son of Peleth, from the tribe of Reuben. They incited a rebellion against Moses, involving 250 other prominent leaders, all members of the assembly. They went to Moses and Aaron and said, "You have gone too far! Everyone in Israel has been set apart by the Lord, and he is with all of us. What right do you have to act as though you are greater than anyone else among all these people of the Lord?"

When Moses heard what they were saying, he threw himself down with his face to the ground. Then he said to Korah and his followers, "Tomorrow morning the Lord will show us who belongs to him and who is holy. The Lord will allow those who are chosen to enter his holy presence. You, Korah, and all your followers must do this: Take incense burners, and burn incense in them tomorrow before the Lord. Then we will see whom the Lord chooses as his holy one. You Levites are the ones who have gone too far!"

Then Moses spoke again to Korah: "Now listen, you Levites! Does it seem a small thing to you that the God of Israel has chosen you from among all the people of Israel to be near him as you serve in the Lord's Tabernacle and to stand before the people to minister to them? He has given this special ministry only to you and your fellow Levites, but now you are demanding the priesthood as well! The one you are really revolting against is the Lord! And who is Aaron that you are complaining about him?"

Then Moses summoned Dathan and Abiram, the sons of Eliab, but they replied, "We refuse to come! Isn't it enough that you brought us out of Egypt, a land flowing with milk and honey, to kill us here in this wilderness, and that you now treat us like your subjects? What's more, you haven't brought us into the land flowing with milk and honey or given us an inheritance of fields and vineyards. Are you trying to fool us? We will not come."

Then Moses became very angry and said to the Lord, "Do not accept their offerings! I have not taken so much as a donkey from them, and I have never hurt a single one of them." And Moses said to Korah, "Come here tomorrow and present yourself before the Lord with all your followers. Aaron will also be here. Be sure that each of your 250 followers brings an incense burner with incense on it, so you can present them before the Lord. Aaron will also bring his incense burner."

So these men came with their incense burners, placed burning coals and incense on them, and stood at the entrance of the Tabernacle with Moses and Aaron. Meanwhile, Korah had stirred up the entire community against Moses and Aaron, and they all assembled at the Tabernacle entrance. Then the glorious presence of the Lord appeared to the whole community, and the Lord said to Moses and Aaron, "Get away from these people so that I may instantly destroy them!"

But Moses and Aaron fell face down on the ground. "O God, the God and source of all life," they pleaded. "Must you be angry with all the people when only one man sins?"

And the Lord said to Moses, "Then tell all the people to get away from the tents of Korah, Dathan, and Abiram."

So Moses got up and rushed over to the tents of Dathan and Abiram, followed closely by the Israelite leaders. "Quick!" he told the people. "Get away from the tents of these wicked men, and don't touch anything that belongs to them. If you do, you will be destroyed for their sins." So all the people stood back from the tents of Korah, Dathan, and Abiram. Then Dathan and Abiram came out and stood at the entrances of their tents with their wives and children and little ones.

And Moses said, "By this you will know that the Lord has sent me to do all these things that I have done—for I have not done them on my own. If these men die a natural death, then the Lord has not sent me. But if the Lord performs a miracle and the ground opens up and swallows them and all their belongings, and they go down alive into the grave, then you will know that these men have despised the Lord."

He had hardly finished speaking the words when the ground suddenly split open beneath them. The earth opened up and swallowed the men, along with their households and the followers who were standing with them, and everything they owned. So they went down alive into the grave, along with their belongings. The earth closed over them, and they all vanished. All of the people of Israel fled as they heard their screams, fearing that the earth would swallow them, too. Then fire blazed forth from the Lord and burned up the 250 men who were offering incense.

And the Lord said to Moses, "Tell Eleazar son of Aaron the priest to pull all the incense burners from the fire, for they are holy. Also tell him to scatter the burning incense from the burners of these men who have sinned at the cost of their lives. He must then hammer the metal of the incense burners into a sheet as a covering for the altar, for these burners have become holy because they were used in the Lord's presence. The altar covering will then serve as a warning to the people of Israel."

So Eleazar the priest collected the 250 bronze incense burners that had been used by the men who died in the fire, and they were hammered out into a sheet of metal to cover the altar. This would warn the Israelites that no unauthorized man—no one who was not a descendant of Aaron—should ever enter the Lord's presence to burn incense. If anyone did, the same thing would happen to him as happened to Korah and his followers. Thus, the Lord's instructions to Moses were carried out.

But the very next morning the whole community began muttering again against Moses and Aaron, saying, "You two have killed the Lord's people!" As the people gathered to protest to Moses and Aaron, they turned toward the Tabernacle and saw that the cloud had covered it, and the glorious presence of the Lord appeared.

Moses and Aaron came and stood at the entrance of the Tabernacle, and the Lord said to Moses, "Get away from these people so that I can instantly destroy them!" But Moses and Aaron fell face down on the ground.

And Moses said to Aaron, "Quick, take an incense burner and place burning coals on it from the altar. Lay incense on it and carry it quickly among the people to make atonement for them. The Lord's anger is blazing among them— the plague has already begun."

Aaron did as Moses told him and ran out among the people. The plague indeed had already begun, but Aaron burned the incense and made atonement for them. He stood between the living and the dead until the plague was stopped. But 14,700 people died in that plague, in addition to those who had died in the incident involving Korah. Then because the plague had stopped, Aaron returned to Moses at the entrance of the Tabernacle.

Then the Lord said to Moses, "Take twelve wooden staffs, one from each of Israel's ancestral tribes, and inscribe each tribal leader's name on his staff. Inscribe Aaron's name on the staff of the tribe of Levi, for there must be one staff for the leader of each ancestral tribe. Put these staffs in the Tabernacle in front of the Ark of the Covenant, where I meet with you. Buds will sprout on the staff belonging to the man I choose. Then I will finally put an end to this murmuring and complaining against you."

So Moses gave the instructions to the people of Israel, and each of the twelve tribal leaders, including Aaron, brought Moses a staff. Moses put the staffs in the Lord's presence in the Tabernacle of the Covenant. When he went into the Tabernacle of the Covenant the next day, he found that Aaron's staff, representing the tribe of Levi, had sprouted, blossomed, and produced almonds!

When Moses brought all the staffs out from the Lord's presence, he showed them to the people. Each man claimed his own staff. And the Lord said to Moses: "Place Aaron's staff permanently before the Ark of the Covenant as a warning to rebels. This should put an end to their complaints against me and prevent any further deaths." So Moses did as the Lord commanded him.

NUMBERS 16:1–17:11

+ What complaint did Korah, Dathan, and Abiram have? To whom did they complain? About whom were they really complaining?

+ What did God tell Moses and Aaron to do? What was their response?

+ Because of this insurrection, who else began to complain? What was their complaint?

+ Compare the way the Lord dealt with Korah to the way He dealt with the whole community. What role does Moses have? What role does Aaron accept?

+ Discuss how God settled the murmuring and complaining against the leadership.

+ What two warnings come from these rebellions? How are they memorialized?

FIND GOD'S WAYS FOR YOU

+ Remember a time when you were criticized for your leadership, position, or authority. What effect did it have on you personally? How did it affect those around you?

+ Now remember a time when you complained about someone else's leadership, position, or authority. How did it affect others? Looking back, have you gained any insights into yourself? your motives?

In everything you do, stay away from complaining and arguing, so that no one can speak a word of blame against you. You are to live clean, innocent lives as

children of God in a dark world full of crooked and perverse people. Let your
lives shine brightly before them.   PHILIPPIANS 2:14-15

✦ What are you to do about complaining and arguing? Why?

STOP AND PONDER

I urge you, first of all, to pray for all people. As you make your requests, plead
for God's mercy upon them, and give thanks. Pray this way for kings and all
others who are in authority, so that we can live in peace and quietness, in
godliness and dignity. This is good and pleases God our Savior, for he wants
everyone to be saved and to understand the truth.   I TIMOTHY 2:1-4

CALLED UPWARD

SEEK GOD'S WORD FOR TRUTH

Read the following passage:

In early spring the people of Israel arrived in the wilderness of Zin and camped
at Kadesh. While they were there, Miriam died and was buried.

There was no water for the people to drink at that place, so they rebelled
against Moses and Aaron. The people blamed Moses and said, "We wish we
had died in the Lord's presence with our brothers! Did you bring the Lord's
people into this wilderness to die, along with all our livestock? Why did you
make us leave Egypt and bring us here to this terrible place? This land has no
grain, figs, grapes, or pomegranates. And there is no water to drink!"

Moses and Aaron turned away from the people and went to the entrance
of the Tabernacle, where they fell face down on the ground. Then the glorious
presence of the Lord appeared to them, and the Lord said to Moses, "You and
Aaron must take the staff and assemble the entire community. As the people
watch, command the rock over there to pour out its water. You will get enough
water from the rock to satisfy all the people and their livestock."

So Moses did as he was told. He took the staff from the place where it was
kept before the Lord. Then he and Aaron summoned the people to come and
gather at the rock. "Listen, you rebels!" he shouted. "Must we bring you
water from this rock?" Then Moses raised his hand and struck the rock twice
with the staff, and water gushed out. So all the people and their livestock
drank their fill.

But the Lord said to Moses and Aaron, "Because you did not trust me
enough to demonstrate my holiness to the people of Israel, you will not lead
them into the land I am giving them!" This place was known as the waters of
Meribah, because it was where the people of Israel argued with the Lord, and
where he demonstrated his holiness among them.

While Moses was at Kadesh, he sent ambassadors to the king of Edom with
this message:

"This message is from your relatives, the people of Israel: You know all the hardships we have been through, and that our ancestors went down to Egypt. We lived there a long time and suffered as slaves to the Egyptians. But when we cried out to the Lord, he heard us and sent an angel who brought us out of Egypt. Now we are camped at Kadesh, a town on the border of your land. Please let us pass through your country. We will be careful not to go through your fields and vineyards. We won't even drink water from your wells. We will stay on the king's road and never leave it until we have crossed the opposite border."

But the king of Edom said, "Stay out of my land or I will meet you with an army!"

The Israelites answered, "We will stay on the main road. If any of our livestock drinks your water, we will pay for it. We only want to pass through your country and nothing else."

But the king of Edom replied, "Stay out! You may not pass through our land." With that he mobilized his army and marched out to meet them with an imposing force. Because Edom refused to allow Israel to pass through their country, Israel was forced to turn around.

The whole community of Israel left Kadesh as a group and arrived at Mount Hor. Then the Lord said to Moses and Aaron at Mount Hor on the border of the land of Edom, "The time has come for Aaron to join his ancestors in death. He will not enter the land I am giving the people of Israel, because the two of you rebelled against my instructions concerning the waters of Meribah. Now take Aaron and his son Eleazar up Mount Hor. There you will remove Aaron's priestly garments and put them on Eleazar, his son. Aaron will die there and join his ancestors."

So Moses did as the Lord commanded. The three of them went up Mount Hor together as the whole community watched. At the summit, Moses removed the priestly garments from Aaron and put them on Eleazar, Aaron's son. Then Aaron died there on top of the mountain, and Moses and Eleazar went back down. When the people realized that Aaron had died, all Israel mourned for him thirty days.   NUMBERS 20

✦ Describe the mood of the camp. What steps do Moses and Aaron immediately take?

✦ Compare the instructions God gave to Moses and Aaron with what the two men actually do. Any conclusions?

✦ What instructions are given to Moses and Aaron when the whole community arrived at Mount Hor?

✦ Contrast Moses' and Aaron's actions this time with their previous actions.

✦ What reasons are given for Aaron's not getting to enter the Promised Land?

✦ What evidence do you find that God kept His promise to Aaron about the priesthood being kept in his family? How would you characterize Aaron at the end of his journey?

FIND GOD'S WAYS FOR YOU

+ What are some reasons we fail to follow instructions?

+ How do you handle personal disappointments?

God has not given us a spirit of fear and timidity, but of power, love, and self-discipline. 2 TIMOTHY 1:7

+ When we believe in Jesus, what is available to us for navigating though life's dilemmas and disappointments?

STOP AND PONDER

That is why we have a great High Priest who has gone to heaven, Jesus the Son of God. Let us cling to him and never stop trusting him. This High Priest of ours understands our weaknesses, for he faced all of the same temptations we do, yet he did not sin. So let us come boldly to the throne of our gracious God. There we will receive his mercy, and we will find grace to help us when we need it. HEBREWS 4:14-16

BOOK TWO

THE WARRIOR

A NOTE TO READERS

Bible scholars differ in their opinions as to whether the Caleb whose genealogy is listed in 1 Chronicles 2 is the same Caleb who scouted out the Promised Land with Joshua in Numbers 13. We know that Caleb the scout had a daughter named Acsah (Joshua 15:16), and the Caleb of 1 Chronicles 2 also had a daughter named Acsah (2:49). This correspondence has prompted the author to choose, for the purposes of this story, the view that they are indeed the same person. With this interpretation, references to "Caleb, son of Jephunneh" are taken to mean "Caleb, descendent of Jephunneh."

ONE

"Run!"

No one heard, so Kelubai put his fingers in his mouth and gave a shrill whistle. His relatives raised their heads. He pointed at the darkening sky. They looked up and stared. *"Find cover!"*

Men, women, and children dropped their hoes and scattered. Kelubai followed. Farthest out in Pharaoh's field, he had the longest distance to run. The black swirling clouds moved with frightening speed, casting a cold shadow over the land. Was it the great lion of God that let out such a rumbling roar from that blackness? Screaming, hands over their heads, people ran faster.

A shaft of jagged light flashed and struck the middle of the barley field. Flames shot up from the ground and the stalks of ripened grain caught fire. Something hard struck Kelubai in the head. Then another and another, like small pebbles hurled at him from an open hand. And the air grew cold, so cold his breath came like puffs of smoke as he panted. His lungs burned. Could he make it to cover before one of those bolts of fire struck him down? He reached his mud-brick house, swung the door shut, and leaned against it.

Gasping for breath, he saw his wife, Azubah, crouched in the corner, their two older sons cowering beside her as she held their third son squalling at her breast. His older boys, Mesha and Mareshah, stood wide-eyed but silent. Their mother, Kelubai's first wife, would not have been as quick to give in to hysteria. She had faced death—giving Mareshah life—with more fortitude than Azubah now showed in the face of this storm.

Tears streaked her frightened face. "What is that noise, Kelubai? What's happening?" Her voice kept rising until she was screaming even louder than the babe. *"What's happening?"*

He grasped her shoulders and gave her a hard shake. "Hush!" He let go of her and ran his hands over his sons' heads. "Be quiet." He kissed each of them. "Shhhh. Sit still." He gathered them all close, shielding them with his body. His own heart was flailing, threatening to burst its bonds of bone and flesh. Never had he felt such terror, but he needed to be calm for their sake. He fixed his mind upon his family, soothing, encouraging. "Shhhh . . ."

"Abba." His oldest son, Mesha, pressed closer, his fingers grasping Kelubai's robe. "Abba . . ."

Hard pounding came against the house, like a thousand fists hitting at once. Azubah ducked her head, seeking the shelter of his shoulder. Mesha pressed close. Hard white stones flew in through the window. Curious, Kelubai rose. When his wife and sons protested, he set Mesha beside Azubah. "Stay calm. See to Mareshah." Kelubai could not depend on Azubah to comfort them. They were not her sons, and she would always hold her own flesh and blood more dear.

"Where are you going?"

"I just want to see."

"Kelubai!"

He held up his hand, commanding her to silence. Edging across the room, he reached out to take up one of the stones. It was hard and cold. Turning it in his hand, he examined it. It became slippery. Frowning, perplexed, he put it to his mouth. He glanced back at his wife and sons. "Water!" He picked up several more and brought them to Azubah and his sons. "Taste it." Only Mesha was willing. "It's water. Water hard as a stone!"

Shivering, Azubah pressed back farther into the corner. "What manner of magic is this?" When a burst of light exploded outside the window, she screamed; the boys cried hysterically. Kelubai snatched the blankets from the straw pallets and draped them over the children. "Stay down."

"You can't go out there. You'll be killed!"

He put his hand gently over her mouth. "Do not make matters worse, woman. Your fear is a contagion they can ill afford." He looked pointedly at the boys.

She made no sound, though her eyes were wide with fear. She drew the boys closer, drawing the blankets tighter, covering her head as well.

Animals bawled and screamed, their hooves pounding as they tried to run. Kelubai was thankful he had brought his team of oxen in early or they would be lost with the others. He rose and edged near to the window, staying back while looking out. An acrid smell drifted in the cold air amid the pounding. The fields of flax that had just begun blooming were now in flames. Months of hard labor were going up in smoke.

"It's *Him*, isn't it?" Azubah said from her corner.

"Yes." It must be the same God who had turned the Nile to blood, brought on a plague of frogs, then gnats and flies, death to the livestock, and boils to all but the Hebrews in Goshen. "Yes. It's *Him*."

"You sound pleased."

"You have heard the stories I have. A deliverer will come."

"Not for us."

"Why not for us?"

"What are you saying, Kelubai?"

"Something my grandfather said to me when I was a boy." He came back and hunkered down before her and their sons. "A story passed down from our ancestor Jephunneh. He was a friend of Judah, the fourth son of Jacob, the patriarch of the twelve tribes." Kelubai remembered his grandfather's face in the firelight, grim, scoffing.

"I don't understand. We have nothing to do with the Hebrews."

He rose, pacing. "Not now. But back then, there was a connection. Judah's sons were half Canaanite. Two were said to have been struck down by this God. Shelah was the last one, named for Shelahphelah, the land in which he was born: Canaan. Two more sons were born to Judah by a woman named Tamar, also a Canaanite. And then he returned to his father's tents. This was during the time of the great famine. Everyone was starving, everywhere except here in Egypt. Then unbelievably, Judah's brother Joseph became overseer of Egypt and subject only to Pharaoh. Imagine. A slave becoming second only to Pharaoh. A great and mighty God had a hand in that!"

He looked out the window. "When the Hebrews arrived, they were welcomed and given the best land: Goshen. Jephunneh was descended from Esau, Judah's uncle, and he was a friend of Abdullam as well. So he gained the ear of Judah and made a pact in order to provide for our family. That's how we became slaves, theirs at first, farming land and growing crops so that the Hebrews were free to shepherd their growing flocks. It was a loathsome alliance, but necessary for survival. And then things turned around. Other rulers came. We were still slaves, but so were the Hebrews, and with each passing year, Pharaoh's heel bore down harder upon them than us."

"Why?"

He looked at her. "Who knows?"

Jealousy? Spite? More likely because they were fruitful and multiplied. One patriarch and twelve sons now numbered in the hundreds of thousands. There were as many Jews as there were stars in the heavens! Pharaoh probably feared if the Hebrews had wits and courage enough, they could rise up, join with Egypt's enemies, and gain their freedom. They could become masters over Egypt. Instead, they wailed and moaned as they worked, crying out to their unseen God to save them, and thereby making themselves the brunt of contempt and mockery.

Until now.

Kelubai looked up at the roiling dark sky in wonder. He could not see this God, but he was witnessing His power. The gods of Egypt were as nothing against Him. In the distance, the sun shone over Goshen. It would also seem this God could make a distinction between His people and the enemy. Pressing his lips together, Kelubai watched the fire sweep across the fields of barley. It had just come to head, harvest so close. Now, all lost.

There would be another famine after this night, and his family would suffer.

Unless . . .

A thin thread, a distant connection might be just enough to change everything.

Kelubai took a pellet from the sill. He rolled it between his fingers and popped it in his mouth. The stone was hard and cold against his tongue, but it melted warm and sweet, refreshing. His heart swelled at the sound and fury around him. He rejoiced in it. The God of the Hebrews could turn water to blood and call forth frogs, gnats, flies, and disease. Wind, water, fire, and air obeyed Him. Here was a God he could worship. Here was a God not carved by human hands!

Cupping his hands, he held them outstretched. His palms stung as the hard pellets struck, but he held his hands steady until a small pile had gathered. Then he tossed them back into his mouth and chewed the ice.

✦   ✦   ✦

Kelubai gathered his relatives. "If we are to survive, we must go to Goshen and live among the Jews."

"Live among the people Pharaoh despises? You're out of your mind, Kelubai!"

"The wheat and spelt are still growing. The gods of Egypt protected them. We still have those fields left."

Kelubai shook his head. "For how long?"

"The gods are at war, Kelubai. And we had best stay out of their way."

"What say you, Father?"

Hezron had been silent since the discussion began. Troubled, he raised his head. "It has been generations since our ancestor Jephunneh followed Judah from Canaan. The Hebrews will have long since forgotten how and why we came here."

"We will remind them we were once close friends of Judah."

"Close?" Kelubai's oldest brother, Jerahmeel, snorted. "A friend of a friend?"

"Father, did you not once say your father said his father's father took a Hebrew woman to wife?"

Ram was quick to follow their older brother's lead. "And how many years ago was that? Do you think the Hebrews will care that we have one of their women in our line? Ha! What use is a woman? What was the name of her father?"

Kelubai scowled. "Have you forgotten? The Hebrews came to us for straw when Pharaoh would not provide it."

"Straw we needed for our oxen."

Kelubai looked at Jerahmeel. "I gave all I had."

"Is that why you came to me for fodder for your animals?"

"Yes, it is. And now, if you but look around, you'll see there's nothing left for the animals to eat. Except in Goshen! There is pasturage there." Kelubai looked at his father. "And we have traded grain for goats. These are alliances we can build on."

"Alliances could bring the wrath of Pharaoh down upon us!" Jerahmeel stood, red-faced with impatient anger. "What protection will we have against his soldiers? No alliances. We must stay out of this war."

"Are you blind? Look around you, my brothers." Kelubai thrust his hand toward the barley and flax fields, flattened by hail, blackened by fire. "We're in the *middle* of the battlefield!"

"Pharaoh will prevail."

Kelubai gave a mirthless laugh. "Pharaoh and all his gods put together have not been able to protect Egypt from the God of the Hebrews. A river of blood, frogs, gnats, flies, boils! What will the God of the Hebrews send next?" He leaned forward. "We have heard the Hebrews wail for their deliverer. And their deliverer has come. Let us make Him ours as well."

"You mean Moses?"

"Moses is a man. He is but God's spokesman, telling Pharaoh what the God of the Hebrews has told him to say. It is an almighty God who destroyed our fields yesterday, and it is this God who will deliver His people."

"No." Jerahmeel glowered. "No, I say. *No!*"

Kelubai clung to self-control. Exploding in anger at his brother's stupidity would not convince their father to leave this place of desolation. He spread his hands and spoke more quietly. "What if we are left behind? What happens when Pharaoh and his officials are hungry and need grain? Will he say, 'My foolishness has brought destruction upon our land'? No, he won't. He'll send his soldiers to take whatever is left. The sacks of grain we have winnowed from our labors will be stolen from us. But we can take these stores with us to Goshen as gifts. All of the wheat and spelt."

"Gifts?"

"Yes, Ram. Gifts. We must align ourselves with the Jews. And we must do it now."

Kelubai felt his father's eyes upon him. He met that troubled stare with a look of fierce determination. "If we are to survive, Father, we must act *now!*"

His father looked at his other sons. "Perhaps Kelubai is right."

Flushed and angry, they protested, everyone talking at once. But no one had another solution to protect them from impending disaster.

"If Pharaoh hated the Hebrews before, he hates them all the more now."

"He'll be sending soldiers to Goshen again."

"Would you have the king of Egypt turn his hatred upon us as well?"

"Father, we had best stay out of this."

Kelubai had talked all morning and been unable to convince them. He would *not* waste any more time. He stood. "Do as you will, my brothers. Stay in your huts. Hope that whatever plague comes next will leave your barley untouched. As for me and my house, we'll be in Goshen before the sun sets, before another plague is upon us, a worse one than the last!"

His brothers all protested. "Better to wait and see what happens than be a headstrong fool."

Kelubai glared at his older brothers. "Wait long enough and you'll all be dead."

+ + +

By the time Kelubai returned to the land over which he had charge, Azubah had loaded the oxen with the plowshares, the pruning hooks, and the remaining sacks of grain from last year's harvest. Stacked on top were all the family possessions. Mesha would see to the small flock of goats that provided milk and meat.

Kelubai noticed a small wooden cabinet lashed to the side of the cart. "What's this?" he asked his wife, although he knew all too well.

"We can't leave our household gods behind."

He untied the box. "Have you learned nothing these past weeks?" Ignoring her shriek, he heaved the container against the wall of his empty hut. The cabinet burst open, spilling clay idols that smashed on the ground. He caught her by the arm before she could go after them. "They're useless, woman! Worse than useless." He took the rod from Mesha and prodded the oxen. "Now, let's go. We'll be fortunate if we reach Goshen before nightfall."

Others were heading for Goshen; even Egyptians were among those with their possessions on their backs or loaded in small carts. Squalid camps had sprung up like thistles around the outer edges of the humble Hebrew villages. Kelubai avoided them and went into the villages themselves, seeking information about the placement of the tribe of Judah. They camped away from everyone.

On the third day, he approached a gathering of old men in the middle of a village, knowing they would be the elders and leaders. Several noticed his approach and studied him nervously. "I am a friend come to join you."

"Friend? I don't know you." The elder glanced around the circle. "Do any of you know this man?" There was a rumble of voices as the others agreed that Kelubai was a stranger to all of them.

Kelubai came closer. "We are connected through my ancestor Jephunneh, friend of Judah, son of Jacob. Our people followed your family from Canaan during the great famine. We were your servants for a time."

"What is your name?"

"Kelubai."

"*Caleb*, he says." *Dog*. Some laughed, not pleasantly.

Kelubai felt the heat pour into his face. "Kelubai." He spoke slowly; his gaze went to each man in the circle in an unhurried clarification.

"Caleb," someone said again, snide and unseen.

And then another, "No doubt a friend of Egyptians."

Kelubai would not let insults or his temper rule his judgment. "I am your brother."

"A spy."

They seemed determine to insult him, these men who had been slaves all their lives.

Kelubai stepped inside the circle. "When the heel of Pharaoh came down upon you, our family continued to barter grain for goats. When Pharaoh denied you straw to make bricks, I gave all I had. Do you so quickly forget those who help you?"

"A little straw does not make you a brother."

These Hebrews were as hard to reason with as his own family. Kelubai smiled mirthlessly. That alone should be a sign that they were blood related. "I am a son of Abraham, just as you are."

"A claim not yet established."

He faced the elder who spoke and inclined his head. "I am descended from Abraham's grandson Esau, and Esau's eldest son, Eliphaz."

Another snorted. "We have no commerce with Esau's spawn."

"See how *red* his face is." *Edom*.

Kelubai's hackles rose. How did they come to be so proud of Israel, the trickster, who cheated his brother, Esau, out of his birthright! But he held his tongue, knowing it would not serve his purpose to argue that cause before this council of men. Besides, Israel might have been a deceiver, but Esau had been less than wise.

Someone laughed. "He has no answer to that!"

Kelubai turned his head slowly and stared into the man's eyes. The laughter stopped.

"We are sons of Israel." The elder spoke quietly this time, his words fact, not insult.

Did they think he would back down? "I am a son of Abraham, who was called by God to leave his land and go wherever God would take him."

"Is he speaking of Abraham or himself?"

"The dog thinks he is a lion."

Kelubai clenched his teeth. "As Abraham was called out of Ur, so too have we been called out of Egypt. Or do you think Moses speaks his own words and not the words of God?"

Kelubai might not be as pure in blood as they, but his desire to be counted among God's people went far beyond blood. It came from the very heart and soul of him. Could these men say the same, when they bowed down in worship one day and rose up in rebellion the next?

The old man assessed him. Kelubai felt a prickling of apprehension. Finally the elder held out his hand. "Sit. Tell us more."

Kelubai accepted the invitation. The others in the circle watched him closely, mouths tight, making it clear a hearing was not a vote of trust. He must choose his words carefully so he would not offend anyone. "You have good reason to be suspicious of strangers. Every time the Lord your God sends His prophet Moses to Pharaoh and another plague strikes Egypt, Pharaoh hates you all the more."

"We have had more trouble since Moses came out of the desert than we had before!"

Surprised, Kelubai glanced at the man who spoke. "What Moses says comes to pass. This is proof he is what he says he is—a messenger from God."

"He brings more trouble upon us!" the Israelite insisted.

Kelubai might as well be talking to his father and brothers. "Your animals survived the pestilence. Did any of you suffer boils? The hail and fire did not touch your lands. The God of Abraham is protecting you."

"And you want that protection for yourself. Isn't that the real reason you have come here and tried to worm your way into our tribe?"

"It is not *your* protection I seek." Clearly, some sitting in their council did not believe in the God who was fighting for their salvation. "You have as little power in yourself as I have." Kelubai drew a slow breath, and focused his attention on the elder who had invited him to sit. Here, at least, was a reasonable man. "I am a slave of Egypt. All my life I have worked for taskmasters, and all my life I have dreamed of freedom. And then I heard that the Nile had been turned to blood. I went to see for myself, and saw frogs as well—by the thousands—come up from the river into Thebes. Then gnats and flies by the millions! I saw oxen drop dead in harness because my neighbors did not heed the warning and bring the animals inside. Members of my family suffered from boils just as the Egyptians did. And a few days ago from the window of my hut, I watched the wheat fields in which I've toiled for months beaten down by stones of water and set aflame by spears of fire from heaven!"

At least they were silent now, all eyes on him, though some most unfriendly. "I *believe* Moses. Every plague that has come upon the land of Egypt weakens Pharaoh's power and brings us closer to freedom. The God who promised to deliver you has come, and He has shown He has the power to fulfill His Word!" He looked around the circle of elders. "I want—" he shook his head—"no. I *intend* to be counted among His people."

Some grumbled. "Intend? Such arrogance!"

"Honesty, not arrogance."

"Why bother to speak to the council at all?"

"I want to be shoulder to shoulder with you in whatever lies ahead, not nose to nose."

Others said what did it matter if this Edomite and his family camped nearby? Hundreds of other people, Egyptians included, had put up tents around the village. What did one more man and his family matter as long as they brought their own provisions with them? Besides, wouldn't having such numbers around them afford a hedge of protection if Pharaoh sent his soldiers? They talked among themselves, argued, worried, fretted.

Kelubai sat and listened, measuring these men with whom he would be aligned. He had expected the Hebrews to be different. Instead, they reminded him of Jerahmeel and his younger brothers squabbling and carping, assuming and fearing the worst would happen. One would think they wished Moses had never been sent to Pharaoh to demand the slaves be released. One would think it would be better to go on making bricks for Pharaoh than risk even the hope of freedom!

Was it not a mighty God directing events that would open the way to salvation?

The old man, Zimri, watched Kelubai, his gaze enigmatic. Kelubai looked into his eyes and held his gaze, wanting the elder to know his thoughts. *I am here, Zimri. These men can ignore me, but neither they nor you will drive me away.*

It was hours later and nothing decided when the men began to disperse. God was ever on their lips, but clearly they did not trust the signs, nor the deliverer. When Kelubai rose, he saw Mesha waiting for him in the shadows between two huts. Smiling, he headed toward him.

"Caleb!"

Hackles rising, Kelubai turned and faced three men he knew to be his enemies. He remembered their names: Tobias, Jakim, and Nepheg. It was always wise to identify your enemies. Jakim raised his hand, pointing at him. "You don't belong among our people, let alone among the elders."

"I came to make a petition."

"Your petition has been rejected."

They spoke boldly now that the others were gone. "I will wait to hear what the entire council has to say." Not that it would make any difference. He was here to stay whether they liked it or not.

"We say, *Caleb*, stay outside the boundaries of our village if you know what's good for you. We don't want outsiders among us." They walked away.

"They called you a dog, Father!"

Yes, they had cast him among those wretched animals that lived on the outskirts of settlements, living off the scraps from the garbage heaps. He saw the shame in his son's eyes, anger flaring in his youthful confusion. More stinging was the unspoken question Kelubai saw in his son's eyes: *Why did you allow it?*

"They don't know me yet, my son."

"They insult you." Mesha's voice trembled with youthful fury.

"A man who gives in to anger might as well burn his house down over his head." He could swallow his pride when his family's survival was at stake.

Mesha hung his head, but not before Kelubai had seen the tears building. Did his son think him a coward? Time would have to teach the truth. "A wise man picks his battles carefully, my son." Kelubai put his arm around Mesha and turned him toward their camp on the outer edges of the village. "If they call me Caleb, so be it. I will make it a name of honor and courage."

+ + +

The family remained on the periphery of the villages of Judah, but Kelubai stayed close whenever the council met and therefore heard whatever news came at the same time the Judeans did. And news did come by way of Levite messengers from Moses and his brother, Aaron. Pharaoh had hardened his heart again; another plague was coming. It would not touch Goshen, but would lay waste to Egypt.

"We must go back and warn your father and brothers!"

Kelubai knew what his wife really wanted was to go back, to be away from these Hebrews who would not speak to her. "I warned them already. We will wait here and make a place for them."

"What makes you so sure they'll come?"

"They aren't fools, Azubah. Stubborn, yes. Frightened? As am I. No, we remain here. I left my words like seeds. When they have been plowed under and more plagues rain down upon them, what I said will take root and grow."

The next morning, he went to the edge of Goshen and watched the cloud of locusts come. They darkened the sun. The noise was like a rumbling of chariots, like the roar of a fire sweeping across the land, like a mighty army moving into battle. The locusts marched like warriors, never breaking ranks, never jostling each other. Each moved according to the orders of the Commander, swarming over walls, entering houses through the windows. The earth quaked as they advanced and the heavens trembled. The ground undulated black. Every stalk of wheat and spelt, every tree was consumed by the advancing horde God had called into battle.

It won't be long now, Kelubai thought, watching the road for his father and brothers.

Kenaz came alone. "Jerahmeel rages against the god of the Hebrews for destroying the last of his crops."

"And Father?"

"You know Father cannot leave without his eldest son."

"And Jerahmeel will not come because it was *I* who suggested it. He is the fool!"

"You did not suggest, Kelubai. You commanded. Your manner did not sit well with our brothers." Kenaz smiled. "Since I am the youngest, it matters not what I think or whom I follow."

"You're wrong about that, my brother. You've shown courage by coming of your own free will, rather than bending to the will of those older and fiercer, but far less wise, than you." He looked toward the west. "If Pharaoh does not let the Hebrews go, there will be another plague, and another. Jerahmeel will change his mind."

+ + +

Trading and bartering for goatskins, Kelubai enlarged his tent enough to shelter his brothers and their families when they came.

Another plague did come, one of darkness upon the land of Egypt. But when Moses and Aaron returned to Goshen, they brought ill tidings of Pharaoh's fury. He would *not* allow the people to go with their flocks and herds, and he had threatened Moses that if Pharaoh ever saw him again, he'd kill him.

When Kelubai stood on the outer edge of the Jewish congregation and heard the instructions given by Moses' messenger, he knew the end was coming. He returned to his camp and told Azubah he must go back and bring their father to Goshen. "You must stay here with her, Kenaz, and keep this camp secure. Now that the darkness has lifted from Egypt, others will come seeking refuge among the Hebrews. Hold our ground against them!"

Hastening to his father's house, he found his older brothers had gathered their families. "Another plague is coming!" Kelubai was thankful the locusts and darkness had made them willing to listen. "I heard with my own ears that all the firstborn sons will die in every family in Egypt, from the oldest son of Pharaoh, who sits on the throne, to the oldest son of his lowliest slave. Even the firstborn of the animals will die."

Everyone looked at Jerahmeel, and he paled. Jerahmeel looked at Kelubai with new respect. "You came back to save my life?"

"We are brothers, are we not? But it is not only your life I want spared, Jerahmeel, but those of your firstborn son and the firstborn of all my brothers. Remember! *Every* firstborn son."

Hezron stood. "We will return to Goshen with Kelubai. Our animals are all dead. What little grain we had hidden away for sustenance was eaten by locusts. There is nothing to hold us here."

They journeyed to Goshen willingly, setting up tents close by Kelubai's camp. He called them together as soon as they were settled. "Listen to what the Lord instructed Moses. Each family is to sacrifice a year-old lamb or goat without defect." The blood would be smeared over the entrance to their tent, and they must remain inside until death passed over them. The lamb or goat was to be roasted with bitter herbs and eaten with bread made without yeast. "We are to wear sandals, traveling clothes, and have walking sticks in our hands as we eat this meal."

When the night of the forewarned plague came, Kelubai, his wife and children, Kenaz, his father Hezron, and fourteen others stood around the fire pit as a goat roasted over the hot coals. Trembling in fear, they obeyed Moses' instructions exactly, hoping everyone inside the thin canopy would survive the night.

Kelubai heard a sound moving overhead, a whispering wind that made his blood run cold. He felt a dark presence press down upon them, press in from the thin leather flap that served as their door. All within the circle held their breath and pressed closer to one another. Kelubai shoved Mesha and Jerahmeel into the center of the family circle. "You die; we all die." Jerahmeel looked around, confused, shaken. When screams rent the cold night air, Azubah grasped Kelubai's robe and hid her face in its folds while their sons hugged close around him. A man screamed, and everyone in Kelubai's shelter jumped.

"We're all going to die!" Some began to weep.

"We won't die." Kelubai spoke with a confidence he was far from feeling. "Not if we put our faith in the unseen God."

Jerahmeel held his oldest son by the shoulders, keeping him close. "We've only goatskin to cover us, Kelubai, while the Hebrews have mud-brick huts and doors."

"Something is out there. . . ."

Fear grew in the room, fanned by more screams from outside. The children whimpered; the circle tightened.

"We must follow the instructions." Kelubai cut meat from the goat. He strove to keep his voice calm. "See to the bread, Azubah." She rose to obey.

"How can you expect us to eat at a time like this?"

"Because the God of Abraham demands it." Kelubai held out a slice of goat meat to his father. Hezron took it. "Give thanks to the God of Abraham for His protection from this plague of death."

Kelubai swallowed his fear and forced himself to eat the Passover meal. *Tomorrow will bring our freedom!*

✦ ✦ ✦

Egyptians came running toward Goshen, crying out, "Leave! Go quickly!"

"Pharaoh has relented!"

"Go as quickly as you can or all of us will die!"

"Hurry!"

"Here! Take this grain as a gift. Plead with your god for my life."

"Take my silver."

"Here is my gold!"

"Pray for us!"

"*Away with you! Hurry!*"

Others clutched at the Hebrews' robes, pleading, "Please, let us walk with you, for we've heard God is with you!"

Kelubai accepted the proffered gifts as his sons stripped down the goat-skin coverings and yanked up the tent poles. He laughed. "Didn't I tell you all that our freedom was at hand?" Who would have imagined that God would make the Egyptians pour offerings upon them as they begged them to leave? Kelubai raised his hands in the air and shouted, "What a mighty God You are!" Laughing joyously, Kelubai heaved the last gift onto his cart. "Our taskmasters shower us with gifts and plead with us to leave!"

Azubah scrambled about, gathering their possessions and tying bundles while calling out to the children to keep the goats close. "Frogs, locusts, pestilence, and death! How do we worship such a God? No one gives without expecting to receive, Kelubai. What will this God ask of us?"

"So far He has asked nothing but that we believe what He says."

"And once we are in the wilderness, what will He ask of us then?"

"If He asked for everything, I would give it to Him."

"Our sons, Kelubai? Would you sacrifice our sons?"

Her fear gave him pause. The great overseers of Canaan were gods who thirsted for human blood. Was the God of Abraham such as these? If so, why had He asked for the blood of a lamb or goat rather than the blood of Israel's sons?

Kelubai prodded the ox, and caught up to his father and brothers who had set off before him. Having no animals or possessions to carry, they could travel faster than he.

Hezron shared his excitement, but Jerahmeel feared the future as much as Azubah. "And how many more will be out there in the desert waiting for us?"

"They will have heard what God has done for us."

"The nations may fear this God, but what reason have they to fear a band of slaves?"

Kelubai waved. "We are more than a band, brother. Look around you! We are thousands upon thousands."

"Scattered in a dozen tribes, with stragglers who cling like ticks. We are not a nation. We have no army."

"What need have we for an army when the God of heaven and earth fights for us? When people hear what has happened to Egypt, they will flee before us."

"Where do you come by this faith in a God whose people call you *dog*?"

Kelubai grinned coldly. "I've been called worse."

+   +   +

The ragged mass traveled by day and night, moving south, away from the trade route. Deeper into the wilderness they moved before turning east, pressing between the high walls of a great wadi that spilled into the Red Sea. And there the masses huddled in family groups, crying out to Moses to save them when news came that Pharaoh and his army were not far behind them.

"Now see what you've done to us, Kelubai!" Jerahmeel ranted. "Had we stayed in Egypt our lives and the lives of our children would be safe."

Thousands screamed and wailed in terror when they realized they were blocked from all possible escape.

Kelubai lowered his head against the wind and pushed. "Stay in close with the Judeans." Wind whipped at his robe, stinging his face with sand and drops of salt water. "Stay together!" He hauled his wife and sons closer as a cloud caught flame. Raging overhead, it swirled into a pillar of fire that closed the wadi and stopped Pharaoh's chariots from racing out onto the spillway.

"They're moving!" Azubah cried out.

And so the multitude pressed forward as the sea opened before them clear to the other side, revealing the path of salvation. Some people ran down the slope. Others, burdened with possessions, moved slower. Kelubai shouted for Azubah to run ahead and take their sons with her while he followed with the oxen and cart. His father and brothers stayed with him, grabbing sacks to lighten the load and make the way swifter. Thousands came behind, pressing tight, moving down the road through the sea. When he reached high ground, Kelubai found his family waiting among the Judeans.

The pillar of fire had lifted, and Pharaoh's army raced out onto the sand and down into the pathway God had opened. Kelubai spotted Zimri among the stragglers. The old man, pale with exhaustion and sagging beneath the weight of a sack lumpy with possessions, struggled up the slope, his son, Carmi, helping him. Kelubai ran to them, grasped the pack, and supported the old man as they made their way up the hill.

"The chariots are coming," Kenaz shouted, reaching them and taking the pack. "They're coming! Hurry!"

A rushing sound and screams came from behind, and Kelubai felt a cold wet blast at his back. He fell forward onto his face and then felt hands upon him, dragging him up, shouting. Kelubai dug his heels into the wet ground and pushed, dragging Carmi up the slope. Lungs heaving, Kenaz flung the sack onto dry ground. Zimri was helped up, frightened but uninjured.

"They're gone." Kenaz stared out over the sea, searching. "All of them, gone."

The multitude was silent, staring out at the rippling sea as bodies of the Egyptian soldiers washed up along the shore.

Kelubai stood beside Zimri and Carmi. "Praise be to the God who saved us."

The old man was still pale, but he had regained his breath. He gripped Kelubai's arms for support. "My thanks, Caleb." For the first time, the term was spoken without derision. Caleb. *A new name for a new alliance. So be it.*

The old man's hands tightened. "Make your camp next to mine." His son, Carmi, grinned and slapped Caleb on the back.

✦   ✦   ✦

Before three days had passed, jubilation became complaining when the desert water was found to be bitter and undrinkable. Moses prayed and cast tree bark into the pond, enabling people to quench their thirst before traveling on to the date palms of Elim. Some would have been content to stay, but God had told Moses to lead His people into the wilderness. Why? was the common cry. Why didn't God lead them to green pastures and still waters instead of heading them out into an arid wasteland of sand and rock? Thirst and hunger soon set in, and the people complained for meat, as though God were a heavenly servant meant to give them whatever they craved. Moses prayed and God sent quail into the camp, so many that no one could walk without stepping on them. But in the morning, a greater miracle came when God gave them the bread of heaven to sustain them. Instructions were given to collect only enough for one day and no more.

Caleb knelt, picked up a few white flakes, and let them melt on his tongue. They were sweeter than anything he had ever tasted and held the slightest moisture of dew. When he had filled his clay jar, he rose and looked up at the cloud overshadowing the huge camp. It did not move with the air currents as other clouds did, nor disappear over the course of a hot day. It remained with the people, thick in portions, with fingers of gray-white, as though the mighty hand of God Himself shaded the Israelites and fellow travelers from the killing heat of the desert sun. Freedom, water, food, shelter. Was there anything the Lord had not given them?

Overwhelmed with emotions he could neither understand nor define, Caleb raised his omer high, tears streaming down his face. "How do I worship You, Lord? How do I give thanks for my life? How am I to live from now on? Nothing is the way I imagined it would be, oh, Lord!"

Life had become confusing. Freedom was not the simple matter he had dreamed. As a slave, he knew what the day would hold and how to get through it. Now, he didn't know what the next morning would bring. Every day was different. He didn't know where he would camp or for how long or why a particular place was chosen. He pitched his tent near Zimri's each evening, but there were always others around them, strangers vying for a better position. How was he any different from all these others, ambitious for themselves and their families, craving something better than what they had always known, demanding more now that freedom had come and brought with it the reality of daily decisions that had always been made for them. Caleb had liked to think of himself as more shrewd, more able to find his own way, but realized now that he was the same as all the others. He had been born and reared in a mud hut and lived all his life on one small plot of land he worked for Pharaoh's benefit. Now, he was in constant turmoil, out of his element. Instead of dwelling in one place, he traveled great distances and lived in a tent like a desert nomad. This was not the life he had imagined.

Tense, irritable, fighting against the confusion of his new life, fighting to keep his relatives together and in some semblance of order, he felt more shame than joy. At times, they behaved like a pack of wolves, growling at one another, fighting over scraps.

"Where are we going, brother? I thought we were supposed to be heading for Canaan, and we're in the middle of the wilderness!"

Every day had its squabbles and challenges. How did Moses hear the voice of God through the cacophony of voices raised in constant question and complaint?

Caleb struggled within himself, too.

In his heart, he cried out to God. *I don't want to question Your ways, Lord. I want to go with thanksgiving and without hesitation where You tell us to go. I want to set off into the unknown the way Moses does—head up, staff in hand. I don't want to look back with longing on the life I've known. Oh, God, help me to remember how unbearable it was and how I longed to be free. Is it possible for You to change a man? If so, change me!*

"Caleb!"

At the sound of Jerahmeel's annoyed voice, Caleb lowered the omer and held it against his chest, eyes closed, teeth clenched.

"We're on the move *again!* Though who but Moses can guess where we're going this time. As if there's a better place than this to rest . . ." Jerahmeel's complaining faded as he stalked away.

The cloud was moving now. In its changing shape, Caleb imagined its folds like an eagle with outspread wings, floating, head down watching them, not as prey but as sheltered offspring.

"*Caleb!* Are you going to just stand there? They're *moving!*"

And will You please change a few others as well?

✦ ✦ ✦

The people rose up in anger when they reached Rephidim, for there was no water. Caleb and his wife had given their water to their sons, and were as thirsty as everyone else. His relatives gave him no rest.

"It was your idea to follow this God. . . ."

"Where's the better life you promised?"

"I'm thirsty, Abba."

"How long before we get there?"

"Ask your abba where *there* is."

Caleb left them and sat among the rocks at the base of the high mountain. If he was going to die, he wanted to do it in peace and not surrounded by grumbling Israelites or relatives blaming him for every discomfort. Still, he heard the multitude crying out in the distance. Pressing his hands over his ears, he tried to shut out the angry shouting. His own wrath mounted, his heart pounding fast, his blood rushing hot and heavy.

How soon they all forget what You can do! You made the Nile run with blood. You brought forth plagues; You killed Egypt's livestock with pestilence. You covered the people with boils, destroyed the land with hail and fire, and killed the firstborn from Pharaoh on down, all the while sparing the animals and lives of those who belong to You. And still that madman Pharaoh changed his mind and came after us!

But You opened the sea, made a dry pathway across, then closed it again over Pharaoh's army, washing them away like dust before a windstorm. The sea. The Nile. The river of life . . . no. No! Who but a fool would long for that place of slavery and death?

Water, Lord. Please. Water is a small thing, but we will die without it. Oh, hear us, God who commands the heavens and the earth. Help us!

Tongue parched, throat closing, his skin so dry he felt his body shrinking, he closed his eyes. If not for the cloud overhead, Caleb knew he would have perished already, baked in the heat, dried out like a Nile fish on a rack.

Why am I still alive? What is the purpose in all this suffering? I don't understand You. Did You set us free only to allow us to die of thirst? It makes no sense. Water, Lord. Oh, God of might and mercy, please, give us water. I don't believe You brought us out here to die. I don't believe it. I won't believe it!

The cries of the mob suddenly changed to screams of excitement and exultation. Trembling from weakness, Caleb stood and took a few steps so he could see what was happening. Water gushed from a rock in the side of the mountain, forming a stream that raced down and pooled. Thousands sank to their knees and fell forward onto their hands to thrust their faces into the water and drink like animals. Another miracle! Another, just when they needed it most.

Stumbling, Caleb made his way down the rocky slope. Pressing his way through the celebrants, his gaze never leaving the rock that flowed water, he squatted, cupped his hands, and drank. The Rock itself was the well of life-giving water. The stream flowed straight from the stone, fresh and clear and cool. As Caleb drank deeply, he felt his body renewed, strengthened, revitalized. Closing his eyes, he held the precious water and washed his face, longing to immerse himself in it.

As the people were quenching their thirst, Caleb heard shouting.

"The Amalekites are attacking! They are killing the stragglers!"

Moses called for Joshua. People cried out again, frightened this time.

"They'll soon be upon us!"

"We have no army to fight against the Amalekites!"

Caleb rose, dripping, and ran to his camp. He rummaged through the possessions he had brought from Egypt until he found his scythe. "Come on." He raised his farm implement and called to his brothers. "Fight for our brothers!"

"We're not soldiers." Jerahmeel stood back. "We're farmers."

Caleb faced him, angry. "Should not a farmer fight for his neighbors?"

"Who is my neighbor?"

There was no time to stand and argue. People were dying! Turning his back on his father and brothers, Caleb ran after Joshua. Others had gathered with Moses' young servant. Moses had already given instructions and now climbed the mountain, his brother, Aaron, on one side and his friend Hur on the other.

Caleb peered through the crowd to the man in its center. Joshua looked so young and nervous. The men around him were tense, shifting, uncertain. Caleb felt uneasy. What did he know about fighting against a trained enemy?

He remembered what God had done for them already. The Lord, He would protect them. The Lord, He would give them victory. *I will believe that. I will set my mind upon Him. I will proclaim my faith before these men loud enough that they will all hear and know I am for the Lord!*

"Let me through!" Lowering his head, Caleb shoved his way through the crowd until he stood before Joshua. "We are God's to command, Joshua. And the Lord has designated you to lead." Caleb looked around and raised his voice. "God will fight for us! He did not bring us out into this desert to be picked off by cowardly marauders who kill the weak and helpless, nor by any who bow down to false gods!" Baring his teeth in a grin, Caleb stared Joshua in the eye. "Command us as God commands you. The battle is the Lord's!"

Joshua's eyes shone with sudden fierceness. He let out a shout and the others joined with him.

And so they went out into battle armed with farm implements and threshing tools, while three old men stood on the mountain praying.

And God gave them victory.

After the triumph came the lingering stillness. Caleb waited along with thousands of others camped at the base of the mountain while Moses went up to meet with the Lord. Days passed, and long nights of quiet and question.

Waiting proved a greater test than taking up arms against the enemy.

TWO

✦✦✦✦✦✦✦

Caleb sat in misery, staring up at the mountain. *Here I sit, coward that I am, an outsider again*. He hung his head.

Washed, adorned in clean garments, consecrated, he had stood with the multitude, eager to hear the Lord. He had heard God blow the shofar blast. The sound of it, long and heavy, had rattled his chest. A consuming fire had flared from the mountaintop, along with a thunderous roar. He had fled in terror. Like stampeding sheep, thousands had run. And like the others, he had cowered at a distance. Let Moses listen to God and tell them what He said.

Moses was on the mountain again, but this time he had taken the elders with him, including Zimri from the tribe of Judah. Joshua, too, had been summoned.

Mortified by his own cowardice, Caleb spoke to no one. He knew he had missed his chance to be close to God. Covering his face, he wept.

When Aaron and the elders returned, Caleb went to hear what Zimri had to tell the sons of Judah.

"We saw the God of Israel; under His feet there was a pavement of sapphire, as clear as the sky itself." Zimri shook with excitement, his eyes shining. "And He did not stretch out His hand against us. We ate and drank in praise of Him. And then the Lord called Moses up the mountain. God will give him the laws we are to live by."

"Where is Joshua? What happened to him?"

"Joshua went up the mountain with Moses. We could see them both as they went up. Then they stopped and waited for six days. On the seventh, the mountain caught fire and Moses went into the cloud and disappeared. Joshua is still up there waiting for him."

"Are Moses and Joshua alive?"

"God only knows."

"Before Moses went up, he told us to wait, and we did wait."

"Did they take anything up with them? Food? Water?"

"Nothing."

Days passed, then weeks. The people grew restless. Moses was surely dead. Why were they still camped in this desolate place? Why didn't they return to Egypt? They need not fear going back now. Surely, after all the plagues, the Egyptians would be in fear of them?

"Why should they fear us?" Caleb remonstrated with his family. "*We* did not bring the plagues. *God* did!"

"We should get out of here before he decides to kill us the way he's killed Moses."

"We don't know that Moses is dead."

Jerahmeel stood. "He's been gone a month, Caleb! He's an old man, and he went up that mountain without food and water. What do you think has happened to him?"

"He lived in Midian forty years before he returned to Egypt. That old man knows how to survive in the desert."

Hezron stood between them. "Kelubai, you were right in leading us to Goshen. We are free from slavery. But now, it is time to go back to Egypt or go on to Canaan. We cannot stay here forever."

Caleb clenched his hands. "Why not? We have water. We have manna."

"What sort of a life is this?" Jerahmeel raged. "I'm sick of manna. The sweetness of it sticks in my throat."

"In Egypt, you never knew from one day to the next if you would have bread to eat!"

Jerahmeel turned to the others. "We should go back to Egypt. They fear us. Even the gods fear us. We can fashion gods and show that we have returned as brothers."

Caleb sneered. "Return to gods who had no power to protect themselves?"

"And what good is this god doing for us now? We sit and wait. Weeks we have waited. Are we to live the rest of our lives at the base of this mountain?"

"Go then, and see how far you get without His protection."

"We won't be going alone, Caleb. Everywhere I turn, others are saying the same thing I am saying. Even that old man you follow around, Zimri, has gone with others to speak to Aaron."

"And what does Aaron say?"

"At first he said to wait. Now he says nothing."

Caleb went outside. He couldn't abide the air inside the tent any longer. He looked up at the mountain. Nothing had changed. The cloud remained, surges of light flashing from within. Why would God kill Moses? What sense did that make? And yet, if the old man hadn't died, why did he linger up there? And where was Joshua?

He clenched his fist. "I will not believe You brought us out here only to abandon us. I won't believe it."

"Kelubai?"

Azubah stood at the doorway. She came to him hesitantly, her gaze troubled. "Why are you so determined to believe in this God?"

"What is the alternative?"

"Return to Egypt."

"Yes, and I would rather my sons die here than go back to that place of death."

"It will be different this time, Kelubai."

"Woman, you speak of things you do not understand."

Her chin jutted. "Ah, yes, as you understand this God. As you understand why we must remain here, day after day, waiting for no one knows what."

"You would do better to listen to me rather than my brother."

"I listen to you, but you would do better to listen to your father." She went back into the tent.

Frustrated, Caleb walked away into the night. How he longed to climb that mountain and find out for himself what had happened to Moses. But there was a boundary set; the mountain was sacred ground. He would not set foot upon it.

Wandering among the clustered camps, Caleb heard others talking. Jerahmeel had spoken the truth. He was not the only man counseling a return to Egypt. It was near dawn when he returned to his tent, exhausted and disheartened, and went to bed.

Azubah awakened him. "Messengers came through camp, my husband. Aaron has called for the men to bring him a pair of gold earrings from each wife, son, and daughter." She had already collected the earrings in a cloth.

"What for?"

"Does it matter? Your father and brothers wait outside."

"Hurry!" Jerahmeel appeared at the entrance to the tent. "Baskets are set outside Aaron's tent, and they are overflowing with gold earrings. Some put in necklaces and bracelets."

"Give whatever you want." Angry, Caleb turned over on his pallet. He was too tired and despondent to care why Aaron had asked for gold.

He found out soon enough. Word spread. All were to come and worship before the Lord. Caleb went eagerly, his family with him. Shocked, he found himself standing before a golden calf much like those he had seen in Egypt. This one was far from the svelte beasts set upon pedestals in Egypt. "Where did it come from?"

"Aaron made it for us."

"Aaron?" He couldn't believe Moses' brother would make such a thing. But there he was, standing before the gathering, presiding over it, calling for offerings to the God who had brought them out of Egypt.

This cannot be! Confused, Caleb drew back.

The people bowed down and presented offerings. Azubah and Caleb's sons, his brothers and father went forward. No one trembled and shook before this god. Instead, they rose up to laugh and dance and celebrate. Aaron proclaimed a feast. Caleb didn't know what to do. Sick and confused, he returned to his tent.

Music filled the camp. Then shrieking and laughter. Azubah came in and lay down beside him, her eyes dark. She smelled of incense and tasted of wine. "This is better, isn't it?" She moved over him, wanton, eager.

Caleb caught his breath. Maybe it was better not to think about a God he couldn't understand. But, somehow, this didn't feel right. He wanted to push her away, but she kissed him. His senses swam. She was his wife, after all. Surely, there was nothing wrong in this. Maybe it was better not to trouble himself with inexplicable feelings of shame and guilt. "Azubah . . ."

"Love me."

Why should he feel guilty? Maybe it was better to live and not think at all. *God, God.* No. He would not think of God right now. Not now. Grasping Azubah's flowing hair, he took what she offered, surrendering himself to the fire in his belly. Passion rose, crested, and evaporated, leaving in its wake a sense of shame and bewilderment. Caleb lay in the darkness, with Azubah, sated, asleep beside him. Never had he felt so unclean.

The camp was in an uproar. "What's going on now?" His wife slept on, the effects of the wine deadening her to sound and light. She would have a headache when she awakened. Caleb dressed and went outside.

Moses had returned! He strode through the camp, shouting.

"He destroyed the stone tablets!"

Caleb caught hold of a man running away. "What stone tablets?"

"The ones on which God wrote the laws we were to follow!"

Caleb ran toward the screaming. Moses climbed onto the platform and pushed the calf off its stand. "Burn it." His face was red, his eyes filled with wrath. "Grind it into powder. Spread it over the drinking water."

The people were out of control, some drunk and unwilling to give up their pleasure taking, others screaming defiance.

Caleb felt the gathering storm. Aaron was running. He shouted, and others from his tribe of Levi raced to stand behind Moses. Some had swords and drew them.

With sudden understanding, Caleb cried out. He saw his sons among the crowd gathering against Moses.

"Mesha! Mareshah! Jesher! Come out from among those people. Shobab! Ardon! Come to me. Hurry!" His sons wove their way through the crowd, eyes wide. He ran to meet them, grabbed them, and dove to the ground. When they cried out in panic and tried to rise and run, he yanked them down. "Bow down before the Lord. Bow down!"

Screams of rage and death came all around him. Someone stepped over him. Metal struck metal, words exchanged, a gurgling cry, a thud. His heart pounded. Reason kept him on his face. "Forgive us, Lord. Forgive us. God, forgive us."

If this was Moses' fury vented, what could God in His wrath do?

When a man fell dead beside them, Ardon screamed and tried to rise. Caleb yanked him down again, sliding half over him to hold him to the ground. "Mercy, Lord! Mercy!" His sons sobbed in terror. "Pray for forgiveness! Pray!" Caleb ordered them.

"God, forgive us . . ."

"God, forgive . . ."

Would the Lord hear such soft cries amidst the chaos of terror surging all around them?

The battle was soon over. Sobs and wailing rose.

Jerahmeel lay dead near his tent. So, too, another brother. Their wives lay dead nearby. Hezron sat at the opening of his tent, rocking back and forth, face ashen, his garments torn in grieving. When Azubah came outside, bleary-eyed, and saw what had happened, she wailed and threw dust into the air. Silent, Caleb commanded his sons to help him carry the bodies outside the camp for burial.

Would his family blame him for the deaths? Would they cry out against him because he had fought so hard to come with the Israelites and follow after their God? Would they want to turn back now?

When he returned to his tent, he found everyone silent. No one looked at him, not even his wife and sons. "You blame me for their deaths, don't you?"

"We should have turned back when we had the chance."

"Turned back to what, Father? Slavery?"

"*My sons are dead!*"

My brothers, Caleb wanted to add, but he hunkered down and spoke gently. "We must give honor only to the God who delivered us."

"Should we not have choice in which god we worship?"

He looked at Azubah. "Will my own wife turn against me? Not one, not *all* of the gods of Egypt could stand against the Lord God of Israel." She disgusted him. He disgusted himself.

"Aaron made the golden calf and Aaron still lives."

"Yes, Father, because he ran to Moses when asked where he stood. Had my brothers bowed down before the Lord, they would still be alive. But instead, they chose to defy God and Moses. They chose death over life."

The old man sobbed.

Mourning deeply, Caleb removed his jewelry. As he lifted an amulet from his neck, he looked at it and went cold. Why had he not noticed it was the Star of Rompha? He wore the cobra Ra on his arm, a lapis scarab set in solid gold on his finger. Shuddering, he yanked off every piece of jewelry he wore. "Take off everything that honors another god." They did as he said, casting off gifts the Egyptians had poured upon them. "It's a wonder we aren't all dead!"

+ + +

Moses had chiseled out two more stone tablets and gone back up the mountain to plead with God on the people's behalf. When he returned, his face shone like the sun. Until he covered his face with a veil, no one had courage enough to go near him, not even his brother, Aaron. Moses had not returned empty-handed; he brought back the Law written by God's hand upon the tablets, and plans for a tabernacle and holy items including an ark to contain the Law. God had chosen two men for the task of building the Tabernacle: Bezalel and Oholiab. Offerings were needed for the construction, and the people responded. Had not God provided what was needed by the gifts the Egyptians had given the Israelites? The people merely gave back a portion of what God had already given them.

Caleb gave the best of what he had.

"Enough!" Moses' servants said. "We have enough!"

Everyone worked. Even Azubah. She joined other women of the family and wove fine cloth. Caleb's remaining brothers helped keep the fires burning so the gold and bronze could be melted. Caleb worked hard, honored to be assigned any task alongside the sons of Judah. But he knew alliances weakened under stress. He had to find another way to be grafted in among these people.

Young women wore mourning clothes. Many had lost fathers and brothers on the day of God's retribution for the golden idol. Caleb saw in them a way to solidify his family's connection to the tribe of Judah.

He approached his father and brothers. "We must strengthen our alliance with Judah."

"How?" Kenaz spoke with willingness.

"Take wives from among the sons of Judah."

Caleb took a second wife, Jerioth. His father and Kenaz followed his lead, as did the others over the next months.

Each morning, Caleb listened eagerly to the laws God had given Moses. He wanted to please the God of heaven and earth. Though the task of following the numerous laws was daunting, he felt hedged in from all sides, safe under the watchful eye of God.

Know my heart, Lord. Know that I desire to please You.

When the Tabernacle and holy items were ready, Caleb stood amidst the multitude, shoulder to shoulder for the dedication ceremonies, praying that God would be pleased with their work. He did not hold a place in the front, so he had to stretch up to see, and strain to hear what was said. Giving up, he kept his gaze fixed upon the cloud. When it moved, his heart fluttered and then pounded. In awe, he drew in his breath and held it. When the cloud came down and filled the tabernacle, there was weeping in joy. Caleb shouted praise to God.

The joy was short-lived.

"Aaron's sons are dead!" People shouted and wept. Some ran.

"What happened?"

"They were consumed by fire!"

"Why?"

Caleb heard later that they had scorned the law of the Lord and offered incense in a manner other than that which God commanded. Fear gripped Caleb. If God would kill Aaron's sons, He would not tolerate sin among any of His people. Caleb was afraid to turn to the left or right of what the Lord commanded.

Zimri represented Judah among the seventy elders instructing the sons of Judah. Whenever the old man sat to teach the laws Moses had received from the Lord, Caleb was there, listening more intently than the younger men who gathered.

As the people moved toward the Promised Land, more trouble brewed. The Egyptian rabble traveling with them complained about the manna. They longed for the fish, cucumber, melons, leeks, onions, and garlic of their homeland. "We are sick of nothing at all to eat except this manna!" The Israelites took up the rebellious whining. Even the sons of Judah began complaining.

"These people have learned nothing." Caleb kept his wives and sons inside the tent. "Do they think the Lord does not hear their carping?"

Jerioth said nothing, but Azubah argued. "I am as sick of the manna as they are. I can barely swallow it without gagging on the sweetness of it."

"You try my patience, woman. When will you learn to give thanks for what God has given us?"

"I am thankful, but must we have the same thing day after day?"

"You lived on barley cakes and water in Egypt and never once complained."

"Yes, but this God could give us anything and everything we want. Why does He withhold a *feast* from heaven and instead make us grovel on our knees every morning for one day's portion of manna? I'm sick of it—sick of it, I say. I wish we had never left Egypt!"

Then God sent quail and a plague.

Azubah feasted on roasted birds and died.

Remembering her as a young bride and mother, Caleb grieved. Leaving Jerioth in camp to tend the baby, he and his other sons carried Azubah's body outside the camp. They buried her among thousands of others.

Weeping, Caleb went down on his knees and stretched out his hands, his gaze fixed upon the cloud. *Why won't they listen, Lord? How is it I believe and so many don't? They saw the plagues of Egypt. They walked through the sea. They saw the water come from the rock. They've eaten the manna. Why, Lord? Why won't they believe?*

Thirty days after Azubah's death, Caleb sought another wife from among the daughters of Judah left fatherless.

Zimri advised him. "Ephrathah would be a good choice."

The Hebrews overhearing the conversation exchanged smiles, and Caleb suspected that no one else wanted the woman. So be it. He would do whatever necessary to solidify his family's alliance with Zimri, even if it meant taking some loathsome woman off his hands.

"I will make arrangements for the bride-price."

Several men laughed low and bent their heads close to whisper. Zimri gripped Caleb's arm. "Do not take heed of those who only take notice of the surface."

Ephrathah was brought to his tent. When Caleb lifted her veil, his suspicions were confirmed. He treated her with consideration if not affection.

✦　✦　✦

Another rebellion arose, this time between the high priest, Aaron, and Miriam over Moses' Cushite wife. The Lord struck Miriam with leprosy and then healed her when Aaron pleaded for her. Even so, the law required Miriam to spend seven days outside the camp. Everyone waited for her return, for she was held in high esteem as the sister of Moses, the one who had watched over him as he drifted on the Nile and then been bold enough to speak to Pharaoh's daughter about his need for a wet nurse. The cunning girl had brought back their mother to tend him.

✦　✦　✦

Caleb loved to listen to Ephrathah's stories. She knew the history of her people in a way he had never heard it. She was more eloquent than Zimri and the elders! Every bit of information he could gather helped him pry into the boundaries of his adopted tribe. He smiled as his sons leaned in close, listening hungrily. This new wife of his had the gift of storytelling. Seeing her more clearly, he cherished her. Ephrathah was as stubborn in her faith as he. Even Jerioth, about to bear her second child, deferred to Ephrathah.

"Moses drifted among the crocodiles and serpents." Ephrathah moved her hands sinuously as she told the story of Moses. "Even the wise ibises paid no attention. Israel's deliverer was within their reach, and they did not know. And where did the Lord take the babe, but straight into the arms of the daughter of His enemy, Pharaoh. Moses' sister, Miriam, came out of hiding then and said the baby needed a wet nurse and would the lady like her to fetch one. Of course, she did, having no milk to offer. And so it was that Jochebed, Moses' own mother, received her son back again." Ephrathah laughed. "The Lord laughs at His enemies, for they have no power against Him."

Caleb drew Ephrathah close in his arms that night. He whispered into the curve of her neck, "You are worth your weight in gold."

✦ ✦ ✦

Zimri and the other elders of Judah called the heads of families together. Moses had called for twelve spies to enter Canaan, one from each tribe. Judah must choose a representative.

Dozens of men volunteered, Caleb among them. Though he quaked at the thought of entering Canaan without the Lord overhead, he knew if he was chosen, he and his family would hold a place of honor from this time forward. "Let me. I'm not afraid. Send me!"

Everyone started talking at once and no one heard him but those standing close. They sneered. The elders were calling for discussion.

"It should be a young man without wife and children on such a journey."

"There is no guarantee the man will return alive."

"There are giants in the land. Descendants of Anak."

At that, some men changed their minds about volunteering.

Voices grew louder. "Let each family offer one, and we will cast lots to see who the Lord will send."

If that happened, Caleb knew he stood no chance. He shoved into the circle. "I will go." His sons would have a place among God's people even if he had to sacrifice his life to make certain of it.

The gathering fell silent. Several looked to Zimri.

The old man shook his head. "No."

Caleb faced the old man he had saved. "Why not?" He looked around the circle. "I don't see all that many jumping at the chance to go."

"You have two wives and sons."

"Not to mention the rabble who came with him!" another called out from the back.

Caleb seethed, but forced himself to offer a wry smile. "Why not send the dog if he's so eager to sniff out Canaan?" Some laughed at Caleb's challenge. Others called out agreement. "What do you say? Will you send the Caleb?" A cry of agreement rose amidst the laughter. Caleb laughed loudest, determined. "Mock me if you will, but send me. If I die in Canaan, what have you lost?"

"Nothing!"

"Enough!" Zimri shouted. "Hear me." The men grew quiet. "Moses has called for men who are leaders. He is no leader who mocks his brother." Caleb felt the heat surge into his face and then realized Zimri's scowl was directed at the man who had started the baiting. The offender lowered his gaze. Zimri looked at the others. "Who will represent Judah on this perilous errand? Step forward if you're willing. Otherwise, be silent."

Emboldened by Zimri's defense, Caleb stepped into the center of the circle. "Send me."

"You are not equipped."

"Did I not go into battle beside Joshua against the Amalekites?"

"You are my friend, Caleb, but you are not . . ."

"Full-blooded." Another man finished what Zimri was too kind to voice.

Caleb's face flushed hot as he looked between the elders. "Did I not hear you just call me brother?"

"We have an alliance with you, but it must be a Judean by birth that should go on our behalf."

That these words should come from Zimri hurt deeply, for he had thought him an ally. "And where is he?" Caleb swept his hand toward those standing silent.

Zimri frowned. "You are not a young man, Caleb."

"I am forty years old, and I come with forty years of life experience." He turned his back on Zimri and walked the circle, pausing to look into the face of each man he passed. "Do you want to go? Do you? Come on! Step forward if you're willing to face the Anak." No one held his gaze for long. "The man who goes into Canaan will not just be looking at the enemy we must fight, at their city walls and weapons, but at the land itself. Should Judah not have the best? All of you here were brick makers and shepherds. I was a farmer. I made my living off the land. To have good crops, you need good land. I offer myself as your servant. *Send me.*"

Everyone started talking at once again.

"Let God decide," someone called out, and others joined in.

Zimri and the elders commanded order again and called for a lottery. "One man from each family must bring a lot. We will let the Lord decide."

And there was an end to further discussion. Grim and despairing, Caleb had his name etched upon a bone and tossed it into the growing pile. The census had counted 74,600 men twenty years and older in the tribe of Judah. There would be thousands of lots cast before the choice was known. The lots were shaken and cast and the elimination process began. It would take the rest of the night, if not longer.

Ephrathah tried to soothe him, but Caleb went off by himself and sat looking up at the pillar of fire swirling in the night sky. He spread his hands, palms up. He had no words to express his longing. *I am as afraid as*

*any man to go into Canaan and walk among the giants who live there. But I
fear more not being counted among Your people. Do not allow them to set me
aside. Please don't reject me, Lord. Purify my blood. Make me a son of Israel!*

He covered his head. "I know I am not fully Hebrew, Lord. I know Esau's
blood runs in my veins. But even so, Lord . . ." He lifted his head, tears
streaming down his cheeks. "You are my God. You and only You. There is
no other."

He knew there were many who disliked him, who thought he was proud
and ambitious, a thorn in their sides. Some wished he would turn around
and go back to Egypt. They saw him as a growling, groveling dog on the
edge of the camp. And didn't he behave like one, barking constantly for
what he wanted? A place among God's people! He groaned. Who was he
to think himself worthy to represent the tribe of Judah? Surely the Lord
looked down and saw him for the cur he was. He hunched against the rock,
too depressed to go back to camp.

Dawn came and went. It was midday before he returned to his tent.

Zimri was there in the shady entrance of Caleb's tent, sipping a drink
Ephrathah had just replenished.

Caleb sat with him. "I'm sorry I put you in an awkward position, Zimri.
I had no right to demand that I be chosen to represent Judah. I'm not worthy."

The old man opened his hand. Caleb's lot lay on his palm.

He took the lot and turned it over and over in his hand. "You removed
it from the pile."

"I did."

Caleb felt as though he had been kicked in the gut. It was a moment
before he could speak. "I thought being counted in the census at least gave
me the right to take part in the lottery."

"You misunderstand me, Caleb."

"So it would seem." Caleb looked out at the other tents clustered close.
He did not want Zimri to see his deep hurt. Angry words rose, but he held
them back. Rash speaking would cause a permanent rift between them,
and Caleb had few friends among the sons of Judah as it was. "Who won
the lottery?"

"You are the only man I know who would see it as winning."

Caleb gave a bleak laugh. "Who is God sending?"

"Who do you think?" The old man stared at him. After a moment, he
smiled faintly. "It would seem among all the men of Judah, God has chosen
you to represent us."

Caleb felt gooseflesh rise up and down his back and arms. First joy, then
terror, filled him. He released his breath unevenly.

Zimri laughed. "Wonders never cease, my friend. This is the first time
I've seen you speechless." He rose. "Report to Moses and he will give you

further instructions. Whatever you need, Caleb, anything, you have only to ask. The men of Judah will give it."

✦ ✦ ✦

When Caleb saw Joshua among the other spies, he pressed his way through the men gathered. "Ah, my young friend." Caleb grinned. "Let an old man travel with you. Between us, we will have the impetuousness of youth and the cunning of age on our side."

Joshua laughed. "I wondered if Judah would send you."

They clasped hands. "God sent me."

"I would meet your friend, Joshua."

Caleb would know that voice if it had spoken to him in darkness. Heart hammering, he turned and bowed his head low to Moses. He had never been this close to God's chosen prophet. Aaron, dressed in the garments of high priest, stood behind his brother, forgiven and restored by God.

"Do not bow low before me." Moses put his hand upon Caleb. "I am but a man."

Caleb straightened. "A man, yes, but God's anointed prophet who speaks the Word of the Lord. You have pleaded for our lives when we deserved death. And God granted us mercy. May the Lord grant you long life and teach us obedience."

Joshua grasped his shoulder. "This is Caleb of the tribe of Judah."

"Ah, yes. I saw you fight alongside Joshua against the Amalekites."

Stunned that he had been noticed, Caleb received his blessing.

Moses gathered the men. "The Lord told me to send out from the people men to explore the land of Canaan, which He is going to give to us. Go northward through the Negev into the hill country. See what the land is like and find out whether the people living there are strong or weak, few or many. What kind of land do they live in? Is it good or bad? Do their towns have walls or are they unprotected? How is the soil? Is it fertile or poor? Are there many trees? Enter the land boldly, and bring back samples of the crops you see."

After praying for them and blessing them, Moses and Aaron left them alone to make their plans for departure.

The men agreed to meet at dawn and leave together.

Caleb, with ideas of his own, returned to his tent to make preparations.

When he arrived at the agreed meeting site the next morning, the others stared and spoke in derision. "You look like an Egyptian trader."

Caleb grinned. "Good." Dressed in finery, he held the lead rope of three donkeys laden with trade goods donated by the men of Judah, and another with a saddle, but no rider. "This is the best way to get inside the walled cities and take a good look around."

"*Inside* the walls? Are you out of your mind?"

"We can see all we need to see from the outside."

It was too early to argue. "You go your way, and we will go ours." He tossed the reins to Joshua, then tapped the flank of his mount with a stick and set off. Once away from Kadesh and the multitude and camped the first night on their own in the wilderness of Paran, he would be able to speak with these men. Perhaps then they would listen. The others came along behind, mumbling.

Joshua rode alongside him. "What do you have in mind?" He did not look comfortable mounted.

Caleb swung his leg off the donkey. Joshua dismounted and they walked together. "Here is how I see it, Joshua. We need to find out everything we can about Canaanite defenses, and you can't do that by skirting around a city. You have to go inside and see what war machines they have, if any, how strong their walls are, where the weak points exist."

"How does a farmer come to know anything about warfare?"

"I don't know much, my friend, but I have learned to observe everything around me. We listen to the wind and watch the movement of the stars and passing of seasons. I think there may be more than one reason for each command the Lord gives us."

Joshua tilted his head. "Go on."

"We know God fights for us. He destroyed Egypt with the plagues and opened a sea to give us safe passage out of Egypt. We know He has promised to give us Canaan. But we continue to test Him. It seems part of our nature to rebel against the Lord. Who knows what tomorrow may bring, Joshua. But there may be more than one reason why God sends us to view the land and people." Caleb smiled bleakly. "If we fail again, what will God have us do?" Or what would God do to them?

"We won't fail."

"I have faith in God, my friend, but little faith in men."

They camped on the desolate southern edge of the wilderness of Zin. When they reached the dry mountain terrain of the Negev, Caleb thought it wise to split into smaller groups.

"We're safer together."

"Two men can move more quickly than twelve, and six groups will see more of Canaan than one."

"There is that to consider." Joshua's face shone bronze in the firelight. "And another. If we come as one, we will draw attention to ourselves, and the Canaanites may view us as a threat. If we travel in pairs, we can melt in, mingle. Take note of everything you see. Join others traveling and listen. We will meet here and make the journey back together."

Caleb had another idea. "Wherever you go, speak of what happened in

Egypt. Spread the news that the Lord God of Israel overcame the gods of Egypt and delivered the Hebrews from slavery."

The others spoke in protest. "We may be questioned by leaders if we do that."

"The less we talk about what God did to Egypt the safer for us."

Even Joshua looked troubled by Caleb's suggestion. Caleb tried to reason with them. "God called for leaders from among the tribes of Israel. Men of courage! You are all younger than me, but where is the fire of youth? Didn't you hear what Moses said? The Lord has given us the land already. Canaan is already ours. We are being sent merely to see and report to the people the great gift God has given us."

"Do you really think we'll just stroll into Canaan and the inhabitants will flee before us?"

"If they know the God who is with us, yes! With the Lord on our side, who will dare come against us? Let the Canaanites know what has befallen Egypt so that the fear of the Lord will fall upon them. Then they will run from us when Moses leads us into Canaan."

Shaphat of Simeon stood. "A bold plan, Caleb."

Shammua of Reuben shook his head. "A little too bold, in my opinion."

"Should we not be bold? Look to the Lord who . . . ."

"Look things over!" Palti of Benjamin said. "That's what Moses said. That's all he said."

They ignored him.

Nahbi of Naphtali gave a grim laugh. "That's *all* I plan to do."

"What good if we get ourselves killed?" Ammiel of Dan wanted to know.

Joshua looked across the fire at Caleb. Caleb gave him a hard stare. *Why do you say nothing? You, who have stood beside Moses. You, who have seen closer at hand than any of us the power of the Lord.*

The others talked on around them. "No one has to die if we keep out of the cities and stay off the roads."

"Stay low and listen," Caleb said in disgust. "Be like a lizard in the dust."

Shaphat's eyes flashed. "You are not our leader, Caleb. We will each do what is best in our own eyes."

Igal of Issachar, Gaddi of Manasseh, and Asher's Sethur agreed.

"You don't have to say much to plant fear in the minds of men, do you?" Caleb looked around the gathering, jaw clenched.

"We were not sent to be foolhardy. You're going to get yourself and anyone who travels with you killed!"

Caleb glared at Joshua. He looked up to the heavens. "These are the leaders of Israel?" He rose abruptly, unable to stomach any more, and went out into the night. He wanted to shout out his frustration at their timidity, but instead sat alone, thinking about God. He missed the swirling cloud of protection, the Word of God given through Moses. Even now that he had been chosen by God to stand among these men, Caleb felt like an outsider. Had he nothing in common with them? God's chosen! Cowards, every one.

He didn't understand Joshua's reticence. The young man had fought valiantly against the Amalekites. He was no coward. So why did he sit in silence, watching and listening, not an idea in his head?

Am I wrong, Lord? Should we creep along, peering over rocks and from behind trees? Should we tiptoe through the land? Should I go back to the fire and give in to their plans? I can't do that. I can't!

If I sit with them and take their counsel, I will give in to fear. I will cower before the Canaanites as I did the Egyptians. Who then will be master of my life but fear itself? Lord, You alone are to be feared. You are the One who holds our lives in Your hands.

Joshua joined him. "We leave at first light." He looked up, scanning the night sky. "They will go in three groups."

"Three groups and one alone."

"You and I will travel together."

"Did you decide that all by yourself, Joshua?" Caleb gave a cold laugh as he stood and faced him. "Or did the others decide for you? Did you all cast lots around the fire?"

"I needed to hear everyone's plan and then lay them out before the Lord to seek His guidance."

Temper snuffed by Joshua's words, Caleb rubbed the back of his neck. "Forgive me, brother." He gave a self-deprecating laugh. "No wonder God chose you to stand at Moses' side."

"I have much to learn, Caleb, but the Lord has said, 'Do not be afraid.'"

Caleb turned the younger man back toward the light. "Then we will not be afraid! We will cast out our fear of men, and fear only the Lord who holds our lives in His mighty hand."

✦   ✦   ✦

The rugged mountains and wadis of the Negev made travel difficult. Two of the groups decided they would head for the foothills to the west, traveling in the forests below the ridge country. Caleb was relieved they were finally willing to venture out.

Caleb and Joshua moved farther north until they encountered towns of stone built on hilltops. They spent the night outside the walls of Kiriathsepher, paid tariffs so they could trade, and set out wares at the marketplace the next day.

Caleb fought his fears as he watched the Hittite men. They stood a head taller than he and were heavier muscled. Armed and richly dressed from the cone helmets and thick braided hair and trimmed beards to their finely woven, colorfully patterned garments and leather-covered feet, they walked with an air of power and confidence. The women, too, were comely and bold.

"You do not speak as we do." A woman looked him over. "Where are you from?"

He noticed her interest in a gold and lapis bracelet, and picked it up. "Egypt. A ruined country." He held the bracelet out and named his price—grain, olive oil.

Others milled around the jewelry, bargaining. "Will apricots do? Or almonds?" Caleb agreed to a measure of both.

The first woman returned quickly with the necessary staples. Her eyes glowed as she slipped the bracelet on. "I got the better bargain." She laughed. "Grain we have in plenty, and olive oil, but nothing so grand as this." She caressed the gold and lapis. "What did you mean when you said Egypt is ruined?"

"The plagues."

"What plagues?" Another heard the dread word.

"The God of the Hebrews made war against the gods of Pharaoh. The Nile turned to blood. Frogs and flies swarmed over the country. Then locusts came and ate the crops. Fire from heaven burned what remained. Pestilence killed the cattle, sheep, goats, camels. Even as we began starving, an outbreak of boils struck everyone, even the house of Pharaoh, and then the worst came to pass. Have you ever had a boil?"

"No."

"Such pain and misery, you can't imagine. And the scars. Horrible."

"Scars?" The woman's eyes went wide with alarm. "You said that wasn't the worst. What could be worse than beauty destroyed?"

"Tell us." Another came close.

"What did you mean by the worst?"

"How could it be worse than what you have described?"

"The Lord God of Israel struck down every firstborn male from Pharaoh's house to the lowest servant, and even among the animals."

"Do you hear what this man says?" The woman called for others to listen. A crowd of men and women gathered.

"How did you survive?"

"We escaped death by the skin of our teeth." Caleb noted the weapon the man wore. "May I have a look at that sword?"

"Why? You have swords in Egypt."

"I have never seen anything so grand."

Proud, the man drew it, taunting Caleb for a moment before offering a closer look. Caleb took it carefully. "Such an honor." He flattered the owner as he studied the shape of the blade, tested the weight and balance, while the man laughed among his friends.

Caleb handed the sword to Joshua, who studied it as well and handed it back to the Hittite. "Perhaps it is a good time to expand our territories," the man said as he slipped the sword into its scabbard. "We will tell our king of Egypt's weakened state."

Caleb and Joshua took turns walking around the town, and then packed up their remaining wares and moved on.

"They have more gods than Egypt."

"Baser ones." Caleb couldn't hide his disgust. "Here I am, a stranger to their city, and one of their women invites me to please Astarte by lying with her."

"At least it was not Anath calling for your blood. These people bow down to gods who consume children in fires and call for men and women to fornicate upon their altars. Did you notice how little surprised those women were when you told them about the tenth plague and death of the firstborn? Some in Canaan cast their firstborn sons into the fire to appease Molech."

They traveled on to Kiriath-arba, a city inhabited by the sons of Anak, a descendant of giants. The land was good, the city walled and fortified. Altars stood on every corner, the largest in the middle of town. Caleb saw crowds gather to watch a man and woman writhe upon an altar, crying out for Baal to awaken and bring fertility to their land. Lust swept like fire among them. The more Caleb saw of these people, the more he despised them for their debauchery and wickedness. There was no limit to the grotesque worship they performed for their gods—even to burning their own children.

He and Joshua traveled to a Jebusite city on the mountaintops, then on to Ai and Shechem until they reached Rehob in the far north. Turning south once again, they made their way down the mountains and traveled along a great rift and the River Jordan. Jericho loomed before them.

They followed the trade road into the mountains again, meeting the others at the prearranged point near Kiriath-arba. They all agreed that the land was everything God had promised, a land of milk with its flocks and herds, and of honey among the fruit trees and wheat fields and olive groves and vineyards. They had all tasted of it.

When they came through the valley, Caleb and Joshua cut a single cluster of grapes so large they had to carry it on a pole between them. "Go get some of those pomegranates," Joshua called to the others.

"And some figs!" Caleb shouted. He laughed. "The people will never believe the abundance until they see it with their own eyes. Even what we bring back will not tell them of the riches of the land God promised us."

Forty days had passed, and Caleb couldn't wait to get back to Kadesh. As soon as the people heard and saw proof that everything God had said was true, the sooner they would come back. God would help them drive out the evil inhabitants so the twelve tribes could reclaim the land Jacob's and Caleb's ancestors had left four hundred years ago.

Not once did it occur to Caleb that the people might not listen.

+   +   +

"The spies are returning!" People hailed them. "They're here!" Men, women and children ran to them, gathering alongside, walking with them as they entered the camp. They exclaimed at the cluster of grapes. "Have you ever seen anything like that in your life?"

"This is just a small sample of what God is giving us," Caleb boasted in the Lord. "Forests, wheat fields, orchards, flocks of sheep and herds of cattle."

"And the people? What are the people like?"

"Tall," Palti said.

"Fierce. Warriors, all of them," Ammiel reported as he walked in.

Annoyed, Caleb called out loudly, "They are no threat for the Lord our God!"

Moses and Aaron and the seventy elders were waiting for them before the Tabernacle. Joshua and Caleb turned the pole so they approached straight on with the immense cluster of grapes suspended between them. Caleb grinned at their expressions and laughed with joy. Thousands came, pressing in, talking among themselves in excitement, peering at the men and the samples of the fruit of the land.

Moses raised his hands for silence. "Tell us what you learned."

Shaphat spoke quickly, joined by Igal, Palti, and Ammiel. "We arrived in the land you sent us to see, and it is indeed a magnificent country— a land flowing with milk and honey. Here is some of its fruit as proof. But the people living there are powerful, and their cities and towns are fortified and very large. We also saw the descendants of Anak who are living there!"

"Giants!" A ripple of alarm spread out among the gathering.

"The Amalekites live in the Negev."

"And the Hittites, Jebusites, and Amorites live in the hill country."

"The Canaanites live along the coast of the Mediterranean Sea and along the Jordan Valley."

The people grew restless, fear spreading through the crowd. "Giants . . . fortified cities . . . Anak . . ."

Caleb stepped forward and raised his hands. "Quiet. Listen, all of you." He did not shout. He knew he must hold his temper and speak as a father would to frightened children. "We were not sent to find out *if* we could take the land. The Lord has already given the land to us. All we have to do is obey Him. You remember what the Lord did to Egypt. Let's go at once to take the land. We can certainly conquer it!"

The other spies spoke loudly, breaking in on his appeal. "We can't go up against them!"

"They are stronger than we are!"

"Listen to us!"

"What do we know about war?"

"We are only slaves!"

"They are seasoned warriors!"

Caleb shouted over them. "We can take the land! Don't be afraid of those people."

"Don't listen to this man. He's not even a Hebrew!"

Men cried out. "He stands for Judah! Caleb stands for Judah!"

Emboldened, Caleb shouted louder. "It is a beautiful land. Green fields and hills, cities already built and ready for us to take!"

"The land we explored will swallow up any who go to live there!"

"All the people we saw were huge!"

"We even saw giants there, the descendants of Anak!"

"We felt like grasshoppers next to them, and that's what we looked like to them!"

"The land is ours!" Caleb cried out. "The Lord has already given it to us!"

Moses called for order. He looked old and tired as he told the people to return to their tents and allow the elders to talk among themselves. He and Aaron turned away, dejected, and the elders followed. The people cried out their disappointment and wandered away, weeping.

Furious, Caleb grabbed Joshua by the arm. "Why didn't you speak up? Why did you stand silent?"

"There are two million people and ten shouting to be heard. They wouldn't have heard me."

"You know as well as I do the land is ours. God said He would give it to us. Where is your faith, Joshua? Where is the courage I saw in the battle against the Amalekites? Where is that assurance I saw in Canaan? Those others are cowards. We cannot let them sway the people. You hold a high position. People will listen to you! Are you going to speak out or not? Decide, Joshua! Will you lead the congregation or follow?"

"I'm not the leader, Caleb. Moses is."

"For now, yes. And as his assistant, you can speak to him. But will you have the guts to do so? Why do you think God placed you beside Moses? Think, man. When Moses goes to his fathers, who will stand in his place? His half-Midianite sons? Korah, who would like to take us back to Egypt? God is preparing *you* to lead. How is it I can see it and you can't? For God and the sake of the people, *stand and be heard!*" Caleb let go of the younger man and strode through the camp to his tent.

When he ducked and entered his tent, he found his entire family sitting in a circle. He could feel their tension, see their doubt. Only Ephrathah's eyes shone with something other than fear. "Tell them what you saw, my husband. Tell them about the Promised Land."

And so he did, relieved as he saw their fears turn to hope and then excitement. He reminded them of what God had done to Egypt in order to deliver them from slavery. "He is a mighty God. Nothing is too difficult for Him. But we must trust Him. We must be ready so that when He tells us to go into Canaan, *we go!*"

With Ephrathah's encouragement, they kept him talking about the beauty of Canaan most of the night.

But outside his tent, beyond his cloistered family members, out there among the thousands upon thousands, the seed of fear had taken root and was spreading its malevolent tendrils through the camp, stifling anticipation, smothering joy, and bringing a wave of murderous wrath.

✦ ✦ ✦

When Caleb finally stretched out to rest, he slept fitfully. People wailed in the distance. He awakened once to shouts in the darkness. What had the people expected? That the Lord would wipe out everyone *before* they reached the borders of Canaan, so they could enter unoccupied land? He got up before sunrise, washed, and dressed in his best clothing.

Ephrathah heard him moving about the tent and rose. She awakened the others. "Hurry. We must go with your father. Come, Jerioth. We must stand behind our husband."

Caleb pushed aside the curtain. "Stay here." Both women were pregnant, and he didn't want any harm to come to them or the babies they carried. "The people are angry. I don't know what will happen. It's best if you both remain here rather than be caught up in their rebellion."

"What would you have us do?"

"Pray to the Lord our God that the people will listen and obey the Lord."

Thousands were coming from every area of the camp, marching and shouting. Caleb ran ahead and pressed his way through those who had already gathered before the Tabernacle. He shoved his way through the crowd and broke free at the front, running to stand beside Joshua. "We have to stop them from rebelling!"

"What have you done to us, Moses?"

"We wish we had died in Egypt!"

"Or even here in the wilderness!"

"Why is the Lord taking us to this country only to have us die in battle?"

"Our wives and little ones will be carried off as slaves!"

"We should go back!"

Elders from the tribes came to the front, the ten other scouts among them. Red-faced men shouted, "Let's choose a leader and go back to Egypt!"

Crying out in fear, Moses and Aaron dropped to the ground before the people. Caleb understood, for he felt the change in the air around him. It was not just fear of the people that made them prostrate themselves. Were the people so foolish they didn't know the Lord heard them crying to go back to the land from which He had delivered them? to go back to slavery? to go back to false gods and idols?

Caleb let out a cry and ripped his garment. While Moses and Aaron covered their heads in fear of what the Lord would do, Caleb dove into the fracas, shouting with all his strength, "Listen, you people! Listen! The land we explored is wonderful land!"

Joshua shouted with him. "If the Lord is pleased with us, He will bring us safely into that land and give it to us!"

Caleb strode toward the elders and scouts, pointing at them. "Do not rebel against the Lord, and don't be afraid of the people of the land."

"They are only helpless prey to us!" Joshua shouted. "They have no protection, but the Lord is with us!"

"*The Lord is with us!*"

"Don't be afraid of them!"

Korah stepped forward. "Don't listen to this *Caleb!* He and Moses' lackey would lead you into a land filled with enemies who have the power to slay your little ones."

"Do you want to be slaughtered?"

"No!"

"*Stone them!*"

Caleb saw the hatred in the people's faces, the fury growing past reason as they scraped around on the ground for rocks and pebbles.

Is this where my faith has led me, Lord? To death? Then let it be.

Screams rent the air and people scattered, for the cloud moved, changing color as it rose, spread, compressed, descended, and stood between the people and Caleb and Joshua. Caleb threw himself to the ground, covering his head in terror. Joshua lay beside him, crying out to God not to kill everyone.

Moses cried out, too. "*Oh, Lord, no!*" Moses was on his feet, hands raised, pleading frantically. "What will the Egyptians think when they hear about it?"

About what? Caleb's heart pounded. He felt the presence of the Lord, the rising wrath, the chill of death close at hand. He shook violently and clutched the earth.

"The Egyptians know full well the power You displayed in rescuing these people from Egypt!" Moses cried out to the Lord. "They will tell this to the inhabitants of this land, who are well aware that You are with this people. They know, Lord, that You have appeared in full view of Your people in the pillar of cloud that hovers over them. They know that You go before them in the pillar of cloud by day and the pillar of fire by night."

Never had Caleb heard Moses speak so fast. He felt judgment at hand. *Oh, Lord, have mercy upon us. Speak faster, Moses. Plead for us. God hears your voice. Without you, the Lord will kill us. My children! My wives!*

"Now if You slaughter all these people . . ."

People screamed and scattered.

" . . . if You slaughter all these people, the nations that have heard of Your fame will say, 'The Lord was not able to bring them into the land He swore to give them, so He killed them in the wilderness.' "

Wailing rose. Thousands of voices cried out in terror, "Save us, Moses!"

Caleb wanted to rise up and scream to the people, "Cry to the Lord, for it is He who saves!" Were they still so foolish they could not hear Moses' pleading? "Cry out to the Lord for forgiveness."

"*Please*, Lord, prove that Your power is as great as You have claimed it to be." Moses held his hands high. "For You said, 'The Lord is slow to anger and rich in unfailing love, forgiving every kind of sin and rebellion. Even so He does not leave sin unpunished, but He punishes the children for the sins of their parents to the third and fourth generations.' Please pardon the sins of this people because of Your magnificent, unfailing love, just as You have forgiven them ever since they left Egypt."

Moses went down on his face before the Lord, and there was silence, such a silence that Caleb's ears rang with it. And then he thought he heard a still, quiet Voice whisper his name like a breath of warm, life-giving air. He strained mentally toward that Voice, listening intently, yearning to hear it again, so soft and loving but with the power of Almighty God behind it. But it was not for him to hear more. Not yet. Not now.

Stretching out his arms on the ground, his face in the dust, Caleb prayed. *Lord, Lord, if You slay me now because I failed to convince these people of what I saw, I will die happy because it is by Your hand my life ends.*

The glorious presence of the Lord lifted. Moses sobbed in relief.

Caleb raised his head as the old man rose slowly to his feet, trembling, tears running into his white beard. But when Moses looked out at the people, his eyes blazed. Caleb felt fear then, a fear that welled up inside him and made his stomach quiver, sweat bead, his mouth go dry.

"Listen, all of you, and hear the Word of the Lord!" The power of the Lord was behind Moses' voice and it carried like a storm.

Caleb moved quickly so that he was standing beside Joshua again. The other ten scouts did not join them, but remained among the elders of their tribes. There might as well have been a chasm between them. On one side stood six hundred thousand men who had chosen to fear the enemy rather than follow their trusted Friend. They had chosen to speak against the One who had saved them and provided for them every day since they had been rescued from slavery. On the other side stood Caleb and Joshua, two strong voices of reason not heeded.

The people came closer, but rebellion still shone in their eyes. The elders of each tribe came to the front with their scout. Caleb looked out at them and wondered how they could think the threat was past, that the Lord would do whatever Moses asked.

We deserve nothing, Lord. After all You have done for us, and this is what the people decide.

"Hear the Word of the Lord!" Moses' voice went forth like fire. " 'I will pardon them as you have requested. But as surely as I live, and as surely as the earth is filled with the Lord's glory, not one of these people will ever enter that land.' "

The Promised Land was lost to them. While many cried out in relief, Caleb cried out in grief and fell upon his face again. He drew his knees up under his body and threw dust on his head. Imagining the ten scouts, he pounded the earth with his fists and wept bitterly.

Moses' voice rose, hot with anger, weighed with grief.

" 'They have seen My glorious presence and the miraculous signs I performed both in Egypt and in the wilderness, but again and again they tested Me by refusing to listen. They will never even see the land I swore to give their ancestors. None of those who have treated Me with contempt will enter it.' "

Moses paused and then spoke tenderly. " 'But my servant Caleb . . .' "

My servant Caleb . . . The Voice again, so tenderly calling him. **Caleb, My servant . . .**

Caleb raised his face to the heavens. Moses spoke, but it was the Lord's voice Caleb heard. **Caleb is different from the others. He has remained loyal to Me, and I will bring him into the land he explored. His descendants will receive their full share of that land.**

Caleb bowed his face to the ground. *Unworthy, Lord, I am an unworthy dog. What of Joshua?*

" 'Now, *turn around,*' " Moses said in the power of the Spirit, " 'and don't go on toward the land where the Amalekites and Canaanites live. Tomorrow you must set out for the wilderness in the direction of the Red Sea.' "

The people wailed, but some stood their ground.

"No. We want our land."

Caleb covered his head. It was never *their* land. It had always been the Lord's land. And it was the Lord who would have placed them there as He had placed Adam and Eve in the Garden of Eden. *Why do men always refuse to listen and act upon what the Lord says? Lord, give me the heart to hear and the courage to obey.*

"Thus says the Lord, 'How long will this wicked nation complain about Me? I have heard everything the Israelites have been saying. You will all die here in this wilderness! Because you complained against Me, none of you who are twenty years old or older and were counted in the census will enter the land I swore to give you. The only exceptions will be Caleb and Joshua.

"'You said your children would be taken captive. Well, I will bring *them* safely into the land, and they will enjoy what you have despised. But as for you, your dead bodies will fall in this wilderness. And your children will be like shepherds, wandering in the wilderness forty years. In this way, they will pay for your faithlessness, until the last of you lies dead in the wilderness.'"

The people drew back from Moses as he came forward, hands spread, his voice carrying over the throng. "'Because the men who explored the land were there for forty days, you must wander in the wilderness for forty years—a year for each day, suffering the consequences of your sins. You will discover what it is like to have Me for an enemy.'"

Gagging violently, Palti fell to the ground in convulsions. People screamed and withdrew as Palti bit off his own tongue. People ran from Shaphat, who dropped where he stood among the elders. Igal and Gaddiel pitched over. Ammiel ran, Gaddi on his heels, but both fell as though struck by invisible arrows. Sethur and Nahbi, Geuel and Shammua died as Palti did.

Of the twelve who had explored the land, only Caleb and Joshua stood untouched by God's judgment, for they hadn't spread lies about the land and its people.

Caleb shook as the Lord took swift vengeance. The people scattered, but still God's hand of judgment was upon them, and many others died that night.

In the morning, hundreds went out with their weapons to take Canaan. "Let's go," they said. "We realize that we have sinned, but now we are ready to enter the land the Lord has promised us."

"What are you doing?" Moses ran after them, Joshua with him. "God has told us to turn back to the Red Sea!"

"We're not going back to the Sinai. The Lord said He would give us the land, and we're going to take it."

But Moses said, "Why are you now disobeying the Lord's orders to return to the wilderness? It won't work. Do not go into the land now. You will only be crushed by your enemies because the Lord is not with you. When you face the Amalekites and Canaanites in battle, you will be slaughtered. The Lord will abandon you because you have abandoned the Lord!"

"Who are you to tell us to stay here? We're sick of you telling us what not to do and what to do. We *will* take the land. God *will* help us."

Caleb stood at the edge of camp, watching several of his friends head north for Canaan. They had fretted and argued all night, and finally convinced themselves they could do it. They thought there was power in their dream, power to reach out and grab what they wanted for themselves.

He had heard his brother say, "If we just believe we can do it, it will happen."

They assumed God would give in to *their* desire and bless *their* endeavors. Faith in God would have given them everything they ever hoped to have, but faith in themselves would bring them death.

Caleb shouted after them, "When will you learn to obey the Lord?"

One of his brothers shouted back, "Come with us, Caleb. When will you learn it is not the Lord who speaks, but Moses! And who is he to tell us what to do?"

Helpless, angry, Caleb stood his ground. "Fools! All of you!" His eyes hot, Caleb dropped to his knees and hung his head. Someone gripped his shoulder.

Joshua watched the rebels. "When they are dead, the others will heed the Word of the Lord."

Caleb gave a laugh of despair. "Do you really think so? Like begets like. Their children will be just like them."

"Your voice is filled with hatred."

"I hate those who hate Moses. To hate God's prophet is to hate God Himself. I hate them with a passion almost as great as my love for God!"

"Brother . . ."

"It sears my heart," Caleb cried out in wrath. "We were so close. So close! And their faithlessness has stripped us bare. Now, you and I must wait forty years to enter into the land God gave us. Forty years, Joshua! My sons and little ones will suffer in the desert because of them. Our wives will die without ever seeing what you and I saw." He grasped Joshua's garment. "And I see it in your eyes, too, my friend."

"It chews at my soul. What must we do about it?"

Caleb gripped the robe over Joshua's heart. "Go back." He shut his eyes and spoke quietly, in despair. "Go back to the last place where we rejoiced over God our Savior. Go back to the Red Sea and begin again."

And God preserve us, may we continue in faith this time.

THREE

The congregation hadn't even traveled toward the Red Sea for a day when another rebellion broke out, this time led by Korah, a Levite who blamed Moses for the deaths of those who had gone into the Promised Land. He scorned Aaron as high priest and roused others to think likewise. Two hundred and fifty Levites stood with Korah, determined to preside over worship. Moses told them to stand at the entrances of their tents with censors of burning incense the next morning and the Lord would decide.

Struck by fire from the Holy of Holies, Korah and his rebels died horribly. The earth opened with a roar and swallowed them, along with their households. Tumbling down into the yawning jaws of Sheol, they screamed, as the jagged edges of the precipice closed over them like the teeth of a lion.

And still, it was not enough to put an end to the stubbornness of hearts baked and hardened to stone beneath the sun of Egypt's profane and profligate gods.

"Stay away from the people." Caleb kept his wives and children inside the tent. "Stay out of it." He could feel the heat of rebellion building all around him, even in the tribe of Judah as people wailed and cried out through the night.

"I can't bear it!" Ephrathah covered her ears.

The people rose up again, and accused Moses of killing God's people. The glory of the Lord appeared and struck the camp with plague. Men and women blaspheming God and His prophet dropped dead where they stood. Ten, a hundred, a thousand, thousands upon thousands. The rebels could not run and hide, for God knew them and sought them out for destruction. Moses cried out for mercy and sent Aaron running to burn incense to atone for the people. Aaron ran to do what was asked of him, and stood between the living and the dead.

Finally, the people were silent, too afraid to open their mouths lest another plague fall upon them. Too late, they remembered what the Lord had done in Egypt. If not for Moses and Aaron, they would all be dead.

Caleb came out of hiding to help carry Judah's dead from the camp. But he knew it wasn't over. "I can see it in their eyes."

Ephrathah put her arm around him in the darkness of their tent. "What do you see, my love?" She pressed into the shelter of his arm.

"Wrath. But it isn't for those who rebelled against the Lord, but against God Himself for holding true to His word." It was as though the muddy waters of the Nile still ran in their veins, his included, for Caleb knew sin dwelt in him. He loved these men who had become his brothers. He loved them, and yet, he hated them, too. When he heard a man grumbling close by, he could have so easily raised his hand against him and struck him down. Resentment rose, bringing with it a lust for vengeance.

My heart is a storm within me, Lord. You are my God! Let nothing stand between You and me. Sin crouches at the entrance of my heart waiting to devour me. And I must fight against it. Oh, God, how I must fight against the fire in my blood! Their faithlessness kept me and my sons from Canaan. Help me not to hate these people. Help me to stand firm beneath the cooling spring of Your living water so that I may obey Your every command whether I understand or not.

But the grumbling persisted, low, an undercurrent that still pulled at the souls of some, sucking the hope from God's promises.

Bowing his head, Caleb gripped the hoe he used to dig graves until his fingers hurt.

Help me, Lord. Oh, God, help me not to give in to my wrath.

✦   ✦   ✦

The multitude followed the Lord and Moses back to the Red Sea, and then the wandering began. No one knew how long they would remain in one place. Caleb kept his eyes on the cloud, for when it rose, so too did he and his family members. "Rise up. The Lord is on the move. *Rise up!*"

Jerioth bore another son. Caleb named him for the place where God allowed them to camp. When Ephrathah bore a son, Caleb lifted him high before the cloud of the Lord. "His name will be Hur."

Hezron stood bent over his staff. "Another name not of our family." The years were heavy upon him, and the grief of sons lost spawned bitterness and hatred.

Caleb did not weaken. "Hur and Aaron held Moses' arms up while Joshua went out against Amalek. So shall my son support those who are chosen of God to lead the people." He held the babe against his heart. "My sons shall choose honor over shame."

"May they grow strong in faith like you, but have Moses' compassion." The old man walked away.

Caleb kept his sons close, even in the midst of Judah, not wanting them to mingle among those who still looked back toward Egypt and sighed.

Zimri sought him out. "We need you in the council of elders."

"To what purpose?" They had never listened to him before.

"Your enemies have died, my friend, many in the plague."

Caleb lifted his head. "And should I mourn them?"

"You heard their screams just as I did. I lost sons that day. Have you no pity for me or those the Lord killed?"

"It was their own faithlessness that brought them down."

"Dreams too long delayed in coming."

Even Zimri was blind. "It was not a dream! The land was there as God promised, ripe as the grapes and pomegranates Joshua and I brought back to you. And your fear hardened your heart against the Lord."

"My sons, my sons. Only Carmi and his son are left."

Caleb saw the appeal in the old man's eyes, but would not give in to it. "Faithless still, Zimri. You make excuses for blasphemers. You have heard the Law. Love the Lord your God with all your heart and all your soul and with all your might. You and the others still hold fast to flesh and blood."

"You resent us so much?"

"I resent the years of waste."

Zimri looked at the young men playing games. His mouth drew tight. "You will go in to that which we have been denied."

"Yes. When I'm *eighty*. When my infant sons are as old as I am now. Mesha and Mareshah will be older still!"

Zimri hung his head.

Caleb turned away, but Zimri grasped his arm. "We *need* you." He looked up, his eyes moist. "My grandsons need you."

So Caleb went to the council of elders. "You want to hear what I have to say? So be it. Stop talking among yourselves and *listen* to the Lord God who brought you out of Egypt. It is too late to look back on what could have been. We must look forward to the promise God has given us. Yes. You will all die! But your sons will go into Canaan—if they learn to obey the Lord. When you come together, judge cases wisely according to the Law. When you gather, speak of the miracles you saw in Egypt. Speak of the opening of the Red Sea; speak of the water that came forth from the rock. Give thanks over the manna you receive from God's hand each morning. Give thanks for the pillar of fire that protects us by night. Confess to your sons and daughters that it is by our own sins that we wander in this desert. It is because we did not trust in the Lord that they must live as nomads! Let them see us humble ourselves before the Lord so that they will learn *He is the Lord our God!* We failed to obey. We must teach our sons to succeed."

Silent, the men looked to Zimri and he spoke for them all. "We agree, Caleb. Only promise you will lead them."

Caleb looked around the circle. Still, after everything, they failed to understand. "No. I will not. For the Lord our God will lead them!"

+ + +

The men sent their sons to Caleb, who pressed them hard. He walked down their ranks.

"We no longer have fields to plow and plant, nor crops to harvest, for the Lord has given us all we need. You do not have to toil in the sun making bricks as your fathers did before you. But you will not spend your days in idleness! The Lord is a warrior, the Lord is His Name!"

"The Lord is a warrior, the Lord is His Name!" his sons called out. The others joined in.

"Again. And mean it!"

They shouted.

"We will all learn to be warriors as well." He set courses for them to run to make their bodies strong and fast. He planned games to test their agility and strength. He drilled them and drilled them. The older men watched and died as their sons trained.

Caleb's sons and the others with them were sprouting up like ripe stalks of wheat. But Caleb wanted them strong and unwavering. "You will not bend with every wind that blows down upon us. There were cedars in Canaan, towers of strength. So shall we be. We will stand firm in the power of the Lord our God!"

Whenever the Lord settled the people in a place with wood, Caleb sent out his sons to gather it and build up the fires. The clang of metal against metal and hiss of steam was heard around his camp as he beat his plow-shares into swords and his pruning hooks into spears. Through trial and error, the young men learned to wield the weapons and hit the mark with bow and arrow. The shepherds among them taught others how to use the sling and stones.

"Keep your eyes on the Lord," Caleb taught them. "Be ready to set out the moment the cloud lifts from the Tabernacle." He taught the boys and young men to run at the first blast of the shofar, rewarding those who were first to have their camps ready for the journey to the next site.

"Rise up! *Rise up, O Israel!* The Lord is on the move!" And so they all learned to do, not reluctantly but swiftly, pulling down tents, rolling, packing, setting out to wherever God led them.

One of Caleb's sons was always on watch. For he wanted Judah close on Moses' and Aaron's heels, within sight of Joshua who would one day lead.

+ + +

Caleb and Joshua often worshiped together and then went to a high place that gave them an overview of the camp. Thousands of tents spread out over the desert plain beneath a canopy of cloud. Smoke rose from cook fires. Children ran between the tents; old men gathered at entrances while women served. Where Judah camped, young men sparred and raced against one another. In the distance, shepherds moved flocks of sheep and herds of cattle closer for the night.

The air began to change. Caleb held his breath and watched the transformation of cooling cloud to swirling pillar of flame. It never ceased to amaze him. "Shadowed by day, warmed by night. Our Lord is ever merciful."

Joshua made a sound of agreement. "You are training Judah's sons to become fierce warriors."

Caleb could detect neither approval nor reprimand in Joshua's statement. "All the sons of Jacob should train to be warriors."

"I've been praying on the matter."

"And what does the Lord say?"

"He speaks to Moses, not to me." Caleb felt Joshua's restlessness and knew he had more to say. After a long moment, Joshua glanced at him. "Nothing has been said one way or the other, which gives me great cause to wonder."

"About what?"

"Whether it is right to train for battle."

"When the Lord sends us into Canaan, Joshua, we must know how to fight. Do you think it a sin to train soldiers?"

"The Lord said the land is ours."

"Yes. The victory is already decided, but our work has yet to be done. Do you think the Lord would have us recline on mats and sleep for the next forty years?"

"Our work is to believe, Caleb."

"Yes, Joshua, but faith is proven by action. The ten scouts who went with us into Canaan believed in God, but they refused to act upon their faith by leading their brothers into Canaan." He sneered. "Perhaps they would have had the courage had God crushed the walls of the fortified cities and obliterated the people *before* extending the invitation to us to occupy the land."

"You have no compassion for them."

Caleb clenched his teeth.

"They suffered for their lack of faith, Caleb."

"Their lack of faith could grow within our ranks. Inactivity breeds rebellion. We must do something. What better than to prepare for the battle ahead?"

"You speak as though we are soldiers or charioteers. We are slaves."

"We *were* slaves. Now we are free men with God's promise of a future and a hope. The children born to us in the wilderness will never have known the yoke of Egypt. They will be born beneath the canopy of God. They will walk in His presence every day of their lives. Perhaps it is for us who spent most of our lives bowing down to others to learn to be like our children. If I am bound to anyone as slave, it is to the Lord our God. You must not weaken, Joshua. You must not allow yourself to look back, but up." He pointed to the pillar of fire. "And out to what is before us." He pointed north to Canaan.

"It is the wandering that wears upon me."

"As it wears upon us all. But it is a training ground, too." Caleb looked toward the horizon. Would God rise up tomorrow and lead them somewhere else? Only the Lord could lead them through this wasteland and bring them to water. "We may believe we wander aimlessly, my friend, but I am convinced God has a plan. I must believe or I would despair. We were judged and now we live with the consequences of our sins, but surely this isn't all about punishment. Every day we keep our eyes upon Him, we are learning to move when He moves."

"It is punishment."

"Yes. Yes." Caleb grew impatient. "But it is also opportunity." He had thought much about it over the past weeks. "Perhaps God always has more than one purpose. He judged us righteously, but He shows us mercy. He gives us the Law on which to fix our minds and hearts, a Law that sets me at war within myself. And God told us to sacrifice every morning and evening. The smell is a constant reminder. He knows us so well. He gives us food and water to sustain us. He directs our every step. When the Lord rises up, we strike our tents and follow. When He returns to the Tabernacle, we camp and wait. In Egypt, our taskmasters did our thinking for us and we responded like beasts of burden. Now, we must think as men. We are not animals that graze at whatever pasture is available to us. We are faced with choices. Do we grumble among ourselves, or walk the path God has given us?"

Caleb pointed northeast. "That land is ours. Right now, it is filled with people who bow down to false gods and practice all manner of evil. Every man, woman, and child is corrupt and rotten with sin. You saw how they worshiped their gods, casting babies into fire and fornicating on altars in the middle of town and under every spreading oak. They practice worse abominations than Egypt all puffed up and spread out like a cobra. The Lord sent us into the land as scouts to see what we would be up against. We saw. We know. Now, we must prepare to do battle."

Joshua said nothing. Silence had never sat well upon Caleb. He had no reason to doubt Joshua's courage, but he wished he knew what was going on in his mind. "We have fought battles before, Joshua. The Lord didn't tell us to sit by and watch while He destroyed the Amalekites. He sent us into battle against them."

"Moses prayed."

"And God answered by giving us victory."

"Sometimes we are called to do nothing more than pray, Caleb."

"Yes. But is it wise to assume the Lord will destroy Canaan with plagues first and then send us into the land? Or wiser to train and prepare for whatever God asks of us?" Even if the Lord told them to stand and watch, the work would not be wasted if they were prepared to do whatever God asked of them.

"You have already made up your mind about what we should do."

Caleb looked down at the camps spread upon the plain. Where the tents of Judah were positioned, youths fought mock battles. After each rally, they backed off and began again. "Are you trying to change it?"

"Where is prayer in all this strife?"

"Strife?" Caleb's jaw tightened. "There is less strife among the Judean boys who train than I've witnessed among the other tribes who do little more than gather manna every morning, then sit on their haunches and talk the rest of the day. Aimless talk leads to whining and complaining and rebellion. And as to prayer, it comes first. No one lifts a hand or a weapon until after morning sacrifices and the reading of the Law."

Joshua's mouth curved wryly. "But you are partial."

His temper bubbled. "Partial?"

"You show particular attention to certain men."

Why was Joshua pressing him so? Why didn't he just speak what was on his mind? "What are you getting at, Joshua?"

"You train the sons of Judah."

"Of course."

"You have other allegiances."

Caleb felt the heat surge into his face. Did he mean Edom? Caleb stared hard at Joshua through narrowed eyes. "My only allegiance is to the Lord who told me I will go into the land. When that day comes, I want my sons beside me, ready to destroy *anyone* or *anything* that stands in the way of our inheritance."

Joshua put his hand on Caleb's shoulder. "But you are *Hebrew*, my friend. A son of Abraham, and all these others are our brothers."

"Why bait me? Speak your mind."

"What has been in your mind has been on mine as well. We must train for battle. What troubles me is the way we're going about it. Scattered groups, scattered efforts. One day we may be at one another's throats rather than set against the enemies of God."

The vision caught Caleb's heart. He gripped Joshua's arm. "Then unite us!"

"It is not my place to do that."

"Then speak to Moses. The Lord brought twelve tribes together and brought them out of Egypt. Surely He wants us to be one flock and not twelve.

Moses can also train us. He grew up in the Egyptian court among the princes. Much of his education must have centered on tactics and weaponry. And you are closer to him than his own sons, close enough to pose the question."

"You would have me be presumptuous?"

"If you do not ask, you will not receive an answer."

"And what if he says no?"

Caleb did not want to speak rashly. He looked out over the thousands of tents. He could see the banners of each tribe, the space between, boundaries. "Look at us. You are correct. We are scattered in our thinking. God is trying to bring us together through the Law—one mind, one heart, one promise that gives us hope. We cannot be twelve tribes encamped around the Tabernacle. We must become one nation under God! And every nation has an army. Let us build an army for the Lord." He looked into Joshua's solemn face. Joshua had aged greatly during the last months. Love for the people weighed heavily upon the younger man's heart.

"Speak to Moses, Joshua. Tell him what is on your mind and heart. I'm surprised you haven't already done so."

"He is troubled in spirit and prays unceasingly for the people."

"Who are vain and bored and need something to occupy them. *Ask!* You know what Moses will do."

"He will go to the Lord."

Caleb laughed joyously. "Yes!" He slapped Joshua hard on the back. "And then we will know if the fire in our blood was placed there by our own pride or by God's Spirit."

+   +   +

The years passed slowly as the Israelites moved from place to place in the wilderness. The slave generation died one by one as the children grew taller and more robust. Families were left without patriarchs and matriarchs, then without aunts and uncles.

Caleb faced constant sorrow as he watched friends and family members die. Zimri was the first, followed soon after by Hezron. Some died embittered and unrepentant. Others grieved over their lack of faith and its cost to their children. Zimri's son Carmi sat on the council now with Caleb. They became good, if not close, friends.

When Caleb walked among the tents, those of his generation watched him pass. Some stared with resentment, others with burning envy, precious few with a respectful nod of greeting. The camp was in constant mourning, over loved ones dying as well as over the sin that kept them from the Promised Land.

Boys clamored around Caleb wherever he went, eager to join in the training. He tested their knowledge of the Law first. "It is not enough to want to fight. All men have it in them to fight! You must know the One who leads you into battle."

"Moses!"

"And Joshua!"

Caleb knew what both men would say to that. "Go back to your tent. You're not ready." They came to him with the fire to fight, but without faith and knowledge. The Lord was their commander. They must prepare their hearts and minds to follow His will. Not a man's. Not even his.

The seventy elders died and were replaced by younger men who lived with the cost of their fathers' sins. They listened to Moses' counsel and acted upon it, choosing wise men who loved the Lord to judge the people. One by one, the men who grew up in the fear of Pharaoh died off and were replaced by men who grew up in the fear of the Lord.

The camps moved with the precision of an army. When the cloud rose, so too did the people, often even before the shofar blasted. The people were learning day by day, week by week, month by month, year by year to keep watch and follow the Lord.

The old moaned and mourned, grumbled and groaned, and died.

The young praised and practiced, rejoiced in and reverenced God, and lived.

✦ ✦ ✦

During the thirty-eighth year of wandering, Caleb was called to the tent of Kenaz. His brother lay dying. Caleb sat beside him, grieving this loss more than any other.

Kenaz smiled weakly. "I thought, perhaps, the Lord had forgotten about me, and I might sneak into the Promised Land among my sons and grandsons. . . ."

Caleb couldn't speak. He gripped Kenaz's hand between his own.

"I have watched you, my brother." Kenaz's voice was barely a whisper. "You sit at the entrance of your tent and fix your eyes upon the pillar of fire. And God's fire is reflected in your eyes, my brother."

Caleb bowed his head, tears flowing.

"We should've listened . . ." Kenaz sighed. His hand went slack between Caleb's.

Two days later, Jerioth died, and a month later Caleb awakened to find Ephrathah dead beside him. A cry rose from his throat as he tore his clothing and went out to throw dust in the air. He didn't speak a word to anyone for a month.

Never had Caleb felt such a weight of grief upon him, and rebellion rose up with it, unbidden and unexpected. He ran to the Tabernacle and prostrated himself before the Lord. *Kill the evil within me, Lord. Kill it before it takes root and grows.* He did not leave the Tabernacle for three days. Still grieving, he rose with a peace beyond understanding. *The Lord, the Lord is my strength. He is my high place, my comfort.*

The next morning, the cloud moved and Caleb had his tents struck, packed, and set out to follow. When the Lord stopped, the Tabernacle was set up and the tribes took positions around it, this time at an oasis with date palms. As Caleb returned to the courtyard of the Tabernacle, he rested in the Lord's presence rather than warring within himself. Better was one day in the court of the Lord than a thousand elsewhere.

He mourned for Ephrathah, but went back out to train the young men for battle. A new generation had come to manhood, with sons coming up behind them. Caleb felt renewed strength flood through his body, as though the Lord had given him back the time and strength the wilderness had taken from him.

The forty years were almost over. Their wandering was almost at an end.

+ + +

The Lord led the Israelites to Kadesh a second time. Caleb gathered his sons and their sons around him. "This is where the people waited while Joshua and I went into Canaan. This is where the people rebelled against the Lord." He made fists. "Listen this time. Listen and obey."

He awakened each morning, prepared to go on, to move closer, to have that which God had promised him. Land of his own, a place to plant crops, a place where he could rest beneath his own olive tree and sip the fruit of his vines.

But the waiting wasn't over.

Moses' sister, Miriam, died. Shocked, the entire camp mourned her death as they would a mother. Something broke within the ranks and a mob cried out against Moses, for once again there was no water.

"The Lord will provide!" Caleb shouted, but no one listened. He went into his tent, and sat, head in hands.

If I stay out there, Lord, I will kill someone. I will draw my sword and not stop until You strike me down! Will we never change? Are we destined to rebel against the Lord God Almighty all our lives. Israel! The name itself means to wrestle with You. Is that why You called them that? This generation is the same as the last. Rebellion against God is in the blood!

Cries of jubilation came. He arose and went out to find water pouring from a rock. The people shouted and sang and splashed the water over themselves. The waters were called Meribah because this place was yet another where the Israelites had quarreled with the Lord. But after that day, Moses looked old and sick, and spoke hardly at all.

Moses sent messengers to Edom requesting passage through their land,

and Edom answered with the threat of war. Caleb was filled with shame. Were the Edomites not brothers? They—like Caleb—were descended from Esau. Caleb despised the blood that ran in his veins.

Once again, Moses sent messengers with assurances that the people would stay to the King's Highway and not tread upon any field or go through any vineyard or even drink water from any well, but merely pass through to the land God had given them. Not only did the Edomites refuse, they came out with an army ready for battle.

"Tell Moses we are ready to fight!" Caleb told Joshua. "Send us out to deal with these people. Let none stand in the way of the Lord God of Israel!"

"They are brothers, Caleb."

"They reject us. Let us annihilate them! They are betrayers and blasphemers."

"They are descendants of Abraham as we are."

"They are a wall between us and God's promises!"

"Caleb—"

"Do not excuse them, Joshua. Men must choose. And they have chosen death!"

"You are my brother and friend, Caleb. Remember the Law. Vengeance is the Lord's."

The words pierced Caleb and cooled his anger. But his temper and impatience rose again when Moses prayed and then turned away from Edom and set out to return to Kadesh.

"Kadesh!" Caleb ground his teeth. "Will our faith take us no farther than Kadesh?" When the people rested, he went to the Tabernacle and spent the night on his face in the dust. *Why, Lord? Why must we show mercy?*

They moved on to Mount Hor and made camp. Moses, Aaron, and Aaron's son Eleazar went up the mountain. Caleb's impatience was eating him alive. He practiced with his sword. He paced. He pondered. *Lord, Lord! When? The slaves are all dead! Your judgment has been fulfilled!*

Only Moses and Eleazar came down.

When word spread that Aaron was dead, shock spread through the camp and the people went into mourning. No one had expected God to take Aaron. Thirty days passed before the cloud rose and the people followed Him along the road to Atharim.

Shouts and screams came from the distance. Armed and ready to fight, Caleb shouted for his sons. But it was already too late. Canaanites living in the Negev, led by the king of Arad, had attacked and taken captives. The people mourned and raged. It had happened so quickly, no one had expected it.

Caleb's wrath boiled over. "Give us leave to destroy them."

"It is not my decision," Joshua said.

"Will you never stand and cry out to the Lord as Moses does?" Caleb strode into the courtyard of the Tabernacle. "*Lord!*" People stopped moving and stared. "Lord, send us." No one spoke or even dared breathe. "Deliver these people into our hands and we will destroy their cities!"

Moses rose from his knees and came toward him, face haggard. Caleb stood his ground. "Forty years we've wandered because we did not have the faith to go into the land. Will we lack faith again? The Lord said the land is ours. Don't tell me the Lord wants us to be attacked and made slaves again. I won't believe it!"

Moses' eyes caught fire. "The Lord has heard our plea and given the Canaanites over to us. 'Go!' saith the Lord. 'Go and destroy them and their towns. Leave nothing standing and no one breathing! Go in the name of the Lord.'"

And Caleb and Joshua did.

The place came to be known as Hormah: "Destruction."

+   +   +

When Moses led the community back toward the Red Sea in order to take the route around Edom, Caleb had to turn his mind to daily training rather than give in to his growing tension and impatience to reach Canaan. When he heard grumbling, which came more often since the victory over the king of Arad, he reminded the people of what Moses had said: "The Edomites are sons of Esau, and therefore our brothers."

"Brothers who treat us like enemies!" Jesher was as eager to fight as his older half brothers Mesha and Mareshah.

"It matters not how they treat us." Caleb reined his sons in like young stallions. "We must do what is right."

"Anyone who stands in our way stands in the way of the Lord!"

Caleb felt a prickling of apprehension. He grasped Mesha by the shoulder. "Who are you to presume you know the will of God?" He dug his fingers in until his son winced. "It is Moses who speaks God's Word, and it is Moses who says we must go around Edom." He let go of his son and looked around the tent at the five others. "You would all do well to remember that, whether we like it or not, Esau's blood runs in our veins."

They couldn't quibble about Edom, so they focused their anger and impatience elsewhere.

"We never have enough water!"

"I'm sick to death of this manna."

"When will we have something else to eat?"

Beneath the surface of their complaints was a lusting for vengeance upon Edom and what they believed was a needless delay to the gratification of entering the Promised Land. The people coiled in small groups of malcontents, hissed and struck at Moses, forgetting how he had loved and prayed for them every day, all day, for forty years.

+ + +

Reaching for some firewood, Caleb felt a sharp sting. Sucking in his breath, he drew back his hand. A snake hung from his arm, fangs sunk deep into the tendons of Caleb's wrist. Pain licked through his veins. Some women screamed.

"Get back!" he cried out as he shook his arm. Rather than shaking free, the serpent's tail curled around his arm and tightened.

Caleb grasped the head and yanked the snake free, tossing it away from him. It coiled for another strike. Caleb's grandson Hebron drew his dagger and sliced off the snake's head. As its body writhed in the dust, Caleb crushed the head with his heel. Then, losing strength, he went to his knees.

The poison worked quickly. Caleb felt his heart pounding faster and faster. Sweat broke out and a wave of nausea gripped him. Someone held him gently and laid him down. "No," he rasped. "Get me up . . ."

"Father!" Mesha grasped him. Jesher and Mareshah came running, Shobab just behind them. They were all talking at once, no one listening. He saw fear in their eyes. Confusion.

"A snake bit him!" a woman sobbed. "It was in the wood. He—"

Vision blurring, Caleb grasped Mesha's belt. "Help me up . . ." He had to get to the Tabernacle. He had to see the pole with the replica of the poisonous snake attached to it. The Lord had promised that anyone who was bitten would live if he simply looked at it!

"Help him! Hurry!" Everyone cried out at once. His sons grabbed him by the arms and hauled him up. Mesha and Jesher supported him between them. He tried to walk, but his body betrayed him.

"He can't use his legs!"

"He's going to die!"

"Lift him!"

"*Hurry!*"

Four of his sons carried him, shouting as they wove their way through the tents. It seemed to take them forever. Were they so far from the Tabernacle?

"It's Caleb!" people cried out in alarm.

"Get back! Get out of our way!"

Caleb struggled for air. "Lord, You promised . . ." He could say no more.

"Father!" Mesha was crying.

I have come too far, Lord, to die now. You promised.

"Put him down!" someone said.

His sons lowered him to his knees, but he couldn't hold his head up. He couldn't breathe to tell his sons how to help him.

Oh, Lord, You know how many times we've broken our word to You, but You have never broken Your word to us. You said I would enter the land.

Caleb crumpled face-first into the dust. Hands fell upon him again—so many hands, so many voices, shouting, crying.

Pray. Someone, pray.

"Caleb!" People surrounded them. "It's Caleb!" They blocked the sun.

"Get back!" Joshua's voice this time. "Give him room to breathe."

"Lord, Lord . . ." Caleb recognized Hur's voice, felt himself being rolled onto his back. "Don't take him from us, Lord."

Caleb lay on his back, the cloud above him, anguished faces surrounding him. He couldn't raise his head. He couldn't raise his hand to grab hold of someone and pull himself up. His throat was closing, his lungs burning.

He felt Hebron lift his shoulders and prop him up, bracing him. "Open your eyes, Grandfather. Look up. The pole is right before you."

"Breathe, Father! Breathe!"

"He's dead!" someone shrieked. "Caleb's dead!"

People wailed.

With his last bit of strength, Caleb opened his eyes . . . but he could see nothing. Darkness closed in around him. "Look," Moses had said. "Look and believe and you will live!" *You are my salvation, Lord. You alone.*

Spears of light came, driving the darkness back. His vision cleared. Above him was the pole with the bronze snake.

You are the Lord. You are Rapha, the Healer. Your Word is Truth.

Caleb's lungs unlocked and he drew in a deep breath. His heart slowed. His skin cooled. He came up through the shadow of death, shaking off the fettering hands until he was able to stand in the midst of the people. "Death, where is your sting?" he shouted.

His sons laughed in relief and thanksgiving.

Caleb raised his hands. "The Lord, He is God."

Shaken, tears in his eyes, Joshua cried out with him. *"The Lord, He is God!"*

Those surrounding them joined in shouting praises to the Lord, who kept His word.

✦   ✦   ✦

They moved from Oboth to Iye-abarim in the desert facing Moab toward the sunrise. Then they moved on to Zered Valley and farther to camp along the Arnon River on the border between Moab and the Amorites. The Lord led them to Beer and gave them water so they could cross the desert to Mattanah and on to Nahaliel, Bamoth and the Valley of Moab where the top of Mount Pisgah overlooked the wasteland.

Moses dispatched messengers to Sihon, king of the Amorites, requesting safe travel through his territory and also sent spies to Jazer. In response, Sihon mustered his entire army and marched out into the desert against Israel.

This time, the Lord sent them out. "Put the Amorites to the sword and take over his land from the Arnon to the Jabbok!"

At the blast of the shofar, Caleb raised his sword and let out a battle roar. Others joined in until the earth shook with the sound. Joshua led them into war. As they ran at the fortified city of Heshbon, Caleb shouted to his sons. "Destroy these people of Chemosh!" Chemosh, the false god who demanded the blood sacrifice of children.

The Israelite boys and young men Caleb and Joshua had trained were now warriors eager to fight for the Lord their God. They overran Heshbon, breaking down its walls, smashing its idols and altars, and burning everything that was left. They did not withhold their hand, but cut down every citizen who remained to fight. From Heshbon, they moved on to the surrounding settlements, clearing out the Amorites from their towns and land. The vultures feasted.

Survivors fled along the road to Bashan and enlisted the help of King Og, who marched his whole army out to meet Israel at Edrei.

"Do not be afraid of them," Moses shouted. "Fear not, for the Lord God has handed them over to you, Og and his whole army and his land!"

When the day was over, not one Israelite had fallen, but Og, his sons, and his entire army lay dead upon the field of battle. Stained with blood, Caleb stood with his sons among the twisted, tangled bodies of the slain. He heard the jubilation of the men around him as they congratulated one another on their victory. Did they really believe their own strength had brought victory?

Caleb looked at the young men he had trained and wanted to grab them by the throat. They now knew how to fight, and they had the will to destroy. But they were forgetting the most important lesson he had tried to drum into their thick heads every day from the time they began training: Love the Lord your God with all your heart, mind, soul, and strength!

Panting, Caleb drove his spear deep into the earth that now belonged to Israel. Thrusting his hands into the air, he shouted with all his might, *"Lord! Lord! All praise to the Lord!"*

His sons were the first to join in. One by one, others took up the cry until the sound swelled by thousands.

Make them remember, Lord. Write the truth upon their hearts.

+ + +

Israel camped on the plains of Moab along the Jordan across from Jericho. Caleb heard reports that Balak, king of Moab, was gathering forces and sending out messengers to Midian and other peoples of Canaan. "He intends to make an alliance with neighboring nations to keep us out."

"He won't succeed," Caleb vowed, pacing in front of his tent. He couldn't put his worry into words, and Joshua would wait upon Moses to make a decision. "I don't trust the Midianites. Something is wrong. I feel it."

"What?"

"They're too friendly."

"They are related to Moses' family."

Caleb knew as well as everyone else that Moses' wife Zipporah had been a Midianite, and her father, Jethro, had been a chieftain. When the Lord had brought the Israelites out of Egypt, Jethro had met Moses at the Mountain of God and returned to him Zipporah and Moses' two sons. Jethro had even advised Moses on selecting men from among the tribes to help him judge the birthing nation. A wise man, Jethro.

"Jethro was a man of honor, Joshua, but Jethro is long dead. Zipporah is not even a memory to these people, and Moses' sons are trained up in the ways of the Lord. They have nothing in common with their relatives who bow down to Baal."

"You judge them harshly, Caleb. Moses says to treat them as brothers."

"The women do not act like sisters. Have you sent anyone to see what's going on in Shittim?"

Joshua frowned. "No."

"Perhaps you should. Perhaps you should discuss these concerns with Moses. Perhaps he should pray and ask God why these Midianites are so friendly and if we should have commerce with them." He had failed to keep the impatience out of his voice.

Joshua glowered. "Moses is our leader. Not I."

"Does that mean you can't think for yourself?" Caleb watched the color surge into Joshua's face and his eyes darken. "Some of the men are leaving camp and going over to the Midianite settlements. Did the Lord tell us to mingle with these people? At one time, a long time ago, Moses had reason to trust the Midianites. I am asking if they are trustworthy now."

"If an opportunity arises, I will ask."

"Make the opportunity!"

Caleb left before he said harsher words. He called his sons together and their sons. "You will not talk with the Midianites or have anything to do with them."

"Has Moses ruled on the matter?"

Caleb turned to Ardon. "I have ruled on this matter, and I am your father."

They had learned not to argue with him. No further questions were asked.

But others training with Caleb's sons did as they pleased, spending their leisure hours visiting with Midianites. They brought back stories of how friendly and how beautiful the young women of Midian were. Moses had married one, after all. Was it any wonder they were so attracted? And the feasting that went on beneath the spreading oaks was unlike anything they had experienced in their desert life. Caleb came upon young men gathered tightly, whispering, laughing, eyes bright, cheeks flushed. "You should come and see for yourselves."

His sons wanted to go and pressed Caleb daily for permission.

"Everyone is going. We're the only ones who show such a lack of hospitality to Moses' relatives."

"You will not go over to them."

"Carmi lets his son go."

"And Salu."

"Salu is a Simeonite. You answer to me. And I say no. If you ask again, I will find work to keep you so tired you won't be able to stand, let alone think about Midianite women or their feasts!"

Despite Caleb's warning, some of the Judean men went to visit the Midianites. They didn't return until late. Several missed morning worship. One collapsed during training exercises. Caleb had no sympathy or patience. "Get your face out of the dirt."

The young man struggled to his feet, sallow, trembling, unable to look Caleb in the eye.

"Go back to your tent, Asriel." Caleb glowered in disgust. "Go! Now! Before I beat you into the ground!" He watched the young man stumble away. Turning to the others, he pointed after Asriel. "Can any man in that condition stand against the enemy? That is what happens when you stay out all night. You are worse than useless. You will cost the lives of your brothers! Never forget we serve the Lord, the God of Israel. And we are preparing to enter Canaan at His command. Our inheritance is over there." He stretched out his arm. "The Canaanites will not throw open their gates to welcome us. Balak is building a force against us. We do not have time to dance and sing and feast with Midianites."

"The Lord has sent a plague upon us!" the people cried out.

The people wailed, mourning the young men who were dying. "Why?" a mother cried. "We have done everything God asked of us, and now He kills our children! Why?"

✦ ✦ ✦

Asriel died. He was the first of many. None of Caleb's sons were sick, but he questioned them anyway, pressing until they told him what others had told them about the Midianites and their comely young women and the feasts that went on beneath the spreading oaks.

"No wonder God is killing us." Caleb wept. "We have sinned against him." Caleb looked at Joshua, sitting beside Moses, with the other elders gathered to discuss the plague that was spreading through the camp. Hundreds had died, and hundreds more fell ill every day.

"How have we sinned?" someone asked.

"The Midianites."

"They are our friends," another insisted.

"What friendship do we have with those who worship idols? Remember Egypt!" Caleb had to remind himself that the men gathered here had no recollection of what had happened there other than what had been told to them. They were the sons of those who had come out of slavery. "The Moabites and Midianites know we belong to the God who destroyed Egypt with plagues. They know we serve Him. They are cunning enough to realize that they must drive a wedge between us and the God we serve. So they send their beautiful young women to entice our young men into Baal worship. These women were sent to turn the hearts and minds of our sons away from God! And God is judging us for our unfaithfulness."

"I've seen nothing of that sort in our camp."

"Or ours!"

"Will we always be like this?" Caleb shouted, furious. Would they never understand? "Talking and talking. And still you fail to understand. God does not send a plague without cause. He does not punish without reason. We must examine ourselves so that we can repent!"

Moses leaned close to Joshua and spoke to him. Joshua nodded his head and whispered back. Agitated, others began talking at once.

"Salu," Caleb said loudly, "my sons tell me that your son Zimri visits the Midianites."

Salu the Simeonite looked less than pleased to be the center of attention. "He goes to tell them of our God."

"He brought a girl back with him," another added.

Moses' head came up. Joshua stared.

Salu shook his head. "No. You're wrong."

"I was on my way here when I saw your son with her," the man said. "I stopped him and asked what he was doing. He said he wanted all his friends to join him in a celebration, and this woman, Cozbi, had come to encourage us. He said she is the daughter of one of the Midianite chieftains. Zur, I think is his name."

"Invite his friends to a celebration?" Men looked at one another. "What did he mean by that?"

Abruptly, Phinehas rose and strode away from the gathering of elders. His father, Eleazar, high priest and son of Aaron, called after him. Phinehas didn't answer. He went into his tent and came out with a spear in his hand.

Caleb rose, staring after him. His heart raced. The son of the high priest looked neither to the right nor to the left as he strode toward the tents of

Simeon. Caleb had never seen such an expression of wrath on a man's face, even in battle.

Moses' eyes went wide. At a word, Joshua was on his feet and following the high priest's son, Caleb right on his heels.

"What's the matter?" The others clamored to their feet. "What's happening?"

Phinehas broke into a run, spear high in his fist. He gave no battle cry as he charged. People scattered before him.

Caleb and Joshua ran after him, others falling in behind them. Among the tents of Simeon rose sounds of celebration. A circle of men and women stood around the entrance of a tent, staring, restless, moving, pressing in and leaning forward to see more.

"Get back!" At Joshua's shout, the people parted like a sea, exposing the debauchery that had so excited them. Some ducked their heads and ran, diving into their tents to hide themselves.

Phinehas entered the tent. With a loud cry, he planted his feet on either side of the couple writhing upon the mat, raised the spear in both hands, and brought it down with his full strength. The Midianite girl had seen him and screamed. Too late, she tried to kick back from beneath Salu's son, still in the throes of violent passion. Phinehas bore down on the spear, driving it through them both, pinning them to the ground. Salu's son died quickly, but Cozbi clawed and shoved, kicked and screamed, pressing her heels until blood spilled from her mouth. Phinehas held the spear until there was no movement, then let go and backed away, gasping for breath.

Moses ordered the Israelite sons to stay away from the Midianite camp. No further contact was to be made with the Midianites. Eleazar made atonement for the people who stood silent in fear of the plague. How many more would die before the Lord took mercy upon them?

"From this day forth," Moses told the people, "treat the Midianites as enemies. Kill them! They treated us as enemies." He called for a census. Twenty-four thousand had died in the plague. Still, Israel's numbers had increased since the first census before the Mountain of God.

Only two men remained from the generation of slaves who had been delivered from Egypt: Joshua from the tribe of Ephraim and Caleb of Judah.

✦   ✦   ✦

"The Lord has called for vengeance on the Midianites!" Moses told the people. "Arm one thousand men from each tribe and send them into battle." Phinehas would lead them into battle, taking with him the holy items and the trumpets for signaling.

Whispers of alarm went through some ranks. Twelve thousand against hundreds of thousands? They would be slaughtered!

Faithless. Even now, faithless. "The Lord is with us!" Caleb shouted.

"Fear no man!" Joshua called out, raising his sword.

After years of drilling and practicing, the young men were eager to fight and prove themselves in battle. Everyone wanted to go. Caleb called for a lottery to eliminate all but the one thousand men God would assign to fight for Judah. His sons were among them. They stood ready, dressed for battle, swords in hand, shielded by their faith in the living God they served. They had received the Lord's instructions. Now it remained to be seen if they would obey and receive the victory.

Caleb found himself left behind with the other leaders of the community, Joshua among them. Neither was at ease with the waiting.

Caleb heard the shofar blast in the distance and then the war cries of twelve thousand men going into battle. He longed to run with those men, to wield his sword, to kill God's enemies. But he waited with Joshua and the multitude. Let the younger men be tested.

Hour after hour passed. Moses prayed. Joshua prayed. Caleb tried, but his mind was in the midst of that battle, hands clenched, and sweat pouring. His sons had gone out to battle. His sons!

Don't let them fail, Lord. Hold them to their word. Keep their minds fixed upon You. Keep them faithful.

Forty years he had waited to enter the Promised Land. Forty years he had wandered with the sons of those who had refused to listen to his report about Canaan.

Messengers arrived. The Midianites had been conquered; the five kings—Evi, Rekem, Zur, Hur, and Reba—killed, as well as Balaam, King Balak's advisor. The men were returning in triumph.

Caleb noticed Moses' anger and joined Joshua and Eleazar, the high priest. "What's wrong?"

"The men are bringing back captives."

Fear gripped Caleb. Would the Lord send yet another plague upon them?

Herds of cattle and flocks of sheep and goats were being driven toward the camp, and Caleb could see carts of plunder and men carrying all manner of goods they had taken from the Midianite cities and villages.

"Why have you let all the women live?" Moses cried out against them. "These are the very ones who followed Balaam's advice and caused the people of Israel to rebel against the Lord at Mount Peor. They are the ones who caused the plague to strike the Lord's people. Now kill all the boys and all the women who have slept with a man. Only the young girls who are virgins may live; you may keep them for yourselves."

Those who had fought in the battle were commanded to remain outside of camp. They were to wash themselves and their clothing and everything made of leather, goat hair, or wood. All gold, silver, bronze, iron, tin, and lead were to be put through the fire. Every idol and item bearing the emblems and symbols of pagan gods would be melted down. The spoils were divided among the soldiers who had taken part in the battle and with the rest of the community. One out of every five hundred persons, cattle, donkeys, goats, and sheep was given as tribute for the Lord and placed in the care of the Levites.

Caleb's sons returned to their tents with their share of plunder. He stood as they approached, heat surging into his face, every muscle taut. Mesha and Mareshah stood before him with the confidence of soldiers who had returned from a great victory. And indeed it had been. Not one Israelite had fallen.

"We have brought you presents, Father."

"I asked for nothing." Nor did he want what they had brought back to him.

"You have not had the comfort of a woman since Jerioth and Ephrathah died."

"And you think I will take a Midianite as my wife? I am the one who told you to have no commerce with them!"

"These girls are no longer Midianite. They belong to us now. If you will not have them as wives, take them as concubines."

"They know nothing of who we are or what we've been through. Nor of the God we serve."

"Then teach them as you taught us," Mareshah said gravely.

Mesha stepped closer. "We must increase our numbers, Father. And you need women to accomplish that." He grasped one of the girls by the arm and yanked her forward. "She is young, healthy, and gave us no trouble. Do with her what you will." He pushed her forward.

The girl looked at Caleb with calf eyes. He could see nothing in her expression to give him any idea of what she was thinking. He thought of the young Midianite women laughing and beckoning to the men he had trained, leading them away like lambs to the slaughter. Twenty-four thousand had died because men had been easily seduced into Baal worship. The girl had slender curves and smooth olive skin. She would become a beautiful woman. He put his hand to his sword and drew it.

Though the girl's lips parted, she didn't speak. Closing her eyes, she knelt and bowed her head.

"It would be a waste to kill her, Father." Mesha made no move to stop him.

"Do you mock me?" Caleb was eighty years old.

"All those who called you a dog are dead. You are respected by all who know you. And you are my father. You would have led us into battle if God had called you to do it!" Mesha said.

"Moses said we were to keep the virgins." Mareshah spoke quietly.

Hur stretched out his hand and drew another comely young woman forward. "You deserve the best of our portion." The second young woman knelt beside the first, trembling.

Mesha gripped Caleb's sword arm. "They are yours, Father. Make good use of them for all our sakes."

Left alone, Caleb stood over the two young women, sword in hand. *Judgment or mercy, Lord. What do I do?*

He waited, longing for a word, a sign, from the Lord. He studied the two before him. One finally raised her head and looked at him. Her dark eyes shone with fear, but she did not beg for her life. The other girl, still trembling violently, began to sob.

Caleb thought of the countless times God had shown mercy to him and to the people. Was it only accident or circumstance that had plucked these two young women from their foul culture and placed them here in the midst of Israel? Or did God have a plan for them, too?

"I am Caleb." He put his hand over his heart. "Caleb."

The girl who was looking at him placed her hand over her heart. "Maacah." She touched the bowed head of her sobbing companion. "Ephah."

"Life and death are before you. If you learn the law of God and obey, you will live."

Maacah frowned, perplexed. She spread her hands and shook her head.

Caleb scowled. Of course she could not understand his language. But she must learn the most important thing, language barrier or not. "The Lord." He spoke firmly, with a nod of expectation. "The Lord!"

She understood. "The Lord." She spoke hesitantly, then drew up the girl beside her. She spoke to her. Then they both spoke together. "The Lord."

It was not enough to repeat what he said. They must understand he was not speaking of himself, but of the One they must learn to serve. Caleb stretched out his arm, pointing toward the Tabernacle, where the Ark of the Lord was hidden in the Holy of Holies. "The Lord. The Lord, *He is God!*"

Maacah's beautiful dark eyes widened. "The Lord." She spoke in awe. Her expression gave Caleb cause to hope. If these two young women learned that, they would have learned more than the people who had wandered and died in the wilderness.

"The Lord, He is God."

The two young women repeated Caleb's words.

Caleb sheathed his sword. He called to one of his granddaughters. He pointed at each of the young women his sons had given him and gave their names. "See that they learn our language. Then they will learn the law of God."

He would not have anything to do with them until they did.

FOUR

✦❖✦❖✦❖✦

"When you cross the Jordan River into the land of Canaan, you must drive out all the people living there."

Caleb stood in front of the tribe of Judah, listening to Moses give the Lord's instructions. This should be a day of exultation, but he felt weighed down. Forty years had passed. The wandering was over. And he was an eighty-year-old man. But it was not the years that burdened him. It was the responsibility for these people.

"You must destroy all their carved and molten images and demolish all their pagan shrines." Moses' voice carried. "Take possession of the land and settle in it, because I have given it to you to occupy. You must distribute the land among the clans."

Caleb had been placed in charge of all of Judah.

"If you fail to drive out the people who live in the land, those who remain will be like splinters in your eyes and thorns in your sides. They will harass you in the land where you live. And then the Lord will do to you what He plans to do to them!"

Time passed quickly as Moses reminded them of the plagues of Egypt and their own sins. "Hear, O Israel! The Lord is our God, the Lord alone. And you must love the Lord your God with all your heart, all your soul, and all your strength. And you must commit yourselves wholeheartedly to these commandments I am giving you today. Repeat them again and again to your children. Talk about them when you are at home and when you are away on a journey, when you are lying down and when you are getting up again. They are life to you. Make no treaties with the people of the land and show them no mercy. Do not intermarry with them."

Moses spread his hands as though he would embrace all of them. "I am now one hundred and twenty years old and am no longer able to lead you. The Lord has told me that I will not cross the Jordan River."

The people wailed and cried out in protest. Caleb clenched his teeth, tears spilled into his beard, his throat was tight and on fire. He looked at Joshua, standing tall beside Moses, his face set.

Moses raised his voice and through it came the voice of God. **The Lord your God Himself will cross over ahead of you!**

The people grew quiet again, grieving, yet obedient.

"The Lord will destroy the nations living there, and you will take possession of their land. Joshua is your new leader, and he will go with you, just as the Lord promised."

Eleazar the high priest anointed Joshua, after which Moses laid hands upon him and commissioned him to carry out the Lord's commands. Then raising his hands to the cloud overshadowing them, Moses sang Israel's history. He sang blessings upon them. And then he dismissed the congregation.

"He's gone." Joshua's voice was thick, fear glistening in his dark eyes.

"Gone where?"

"Up Mount Nebo." Joshua wept like a boy who had lost his father.

Caleb could not give in to tears, not if he was to be of any help to Joshua. "He will see the whole of the land God is giving us from there. He will see from Gilead to the Negev, from the Jordan Valley and Jericho as far as Zoar."

"I had hoped."

"We assumed Moses would be there, Joshua. We didn't understand that you and I would be the only men from our generation to enter Canaan."

"There will never be another prophet like Moses. No man will ever do the miraculous signs and wonders the Lord sent him to do in Egypt!"

"Until the One Moses said would come, the One who will fulfill the Law." But Caleb knew what lay beneath Joshua's words. "The Lord has appointed you to lead His people Israel. And lead you shall!"

Joshua put his hands over his head as though to hide from God. "I tremble at the thought."

"Fear of the Lord is the beginning of wisdom, my friend." Caleb sat down beside him. "When our time of grieving is over, God will tell you what to do. And whatever it is, I will stand with you."

+   +   +

Caleb spent most of the day at the Tabernacle, close to Joshua, who was closeted in prayer. *Lord, help him. Be with him as You were with Moses. Tell him what he needs to know to lead us into our inheritance.*

They ate together in silence, pondering the days ahead, uncertain of how to proceed, where to start. For once, Caleb did not press his friend. He waited, knowing the day would come when the Lord would speak to Joshua as He had spoken to Moses.

Joshua rose and stood at the entrance of his tent. He stared out at Jericho looming on the other side of the Jordan, immense, fortified, a closed gate into

Canaan. "Bring me two good men, Caleb." He spoke with an assurance Caleb had not heard before. The Lord had spoken to him! "Men other than your own sons. I'm sending them in to look over the land, especially Jericho."

"Done."

When the young men had left on their errand, Caleb tilted his head. "What else did the Lord say to you?"

"Be strong and courageous." Joshua smiled grimly. "He said that many times."

"We all need to hear it." No man was eager to be in the middle of a bloodbath.

"We must be very careful to obey all the laws Moses gave us, Caleb. We must follow everything the Lord says."

Caleb knew Joshua meditated on the Law day and night. "Anything else?"

"The Lord promised to be with me wherever I go."

Caleb's spirit rose like an eagle, wings spread. "Where you are, there shall I be!"

"I need to speak with all the officers."

Caleb sent messengers and the men came quickly, ready to do whatever Joshua told them. "Tell the people to get their supplies ready. The Lord has said that three days from now—" he pointed out the spot on the map Moses had prepared—"we cross the Jordan here. We will take possession of the land the Lord our God has given to us."

Even the Reubenites and Gadites, who had asked to remain on the east side of the Jordan, prepared to go in and fight for their brothers. "Whatever you have commanded us, we will do, Joshua. Wherever you send us, we will go."

Everyone worked and prepared with practiced precision. The years in the wilderness, of watching the cloud rise up, move, and settle, had trained the people to move quickly when so commanded. The defeat of the kings Sihon and Og encouraged them. Balak, king of Moab, had withdrawn now that Balaam and the five kings of Midian who had listened to his counsel were dead. Israel stood ready, eager to obey the Lord's command to take the land.

The spies returned with good news. "The Lord will certainly give us the whole land! Rahab told us the heart of every man in Jericho is terrified of us."

"Who is Rahab?"

"A prostitute." She had brought them into her house and made them swear by the Lord their God that they would save her and her family from the coming destruction.

Caleb's heart sank. Already, compromise. And then he thought of his two concubines and prayed, *Let this woman, Rahab, worship and adore You, Lord, as Maacah and Ephah have.*

"She protected us from the king's men and told us the way of escape. We might not have made it out alive without her."

Joshua asked no further questions. "Then you will see that you keep the vow you made in the name of the Lord. Gather the people tomorrow morning. I will give them the Lord's instructions."

As the men filed out of the tent, Caleb remained behind in case Joshua wanted to discuss plans and go over the maps again.

Joshua sat and beckoned him to do likewise. "We will cross the Jordan in two days. I didn't want to say anything to the officers. Not yet."

Caleb didn't have to ask why. The river was at flood stage, and no one in Israel knew how to swim or build rafts or a bridge. "I'm sure the Lord told you how we're to get across."

"No, He didn't. He only said the priests are to carry the Ark and the people are to follow a thousand feet behind."

Feeling a quiver of alarm, Caleb wondered what they would do once they reached the floodwaters. And then he remembered and laughed. "Do not be afraid, my friend! Do not be discouraged." He grinned. "A river is but a small matter to the God who opened a sea."

✦   ✦   ✦

"Gather around!" Caleb beckoned his sons and their wives and their children. They came eagerly. Ephah and Maacah were among his family members now, grafted in, warmly accepted, and held accountable to God. He told all of them of Egypt and slavery and how the Lord had sent Moses to deliver them. He told them of the plagues upon Egypt and about the miracles of protection God provided for His people. "You have heard your history from Moses' own lips, and you have heard it from mine as well. And so you will hear it often for as long as I live. And you must tell your children and your grandchildren so they will not forget."

Caleb reminded them of the sins committed that had brought God's judgment upon his generation. "Sin crouches like a lion waiting to devour you. You must resist it. You must obey the Lord. Do whatever He asks of you, no matter how difficult." He reminded them of the sins that had cost the lives of twenty-four thousand. "Your sins bring death to those you love. You must keep your eyes on the Lord. Not just tomorrow or until we have taken the land God has promised us, but *always*. Serve the Lord with gladness. Stand in His presence with thanksgiving! Our hope and our future are in Him."

His sons leaned in closer, eyes ablaze, tense. They had spent their lives preparing for the day at hand.

"Tomorrow you will hear the Word of the Lord from His anointed. Joshua will tell us what we are to do. Obey him as you would obey the Lord."

And thus they did.

The people consecrated themselves. They waited until the priests carrying the Ark were one thousand feet ahead of them and then followed. When the priests came to the Jordan River, they stepped down into it. A sound of wind came and the water rolled back, leaving dry land where water had rushed. The priests stood in the middle of the empty riverbed, holding the Ark, as men, women, children—over a million of them—crossed over. When the entire nation stood on the west bank of the Jordan, Joshua sent one man from each of the twelve tribes back, each for one river stone. He stacked them there at Gilgal on the eastern border of Jericho.

"In the future, your children will ask, 'What do these stones mean?' Then you can tell them, 'This is where the Israelites crossed the Jordan on dry ground.' For the Lord your God dried up the river right before your eyes, and He kept it dry until you were all across, just as He did at the Red Sea when He dried it up until we had all crossed over. He did this so that all the nations of the earth might know the power of the Lord, and that you might fear the Lord your God forever."

+ + +

"Joshua cannot have heard right, Father."

"The Lord commanded that we all be circumcised, and so we shall. I'm ashamed I did not think to do it years ago when you were boys."

"No one has been circumcised, not in forty years! We should wait."

"Wait?" Caleb glowered at his sons. "When God gives a command, we obey. We don't *wait*."

"Be reasonable, Father! We're camped within sight of Jericho. If we submit to this mutilation now, we won't be able to defend ourselves."

"Mutilation? You call the sign of the covenant between God and us a mutilation?" He watched the color drain from his son's face.

"I spoke rashly. Forgive me."

"It is God's forgiveness you need." He fixed his eyes upon each of his sons and grandsons. "Are you afraid of a small knife in the hands of a priest?" They all shook their heads, denying any fear.

Shobab laughed, self-deprecatingly. "*Yes*. I'm afraid."

"As am I," Caleb said.

"You?"

"Let it be a comfort to know that your father will be in line for circumcision tomorrow."

They all began talking at once. His words had not served to calm them, but caused even more agitation.

"Father . . ." Shobab pointed feebly. "Mesha is right. What is to keep the

Canaanite warriors from coming out of Jericho and slaughtering us while we mend?"

"God has been with us every day, and you can ask such a question?" Restraining his anger, Caleb spoke slowly, quietly, empathically. "The Lord is our shield and strength. He will watch over and protect us. We have nothing to fear."

When the circumcisions were completed, Caleb retired to his tent. Racked with pain, he lay upon his pallet. When fever came upon him, he couldn't sleep. Now that they had crossed the Jordan, the manna had stopped raining from heaven. His concubines, Ephah and Maacah, knew how to prepare meals from the provisions the land offered, but Caleb missed the manna. Gone was the sweetness God had given them.

Joshua came to see him. "Don't get up, Caleb."

Drained by the fever, Caleb remained upon his cushioned pallet. He chuckled bleakly. "You are blessed among men." Joshua had been circumcised as a baby. Few among the Jews had continued the practice once they were enslaved by the Egyptians. "How are the others faring?"

"Better than you, old friend."

Caleb grasped Joshua's extended hand and pulled himself up. "Youth has its advantages." Wincing, he waved Maacah away and walked . . . slowly . . . tenderly . . . outside. It was the first time in three days that he had been outside his tent. He squinted at the bright sunlight. "The Lord has given you His plan. When and how do we take Jericho?"

"Tomorrow at daybreak . . ." Joshua told him God's plan.

Astounded, Caleb went over the plan again. "We are to be silent?"

"Yes."

"No war cry."

"No one is to speak."

"And then we march around the city? Nothing more?"

"For six days. The Ark will go before us, followed by seven priests carrying shofars. On the seventh day, they will blow them and we will shout as we march around the city *seven* times."

Caleb looked at the walls of Jericho. Not since leaving Egypt had he seen such a well-fortified city. "And God said the walls will collapse?"

"Yes."

The plan was preposterous. It was ridiculous! No man in his right mind would ever have thought up such a thing. Caleb laughed in praise. "All the world will hear of this. People will talk about what God did at Jericho for thousands of years to come!"

"Then you believe it will happen?"

"Of course I believe it." Caleb's laughter died. "You don't?"

"Yes, *I* believe. But will the men?"

Caleb understood Joshua's trepidation. It had not been that long ago when some had gone after other gods at Peor. Twenty-four thousand had died during the plague God sent to discipline them. "They'd better."

From the time of the Garden of Eden, the seed of rebellion had been planted deep in the hearts of men. It was there the real battle raged.

+ + +

On the first day of marching, Caleb concentrated on putting one foot in front of the other. He throbbed with pain and gritted his teeth, determined to make it around the city and back to his tent with his head high. On the second day, he moved less stiffly and noticed the soldiers on Jericho's battlements staring out. On the third day, some mocked. By the fifth day, men and women were laughing and shouting blasphemies from the wall. Even children had joined in.

His sons and grandsons did not speak when they returned to camp, but their wrath showed in the way they yanked off their belts and swords. Caleb watched them, smiling secretly, thanking God. The days of suffering from the circumcision were over. Each day renewed and built their strength. And each day the Canaanites added fuel to the fire that would consume them.

Let it build. Hold that anger in. Hold it in until the last day—the day of the Lord!

When the seventh day came, Caleb was at full strength, his blood on fire. The men no longer marched with quiet reserve. They pounded their feet into the ground. *Boom! Boom! Boom!* Each time around the city, the tension grew. The men on the walls of Jericho stopped laughing. Seven times the army of Israel marched around the city, shofars blowing. And then they stopped and turned inward.

The blast came—long and loud. Caleb's heart rattled; his blood raced. The air of retribution filled his lungs. He released it with a mighty shout. *"For the Lord!"* Thousands joined in until the sound was deafening, terrifying.

God's promise was fulfilled before their eyes. The great walls of Jericho shook with the sounds of the shofars and their battle cries. And as the walls shook and cracked, the Israelites shouted all the louder for the Lord. The walls collapsed, stones and rampart soldiers tumbling, dust rising with the screams.

Raising his sword high, Caleb ran with Joshua, and like a tidal wave, thousands upon thousands came with them, sweeping across the plain, straight for the city. The sword in his hand had once been a scythe, and he swung it to the right and left, cutting down Canaanites like stalks of wheat. Men, women, young and old, cattle, sheep, donkeys—nothing that breathed survived.

Panting, Caleb stood in the center of the vanquished city. "Remember your orders. All the silver, gold, bronze, and iron are sacred to the Lord and must be taken into His treasury. Destroy the rest! *Burn the city! Burn everything in it!*"

✦   ✦   ✦

Jericho was still smoldering when Joshua sent spies to Ai, near Beth-aven. It lay to the east of Bethel, where Israel's ancestor Jacob had seen the ladder into heaven and the angels going up and down. The spies returned within a short time.

"It's not like Jericho. Not all our people will have to go up against it. Send two or three thousand men to take it. There's no need to tire the people over the few in Ai."

Joshua considered and then nodded. "Go and do so." As soon as the messenger left, Caleb leaned over the maps made from their first sojourn into Canaan forty years earlier. Joshua laid out God's plan to conquer Canaan.

✦   ✦   ✦

"The men are returning from Ai." The breathless messenger looked ashen. "And they're bringing wounded and bodies!"

Caleb ran out to find his sons. Shobab was wounded. Mesha wept. "We thought it would be so easy after Jericho, but the men of Ai routed us! They chased us from the city gate as far as the stone quarries. The arrow hit Shobab while he retreated to the slopes. We ran!" He sobbed. "Ardon didn't make it, Father. He's dead!"

"My son? My son . . ." Caleb wept. How could this happen? How?

Joshua cried out at the news and tore his clothes. He went straight to the Tabernacle and fell facedown on the ground before the Ark of the Lord.

Caleb stood outside waiting, trembling. What had gone wrong?

The people began gathering—a dozen, a hundred, a thousand. Those who had lost sons and husbands wailed and threw dust over themselves.

Joshua came outside within moments, his face ashen. "We have violated the Lord's covenant."

Caleb felt cold. "When? How? Who?" Fear gripped him. What would God do to them? What plague would come upon Israel? What retribution for unfaithfulness?

"Someone has stolen things devoted to the Lord and then lied and put these things among their own possessions. Until this is settled, we can't stand against our enemies." Joshua's voice kept rising. "Consecrate yourselves!" he shouted to the people. "Present yourselves before the Lord tomorrow, tribe by tribe, clan by clan, family by family. The one who is caught with the devoted things will be burned, along with everything that belongs to him!"

Caleb gestured for his sons and grandsons, their wives and his concubines to return to their camp. He studied each one of his sons and grandsons. He looked at his concubines. He hated the feeling of distrust welling within him, the wrath and frustration, the fear of knowing someone who belonged to him may have brought God's wrath upon the entire nation. But who would dare steal from God? "God will tell us who the guilty man is. And whoever he is, he will die." *Don't let it be one of my sons or grandsons.*

No one said a word, but Caleb saw that his own feelings were reflected in their eyes. They looked at one another, questioning, wondering, afraid. Until the guilty party was found, everyone would be suspect.

No one slept that night. *Not one of my sons or grandsons, Lord. Let it not be anyone from Judah.*

In the morning, Eleazar the priest stood with Joshua as the tribes came forward one by one. The Reubenites passed by, then the Simeonites. Judah was halted. Caleb wanted to sink into the ground in shame. As the other tribes moved back from them, Judah came forward clan by clan. Caleb went first, followed by his sons, grandsons, and all their wives, concubines, and children. They were not stopped. But Caleb felt no great relief. *Judah, oh, Judah. Leader among your brothers! Are you leader in sin as well?* The Shelanite clan passed by, then the Perezites.

When the Zerahite clan came before Eleazar and Joshua, they were halted. Joshua commanded them to come forward by families.

Caleb watched Eleazar and knew the moment God revealed the guilty man: Achan, son of Carmi, son of Zimri. Caleb hung his head and wept. Achan and Ardon had played together. They had trained together, laughed together, gone out to battle together.

"It is true! I have sinned against the Lord, the God of Israel." Achan spoke quickly, pacing and sweating in fear before Joshua and Eleazar, turning to his Judean brothers. "I saw a beautiful robe imported from Babylon, two hundred silver coins, and a bar of gold weighing more than a pound. I wanted them so much that I took them. They are hidden in the ground beneath my tent, with the silver buried deeper than the rest."

"Go!" Joshua gestured to two assistants, and they departed. Everyone waited until they returned with the beautiful multicolored, woven, embroidered robe; the silver; and the gold. The silver and gold were given to Eleazar and the priests to spread out before the Lord.

Joshua turned to Caleb, his eyes filled with sorrow. "We must take Achan and all that belongs to him to the valley."

As head of Judah, Caleb obeyed the command. Achan did not go easily. "I'm sorry! I didn't mean to do it. I don't know what got into me! It's just a robe and some silver and gold. Is that reason enough to kill me and my entire family? Caleb, help me. My grandfather and father were your friends. The council will listen to you. *Help me!*"

Grief and disappointment fueled Caleb's rage as he backhanded Achan, who fell to his knees begging. Pity caught at Caleb, but he dragged him up. His son Ardon had died because of this man's sin. So had thirty-five others! Caleb thought of their widows and children as he propelled Achan ahead of him. He would not listen to Achan's excuses or his pleas for mercy. He closed his ears to the sobs of Achan's sons and daughters as others pressed them along after their father. Even the man's cattle, donkeys, and sheep were driven into the valley, and his tent and all he had were cast down around him.

"Spare my children!" Achan screamed, weeping. "At least my sons so that my name will . . ."

"Why have you brought trouble on us?" Joshua's voice carried so that all those standing around the rim of the small valley heard. "The Lord will now bring trouble on you." He took up a rock. Caleb did likewise, gripping it tightly, palm sweating, tears filling his eyes.

Achan's screams were abruptly silenced, as were those of his sons and daughters. The animals were not so easily killed. When everything that breathed was dead, the remains and all Achan's possessions were torched. Then stones were piled up in a heap.

Silent, the people dispersed.

Caleb returned to his tent with his sons and grandsons. Some wept. Others were quiet. Some questioned.

Caleb stood firm. "Achan had to die!"

"Yes, but did his children?" One of the women wept.

Caleb felt every day of his eighty years. "They knew. Don't you understand? They all knew. Achan buried inside his tent what he stole from God. Do you think his sons and daughters didn't know about it?" He swept his arms wide. "Could I dig a hole here and my family not see it? No! Achan's sons and daughters saw what he did and said nothing. They forsook the Word of the Lord and followed their father. They were all guilty!"

"He loved Ardon like a brother." Shobab shook his head. "They were friends from childhood. You heard what he said. He wasn't thinking clearly when he took those things. It all happened in the heat of battle. He didn't mean to sin . . ."

"*Do not pity him!*" Tears streamed down Caleb's face. "Achan knew he sinned. It took time to smuggle those things out of Jericho. It took time to hide them. He thought he could steal from God and no one would know, and Ardon died at Ai because of him. To show him pity is to rebel against the Lord's judgment. Think of Ardon and the thirty-five others who died because of one man's greed. We grieve and suffer now because of Achan. He had herds of cattle and flocks of sheep. His sons rode on donkeys like young princes. God had given him wealth. Was he satisfied? No! Was he thankful? No!" He spit in disgust. "Your brother and the others died because Achan wanted a robe, a few silver shekels, and a wedge of gold!"

For forty years, he had taught and counseled his sons and grandsons. Did they still not understand? "You *must* obey the Lord. Whatever He says, you must do. God gave us the Law to protect us, to teach us how to live righteously before Him. The battle belongs to the Lord. We are to be holy as He is holy!"

"How can we do that, Father?" Hur, the only son of his beloved Ephrathah, leaned forward. "You know we love you and respect you." He held his hands out. "We all strive to do whatever you ask of us because we know you live for God. But I want to know, Father. How is it possible to be holy like God? How can we keep every law laid upon our backs? I try. God must know I try. But I fail."

Caleb saw the anguish in his son's eyes. He saw the others were troubled as well.

"Yes." He let out his breath slowly. "Yes, we all fail." He banged his chest with his fists. "But inside, we fight to do what the Lord wills. We must fight our inclinations!" They listened more intently now than they had for a long time. "The battle is not over what's out there. The battle is within us, always within us."

Achan had been judged rightly, and now they must forget their sorrow and their losses and move forward. With God!

"If you can only remember one command, my sons, let it be this: Love the Lord with all your heart, mind, soul, and strength. If you can do that, God will show you that all things are possible with Him." Caleb spread his hands. "Say it with me." And they did. "Say it again." And they did, louder. "*And again!*" And they shouted it.

"Say it every day for the rest of your lives, and live by your word." Bowing his head, Caleb prayed a blessing upon them.

+ + +

"Hide in ambush close behind the city and be ready for action." Joshua pointed to the map. Caleb studied the markings so he would know where he would hold the men. Joshua straightened. "When our main army attacks, the men of Ai will come out to fight as they did before, and we will run away from them. We will let them chase us until they have all left the city. For they will say, 'The Israelites are running away from us as they did before.' Then you will jump up from your ambush and take possession of the city, for the Lord your God will give it to you."

"And when we have the city in our hands?"

"Set the city on fire, as the Lord has commanded. You have your orders."

Caleb led the men by night to their position behind the city. They waited until early the next morning when a messenger reported that Joshua had mustered his men and was on the move. From his position, Caleb could see Joshua's army approach the city and form in front of it, setting up camp north of Ai, with a valley between them and the city. With Caleb's five thousand men to the west of the city, the men of Ai would be boxed into that valley with no escape.

Shouting arose as warriors poured from the gates of Ai, chasing Joshua and his army toward the desert. Caleb snapped his fingers and several messengers ducked down beside him. "The men of Ai are in pursuit of Joshua. Alert the men!" The men of Ai raced across the valley, leaving the gates of the city open and unguarded. Spotting Joshua, Caleb waited, teeth gritted, for the sign.

And then it came. Joshua pointed his javelin toward Ai.

"Now!" Caleb shouted and rose up. Those under his command followed him up the slope and in through the city gates. People screamed and ran, but didn't get far. "Torch the city. Hurry!" Fires were set and the buildings took flame, smoke billowing into the sky. "To the battle!"

Caleb mustered his men. The warriors of Ai were in full retreat into the valley, but they couldn't escape for five thousand Israelites blocked them. "*For the Lord!*" Sword raised, Caleb ran toward the warriors of Ai. "For the Lord!" Thousands responded.

The valley became like a bowl of blood. Every warrior of Ai died there. Joshua took the king of Ai and hung him on a tree until evening, then ordered his body taken down and thrown on the burning city gate.

They built two altars of uncut stones, one on Mount Ebal and another Mount Gerizim. "Gather the people." When all the men, women, children, and aliens living among them were brought near, Joshua read the law God had given Moses to write. Not a word was left out.

The blessings and the curses were heard clearly from one mountain to the other. No one would ever be able to say they had not heard the Lord's warnings of what would happen if men failed to obey Him.

+   +   +

"Who are you?" Caleb narrowed his eyes as he studied the ragged delegation of men, their donkeys loaded with worn-out sacks and cracked and mended wineskins. "Where did you come from?" A long distance from their appearance, for their sandals were patched.

"We are your servants. We have come to make a treaty with you."

Some of the younger men had gathered around to watch. "They might live near us. How can we make a treaty with them?"

Eleazar raised his hands. "Let them speak!"

Joshua looked them over. "Who are you and where do you come from?"

"We are your servants. We have come from a distant country because of the fame of the Lord your God. We heard reports about Him and all that He did in Egypt, and what He did to the two kings of the Amorites east of the Jordan, Sihon and Og. Our elders told us to take provisions and come and meet with you." The speaker reached into his pack.

Caleb drew his sword. A dozen others did the same.

The man's eyes went wide. "I only want to show you what has become of our provisions."

"Back away." Caleb stepped forward and looked in the pack.

"That bread was warm and fresh when we left our home." The man put his hand on the wineskins. "And these new and filled."

Caleb tore off a piece of bread. After a taste, he spit it out. "Dry. Moldy." But he still didn't trust them.

"We'll make a treaty with you."

Joshua and most of the elders were in agreement.

Caleb was not so easily convinced. "The Lord said to make no treaties."

"Yes." Joshua grew impatient. "But we must not be too quick to judge and wipe out people. The Lord meant no treaties with those of the land. These men are from a distant country. We have no reason to be at war with them."

"Then why do I feel this unease in my gut?"

Joshua slapped him on the back. "Perhaps it is the bread you just ate."

Others laughed, friends of old. Overruled, Caleb kept silent.

The delegation left soon after the treaty was made. Three days later, Israelite warriors sent to scout out the land returned, red-faced and raging. "They're Hivites from Gibeon! Those clothes they wore were a ruse. We did not attack because we signed a treaty with them."

Caleb exploded in anger. "They made fools of us!"

"Of me." Joshua was pale with mortification. "I did not inquire of the Lord. I did what I thought was right."

"Well, you had better pray now, my brother, because we are in trouble. The people are not happy about what we've done."

The people grumbled. "God said not to make a treaty with these people!"

"What were you thinking?"

"They'll be a thorn in our sides from now on!"

The leaders argued among themselves over what to do.

"*They lied!*"

"We don't owe them anything!"

The tribe of Simeon was eager for blood. "I say we march on their cities and kill every last one of them!"

Those representing the other tribes were as eager for revenge. "That's what the Lord told us to do in the first place."

Joshua shook his head. "We must keep our oath."

Caleb listened to the others all talk at once. They were afraid, and with good reason. The people were angry and casting blame. "Be still!" He spoke loudly, and the others quieted. "We made a mistake in not asking God who those men were. We must not make another. My heart cries out for vengeance just as yours does, but vengeance belongs to the Lord. Listen to Joshua!"

They waited for God's chosen to speak.

"We have given them our oath by the Lord, the God of Israel, and we cannot touch them now. If we break our oath, we will bring God's wrath down upon us."

"So what do we do about them?"

Joshua called the people to order and told them the way of the Lord.

And then he summoned the Gibeonites. "Why did you lie to us?"

"We did it because we were told that the Lord your God instructed his servant Moses to conquer this entire land and destroy all the people living in it. So we feared for our lives because of you. That is why we have done it. Now we are at your mercy—do whatever you think is right."

Whatever you think is right. Caleb seethed. These people knew the oath could not be broken without incurring God's wrath. The Gibeonites had counted on it.

The people grumbled. A wave of fury could be felt until Joshua reminded them that the Lord would hold the nation to their oath. He faced the frightened Gibeonites. "You are under a curse. From this day forth, you will never cease to serve as woodcutters and water carriers for the house of my God." They bowed before him and departed.

The camp was quiet that night.

God's enemies would now retain a toehold in the land for generations to come.

✦ ✦ ✦

Summoned by messenger, Caleb hurried to Joshua's tent. One look at Joshua's face and Caleb knew something was wrong. "What's happened?"

"The Gibeonites have sent word they need our help. The Amorite kings of Jerusalem, Kiriath-arba, Jarmuth, Lachish, and Eglon have moved against them."

"It's bad enough that we have to allow those people to live. Now we have to defend them?"

They gathered the entire Israelite army and marched all night to rescue Gibeon. In the morning they took the attacking armies by surprise.

"Look," Caleb cried out. "The Lord is with us!" The enemy was in confusion, bumping into one another in their haste to flee. The battle raged.

"Joshua! Joshua!" A young warrior panted before him. "The kings! I saw all five of them go into a cave."

"Roll large rocks up to the mouth of it and post guards. Don't stop fighting! Pursue your enemies. Attack them and don't let them reach their cities."

Frustrated, Caleb assessed the numbers and the lay of the land. There were not enough hours in the day to complete the work God had given them. He sought out Joshua, who stood on the highest hill overlooking the battle, and voiced his concern. "We won't have the time to finish them. The sun is already overhead!"

Joshua shared his agitation. "We need more time! More time!" He raised his hands and cried out in a loud voice, "Let the sun stand still over Gibeon, Lord, and the moon over the valley of Aijalon!"

They joined the battle. As Caleb swung his sword from the right to the left, Amorites fell before him like stalks of wheat before a reaper. He kept on, cutting down any man who came against him, until he could no longer number those he had killed. His arm did not weaken, and the sun seemed to remain overhead! But how could this be? Hour after hour, the sun remained in the middle of the sky, blazing down upon the battlefield.

"The Lord! The Lord, He is with us!" Exultant, Caleb let the fire within him blaze. Surely all the nations would see that the Lord God of Israel had power not only over all creation but over time itself. No one could fight against God and win!

The Amorites fled, and Caleb and Joshua raised their swords. "After them!"

The Israelites pursued the enemy up to Beth-horon, but before they caught up with them, the Lord cast hailstones the size of a man's fist from heaven. Caleb saw men struck in the head and back, crashing to the ground. Battered and bloody bodies lay along the road. So many were strewn along the way that Caleb knew the Lord had killed more by hail than he and the others had killed by the sword.

The army camped at Makkedah, and reports began coming in from the captains. "The Amorites were destroyed. Only a few managed to make it to their cities."

Thankful that God had given them one more full day of sunlight during which to fight, Caleb was still not satisfied with the outcome. "And those few who escaped will be a thorn in our side if we don't hunt them down and destroy them."

"We have the kings in the caves," Joshua reminded him.

The order was given to open the cave and bring the kings out. When a contingent obeyed, the kings appeared, blinking at the bright sunlight.

For all their grand apparel and lofty plans to annihilate Israel, they were thrown to the ground before Joshua. He called for the commanders to come forward. "Put your feet on the necks of these kings."

Caleb motioned for Mesha to put his foot on the neck of Adoni-zedek, king of Jerusalem.

"Do not fear these men." Joshua drew his sword. "They fled the battle and hid in this cave." One by one, he struck and killed them. "Hang them on the trees until evening," he ordered. "Then throw their bodies into the cave. Tomorrow we take Makkedah!"

Swords were raised, and the sound of triumph rang.

But Caleb wondered why nothing much was said about what the Lord had done for them that day. Joshua could talk of little else, and Caleb's own heart sang praises. But what of the younger men, the captains and those in their charge? God had provided the people with manna and water in the desert for forty years. In all that time, their clothes and shoes had not worn out. God's presence and protection had been with them in the cloud and pillar of fire. Had they all become so accustomed to miracles that the Lord's stopping the sun seemed a small matter?

Caleb wondered about the days ahead. Victory sang in the air. The Promised Land smelled sweet with the blossoms of fruit trees, fields of grain, vineyards, and olive trees. But was taking the land their only goal?

Lord, don't let us become complacent. Don't let us become so used to miracles that we fail to recognize and give thanks and praise for what You do for us. Sometimes You are so vast, Your ways so incomprehensible, that we fail to see You at all. And You are here. You are over us and behind us. You go before us and are our rear guard. You breathe life into us.

Let us never forget that we are but dust without You, only chaff to be blown away by the lightest breeze that may come against us.

+ + +

Makkedah fell and the Israelites left no survivors. Libnah, Lachish, Eglon, Kiriath-arba, and Kiriath-sepher met the same fate. The Lord's command to destroy all who breathed was carried out. But some fled to the north and to the coastlines.

The Amorites, Hittites, Perizzites, Jebusites and Hivites joined forces at the Waters of Merom.

"They have a huge army!" The scout's eyes were dark with worry. "And thousands of horses and chariots. There are too many for us . . ."

"How many is too many for the Lord, Parnach?" Caleb drew the tent flap back. "You're dismissed."

The young man flushed and departed quickly.

"Perhaps we should rethink our battle plan," said Joshua.

Our battle plan? Joshua looked tired. So were they all. They had been fighting for months, taking one city after another, putting thousands to the sword. "We never fight by *our* battle plan, Joshua. You know that better than any man. Inquire of the Lord. He will tell you again what we must do."

"How many times must the Lord say to me, 'Have no fear' before I have no fear?"

Caleb frowned. "You are not a coward, Joshua."

Joshua gave a grim laugh. "The Lord knows differently."

"If you are a coward, so are we all. Not a man among us is without fear, my friend. Brave men do what the Lord commands despite their fear. As you have done, and so shall the Lord tell you to do again."

"You are the fiercest man I've ever known, Caleb. I've never seen you waver, even when cutting down women and children."

"Because I fear God more than men. But I am sick after every battle."

"I find that hard to believe."

"Ask Maacah. Ask Ephrah." Killing women and children was a difficult thing to do. "I must remind myself continually of what I saw during those forty days we traveled through this land as scouts. Remember their festivals, the debauchery, the perversion, the way they sacrificed their children to their gods? Even the children acted out what they saw their parents doing. We told them the stories of our God, how He destroyed Egypt with plagues, how He provides for His people. Have they changed? When we went into Jericho, what did we find but altars like those we saw all over Canaan. Rahab said the people were afraid of us, but do they fear God? No! Forty years, Joshua. The Lord is merciful to those who repent and cry out to Him. Have these people done that?"

Caleb clenched his fist. "I have to remind myself of these things every time I draw my sword. I have to remind myself of what God requires of me. We all must remind ourselves that God is on our side. As long as we obey His Word, He will protect us and give us the victory. As long as we obey."

"That preys upon my mind. How long will our people obey? We have seen that their hearts are easily seduced."

"And that is precisely why the Lord told us to get rid of these people, to be a scourge and cleanse the land of them. We erred with the Gibeonites, Joshua. We must never make that mistake again."

Joshua's eyes shone. "We won't. Not as long as I live. I will inquire of the Lord and we will follow Him."

Caleb smiled.

"There is momentum in these battles, Caleb, like a great stone rolling down a mountain. The Canaanites, Amorites, and all the rest flee before us because God hardened their hearts. Their opportunity to repent has passed. And God is using us to carry out His judgment against them."

"Yes, Joshua, but we must not forget that we could share the same fate if we ever turn our backs on the Lord."

God had told them He would bring the curses to bear upon them and they would be cut down by the sword and scattered across the face of the earth.

+ + +

"For the Lord!" Caleb led Judah's charge into battle at the Waters of Merom. Joshua was at the head of Israel's divisions. The army of Amorites, Hittites, Perizzites, Jebusites, and Hivites fell before the ferocity as the Lord gave them into the hand of Israel. The allies split, retreating.

Caleb cut down all those who stood against him. His arm swung to the right and then the left, hacking through any Amorite or Hittite who came at him. He saw others run. "Pursue them!" he shouted and the Hebrews went after them.

Bodies lay all along the way to Greater Sidon, to Misrephoth-maim and to the Valley of Mizpah on the east. Hamstrung horses screamed. Chariots burned. One by one, cities fell. The Israelites followed the command to leave no survivors. They left the uninhabited dwellings and cities on their mounds and moved on to Hazor and King Jabin, the man who had gathered the other nations against Israel. And the city fell.

"Here he is!" Caleb threw King Jabin at Joshua's feet. When the Amorite king tried to rise, Caleb put his foot on his back.

"We wait—" Joshua drew his sword—"until every man, woman, and child in his domain has reaped the Lord's wrath."

When the city was silent, Joshua drew his sword. "For the Lord." He sliced through Jabin with one powerful sweep of the blade. Caleb stood near enough to be splattered by the blood as the Amorite king died.

The men cheered in victory.

"Hazor has well-built walls, fine dwellings, and cisterns."

Caleb knew what they were thinking. After years of living in tents, how easy it would be to move into those houses and live in comfort. Hadn't he been tempted by the same things? But there were other things to consider. "There is an altar to Baal at the center and an Asherah pole. I did not enter a single household where there was not some kind of idol."

The officer from Simeon glared at Caleb. "We can put everything through fire as we have before."

Cattle lowed and sheep bleated as they were herded toward the valley. Israel's flocks and herds were growing with every battle they fought. Even in their dreams, they had not imagined the wealth God had given them.

Caleb thought of the blood on the altar in the center of Hazor. "What does the Lord say about *this* city?"

Joshua walked away from them. When one of the men started to follow, Caleb blocked him. "Let him inquire of the Lord."

The commanders all talked at once. What they wanted was clear.

Caleb stilled his impatience. "Jabin gathered the nations against us."

"Jabin is dead!"

"Yes, I know he is dead. And Hazor stands as a monument to his rebellion."

"We'll rename the city. We can burn all the idols and smash the Asherah pole and the altars of Baal."

"Should we bring our children to live in a city founded upon sin?"

"You would tear down every one of these towns, Caleb. You are a destroyer!"

"I saw what they did on those altars. In forty years, I have not forgotten."

"We didn't see it, Caleb. We aren't plagued by such memories. We can—"

"Be silent!" Caleb commanded. Joshua was returning. "What does the Lord want done, Joshua?"

Joshua came toward them, wrath in his eyes. "Burn it. The Lord says burn it. *Leave nothing standing!*"

Caleb called out the order. Men ran to obey, tearing down the gates and setting a torch to them. The crackle of flames filled the air along with billowing smoke. Caleb strode through the city, making certain the dwellings were set on fire. He shouted to several men and ordered them to help him topple an Asherah pole. The stench of burning flesh filled his nostrils until he was nauseated.

As he went out, he drew in fresh air and thanked God for leading them away from temptation. Hazor had been a place of death long before God's wrath brought the Israelites to the gates of the city.

✦   ✦   ✦

Caleb cleaned the blood from his sword, then began the slow work of sharpening it. How many men had he killed in the last three years? How many more would he have to kill before God's enemies were removed from Canaan? He ran the stone along the blade in one long smooth stroke. He had met with Joshua last night and come away grim with resolve.

"The Lord has told me there are still large areas of land to be taken over," Joshua had said.

"What areas?"

"All the regions of the Philistines and Gershurites; from the Shihor River on the east of Egypt to the territory of Ekron on the north."

"Gaza and Ashdod?"

"Yes, and Ashkelon and Gath as well. From the south, all the land of the Canaanites, from Mearah of the Sidonians as far as Aphek where the

Amorites still live, the area of the Gebalites; and all Lebanon to the east, from Baal-gad below Mount Hermon to Lebo-hamath."

The years stretched before Caleb. Would he ever plow the soil or plant seed again? Would he watch his crops grow? He couldn't speak.

Joshua pointed as he spoke.

"The Lord Himself will drive the Sidonians out of the mountain regions from Lebanan to Misrephoth-maim. This land will be allocated as an inheritance and divided among the nine tribes and the half tribe of Manasseh."

Even as the fighting continued, the Israelites took possession of Canaan, dividing up the land according to the boundaries set by the Lord. The Reubenites and Gadites had received their inheritance, their clans and families establishing themselves in the area taken from Sihon and Og. The tribe of Reuben held the towns of the plateau and the area once ruled by Amorites at Heshbon. The boundary was the Jordan River.

Gad received all the towns of Gilead and half the Ammonite country as far as Aroer near Rabbah. Their territory ran up to the end of the Sea of Galilee. Manasseh's territory included Bashan and all the settlements of Jair. Sixty towns!

God assigned the other inheritances, and the areas were marked out on a map. Judah's allotment was in the heart of Canaan, including the mountain where Abraham had taken Isaac and made ready to offer him to the Lord in obedience to God's command, but the Lord had called out to him to withhold his hand from the boy and provided the offering Himself.

"Are you all right, Caleb?"

"I'm growing old."

Joshua's face softened. "Our day will come, my friend."

"Will it?" Caleb bowed his head in shame. Who was he to question God? *Forgive me, Lord. It's only that* . . . He stopped the thought. *Forgive me!* He fought against the despair filling him. He had spent forty years wandering in the wilderness because of the faithlessness of his generation. And now he was spending his last years fighting a war and allotting the land to the sons of the very men whose sin had kept him out of the Promised Land all those years. The Lord would keep His promises, but that did not mean all would be as Caleb had hoped.

Canaan was a land of mountains and valleys, pasturelands and rippling streams. Blossoms scented the air and hummed with the bees that made honey, as cattle and sheep and goats on a thousand hills grazed and grew fat, providing milk and meat in plenty. The olive trees were loaded with their fruit, as were the apricot, pomegranate, and palm trees. Grapevines spread plentifully across the ground, bearing clusters enough to feed an entire family. The land of milk and honey!

Everything the Lord had said came true. The richness of Canaan made

Caleb's head spin with dreams and longings he knew he must not dwell upon, for the Lord had not released him from his call to stand at Joshua's side. He must continue to wage war against the idol worshipers who had polluted the paradise God had created.

He must not question.

But sometimes the ache in his heart seemed past enduring. *Lord, Lord, help me!*

"The Lord will keep His promise, Caleb."

"He already has. The Lord promised that I would enter Canaan. And He has kept that promise." He looked away so that Joshua would not see the moisture growing in his eyes. Dropping his chin, he cleared his throat softly and waited a moment more before he could trust his voice. "God did not say I would return to farming."

FIVE

"When do we get *our* land, Father? How long do we have to fight and place others first before we get our own inheritance?"

Caleb had struggled with these same questions over the past year. It wouldn't do to join in his sons' yearning. Joshua had not released him yet. "Our opportunity will come."

"*When?*"

"When Joshua says it is time."

"Joshua will never say it's time, Father. He needs you!"

"Do not speak as a fool. Joshua doesn't *need* me. The Lord is with him."

"He will never release you, Father. Not until you ask him to let you go."

Was that what they thought? "Joshua and I stood together against the unfaithful generation. We stand together now. He speaks for the Lord." Frowning, he watched his son Hur pour himself another cup of wine. Perhaps it was too much wine that roused their impatience this day. "My sons . . ." Caleb spoke gently, hoping to snuff out the sparks that could so easily take flame. "We may be twelve tribes, but remember, we are all sons of Jacob. We must work together to take the land. Together, we are strong in the Lord. Divided, we weaken."

"Yes." A young voice spoke boldly. "We must wait upon the Lord."

"Hush, Hebron!" Jesher glowered. "Who are you to remind us of the Lord?"

Hebron's face reddened, but he was wise enough not to pursue the argument. Caleb studied his young grandson. At least one among these young lions had a heart for God. "Hebron speaks wisely."

"Hebron speaks as a boy with his whole life ahead of him." Jesher's eyes flashed. "What of you, Father?"

"Ah. So you cry out for my sake?" He mocked them. "Is it a cave you hope to claim? A place to put my bones?"

"We have waited long enough!" The others called out agreement.

"Manasseh, the Reubenites, and the Gadites haven't cleared their land of the enemy. When they do—"

"When they do?" Mesha rose, impatient. "They never will."

Caleb's face went hot. "Do not speak ill of your brothers." As each year passed, his own impatience grew. He did not need his sons to fan the blaze of sin.

"I speak the truth, Father, and well you know it."

His other sons joined in the argument. "Those tribes are not eager to aid us."

"They gave their word," Caleb reminded them in a hard voice. "And God will hold them to it."

"They long to return to their flocks and herds on the east side of the Jordan."

"If Moses hadn't made them take an oath, they wouldn't be helping us now. And they took that oath because they knew they'd all die if they didn't."

"They're half-minded, looking east rather than fully committed to the battle before us."

"Judah is like a lion, and you are the greatest lion of all, Father. Why must we be the last tribe to receive an inheritance?"

"*Enough!*" His sons fell silent before his anger. Caleb clenched his teeth, and breathed out slowly before speaking again. "You call me a lion, and so I must rule this pride. *Listen. All of you!*" He waited for their full attention and spoke slowly, fervently. "We must encourage the others to fulfill the Word of the Lord. We must clear the land of every pagan. If we fail in this, the Canaanites, Amorites, Hittites, and all the rest will be stumbling blocks for generations to come!"

"We will drive them from our land, Father. We will kill them!"

"It is these other tribes who do not seem intent on getting the work done." Mesha leaned toward Caleb, eyes hot. "If we wait, we will have nothing!"

Caleb grabbed Mesha by the throat. Mesha grabbed his wrist, but could not break free. Caleb dug his fingers in until Mesha's eyes rolled back, then let him go. Mesha rasped, coughed.

"If you ever speak rebellion against the Lord again, I'll kill you." Caleb turned his face from Mesha and looked at each of his sons, one at a time. "Don't make the mistake of thinking I'll spare my own household!"

There was silence in the tent. No one moved. Not even the women standing by, ready to serve.

Shobab, ever the peacemaker, spread his hands in a conciliatory gesture. "We ask only that you pray about it, Father. Your heart is pure before the Lord."

"Pure?" Caleb sneered. "No man has a pure heart." Not even Joshua could boast such a thing. Caleb exhaled slowly. They were so quick to battle. Should any man take pleasure in shedding the blood of an enemy? No! Did God take pleasure in killing? Never! Caleb could not help wondering if there would come another day when Israel would be an enemy of God and the judgment would come upon them. These sons of his had only been in the Promised Land four years, and already the bones left in the wilderness were forgotten.

I will not forget, Lord!

He would not allow himself to believe he was impervious to sin, that it could not draw him into deceit and bring him down as it had brought down other men better than he. Moses, for one.

"I have prayed, Shobab. I continue to pray. I see what you all see, and long for our land as much as—if not more than—you do. But we *must* wait upon the Lord! We *must* do all according to God's plan and not our own. If we go after what we want now, we are even less than these brothers you speak against. Without the Lord on our side, we have no hope or future."

Caleb felt compassion within his anger. Some of these sons were now older than he had been when he first set foot in Canaan forty-four years ago. They saw the land as he had then, a fulfillment of God's promise, a place of milk and honey. But it was also a place that ran deep with the corruption of the people who had dwelt upon it. The land must be cleansed first, and then it would become what God meant it to be: a land and people ruled by the God of heaven and earth. And all the nations of the earth would see the difference between His ways and those of men.

These sons, so much like him, thought only of land and houses, a place to rest. Surely God's plan was greater than to sit beneath an olive tree and enjoy the fruit of the land. Caleb was convinced God's plan was greater than any man could imagine. Judah was like a pride of lions. And Caleb must be the strongest lion among them. He must do battle against them for their sake.

"I did not wander for forty years in the wilderness and oversee your training so that we would become like a pack of wolves, thinking only of ourselves!" Caleb raised his fist. "We shall lead the other tribes as God bids us lead them. Let them see Judah wait. Let them see Judah fight so that others might claim their inheritance first."

Reaching out, he rested his hand gently on Mesha's shoulder. "Let them see this pride of lions show humility."

✦   ✦   ✦

Caleb dreamed again of the hill country. Hunkering down, he took a handful of soil and rubbed it between his fingers, letting it sift and drop. Above him was Kiriath-arba with its high gates and fierce warriors.

Let me have them, Lord. Let me vanquish them.

Go, My servant. Take the land.

Startled awake, Caleb sat up. His heart drummed. A strange prickling sensation made every hair on his body stand up. "Lord," he whispered. "So be it." He stood, dressed, and called for his servant. "Rouse my sons and tell them to gather Judah."

The men came and stood waiting for his instructions. "We go to Gilgal." He did not have to say more. The men cheered.

Caleb led the sons of Judah up the hill. One of the men standing before Joshua's tent ducked inside. Joshua came out. He moved toward Caleb, and clasped arms with him. He looked past him to the men and then released Caleb. "Speak, my friend. Why have you come?"

"Remember what the Lord said to Moses, the man of God, about you and me when we were at Kadesh-barnea. I was forty years old when Moses, the servant of the Lord, sent me from Kadesh-barnea to explore the land of Canaan. I returned and gave from my heart a good report, but my brothers who went with me frightened the people and discouraged them from entering the Promised Land. For my part, I followed the Lord my God completely. So that day Moses promised me, 'The land of Canaan on which you were just walking will be your special possession and that of your descendants forever, because you wholeheartedly followed the Lord my God.'"

Joshua nodded gravely. "I remember well."

Caleb, too, remembered. The memories came with a rush of sorrow. They had been bound together because of their faith, two men against a nation. Had God not stood as a wall between them and the sons of Israel, he and Joshua would have been stoned to death. He remembered the forty days of traveling with Joshua, how they had entered the towns and pretended to be traders, how they had talked to the people of the land, telling them of the plagues of Egypt, the Red Sea opening, the cloud and pillar of fire that sheltered them. They had given warning. None had listened.

Joshua had been a young man then, untried, eager to serve Moses, never ambitious for the position God would give him. When it had come and Moses had laid his hands upon Joshua's shoulders and the burden of the people with it, Caleb had seen the fear in his eyes and wondered at God's choice. But God had been faithful. God had molded Joshua into the leader He had intended him to be. And God had brought them into the land He had promised them.

It struck Caleb's heart how much he would miss this man so many years younger than he. They had stood together over the past forty-five years. Now, they must separate and take possession of the land God had given each of them. They must wipe Canaan clean, build homes, establish their sons. They could no longer sit together and talk or walk through the camps after evening sacrifices. Time was a cruel master. Still, they would see one another when the tribes came together for Passover at the place the Lord would establish. Surely their friendship would stand despite the distance.

O Lord, watch over and protect Joshua. Keep him strong of heart, mind, soul, and body.

Israel's captain had aged in the past five years. How much, troubled Caleb. But he could not turn away from what the Lord had called him to do: Take the hill country.

"Now, as you can see, the Lord has kept me alive and well as He promised for all these forty-five years since Moses made this promise—even while Israel wandered in the wilderness. Today I am eighty-five years old. I am as strong now as I was when Moses sent me on that journey, and I can still travel and fight as well as I could then. So I'm asking you to give me the hill country that the Lord promised me. You will remember that as scouts we found the Anakites living there in great, walled cities. But if the Lord is with me, I will drive them out of the land, just as the Lord said."

Moisture filled Joshua's eyes. They both had known this day would come. It had to come. Joshua nodded solemnly. "Kiriath-arba is yours, Caleb."

Caleb's heart quickened with joy.

Joshua grasped Caleb's arm and turned him to face the sons of Judah. He raised his voice so that all could hear. "Kiriath-arba belongs to Caleb!"

Caleb's sons rejoiced, as did the others. They didn't understand that they'd face the greatest test of their lives, but the Lord would be with them. The Lord would shine His face upon them and give them victory, if only they stood firm in their faith. For without the Lord, they wouldn't be able to stand against those who dwelt in Kiriath-arba.

Joshua clasped Caleb's hand in a hard grip. "That place has always been yours, and so it always shall be."

It had been Kiriath-arba who had set fear in the hearts of the other ten spies and made them feel like grasshoppers.

Kiriath-arba, the city inhabited by giants.

+   +   +

"For the Lord!" Caleb raised his sword and Mesha blew the shofar. Caleb and his sons led their warriors against the Anakites, who, brash and arrogant, had mocked the Lord God of Israel and come out against Judah.

"For the Lord!" Caleb felt the strength flow into him even as the words burst from his lips. He ran with the strength of youth, feeling he could soar on eagle's wings to the top of those hills. His sword rang as it blocked an Anakite's swing. Turning, Caleb drove his shoulder hard into the man's stomach, sending him back just enough that he could drive his sword up beneath the chest armor, straight into his heart. Caleb yanked his sword

free as the man crumpled. Stepping over him, he shouted the battle cry again and kept going.

The cave of Machpelah would no longer be in the possession of idol worshipers and blasphemers. He struck down two more Anakites as they came at him. The burial place of Abraham, Isaac, Jacob, and their wives would once more be held by Hebrews! He hacked into an Anakite's thigh, tumbling him, cleaving his skull as he tried to rise.

The hillsides reverberated with the cry, "For the Lord!" Caleb and his sons and the men of Judah surged up the hill, driving into the Anakites. The warriors who had once made Israel quake and refuse to enter the Promised Land melted in fear and tried to run. Caleb cried out to his sons. "Don't let them escape the judgment of the Lord!" The Anakites were pursued and cut down until the four hills on which the city stood were strewn with the dead.

Arba, the king of Kiriath-arba, was hedged in. One by one, the Anakite warriors fell.

"The king," Mesha shouted. "We have the king!"

Caleb came at a run, bursting through the lines. "*There is no king but the Lord our God!*" He brushed his son aside.

Mesha tried to block him. "What are you going to do?"

Caleb saw the fear in his son's eyes. "I'm going to kill him."

"We'll do it, Father."

"Stand aside."

Cornered, Arba glared, teeth bared. He held his mighty sword in huge hands, swinging it back and forth, spitting insults and hissing blasphemies.

Caleb strode toward him. "*Lord, give me strength!*" At his cry, his sons lowered their swords. The men of Judah held their ground and watched.

"Come to me." Arba jerked his chin up. "Come to me, you little red dog."

And Caleb came in the strength of the Lord. With one swing, he severed Arba's sword arm. With the second, he sliced along the base of Arba's chest armor so the Anakite's innards spilled out. As Arba fell to his knees, Caleb swung one last time, and sent the enemy of God into the dust.

"Cleanse the city!"

The men of Judah poured through the gates, killing every citizen, from the oldest to the youngest. They broke down the pagan altars and burned them. Household gods were put through fire, melting down the gold so the images were destroyed. The best of everything was then set aside to be delivered to Joshua for the Lord's treasury.

Caleb stood on the highest of the four hills and surveyed the land the Lord had given him. This ground on which he stood was rich in history. During his first visit, he had heard that Kiriath-arba was the oldest city in the hill country, an ancient dwelling place for Canaanite royalty, founded seven years before Tanis in Egypt. Somewhere nearby was the cave of Machpelah that served as the burial place for Abraham, who had been called out of Ur by the Lord. With him were buried his wife, Sarah, who had born the son of promise, Isaac, who married Rebekah and fathered Jacob, who had twelve sons and came to be known as Israel—one who contends with God.

Heart full, Caleb raised his hands to the Lord like a child asking to be lifted up. The strength that had pulsed through him for the battle had waned, leaving in its wake gratitude and praise.

"This place shall no longer be called Kiriath-arba." He thought of Abraham, first in faith, and knew the name it should bear. "It shall be called *beloved of God*."

Hebron. Like his grandson.

+   +   +

"You look well, my friend."

Caleb heard the tremor in Joshua's voice and could say nothing. He grasped his arms. They kissed both cheeks in greeting. Joshua did not look well. Caleb stood to one side. Joshua reached out, gesturing for him to remain close at his side as he always had.

The other elders, leaders, judges, and officials presented themselves. Joshua had summoned all Israel to Shechem, where Joseph's bones had been buried in the tract of land Jacob had bought from the sons of Hamor, the father of Shechem.

As Caleb watched, unease filled him. Perhaps he should have paid closer attention to what was happening with the other tribes. Since gaining permission to take the hill country, he had concentrated on nothing else. With Hebron now in his hands, he had made plans to put his hand to the plow again and sow crops. Surely it was time.

"The Lord has given us rest from all our enemies." Joshua spread his hands. "I am an old man now."

A faint rumbling rose from the men. Caleb frowned, studying Joshua's face. He seemed distressed, more distressed than he had seen him since the night he had fully realized God had chosen him to lead the people. Caleb turned to the others. "Be quiet. Joshua has called us here on matters of great importance."

Joshua nodded solemnly. "You have seen everything the Lord your God has done for you during my lifetime. The Lord your God has fought for you against your enemies."

As Joshua continued, speaking slowly, with great deliberation, Caleb felt the impatience in those around him. He could almost hear their thoughts: *Why is Joshua telling us the same things he has told us countless times before?*

"So be strong! Be very careful to follow all the instructions written in the Book of the Law of Moses." Joshua reminded them once again of how God had brought them into the land He had promised them, driven out the enemies before them, how it had not been their swords and bows, but God's power, that had given them the land in which they now lived, eating from vineyards and olive groves they did not plant.

"Every promise of the Lord your God has come true. Not a single one has failed!"

When Joshua looked at him, Caleb was caught by the sorrow he saw in his friend's eyes. There was a deeper purpose for this gathering, a solemn assembly. "I am old," Joshua had said. Caleb had smiled at that. For he was older still.

"But as surely as the Lord your God has given you the good things He promised, He will also bring disaster on you if you disobey Him. He will completely wipe you out from this good land He has given you. If you break the covenant of the Lord your God by worshiping and serving other gods, His anger will burn against you."

Caleb closed his eyes and bowed his head. *Have we sinned, Lord? Is that why You give this warning? Are there some among us who are already turning away?*

"So honor the Lord and serve Him wholeheartedly. Put away forever the idols your ancestors worshiped when they lived beyond the Euphrates River and in Egypt. Serve the Lord alone." Joshua's mouth twisted in derision. "But if you are unwilling to serve the Lord, then choose today whom you will serve. Would you prefer the gods your ancestors served beyond the Euphrates? Or will it be the gods of the Amorites in whose land you now live?" His mouth softened and he looked at Caleb again, eyes shining. "But as for me and my family, we will serve the Lord."

"We would never forsake the Lord and worship other gods!"

The others joined in Caleb's answer.

Hebron rose. "For the Lord our God is the one who rescued us and our ancestors from slavery in the land of Egypt."

"He performed mighty miracles before our very eyes!"

"As we traveled through the wilderness among our enemies, He preserved us."

"It was the Lord who drove out the Amorites . . ."

". . . and the other nations living here in the land."

Caleb held out his hands. "So we, too, will serve the Lord, for He alone is our God." *May the Lord hear our words and hold us to them. And may Joshua be comforted.* He had never seen Joshua so grim, so tired, so *old*.

"You are not able to serve the Lord," Joshua continued, "for He is a holy and jealous God. He will not forgive your rebellion and sins."

"No!"

"If you forsake the Lord and serve other gods, He will turn against you and destroy you, even though He has been so good to you."

"No!" Caleb cried out in anguish. "We are determined to serve the Lord!"

"You are accountable for this decision." Joshua spoke in a quiet, fierce voice. "You have chosen to serve the Lord."

"Yes!" the men cried out. "We are accountable!"

"All right, then—" Joshua clenched his hands—"destroy the idols among you, and turn your hearts to the Lord, the God of Israel."

Shock ran through Caleb. *Idols among us?* He glanced around. He saw men lower their eyes, others pale. He thought of Achan and how easy it would be for someone to hide an idol among his possessions. He turned back with a fierce anger. If he had to search every household himself, he would do so.

The people heard the message of the Lord and made a covenant there at Shechem. Joshua drew up for them the decrees and laws so that no one could say they did not know what God required of them. Everything was recorded carefully in the Book of the Law of God. Joshua took a large stone and set it up there under the oak near where the Ark of the Covenant rested. "This stone has heard everything the Lord said to us. It will be a witness to testify against you if you go back on your word to God." Joshua sent the people away, each to his own inheritance.

+ + +

Caleb lingered. It had been years since he had walked with Joshua. Their steps were slower now, more deliberate. Though their bodies were weakening, their friendship remained strong.

"I am filled with sorrow over the people, Caleb."

"That they will lose faith?"

"Yes. And resolve."

"We have given our vow, Joshua."

Joshua let out his breath and shook his head. He smiled sadly. "Not all men keep their vows as you do, my friend."

"The Lord will hold them to it."

"Yes, and they will suffer."

Troubled, Caleb paused. "Let an old man rest."

Joshua stood on a knoll overlooking the fertile lands around Shechem. "I feel the seeds of rebellion growing."

"Where? We will uproot them!"

"The seeds are in the heart of every man." He gripped his garment in a tight fist. "How do we change that, Caleb?"

"We have the Law, Joshua. That's why God gave it to us."

"Is it?"

"Isn't it?" Caleb wanted to shake Joshua out of his grim reverie. "The Law is as solid as the stones on which God carved it. It is the Law God has given us that will hold us together."

"Or drive us apart. All men are not as passionate about doing right as you are, Caleb. Most are eager to live in peace, even if that means compromise." Joshua spoke firmly, not as an old man whining over past days and faint worries of the future.

"What do you want me to do, Joshua? Speak openly."

"I want you to do what you have always done. Have faith in the Lord. Stand firm. Speak out when you see men weaken." He gripped Caleb's arm. "*Keep watch!* We are still at war, Caleb, though the enemy appears vanquished. We are at war and retreat is impossible."

+ + +

Sitting in the shade of his olive tree, Caleb spotted a man running up the road. He felt a deep stirring. Closing his eyes, he bowed his head.

"Where is Caleb?" a breathless voice shouted. "*Caleb!* I must speak with Caleb!"

Sighing, Caleb rose. "I'm here."

The young man ran up the hill to him. Caleb knew him well though the years had altered him. "Ephraim, aren't you?"

"Ephraim's son, Hirah."

"I remember when your father was a boy. He followed Joshua around like a pet lamb. We——"

"Joshua is dead!"

Caleb fell silent. He couldn't take it in, didn't want to, closed his ears to it. No, not Joshua. Joshua was fifteen years younger than he. Joshua was God's anointed leader. Joshua!

"Joshua is dead." The boy dropped to his knees, hunched over, and wept.

Anguish filled Caleb and he uttered a loud cry, then tore his garments.

Oh, Lord, my friend, my friend! What will happen to Israel now? Who will lead these stubborn people? Who, Lord?

Even as the thoughts came to him, shame filled him. Who else but the Lord had led them? Who else but God Himself could be king over such a nation as Israel?

Forgive me, Lord. After all these years, I should know better than to ask such questions. Forgive me. Help me stand firm.

Caleb put his hand on the boy's head. "Rise up, Hirah. Tell me everything."

Joshua had been buried at Timnath-serah in the hill country of Ephraim north of Mount Gaash. The boy bore other grievous news. Eleazar, son of Moses' brother, Aaron, was ailing at Gibeah.

Caleb took Hirah to his home and gave him food and drink. "How have the tribes taken the news?"

"With confusion. No one knows what to do now that Joshua is dead."

Caleb scowled. "We do what the Lord has told us to do. We cleanse the land of idol worshipers and keep our covenant with Him." It had not been that many years since they had made the covenant with Joshua at Shechem. Had they forgotten everything he had said to them already?

"We are preparing to travel to Shechem for Passover. The Lord will make His will known to us. Go now, in peace."

Caleb's sons made preparations for the journey, including in the provisions plunder they had collected from the hill country villages they had conquered. Caleb wondered if they were more interested in trade than in worship. When they arrived, there was sorrow mixed with jubilation. Joshua and Eleazer were well remembered, but as the council met and men talked, Caleb realized now much work there was yet to do. Why had it been so long left undone? The tribes had received their inheritances, and still they failed to drive all the Canaanites from their land. Worse, the tribal elders were in confusion over Joshua's death.

"Who will be the first to go out and fight for us against the Canaanites?"

"How do we decide?"

What manner of men were they? When had *they* ever decided anything?

At least Phinehas, son of Eleazar, high priest of Israel, remembered. "The Lord decides!"

Lots were cast and God's answer came swiftly.

"Judah." Phinehas stood. "Judah is to go and fight. The Lord has given the land into their hands."

Once, Caleb would have been exultant. Now, he stood silent, grim with resolve while his sons and the men of Judah shouted their response. Too many in Israel lacked the faith to take and hold their land and keep it purified. Did they think Judah could do for them what God had told them they must do for themselves? Some had allowed the pagans to remain pocketed in fertile valleys or nestled in ravines. The Lord had said these idol worshipers would be like thorns in Israel's side if allowed to remain. *None* must remain.

His sons came to him. "We have made an alliance with our Simeonite brothers. If they will come up into the territory allotted to us to fight against the Canaanites, we will in turn go with them into theirs."

"Did you inquire of the Lord about this alliance?"

"They are our brothers, Father. Hasn't the Lord said from the beginning that we are to come alongside one another? Didn't you say—"

"Has every man among you forgotten what happened when we did not inquire of the Lord over the Gibeonites?"

"These are our brothers!" Mesha said.

Caleb raged. "And the Lord said *Judah* is to go! The Lord has given the land into *Judah's* hand."

They all talked at once, rationalizing and justifying their decision.

"Enough." They might as well have kicked Caleb in the stomach. Simeon! These brothers used their swords as implements of violence. Even Jacob had said not to enter into their council or be united in their assemblies, for they were cursed because of their anger and cruelty. As was Levi. The Lord had dispersed the Levites among the tribes as priests, but what of the Simeonites? How would the Lord disperse them? And what trouble would arise if Judah aligned with them?

"When will you learn we must heed the Word of the Lord and follow Him only?"

When men made their own plans, disaster was sure to follow.

+   +   +

Judah attacked the Canaanites at Bezek and the Lord was with them. They struck down hundreds, then thousands.

Bloodied by those he had cut down, Caleb spotted the king of Bezek with his circlet of gold. "There is Adoni-bezek." He hacked his way toward the Canaanite king, and saw the man flee the raging battle. "Don't let him escape!"

Some of the men of Judah went in pursuit. Caleb did not leave the battlefield, but roused the men of Judah and Simeon to destroy the enemies of God. Ten thousand were cut down before they could scatter in retreat. When Caleb saw Adoni-bezek, he was appalled. The man's thumbs and big toes had been chopped off. The conquered king stumbled and fell, sobbing in agony.

Caleb raged. "What have you done?"

Shelumiel, leader of the Simeonites, spoke, head high, chin jutting. "What he deserves! We have done to him what he did to the seventy kings who ate scraps under his table."

Moaning in the dust, Adoni-bezek cried out, "God has paid me back."

"Kill him," Caleb ordered. Surely there was more mercy in killing him outright than torturing and mutilating him.

"We will kill him!" Shelumiel looped a rope around the Canaanite's neck. "When we're ready." The men of Simeon laughed at the man's plight. He was led up the mountain. When he fell, they dragged him. He was given only enough water to keep him alive. When the army arrived before the city of Jerusalem, Adoni-bezek was brought up before the men and stood before the walls. Shelumiel executed him there so the Jebusites could witness his death.

Furious, Caleb ordered them to leave. "Go home. Go back to your own land!" He wanted no part of these men.

"What are you talking about? We've come to help you. You can't destroy these people without us."

"The Lord said *Judah* was to go up. Not Simeon! Would you rebel against the Lord with whom you just renewed a covenant?" Caleb looked at Adoni-bezek's body. The Lord had said to kill the Canaanites, not torture them. "Go south and fight for your land."

"You made an alliance to help us!"

"We will help you *after* we have taken Jerusalem."

The Simeonites departed, but his sons were not pleased. "How are we going to deal with the Jebusites without more men?"

Caleb was angrier with the men of Judah than with the Simeonites. "We do not *need* more men. The Lord is our strength. Trust in *Him*. Do not put your faith in men. Our victory does not depend on the number of warriors, or how many horses or chariots, *but on the power of the God who delivered us from Egypt!*"

Rallied, the men cried out to the Lord to give them help. But Caleb wondered then what the future held.

Joshua had been right in speaking to Israel that last time in Shechem. Joshua had seen the way things were going.

And now, Caleb feared he saw as well.

+   +   +

The gates were breached, the walls scaled, the men on the battlements killed. Screams rent the air, carrying across the narrow valley in which a grove of olives grew. Every man, woman, and child who had not fled before the onslaught of Judah died within the walls. "Burn it!" Caleb commanded, and men ran with torches, setting houses, altars, and piles of wooden household gods on fire.

The army of Judah headed south and joined forces with Simeon. They fought against and defeated the Canaanites. Simeonites settled in Beersheba, Hormah, and Arad.

Judah turned north once again, fighting against the Canaanites who had come back into the hill country during their absence. Judah took the Negev and the western hills, and returned to Hebron in force, destroying the remnant of Anak who attempted to reclaim it.

"They keep coming back!"

"They're like a plague of locusts!"

Judah's army drove out the Canaanites from the hill country, killing every one of them they found. Only Caleb sent his men in pursuit of those who escaped. "The Lord was clear. If you don't finish them, they will keep coming back. Now, go after them and destroy them completely."

They obeyed until the winter months and then returned to their homes. They were tired of fighting. They wanted to celebrate their victories and tell tales of their great feats. They praised the Lord, too, but mostly they talked of what they had accomplished over the years of fighting. Areas remained unconquered; enemies hid, plotted, and spread in the recesses of the hill country.

"We will finish the work when spring comes."

When spring came, the people of Judah planted crops.

"Next year we will finish the job."

And with each year sin grew.

+   +   +

Triumph gave way to complacency.

The Benjamites failed to hold Jerusalem. The Jebusites poured back into the city and the Benjamites could not dislodge them.

The tribe of Manasseh chose not to drive out the people of Beth-shan or Taanach or Dor or Ibleam or Megiddo nor the surrounding settlements. Instead, they made the Canaanites forced labor.

The tribe of Ephraim did not succeed in driving out the Canaanites living in Gezer.

The tribe of Zebulun allowed the Canaanites to live in Kitron and Nahalol. They did not follow the example of Manasseh, but made alliances with the people of the land and began adopting their ways.

The tribe of Asher did not drive out those living in Acco, Sidon, Ahlab, Aczib or Helbah, or in Aphek or Rehob. Asher dwelt among the people of the land.

The tribe of Naphtali left the inhabitants in Beth-shemesh and Beth-anath living in peace, and lived among them.

+   +   +

"We can't drive them from the plains, Father."

"You must rely upon the Lord."

"We have prayed."

"We have fasted."

"We have done everything we can think to do. And we cannot drive them out."

"They have iron chariots, Father."

"At least, we hold the hill country. We hold Hebron securely. That was our own inheritance."

"And for how long will we hold it if we allow God's enemies to live?"

Caleb hung his head in shame. "We have failed to do what the Lord told us to do."

"We have fought!"

"Some have died."

"The Lord is not protecting us! He is far from us!"

"Because we have sinned!" Caleb cried out in anger. "Because you lack the faith to follow the Lord."

"How have we sinned, Father? Tell us. We have worshiped the Lord just as you have."

"I have scars to show for my faith, Father! And so do countless others. I have grandchildren. I want to have time to enjoy my inheritance. Don't you?"

"We don't need the plains, Father. We have enough land here in the hill country."

Caleb could not believe what he was hearing. "We will be at war until the enemies of God are all dead like the generation who perished in the wilderness. You cannot give up. You must arm yourselves."

"We are tired of fighting!"

"We can do no more in the plains!"

"And what of Hebron?"

Mesha gazed at him, defeated. "Don't you remember, Father? Hebron no longer belongs to Judah. Joshua and the others gave it to the Levites as a city of refuge. The Kohathite clan can take care of themselves."

"Naked we come into this world, Mesha. Naked we go out of it." Caleb had been surprised when Joshua named Hebron as a city of refuge, but Joshua had done only what the Lord had told him to. Caleb had known then that he could think upon it in either of two ways: resentment, allowing bitterness and envy to grow and spread their killing vines . . . or gratitude. He chose to be thankful that God had wanted Hebron, Caleb's city, to be counted as a city of refuge.

Unfortunately, not all his sons had been able to accept the loss, or been completely content living in the surrounding villages.

"Hebron was never ours, my sons. God gave it to us, and we have given it back to Him."

"It was to be your inheritance forever, Father."

"Some of our men died in taking that city from the Anakites. It was *our* blood that was shed for that city."

"The Lord was with us."

They all talked at once.

Mesha spoke for all. "We will rest for a while, and if they attempt to come up into the hill country, then we will fight again."

Wine flowed freely, made from grapes that came from vines they did not plant, vines the Lord had given them.

Shobab sighed. "I've yet to plow a field."

Fields the Lord had given them.

"Or plant crops," Mareshah agreed.

Caleb thought of the grain that had been harvested the first years they had come into the Promised Land. The Lord had brought them in when there was a bounty of food, theirs for the taking.

"Will you know how to plant crops?" one joked.

"I can learn."

Would they ever learn what was important?

"I have work to do on my house."

What about the work God had given them to do?

"It's time for my son Hebron to take a wife."

"I have a daughter he can marry."

The men, young and old, laughed and talked on around Caleb. He rose, knowing they would take little notice of him now. They were too busy making plans for themselves. He went outside and raised his head.

Oh, God, forgive them. They know not what they do.

SIX

Caleb hobbled toward a flat stone near an ancient olive tree where he often sat overlooking the orchard and vineyard. "Come, my sons. Come. We must make plans to secure the hill country. We cannot stop the advance."

"We can't now, Father." They raised their hoes in a gesture of solidarity. "We have work to do."

Caleb's mouth tightened. He and his sons had driven out the three Anakites—Sheshai, Ahiman, and Talmai—from Hebron, but when they advanced upon Kiriath-sepher, Caleb had been too weary to go with them and they had left the work undone. Thus, the Canaanites had trickled back in like a leak in a roof. His sons, complacent, had forgotten the warnings of the Lord.

He heard his sons' grumbling. *Doesn't he ever get tired of fighting? War, war. We've had enough of war. It's time to enjoy the land we've taken. We will hold what we have.*

Oh, they knew what he was going to say. Hadn't they heard everything a hundred times before? They wanted to plow and plant seed, to enjoy the land they had taken. So what if a few Canaanites came back. *Peace, we want peace!* But they would have none. God had warned them. They just wouldn't listen.

Leaning on his walking stick, Caleb felt defeated. The spirit within him still rose to the challenge, but his body had given out. And there was no one to rally these sons of his, no one to lead them. Ever since they had reconquered Hebron, only to find it given to the Levites as a city of refuge, they had ceased listening to him.

Mesha's resentment grew with each year he tilled the soil. Caleb grew weary of hearing the same complaints over and over again. "We fought for five years to settle the tribes. And then, our turn came and we had to take the land by ourselves! And then what happens? The biggest and best city we have is handed over to the Levites and we get the surrounding villages!"

Patiently, Caleb would explain again. "Hebron is the best of what we have. And the Lord gave it to us. Is it not right that we give God the best? Do you think we could have taken Hebron by ourselves? God gave it to us. He is the rightful owner! You cannot offer a village as a city of refuge."

Still their whining continued. "A village would have sufficed!"

"We pay in blood and the Levites reap the benefits!"

What was wrong with these sons of his? Had they set their hearts against the Lord their God? Had they forgotten already the commandments by which they were to live?

Ultimately, they gave up Hebron, then concentrated on claiming the surrounding villages and pasturelands. They drove the Canaanites out, killing every one of them that did not flee the hill country. No more was said about Hebron, but Caleb saw how they looked toward it. Their resentment spread like mildew, seeping into the cracks and walls of the houses in which they now lived, houses they had not built, but God had given them. It seemed against their very nature to be grateful for the gifts God had given them.

As the months and years wore on, Caleb's sons turned their strength and thoughts to the orchards and vineyards, flocks and herds. They prospered, but were not content. They didn't listen to their father as they had when they were boys. They no longer hung upon his every word, nor followed his instructions, nor strove to please him and, in doing so, please God.

Often, Caleb thought back with strange longing to those hard years of wandering in the desert. The people had learned to rely upon the Lord for everything—for food, for water, for shelter, and for protection from enemies who watched and waited. Now that they had conquered the Promised Land and settled in it, life had become easier. The Israelites had relaxed their vigil, dozed in the sunshine, forgotten that faith was more work than tilling the ground.

Like so many others in Israel, his sons were doing whatever was right in their own eyes. And Caleb grieved over it, trying each day to draw them back to what they had been when times were harder. But they did not want to come or listen. Not anymore. It was by God's grace that they continued to prosper, but they had been warned when the blessings of steadfast faith and cursings of rebellion had been read to them from Mount Gerizim and Mount Ebal. Oh, they kept the Sabbaths, but without joy. What God had given them now ruled their days and nights.

When Caleb prayed with them, he felt their impatience. *Get it done and said, Father, and let us be about our work!* He could almost hear their thoughts. *Must we listen to another rambling prayer of praise from this old man?*

Oh, they loved him. He had no doubt of that. They saw to his every need and made sure he was pampered and petted. But they thought his time was over and theirs had begun. They thought he couldn't teach them anything they didn't already know. They thought times were different now.

All true, but some things must stay the same. And it was this he tried to tell them. And it was this they refused to hear.

The slippage had already begun, like a few pebbles trickling down a hillside with a boulder now and then. The people neglected the things the Lord had told them to do. The Canaanites had not been driven from every valley in the region. A few had returned, tentative at first, with words of peace and offerings of friendship. The men of Israel were too busy enjoying the milk and honey of the land God had given them to see the danger in allowing God's enemies to return and settle in small encampments. The Canaanites vowing peace gnawed like termites at the foundations God had laid.

How could his sons have forgotten what happened at Shittim? Men were easily enticed into Baal worship. *A beautiful young woman beckons, and a foolish man follows like a lamb to the slaughter.*

God demanded that His people live holy lives and not intermingle with those who had corrupted the land. All his sons could see were the healthy vines, the orchards, the houses, the wells of water. They failed to uproot and destroy every enemy of God, and now Canaanites were springing up here and there, like poisonous weeds, and their evil ways with them.

His sons and the other men of Judah had yet to take Kiriath-sepher. The fortified city was still infested with Canaanite vermin.

Caleb's twelve sons and their many sons plowed and planted, tended and harvested, believing their efforts made the difference between prosperity and poverty. And each year, they had to work a little harder.

"It is not by your strength and power that you conquered this land, but by the Spirit of the Lord!" Caleb told them.

"Someone has to plow, Father. Someone has to plant the seed."

"But it is the Lord who waters, my sons. It is the Lord who gives the sunlight and makes things grow."

"Things grew here long before we came. Canaan was a treasure trove *before* we entered it."

Caleb felt his skin prickle with alarm. He had heard that some of his sons were going after other gods. Mesha's words confirmed it. "God made it prosper. He prepared this land for us."

"So you say."

They listened less with each passing year. And like this morning, they prayed the same prayers they prayed every day, and then went off to live life on their own terms.

"Good morning, Father."

Startled from his grim thoughts, he turned. Acsah, his only daughter, the last child of his loins, came to him and slipped her arm into his. She had Maacah's dark eyes and olive skin and his red hair. *Edom,* some called her when they thought his back was turned and he couldn't hear. Had her mother sent her to tend him?

"Do you think I need help to the rock?"

"You have that look again."

Annoyed, he shook off her support and made his way toward his destination. Every joint in his body ached. His legs felt like tree trunks sending roots into the ground. Stooped, he gritted his teeth against the grinding pain and jabbed his walking stick into the ground. One deliberate step at a time.

Acsah strolled at a leisurely pace beside him, her hands clasped behind her back. He glowered at her. "Don't hover like a mother hen!"

"You're in a fine mood this morning."

Because he had fixed his gaze upon her, he stumbled. He caught himself, but not before he had seen her quick movement. His heart thundered in fury. "What would you do? Throw yourself on the ground to cushion my fall?"

"Should I stand by and watch my father dive headfirst into the ground?"

"You have work to do. Go do it."

She looked away and blinked. "I've been to the well."

Women were always too quick to tears. He didn't soften. "There are other things to do besides water the sheep and goats."

Eyes flashing, her chin came up. "Then give *me* the sword and let *me* do it."

He gave a derisive laugh and hobbled on. Maybe if he ignored her, she would go away. He groaned as he eased himself down on the flat boulder.

Lord, I can't get my sons to sit for an hour and listen to me, but this girl digs in like a tick.

Sighing deeply, he hunched in the shade of the ancient olive tree. Acsah sat within the cool circle of shade. He peered at her, still irritated. "It's time you were married." She would scurry off at that. She usually kept her distance for a few days when he mentioned her future.

"There's no one worthy enough to marry me."

"Oh!" He laughed outright at that. "You don't think much of yourself, do you? A half-caste Canaanite whelp."

Her olive skin reddened. She turned her face away.

Caleb clenched his teeth. "It's time you covered your hair."

She looked back at him. "It's time for a lot of things, Father."

"You're not a child anymore. You're—" he frowned—"how old are you?"

She stared at him without answering.

Anger bubbled up inside him. "Don't think my arm isn't long enough to deal with you."

Acsah rose gracefully and sat near enough that he could backhand her. "Anything to make your life easier, Father."

He raised his hand. She didn't draw back. He watched the pulse throb in her throat. Anger or fear? What did it matter? Releasing his breath slowly, he lowered his hand. He ignored her. The silence lengthened, but not comfortably. He cleared his throat; the sound came like a low growl. She raised one brow. He closed his eyes. Maybe if he pretended to nap.

"What were you going to say to my brothers?"

His mouth tightened. He opened one eye. "Ask them. They could tell you word for word what I was going to say. The same things I always say; the same things they always ignore."

"If you were going to tell them about the plagues of Egypt and the wandering in the wilderness, you tell the stories better than they do."

"They are not stories! I lived through those times."

"I wish I had."

He ignored the longing in her voice. "Did your mother tell you to come out and humor me?"

"Do you think I need my mother to command me to sit with you? I love you, Abba!" She looked at him, unblinking, and then bowed her head. "If I heard your stories a thousand times, Father, it would not be enough."

He said nothing and she looked up. He saw the yearning in her dark eyes, the intensity of her interest. Why was it that this girl, daughter of his concubine, had such a passion for God when his sons had so little? Overcome by despair, he cried out bitterly, "Go away. Leave me alone." What use was a girl?

She rose slowly and walked away, shoulders slumped.

Caleb regretted his harshness, but did not call her back.

The day wore on, the same as every other. Everyone had things to occupy their time and their minds. Except Caleb. He sat and waited for time to pass, waited for the sun to cross the sky and dip red-gold, orange-purple into the west. Right now, it was overhead and beating down. He wished for a cooler place, but was too weary to get up and make his way back to the house.

Caleb watched Acsah work with the wives of her brothers and half brothers. She did not seem interested in their conversation. They talked around her. They laughed. Some leaned close and whispered, eyes upon her. Caleb tried not to think about it. He tried not to let it bother him that his daughter was treated like an outsider. Even after all these years, he remembered how he had felt.

When he dozed, he dreamed of Egypt. He stood before his father again, arguing. "This is a God of gods, a Lord of lords. Wherever He leads, I will follow." When he awakened, he felt an ache in his heart so deep he had to breathe around it.

Acsah came with bread and wine. "You haven't eaten since early this morning."

"I'm not hungry."

She left it for him anyway.

After a while, he dipped the bread into the wine. When it was softened, he chewed slowly until it was a sodden mass he could swallow.

Acsah came again, bringing his great-grandchildren with her this time. "Come, come, children. Listen to Abba tell of the plagues of Egypt and the opening of the Red Sea." She sat them around him and took a place herself on the outer edge of the gathering. Gratified, Caleb spoke of the events that had shaped his faith and molded his life. It was not a quick telling, and one by one, the children rose and went away to play, until only Acsah remained.

He gave a weary sigh. "You're the only one who cares to listen."

Her eyes filled. "I wish it were not so."

His sons were returning from the fields, their hoes across their shoulders, hands draped over them. They looked weary, discontent. He looked at Acsah, still waiting, hope in her eyes. "How is it that you alone hang upon every word about the Lord our God?"

"I don't know, Father. Where did your faith come from?"

+   +   +

Acsah's answer remained in Caleb's grieving mind. How had he come by his faith? Why was it he could not instill faith in his sons?

He lay awake upon his cushions all night, thinking. How was it that he alone among all his family members had known there was only one God with power, that all the others were counterfeit? He had grown up with the idols of Egypt, given libations and prayers as did his mother and father and his brothers and their wives. Yet, the moment Moses had returned from Midian, Caleb had known his life would never be the same. He had witnessed the plagues and known without doubt that the God of Moses, the God of Abraham was all-powerful. All the gods of Egypt could not prevail against Him, for they were nothing more than the pathetic conjuring of men's imaginations.

Faith had come to him like a flash of sunlight, a joy in his heart. *Here is a God I can worship! Here is a God I can follow with confidence and rejoicing!*

But faith had not come to his family members in the same way—reason and necessity had drawn them. Crops beaten down by hail and burned by lightning, animals dead from disease, boils making the Egyptians moan in agony, Caleb knew it had been fear that made his family listen at last to his reasoning and follow him to the Hebrew encampment. They'd never shared his excitement or joy at being in the Presence of the cloud or pillar of fire. They'd never stood in wonder and stared at the swirling canopy of light and shadow.

They followed in dread.

They obeyed out of fear.

They gave offerings because the Law required them to do so.

Surely my faith came from You, Lord, and I can't boast in it. It was born in an instant. My eyes and ears were opened. My heart beat as though for the first time. My lungs filled with the air of thanksgiving. I wanted to be counted among Your people. I wanted to live a life that would please You.

Why not my sons? Why only Acsah, a girl, last and least among all my offspring?

He wearied himself asking the questions. Whatever the reason, Acsah believed as strongly as he did. She yearned to be close to God the way he yearned. But instead of encouraging her faith, he had assumed she was patronizing him. He had been irritated at the thought of his concubines and sons humoring him, thinking he was an old man and should have someone to watch over him.

But Acsah's faith was genuine.

Only last year, when they had gone up to Jerusalem to the solemn assembly of Atonement Day, Caleb had watched her gather olive and myrtle branches and palm branches while his sons were off celebrating with their friends.

"Where is Acsah?"

"Am I my sister's keeper?"

Maacah slapped Sheva. "Go and find her. And you, too, Tirhanah." She gestured to her sons.

"She is building a booth," Caleb said.

Maacah had looked at him, perplexed. "Did you send her?"

He could see that his concubine wondered if he had lost his mind. "No. She went of her own accord."

"But why?"

He looked at his sons. "Atonement Day is followed by the Festival of the Booths."

"We haven't lived in booths since Joshua died, Father."

"No one does that anymore."

Caleb roused. "It would be good for you to remember why we wandered in the wilderness for forty years and had to live in booths!"

Into the tense silence that followed, Maacah spoke gravely. "An unmarried girl has no business living outside her father's house." His sons went to bring her back. He remembered how Acsah had fought and then, defeated, had wept.

Now they lived in a garden of God's making, and the wilderness was forgotten. So, too, were the lessons they had learned there.

Caleb knew he must do something before it was too late.

+ + +

I am an old man, Lord, and I cannot fight anymore. My words no longer fire men's blood. The sin in our lives is a greater threat than our enemies! We have not completed the work You set before us. I look around me and see how complacent my sons have become, how complacent the people.

We rebuild towns, but step over the rubble in our lives. We make friends with those who despise Your Name. I don't know what to do. I'm tired, worn down by despair, worn out by age. I can barely rise from my pallet now or eat my food. Servants tend me. But my mind, Lord, my mind still races. My heart still pounds out praises to Your name!

"He's crying again."

Caleb sat with his back resting against cushions propped up to support him. Was he crying? Tears seemed to come without warning these days. His body was feeble. Did they think his mind was as well? He listened to his sons talk around him. He hadn't spoken in days, his thoughts focused on God. Perhaps his silence now would cause them to open their ears when he did decide to speak again. If he did. He would say nothing until the Lord told him what to do. For now, let them wonder. He was beyond explanations, weary of trying to convince them to pursue God's will.

I wait upon You, Lord. Until I take my last breath, I wait upon You. Tell me what I am to do about my sons.

Acsah came near. She rested her hand upon his shoulder and knelt beside him, a bowl of brown muck in her hand. He scowled as he looked at it. The few teeth he had left were worn down and caused him pain. He was reduced to eating finely chopped meat and mashed vegetables. He couldn't even tell what she was offering him.

She placed the bowl in his hands. "Please, Father, eat a little. You need it to keep up your strength."

It would do no good to tell her that he had lost his sense of smell and taste and that to eat this slop tested his will.

"What ails Father?" Hur studied him from across the room.

Moza shrugged. "He's old; that's what ails him." He called to Acsah and held his cup up so she could replenish his wine.

Haran ate a date. "He hardly eats."

"He's not leading an army anymore."

"He hasn't said a word in days."

Acsah poured wine into Caleb's cup. "Perhaps he's tired of speaking and being ignored."

Her older brother Sheber scowled. "Go about your business, girl, and leave the men to theirs."

Caleb clenched his jaw. It wasn't the first time he had heard his sons speak to their sister with such disdain. Even some of his sons' wives treated her like an outsider, a servant at best. And Acsah had more faith than all of them combined.

"Perhaps his mind is going." Sheber did not appear much distressed at the possibility.

"The people still revere him. If his mind is going, we should keep quiet about it and not shame him."

Caleb felt his sons studying him. He didn't raise his head or look at them, but ate slowly with a trembling hand.

"He's praying." Acsah again, quietly, tenderly.

"For seven days straight? No man prays that long."

"Moses was on the mountain forty days and forty nights."

Sheber waved his sister off. "*Moses*. Yes. Our father believes in God, but Father was a warrior, not a prophet."

"God chose him after Joshua—"

"Hush, girl! Go feed the goats." Shaaph gestured. "Go card wool. Get out of our hair."

Caleb heard the clatter of crockery and stomping feet.

"Maybe Acsah is right. Maybe he is praying."

"We're at peace. We're prospering. What is there to pray about now?"

Caleb lost what little appetite he had. Shaking, he leaned forward to put his bowl down.

"You'd better take that from him or he'll spill it all over himself."

Hebron took the bowl and set it aside.

"I've never seen him pray longer than a few hours at one sitting." Tirhanah squinted at his father.

"We should do something about Acsah."

"What about Acsah?"

"We should find her a husband."

"Mesha's youngest daughter is a year younger than our sister, and she's married and has a son. Acsah needs sons."

"She has four brothers. She doesn't need sons."

"Besides, she's needed here."

His sons were silent just long enough for Caleb to know they were looking at him. The heat of anger surged into Caleb's face, but he did keep his silence.

Replete from the sumptuous meal, Sheber leaned back with a belch. "She's content."

Content? How little they knew or cared about their sister.

"Just leave her be. If she wants to get married, she'll say something to Father about it and he can decide what to do about her."

It was easy to see they all assumed he would do nothing because of the convenience of her tender care. He kept his head down, pretending to doze.

Let them think he was a tired old man, hardly able to chew his bread. One by one, his sons rose and went out to whatever work or pleasurable activities they had planned for themselves.

Acsah returned and knelt beside him. She tore off some bread and dipped it into the wine and held the morsel to his lips. "Just a little, Father, please. Don't give up."

He looked into her eyes. The others no longer needed him. They were moving on with their lives, moving ahead without any thought of him. But she was different. She was determined to keep him going. Why? *Oh, Lord, I'm tired. I'm sick at heart. Don't let me live long enough to see my sons all turn away from You. Let me die before that day comes.* Unable to stop the tears, he bent his head and let them come, shoulders heaving.

"God of mercy and strength . . ." Acsah spoke softly, weeping as she prayed fervently. For him. "Give Father back his strength, Lord. We need him. If he lays down his head now, what will become of our people? Who will rise up to shout Your name? Who will . . . ?"

Caleb's tears ceased as he listened to his daughter. His mind opened wide, as though a hand drew aside a curtain so that he could see clearly. Did his sons love him as she did? Did they listen to him with open mind and heart, absorbing the lessons he had to teach as though his words came from the Lord Himself? *Acsah. Sweet Acsah.* A future and a hope lay before him. This girl was more like him than all his sons combined. They caused him endless grief; she lived to please him. She alone stood straight among others who bent with the wind.

"Then give me the sword!" she had cried out to him once.

A sword.

His burden lifted and he let out his breath in a long sigh. "Acsah." Trembling, he rested his hand upon her. "God has answered us."

She raised her head, eyes red and cheeks pale from weeping. Catching her breath, she sat upon her heels, eyes brightened. "What did He say, Father?" Tiny bumps rose on her arms and she leaned toward him, eager to hear.

"I must find you a husband."

She blanched. "No."

"Yes."

Her tears came again, in a storm of anger this time. "Why?" She glared at him. "You made it up. God said no such thing!"

Caleb caught her face between his hands and held her firmly, trembling. "I didn't make it up. You are to marry. Now, tell me who it is to be. Give me the name."

Her eyes went wide. "I don't know."

He opened his heart wide and sent up a prayer like an arrow to heaven. *Who, Lord? Who is to be my daughter's husband?*

Ask her.

If she didn't know the name, she must know other things. But what? What?

"Father, don't upset yourself."

"Hush." He must look wild in his frustration. He released her with a pat on her cheek. "Let an old man think." *Lord, what do I ask? What?* And then it came to him. "What sort of man would you want?"

"I have not thought about it."

"You must have thought about it. Now, tell me."

"I see the sort of men there are, and I want none of them. Why would I want any one of them to be my husband? I would rather die than—"

"Answer the question. What would it take to make you content? to bring you joy. Think!"

She clenched her hands until her knuckles were white. "Someone who loves God above everyone and everything else. Someone who keeps the covenant. Someone who doesn't look away when God's enemies move back into the land God gave us. Someone who hears God when He speaks. A man with a warrior's heart." She glared at him through her tears. "*Someone like my father!*"

He smiled ruefully. "Someone far better than your father, I think. You want a prophet."

"Nothing less." Her eyes were as fierce as a lioness's. "If I have any real choice in the matter."

"Go and fetch me your brothers."

Her defiance withered. "No, Father, please . . ."

"Do you trust me?"

She bit her lip.

He gave a curt laugh. Why *should* she trust him? Had he ever put her interests above his sons'? His eyes had been so fixed upon them that he had neglected to think much about her. But she had gleaned the Word of the Lord. She had taken up hope and held it close, nourishing her soul upon it.

"Father, let me stay with you." Tears slipped down her cheeks. "Let me serve you." She bowed her head.

He tipped her chin. "Acsah, my child. Do you trust *God?*" He already knew the answer, but wanted to hear it from her lips.

"Yes."

"Then trust in Him and go fetch your brothers. God knows the plans He has for you, and it is for your future and *our* hope."

Resigned, she rose to obey.

Caleb lifted his hands to the heavens. *In my distress, I cried out to You, Lord. And You answered.*

A leader would rise because of his daughter. And an army would go out and be victorious.

+ + +

Caleb looked out over the field of faces who had come at his summons. Not all the families of Judah were represented, but that didn't matter. God would have His way. Somewhere among these men was a man God would call to arms. Perhaps he had already sensed God's leading, and been troubled and unsure why. But what lay before Caleb now was certain. The one who listened and acted upon what was said today would be the one God would use to judge Israel.

The men talked among themselves, and Caleb did not have the wind to shout anymore. His sons stood around him, his grandson Hebron giving him support. How would they take what he had to announce? He nudged Hebron. "Call them to order."

"Silence! Let Caleb speak."

The men fell quiet.

Caleb gestured for them to come closer and they did.

"I am an old man and can no longer lead you in battle. Another must rise to take my place."

"What of your sons? What of Mesha? or Hur?"

Caleb held his hand out and they fell silent again.

"Even now, the Lord is preparing one to lead us. Even now—" he looked at the faces of the men gathered close—"one of you . . ." His eyes were not as they once were and his vision was blurred. "I have called you here to remind you of the work yet to be done. Canaanites still inhabit Kiriath-sepher. God told us to take this land and drive the inhabitants out. God's enemies are emboldened by our lack of action. We must finish the work God gave us to do. We did not enter into the land to make peace with God's enemies, but to destroy them!"

Some of the men shouted in agreement, but his sons were not among them. Perhaps the one whom God had called here would renew the vision and quicken the spirit to obey the Lord. *Let it be so, Lord. Let it be so!*

"Father." Hur bent close. "Is that all you wish to say?"

They were so impatient, so eager to be about their own business. They had no time for contemplation.

"No." Caleb had so much more to say, words they had heard so many times before. They were like their fathers before them, slow to obey the Lord, quick to forget Him. If he said what he had said so many times before, they would not listen. *Lord, how do You bear us? It is a wonder You didn't wipe us from the face of the earth after we tested You so many times in the desert!*

Wrath fired his blood, but wisdom made him speak briefly. "The Lord God of Abraham, Isaac, and Jacob gave me the hill country. My sons have claimed their portions and have settled their families upon it. But there is still land to conquer, land God gave me that has not yet been claimed. I give the Negev to my daughter Acsah as her inheritance."

He heard the hiss of the drawn breath of his sons.

"Acsah?"

Caleb raised his voice. "The daughters of Zelophehad stood before Moses and Eleazar and the leaders and the entire congregation, and were given land to possess among their father's brothers. I have many sons. Mesha, my firstborn, has received his double portion. A son has been raised up for Ardon, killed in battle, and he has received his portion. The others have their portions of the land we have taken. But the Lord God gave me the Negev as well, and Kiriath-sepher is once again in the possession of the Anakites. The portion not yet conquered shall belong to my daughter, whose faith is like a fire within her. Mighty men shall come from her!"

He jammed his walking stick into the ground and stepped forward. "Hear me, sons of Judah. I will give my daughter Acsah in marriage to the man who attacks and captures Kiriath-sepher!"

✦   ✦   ✦

Caleb heard running feet and struggled to raise himself on his pallet. Acsah hastened to him and helped him sit up, pressing cushions behind him.

He heard a man speaking breathlessly outside. "Come!" Caleb called. "Enter in!" He put his hand over Acsah's. She was trembling and pale, her eyes huge and dark.

Hur's son Salma came in, face streaked with dust and sweat. He went to his knees and bowed low. "Kiriath-sepher is in our hands. The Anakites are no more!"

Caleb sat up straight, shaking violently from the effort. "Who led?"

"Othniel!" The boy raised his head, eyes shining. "Othniel, son of Kenaz!" He stood and raised his hand. "He broke through their gates and destroyed the enemy. His hand was heavy against them. They fell to his right and to his left. He did not rest until they were no more!" Salma described the battle in detail, his face alight with excitement and triumph. "The Lord our God gave Kiriath-sepher into our hands!"

Caleb saw that Othniel had done more than take Kiraith-sepher. He had fired up the sons of Judah. And if this young man was any indication, perhaps he had even turned Caleb's sons' hearts back toward the Lord. His throat tightened with tears of thanksgiving. Oh, that Kenaz, Caleb's youngest brother, the first among his family members who had followed him to the camp of the Israelites, could see this day. Caleb gave thanks to God that it was one among his own flesh and blood who now stood before Israel and called them back to faith. "The Lord is our strength and deliverer!"

"Blessed be the name of the Lord." Acsah bowed her head.

"Acsah." Caleb placed his hand upon her. She raised her head and looked into his eyes. Hers softened with love and pooled with tears. She took his hand and kissed it fervently. Then she rose and left him.

Caleb gestured to Salma. "I wish to be outside." He wanted to see the comings and goings of those he loved. Salma helped him up. He gave him support as Caleb hobbled outside and sat beneath the shade of the olive tree. He rested his back against the ancient trunk. "My sons?"

"All are well."

"Thanks be to God." Caleb gave the boy his blessing and sent him away. Then Caleb waited and looked out over the hill country. Othniel would come, and would bring Mesha and the rest of his sons and grandsons with him.

A flurry of excited activity gained Caleb's attention. Startled, he saw Acsah come out of his house garbed in wedding finery. Covered as she was with veils, he could not see her face. She spoke to a servant and stood in the sunshine waiting. A donkey was brought to her. She turned to him again and bowed her head in deep respect. She remained that way for a long moment and then straightened. Then she mounted the donkey and rode away.

All had misjudged this girl, including him. She didn't wait for her husband to come to her, but rode out to meet him. She tapped the side of the donkey with a stick so the animal trotted more quickly. He smiled. At least she wasn't dragging her feet and going out with misgivings and hesitance. No, she went out eagerly to meet the man God had chosen for her.

As the distance widened between them and Acsah became smaller, Caleb felt sorrow mingle with joy. Until this moment when he watched her ride away, he had not realized how much comfort he received from his daughter's presence.

Never had he felt so alone.

+ + +

Days passed slowly and then word came that his sons were returning, Othniel at their head and Acsah with them.

"Acsah!" Too weak now to rise from his pallet, Caleb told the servants to take him outside. They lifted him and carried him out and made him comfortable so that he could see the procession coming up to his village. Acsah rode beside her husband, not behind him.

Othniel came to him first and greeted him with the respect due a father. And then, blushing, he asked for a field already producing grain. Taken aback, Caleb thought about it for a moment. It would take time to tame the Negev. Caleb granted his request. Next Caleb's sons came, kissing him and talking excitedly of the battle. They then dispersed to their families.

Othniel went to Acsah and spoke to her. She smiled and put her hands upon her husband's shoulders, alighting gracefully from her donkey. She said something to Othniel. He shook his head. She spoke again and came toward Caleb. She was no longer veiled, but her hair was covered. She had become a woman in the past few days, for there was an air about her that was different. She knelt close to Caleb, her hands loosely clasped in her lap.

"Thank you for granting my husband a field, Father."

Caleb raised his brows. "Did you suggest he ask for it?"

She blushed as her husband had. "We must have grain to sustain ourselves until all the enemies of God are driven from the Negev."

"Provisions." He lowered his head and peered at her. "What is it? What can I do for you?"

She took a deep breath. "Give me a further blessing. You have been kind enough to give me land in the Negev; please give me springs as well."

Caleb smiled. She was shrewd as well as courageous. He'd only thought of the land, not the provisions needed to take it. "The upper and lower springs are yours."

It was time to celebrate, time to feast and give thanks. He watched his sons dance in the firelight and listened to their songs of praise. His daughter danced with the women, her face alight as she twirled and raised her hands.

Caleb dozed for a while, replete and deeply satisfied. When he awakened, the celebration was still going on, the stars twinkling in the canopy of the night sky. He saw Acsah and Othniel standing in the rim of firelight, off by themselves, talking. Othniel lifted his hand and touched her. It was a gesture of tenderness. When Acsah stepped closer and reached up to her husband, Caleb closed his eyes.

Othniel and Acsah came to him before they headed south. He knew it was the last time he would see his daughter, for he was an old man with death fast approaching. When she knelt before him, he held her face between his hands and looked long into her eyes. "Do not weep so."

"How can I not weep?" She fell into his arms and buried her face in his shoulder.

"I have lived a long life and been a witness to God's signs and wonders. Could any man ask for a greater blessing? And now, I hold hope for the future. I hold that hope in you." His arms tightened around her briefly. "Your husband awaits." As she drew back, he cupped her face and kissed her cheeks and forehead. "May the Lord bless you with many God-fearing sons."

She smiled through her tears. "And daughters."

"May all your children be like you."

Othniel helped her to her feet and left his hand lightly upon her, a possessive gesture that pleased Caleb. He knew he had gained something precious, something to be protected and cherished. A wise man who saw what he himself had missed for far too long.

Caleb held his hands out as though to embrace them both. "May righteousness go before you, and the glory of the Lord be your rear guard."

He couldn't watch them ride away. They were followed by Othniel's relatives and some of his own grandsons, eager now to wage war and drive God's enemies from the land.

May they succeed this time, Lord. May they not pause to rest until every last enemy is vanquished!

But Caleb knew men were weak. They were like sheep in desperate need of a shepherd. As long as they had one, they followed. *May all their shepherds be upright, honest men of integrity who will hold fast to Your laws and statutes, Lord.*

We will rise up in faith and then fall into sin again, won't we, Lord? Is that our destiny?

The servants came out to lift his pallet. "No. Leave me here a little longer." He gestured impatiently when they hovered. "Go!" As they turned to obey, he called them back. "Bring me my sword." Troubled, they hesitated. "My sword!"

A young man ran to do Caleb's bidding and brought the weapon back. He bent down reverently, presenting the hilt to Caleb.

Caleb held his sword once more. He remembered a time when he would go into battle with this sword, swinging it to the right and left for hours without tiring. Now, he barely had the strength to lift it. Arm trembling, he used all his will not to drop it. "Go now."

How is it, Lord, that within this aging husk of a body my heart still beats for battle? I remember the day I pounded my plowshare into this sword. I thought a day would come when I would heat it in the fire and place it upon the anvil and make another plowshare. But it was not to be. Even now, I know the battle is far from over.

We cried for a deliverer and You sent us Moses. When Pharaoh refused to let Your people go, You sent plagues upon Egypt. You opened the sea for our escape and closed it over the army of Your enemies. You sheltered us with a cloud by day and protected us as a pillar of fire by night. You fed us manna from heaven and water from a rock. You satisfied my thirsty soul and filled my hungry heart with what is good and lasting.

Caleb dozed in the afternoon sun, his strength seeping, his breath slowing. He saw a temple rise, shining white with gold, glorious. A strong wind came up and blew across the land, and the temple crumbled. People wailed as they were led away in chains. And then another procession back up the mountain and another temple rose, less grand, then walls around it and a man upon the battlements calling out to the workers. "Do not be afraid. Do not grow weary. Finish the work God has given you!" But again, destruction came, again a temple rose, grander still. And light came so bright that Caleb felt pain, such pain, he moaned and clutched at his heart. *Oh, God, oh, God, will You have to do that? You are perfect! You are holy!* And then the heavens darkened, but brightened again, light spreading slowly across the land like a new dawn.

Once again destruction came.

Caleb's soul cried out in agony. His heart broke. *Oh, Lord, will it ever be so? Oh, Lord, Lord!*

The heavens opened and there came One riding a white horse, riding from the swirling clouds, riding swiftly with a sword in His hand, and upon Him emblazoned *Faithful and True, the Word of God.* Armies came with Him, clothed in fine linen, white and clean, following Him. Caleb heard the blast of the shofar. Eager to obey the call to battle, he grasped the hilt of his sword, half rising from his pallet. "Lord! *Yes!*"

King of kings, Lord of Lords!

A myriad singing. "Holy! Holy! Holy!"

Caleb drew in his breath at the blaze of colors: reds, yellows, blues, purples. Light streaming, water rushing, life pulsing.

Wait, and you will see.

Releasing his breath in a long, slow sigh, Caleb let his sword drop to his side. He closed his eyes. For now, he could rest.

For he knew one day he would awaken and rise again in strength.

SEEK AND FIND

❖❖❖❖❖❖

Dear Reader,

We hope you enjoyed this fictional account of the life of Caleb, tribal leader, half-breed, scout, and beloved of God. This powerful story of faith and obedience by Francine Rivers is meant to whet your appetite. Francine's first and foremost desire is to take you back to God's Word to decide for yourself the truth about Caleb—his persistence, his promises, and his source of peace.

The following Bible study is designed to guide you through Scripture to seek the truth about Caleb and to find applications for your own life.

Caleb's walk with God enabled him to trust God even when circumstances screamed "not fair!" His loyalty required obedience at all costs. His trust in God's promises provided calmness in the midst of turmoil. Caleb's faith remained steadfast and growing throughout his life. It energized him in old age to aspire to all that God had promised.

May God bless you as you seek Him for the answers to your life's turmoils and inequities. And may He find you faithful and resolute in your journey with Him.

Peggy Lynch

A SCOUT'S REPORT

SEEK GOD'S WORD FOR TRUTH

Read the following passage:

The Lord now said to Moses, "Send men to explore the land of Canaan, the land I am giving to Israel. Send one leader from each of the twelve ancestral tribes." So Moses did as the Lord commanded him. He sent out twelve men, all tribal leaders of Israel, from their camp in the wilderness of Paran. These were the tribes and the names of the leaders:

Tribe	Leader
Reuben	Shammua son of Zaccur
Simeon	Shaphat son of Hori
Judah	Caleb son of Jephunneh
Issachar	Igal son of Joseph
Ephraim	Hoshea son of Nun
Benjamin	Palti son of Raphu
Zebulun	Gaddiel son of Sodi
Manasseh son of Joseph	Gaddi son of Susi
Dan	Ammiel son of Gemalli
Asher	Sethur son of Michael
Naphtali	Nahbi son of Vophsi
Gad	Geuel son of Maki

These are the names of the men Moses sent to explore the land. By this time Moses had changed Hoshea's name to Joshua.   NUMBERS 13:1-16

✦ The very first mention of Caleb in Scripture is found in this passage. Who was Caleb? What position did he hold?

✦ What would it take to acquire and maintain this position?

Read the following passage:

Moses gave the men these instructions as he sent them out to explore the land: "Go northward through the Negev into the hill country. See what the land is like and find out whether the people living there are strong or weak, few or many. What kind of land do they live in? Is it good or bad? Do their towns have walls or are they unprotected? How is the soil? Is it fertile or poor? Are there many trees? Enter the land boldly, and bring back samples of the crops you see." (It happened to be the season for harvesting the first ripe grapes.)

So they went up and explored the land from the wilderness of Zin as far as Rehob, near Lebo-hamath. Going northward, they passed first through the Negev and arrived at Hebron, where Ahiman, Sheshai, and Talmai—all descendants of Anak—lived. (The ancient town of Hebron was founded seven years before the Egyptian city of Zoan.) When they came to what is now known as the valley of Eshcol, they cut down a cluster of grapes so large that it took two of them to carry it on a pole between them! They also took samples of the pomegranates and figs. At that time the Israelites renamed the valley Eshcol—"cluster"—because of the cluster of grapes they had cut there.

After exploring the land for forty days, the men returned to Moses, Aaron, and the people of Israel at Kadesh in the wilderness of Paran. They reported to the whole community what they had seen and showed them the fruit they had taken from the land. This was their report to Moses: "We arrived in the land you sent us to see, and it is indeed a magnificent country—a land flowing with milk and honey. Here is some of its fruit as proof. But the people living there are powerful, and their cities and towns are fortified and very large. We also saw the descendants of Anak who are living there! The Amalekites live in the Negev, and the Hittites, Jebusites, and Amorites live in the hill country. The Canaanites live along the coast of the Mediterranean Sea and along the Jordan Valley."

But Caleb tried to encourage the people as they stood before Moses. "Let's go at once to take the land," he said. "We can certainly conquer it!"

But the other men who had explored the land with him answered, "We can't go up against them! They are stronger than we are!" So they spread discouraging reports about the land among the Israelites: "The land we explored will swallow up any who go to live there. All the people we saw were huge. We even saw giants there, the descendants of Anak. We felt like grasshoppers next to them, and that's what we looked like to them!"   NUMBERS 13:17-33

+ What instructions were given to the twelve men? How much time did they have to complete their mission?

+ What did the men find? What evidence did they bring back with them?

+ What was the nature of the scouts' report? What was their attitude like?

+ What was Caleb's report? How was his attitude different?

FIND GOD'S WAYS FOR YOU

+ Describe a time you followed the crowd. What was the result? What did you learn?

+ Describe a time you stood alone. What was the outcome? How did you feel?

O Lord, you are my refuge; never let me be disgraced. Rescue me! Save me from my enemies, for you are just. Turn your ear to listen and set me free. Be to me a protecting rock of safety, where I am always welcome.   PSALM 71:1-3

+ What are some reasons why we need not fear standing alone?

STOP AND PONDER

> For I can do everything with the help of Christ who gives me the strength
> I need.   PHILIPPIANS 4:13

WISE COUNSEL

SEEK GOD'S WORD FOR TRUTH

Read the following passage:

> Then all the people began weeping aloud, and they cried all night. Their voices
> rose in a great chorus of complaint against Moses and Aaron. "We wish we had
> died in Egypt, or even here in the wilderness!" they wailed. "Why is the Lord
> taking us to this country only to have us die in battle? Our wives and little ones
> will be carried off as slaves! Let's get out of here and return to Egypt!" Then
> they plotted among themselves, "Let's choose a leader and go back to Egypt!"
>
> Then Moses and Aaron fell face down on the ground before the people of
> Israel. Two of the men who had explored the land, Joshua son of Nun and Caleb
> son of Jephunneh, tore their clothing. They said to the community of Israel,
> "The land we explored is a wonderful land! And if the Lord is pleased with us,
> he will bring us safely into that land and give it to us. It is a rich land flowing
> with milk and honey, and he will give it to us! Do not rebel against the Lord,
> and don't be afraid of the people of the land. They are only helpless prey to us!
> They have no protection, but the Lord is with us! Don't be afraid of them!"
>
> But the whole community began to talk about stoning Joshua and Caleb.
> Then the glorious presence of the Lord appeared to all the Israelites from above
> the Tabernacle. And the Lord said to Moses, "How long will these people reject
> me? Will they never believe me, even after all the miraculous signs I have done
> among them? I will disown them and destroy them with a plague. Then I will
> make you into a nation far greater and mightier than they are!"
>
> "But what will the Egyptians think when they hear about it?" Moses
> pleaded with the Lord. "They know full well the power you displayed in
> rescuing these people from Egypt. They will tell this to the inhabitants of this
> land, who are well aware that you are with this people. They know, Lord,
> that you have appeared in full view of your people in the pillar of cloud that
> hovers over them. They know that you go before them in the pillar of cloud
> by day and the pillar of fire by night. Now if you slaughter all these people,
> the nations that have heard of your fame will say, 'The Lord was not able
> to bring them into the land he swore to give them, so he killed them in the
> wilderness.'"   NUMBERS 14:1-16

✦ Describe the camp atmosphere after the scouting reports. What plans did
the people propose?

✦ When Moses and Aaron fell facedown on the ground, what words of
comfort did Caleb and Joshua offer? What warning did they give?

✦ What specifically demonstrated the faith of Caleb and Joshua?

✦ How did the people respond to the warnings?

✦ Describe God's response to the people's behavior.

FIND GOD'S WAYS FOR YOU

✦ Discuss a time when you were a mediator. Why is this event memorable?

What advice did you offer? What was the outcome? People who despise advice will find themselves in trouble; those who respect it will succeed. The advice of the wise is like a life-giving fountain; those who accept it avoid the snares of death.   PROVERBS 13:13-14

✦ Apply these verses to Caleb and the Israelites. Apply them to yourself.

STOP AND PONDER

Whoever walks with the wise will become wise; whoever walks with fools will suffer harm.   PROVERBS 13:20

GOD SEES

SEEK GOD'S WORD FOR TRUTH

Read the following passage:

[Moses said,] "Please, Lord, prove that your power is as great as you have claimed it to be. For you said, 'The Lord is slow to anger and rich in unfailing love, forgiving every kind of sin and rebellion. Even so he does not leave sin unpunished, but he punishes the children for the sins of their parents to the third and fourth generations.' Please pardon the sins of this people because of your magnificent, unfailing love, just as you have forgiven them ever since they left Egypt."

Then the Lord said, "I will pardon them as you have requested. But as surely as I live, and as surely as the earth is filled with the Lord's glory, not one of these people will ever enter that land. They have seen my glorious presence and the miraculous signs I performed both in Egypt and in the wilderness, but again and again they tested me by refusing to listen. They will never even see the land I swore to give their ancestors. None of those who have treated me with contempt will enter it. But my servant Caleb is different from the others. He has remained loyal to me, and I will bring him into the land he explored. His descendants will receive their full share of that land. Now turn around and don't go on toward the land where the Amalekites and Canaanites live. Tomorrow you must set out for the wilderness in the direction of the Red Sea."

NUMBERS 14:17-25

+ List all you learn about God's character from Moses' prayer.

+ What does this prayer tell you about Moses?

+ What is God's plan for the people now? Why?

+ What new instruction was given to the people?

+ How does God describe Caleb?

+ What is God's plan for Caleb and his family?

SEEK GOD'S WAYS FOR YOU

+ To whom do you turn in crises? Why?

+ What does this reveal about you?

+ How do you think God would describe you?

STOP AND PONDER

> Dear brothers and sisters, whenever trouble comes your way, let it be an opportunity for joy. For when your faith is tested, your endurance has a chance to grow. So let it grow, for when your endurance is fully developed, you will be strong in character and ready for anything.   JAMES 1:2-4

THE FALLOUT

SEEK GOD'S WORD FOR TRUTH

Read the following passage:

> Then the Lord said to Moses and Aaron, "How long will this wicked nation complain about me? I have heard everything the Israelites have been saying. Now tell them this: 'As surely as I live, I will do to you the very things I heard you say. I, the Lord, have spoken! You will all die here in this wilderness! Because you complained against me, none of you who are twenty years old or older and were counted in the census will enter the land I swore to give you. The only exceptions will be Caleb son of Jephunneh and Joshua son of Nun.
>
> "'You said your children would be taken captive. Well, I will bring them safely into the land, and they will enjoy what you have despised. But as for you, your dead bodies will fall in this wilderness. And your children will be like shepherds, wandering in the wilderness forty years. In this way, they will pay for your faithlessness, until the last of you lies dead in the wilderness.

"'Because the men who explored the land were there for forty days, you must wander in the wilderness for forty years—a year for each day, suffering the consequences of your sins. You will discover what it is like to have me for an enemy.' I, the Lord, have spoken! I will do these things to every member of the community who has conspired against me. They will all die here in this wilderness!"

Then the ten scouts who had incited the rebellion against the Lord by spreading discouraging reports about the land were struck dead with a plague before the Lord. Of the twelve who had explored the land, only Joshua and Caleb remained alive.

When Moses reported the Lord's words to the Israelites, there was much sorrow among the people. So they got up early the next morning and set out for the hill country of Canaan. "Let's go," they said. "We realize that we have sinned, but now we are ready to enter the land the Lord has promised us."

But Moses said, "Why are you now disobeying the Lord's orders to return to the wilderness? It won't work. Do not go into the land now. You will only be crushed by your enemies because the Lord is not with you. When you face the Amalekites and Canaanites in battle, you will be slaughtered. The Lord will abandon you because you have abandoned the Lord."

But the people pushed ahead toward the hill country of Canaan, despite the fact that neither Moses nor the Ark of the Lord's covenant left the camp.

NUMBERS 14:26-44

Discuss the camp from God's perspective.

+ What do you learn about the people at this point?

+ What consequences befell the twelve scouts? What exceptions were made?

+ What consequences were exacted on the entire camp without exceptions?

+ What warnings did Moses give to the people? How did they react?

+ What did this reveal about the Israelites' relationship with Moses and with God?

FIND GOD'S WAYS FOR YOU

+ Discuss a time you had to live with the consequences of what someone else did. How did you feel?

+ Share a time when you were spared consequences you deserved. How did that feel?

No discipline is enjoyable while it is happening—it is painful! But afterward there will be a quiet harvest of right living for those who are trained in this way.   HEBREWS 12:11

+ What do we learn about discipline from this verse? What are the conditions for "harvest"?

STOP AND PONDER

Dear brothers and sisters, I plead with you to give your bodies to God. Let them be a living and holy sacrifice—the kind he will accept. When you think of what he has done for you, is this too much to ask? Don't copy the behavior and customs of this world, but let God transform you into a new person by changing the way you think. Then you will know what God wants you to do, and you will know how good and pleasing and perfect his will really is.

ROMANS 12:1-2

THE PROMISE KEPT

SEEK GOD'S WORD FOR TRUTH

Read the following passage:

After the death of Moses the Lord's servant, the Lord spoke to Joshua son of Nun, Moses' assistant. He said, "Now that my servant Moses is dead, you must lead my people across the Jordan River into the land I am giving them. I promise you what I promised Moses: 'Everywhere you go, you will be on land I have given you—from the Negev Desert in the south to the Lebanon mountains in the north, from the Euphrates River on the east to the Mediterranean Sea on the west, and all the land of the Hittites.' No one will be able to stand their ground against you as long as you live. For I will be with you as I was with Moses. I will not fail you or abandon you.

JOSHUA 1:1-5

✦ Who succeeded Moses as camp leader? What is significant about this?

Read the following passage:

When Joshua was an old man, the Lord said to him, "You are growing old, and much land remains to be conquered. The people still need to occupy the land of the Philistines and the Geshurites—territory that belongs to the Canaanites.

"I will drive these people out of the land for the Israelites. So be sure to give this land to Israel as a special possession, just as I have commanded you. Include all this territory as Israel's inheritance when you divide the land among the nine tribes and the half-tribe of Manasseh."

A delegation from the tribe of Judah, led by Caleb son of Jephunneh the Kenizzite, came to Joshua at Gilgal. Caleb said to Joshua, "Remember what the Lord said to Moses, the man of God, about you and me when we were at Kadesh-barnea. I was forty years old when Moses, the servant of the Lord, sent me from Kadesh-barnea to explore the land of Canaan. I returned and gave from my heart a good report, but my brothers who went with me frightened the people and discouraged them from entering the Promised Land. For my part, I followed the Lord my God completely. So that day Moses promised me, 'The land of Canaan on which you were just walking will be your special possession and that of your descendants forever, because you wholeheartedly followed the Lord my God.'

"Now, as you can see, the Lord has kept me alive and well as he promised for all these forty-five years since Moses made this promise—even while Israel wandered in the wilderness. Today I am eighty-five years old. I am as strong now as I was when Moses sent me on that journey, and I can still travel and fight as well as I could then. So I'm asking you to give me the hill country that the Lord promised me. You will remember that as scouts we found the Anakites living there in great, walled cities. But if the Lord is with me, I will drive them out of the land, just as the Lord said."

So Joshua blessed Caleb son of Jephunneh and gave Hebron to him as an inheritance. Hebron still belongs to the descendants of Caleb son of Jephunneh the Kenizzite because he wholeheartedly followed the Lord, the God of Israel. (Previously Hebron had been called Kiriath-arba. It had been named after Arba, a great hero of the Anakites.)

And the land had rest from war.   JOSHUA 13:1-3, 6-7; 14:6-15

+ How did Caleb approach Joshua about Moses' promise?

+ As Caleb laid out his case, what did he offer as past, present, and future evidence?

+ How did Joshua respond to Caleb's request?

+ What proclamation about God does Caleb make that is like Moses?

+ What reason is given for Caleb's inheritance? What does this tell you about his relationship with God?

FIND GOD'S WAYS FOR YOU

+ How do you approach people when reminding them of a promise? How has it worked out?

+ How have you responded when someone has approached you about a promise you made?

If you need wisdom—if you want to know what God wants you to do—ask him, and he will gladly tell you. He will not resent your asking.   JAMES 1:5

+ What advice does this verse offer?

STOP AND PONDER

God blesses the people who patiently endure testing. Afterward they will receive the crown of life that God has promised to those who love him.

JAMES 1:12

THE LEGACY

SEEK GOD'S WORD FOR TRUTH

Read the following passage:

> After Joshua died, the Israelites asked the Lord, "Which tribe should attack the Canaanites first?"
>
> The Lord answered, "Judah, for I have given them victory over the land."
>
> Judah marched against the Canaanites in Hebron (formerly called Kiriath-arba), defeating the forces of Sheshai, Ahiman, and Talmai. From there they marched against the people living in the town of Debir (formerly called Kiriath-sepher).
>
> Then Caleb said, "I will give my daughter Acsah in marriage to the one who attacks and captures Kiriath-sepher." Othniel, the son of Caleb's younger brother Kenaz, was the one who conquered it, so Acsah became Othniel's wife.
>
> When Acsah married Othniel, she urged him to ask her father for an additional field. As she got down off her donkey, Caleb asked her, "What is it? What can I do for you?"
>
> She said, "Give me a further blessing. You have been kind enough to give me land in the Negev; please give me springs as well." So Caleb gave her the upper and lower springs.   JUDGES 1:1-2, 10-15

✦ After Joshua died, the tribe of Judah was selected to lead the taking of the Caananite land. Who was the tribal leader? What significance do you find in this?

✦ What incentive does Caleb offer the man who will secure the area of Kiriath-sepher?

✦ Who accomplishes this feat? How does Caleb keep his word?

✦ How would you describe Caleb's relationship with his daughter? What similarities do you see between the two of them?

Read the following passage:

> After that generation died, another generation grew up who did not acknowledge the Lord or remember the mighty things he had done for Israel. Then the Israelites did what was evil in the Lord's sight and worshiped the images of Baal. They abandoned the Lord, the God of their ancestors, who had brought them out of Egypt. They chased after other gods, worshiping the gods of the people around them. And they angered the Lord. They abandoned the Lord to serve Baal and the images of Ashtoreth.
>
> Then the Lord raised up judges to rescue the Israelites from their enemies.
>
> The Israelites did what was evil in the Lord's sight. They forgot about the Lord their God, and they worshiped the images of Baal and the Asherah poles. Then the Lord burned with anger against Israel, and he handed them over to King Cushan-rishathaim of Aram-naharaim. And the Israelites were subject to Cushan-rishathaim for eight years.
>
> But when Israel cried out to the Lord for help, the Lord raised up a man to

rescue them. His name was Othniel, the son of Caleb's younger brother, Kenaz. The Spirit of the Lord came upon him, and he became Israel's judge. He went to war against King Cushan-rishathaim of Aram, and the Lord gave Othniel victory over him. So there was peace in the land for forty years. Then Othniel son of Kenaz died.   JUDGES 2:10-13, 16; 3:7-11

✦ What happened after Joshua and Caleb's generation died? What did God do to help the people?

✦ Who was Israel's first judge and how did he become a judge? What, if any, similarities to Caleb do you find in him?

FIND GOD'S WAYS FOR YOU

✦ What is Caleb's most outstanding trait? Why do you think so?

✦ In what ways do you identify with Caleb? What have you learned about yourself from this study?

✦ What have you learned about God from Caleb's experiences?

STOP AND PONDER

Dear brothers and sisters, let me say one more thing as I close this letter. Fix your thoughts on what is true and honorable and right. Think about things that are pure and lovely and admirable. Think about things that are excellent and worthy of praise. Keep putting into practice all you learned from me and heard from me and saw me doing, and the God of peace will be with you.

PHILIPPIANS 4:8-9

CALEB THE WARRIOR

Caleb often despaired because of his inability to follow the law that God had given to His people. Hundreds of years later, the apostle Paul would speak of this same struggle:

"I love God's law with all my heart. But there is another law at work within me that is at war with my mind. This law wins the fight and makes me a slave to the sin that is still within me. Oh, what a miserable person I am! Who will free me from this life that is dominated by sin? Thank God! The answer is in Jesus Christ our Lord."   ROMANS 7:22-25

Interestingly, there are parallels between the lives of Caleb and Jesus:

CALEB
+ Questionable birthright
+ Of the tribe of Judah
+ Endured unfair consequences as a result of others' actions
+ War hero of Judah
+ Committed to completing his mission—clearing the land of enemies so God's people might live in it
+ Commander of Israel's army, fighting for God and for his family
+ Believed and relied on the Word of God
+ A prayer warrior armed for battle

JESUS
+ Questionable birthright
+ Of the tribe of Judah (Rev. 5:5)
+ Endured unfair execution as a result of our actions (2 Cor. 5:21)
+ Lion of Judah (Rev. 5:5)
+ Committed to completing His mission—clearing our lives of sin so God Himself might live in us (John 6:56)
+ Commander of the armies of heaven, fighting our spiritual battles (Rev. 19:11-16)
+ Is the Word of God (John 1:1)
+ Is our armor and intercedes for us (Eph. 6:10-18; Heb. 7:24-25)

The same armor that covered Caleb spiritually is available to us today. In his letter to the Christians at Ephesus, the apostle Paul wrote:

> A final word: Be strong with the Lord's mighty power. Put on all of God's armor so that you will be able to stand firm against all strategies and tricks of the Devil. For we are not fighting against people made of flesh and blood, but against the evil rulers and authorities of the unseen world, against those mighty powers of darkness who rule this world, and against wicked spirits in the heavenly realms. Use every piece of God's armor to resist the enemy in the time of evil, so that after the battle you will still be standing firm. Stand your ground, putting on the sturdy belt of truth and the body armor of God's righteousness. For shoes, put on the peace that comes from the Good News, so that you will be fully prepared. In every battle you will need faith as your shield to stop the fiery arrows aimed at you by Satan. Put on salvation as your helmet, and take the sword of the Spirit, which is the word of God. Pray at all times and on every occasion in the power of the Holy Spirit. Stay alert and be persistent in your prayers for all Christians everywhere.   EPHESIANS 6:10-18

BOOK THREE

THE PRINCE

ONE

"We have no weapons!"

"We'll have to find a way to make them."

"How? There isn't a blacksmith in the whole land of Israel to make them. The Philistines made sure of that. Those they didn't murder, they took captive."

Jonathan sat with his father, Saul, beneath the shade of an olive tree. His uncles, frustrated and angry, bewailed the latest Philistine raid.

"Even if we could make swords, what good would they be? Whatever the Philistines' swords and spear tips are made of, they're far superior to ours. Bronze isn't strong enough. It shatters against their blades."

"I choke on my pride every time I have to go down to Aijalon and pay hard-earned shekels to a stinking Philistine so he'll sharpen my plowshare and sickles!"

"If I need an ax sharpened, I have to answer question after question."

Another laughed bitterly. "I need my pitchfork repaired this year, and new points for the ox goad. I wonder how much that will cost me."

Saul stared off toward the fields. "There's nothing we can do about it."

The Philistine outpost at Geba was only a short distance away, and it was the duty of Saul's tribe, the Benjaminites, to keep close watch over it.

"Kish says what we need is a king!"

Saul shook his head. "You know what the prophet Samuel says about having a king."

"The Philistines have kings. That's why they're organized."

"If only Samuel were like Samson. Instead, all he does is blame us for what's happening."

Jonathan looked at his father. "Grandfather Ahimaaz said the Lord our God is more powerful than all the gods of Philistia."

The uncles exchanged sallow looks.

Jonathan leaned forward. "Grandfather Ahimaaz said when the Philistines killed the high priests' sons and took the Ark of the Covenant,

God went to war against them. Their god Dagon fell facedown before the Ark, his head and the hands breaking off. And then the Lord cursed the Philistines with tumors and a plague of rats. They were so afraid they sent the Ark back on a cart pulled by two milch cows and loaded with gold!"

Saul shook his head. "That was years ago."

One of Jonathan's uncles flung a pebble. "God leaves us alone now to defend ourselves."

Jonathan felt confused. "But if the Lord—"

Saul looked at him. "Your mother tells you too many stories about what her father said."

"But they're true, aren't they?"

Another uncle snorted in despair. "It was years ago! When was the last time the Lord did anything for us?"

Saul put his arm around Jonathan. "There are things you don't yet understand, my son. When you are a man—"

"Saul!"

At the sound of Kish's angry shout, Saul removed his arm from around Jonathan's shoulders and stood. "What now?" he grumbled. "I'm here!"

Jonathan's grandfather strode across the partially plowed field, his fine robes billowing around him, the red tinge in his cheeks betraying his temper. His younger sons scattered like chaff before a strong wind, leaving Saul alone to face their father.

Saul came out from the shade. "What's the matter?"

His question fanned the flames. "What's the matter? You have to ask me?"

Saul's face darkened. "If I knew, I wouldn't ask."

"You're out here sitting in the shade, and my donkeys are missing!"

"Missing?" Saul frowned and looked off toward the hills.

"Yes! Missing! Have you no ears that you can hear?"

"I told Mesha to watch over the donkeys."

Jonathan gulped. Mesha was an old man, easily distracted. No wonder the donkeys had gone missing.

"Mesha?" Kish spat in disgust. "Mesha!"

Saul spread his hands. "Well, I can't be in two places at the same time. I've been plowing the field."

"Plowing? Is that what you call sitting under an olive tree, talking with your brothers?" Kish shouted for the rest to hear. "Will we have enough food with all of you sitting around talking?"

"We were making plans."

"Plans for what?"

"War."

Kish barked a harsh laugh. "We would need a king to lead us into war, and we have no king. Where are my donkeys?" He made a fist.

Saul stepped back out of range of a blow. "It's not my fault Mesha didn't do as he was told!"

"You'll lose the oxen next! How long do you think you'll manage without animals to pull the plow? I'll have to put *you* to harness!"

Saul's face reddened. He stalked back into the shade.

Kish followed. "I put you in charge! I didn't want a servant watching over my donkeys! I wanted *my son* watching them!"

"You have more than one son!"

"You're the eldest!" He cursed. "Mesha is an old man and a hireling. What does it matter to him if my property is lost? You're the one to inherit. If you had to put someone over those animals, why didn't you send Jonathan? He would have kept close watch over my property."

Jonathan cringed. Why did his grandfather have to pitch him into the fray? His father's pride was easily pricked.

Saul glared. "You always blame me when anything goes wrong!"

"Father, I'll go look—"

"No, you won't!" both men shouted.

"I'll send one of the servants." Saul turned as if to leave.

Kish yelled, "No, you won't! You'll go yourself. And don't give me excuses! You're not going to sit out here on your backside and wait for someone else to find what you allowed to wander off. Take a servant with you, and go look for the donkeys!" Kish strode back toward Gibeah, still shouting. "And don't even think about riding a donkey. There's only one donkey left, and that one stays here. You can search on foot! And take someone other than *Mesha* with you!"

Saul kicked the dust and muttered. Eyes blazing, he stormed across the field toward home. Jonathan followed.

His mother, Ahinoam, stood in the doorway, waiting for them. The whole town had probably heard Kish shouting out in the field. "I've filled two water bags and stuffed two packs with bread."

His father scowled. "You're so eager to have me go?"

She put her hand against his heart. "The sooner you go, the sooner you will be back."

"I'll go with you, Father."

Ahinoam followed Saul inside the house. "Jehiel knows more about donkeys than any man in Gibeah, Saul. Take him with you. Jonathan can continue the plowing."

"But, Mother—"

She gave Jonathan a quelling look. "With both of you gone, nothing would get done."

"Father, the Philistines may have stolen the donkeys and taken them to Geba." The garrison was not far away. "We should go there first."

His mother faced him. "You're not going. Your father has enough to do without having to watch out for you."

Jonathan's face went hot. "I can use a bow better than any man in Gibeah."

"Your father is going out to find donkeys, not start a war."

"Enough!" Saul snarled. "Pack me enough bread and dried fruit to last me a few days. There's no telling how far the donkeys have wandered."

His wife moved quickly to do his bidding.

Saul muttered and stormed around the room, kicking things out of his way. When he saw Jonathan still standing there, he jerked his chin. "Go and find Jehiel. Tell him to hurry up!"

"I'll go." Jonathan backed toward the door. "But what if the donkeys are in Geba?"

Saul flung his hand into the air. "Then they're gone, aren't they? And Mesha will wish he had done what he was told!"

"They've wandered off." Ahinoam spoke in soothing tones. "That's all that's happened. You'll find them before the sun sets, my love." She shoved more bread into a sack. "The Philistines have more donkeys than they need. Besides, they covet horses."

Saul shouted after Jonathan. "Tell Jehiel I'm ready and waiting on him!"

Jonathan found Jehiel hard at work repairing the wall of an empty sheepfold. "Kish is sending my father out to find some stray donkeys. My father wants you to go with him. He's packed and ready to go."

Jehiel straightened and brushed his hands off. "I will gather what I need and come."

Jonathan followed him. "You could tell my father that the sheep might escape if you don't complete your work. You could say I can serve him as well as you." He had explored the hills and valleys all around Gibeah and even dared go close enough to the walls of Geba to hear the guards talking.

"The sheep are out to pasture, Jonathan, and there are two shepherds to watch over them."

"What if you run into Philistines while you're searching for the donkeys?"

"You needn't worry about your father. We will avoid the Philistines. Even if by mischance we crossed paths with them, I doubt they would bother with two men on foot with little more than some bread and water to steal."

Jonathan sighed.

Before the two men left, Saul gripped Jonathan's shoulder. "Finish plowing the west field. Keep watch over your brothers. You know how they tend to wander."

"I wish I were going with you."

Saul looked past him to Ahinoam. "Soon."

✦ ✦ ✦

Jonathan went out to work in the west field. Not long after his father and Jehiel had left, his mother came out to him. It was not her habit to do so, and he stopped the oxen to wait. "Is something wrong?"

"No. Nothing. Sit with me in the shade and rest a while."

"Father wanted me to plow—"

"I will not keep you from your work for long, my son."

He secured the reins and followed her. She led him to the same tree where he had sat earlier with his father and uncles, listening to talk of kings and war.

Kneeling, she laid out fresh bread, a skin of wine, dried dates and raisins.

Jonathan's brows rose slightly. Perhaps she meant to sweeten words that would sour his mood. His defenses rose.

She looked up at him. "You are still upset that you weren't allowed to go with your father."

"These are troubled times, Mother, and he is too important a man to be guarded by only one servant. What if they meet some Philistines?"

"Your father is looking for donkeys, not a fight."

Women would never understand! "You don't have to look for a fight to find yourself in the middle of one."

His mother sighed. "You love your father, Jonathan. In that, I know your heart is ever in the right place. But you must learn to use your head, my son. I saw you stand and watch your father and Jehiel depart. Did they head for the garrison? Did they go armed to accuse and ready to fight?" She folded her hands in her lap. "You would have urged your father to look in Geba first. Would that be in keeping with protecting your father, or urging him to danger?"

"But that's probably where the donkeys are."

"Just because a lamb is missing doesn't mean it's in a lion's mouth. Jehiel will try to track the donkeys. We can hope the Philistines had nothing to do with them. If they did, then they're gone and that's the end of it."

Jonathan rubbed his face in frustration. "The Philistines take everything they can get their hands on."

"I did not come out here to talk about Philistines or donkeys. God knows where the donkeys are. And if it is God's will, He will let your father find them. I care more about my son than a few beasts of burden." She stood and squeezed his hand. "I came out to tell you I am very proud of you, Jonathan. You have courage. I just want you to live long enough to have good sense."

She leaned down and covered the bread with a cloth. "If all Israel has its way, we will soon have a king like every other nation around us. And what else does a king do but draft sons into the army or make them run before his chariot? Your sisters may one day end up cooks or bakers or perfumers in some palace in Judah's territory, since Judah thinks it must be one of their own rather than a Benjaminite to rule. A king will take the best of our crops and herds and give them to his assistants. He will want a portion of everything we have. These are the things the prophet Samuel told your grandfather and the others who went to Ramah to ask for a king. Samuel speaks the truth. All you have to do is look around you to see—"

"We are at the Philistines' mercy, Mother. Would you have us sit and do nothing?"

"My father, Ahimaaz, was a great man. He said we must trust in the Lord. God is our king."

"God has abandoned us."

"Men who say such things have no faith, and without faith, we have no hope." His mother raised her hands in frustration. "I know, I am but a woman. What could I know?" She raised her chin, dark eyes sparkling. "But I do know that you are my son. You are the grandson of Ahimaaz. Listen to *his* words, not mine. If a man is going to follow God, he must align himself with men of God. Samuel is God's anointed prophet. He speaks God's Word. Listen carefully to what *he* says."

"I wasn't in Ramah." How did she know so much of what was said there?

"I wish you had been. You'd have heard for yourself the words of the prophet rather than hearing your mother repeat what she overheard." She sighed. "I came to say that many things could change and it could happen quickly. While you work in the fields, pray. Ask the Lord what He requires of you."

And what did the Lord want of him but to fight, to drive the idol worshipers from the land?

His mother studied him. Her eyes darkened and grew moist. She shook her head slowly, rose, and walked away.

+   +   +

A day passed, then another, and Jonathan's father and Jehiel did not return. His mother said nothing.

The men gathered at Kish's table and complained about the Philistines; then complained about Samuel's corrupt sons, who were now assigned to rule over Israel. Jonathan sat with his younger brothers—Malkishua, Abinadab, and Ishbosheth—and ate in silence, worrying about his father.

Saul's cousin Abner cut off a portion of roasted goat. "Samuel was not pleased when we met with him at Ramah. He took our request for a king as a personal affront."

Kish dipped bread into the bowl of lentil stew. "He is not long for this world, and we need a man to rule before he goes the way of all flesh. There are none like Samuel in the land."

"All too true! But his sons are despicable."

"They hold court in Beersheba and collect tribute like pagan kings!"

One of Jonathan's uncles reached for a cluster of grapes. "They have been helpful in the past."

Kish gave a harsh laugh. "Only because we paid them larger bribes than those who complained against us! Joel and Abijah cannot be trusted. They are greedy and will turn their rulings to whomever gives them what they want."

"And what they want changes from one day to the next."

"How does a man like Samuel come to have sons like those two?"

"Kish, you convinced Samuel, didn't you, my brother? He said we would have a king."

Kish poured wine. "The question is when? And who will it be? A Judean? So it will be, according to Jacob's prophecy."

"There is not a Judean worthy enough to rule over us!"

"Why not you, Kish? You are rich."

Kish's brothers and sons, equally ambitious for the tribe of Benjamin, were quick to agree.

"You are a leader of Israel."

"The greatest among all the tribes."

"You have influence."

"The other tribes grumble, but it is clear their elders look to our house to rule."

Kish's dark eyes glowed with fire. "I know they look to us, but I am an old man. It will take someone younger and stronger than I, a man of stature who will impress the other tribes enough to convince them to stand behind him."

Jonathan leaned in to listen. There was no man taller nor of more regal bearing than his father, Saul.

"The twelve tribes must be unified. We need a king like the nations around us, a champion who will go out and fight for us."

Jonathan thought of his mother's words about Ahimaaz. Ahimaaz had been killed by Philistines, and Jonathan had few memories of him, other than that he had not been like Kish. Kish was angry. Loud. Always making plans for war. Ahimaaz had taught Jonathan to say, "Trust in the Lord and the power of His strength." Kish believed God helped those who helped themselves. And Kish ruled the men gathered in this room. They all believed that the Lord had left them to protect themselves, and to stand against the Philistines meant they must adopt the ways of the nations around them, nations who had powerful kings and large armies. Some even thought the gods of Philistia were more powerful than the God of Abraham, Isaac, and Jacob. How else could they be so oppressed by the Philistines?

Kish tore off another piece of bread. "Samuel said God will give us what we want."

Every man in the room knew who Kish had in mind. The men had talked often among themselves. Saul stood a head taller than any other man in Gibeah, and he had the famed handsome features of the Benjaminite tribe, descended from the youngest son of Jacob's beautiful and favored wife, Rachel. Men—and women—stared every time Saul attended one of the religious festivals, not that he attended often. He would rather plow, plant, and harvest crops than attend religious services, even though he was required to go three times a year. Saul *looked* like a king even if he had no ambitions to become one.

Jonathan knew it didn't matter what Kish wanted. God would tell Samuel whom to choose.

As much as he loved and respected his father, he could not imagine Saul as king.

But if not Saul, who? Abner? He was an able leader, fierce and uncompromising. Or Amasa, Abner's brother? Both were men of courage and strength, always talking over plans of how they would drive the Philistines from the land if God would just give them a king to pull the tribes together. They could talk, but could they lead?

Jonathan looked around at his relatives. They were all eager for a king, intent upon having one whether Samuel liked it or not. If his father were made king, it would change everything. Jonathan felt a rush of apprehension at the thought that he would then become the heir to the throne.

His mother's words pricked his spirit: *"Trust in the Lord. He is our king."*

Then why didn't the Lord destroy their enemies? Why did He allow the Philistines to oppress them? If God still cared, why didn't He deliver them? He had sent Moses. He had sent others. Every now and then, it seemed the Lord awakened to their need and sent a man to deliver them. But years had passed and no one had come. The only Word they had from God came through Samuel, who said they were at fault.

What was left, then, but for every man to do what was right in his own eyes? For it was certain no one had confidence in Samuel's sons to make decisions with the wisdom and justice of their father.

Jonathan had heard Samuel speak only once, but still remembered how his heart had quickened when the prophet reminded the people how their forefathers had been slaves in Egypt, and how God had sent Moses to deliver them from bondage. God had sent the plagues to free them from Pharaoh, had given the people water in the desert, and rained manna from heaven. God had opened the Red Sea to save Israel and then closed it over Pharaoh's army. Whatever the people needed, God had provided. All the years they wandered in the wilderness and suffered under the blazing desert sun, they had water and food enough. Their shoes and clothing never wore out. When all those who had refused to trust in the Lord died, their children crossed the River Jordan and claimed the land God promised. Canaan, a land of milk and honey.

Samuel said the Lord their God had driven out many of the Canaanites before they came, and then commanded His people to drive out the rest. The Lord had tested them to see if they would follow His commandments with single-minded determination. As long as Joshua, then Caleb, then Othniel lived, they had obeyed. But eventually, the people had grown tired of fighting and had given up trying to wipe the land clean. So what if a few enemies survived in caves and crags? God's people had tried, hadn't they? Surely God couldn't expect more of them than that. It was too much work to hunt the stragglers down and finish them off. What harm to leave them alone? It was time to enjoy the crops, the flocks and herds, the fruit trees ready for harvest. It was time to savor the milk and honey!

But the surviving enemy had been like weeds. They grew quickly and spread.

And now, here were the Philistines—a garrison of them—only a few hills away. These people from the sea were powerful, armed, and arrogant. And they moved farther inland every year. No one in Israel did anything to drive them from the land. No one dared, especially now that not a single blacksmith could be found to forge a weapon. And how could twelve disparate tribes with countless leaders unite and fight against the organized forces that moved beneath the command of a king?

"We need a king like they have. Without a king to unite us, we are defenseless."

"When a king unites us, we won't have to live in fear, wondering from one day to the next whether marauders are going to steal our crops and animals."

Animals!

Jonathan felt a rush of fear. His father had not yet returned. How long did it take to find a few donkeys?

God, please bring my father home safely.

Did God even hear their prayers anymore? *Had* the Lord abandoned them, as some of his relatives claimed? Did the Lord expect them to live by their own strength and cunning?

Samuel said if they returned to the Lord, the Lord would deliver them from their enemies. But Jonathan didn't understand what the prophet meant. How had he left the Lord? The Philistines continued to encroach bit by bit, taking more territory, striking at every weak place, building strongholds. And God did not stop them. He did not intervene and sweep His mighty hand across the land, even though from history, Jonathan knew it would be a small thing for the God who sent ten plagues upon Egypt to send another plague or two upon the Philistines! Why didn't He?

His mother had told him that his grandfather Ahimaaz used to say, "Every trial that comes will strengthen or weaken our faith."

The Philistines increased in number and power every year. They dressed in their fine-colored garments and armor, their thick hair like braided crowns, heads high, armed to kill, quick with mocking laughter and unleashed passion before their idols. They were a sight to see! Did their gods exist? How else did they come by such confidence in themselves and disdain for others? They were the conquerors, making themselves rich off those they oppressed. Israel was stripped while God remained silent.

"The Lord has spoken to Samuel and told him a king will be chosen." Kish put his wine goblet down. "Either he agrees that we need a king, or he no longer plans to rule."

Did Kish mean God or Samuel? Either way, Jonathan felt a chill spread through his blood.

Could his father or any other man effectively rule Israel? Whenever the elders gathered, they bickered. They might believe in God, but they distrusted one another.

Jonathan's mind wandered.

What must it have been like to live beneath God's protection—the cloud by day, the pillar of fire by night? What had the manna tasted like? What must it have felt like to see water streaming from a rock? Jonathan often yearned for days he had never experienced. He felt bereft, soul starved.

He used to dream of studying the Law—perhaps even at Naioth, where Samuel was. The Lord spoke to Samuel. Samuel would know the answers to the questions that often plagued Jonathan. What did it mean to trust and obey God? What action should he take to please Him? Clearly, the offerings did not suffice. God was far off, silent. Did the Lord listen to anyone other than Samuel?

As great a man as Samuel was, as honest and upright a judge, he paled next to stories of Moses, who had brought the Law down from Mount Sinai, and Joshua, who had conquered the land. Those had been days when God ruled as king! God had gone out ahead of them in battle and stood as their rear guard. He had hurled hailstones from heaven! Who could stand against a God like that? He had made slaves into free men and frightened sheep into an army of lions.

But where was the army of Israel now? The mighty warriors who once claimed their inheritance had produced frightened sheep that bleated over scant crops and drying water holes, and lived in fear of Philistine wolves.

What if Kish got what he wanted and lived to see Saul crowned king over Israel? Jonathan felt a rush of fear. His father was a farmer, not a warrior. Even now, he might be dead. It should not have taken this long to find the donkeys.

Jonathan gave voice to his concern. "My father has been gone too long. Can I go and look for him?"

Abner frowned. "Saul *has* been gone a long time."

Kish considered for a moment, then waved his hand. "It is too early to be concerned, my son."

"He's been gone two full days, Grandfather."

Kish gave a bleak laugh. "One day to find the donkeys, one day to sulk, one day to return. If he hasn't come home by the day after tomorrow, then I will worry."

"With your permission, I will go and look for him tomorrow. He could have run into trouble."

"The boy thinks he could take on some Philistines."

Jonathan was thirteen and a man. How long before they saw him as such?

"Be quiet. Should we dismiss a son's love for his father?" Kish's eyes glowed with pride as he studied Jonathan, but he shook his head. "Your father takes his time because he is angry. He'll be home in a few days."

Jonathan wished he could be as certain.

+ + +

Jonathan heard the cry of alarm. One of the shepherds came running across the field. "The donkeys are at the well."

Something must have happened to his father! Jonathan took off running. "Grandfather!"

Kish came out. Jonathan told him about the donkeys, and Kish shouted to the shepherd, "Have you seen my son?"

"No, my lord. I've seen no sign of him."

"Let me go." Jonathan feared they had waited too long already. "Let me go find my father!"

Kish shouted and several men came running.

Jonathan refused to be set aside. "I have to go!"

"Abner will go."

"Let me go with him."

Kish grabbed hold of Jonathan's shoulder. "Go! But do not look for trouble."

They traveled quickly, stopping to ask if anyone had seen Saul and Jehiel. They had been seen, but had gone on. Jonathan and Abner passed through the hill country of Ephraim, through the area around Shalishah, and on into the district of Zuph, following word of them.

Abner looked perplexed. "The seer lives here."

Would his father come all this way to ask Samuel where the donkeys were?

Eyes glowing, Abner entered the town of Naioth. "We'll have news of Saul here. I'm certain of it."

Yes, Saul and his servant had been there. The town was still talking about him.

"Samuel invited Saul to eat with him." Men were still talking about the feast. "Samuel had saved the best portion of the lamb for him."

The best portion? What did that mean? "Why?"

"We don't know, but Samuel seemed to be expecting him."

Jonathan looked around. "Where is my father now?"

"Gone."

Abner's voice was strained with excitement. "What of Samuel? May we speak with him?"

"He left as well."

"Did they leave together?" Abner wanted to know.

One elder shrugged while the other pointed. "No. Saul took the road to Bethel."

Abner grasped Jonathan's arm. "Let's go. We must hurry!"

"What do you think happened?"

"We'll find out when we find your father."

Saul and Jehiel were not in Bethel. Apparently Saul and his servant had entered the town with three others, were given bread, and had taken the road to Gibeah.

"Maybe he found out the donkeys came back," Jonathan said.

Abner laughed strangely. "Or maybe something else!"

They came upon others who had seen Saul and were full of news about what had happened.

"Your father joined the procession of prophets coming down from the high place in Gibeah. He prophesied with them!"

Jonathan's father, a prophet? How could that be?

Others came near to hear what was being said.

"What happened to the son of Kish?"

"He prophesied!"

"What? Is even Saul a prophet?"

Jonathan pressed in among them. "Where is my father now?"

"He's gone up to the high place!"

But by the time they got there, Saul and Jehiel were gone.

"How long ago did they leave?"

"Not long."

Jonathan and Abner ran to catch up. Finally, Jonathan spotted a tall man and a smaller one walking beside him on a distant hill. "Father!" Jonathan shouted and increased his speed. Abner was on his heels.

Saul turned and waited. He embraced Jonathan, pounded him on the back, and grinned.

"We were worried about you and came looking." Jonathan panted.

What was that he smelled on his father? Something sweet. His father's hair was thick with oil.

Saul greeted Abner.

"What happened to you?" Abner demanded.

Saul's expression closed. "I've been looking for the donkeys."

Abner stepped closer. "You ate with Samuel!"

Saul lifted his shoulders and turned toward home. "When we saw the donkeys were not to be found, we went to him. Jehiel had a little money with him as a gift."

"And Samuel took it?" Abner seemed surprised.

"No," Jehiel was quick to say.

"Tell me what happened."

Saul glowered at Abner. "Samuel told me to go ahead to the high place."

Jonathan sensed the subtle change in his father's demeanor. Something momentous had happened, but he was unwilling to explain.

Abner put his hand on Saul. "What did Samuel say to you?"

Saul jerked free. "He assured us that the donkeys had been found." He stared hard at Abner. "And they have, haven't they?"

"Yes."

Without another word, Saul headed toward Gibeah.

Abner turned in frustration. "Jehiel!" He walked with the servant, speaking quietly. The man spread his hands and shrugged.

Jonathan caught up to his father and walked with him.

Saul gave a harsh laugh. "Jehiel knows nothing."

"Is there something to know, Father?"

Saul pressed his lips together.

Jonathan's heart thumped. "I smelled incense—"

Saul flashed him a look. Color surged into his face. "Say nothing of it to anyone. Do you understand?"

"Yes."

Jonathan said nothing more, but he was afraid Kish's prayers might have been answered.

+ + +

Saul refused to talk about his meeting with Samuel. He returned to work and plowed, while Kish and the others speculated on what had happened. Jonathan labored with his father, waiting for him to say something about what had happened in Naioth. But his father said nothing, working in silence, pensive and nervous. Jonathan refrained from pressing him like the others had.

But he spoke to his mother about it.

"Of course something happened," she whispered. "I'm afraid to think what it might have been. Just stay close to your father. Do whatever he asks of you. When he's ready, he'll probably tell you first before the others. I think he'll need you in the days ahead."

"Did he say anything to you?"

"No, but sometimes a man's silence speaks louder than his words."

Kish came out to the fields. "Let the servants do the rest of the plowing, my son. You are too important to do such work."

Saul glowered. "I'm a farmer, nothing more."

"Yes, we are farmers. But you may be called to something greater than that."

"I cannot live your dream, Father."

"We are summoned to Mizpah."

"Summoned?"

"Samuel has sent word that everyone is to gather at Mizpah."

Saul turned ashen. "Why?"

"Why do you think?" Kish was taut with excitement. "Samuel is going to tell us whom God has chosen to rule over Israel."

Saul put his hand to the plow. "Judah will rule."

"Judah?" Kish gave a derisive laugh. "There has not been a mighty man in Judah since Caleb and Othniel died. Judah!"

"It is the prophecy!" Saul didn't raise his head. "Jacob said—"

"And you think that gives Judah the right to rule over us? How many centuries ago was that?"

"Then *you* go! You're the head of our clan! Maybe we'll all get lucky and you'll be king! I'm staying here."

Kish's face reddened. "We *all* go! Samuel has summoned *all* the people. *All* of us! Do you understand?" He shook his head when Saul snapped the reins and bent his strength to the plow. "We leave tomorrow!" Kish shouted after him. He looked at Jonathan. "We leave at dawn!" He strode away.

Jonathan signaled a servant and left him in charge of his team of oxen. He went after his father. Saul paused at the end of the field, and ran a shaking hand down over his face. Jonathan heard him mutter an angry prayer. Saul stood still, staring off into the distance. Jonathan stood near him, waiting, uncertain what to say. "What's wrong?"

Saul gave a bitter laugh. "Why should anything be wrong? Other than everyone is making plans for *my* life!" He gave Jonathan a stricken look. "A man should be able to say yes or no, shouldn't he?"

Jonathan didn't know what to say.

Saul shook his head and looked back over the newly plowed field. "He can't be right."

Was he talking about Kish? or someone else? "Whatever happens, Father, I'll stand with you."

Saul let out his breath slowly. "You won't have any choice." He handed Jonathan the reins and goad and walked slowly toward Gibeah, shoulders slumped.

✦   ✦   ✦

All Israel gathered at Mizpah. Jonathan had never seen so many people in his life! Thousands upon thousands of tents had been erected, and the multitude pressed close, murmuring like the rumble of a storm ready to rain praises on the king God had chosen.

When Samuel came out, not a man, woman, or child spoke. Here and there, a baby cried, but was quickly soothed into silence.

"This is what the Lord, the God of Israel, has declared!" Samuel raised his arms.

Jonathan's heart pounded.

"I brought you from Egypt and rescued you from the Egyptians and from all of the nations that were oppressing you. But though I have rescued you from your misery and distress, you have rejected your God today and have said, 'No, we want a king instead!' Now, therefore, present yourselves before the Lord by tribes and clans."

Samuel watched the clans of each tribe pass by him; the Levites, the Reubenites, the Simeonites and sons of Judah, then the tribe of Dan and Naphtali. The brush and scrape of sandals and bare feet were all that was heard, for no one dared utter a word as the prophet watched and waited for the Lord to tell him who would be king. The Gadites and Asherites, sons of Issachar and Zebulun passed him. Then the half-tribes of Manasseh and Ephraim descended from Joseph. Only the tribe of Benjamin remained.

Jonathan's stomach clenched tight. The closer they came to Samuel, the harder his heart pounded. His father wasn't beside him. He couldn't see his father anywhere. Where was he? He could feel the excitement in the air. Kish strode forward—head high, eyes bright, face flushed. Did he know Saul was missing?

"*Benjamin!*" Samuel called out, and Jonathan's heart leapt into his throat. A rush of quiet voices rippled like water cascading over rock.

"Come forward clan by clan," Samuel told them.

The men of Benjamin obeyed.

Kish looked around. He grasped Jonathan's arm. "Where is your father?"

"I don't know."

"Matri!" Samuel called out.

Kish looked around again, his eyes frantic.

"Kish!" Samuel's voice rang out. "The Lord has appointed Saul king over Israel."

The tribe of Benjamin burst out in cheers and jumped up and down.

"Saul!" Kish turned this way and that. *"Saul!"*

The voices rose—some in triumph, some in question.

Jonathan looked around, searching. *Oh, Father. Father!* Where could he have gone?

Kish's face darkened. He grabbed one of his sons and beckoned the others. "Find your brother! Quickly! Go! Before these cheers turn to jeers! *Go!*"

"Has the man come here yet?" some called out.

Samuel looked grim. "Yes. He has hidden himself among the baggage."

Jonathan felt the blood drain from his face and then flood back until he felt on fire with embarrassment. He ducked his head and wove through the men.

Some began to shout. "Hiding? How can such a man save us?"

"What sort of champion will he be?"

Jonathan ran toward the piles of baggage, as eager to find his father as he was to escape disdain and contemptuous words. Hiding? Surely not! His father was no coward!

Jonathan found his father huddled among the bundles and sacks, shoulders slumped, head in his hands.

"You're the king, Father. The Lord has made you king!"

Saul groaned in misery. "Tell Samuel it's all a mistake."

"God told Samuel it's you. God doesn't make mistakes." Jonathan hunkered down beside him. "You must come." He fought tears, humiliation gathering. What if others saw his father like this? He couldn't bear it. "The Lord will help you. Surely the Lord will not abandon the one He's chosen, even if He abandons the rest of us."

Saul raised his head. When he held out his hand, Jonathan grasped it and helped him to his feet. He could feel his father shudder when someone cried out, "There he is!"

Men surged toward them. They surrounded Saul and Jonathan. Saul covered his fear and straightened. He was a head taller than every other man around him. Handsome and strongly built, he stood like a king among them. Saul was swept along like a leaf on a river until he stood before Samuel.

The prophet held out his hand. "This is the man the Lord has chosen as your king. No one in all Israel is like him!"

Jonathan saw men of Judah sneer and whisper among themselves. Thankfully, the vast majority shouted, "Long live the king!"

"Listen to the Word of the Lord!" Samuel called out to the mass. Saul stood beside the seer, facing the people. Samuel opened a scroll and read from it. Some stood still and listened. Many fidgeted. A few whispered among themselves. Samuel looked out over the people.

"The Lord said a day would come when we would ask for a king. He said to appoint a fellow Israelite; he may not be a foreigner." He faced Saul.

"The king must not build up a large stable of horses for himself or send his people to Egypt to buy horses, for the Lord has told you, 'You must never return to Egypt.' The king must not take many wives for himself, because they will turn his heart away from the Lord. And he must not accumulate large amounts of wealth in silver and gold for himself."

Samuel took a smaller scroll and placed it upon the altar he had made of stones, and then handed Saul the Torah. "Saul, son of Kish, son of Abiel, son of Zeror, son of Becorath, son of Aphiah of Benjamin, you must copy for yourself this body of instruction on a scroll in the presence of the Levitical priests. You must always keep that copy with you and read it daily as long as you live. That way you will learn to fear the Lord your God by obeying all the terms of these instructions and decrees. This regular reading will prevent you from becoming proud and acting as if you are above your fellow citizens. It will also prevent you from turning away from these commands in the smallest way. And it will ensure that you and your descendants will reign for many generations in Israel."

Saul took the scroll and held it at his side like a sword. Samuel turned him toward the people. Saul's jaw locked as he looked out over the thousands upon thousands staring at him. He looked but said nothing.

Jonathan was filled with pride as he observed his father. No one could say that he had coveted the power of kingship. Saul had all the eagerness of a man who had just received a sentence of death. But no man among all Israel looked more like a king than Saul, son of Kish.

Whatever it takes, Lord, help me to help my father, Jonathan prayed. *Give me strength when he needs protection. Give me wisdom when he needs counsel. Put mighty men around him, warriors who fear You and will faithfully serve the king.*

✦ ✦ ✦

Jonathan thought their lives would change, but as soon as the family reached Gibeah, his father turned to his field, leaving without orders those who returned with them and were eager to do the king's bidding. They built camps around the town and waited.

"Are you going to copy the Law, Father?"

"The fields must come first."

Troubled, Jonathan went to his mother. "The seer commanded it, Mother. Surely Samuel will be displeased if Father doesn't do it."

"Saul is king of Israel now, Jonathan, and every king does what is pleasing in his own sight. If your father won't copy the Law, there's nothing you can do about it. Do not waste time arguing with him. As strong as Kish is, has your grandfather ever won a battle with Saul?"

"No."

"Your father had no ambitions to be king, but whether he likes it or not, he is. And whether you want to be or not, you are the prince, heir to the throne."

His mother was shrewd. Everything she said meant something. "What are you saying, Mother? I would prefer you tell me outright."

She spread her hands. "Is it for a woman to tell a man what he should do?"

"All I want is to serve Father."

She folded her hands in her lap and smiled enigmatically. "Then serve him."

Ah. If the Law must be written and his father had no time to do it, then he must.

He went out into the field and asked permission to go to the school of prophets in Naioth. Saul nodded. "Finish the task as quickly as possible and come home." He embraced Jonathan, kissed him, and let him go.

By the time Jonathan returned to the house, his mother had already made preparations for his journey.

TWO

✦❧❀❧❀❧✦

Jonathan unrolled the scroll a little farther, secured it, and carefully dipped his stylus into the ink. He copied each letter, jot, and tittle exactly as it was written in the Law handed down by Moses. His lip was raw from chewing on it, the back of his neck ached, and his shoulder muscles were knotted; but he finished the line, set the stylus aside, and leaned back, wiping the sweat from his forehead.

"Enough for today."

Startled, Jonathan glanced up and saw Samuel watching him. The seer's face was solemn, his eyes glowing with inner fire. Jonathan never felt at ease when he looked into Samuel's face, this man who heard the voice of God and spoke His Word to the people.

As Jonathan stood, Samuel took the scroll, rolled it carefully, placed it inside its covering, and put it away.

"The letter of the Law is important, my prince, but you must also understand what it says."

Jonathan recited, " 'Honor your father and mother. Then you will live a long, full life in the land the Lord your God is giving you.' " He saw the frown that crossed the seer's face and felt heat flood his own. Had Samuel thought him impertinent, or worse—disrespectful? Jonathan wished he had not said something that might be misconstrued as criticism of the prophets' sons, whose reputations were as different from Samuel's as the sun was from the earth. Jonathan swallowed hard, debating. If he apologized, he might have to explain.

"You walked all the way to this school of prophets to copy the Law. Why not one closer to home?"

"You were here, my lord."

Samuel's eyes darkened. "Do not call me lord." He pointed up. "There is only one Lord. The Lord God of Abraham, Isaac, and Jacob, the God of heaven and earth."

Jonathan hung his head. Better to say nothing than to cause more offense.

"Did your father the king send you here?"

How should he answer? He did not want the prophet to know that Saul thought the fields more important than the law of God.

"You won't answer?"

"He gave me permission to come."

"Why is your father not with you?"

Jonathan's heart thumped. "The king has matters of great importance—"

"More important than copying the Law?"

A rebuke! "No. I will give it to him."

Samuel shook his head. "Everyone heard what I said to your father at the coronation at Gilgal. You were standing right there beside him, weren't you?"

"Yes." Jonathan's palms sweated. Was God listening? "You said the king was to have a copy of the Law, read it every day, and carry it with him at all times."

"The *king* is to write a copy of the Law in his own hand."

Jonathan could not promise that his father would take the time to make his own copy. Despite the warriors who had followed Saul back to Gibeah, the king kept to his fields. Maybe he hoped they would grow tired of waiting and go home. But would God allow that to happen? It was one thing to want to be king, another entirely to be called by God to be king.

"Are you afraid to say anything?"

Jonathan looked up at the seer. "I don't know what my father is thinking. He is pressed from all sides. I didn't want to add to his burdens."

Samuel's expression gentled. He held out his hand. "Sit." He approached and sat on the bench with Jonathan. He rested his hands on his knees. "If you wish to honor and serve your father, tell him the truth. If you always speak the truth to the king, he will have reason to trust you, even when he doesn't like what you say."

"As the people trust you."

A flicker of pain crossed the seer's face. "If Saul obeys the Law, the Lord will give him victory over our enemies, and Israel *may* complete the work God gave them to do when they entered Canaan."

"My father will listen."

"It is not enough to listen, my son. One must obey."

Jonathan was certain his father would have come himself to copy the Law if he had not had so many other responsibilities. He worried about preparing the fields. He worried about the quality of the seed. He worried about sun and rain. He had always worried about many things. Now he had the entire nation to concern him. "Can any one man hold the future of Israel in his hands?"

Samuel shook his head. "God holds the future in His hands."

"May I ask you something?" Jonathan hoped Samuel would agree, for one thing had continued to plague him. He couldn't sleep for worrying about it.

Samuel inclined his head.

"You told us at Mizpah that we sinned by asking for a king. Has God forgiven us, Abba? or will His wrath be poured out upon my father? Saul did not ask to be king."

Samuel's gaze softened. "God calls whom He calls, Jonathan. The people have what they want: a king who stands tall among men. The Lord is compassionate upon His people. When we confessed before Him, He forgave us. God knows the hearts of men, my prince. He gave us commandments to follow so that we will not fall into sin. He knew Israel would one day ask for a king, and He told Moses what that king must be: a brother, a man who writes the Law in his own hand, studies it, is able to teach it, and abides by it all the days of his life."

When Jonathan returned home, he would tell his father everything Samuel said.

"You have great confidence in your father, don't you?"

"Yes!" Jonathan nodded. He was proud of his father. "I think I have more confidence in my father than he has in himself."

"He will learn what it means to be a king."

Who else could Jonathan trust but the prophet of God? "Now that he is king, he has enemies on every side. Some of the other tribes cried out against him when God made him king."

"There will always be men who stand against the one God calls to serve Him." Samuel turned and placed his right hand upon Jonathan's shoulder. "Honor your father, my son, but let your confidence be in the Lord our God. I know you love Saul, as well you should. But do not allow your love to blind you. Do not keep silent if you see your father, the king, sin. Learn the Law and counsel the king wisely. You are his eldest son, first show of his strength, and heir to his throne. Much will be expected of you. Seek wisdom from the Lord. Study the Law, and encourage your father to do the same. But do not ever think you can do the work for him. The king must know the Lord our God and the power of His strength."

Jonathan nodded again, accepting every word Samuel said as though it came from God Himself.

"I have watched you work, my son. You wash your hands before you enter the chamber and tremble when you open the scroll."

"To hold the Law is a wondrous thing, Abba, but to copy it is a terrifying task."

Samuel's eyes grew moist. He put his hands on his knees and pushed himself up. "I will look over your work."

"Thank you, Abba."

Samuel patted Jonathan's shoulder. "I wish all men revered the Law as you do."

Jonathan bowed his head, embarrassed. "I must confess I would rather be a student of the Law than a prince."

Samuel put his hand on Jonathan's head. "You can be both."

+ + +

Jonathan returned home with the copy of the Law carefully packed for travel. A small portion of it was tucked into a leather cylinder hidden beneath his tunic. He would keep it near his heart at all times.

How he looked forward to sitting with his father and discussing the Law, plumbing its meanings, relishing the richness of it. Each day that he had worked on making the copy, he had thought how wonderful it was going to be to share it with the king.

He found his father still in the fields, and warriors still encamped around Gibeah, waiting for the king to give them orders. Kish looked haggard. Jonathan overheard his low, heated words to Abner. "I dare say nothing to Saul that can be overheard or these men who wait upon him will think him more of a coward! What is my son waiting for?"

Jonathan was troubled by the talk. God had chosen his father as king. No one could doubt that! God would tell Saul when to act and what to do.

To pass the time, warriors sparred with one another. They trained for war daily while waiting for a command. Saul's habits did not change. He arose with the sun, yoked his oxen, and went out to work. When he returned, he ate with his family and guests.

Jonathan offered numerous times to read the Law to his father, but Saul always said, "Later. I'm tired."

Reaching for more bread, Kish spoke to his son in a quiet, hard whisper. "You must do something or these men will desert you! They will not wait forever for you to take the reins of kingship."

Tense lines appeared around Saul's eyes. "And everything you planned and sacrificed for will be lost. Isn't that right, Father?"

"I didn't do it for me." Kish spoke between his teeth. "I did it for you, for our family, for our people! Do you wait because you're angry with me?"

"No."

"Then what holds you back?"

"I will wait until I have some sign of what I am to do."

"Some sign?" Kish flung the bread down. Realizing others watched, he bared his teeth in a smile and leaned forward for some dates. When the others began to talk again, Kish glanced at Jonathan and then back to Saul. "A sign from whom? What sort of sign do you need other than the crown upon your head and these men who wait to obey your least command?"

Burned by his grandfather's sarcasm, Jonathan leaned over so that he could see past his father. "*God* will tell the king what to do and when to do it."

"A child's faith."

Heat surged into Jonathan's face.

Saul clenched his hand. "My son speaks more wisdom than anyone at this table!"

The room was silent.

Florid, Kish held his tongue. When Saul rose, Kish followed. Jonathan followed both men. "You have barely three thousand men," Kish stormed when they were out of hearing. "The rest refuse to follow a king who hides among the baggage!"

Saul turned, his face as red as his father's. "I felt unworthy to be king of Israel, but you got what you wanted, Father, didn't you?" He waved his hands in the air. "You and all my other ambitious relatives who thirst for Philistine blood!"

"God chose you."

"Convenient of you to remember that."

Jonathan stood, staring at them. It was not the first time he had seen them argue this way.

Kish lowered his voice. "Yes. We wanted one of our own to be king. Judah ruled for a time, but now it is time for the tribe of Benjamin to lead the nation to glory."

Benjamin, the youngest of Jacob's twelve sons. Benjamin, son of the beautiful Rachel, Jacob's favorite wife. Benjamin, Joseph's beloved baby brother. Though smallest among the twelve tribes, they were not least in arrogance!

"You must prove yourself worthy of respect, my son. You must punish those who refused to bring you gifts due a king. You must—"

"*Must?*" Saul glared, the cords in his neck standing out. "I wear the crown. Not you. God told Samuel to place it upon *my* head. Not yours. You have no right to command me to do anything anymore. Offer me advice when I ask for it, Father. If I ever ask. And never forget Jonathan is my heir."

Kish glanced back. Jonathan wondered if his grandfather realized he had been there the entire time. Muttering under his breath, Kish left them. Saul let out his breath and shook his head. "I need to be alone."

When his father left him, Jonathan found a quiet place and a lamp. He took his scroll from its casing and read. Someone cleared his throat softly. He turned.

A servant appeared from the shadows. "Your mother requests the pleasure of your company, my prince."

Rolling the scroll, he tucked it back into its case. His mother. She always knew every word that was spoken in the household.

When he entered his mother's quarters, she was working at her loom. Without looking up, she said, "Your father and grandfather had words." She turned to face him. "When the time comes, you will stand at your father's right hand and help him command his army."

Distracted, Jonathan watched his sisters.

His mother called to them. Merab came quickly, but Michal ignored them both.

"Get your sister out of the wool. It's yet to be carded. She already reeks." She glanced at him, frustrated. "I have so much to say to you."

Jonathan's brothers Malkishua and Abinadab clattered sticks as they sparred like the warriors outside the walls. Jonathan grinned. "Gibeah is alive with men eager to follow the king."

A servant brought his youngest brother, Ishbosheth, to his mother. The infant cried and sucked on his fist. "Saul is first among our people, Jonathan." His mother took the baby. "And you are second. You must be as wise as a serpent. Kish will come to you now with his advice. Listen to him and hold on to what will best serve your father, for that will serve you best as well." Ishbosheth screamed for what he wanted. "And may God grant us peace."

Jonathan left, relieved that whatever else his mother had to say would have to wait until later.

+   +   +

"Someone is coming!" the watchman called out. Jonathan ran to the gate of the city, where his grandfather and uncles had been holding court. Strangers appeared, stumbling with exhaustion, dust covered, faces streaming sweat. Jonathan pressed through the crowd to hear.

"We come from Jabesh-gilead . . ." The city, belonging to the tribe of Manasseh, lay east of the Jordan River, south of the Sea of Galilee in Manasseh's territory. ". . . to ask the king what we must do."

"Give our brothers water." Kish waved his hand. "Quickly, so they can tell us what's happened!"

Warriors gathered as the panting messengers grasped wooden cups and gulped water. "Nahash," one managed before draining another cup. People whispered among themselves: "The snake!" Everyone had heard of the Ammonite king and feared invasion. Refreshed, the messenger addressed Kish and the other city leaders. "Nahash has besieged us. The elders pleaded for a treaty with him, and promised to be his servants, but he said he will only agree if he gouges out the right eye of every man in the city as a disgrace to all Israel!"

If Nahash got his way, Jabesh-gilead would be defenseless for years to come, and an open doorway to the territory of the other tribes of Israel.

Men wailed and tore their clothing. "God has forsaken us!"

Women screamed and wept.

Jonathan saw his father returning with the oxen and ran out to meet him. Saul looked past him at the wailing mob. "What's the matter? Why is everyone crying?"

So they told him about the message from Jabesh. "The snake has laid siege to Jabesh-gilead." One of the messengers had told Saul everything by the time Abner and Kish came toward them.

Saul spread his arms wide and made a sound unlike anything Jonathan had ever heard from any man before. Terrified, he drew back from his father. The people stared and fell silent. Saul's roar made the hair on Jonathan's neck stand on end.

Face fiery red, eyes blazing, Saul threw the yoke off his oxen. He strode to a man who had been chopping wood and took his ax, then cried out as he raised it and brought it down on the lead ox. The animal dropped and jerked with death throes while Saul moved to the second and killed it as well. No one moved; no one uttered a sound as the king of Israel kept swinging that ax until he had dismembered his oxen.

Tunic soaked in blood, ax still in hand, Saul faced the people. Children ducked behind their mothers. Men drew back, even Kish, who stared, white-faced.

"Send out messengers!" King Saul buried his ax in the severed head of the lead ox. He pointed to the carcasses. "This is what will happen to the oxen of anyone who refuses to follow Saul and Samuel into battle! *We muster at Bezek!*"

Grinning, Abner turned and shouted eleven names, ordering them to spread the word. "And tell them a king rules in Israel!"

Jonathan still stared at his father, convinced he had heard the voice of God come out of him. "King Saul!" he shouted, raising his fists in the air. "King Saul!"

Every warrior raised his hands and shouted with him.

+   +   +

Three hundred thousand Hebrews came to Bezek, thirty thousand more from the tribe of Judah. Even those who had turned their backs on Saul and mocked him now waited eagerly for his command! The prophet Samuel stood at Saul's right hand, Jonathan to his left.

Saul spoke to his officers. "Where are the messengers from Jabesh-gilead?"

The question was shouted. Men pressed forward, separating themselves from the throng of warriors. "Here, my lord!"

"Return to your city and say, 'We will rescue you by noontime tomorrow!' Tell the elders to say to the Ammonites that the city will surrender and

Nahash can do whatever seems best." He laughed coldly. The Ammonites did not know the king of Israel had mustered an army. "They will return to their camp and celebrate. It will be the last time, for at the last night watch, we attack!"

Men raised their spears and clubs and cheered. Jonathan grinned in pride. No one doubted his father was king now! Let the enemies of Israel see God's chosen in battle!

"Abner!" Saul beckoned.

"Yes, my lord!"

"Separate the men into three divisions. If one division is destroyed, there will be two others to continue fighting. If two fall, one will be left." Each commander knew the route he was to take.

Where did his father come by such knowledge and confidence? It could only come from the Lord God!

Samuel stretched out his arms before the fighting men. "May the God of our fathers go out before you!"

Jonathan stayed at his father's side as they marched by night the seventeen miles down the mountains and across the Jordan River. Fear tightened his belly, but he let no one know. When the army came near the Ammonite camp, all was quiet, the guards asleep at their posts.

"Now!" Saul commanded. Jonathan and several others raised the rams' horns and blew. Israel's war cry rose to the heavens.

Saul held his sword high. There were only two in all Israel. Jonathan drew the other and raised it. Shouting, the thousands ran full out toward the Ammonite camp where confusion reigned.

When three Ammonites rose up to attack his father, rage fired Jonathan's blood. He cut down one and sliced through another. His father killed the third. Excitement flooded Jonathan's blood.

Jonathan's strength held all morning as he protected his father. Any man who dared try to reach the king of Israel died. By the time the sun was overhead, Nahash and his army lay slaughtered upon the field. Screams from the dying were silenced. The few who survived had scattered before the scourging fire of the Lord.

Thrusting his bloody sword into the air, Jonathan shouted in victory. *"For the Lord and Saul!"*

Others joined in his ecstatic praise.

But the bloodlust of killing Ammonites darkened and turned on those who had mocked Saul the day Samuel declared him king. The Benjaminites shouted, "Now where are those men who said, 'Why should Saul rule over us?' Bring them here, and we will kill them!"

Men who had fought side by side against the Ammonites now turned on one another, voices raised.

Jonathan remembered the Law he had written. "Father!" He had to shout to be heard. "We are brothers, sons of Jacob!"

Saul pulled him back from the fray and cried out, "No one will be executed today!" The throng quieted. Saul looked at Kish and the others and raised his voice for all to hear. "For today *the Lord has rescued Israel*!"

Samuel raised his staff. "Come, let us all go to Gilgal to renew the kingdom."

"To Gilgal!" men shouted. "To Gilgal!"

Jonathan's heart beat with a fear deeper than what he had felt in battle against the Ammonites. These men who turned so swiftly against one another might just as quickly turn against his father. He stayed close to Saul.

The throng of fighting men moved like a giant flock across the hillsides. For years, they had bunched together in small pockets of discontent, bleating in fear and uncertainty, ignoring the voice of the Shepherd, and looking about for one of their own to lead the way. Now, they followed Saul.

Saul had proven himself today, but Jonathan knew his father would have to continue to prove himself over and over again or these men would scatter once more.

God's people were like sheep, but today Jonathan had seen how quickly they could turn into wolves.

✦ ✦ ✦

Gilgal! Jonathan drank in the sight, remembering the history he had written and now wore around his neck. The children of Israel had crossed the Jordan River and entered the Promised Land here. It was on this plain they had first camped and then renewed their covenant with God. It was here the Angel of the Lord had appeared to Joshua and given him the battle plan to take Jericho, the gateway to Canaan.

What better place for his father to be reaffirmed king of Israel! After years of every man living in fear and doing what was right in his own eyes, God had given them a king to unite them!

May You instruct Saul and bless all Israel, O Lord!

Samuel stood at the monument of twelve stones the tribes had brought from the River Jordan to commemorate their crossing over. A sea of warriors stood silent as the old prophet—bent in frame, but still quick in mind and the Spirit of the Lord—spoke.

"I have done as you asked and given you a king. Your king is now your leader. I stand here before you—an old, gray-haired man—and my sons serve you."

Despised by all.

"Here I stand!" Samuel held his arms outstretched. "I have served as your leader from the time I was a boy to this very day. Now testify against me in the presence of the Lord and before His anointed one. Whose ox or donkey have I stolen? Have I ever cheated any of you? Have I ever oppressed you? Have I ever taken a bribe and perverted justice? Tell me and I will make right whatever I have done wrong."

Jonathan felt tears well at the pain in Samuel's voice. All because his sons had brought shame upon his house. *Lord, let me never bring shame upon my father! Let my actions be honorable.*

He stepped forward, unable to bear the pain he saw in Samuel's face. "You have not cheated us, Abba." His voice broke.

Samuel looked at Jonathan.

The people spoke, calling out here and there. "No! You have never cheated or oppressed us, and you have never taken even a single bribe."

Tears streamed down Samuel's cheeks. He turned to Saul. "The Lord and His anointed one are my witnesses today, that my hands are clean." His voice was harsh with pent-up emotion.

"I am witness." Saul bowed his head in respect.

"He is witness! The king is witness!"

"God is witness!" Jonathan cried out.

Samuel's voice steadied when he spoke of Moses and Aaron and the forefathers of all present who had come out of Egypt. His voice filled with sorrow when he spoke of their sins in serving the baals and ashtoreths of the Canaanites rather than the Lord their God who had performed signs and wonders and delivered them from Egypt. The people had forgotten the Lord! And the Lord gave them into the hands of their enemies! Over the years, when they cried out and repented, the Lord sent deliverers—Gideon and Barak, Jephthah and Samson—to rescue them from the hands of evildoers.

"But when you were afraid of Nahash, the king of Ammon, you came to me and said that you wanted a king to reign over you, even though the Lord your God was already your king."

Jonathan hung his head. Had he once given thought to what it meant for God to withdraw from His people so that men could rule themselves? *He calls us His children and we have rejected Him.* Jonathan's throat closed tightly. *Lord! Let me never forget that You are my king.*

Samuel pointed. "All right, here is the king you have chosen. You asked for him, and the Lord has granted your request!"

Jonathan looked up at his father. Saul stood, head high, and looked out over the tribes of Israel. He was no longer the frightened man who had hidden in the baggage. His face was fierce, challenging. The Law felt heavy against Jonathan's chest.

"Now if you fear and worship the Lord and listen to His voice, and if you do not rebel against the Lord's commands, then both you and your king will show that you recognize the Lord as your God. But if you rebel against the Lord's commands and refuse to listen to Him, then His hand will be as heavy upon you as it was upon your ancestors!"

Jonathan put his hand over his heart, feeling the Law encased there. *Mercy, Lord. Have mercy upon us!*

"Now—" Samuel's voice deepened—"stand here and see the great thing the Lord is about to do. You know that it does not rain at this time of the year during the wheat harvest. I will ask the Lord to send thunder and rain today. Then you will realize how wicked you have been in asking the Lord for a king!"

People murmured and shifted nervously. If God sent rain now, the crops would be ruined. Jonathan studied the sky. Clouds were forming; already the sky was darkening.

Saul groaned.

Jonathan knew all his father's hard work would gain him nothing. He shut his eyes. *Lord, we have sinned! I love my father, but we have all done an evil thing in asking for a king. Forgive us.*

Jonathan's heart quickened as clouds swirled. Lightning flashed, followed by a deep rumble that pressed upon him. And then the rain came, cold against victory-heated pride.

Jonathan bowed his head. *You are God! You are the God of Ahimaaz. You are my God and there is no other!*

Saul wailed. "The wheat is ready for harvest. The stalks will get wet. The grain will rot."

Jonathan raised his head and smiled at his father. "The Lord will provide."

Samuel turned and looked at Jonathan, and the sorrow slowly ebbed from his eyes.

Jonathan raised his hands, palms up and felt the drops of rain hit against him—sharp, cold spears. "Wash us, Lord. Cleanse us of sin." *You are king!*

Men screamed. "Samuel! Pray to the Lord your God for us, or we will die! For now we have added to our sins by asking for a king."

Jonathan prayed. "Without You, we can do nothing for Your people. Command us, Lord. Let it be as it once was. Go out before us and stand at our backs."

Lightning flashed again. Jonathan shuddered and dropped to his knees. He bowed his face to the ground, rain drenching him. "Lord, forgive us."

"Don't be afraid!" Samuel called out in a loud voice. "You have certainly done wrong, but make sure now that you worship the Lord with all your heart, and don't turn your back on Him. Don't go back to worshiping worthless idols that cannot help or rescue you—they are totally useless! The Lord will not abandon His people, because that would dishonor His great name. For it has pleased the Lord to make you His very own people."

Jonathan wept. He met Samuel's gaze, filled with compassion and tenderness.

"As for me—" Samuel spread his hands and looked at Saul and then at the multitude—"I will certainly not sin against the Lord by ending my prayers for you. And I will continue to teach you what is good and right. But be sure to fear the Lord and faithfully serve Him. Think of all the wonderful things He has done for you!"

Jonathan came to his feet, remembering all he had copied. God had delivered them from Egypt, given them land to till and plant, children. *You created us, Lord. You gave us life and breath.*

The rain softened, refreshingly cool against his face.

Samuel gazed out over the nation. "But if you continue to sin, you and your king will be swept away."

I am Saul's son, Lord, but I want to be Your man. I want a heart like Samuel's. Undivided. Devoted to You. Lord, Lord, make it so.

+ + +

Saul chose three thousand of the best warriors and sent the rest of the army home. Jonathan wondered why. "Aren't we going to attack the Philistine outposts?"

"I have no quarrel with the Philistines."

No quarrel? "But Father, they've oppressed us for years."

"We have two swords between us and no blacksmiths. That's reason enough not to start a war with them."

Had his father so quickly forgotten the lesson of Jabesh-gilead? "God is our strength!"

"Winning one battle against the Ammonites does not mean we can win a war against the Philistines."

"But the Lord gave us victory over Nahash. We need not return home, tails tucked between our knees."

Abner grasped Jonathan's shoulder, fingers biting in warning. "We will discuss all this as we travel south."

The army camped at Micmash. The king had no plans to attack the Philistine outpost at Geba, even though it was close enough to threaten Gibeah. Jonathan listened at the military counsel meetings, but heard nothing that would solve the threat to his father's reign if the warriors at Geba moved against Gibeah.

So he spoke again. "It is not wise to have enemies so close to our home. Saul is king of Israel, and Gibeah is now center of the nation. What is to stop the Philistines from attacking my father?"

Saul looked at Abner and then at the others for an answer. When they gave none, he shrugged. "I will remain here in Micmash until we see how the Philistines take the news of Nahash's defeat."

What had happened to his father's boldness? Where was the fierce King Saul who had hacked two oxen to pieces and led Israel into battle? "What of Mother? What of your sons and daughters? Gibeah—"

Saul scowled. "You can go there and secure the city. Close the gates and guard the city."

Jonathan blushed. "I can't hide behind the city walls while you're here. My place is beside you against the enemies of God."

"You will go to Gibeah. I have Abner and three thousand of Israel's best to guard me. I'll stay here in Micmash as we plan for the days ahead. You go on home."

Didn't he understand? "The Ammonites are in fear of us. And the Philistines will be as well!"

Kish snorted. "Young blood flows hot with foolishness."

Saul glared at his father and then looked at Jonathan again. "Samuel is no longer with us."

"God is with us," Jonathan said.

"God was with me at Jabesh-gilead, but I do not feel His Presence with me now."

"Father—"

Saul's eyes darkened. "The Philistines are not the cowards the Ammonites are."

Jonathan moved closer and lowered his voice so the others wouldn't hear. "If the Ammonites were cowards, Father, why did we fear them so long?"

Saul's head came up, eyes flashing; but Jonathan knew the fear that lurked behind the king's quick temper.

Kish smiled and patted Jonathan on the back. "There is a time for everything, Jonathan."

Lord, make them see! "Yes, but the time is now. Nahash is dead! The Ammonites are scattered. The Philistines will have heard how King Saul mustered the army and slaughtered the invaders. They were in fear of us before, my king, and they will be again. God is on our side! We have the advantage!"

Abner put his hand on Jonathan's shoulder. Jonathan shook it off.

Saul's eyes glowed. "No one doubts your courage, my son."

Kish's eyes flickered. "But courage must be tempered with wisdom."

Jonathan looked at his grandfather. "I thought you wanted war." He looked around at the others. "Do not dismiss what I say."

"There is a difference between the Ammonites who attempted to take land—" Saul waved his hand over the maps—"and the Philistines who have occupied it for years. They have strongholds."

"It is our land, Father, the land God gave us. It's time we drove them back into the sea from which they came!"

Saul raised his hands. "Using what against them? They have iron weapons. We have two swords. Our warriors carry dull mattoxes, ruined axes, chipped sickles and spears. Even if we had a blacksmith, do I have the shekels to pay to sharpen weapons for an army? And if I did, the Philistines would know we were preparing for war, and they'd come down on us and drown us in our own blood."

"So we wait? We do nothing when they raid our crops?"

"What crops?" Kish ground out. "God destroyed the wheat."

"We wait, my son. We plan."

Fear still reigned in Israel!

Jonathan's father put his arm around him and walked him to the entrance of the tent. "You go to Gibeah with the men I've assigned you. Secure the city."

Jonathan bowed his head and left the tent. He would go to Gibeah and do exactly what his father commanded.

And then he would destroy Geba before the Philistines there had time to attack and destroy his father!

✦   ✦   ✦

Raging, Saul paced before Jonathan, who was still exultant over the defeat of Geba. "What sort of message does it give all Israel when my own son doesn't listen to me?"

"I secured Gibeah."

"And destroyed Geba! You have brought disaster on us all! Did you think killing a few hundred Philistines and burning a small outpost would accomplish anything? You pulled the tail of a lion and now he will turn and devour us! When word spreads of what you did, we will have all Philistia thirsting for our blood! *We are not ready for this war!*"

Jonathan shrank inwardly as doubt squelched his assurance that God had wanted him to attack the outpost. *Was I listening to my own pride?* If they obeyed God, would the Lord not give them victory on every side? Would the Lord not help them rid their land of the Philistines just as He had helped them crush the Ammonites at Jabesh-gilead? "Samuel said—"

"Be silent! I am the king. Let me think . . ." Saul gripped his head. "I didn't expect rebellion from you!"

Abner cleared his throat. "My lord, what order shall I give the men?"

Saul lowered his hands and stared off into space.

"My lord?"

Saul turned, jaw set. "Send out messengers and have them blow the trumpets. Tell everyone I attacked the Philistine outpost." He glared at

Jonathan. "Better if the people think *I* acted boldly than have them know my son acted in haste and without the backing of the king."

Humiliated, his confidence shredded by doubt, Jonathan said nothing.

✦   ✦   ✦

Jonathan went cold when he heard three thousand Philistine chariots had been sighted. Each bore a driver and a skilled warrior equipped with bow and arrows and several spears.

Saul paled. "How many soldiers?"

"Too many to count, my lord. They are as numerous as the grains of sand upon the seashore, and they're already at Beth-aven."

Worse news came the following morning. Some of Saul's warriors had deserted in the night. Terrified by the power of Philistia, others clustered and whispered among themselves. The men of Israel took to caves and thickets, hid among rocks and in pits and dry cisterns.

Saul returned to Gilgal and waited for Samuel. Jonathan went with him, as did a young armor bearer Saul pressed into Jonathan's service. What Ebenezer lacked in size, he made up for in zeal.

Kish, Abner, and the others were full of advice for the king, but the king listened to no one.

Racked with guilt, Jonathan spent hours in unceasing prayer, asking for the Lord's forgiveness and pleading for guidance. Though many cheered the victory at Geba, most were sick with fear and ready to run.

Abner grew frustrated and confronted the king. "We have less than two thousand warriors right now, my lord, and more are deserting every day. You must make a decision."

Jonathan was afraid to give advice. He was afraid to make claims about what God would do. No one could question God's power, but every man alive in Israel questioned whether He would use it for their defense. Worse, Jonathan realized now that his one small victory could precipitate an all-out war. He looked out over the tents and couldn't help wonder how so few could stand against so many. Rather than rallying his father and his army, Jonathan had succeeded only in bringing their fear to the surface and sending thousands into hiding.

What a sight we are! Lord, why is it so hard for Your people to trust You when You've proven Your power and faithfulness to us time after time? Is it because we know we continue to sin? How do we root out the sin in us? Our forefathers didn't listen to You, and now we don't. Only a few days ago, You sent lightning and thunder and rain, and all these men can think about is the ruined crops and what they will eat when winter comes! You are God! You hold our lives in the palms of Your hands!

Fear spread like tares in the wheat until even Jonathan felt the roots of it sinking into his heart. Some of those who had been with him at Geba deserted. Each morning revealed more empty spaces among the camps of Saul's "best of Israel."

The king grew more and more frustrated. "The entire army will scatter before that old man gets here!"

Jonathan shuddered. *That old man?* Samuel was God's prophet, God's voice to the people. "He will come."

"Where is he? Why does he delay? He said he would come in seven days."

"It hasn't been seven days yet, Father."

"Soon, my entire army will have melted away."

Abner did what he could to rally the remaining warriors, but confidence in the king was at its lowest ebb and the prophet's warning was fresh in their minds. Their king had brought trouble upon them. Forgotten was the victory over the Ammonites. All men could think of was the gathering storm of war, the three thousand chariots and multitude of foot soldiers getting ready to destroy them.

Jonathan felt he had to do something to make up for bringing all this on his father. *But what? What, Lord?* No answer came.

Jonathan awakened Ebenezer before dawn on the seventh day. "If my father misses me, tell him I've gone out to wait for Samuel." Jonathan went to the edge of the shrinking camp. Men huddled over their fires, ducking their heads when he glanced their way. He didn't want to think about what they might be discussing.

Because of me, Lord, they've lost hope in Your king.

The sun rose. There was no sign of Samuel. Jonathan worried. Had his actions at Geba caused the prophet trouble as well? What if the Philistines had taken him captive? Or worse, what if they had killed the aged man of God? He broke out in a cold sweat even thinking such thoughts.

Lord, we need him. He speaks Your Word to us. Please protect him and bring him to us. Oh, God, help us. Tell us what You want us to do! I thought I was stepping out in faith, but maybe my father and his advisors are right and I acted the fool. If so, forgive me, Lord. Let the trouble fall on my head and not my father's. Not on these men who shake with fear. Don't abandon us on my account, Lord.

Jonathan's armor bearer, Ebenezer, came running. "The king—" he rasped for breath—"the king wants you with him. He's going to make the sacrifice."

"What?" Jonathan ran as fast as he could, Ebenezer close behind him. When he reached his father's tent, he entered and went cold at the sight of the king wearing a priestly ephod. "No!" His lungs burned. His heart pounded so hard, he thought he would choke. He grasped the Law he wore around his neck. "You can't do this, Father. The Law says only a priest—"

"There is no priest!"

Terrified for all their sakes, Jonathan went to his father. "It's not midday yet, my lord. Samuel *will* come."

Sweat beaded on Saul's brow. "I called for him and he did not come. I can't wait any longer." His face was pale and strained.

"The Lord will not help us if you do this."

"My army! My men are leaving me! What would you have me do?" He looked around at all his advisors.

"Whatever is in your heart to do, my king." They all seemed to agree.

Jonathan looked from Abner to Kish to the others and back to his father. "Samuel will come!" He stepped in front of his father. "Gideon had fewer men than we have, and he defeated the Midianites."

"I am not Gideon!"

"You were a farmer like him. The Spirit of the Lord came upon you, too. You gathered a force of three hundred and thirty thousand warriors and defeated the Ammonites!"

"And where are all my warriors now?" Saul yanked the flap of the tent aside. "Gone!"

"You have more than Gideon had. Nahash and the Ammonites are destroyed!"

"The Philistines are a worse scourge than the Midiantes or the Ammonites." Saul let the flap fall. He groaned, rubbing his eyes. "I never asked to be king. I never asked for any of this!"

"God chose you, Father." Jonathan spoke as calmly as he could, though their fear seeped into him. "Trust in the Lord and in the power of His strength!"

"And what does that mean?" Abner stepped forward. "In practical, tactical terms, Jonathan?"

"God could send lightning bolts on our enemies," Kish agreed. "Why doesn't He?"

Saul turned abruptly. "Where is the Ark?" They all looked at him. "Maybe if I had the Ark with me. The Philistines were afraid of it once. Remember?"

Jonathan felt a knot growing in his stomach. Did his father mean to use the Ark like an idol? "They captured the Ark."

"Yes. And a plague of mice and rats destroyed their crops. The Philistines were sick with tumors. Eventually they sent it back on a cart loaded down with gold." Saul looked at Abner. "How long would it take to bring it here?"

A warrior entered the tent. "There is still no sign of Samuel, my lord."

Abner frowned. "There is no time. You must do something now before all the men are gone." Everyone agreed.

"Don't." Jonathan was a lone voice in the tent. He looked into his father's face. "Wait. Please. Give the seer more time."

Abner shook his head. "You know too little of men, Jonathan. If we wait much longer, the camp will be empty and the king will stand alone. How long do you think your father will survive with just those of us inside this tent to defend him?"

Abner's words swayed Saul. "Bring me the burnt offerings and the peace offerings. We can't ask God to help us unless we give *Him* something."

Jonathan's heart pounded heavily, the pit of his stomach like a hard, cold ball of fear. He drew out the Law. "You mustn't do this, Father. Please, listen. I can show you—"

"Do you not yet understand?" Saul shouted. "I can't wait." His eyes blazed. "I won't wait! Samuel promised he would come. He didn't keep his word!" Saul went outside. "Gather some stones. We'll build the altar right here." He grabbed Jonathan's arm. "You will stand over there. And say no more!" His chin jerked up. "The kings of other nations make sacrifices before their armies. Why shouldn't I?" Saul turned to Abner. "Call the men. They must see what I do. Tell them I am making an offering to the Lord so He will help us."

Jonathan turned to Ebenezer and spoke quietly. "Station yourself where you can see anyone approaching camp. When you see Samuel, run back here like the wind and shout his coming. Hurry!"

"Yes, my lord." The boy drew back from the others, turned, and ran to do Jonathan's bidding.

As the young prince watched his father, he wondered if God would take Saul's fear into account. *Lord, forgive him. He doesn't know what he's doing.*

The men gathering looked pleased by what was about to happen. Had his father read, written, and studied the Law, he would know better than to defy the Lord like this! And those who followed him would know better than to trust their lives to the plans of men.

The sun hovered above the western horizon. A crippled calf was brought to Saul. Why kill a healthy one without blemish as the Law commanded? It seemed that as long as his father had decided to disregard one part of the Law, none of its other instructions mattered either. Jonathan watched as King Saul put his hands on the animal's head, prayed loudly for God's help, and then slit the calf's throat. Jonathan closed his eyes, sickened by the ceremony. Soon he smelled smoke, mingled with the stench of disobedience.

Dismissed, the men went about their duties. Saul looked at Jonathan and smiled, confident again. He went back inside his tent to talk with his advisors.

Jonathan sat, head in his hands.

Ebenezer came running. Face flushed, out of breath, he rasped, "The prophet comes."

Shame filled Jonathan. How could he face Samuel?

Saul came outside. "Come! We will meet him together!" He spread his arms wide and smiled warmly. "Welcome, Samuel!"

Samuel's eyes blazed. His fingers whitened on his staff. "Saul! What is this you have done?"

Surprised, Saul frowned. He looked from the prophet to the men around him. "I saw my men scattering from me—" his eyes narrowed coldly— "and you didn't arrive when you said you would, and the Philistines are at Micmash ready for battle. So I said, 'The Philistines are ready to march against us at Gilgal, and I haven't even asked for the Lord's help!' So I felt compelled—" he swept his hand, taking in his advisors—"to offer the burnt offering myself before you came."

Jonathan looked between the two men. Wasn't his father's sin bad enough without trying to cast blame on the seer?

Samuel's glance took in everyone. "Leave us!"

Jonathan wanted to flee before the wrath that was sure to come.

"My son stays." Saul commanded Jonathan with a gesture.

Jonathan took his place beside his father. He could not desert him now: how could he when Geba had started all this?

Samuel stared at Saul. "How foolish! You have not kept the command the Lord your God gave you. Had you kept it, the Lord would have established your kingdom over Israel forever. But now your kingdom must end, for the Lord has sought out a man after His own heart. The Lord has already appointed him to be the leader of His people, because you have not kept the Lord's command."

Jonathan cringed.

Saul gritted his teeth in anger, but when the prophet turned away, the king took a step toward him. "You turn your back on me, Samuel? You turn your back on Israel's king? Where are you going?"

"I am going to Gibeah." Samuel sounded weary and disheartened. "I would advise you to do the same."

Saul kicked the dust. "Go and tell Abner to count the men we have left."

Tears pricked Jonathan's eyes as he watched the old prophet walk away. "We should follow Samuel, Father."

"After we find out how many men we have left."

Jonathan wanted to cry out in grief. What did it matter how many men stood with a king rejected by God? "Let me speak to him on your behalf."

"Go, if you think you can do any good." Saul turned away.

✦   ✦   ✦

Jonathan ran after Samuel.

Samuel turned when he came near and spoke to those accompanying him. They moved away. Samuel leaned heavily on his staff, his face etched with exhaustion and sorrow.

Jonathan fell to his knees and bowed his face to the ground.

"Stand up!"

Jonathan surged to his feet, trembling.

"Why do you chase after me? Do you mean to use your sword against me?"

"No!" Jonathan blanched. "My father means you no harm, nor do I! Please . . . I came to ask you to forgive me. The blame is mine!"

Samuel shook his head. "You did not perform the sacrifice."

Tears blurred Jonathan's eyes. "My father was afraid. Because of what I did at Geba, all this . . ." He could not see Samuel's expression or guess at what the seer thought. "I'm the one who attacked Geba and brought the Philistines' wrath upon us. When we heard of the forces that are coming against us, the men began to desert. My father—"

"Each man makes his decisions, Jonathan, and each bears the consequences of what he decides."

"But are we not also prey to circumstances around us?"

"You know better."

"Can there be no allowances for mistakes? for fear?"

"Who is the enemy, Jonathan?"

"The Philistines." Jonathan wept. "I don't want God to be our enemy. What can I do to make things right?"

Samuel put his hand on Jonathan's shoulder. "What do you wear against your heart, my son?"

Jonathan put his hand against his breastplate. "The Law."

"Did you write it in your own hand because you thought you would be king someday?"

Jonathan blinked. Had he? Samuel said that Saul's kingdom would not last now. Did that mean Israel would fall? Did that mean the people would all suffer at the hands of their enemies?

"You say nothing."

Jonathan searched his eyes. "I want to say no." He swallowed hard. "But do I know myself well enough to answer?"

"Speak the truth to the king no matter what the others around him say. And pray for him, my son." Samuel released him.

Jonathan longed for reassurance. "Will you pray for my father?" Surely the prayers of a righteous man would be heard by God.

"Yes."

Jonathan grasped hope. "Then the Lord our God will not abandon us completely."

"God does not abandon men, my son. Men abandon God." As the old prophet headed toward Gibeah, his companions joined him.

Jonathan stood watching for a long time, praying for Samuel's safety and for his father, the king, to repent.

+   +   +

Samuel waited in Gibeah while the Philistines encamped at Micmash. King Saul returned to Gibeah and held court under the shade of a tamarisk tree. When no Israelite army came out to meet the Philistines, the Philistines sent out raiding parties. Ophrah was attacked, then Beth-horon. Soon after, they plundered the borderland overlooking the valley of Zeboim facing the desert.

Samuel returned to Ramah. Saul waited for a sign from God or a word of encouragement from the prophet. None came. He grew more sullen with each passing day. His army of six hundred sank into despair. Abner and the other leaders gave advice, but Saul didn't listen. Numerous plans were laid out and then rejected. The king seemed incapable of action. Worse, he became suspicious. "Send someone to keep watch over Samuel. If he goes anywhere, follow him and report back to me!"

"Samuel prays for you, Father."

"So you say, but can I trust him? He said God will choose another."

Reports came in that the Philistines were on the move again.

Jonathan heard all the talk and kept his eyes open. The inactivity wore on him as much as it did the others. Was this what war was like? Long weeks, sometimes months, of waiting? And then the terror and exhilaration of battle?

The Philistines took cruel delight in raiding when and where they pleased, for King Saul sent no one to stop them. Jonathan's father could not get his mind off Samuel's prophecy.

Something had to be done to rouse the king and the men of Israel, something to bring them together as they had been when the Lord gave them Jabesh-gilead!

Jonathan prayed, *Lord, help me. I don't want to make the same mistake I did with Geba!*

If Jonathan did anything, he must do it alone so the blame would fall only on him if he failed.

A Philistine detachment was camped at the pass at Micmash. Jonathan knew the area well. The slippery, thorny cliffs of Bozez and Seneh faced each other. But there was one place above, barely a furrow of land, where one man could hold ground and kill a score of Philistines, possibly more.

Jonathan might die. So be it. Better to die in battle with honor than live in fear of idol worshipers. He rose, shouldered the quiver of arrows, took up his bow, and left the city.

Ebenezer grabbed Jonathan's shield and his own bow and arrows and ran after him. "Where are we going, my lord?"

"To see what the Lord will do."

The boy stayed at his side, but Jonathan wondered if he would be brave enough to follow all the way.

When they were away from Gibeah, Jonathan faced Ebenezer. "Let's go across to the outpost of those pagans. Perhaps the Lord will help us, for nothing can hinder the Lord. He can win a battle whether He has many warriors or only a few!"

Ebenezer's eyes brightened. He grinned broadly. "Do what you think is best. I'm with you completely, whatever you decide."

Jonathan laughed. What would the Philistines make of the two of them?

When they reached the cliff opposite the Philistine encampment, Jonathan surveyed the gap between them and the enemy camp. *Lord, send me a sign that You will give those men into our hands!*

He felt a quickening, a flush of heat rushing through his veins, a *yes, go* rush of confidence. Jonathan pointed. "All right then. We will cross over and let them see us. If they say to us, 'Stay where you are or we'll kill you,' then we will stop and not go up to them. But if they say, 'Come on up and fight,' then we will go up. That will be the Lord's sign that He will help us defeat them."

Either way, they would fight against God's enemies. One way would bring certain death. The other victory.

Ebenezer nodded. "We can hold them off as long as we have arrows, my lord. And then you have your sword!"

Jonathan gripped the boy's shoulder. Whether in the gap or on the cliffs, the boy was as willing to die fighting as he was. Jonathan descended first, setting the pace. Slipping once, he caught hold and regained his footing. "Watch it there, my friend. Move to your right. That's it."

When they had both reached the bottom, Jonathan moved out of the shadows into the open. He planted his feet and lifted his head. Ebenezer joined him.

"Look!" A man laughed from above. "The Hebrews are crawling out of their holes!" Other Philistines joined the watchman. A few warriors peered over the edge of the cliff. One spit. Their laughter echoed between the walls of the cliffs.

Jonathan's heart beat hard for battle. *Lord, please give them into our hands! Let them know there is a God in Israel!*

And the sign came.

"Come on up here, and we'll teach you a lesson!"

"Come on, climb right behind me, for the Lord will help us defeat them!" Jonathan ran at the cliff and started to climb, Ebenezer right behind him. Grasping hold of thick-rooted thornbushes, Jonathan pulled himself up. He found footholds and climbed like a lizard on a fortress wall, trailed by his young armor bearer.

Still laughing, the Philistine warriors moved back from the edge of the cliff. Jonathan could hear them. When he reached the top, he walked forward and took his stand. He grinned at the surprise on the Philistines' faces.

"A couple of boys!"

One of the Philistines drew his sword. "Both about to die!"

Ebenezer took his place near Jonathan.

One of the Philistines guffawed.

In one fluid motion, Jonathan shrugged the bow from his shoulder, whipped an arrow out, set it, and sent it straight and true to its target. The laughing Philistine fell back, an arrow between his eyes. Stunned, the others stared at Jonathan and then let out a battle roar, drew swords, and came at Jonathan and Ebenezer, who shot one arrow after another, and one after another, Philistines fell—twenty in all.

The shouting had roused the others. More shouting came from behind.

With his last arrow released, Jonathan drew his sword and gave his battle cry. *"For the Lord!"* The ground shook as Philistine warriors panicked and ran. Jonathan ran into the confusion and hacked down an officer. Ebenezer grabbed a spear and threw it into a fleeing Philistine. More screams rent the air.

"The shofar blows!" Ebenezer cried out. "The king is coming!"

Jonathan shouted in exultation. Israel was on the move! Philistines ran in terror. Jonathan spotted a few Hebrews among the Philistines. Whether they were men who had gone up to fight with the enemy or were captives did not matter now. "Fight for Israel or die!" Jonathan shouted, and the men turned as one and fought for Jonathan.

"The Ark!" Ebenezer shouted.

Jonathan looked back and saw the Ark. *No!* With a roar, he turned, enraged at the thought of the enemy getting their hands on it again. He ran into the Philistine camp, sword flashing. *No one will ever take the Ark from us!* He cut to the left. *No one will open it and desecrate it!* He cut to the right. *No one will take the Law from us!* He slashed and stabbed. *No one will open the jar and spill out the manna!* He sliced off a warrior's arm and cut off his head. *No one will break the staff of Aaron that sprouted leaves, bloomed, and bore almonds in a day!*

Jonathan screamed in rage as he fought. *"Jehovah-Roi! El Shaddai! Adonai!"* God our King! God Almighty! Lord!

And Philistines ran from him in terror.

From all directions, the Hebrews came. The king's army of six hundred swelled and advanced north from Gibeah. Men of Ephraim pressed in from the south.

Confusion reigned among the Philistines. Some fled toward Aijalon, others to Ophrah, trying to reach Beth-aven, their stronghold, the house of wickedness.

Taking up a spear, Jonathan kept after the Philistines, encouraging the other Israelites who had joined him. They grew weary and faint, and were barely able to keep up with him. When Jonathan entered the woods, he spotted bees swarming over a hole in the ground. "Honey!" He reached out the end of his staff, dipped it into the hole, and brought up a portion of honeycomb. "God provides!" He ate and felt his strength increasing.

Men stopped and watched him, but made no move to take any of the honey.

"Eat!" Jonathan looked around at them, perplexed. "What's the matter with you?" He dipped his staff again and held it out to them. "The honey will strengthen you!"

"We can't!"

"Your father made the army take a strict oath that anyone who eats food today will be cursed. That is why everyone is weary and faint."

Jonathan went cold, and then hot. "My father has made trouble for us all!" Would he have to die for eating the honey? "A command like that only hurts us. See how refreshed I am now that I have eaten this little bit of honey. It is a gift from the Lord!"

"If we eat it, the king will have us killed."

He pressed them no further. His father would excuse him, but would not excuse others. "If the men had been allowed to eat freely from the food they found among our enemies, think how many more Philistines we could have killed!" All the Philistines would have been dead before the day was over.

Jonathan turned away and continued the chase. Those who could, followed.

✦   ✦   ✦

From Micmash to Aijalon, the Philistines fell. Many escaped because Saul's men were too exhausted from lack of food to follow after them. When the Hebrews came upon sheep, cattle, and calves, they fell upon them, slaughtering the animals in the field and cutting away chunks of flesh, their mouths dripping blood as they ate to satisfy their ravenous hunger.

The priest cried out, "Stop what you're doing! You're breaking the Law."

The men did not listen.

Saul built an altar and ordered the men to bring the animals there. "Kill them here, and drain the blood before you eat them. Do not sin against the Lord by eating meat with the blood still in it."

"Do not sin against the Lord." The priest ran, echoing the king's command. "You must not eat meat with blood still in it!"

Sickened, Jonathan turned away. It was too late to undo what the men had done.

Anxiety spread through the camp. The men who had followed Jonathan came to him. "We will say nothing of what you did in the forest."

Jonathan was troubled by their fear. Did they really think the king would kill his own son? Would he? Could he?

Saul summoned him. "So you disobey me again?"

Jonathan's stomach was a cold knot of fear. He felt sweat break out on the back of his neck. Had someone told the king about the honey? The king's advisors looked at Jonathan, their expressions closed, watchful. "You go out to war without my leave!"

Jonathan lifted his head. "God gave us victory."

"You might have been killed! What did you think you were doing, going out against the Philistines with only your armor bearer? Where is he?" Saul looked around. "Why isn't he at your side?"

"He's asleep." Jonathan bared his teeth in a forced grin. "It has been a long day, Father."

Saul laughed and pounded Jonathan's back. "My son! The warrior!" He looked at the men. "He climbs a cliff, kills more than a score of Philistines, all better equipped and more skilled than he, and then he sets the entire Philistine army on the run!" His eyes glowed as he looked at Jonathan. "You bring honor upon your father, the king."

Jonathan saw something dark in his father's praise. "The panic that came upon the Philistines was from the Lord, my king. It is the Lord who rescued Israel this day."

"Yes!" Saul pounded him again. "The Lord." He smiled at the others. "But we've kept them running, haven't we?" He went to a table and unrolled a map. "Let's chase the Philistines all night and plunder them until sunrise. Let's destroy every last one of them. Think of the wealth it will bring me!"

Jonathan thought that unwise. "The men are exhausted. And now that they have eaten, they will sleep as though drugged."

Saul glared at him. "The men will do what *I* say."

And perish for it! Jonathan held his tongue, hoping the advisors would speak sense.

Instead, they all agreed with the king. They said exactly what Saul wanted to hear. "We'll do whatever you think is best. We will go after them and be the richer for it."

Jonathan looked at Ahijah. "Shouldn't we inquire of the Lord?"

The priest took a nervous step forward. "Your son shows your great wisdom, my lord. Let's ask God first."

When the others agreed, Saul shrugged. "Should we go after the Philistines? Will You help us defeat them?"

Ahijah placed his hands over the Urim and Thummin and waited for God's answer.

Saul stood silent.

The men waited.

The Lord did not answer.

+ + +

The night seemed darker to Jonathan. Even as dawn came, he felt no lifting in his spirit. The sun rose and moved slowly across the sky, and with it the echoing words of the soldiers in the woods: *"Your father made the army take a strict oath . . . anyone who eats food today will be cursed."*

Jonathan bowed his face to the ground. *Lord, I took no such oath. I knew nothing about it! Am I still bound by it? Do You refuse to speak to the king because I sinned? Let it not be so. Don't let me again be the one to bring disaster upon the people!*

When he rose, he sat back on his heels. He knew what he must do.

Abner intercepted him. "What do you think you're doing?"

"I must speak with my father, the king."

"And confess about the honey?"

"You know—"

"Yes! I know. I know everything that happens among my men. I have to know!" He pulled Jonathan aside. "No one has said anything to the king. Nor will they."

"I've brought trouble upon him again."

"He made a hasty vow, Jonathan. Should that vow cost the people their prince?"

Jonathan tried to step around him.

Abner blocked his way, eyes flashing. "Do you think the Lord would want the death of His champion?"

Jonathan went hot. "The Lord needs no champion!"

Abner caught hold of Jonathan's arm, holding him back. "What glory would the Lord receive from your death?"

When Jonathan turned away, he saw his father watching from the entrance of his tent.

Eyes dark, Saul came outside and shouted orders. "Something's wrong!" He looked at Abner. "I want all my army commanders to come here."

The men gathered quickly and stood before him.

Saul looked at each of them. "We must find out what sin was committed today."

Jonathan was afraid. Never had he seen such a look on his father's face. The king's eyes burned with suspicion. *Does my father now see me as his enemy?* He felt sick.

"Jonathan and I will stand over here, and all of you stand over there."
Jonathan took his place at the king's side. Would his father kill him?

"We want a king like the nations around us!"

Jonathan's heart began to pound heavily. He had heard stories about the
surrounding nations, how they executed their own sons to maintain their
power. Some even sacrificed them on the city walls to please their gods.
Sweat broke out on his face. *Will my father kill me, Lord? Not my father.*

"I vow by the name of the Lord who rescued Israel that the sinner will
surely die, even if it is my own son Jonathan!"

Jonathan received his answer, but he could not believe it. *No. He cannot
have changed so much.* He looked at Abner, then at the others. The men all
stared straight ahead, not meeting his eyes. Not a man spoke a word.

Frustrated, Saul summoned the entire army. "Someone will tell me!"
When the men were gathered, the king prayed loudly. "O Lord, God of
Israel, please show us who is guilty and who is innocent."

Jonathan looked at his father. He didn't know what to do. If he confessed
now, would his father break his vow or keep it? Either way, Jonathan had
put his father in an untenable position yet again. Fear shook him, for no
good could come from this day!

The priest cast lots. Men and their units were found innocent.

Jonathan felt his father's tension grow with each passing moment.
Moisture beaded the king's forehead. Jonathan could smell the rank sweat
of fear. *He knows! He's afraid it's me! He doesn't know what to do! He won't
kill me. He loves me. He can't kill his own son.*

Saul held out a trembling hand. "Now cast lots again and choose between
me and Jonathan."

Ahijah did so. He looked up, relieved. "It's Jonathan, my lord."

When his father turned, eyes blazing, Jonathan was shocked to see
relief in his eyes, even as they welled with tears of fury. "Tell me what you
have done!"

"I tasted a little honey," Jonathan admitted. "It was only a little bit on
the end of my stick. Does that deserve death?"

"Yes, Jonathan," Saul said, "you must die! May God strike me and even
kill me if you do not die for this." Saul drew his sword.

Jonathan gaped, too shocked to move.

"No!" Officers moved quickly between king and prince. "Jonathan has
won this great victory for Israel. Should he die? *Far from it!*"

Men shouted from every side.

Abner spoke louder than the rest. "As surely as the Lord lives, not one
hair on his head will be touched, for God helped him do a great deed today.
You cannot do this, Saul!"

Jonathan cringed. He saw his father's wrath evaporate. He looked this way and that. Finally, Saul slid his sword back into its scabbard. "My hand will not be raised against my own son." He put his hand on Jonathan's shoulder and dismissed the army.

As they walked away, Saul took his hand away and went inside the tent. Jonathan followed. He wanted to beg forgiveness. Abner and the advisors stood around him.

Saul faced them. "God has destroyed the wheat harvest, but other crops will soon be ready for harvest, and an army needs provisions." He did not look at Jonathan. "We will not pursue the Philistines. We will withdraw to our own land. Tell your units to break camp. We leave within the hour."

"Father—"

"Not now. We will talk later, on the way home."

When the army was on the move, Jonathan walked beside his father. "I'm sorry."

"Sorry." Saul's tone was flat. He stared straight ahead. "Samuel is against me. Is my own son to be my enemy as well?"

Jonathan's heart sank and tears welled. "Had I known of your vow, I never would have eaten the honey."

Saul glanced at him and then looked ahead again. "Jonathan, you are either with me or you are against me. Which is it?"

Never had words hurt so much. "No one is more loyal to you than I."

"It may seem so to you, but if you continue to act on your own as you did at Geba and now Micmash, you will split the nation. Is that what you want? To remove the crown from my head and have Samuel place it on your own?"

"No!" Jonathan stopped and turned to him. *"No!"*

"Keep walking!"

Jonathan fell into step beside him. His father spoke again, without looking at him. "They all stood against me in order to protect you."

Jonathan could not deny it. Men were easily swayed by an act of courage, but it was God—not he—who had brought the victory. "I only meant to rally the men."

"And me?"

Had his actions brought shame upon his father? What could he say to make amends if that were so?

"Samuel said God has already chosen another to be king." Saul looked at Jonathan, frowning. "Is it you?"

Crushed, Jonathan spoke, his voice choked with emotion. "Father, no! You are king of Israel. My hand will never be raised against you!"

Saul's eyes cleared of suspicion. He put his hand on Jonathan's shoulder and squeezed. "We must protect one another, my son. Like it or not, our lives are in peril. Not just our lives, but those of your brothers as well. If anyone takes the crown from us, Malkishua, Abinadab, Ishbosheth, and your sisters will be killed so that my line will be ended. Do you understand? It is the way of kings to destroy all their enemies, even the children that might grow up to come against them."

He squeezed Jonathan's shoulder again and released him. "Don't trust anyone, Jonathan. We have enemies all around us. Enemies everywhere."

It was true Israel was threatened from all sides. The Philistines were along the coast, Moab to the east, Ammon to the north, and the kings of Zobah to the south. It seemed the entire world wanted to destroy God's people! And the fastest way to scatter an army was to kill the king.

But his father seemed to think there were enemies among their own people as well.

"We will unite the tribes, Father. We will teach them to trust in the Lord our God."

Saul was looking ahead. "You will be at my right hand." He kept walking. "We will build a dynasty."

Jonathan glanced at him. Samuel had said—

Saul made a fist. "I will hold on to my power." His arm jerked as he spoke to himself in a low, hard voice. "I will hold on to my power. I will." He let his hand drop to his side and his chin went up. "I will!"

THREE

❖❖❖❖❖❖❖❖

Samuel came to the king with a commandment from the Lord: Go out and destroy the Amalekites who had waylaid and murdered the defenseless Israelite stragglers who had come out of Egypt.

"Here is a chance for glory!" Saul slapped Jonathan on the back. "God will surely bless us!"

And they did have victory. But Jonathan worried, warning his father not to delay in obeying every instruction Samuel had given. "He said to destroy everything!"

"King Agag is your father's trophy." Abner raised his goblet to King Saul. "He is more use to us alive than dead. When all Israel sees him humbled, they will know the only man they need fear is King Saul!"

Jonathan looked between them. "Kill *every* Amalekite, Samuel said, and the animals as well."

His father clapped him on the shoulder. "Celebrate, Jonathan. Stop worrying so much."

"The Law says to love the Lord your God with all your heart—"

"—mind, soul, and strength." Saul waved his hand. "Yes, I know the Law, too."

Did he? He had never written the Law in his own hand, nor listened for long when Jonathan read it to him. "You have not completed—"

"Enough!" Saul slammed his goblet down. Men looked their way. Saul waved magnanimously. "Eat! Drink! Be merry!" He leaned toward Jonathan and spoke in a hoarse whisper. "Take your gloom elsewhere." When Jonathan started to rise, Saul grabbed his arm. "Look around you, Jonathan." Wine splashed from his goblet as he swept his arm wide. "See how happy the men are. We must keep them happy!"

Jonathan saw the fear in his father's eyes, but knew it was misplaced. "It is the Lord we must please, Father. *The Lord.*"

Saul released him and waved him away.

Jonathan went outside and sat staring out over the hills.

What would Samuel say when he came?

He covered his head, ashamed.

✦   ✦   ✦

King Saul led the army to Carmel, taking with him the best of the Amalekites' sheep and goats, cattle, fat calves and lambs. He ordered a monument erected in his own honor. Continuing the celebrations, he displayed the captive King Agag for all to see as he led the army back to Gilgal.

Samuel came to meet him there.

"May the Lord bless you!" Saul opened his arms wide. "I have carried out the Lord's command."

"Then what is all the bleating of sheep and goats and the lowing of cattle I hear?"

Jonathan cringed at the fierce anger in Samuel's voice.

His father glanced at the officers and leaders. "Come! You need refreshment." Saul led the way to his tent, leaving the others behind.

Samuel entered the king's tent. Saul poured wine, but Samuel would not take it.

Flustered, Saul explained. "It's true that the army spared the best of the sheep, goats, and cattle." He looked at Jonathan. Eyes flickering, he turned back to Samuel and added quickly, "But they are going to sacrifice them to the Lord your God. We have destroyed everything else."

"*Stop!*" Samuel cried out. He bowed his head and raised his hands to cover his ears.

King Saul took a step back, his face ashen. "Leave us."

Jonathan went willingly, fear knotting his stomach. He kept watch at the entrance of the king's quarters. He could hear every word.

Samuel spoke. "Listen to what the Lord told me last night!"

"What did He tell you?"

"Although you may think little of yourself, are you not the leader of the tribes of Israel? The Lord has anointed you king of Israel. And the Lord sent you on a mission and told you, 'Go and completely destroy the sinners, the Amalekites, until they are all dead.' Why haven't you obeyed the Lord? Why did you rush for the plunder and do what was evil in the Lord's sight?"

Jonathan's heart pounded faster with each word the prophet spoke.

"But I did obey the Lord!"

Don't argue, Father. Confess!

"I carried out the mission He gave me."

Father, don't lie!

"I brought back King Agag, but I destroyed everyone else. Then my troops brought in the best of the sheep, goats, cattle, and plunder to sacrifice to the Lord your God in Gilgal."

The heat of shame filled Jonathan's face as he listened to his father's lies and excuses.

Samuel raised his voice. "What is more pleasing to the Lord: your burnt offerings and sacrifices or your obedience to His voice? Listen! Obedience is better than sacrifice, and submission is better than offering the fat of rams. Rebellion is as sinful as witchcraft, and stubbornness as bad as worshiping idols. So because you have rejected the command of the Lord, He has rejected you as king."

Saul cried out in fear, "All right! I admit it. Yes, I have sinned. I have disobeyed your instructions and the Lord's command, for I was afraid of the people and did what they demanded. But now, please forgive my sin and come back with me so that I may worship the Lord."

Jonathan held his head and paced, cold sweat beading. It wasn't God his father feared, but men. *Lord, have mercy. Lord, have mercy.*

"I will not go back with you!" Samuel's voice came closer to the opening of the tent. He was leaving. "Since you have rejected the Lord's command, He has rejected you as king of Israel."

Jonathan heard a struggle and the sound of tearing cloth, and his heart stopped. He opened the curtain and saw his father on his knees, clutching at the prophet's torn robe, his face ashen, his eyes wild with fear.

Samuel stared down at him in anguish. "The Lord has torn the kingdom of Israel from you today and has given it to someone else—one who is better than you." Samuel raised his head and closed his eyes. "And He who is the Glory of Israel will not lie, nor will He change His mind, for He is not human that He should change His mind!"

"I know I have sinned," Saul moaned. "But please, at least honor me before the elders of my people and before Israel by coming back with me so that I may worship the Lord your God."

Heart sinking, Jonathan took his hand from the curtain. His father was more afraid of the men who waited outside than he was of the Lord God who held a man's life in the palm of His mighty hand.

Samuel came outside with Saul. If anyone noticed his torn robe, no one spoke of it. Saul pretended everything was all right. He talked, smiled, his gaze moving from one leader to another.

Jonathan's body was taut. He waited. *God does not change His mind.*

"Bring King Agag to me," Samuel said.

Everyone looked at Saul. "Go!" the king said. "Do as he says."

A few moments later, Jonathan saw the Amalekite king walking in front of the guards, head high. Clearly, he thought all the bitterness of death was behind him and he was safe in Saul's care. He gave a nod to Saul and then lifted his head as he looked at Samuel. Was he waiting for an introduction?

Samuel drew the sword from King Saul's scabbard. "As your sword has killed the sons of many mothers, now your mother will be childless." He raised the sword high and brought it down before the Amalekite could move.

Agag's lifeless body crumpled to the ground, his skull cleaved open.

Everyone talked at once. Saul grabbed his sword and jerked it free. He shouted for his officers to dismiss their divisions. They could go home. The Amalekites were no longer a threat. He called to Abner. "We are going home to Gibeah."

Jonathan followed after Samuel. They walked together in silence for a long while, and then Samuel stopped and looked at him. "The Lord is grieved that He made Saul king over Israel." He stood silent and erect.

Jonathan felt the rejection as acutely as though he were responsible for all of his father's sins. His shoulders heaved. Tears streamed down his cheeks.

Samuel stepped forward and grasped Jonathan's arm. "The Lord is your salvation. Blessed be the name of the Lord."

"So be it." Jonathan choked out the words.

Samuel's hold loosened. "I'm going home to Ramah." He walked away, bent in sorrow.

Though he didn't know it then, it was the last time Jonathan would ever see his beloved mentor.

+   +   +

Jonathan saw his father change after that day. In the first of his strange bouts of rage, Saul held his head and ranted. "I will not listen! I will not!" Grabbing a goblet, he threw it against a wall. "Why should I listen to you?" He overturned a table.

Men watched from doorways, ducking back when the king turned in their direction. Jonathan, keeping watch outside his father's chamber, sent them away. He didn't want anyone to see the king like this. The whole of Israel would be in confusion—and easy prey to enemies—if word spread that Saul was mad.

"He says he'll end my dynasty!" Saul's eyes blazed wildly. He ripped his tunic, mumbling. Sweat dripped. Saliva bubbled. "Why should I listen to you when you hate me?" He tore the turban from his head. "Get away from me! Leave me alone!" He swung around. "Abner!"

Abner grabbed Jonathan's arm, his eyes wide with fear. "We must do something for your father or all will be lost."

"I don't know what to do. Talking to him does no good."

"Abner!"

"Speak with your mother," Abner whispered, his voice urgent. "Sometimes a woman knows ways to soothe a man's temper." He turned and entered the king's chamber. "Yes, my lord?"

"Have you sent someone to watch Samuel?"

"Yes, my lord."

"I want someone keeping an eye on him at all times. I want to know every move he makes . . ."

Jonathan went to his mother. She was in new quarters, away from the king, who had taken a concubine. A servant led him into the room and he saw his mother working at her loom. She glanced up with a smile that quickly turned to a frown. "Sit. Tell me what troubles you."

He tried to find words. Looking at the multicolored sash she was making, he forced a smile.

She followed his gaze and ran her hand over her work. "A gift for your father."

"He will wear it proudly."

"Did he send you?"

"No."

She folded her hands. "I've heard about his spells, though you and Abner and the rest try to keep it secret."

Jonathan stood and went to the grated window. He didn't want to imagine what could happen if word spread. His father was at his most vulnerable.

"Tell me what's happening, Jonathan. I have been shut away here with my servants."

"Some men say Father is possessed of an evil spirit." He thought it more likely Saul's guilt racked his mind. "But I think it's something else."

"What?"

"Sometimes, when I hear what he's mumbling, I wonder if God isn't trying to speak to him, and he's hardening his heart and mind against Him." He turned. "I don't know what to do, Mother."

His mother sat with her head down. Then she rose and came to stand beside him at the window. She looked out for a moment and then faced him. "Your father has always loved the sound of a harp. Perhaps if you found someone to play for him when he suffers these spells—" she put her hand gently on his arm—"he might be soothed."

✦   ✦   ✦

Jonathan mentioned his mother's suggestion to his father's servants, who in turn presented the idea to the king. "All right," Saul said. "Find me someone who plays well, and bring him here."

One of the king's servants sent by the tribe of Judah spoke up. "One of Jesse's sons from Bethlehem is a talented harp player. Not only that—he is a brave warrior, a man of war, and has good judgment. He is also a fine-looking young man, and the Lord is with him."

Saul ordered he be sent for.

The boy arrived a few days later with a donkey loaded with bread, a skin of wine, and a goat—all gifts so that the boy's provisions would cost the king nothing. That night, when an evil spirit came upon the king, the musician was summoned from his bed.

At the first sounds of the harp, the king calmed.

"The Lord is my shepherd," the boy sang softly, slowly.

> "I have all that I need.
> He lets me rest in green meadows;
> He leads me beside peaceful streams."

The king sat, pressing his fingers against his forehead.

> "He renews my strength.
> He guides me along right paths,
> bringing honor to His name.
> Even when I walk
> through the darkest valley,
> I will not be afraid,
> for You are close beside me."

Saul leaned back against the cushions as the boy sang. Jonathan watched his father relax and close his eyes. The boy had a clear, pleasing voice, but it was the words of his song that brought peace into the king's chamber.

A man close by whispered, "The boy sings praises to the king."

"No." Jonathan looked at the boy. "He sings praises to God."

The song continued, filling the chamber with words and sound so free and sweet, violent men were calmed.

> "Your rod and your staff
>   protect and comfort me.
> You prepare a feast for me
>   in the presence of my enemies.
> You honor me by anointing my head with oil.
>   My cup overflows with blessings.
> Surely Your goodness and unfailing love will pursue me
>   all the days of my life,
> and I will live in the house of the Lord forever."

As the last words and chords of the harp quivered to silence, Jonathan sighed. Oh, to have such confidence in God! He longed to feel at peace with the Lord. His soul yearned for such a relationship.

"Sing another." King Saul waved his hand.

The boy plucked at his harp. "The heavens proclaim the glory of God," he sang.

> *"The skies display His craftsmanship.*
> *Day after day they continue to speak;*
> *night after night they make Him known. . . ."*

"Look," someone whispered. "The king sleeps."

Jonathan had not seen his father this relaxed in weeks. His own muscles loosened. Everyone in the chamber seemed soothed. When the boy finished his song, the king roused slightly.

"Sing another," Abner told the boy.

The boy sang of the Law this time. The Law is perfect! The Lord is trustworthy. The Law is right and true! The Law carries fearful warning and great reward! Follow it and live!

Listen, Father! Drink it in as you sleep.

> *"May the words of my mouth*
> *and the meditation of my heart*
> *be pleasing to You,*
> *O Lord, my rock and my redeemer."*

The boy bowed his head, plucked the last few chords, and then sat in silence.

Lord, here is one who shares my thoughts.

Saul awakened slowly. "I am pleased with the boy. Send word to his father that I want him to stay here in my service. He can be one of my armor bearers."

"Yes, my lord. I will see to it immediately."

The king went to his bedchamber.

Jonathan called to the Judean servant who was leading the boy outside. "Give the boy quarters inside the palace so that he may be quickly summoned should the king need him."

The servant bowed.

"And give him finer garments. He serves the king now—not a flock of sheep."

+ + +

The Philistines gathered forces at Socoh in the territory of Judah and made camp at Ephes-dammin. And once more King Saul and Jonathan went to war. Battle lines were drawn: the Philistines on one hill, and the Israelites on the other, with the valley of Elah between them.

Where once Israel had fought boldly and routed the Philistines, they now were rooted in fear. Twice a day, once in the morning and later in the afternoon, the Philistine king sent forth his champion, Goliath, a warrior who was over nine feet tall. The man was a giant who wore a bronze helmet and coat of mail and bronze leg armor. What sort of man could wear over one hundred pounds of protective gear and still move so easily? Goliath's shield bearer was not much smaller and led the way as Goliath strode confidently into the center of the valley.

Day after day, Saul and Jonathan and all the rest quaked at the sight of him. They listened and trembled at the sound of the giant's deep voice booming across the valley in defiance. Israel's courage waned before the Philistine's arrogance. The enemy lined up on the far hill facing them and delighted in their humiliation.

"Why are you all coming out to fight?" Goliath roared. "I am the Philistine champion, but you are only the servants of Saul. Choose one man to come down here and fight me! If he kills me, then we will be your slaves."

The Philistine troops hooted and laughed.

Goliath banged his shield with his sword. "But if I kill him, you will be our slaves!"

The Philistines raised their swords and spears and roared their approval. "Where is your champion?" they chanted. "Send out your champion!"

Saul retreated to his tent. "How long must I bear this?" he moaned, covering his ears. "Who will fight for *me*?"

"Jonathan is our champion." One of the advisors looked at him.

Jonathan went cold at the thought of facing Goliath. He couldn't go out against that giant. The man was half again his size!

"No!" Saul turned. "I won't have my son slaughtered before my eyes."

Abner stepped forward. "Offer a reward to any man who will go forth as our champion."

Saul scowled. "What reward would entice a man to certain death?"

His officers all spoke at once:

"Great wealth."

"Give him one of your daughters in marriage."

"Exempt his family from taxes. All these would be his if he can silence that monster!"

"*If*—" Saul wiped the sweat from his face. "There is not a man in our kingdom who can stand against Goliath of Gath!"

"Not to mention the others."

"What others?" Saul's eyes darted from man to man.

"Saph, for one." Abner looked grim.

Another spoke. "And Goliath has a brother equally mighty."

"There are at least four warriors who are said to be descended from Gath."

"Even if we found a man who could kill the Philistine champion, my lord, can their king be trusted to submit? Never!"

"He will send another and another."

"Now you tell me." Saul sank into despair.

Weeks passed, and each morning, the armies again went out into battle position, facing one another across the valley. Each day, the Israelites shouted their war cry. And each day, Goliath came out mocking Israel and their God.

"I defy the armies of Israel today! Send me a man who will fight me!"

No one went out to answer his challenge.

Jonathan wondered how much more the men could bear before they began to desert, going back to hiding out in caves and cisterns. *Lord, help us! Send us a champion who can wipe the sweat of fear from our brows! God, do not desert us now!*

"What's going on down there?" Abner growled, as a disturbance broke out a short distance away.

"Just some men arguing."

Jonathan grew angry. "The Philistines will enjoy that! See to those men!" The last thing they needed was their own men fighting among themselves. Let them focus their anger upon the enemy and not their own brothers. A messenger ran to the ranking officer. A few minutes later, the officer came with his hand on a boy's shoulder.

"This boy is making trouble. He wants to speak with the king."

"You're the harpist." Jonathan frowned. What was he doing here?

"Yes, my lord."

"Come with me."

Saul turned, agitated, as they entered his tent.

Jonathan lifted his hand from the boy's shoulder. Released, the boy stepped forward boldly. "My father, Jesse, sent me with provisions for my older brothers. Eliab, Abinadab, and Shimea came to fight for the king."

"Leave the provisions and go home." Saul waved him away. "This is no place for you."

"Don't worry about this Philistine." The boy took another step forward. "I'll go fight him!"

The military advisors stared. "You?" One of them laughed. "The foolishness of youth. The Philistine is almost twice your size."

Jonathan saw something in the shepherd boy's eyes that gave him hope. "Let him speak!"

The men fell silent. Perhaps they remembered that Jonathan had not been much older than this boy when he climbed the cliff to Micmash and God used him to rout the entire Philistine army! The boy looked at Jonathan, eyes glowing with recognition and respect.

Saul looked the boy over. "You think you can become Israel's champion?" He shook his head. "Don't be ridiculous! There's no way you can fight this Philistine and possibly win! You're only a boy, and he's been a man of war since his youth."

Flushed with anger, the boy would not be turned away. "I have been taking care of my father's sheep and goats. When a lion or a bear comes to steal a lamb from the flock, I go after it with a club and rescue the lamb from its mouth." He reached out as though demonstrating. "If the animal turns on me, I catch it by the jaw and club it to death." He hit his fist against the palm of his hand.

The advisors snickered. Jonathan silenced them with a look.

"I have done this to both lions and bears, and I'll do it to this pagan Philistine, too, for he has defied the armies of the living God!"

The boy understood what the king and advisors didn't. The monster not only mocked the king and his army, but insulted the Lord God of heaven and earth!

"The Lord who rescued me from the claws of the lion and the bear will rescue me from this Philistine!"

Saul looked at Jonathan. Jonathan nodded. Surely the Lord Himself was with the boy as the Lord had been with his father at Jabesh-gilead and with him when he climbed the cliffs at Micmash. How else could the boy be filled with such fire and confidence?

"All right, go ahead," Saul said. "And may the Lord be with you! Bring my armor!" Saul dressed the boy in his own tunic and coat of arms. He put the bronze helmet on his head. The boy sank lower with each piece added. Finally Saul handed over his sword. "Go. And the Lord be with you."

Jonathan frowned. The boy could hardly walk in the king's armor. The sword bumped clumsily against his thighs. When he tried to draw it from the scabbard, he almost dropped it.

Abner stared, appalled. "Will we send a child to do a man's work?"

Jonathan glared. "Would you have the king go? I'm too much of a coward! How about you, Abner? Are you willing to go?" He looked round at the others. "Is any one of us courageous enough to stand and fight Goliath?"

The boy handed the sword back to King Saul. "I can't go in these." He removed the helmet and armor and fine tunic. "I'm not used to them." He pulled a sling from his belt and went outside.

All the men talked at once.

Jonathan went out and saw the boy heading for a dry creek bed. He stooped and weighed stones in his hand. He decided on a round, smooth stone and placed it in the pouch of his shepherd's bag.

"What's your name?"

The boy straightened and bowed his head in respect to Jonathan. "David, my lord prince, son of Jesse of Bethlehem."

"You do know Goliath has a brother?"

"Does he?" David selected another stone.

"There are said to be three other giants of Gath among the Philistine ranks."

David picked up three more stones, added them to his shepherd's bag. "Is there anything else I need to know?"

Jonathan felt an assurance he hadn't felt since Micmash. "God is with you!"

David bowed low, and then walked toward the valley floor.

Jonathan ran back up the hill to stand with his father and watch.

Saul stood, shoulders slumped, dejected. "I have sent that boy out there to die."

"Let's watch and see what the Lord will do."

The Hebrew warriors moved to stand in battle array, murmuring as David walked down into the valley with nothing but his sling, a pouch of five smooth stones, and his shepherd's staff.

A commotion started in the line as David's relatives saw him striding down the hill. "What's he doing? Get out of there!" The officers ordered silence.

Jonathan looked down into the valley again. He prayed fervently. "God, be with him as You were with me at Micmash. Let all Israel see what the Lord can do!"

Goliath and his armor bearer advanced, shouting in disgust. "Am I a dog, that you come at me with a stick? May Dagon curse you!" The Philistine spat curses by all the gods of Philistia on the boy and all Israel while the Philistine warriors laughed and banged their shields.

Jonathan clenched his hand.

"Come over here, boy!" Goliath sneered. "I'll give your flesh to the birds and wild animals!"

"We come to this!" Abner groaned.

Jonathan waited and watched, praying as David stood straight and faced their enemy, his youthful voice carrying. "You come to me with sword, spear, and javelin, but I come to you in the name of the Lord of Heaven's Armies—the God of the armies of Israel, whom you have defied."

Goliath roared with laughter, the Philistine warriors joining him.

David walked forward. "Today the Lord will conquer you, and I will kill you and cut off your head. And then I will give the dead bodies of your men to the birds and wild animals, and the whole world will know that *there is a God in Israel!*"

David put a stone in his sling and ran toward Goliath.

Jonathan stepped forward. Could he hear the *whir* of the shepherd's sling? Or was it his own pulse that hummed in his ears, his heart pounding with every step David took? The boy's arm shot out and the sling dropped in his hand.

Goliath staggered back, a stone embedded in his forehead. Blood gushed down his face. He spread his feet, trying to keep his balance. Then he toppled like a tree.

Both armies stood in stunned silence. Goliath's armor bearer fled from David, who raised Goliath's sword and, with a shout, brought it down. Grabbing Goliath's severed head by the hair, the shepherd boy held it up for all to see. *"For the Lord!"*

Exultant, Jonathan drew his sword and held it high, answering. *"For the Lord and Israel!"*

Fear vanquished, King Saul and Jonathan led the charge, and once more the mighty Philistines fled in terror before the army of the Lord.

✦   ✦   ✦

When the battle was won, Jonathan searched for David. "Where is he?"

Saul shook his head. "I don't know. When Abner brought him to me, the boy was still holding Goliath's head! But he's gone."

"His name is David, Father. He is the youngest son of Jesse of Bethlehem."

"I know. The same boy who has been in my household for months strumming his harp and singing in my chambers." Saul laughed a bit uneasily. "Who knew he had such a fierce heart!"

"He fights for the Lord and his king." Jonathan laughed with excitement. "The whole world will hear of what he did today. I've got to find him." He wanted to know more about this boy God had used so mightily.

"Abner is finding quarters for him," Saul called after him. "We will want him close."

"He'll make a fine bodyguard!" Jonathan raised his sword in the air and went off to find him.

When Jonathan spotted David among the men of Judah and shouted, David turned. Jonathan spread his arms and gave an exuberant cry of victory.

David bowed low. "My lord prince."

Jonathan grabbed the boy's arm, shaking him slightly. "I knew the Lord was with you!"

"As He was with you at Micmash, my prince. My brothers talked of nothing else for months!"

"Come. Walk with me." David fell into step beside him. "You will be handsomely rewarded for what you did today."

"I ask for nothing."

"You will have a command of your own."

David stopped, his eyes going wide. "But I know nothing of leading men."

Jonathan laughed and ruffled David's curly hair. "I will teach you everything I know."

"But I'm only a shepherd."

"Not anymore." Jonathan grinned. "You will write songs that lead us into battle."

"But it was the Lord who won the victory. The Lord was my rock. The Lord delivered me from the hand of Goliath!"

Jonathan faced him. "Yes! And it is such words from your lips that will turn men's hearts to God." Jonathan would no longer be a lone voice in the king's court. "They saw." Here was a boy who believed as he did. "They will listen to you."

David shook his head. "May those who witnessed what happened today know they can trust in the Lord!"

"I know what you felt when you went out there. I felt it once when I climbed the cliffs at Micmash." Jonathan looked up. "I would give anything to feel the presence of the Lord again." Anything and everything!

"I dreamed of fighting for King Saul, but my brothers just laughed at me."

"They won't laugh anymore."

"No, but I'm not sure they would follow me either."

"Would they follow a king's son?"

"Of course."

"Then we will make you one."

"What do you mean?"

Jonathan stripped off his breastplate and tossed it. David caught it against his chest and stumbled back. Jonathan yanked his fine tunic off and thrust it at David. "Put it on."

David stammered.

"Do as I say." Jonathan removed his sword and scabbard and fixed it around David's waist. Last, he gathered up his bow and quiver of arrows and gave them to him as well. "We are now brothers."

David blinked. "But what can I give you?"

"Your sling."

Fumbling, David finally managed to yank it from his belt. He held it out to Jonathan, flustered. "You do me too much honor, my prince."

"Do I?" Of all the people he had met since his father became king of Israel, he had never wanted one to be even his friend. He wanted David to be his brother.

"You are the crown prince, heir to King Saul's throne."

If only my father had a heart like this boy. What a king he would be!

Jonathan clasped David's hand. "From this day forth, you are my brother. My soul is knit to yours in love. I swear before the Lord our God, my hand will never be raised against you."

David's eyes shone with tears. "Nor mine against you!"

Jonathan turned David toward camp. He slapped his back and gave him a playful shove. "Come. We have plans to make! We must drive God's enemies from the land!"

+ + +

"Promote a boy above others twice his age and skill?" Saul stared at Jonathan, incredulous. "Are you mad?"

"Why not? Am I not a commander? I've already seen to it, Father."

"You are *my son*, the prince of Israel! He is nothing more than a shepherd boy who had a little good luck with sling and stone!"

Good luck? "God was with him yesterday, Father." When his father scowled, Jonathan looked at Abner and the officers and advisors. "Is there any man here who would argue that David is our champion? We can't leave him without distinction." They were silent. "Say something. Or are you afraid to give sound advice to the king?" Jonathan turned away in disgust. "Can we talk alone, Father? Let's walk through the camp."

The king went outside with him. Men bowed as they walked among the tents. "Every man here speaks about how David went into the valley of death and slew the giant! Honor him, Father. Let the nations hear how one Hebrew shepherd boy is better than an army of Philistines!"

Saul spoke without turning his head. "What do you think, Abner?"

Abner was always near the king, guarding him.

"The men will be pleased, my lord."

Saul looked at Jonathan. "You don't merely admire his courage, do you? You like him."

"As should you, Father. The Lord used David to give you the battle. Keep him at your side, and we will have victory after victory."

Saul lowered his eyes and stiffened. His head came up. "Where is your sword?"

"I gave it to David."

"You did *what?*"

"I gave him my tunic also, and my bow and belt as well."

"What else did you give this upstart? Your seal ring?"

Jonathan face went hot. "Of course not!" He held his hand out to prove it. "I adopted him as my brother. I made him your son."

"Without asking me? What did you think you were doing to show him such honor!"

"Who better to show honor to, Father?" Jonathan went cold at his father's look. "You are the Lord's anointed. David fought for the glory of the One you serve."

Saul's eyes flashed. He opened his mouth and clenched his teeth, deciding not to say whatever had come into his mind. Breathing hard, he looked away, staring out over the thousands of tents. "He didn't fight for me."

"David is your servant."

"And best to keep him as such." A muscle tightened in Saul's jaw. He released his breath slowly. "But perhaps you're right. He has proved himself useful. Let's see what else he can do." He grew annoyed. "Hear how they all celebrate the victory! Do you remember how they called out *my* name in Jabesh-gilead?"

"And at Gilgal," Abner reminded him.

"May they never forget." Saul turned and walked away.

✦ ✦ ✦

Jonathan looked over his shoulder as he ran. He laughed. "Come on, little brother! You're faster than that!"

Straining, David gained a little. Jonathan stretched out, his feet flying across the ground. He leapt over several bushes and reached their goal well before David.

Gasping for air, David went to his knees. "You fly like an eagle!"

Panting, Jonathan bent at the waist, dragging in air. He grinned. "You almost beat me."

David lay back on the ground, arms spread. "Your legs are longer than mine."

"A rabbit can outrun a fox."

"If it's cunning. I'm not."

Lungs burning, Jonathan leaned against a boulder. "Excuses. Your legs will grow. Your strength will increase."

David laughed. "I'd be faster if my life depended on it."

Jonathan walked around, hands on his hips, waiting for his heart to slow and his body to cool. "You were much faster this time. One day you will keep up and maybe pass me by."

Sitting up, David dangled his hands between his knees. "You outrun me. You're an expert with bow and arrow. You can throw a spear twice as far as I can."

Someone shouted from a distance. Abner.

Jonathan gave David a hand up. He looped his hand around David's neck and rubbed his curly hair with his knuckles. "All in good time, my brother. All in good time."

✦ ✦ ✦

Women ran out to meet the returning warriors. They sang and danced around them, beating on tambourines and strumming lutes. They filled the air with songs of praise.

"See how they love you!" Jonathan laughed at the look on David's face as a girl danced by, flashing him a smile. "You're blushing!"

"I've never seen girls like these!" David watched them whirl around him. "They're beautiful!"

"Yes. They are." Jonathan admired several as he headed for the city gates.

Men, women, and children cheered as Saul led them into Gibeah. The king's household swarmed around Saul. Jonathan spotted his mother and grabbed David by the arm. "My father promised one of his daughters to the man who killed Goliath. You must meet my sisters. I recommend Merab. She's older than you, but much wiser than Michal."

David dug in his heels. "Jonathan, no! I am unworthy!"

"Better you than some old warrior with other wives and a harem of concubines!" He called out to his mother. She turned, smiling, stretching up to look for him. Jonathan pressed his way through the crowd, receiving congratulations and pats of welcome. When he finally reached her, he introduced David, "the giant killer."

"You are to be praised," she said.

Michal stared at David, moon-eyed and blushing.

David fidgeted. "What I did against Goliath is nothing compared to what the prince did at Micmash."

"My son is a very brave man." Jonathan's mother smiled.

"The bravest! It is an honor to serve King Saul and our prince."

"You are from Judah, are you not?"

"It was your recommendation that brought David to us, Mother."

"The boy who sings and plays the harp." She blinked, her face going pale.

David bowed in respect. "It will be my pleasure to sing for the king whenever he wishes. I am his servant."

"Father made David a ranking officer. He's earned other rewards as well." He looked at Merab. "He should be introduced to his future wife."

David cringed with embarrassment.

Jonathan's mother refused to meet his eyes. "Doesn't the Law state that men must take wives from their own tribes?"

Mortified, Jonathan stared. Had his mother meant to reprimand him and the king as well as insult David?

David stammered. "I-I would never count myself worthy to marry one of the king's daughters." Some of David's relatives called out to him, trying to reach him. "May I go, my lord?"

"Yes."

David ran.

Jonathan glared at his mother. "Did you mean to insult him?"

"I merely spoke the truth, Jonathan."

"The truth is that Father gave his oath. And who better for Merab than the champion of Israel, Mother?"

"Where are you going?"

"To find David and bring him back. He will be at the king's table tonight, along with all the high-ranking officers."

✦   ✦   ✦

The warriors dispersed. As they rejoined their families, Saul welcomed his relatives, officers, and advisors to a feast of celebration. Everyone ate his fill and talked of the battle. David sat across from Jonathan, facing the king. As the evening wore on, Saul leaned back against the wall and took a spear in his hand. His thumb rubbed against the shaft.

"David, will you sing for us? A song of deliverance."

A harp was handed from man to man until it reached David. He leaned over it and strummed softly. Men stopped talking to listen. The king closed his eyes and leaned back.

A servant picked his way across the room as David sang and leaned down to whisper to Jonathan. "Your mother, the queen, requests the pleasure of your company."

Surprised, Jonathan rose. His mother never interrupted him. "Father, may I be excused?"

"Go." Saul didn't open his eyes.

David continued to play.

The servant led him through the palace and into a large room where his mother sat weaving

Smiling, she rose and came to him. "About your friend, the shepherd boy."

Jonathan bristled. "*David*, Mother. His name is David. It's a name you should remember. I made a vow of friendship with him. He is my brother and due the same respect given me." When she said nothing, he felt impelled to go on. "Our friendship will solidify the ties between Judah and Benjamin."

"The tribes have been linked in friendship since the time of Joseph, my son. Judah, fourth son of Jacob, offered to take Benjamin's place as a slave in Egypt. I know our history, too, Jonathan. A rivalry grew between the tribes. When the people demanded a king, the Judeans were quick to remind us all that Jacob prophesied the scepter would never depart from their hands."

"Saul is king of Israel."

"And Judah bows down grudgingly."

"They stood with Saul at Jabesh-gilead. They celebrated his coronation at Gilgal. They were with us at Micmash and—" When she held up her hands, he stopped. Honor your father *and* mother, the Law said.

"You are too trusting, Jonathan."

He would never be able to explain to her how his soul was knit to David's. How could he when he didn't fully understand himself? And so, he used reason to try to convince her. "What better way to end rivalry than by the king's giving one of his daughters in marriage to his opponent's son?"

"The Law says—"

Jonathan sighed heavily. "I know, Mother. No one reminds my father of the Law more often than I. But even more important here is the fact that he made a public vow and must make good on it. A king is only as good as his promises."

Shaking her head, she walked to the window and looked up into the night sky. "Your father was not pleased by the songs the people sang as he entered the gates today."

"The people sang praises to their king."

She looked back at him. "And praised your friend more. 'Saul has killed his thousands, and David his ten thousands!' You should have seen your father's face."

"I didn't notice."

"No, you didn't. You need to notice, Jonathan. You need to keep close watch." She looked out the window again and spoke softly. "I fear a storm is brewing."

+ + +

Jonathan knew the truth of his mother's words when he returned to the gathering and found everything in disarray.

"Where's David?"

"Gone." Abner looked shaken.

Counselors clustered near Saul, talking in low voices. "He oppresses me!" Saul shouted. "A boy, that's all he is! Why do the people make so much of him?"

"What happened?"

"Your father lost his temper and threw a spear. That's all. If he'd meant to kill David, he would have."

"He threw a spear at David? *Why*?"

"You know how things are."

Jonathan found David sitting at a fire among his relatives. When Jonathan entered the circle of light, cold eyes fixed on him, but David rose quickly. "My prince!"

"I heard what happened."

David drew him away from the others. "Your father tried to kill me. Twice he hurled a spear at me." David gave a nervous laugh. "I thought it wise to leave before the king pinned me to the wall."

"You've seen him when the evil spirit comes upon him. It's why you were summoned to the palace."

"My songs did not soothe him tonight."

"Sometimes my father says and does things he would never do if . . ." If what? If he was in his right mind? If he was not tormented by guilt and fear? Jonathan could not say these things to David. "He drank a lot of wine tonight." He smiled wryly. "Maybe he thought you were a Philistine." It was a bad joke.

They went up the ladder to the top of the wall and leaned against the railing, looking out over the land. Jonathan shook his head. "My father is a great man, David." He felt the leather case containing the Law thump against his chest. "But I wish he would listen to me."

"My father doesn't listen to me either. Nor do my uncles and brothers." David rested his chin on folded arms. "Even though I now outrank them."

"Every man in Israel should learn the Law. If they knew the Lord they served, they wouldn't be so afraid of the nations around us. They'd stop trying to live by the customs of our enemies." Did any of them realize that the Scriptures said God would detest them if they did that? Did they remember that God had warned them that the land itself would vomit them out?

"Maybe someday." David sighed. "My father said the Law is too much to learn and takes too much time away from the sheep."

Jonathan remembered how his own father had preferred plowing fields rather than digging into the Scriptures.

"I have often dreamed of going to Naioth." David smiled as he gazed at the night sky. "Those who attend the school of prophets are the most fortunate of men. What could be more exciting and wonderful than to spend your life reading and studying the Law?"

Jonathan looked at him. He had felt the bond between them at the valley of Elah. And it had grown stronger every day since. It was as though the Lord Himself had knit their hearts together. "I copied the Law at the school in Naioth."

David straightened, eyes wide. "You have a copy of the Law?"

Jonathan smiled and nodded slowly. He could see the sheen of excitement in David's eyes. Hadn't he felt the same thing: a hunger to know the Lord, an insatiable appetite to eat and drink the Word of God as his life's sustenance?

"All of it?" David stared in wonder.

"Every word of it." Jonathan took hold of the woven leather strap and drew the leather casing out from beneath his tunic. "I have part of it right here. Samuel oversaw my work to make certain every jot and tittle was exact."

David's eyes glowed. "Oh, what treasure you hold in your hand."

Jonathan pushed away from the wall. Smiling, he rested his hand on

David's shoulder. He jerked his head. "What do you say we find ourselves a lamp and get my scrolls?"

They read the Law until they were too tired to see the words. Exhausted, David went out to his relatives and Jonathan returned to the palace. When he stretched out on his bed, he closed his eyes.

Finally, he had found someone who loved the Lord like Samuel did, a friend who was closer than a brother.

Jonathan smiled. He fell asleep exhausted. Content.

✦ ✦ ✦

The Philistines raided once again, and Saul sent David out to fight. Jonathan heard reports of David's success, and was pleased. Jonathan fought well also and drove the Philistines off tribal lands. Returning to Gibeah, he dined with his father.

"I heard David had another victory."

Saul's mouth was flat and hard. "Yes."

"Have the wedding arrangements been made?"

Saul was eating grapes, the muscles in his jaw bunching hard as he ground his teeth. "I'm still thinking about it."

Jonathan lost his appetite. "You gave your oath. The man who killed Goliath was to have wealth—"

"He is growing wealthy on plunder."

"Tax exemptions for his family—"

"So Jesse sends me a few sheep; why should I decline?"

"And your daughter in marriage."

"I offered him Merab, and he declined."

"He felt unworthy."

Saul gave a harsh laugh. "Or that impudent Judean thinks my daughter's not good enough for him."

Jonathan stared. "You know that's not true."

"David!" Saul spat the word as though it were a foul taste in his mouth. "So much humility!" He sneered and ripped a hunk of meat from the roasted lamb. "I have given Merab to Adriel of Meholah. She leaves day after tomorrow."

Jonathan felt the words like a punch in his stomach. "When was this decision made?"

"What does it matter to you when the decision was made? I am the king!" He threw the meat back onto the platter. "Judah is already an ally." He wiped his greasy hands on a cloth. "Meholah's clan was in question. They are now allies. It was a good decision."

Jonathan was too angry to speak.

His father looked at him. "Do not try me, Jonathan. I know David is your friend, but I understand our people better than you do! I must make alliances."

"You would have made an alliance with Judah by giving Merab to David. Do you think they will be pleased that you've forgotten the promises you made at the valley of Elah?"

Saul's face reddened. "They know I offered Merab to him. I kept my promise."

Jonathan knew he could not let the subject go. Bridges had to be built, not torn down, between the tribes. He waited for his father to finish his meal and drink some wine before he broached it again. "Michal is in love with David."

His younger sister would not make as good a wife as Merab, but what she lacked in sense she made up for in beauty. The marriage would bring Benjamin and David together, and if his sister bore David's sons, they would be added to Saul's household. But most important, the marriage would confirm the king's honor.

"She is?"

"She told me today that he is the most handsome man in all Israel."

Saul chewed, eyes gleaming. He made a gruff sound and drank more wine. "What's to keep him from declining Michal as he declined Merab?"

"He won't if you make it clear you think him worthy to be your son. He paid the bride-price when he killed Goliath."

"The bride-price." Saul raised his head. "I had not thought about that."

"So you will offer Michal."

"Of course." Saul plucked some grapes and tossed one into his mouth. He leaned back, a smug smile curving his lips.

+ + +

David returned to Gibeah. Jonathan was kept so busy with matters of state that he had no time to see him. And when he did, David was preparing to leave again. "Pray for me, my friend!" David clasped Jonathan's arms in greeting. He was trembling with excitement. "I have just spoken to several of the king's attendants and I may become your brother yet!"

"You are already my brother." Jonathan was delighted his father had followed through with his decision to give Michal to David.

David released him and they walked together. "I'm leaving in an hour."

"Leaving? For where?"

"The king announced the bride-price for your sister Michal. And I have until the new moon festival."

"David!" Jonathan called before he went far. "What price did the king set?"

"One hundred foreskins!"

One hundred kills—and proof they were uncircumcised Philistines.

Jonathan was dismayed, for it was another indication that his father was adopting the customs of surrounding nations. The Egyptians lopped off hands and collected them as trophies to prove how many they killed. The Philistines took heads. Jonathan wondered if his father understood that he might be sending David to his death. And if Israel lost their champion, what then? Would they lose their faith as well? By all that was right, Michal already belonged to David because of the king's promise.

But maybe his father was right. David was eager to prove himself worthy.

Lord, protect him. Go before him and be his rear guard. And may Michal prove herself a worthy bride when David returns!

+ + +

Jonathan was in council with his father and the advisors when cheers came from outside. Saul raised his head in irritation. "What is going on out there?"

The city was in an uproar of excitement. "David!" The people shouted. *"David!"*

Saul's face darkened for a moment, and then he rose. "Your friend returns. Go and greet him." He looked at the others. "We will follow."

Jonathan ran. He laughed when he saw David, for no one had to ask if his quest had been successful. A bloody sack was in his hand. "You did it!"

"Two hundred." David held up the sack.

"May the Lord be with you every day of your life! Michal will be dancing when she hears the news." Most likely she already had. His sister would be blessed with a husband who could protect her. He saw his father come outside. "Come, David! The king waits!"

Jonathan brought his friend to Saul. "Two hundred foreskins, Father. Twice what you asked for!"

David bowed low and held the sack out to the king. "The bride-price for your daughter, my king."

A muscle twitched below Saul's right eye, and then he smiled broadly, held his arms wide. "My son!"

As the king engulfed David in his arms, the people went wild with joy.

+ + +

Preparations were quickly made for the wedding. As David's best friend, Jonathan took care of overseeing the details. There would be food for thousands and wine to wash it down. The king was glum, but the prince spared no expense. After all, the daughter of the king was marrying Israel's champion. The tribes of Benjamin and Judah would become allies forever.

No one tried to convince Jonathan otherwise.

Jonathan put the groom's crown on David's head. "You're ready." He put his hand firmly on David's shoulder. "Stop shaking."

David's forehead was beaded with moisture. "I have followed the Law since my youth, Jonathan, but I feel ill-prepared for marriage." He raised his brows.

"Michal is not an enemy, my friend. And she loves you."

David blushed. "We'll see how she feels about me tomorrow morning."

Chuckling, Jonathan gave him a shove toward the door.

Michal had never looked more beautiful or joyful than when she stood beneath the canopy with David. Her dark eyes glowed as she looked at him. When David took her hand, a pulse beat in her throat. People smiled and whispered among themselves.

Representatives from all the tribes came to the wedding, Judah in full force. Campfires dotted the landscape around Gibeah. The sound of harps and tambourines drifted through the night, along with the people's laughter.

King Saul announced his gift at the banquet: a house near the king. David was stunned and grateful by such a show of generosity, and praised the king for it. Saul raised his goblet of wine. The people sang and danced.

Jonathan leaned close. "The people are pleased, Father."

King Saul sipped, watching the festivities over the rim of his cup. "Let us hope we have not sown the seeds of our own destruction!"

FOUR

❖❖❖❖❖

Jonathan found it difficult to concentrate on Michal's litany of complaints, having just come from a tense meeting with his father. The next time his sister requested a visit with him, perhaps he should refuse.

Michal might adore David, but she whined endlessly about the burdens of David's responsibilities. Jonathan was thankful not to have a wife. How hard it must be for David to concentrate on Philistine threats when the most immediate threat was a tantrum in his own home.

"I wish he wasn't Israel's champion. If he was an ordinary soldier, I'd be delighted," she grumbled.

Jonathan knew better.

"At least then he could stay home a year! No one would miss him!"

Lounging, Jonathan considered her. "You and David have had a month without interruption." Long enough to conceive a child. "Now, the king wants him back on duty. Complaining won't alter the needs of the nation, Michal."

"Every time a village is raided, it's my husband who has to go out again. Why can't you be the one to go all the time? You have no wife."

Jonathan would like nothing better, but the king often sent him on other errands, especially to speak for unity among the tribes. "You should be proud of David."

"I am proud. But . . ."

Here it comes.

"You know the Law better than anyone, Jonathan. Doesn't it say when a man takes a new wife, he isn't to go off with the army or be charged with *any* duty other than to give happiness to her?"

He smiled cynically. "I'm delighted you're taking an interest in the Law, though you have dubious motives. You cannot choose one Law and ignore all the rest."

Her eyes blazed. "I'm not happy! It says I'm to have my husband long enough to be happy."

And how long would that take? "You're a daughter of the king of Israel. Shouldn't you be thinking of what is best for our people?"

Chin tipping, she looked away. "It's not fair!"

"Is it fair that the Philistines strip the poor of their sustenance? Of all our commanders, David has the most success against our enemies. The king is wise to use him."

"Or would you rather have the war come to our doorstep?" David spoke from the doorway.

Michal glanced up, blushing. Embarrassed, she grew angry. "You would think my father wanted you dead the number of times he sends you out!"

Jonathan rose in anger. "Only a fool speaks such nonsense!"

"A fool?" She glared up at him. "It's true, Jonathan! The only fool around here is—"

"Be quiet!" David said.

"You spend more time with my brother than you do with me!"

Red-faced, David came to her, drew her up, and led her aside. He kept his voice low as he leaned close and spoke to her. Any other man would have slapped her. Jonathan was pleased that his friend was forgiving. Hopefully, Michal would appreciate her husband's patience and compassion. Her shoulders slumped. She bowed her head. She sniffled and wiped her eyes. He tipped her chin, kissed her cheek, and spoke again, and she left the room.

David faced Jonathan, clearly mortified by his wife's behavior. "My servant will see her home. I'm sorry, Jonathan. She doesn't mean the things she says."

"Why are you apologizing? My sister is the one who can't hold her tongue."

"She's my wife, Jonathan."

"A rebuke?"

David looked uncomfortable.

"Sit. Relax." Jonathan smiled. "It speaks well of you that you are protective of your wife. She is right about the Law, my friend. It does call for a bridegroom's year at home to make a woman happy, and the way to do that is to fill her with child." Unfortunately, the king had no intention of following that particular law. He feared the Philistines more than God.

"I'm trying."

Jonathan laughed. He rose and slapped David's back. "Come, my friend. Let's look over the maps." They spent the next few hours in deliberation, discussing tactics and making plans. A servant came with refreshments.

David tore a piece of bread and dipped it in his wine. "Why haven't you taken a wife, Jonathan?"

From what Jonathan had seen of David and Michal's turbulent

relationship, he was not eager to add a woman to his household. "I have no time for a wife."

"You will need an heir. And a woman gives comfort to a man."

Was Michal a comfort to David? Physically perhaps, but what about a man's other needs? Peace and quiet, a place to rest from trouble. "A contentious woman is worse than a bleating goat outside the window."

"You like women."

Jonathan grinned. "Ah, but they do not dance and sing around me as they do you."

"They dance and sing around me because I am one of them, a common man, a shepherd, youngest of my father's sons. But you, Jonathan. You stand as tall as your father, and from the gossip I hear, the women find you even more handsome. And you are the prince, heir to the throne of Israel. They wait at the gates in hope you will look at them, and when you do, they blush. You could have any woman you want, my friend."

Jonathan knew women liked him. And he liked women. "There is a time for all things, David. Right now, Israel is my beloved. The people are my wife. Perhaps when we have peace—"

"It may be years before we have peace. The Lord said it is not good for a man to be alone."

Jonathan sometimes longed for the comfort of home and family, but other matters must take precedence. "When a man loves a woman, his heart is divided. Remember how Adam sought to please Eve when she offered him the apple? He knew the Lord forbade it and took the fruit anyway." He shook his head. "No. Israel holds my heart. When God's enemies are driven from our land, then I will take a wife." He grinned. "And I will stay at home for a full year to make her happy."

+   +   +

They met each day, going out into the field for a few hours of practice with their weapons. Jonathan cherished the time with his friend and knew David felt the same. Out in the open, beyond the gates and houses, they could talk as they shot arrows and threw spears while their young servants retrieved them.

"Even with your success, we're still far from winning the war." Jonathan sent his arrow winging to the target. "The Philistines keep coming like waves from the sea. We have to stem the tide."

"And how do we do that?" David hurled his spear farther than the last time and hit just off center.

"Philistine weaponry is far superior to ours."

"We strip the dead of their weapons."

"That's not enough." Jonathan shook his head. "When those weapons are damaged, we don't know how to repair them. We can't forge swords like theirs. And their spear tips and arrows go through bronze." He took a handful of arrows from Ebenezer and dropped them into the quiver on his back.

"What's your idea?" David hurled another spear.

"Find men willing to go to Gath."

"And trade for the secret?" David asked.

Jonathan shot another arrow straight to the target. "The Philistines are too shrewd. They won't share their knowledge easily. Someone would have to go and gain their trust in order to learn how to make their weapons."

"A pity they know I'm the one who killed Goliath."

"You'd be the last one they'd welcome."

"What about those men who lived among them before Micmash? They've returned to the ranks of Israel, but maybe a few of them would agree to go back and—"

"I don't think they'd be trusted either. Would you trust a man whose loyalty was swayed whichever way the battle went? I don't trust them." Jonathan shot another arrow straight and true. "Move the target back! It's too easy." He turned to David. "The Lord could destroy all our enemies with one breath, David, but He told *us* to clear the land. I believe He did that to test our loyalty to Him. Would we do as He said? Our forefathers did for a generation and then lost sight of the goal—and of God."

The servant called out that the target was ready, and Jonathan turned and shot his arrow.

"Dead center!" the boy shouted and gave a whoop.

"Move it back again!" Jonathan raised his bow. "We must teach the people to pray and then fight, but it would also help if we had stronger swords!"

✦ ✦ ✦

Jonathan and David went out together to hunt Philistine raiders. Camped beneath the stars, David picked at the strings of his harp, playing a song of celebration over their enemies. "Why is it you never sing, Jonathan?"

Jonathan smirked. "God gives each of us gifts, my friend. Singing isn't one the Lord saw fit to give me."

"Every man can sing. Sing with me, Jonathan!" Some of the men joined him in urging the prince to give it a try.

Laughing, Jonathan decided there was only one way to convince them. David's eyes flickered, but he said nothing. The other men sang louder, some grinning. When the song was over, Jonathan lay back and put his arms behind his head.

David continued to play his harp, trying out new chords and fingerings.

"The king will like that," Jonathan said.

When they returned to Gibeah and dined with the king, Saul ordered David to sing for him. "Sing a new song."

The chamber filled with beautiful music as David strummed gently and plucked at the instrument. Only he could bring sounds of such sweetness and words of grace. But when David started to sing, Jonathan grinned.

"Make a joyful noise—" David grinned back at him before continuing.

✦   ✦   ✦

After several weeks of chasing Philistines and strengthening outposts, Jonathan returned to Gibeah to learn that David had routed another band of raiders and sent them running for their lives.

His father summoned him. Jonathan expected to find the king well pleased. Instead, Saul paced, livid, while his advisors stood about watching uneasily. What had caused the foul mood this time? Nothing but good news had come in from all fronts, the most glorious from David's.

Abner closed the door behind Jonathan. "We are all here, my lord."

Saul turned. "I want David killed."

Jonathan froze, staring. What madness was this?

"This Judean threatens my rule! Did you hear the people shouting his name yesterday when he approached the gates of *my* city?"

Jonathan shook his head, unable to understand his father's fury. "Because he sent the enemy running."

"You understand nothing! You call my enemy *your friend*!"

Heat surged into Jonathan's face, his heart bounding in alarm and anger. "David is your friend as well, my lord. And your son, by marriage to Michal!"

Saul turned away from him. "If we allow this shepherd to continue to gain power, he will assassinate me and take the crown for himself."

Jonathan looked at the others in the room. Would no one speak sense to the king? Abner returned his gaze, nodding. "David could become a threat."

"Have you ever seen evidence of an insurrection?"

"By the time there is evidence, I'll be dead!" Saul raged.

Jonathan extended his hands toward his father. "You couldn't be more wrong about David. He has no ambitions other than to serve you."

"He steals the people's affection!"

"The people love you! They cry out your name as well as David's, Father."

"Not as loudly. Not as long."

Jonathan glared at the others. Would they let suspicion grow in Saul because they were afraid to speak the truth? David was Saul's greatest ally! "Are the Philistines not enemies enough for you? We need not invent one in our midst!"

Abner spoke for the rest. "An enemy in our midst can do the most damage."

Jonathan knew he would have to find a way to speak to his father alone, for these men would say anything to please the king. They were too influenced by Saul's fears and unwittingly fanned the fire of his wounded pride by agreeing with him.

But until he could draw Saul away from these men, Jonathan had to make certain David was removed from harm's way. He found David in a meeting with his officers. "We must talk. Now."

David led him into another room. "What is it, Jonathan? What's wrong?"

"My father is looking for a chance to kill you."

David paled. "Why?"

"He's having one of his spells. You've seen it before. It will pass."

"I pray that you're right!"

"Tomorrow morning, you must find a hiding place out in the fields." Jonathan took his arm and told him where to go. "I'll ask my father to go out there with me, and I'll talk to him about you. Then I'll tell you everything I can find out. But you must take no chances, my friend. Some of the king's advisors see enemies where there are none."

+   +   +

Jonathan joined his father before the morning meal.

Saul looked exhausted and drawn, dark shadows beneath his eyes. When he reached for his goblet of wine, his hand trembled.

"You did not sleep well." And no wonder if all the king could think about was the rise of an adversary. Jonathan intended to clear his father's mind of those fears.

Saul scowled. "How could I sleep with my kingdom in jeopardy?"

Placing the bowl of honey close, Jonathan tore off a hunk of bread and offered it to his father. Saul took it, still frowning, pensive. Men stood in the antechamber, waiting for an audience with the king. Jonathan needed to get his father away from the palace and out into the open air for a while. "Remember how we cleared fields together, Father?"

Saul made a soft sound, gazing off toward the windows.

"The fields are almost ready for reapers. The Lord has blessed us with a good harvest this year." He offered his father dates. "It's been days since you left the palace." And the company of his advisors. "You've worked hard for your people, Father. Surely you are allowed a walk in the fields of the Lord."

Rising, Saul glowered at the men approaching. "Go away."

Servants backed away.

Jonathan hadn't expected it to be so easy.

They walked half the morning and sat beneath one of the olive trees.

Saul sighed. "I miss this."

"I would speak to you of your command yesterday, Father."

"Which one?"

"The one you issued to kill David."

Saul turned his head and looked at him. "Is that why you brought me out here?"

"Yes. And no."

"Which do you mean?"

"I see how burdened you are. Not a week goes by that we must send men out to protect our land from raiders. And the tribes constantly bicker among themselves over petty things. But remember, they all assemble at your command, my lord." He looked into his father's eyes. "You know I love you. You know I honor you. Do you trust me?"

"Yes."

"The king must not sin against his servant David. He's never done anything to harm you. He has always helped you in any way he could. Have you forgotten about the time he risked his life to kill the Philistine giant and how the Lord brought a great victory to all Israel as a result? You were certainly happy about it then."

Saul's shoulders slumped. "No. I will never forget it."

"Why should you murder an innocent man like David? There is no reason for it at all!" He spoke gently, wanting to remind his father of what was right, hoping to turn his mind from the advice of cowards. "If there is any man in the kingdom you can trust more than me, it is your son-in-law David."

Saul grimaced as if in pain. "When I hear what he accomplishes—" He shook his head.

"Everything David has accomplished is for the Lord's glory and yours, Father. He is your faithful servant." Jonathan wanted to speak more of David's achievements, but worried they would distress rather than comfort his father. "With all due respect for your advisors, Father, they are frightened men. Let wisdom rather than fear reign over Israel."

Leaning his head back against the gnarled trunk of the olive tree, Saul closed his eyes and sighed.

Jonathan remained silent. He did not want to press his father as other men did. He looked out over the fields and then up at the blue heavens.

"You are my eldest son, Jonathan, the first show of my strength as a man. The people hold you in high regard. When I die, the crown will pass to you."

"God willing."

When Saul glanced at him, Jonathan felt his heart fillip. He had not meant to remind his father of what Samuel had said.

"I wonder what God was thinking when He chose me to be king."

Jonathan relaxed. "That you were the man the people wanted."

"Yes." Such bleakness. "The people wanted me. Once."

"They still do. You need not worry, Father." *Lord, let him hear my words.* "The people will always love a king who reigns with wisdom and honor."

"Their love is like the wind, Jonathan, blowing east one day and west the next."

"Then you must steady them with a calm spirit."

"I'm tired."

"Rest a while now. I'll keep watch."

And Saul did. He slept several hours while Jonathan remained with him in the olive grove. When servants came to check on the king, Jonathan motioned them away. Every man needed to rest, especially a king.

When his father awakened, he smiled. "I dreamed I was a farmer again."

"The Lord has called you to another purpose."

His father started to rise. Jonathan got to his feet and extended his hand. Saul clasped it and pulled himself up. "You're not a boy anymore." He smiled slightly. "I keep forgetting." He put his hand on Jonathan's shoulder. "As surely as the Lord lives, David will not be killed."

Jonathan bowed low. "May the Lord reward your wisdom, Father."

"We can hope so." Saul saw his servants coming. "I have things to do." He walked toward them.

Jonathan went out farther into the fields. "David!"

"I am here." David came out of hiding and walked toward him. It hurt Jonathan to see his friend so tentative. He smiled when he came closer. "I can see by your face that you believe things went well with the king."

Jonathan put his arm around his friend's shoulders. "There is no need for you to look uncertain, my friend." He released him. "Come. I will take you to him. You will see for yourself that things will be as they were before. Bring your harp."

✦   ✦   ✦

Things were indeed better between the king and his champion. Jonathan saw the peace David brought the king with his songs of deliverance. For a time, the Philistines were quiet and Gibeah basked in the sun. Jonathan would look back on those days as the most peaceful he had known. He and David spent long hours together, poring over the Law, discussing it. No one else among their friends and relatives shared their fascination.

"Until I faced Goliath, my brothers thought I was fit only to watch sheep. No matter what I said, they accused me of something. That day in the valley of Elah, Eliab said I was conceited and wicked for speaking out."

"They didn't know you very well."

"I wonder if they ever will." An expression flickered across David's face and was gone, a grimness Jonathan had not seen before.

Jonathan lifted a jug of fresh water and filled his goblet. "How wonderful and pleasant it would be if all brothers could live together in harmony!" He drank deeply and set his cup aside. "That's my one dream, David, the work I believe God intends for me. To help my father bring the tribes together. We cannot be scattered flocks bleating at one another. If we are to conquer our enemies, we must unite with our brothers and stand firm behind God's anointed king. We must remember our covenant with the Lord, for that covenant with God is what will hold us together."

"You are blessed." David smiled. "You have a copy of the Law with you wherever you go."

If only his father the king had made a copy of the Law for himself. If only Saul had taken the command seriously, perhaps he would not have sinned. And if his father had studied the Law, he would know that the Lord was slow to anger and quick to forgive.

"However many days God gives me upon this earth, David, it will not be enough to know all that He has for us in the Law. It is new every morning that I read it. I wish the Lord in His mercy would write it upon our hearts, for it seems to me, our minds are not able to absorb the lengths and depths of the love God has for us as His chosen people."

✦   ✦   ✦

Yet again, Saul sent David out to fight, and he struck the Philistines with such force that they fled before him. He returned in triumph and the city and countryside celebrated. The king and his officers, David and Jonathan among them, feasted in the palace. Outside, warriors sang songs of victory written by David.

Many of the officers drank heavily. "Sing us a song, David!"

"Yes! Sing us a song!"

David looked at King Saul.

Jonathan felt the air growing thinner. He waited for his father to speak, wondering why he sat with his back against the wall, a spear in his hand, daydreaming. "Father?"

"Yes—" Saul waved his hand—"sing."

David's servant brought him the harp. As the chamber was filled with his playing, one of the advisors remarked, "He casts spells with his music."

Saul's gaze shifted.

Jonathan glared at the man. "I believe you have duties elsewhere." The advisor glanced at the king, but Saul said nothing. Jonathan did not take his gaze from the man until he excused himself, rose, and left the room.

Relaxing back onto the cushions, Jonathan listened to David singing:

"Give to the Lord the glory He deserves!
Bring your offering and come into His courts.

> *Worship the Lord in all His holy splendor.*
> *Let all the earth tremble before Him."*

Men clapped when he plucked the last chords. The king smiled and nodded.

A servant bent close to Jonathan. "Your mother requests your presence, my lord prince."

Surprised, Jonathan asked his father's permission to leave. It was not his mother's custom to ask for him. "Go." Saul barely glanced at him, his gaze still fixed upon David as he began to play another song.

Jonathan's mother had lavish quarters now, and servants to wait upon her every need. When he entered, a pretty servant girl bowed before him and ushered him into his mother's chamber.

She was reclining on a couch, cheeks sallow. "I am sorry to take you away from your celebration, my son."

"You're ill," Jonathan said, alarmed. "Why wasn't I told?"

"I'm not so ill that anyone should know. Bring my son a cushion, Rachel." Jonathan sat and took his mother's hand. "What do the physicians say?"

His mother patted his hand as if he were a child. "The physicians know nothing. I just need rest. Jonathan, I would like you to meet Rachel, daughter of my second cousin. Her father is a scribe."

Jonathan glanced at the blushing girl. She was very pretty.

His mother nodded and the girl slipped from the room. "She's pretty, don't you think? And she comes from a good family." When his mother struggled to sit up, Jonathan got up to help her. "I'm comfortable now. Sit." She smiled. "Rachel's father knows Samuel."

"You asked to see me. Why?"

"I should think it's obvious." She pressed her lips together. "You should marry, my son, and soon."

"This is not the time."

"What better time is there? You are far older than your father was when we married."

"Mother, my responsibilities leave me no time for—"

"David is married. You pressed for that match, didn't you? And he's younger than you are."

Amused, Jonathan shook his head. "I suppose every mother wants her children settled." He leaned toward her, wanting her to rest and not worry. "David's marriage to Michal strengthens the bond between our tribe and Judah, Mother. And besides, what better man could there be for your daughter than Israel's champion?"

Her eyes darkened. "You are Israel's champion, my son. You were scarcely older than David when you routed the Philistines at Micmash. Though many years have passed since then, the people have not forgotton. There are equally good reasons for you to marry, Jonathan."

He felt the tremor in her hand. "Why are you pressing this, Mother?"

Her eyes welled with tears. "Because I don't know from one battle to the next if my son will be killed." Her voice broke. "Is it too much to ask that I hold a grandchild in my arms?"

"Michal and David—"

"No!"

He frowned, troubled by her vehemence.

She sat up and leaned toward him. "Marry and have sons of your own, Jonathan. You and your brothers must have sons to build up Saul's house."

"Why are you so adamant now?"

"We must increase in numbers."

"You have more faith in me than I have in myself if you think I can increase the population—"

"It's not a laughing matter."

He sighed. "No. But it's not the right time either."

"I—"

"No, Mother."

"If it pleases the king for you to marry . . ."

"If it were on his mind, he would have suggested it himself. And if he does now, I'll tell him his wife has put him up to it." Jonathan kissed her cheek and rose. "You and David—"

Her head came up. "What about David?"

"He agrees with you. He told me the Scriptures say it is not good for a man to be alone, that he should have a wife." He tilted his head at her expression. "Why does that surprise you?"

"If you won't listen to your mother, perhaps you should listen to your friend."

"Later, perhaps."

✦   ✦   ✦

Jonathan awakened abruptly from a sound sleep and heard Michal's voice. "I don't care if he's asleep! I must see my brother! *Now!*"

Jonathan sat up and rubbed his face. He had slept fitfully, awakened by strange dreams. Violence in the city. Philistines on the rampage. The walls breeched. Twice he had lunged up, grabbed his sword, and gone to the window, only to find Gibeah quiet.

His servant stood in the doorway. "My lord, I'm sorry to awaken you. Your sister—"

"I heard her. Tell her I will be with her in a moment." He stripped off his tunic, splashed water on his face, and toweled dry. Donning a fresh tunic and robe, he went out to her.

Michal paced, her face splotched from crying, her eyes wild. "Finally!"

She reminded him of their father in one of his moods. "What's going on?" It was then he noticed the bruise on her cheek.

"Father hit me! You have to speak with him. He was so angry I thought he would kill me!" She sobbed. "He's out of his mind! You have to help me!"

He felt a sudden fear. "Where's David?"

"*Gone!*"

He took her hands and made her sit. "Gone where, Michal?"

"I don't know where. Running for his life. He's gone! And I'm left to face the king!" She cried like a frightened child and shrieked at him, "It's all your fault, Jonathan!"

"How is it my fault?"

"My husband would still be home in bed with me if you'd stayed at the feast! Why did you leave?"

"Mother asked for me."

She gulped air and used her shawl to wipe her eyes and nose. "She's dying of a broken heart because Father took that girl Rizpah to his bed. He doesn't care about her anymore."

Jonathan hadn't been pleased when he heard about it. "Mother is still his queen, Michal, and the mother of his children."

She rose, frustrated. "I didn't come to talk about her problems. After you left the celebration the evil spirit came upon Father again. You know how he is when that happens."

All too well.

"He was sitting with his spear in his hand."

A kingly pose after a great victory.

"One minute he seemed fine, and the next, he was hurling his spear at David! He drove it into the wall! David eluded him and came home. He thought Father's advisors would calm him down, but when I heard what had happened I knew Father was determined to kill my husband. I told David if he didn't leave Gibeah, he would be dead before morning. And I was right! He wasn't gone more than a few minutes when Father's men came. I told them David was ill. So they went back to the king, but Father sent them again with orders to bring David, sick or not! Aren't you going to ask how David got away?" She clenched her hands. "I let him down from the window. Then I took one of my idols and laid it in our bed. I covered it with a garment and put some goat's hair on its head." She laughed wildly. "Wasn't that clever of me? Wasn't it?"

"Yes." Jonathan was revolted at the thought of his sister's having idols in the house.

"And then Father's men came again. When they found David wasn't there, they brought *me* to the king instead. And Father accused me of deceiving him and sending his enemy away so that he could escape. His *enemy*! Oh, Jonathan, I thought he was going to have me executed for treason!"

Jonathan forced himself to speak calmly. "He would not kill his own daughter, Michal."

She grew angry. "You didn't see his face. You didn't look into his eyes. I told him David threatened to kill me if I didn't help him get away."

Jonathan drew back and stared.

"Why are you looking at me like that?"

"What sort of wife betrays her husband with such a lie? David wouldn't hurt a hair on your head!"

"Father was ready to lop it off!"

"How you talk! You're here, Michal. Alive and well. No guards with you. Whatever storm you imagined has probably already passed."

She flew to her feet, her face contorted with anger. "You're wrong! Sometimes I wonder if you even know our father. You're so determined to see the good in everyone."

"And you're even quicker to seek faults in everyone."

Her neck stiffened. "Maybe you're wrong about David, too. Did that ever occur to you? Your fine friend didn't stay around to protect his wife, did he? He left without a second thought. Did he stop to think what would happen to me?"

"You took care of yourself, didn't you?"

"I hate you! I hate you almost as much as I hate—"

Jonathan gave her a hard shake. "Lower your voice!"

Michal sagged, weeping, her head resting against his chest. "What am I going to do without him? I love him! I don't want to be a widow."

Jonathan thought of David running for his life. "Where was he going?"

She pushed away. "How would I know? To his family, I suppose. I don't remember. Bethlehem." She wilted onto a cushion and covered her face, her shoulders shaking with sobs. "Will you speak to Father for me? Please, Jonathan. I'm afraid of what he'll do."

✦   ✦   ✦

Jonathan wondered if his sister had exaggerated everything, for the king was in a good mood the next day. "You retired early last night, my son. Were you unwell?"

"Mother summoned me. Is everything all right?"

"Yes! Of course. Why wouldn't it be?"

"Michal came to my house last night."

Saul scowled. "Your sister invents trouble. Speak no more of her." He waved his hand, as though to slap the subject away. "What of your mother? Why did she call you away from the celebration?"

He leaned close and spoke softly so the advisors would not hear. "She thinks it's time I marry."

"Does she?" Saul's brows rose. He considered the thought and then nodded. "Not a bad idea. We should find you a suitable young woman."

Jonathan knew what *suitable* would mean to his father: a bride to bring an alliance. "She must be from the tribe of Benjamin, Father. As the Law requires."

Saul's expression changed. "It will have to wait." He put his arm around Jonathan's shoulder. "The Philistines plundered another village." They reviewed the reports together.

Jonathan pointed out his strategies. "With your permission, I'll take David with me."

The king looked thunderous. "And share the glory?" He shook his head. "Not this time."

"It is not glory I seek, Father, but an end to this war. We can't give the Philistines a single village or field. We must drive them out of the land or we will never have peace."

"Call out your men and go!" Saul turned his back. "I have other plans for David."

✦ ✦ ✦

Weeks passed with some minor skirmishes, but Jonathan didn't find the multitude of Philistines reported. Something was wrong.

He returned to Gibeah and learned that his father had gone to Ramah. "Did Samuel call for him?"

"No, my lord. The king sent men to Naioth in Ramah to summon David, but he was no longer with Samuel."

David had been with Samuel?

"Twice more, the king sent men, but the Spirit of the Lord came upon them and they prophesied in Samuel's presence. So the king went himself. And then the Spirit of the Lord came upon him as well and he prophesied."

Strange happenings indeed, but Jonathan grasped hope. Perhaps his father had repented!

Let it be so, Lord! Let it be so!

✦ ✦ ✦

Jonathan rose early to read the Law, then went out to practice with his bow. David came out of the rocks and called to him. Jonathan ran to meet him.

"What have I done, Jonathan? What is my crime?"

Jonathan remembered Michal's visit in the night. Perhaps he had dismissed her too quickly. "What are you talking about?"

"How have I offended your father that he is so determined to kill me?"

"That's not true!" Jonathan grasped his arms. "You're not going to die!"

"The king tried to pin me to the wall with his spear. If not for Michal, I'd be dead. I hid at the stone pile. I could think of nothing else to do but go to Samuel and ask his help. The king sent three parties of men after me and then came himself."

"And made peace with Samuel. I heard. All is well. He prophesied. He has turned back to the Lord!" The king had not seen Samuel since the debacle at Gilgal. His father had loathed the very mention of Samuel's name. All that must have changed!

David shook his head, anguished. "I'm running for my life, Jonathan. You're the only one I can trust, the only hope I have of finding out why the king is so determined to kill me!"

Jonathan felt how David trembled from exhaustion and fear. Was everyone going mad? "Rest. Here. Eat some grain." He took the pouch from his belt. "Drink." He gave him the skin of water. "All this is a misunderstanding. Look, my father always tells me everything he's going to do, even the little things. I know my father wouldn't hide something like this from me. It just isn't so! You know how he is sometimes. His moods pass. A spear thrown in a fit of temper doesn't mean the king is plotting to murder you. Why would he do such a thing? Your victories rally the armies of God." But a niggling worry took hold of him even as he spoke. *Let it not be so, Lord.* "No! It's not true!" He refused to believe it.

"Jonathan, your father knows perfectly well about our friendship, so he has said to himself, 'I won't tell Jonathan—why should I hurt him?' But I swear to you that I am only a step away from death! I swear it by the Lord and by your own soul!"

David's fear was real, and he must be proven wrong. "Tell me what I can do to help you."

David looked around, a hunted look on his face. "Look, tomorrow we celebrate the new moon festival. I've always eaten with the king on this occasion, but tomorrow I'll hide in the field and stay there until the evening of the third day. If your father asks where I am, tell him I asked permission to go home to Bethlehem for an annual family sacrifice. If he says, 'Fine!' you will know all is well. But if he is angry and loses his temper, you will know he is determined to kill me." His voice broke with pent-up emotion. "Show me this loyalty as my sworn friend—for we made a solemn pact before the Lord—or kill me yourself if I have sinned against your father. But please don't betray me to him!"

"Never!" Jonathan exclaimed. "You know that if I had the slightest notion my father was planning to kill you, I would tell you at once." Surely David was wrong. Surely Michal had exaggerated. His father had seemed himself the next morning he spoke with him.

But why did he send me away?

And the reports were incorrect. All that wasted time.

Or was it?

"How will I know whether or not your father is angry?"

"Come out to the field with me."

They walked across the hills together. They had spent many hours out here practicing with bow and spear, running races.

"Do you believe me, Jonathan?"

"I don't know what to believe." He turned to David. "But I can tell you this. I promise by the Lord, the God of Israel, that by this time tomorrow, or the next day at the latest, I will talk to my father and let you know at once how he feels about you. If he speaks favorably about you, I will let you know. But if he is angry and wants you killed, may the Lord strike me and even kill me if I don't warn you so you can escape and live." He clasped David's hand. "May the Lord be with you as He used to be with my father."

Jonathan knew David had no ambitions to take the throne, but he was not so certain about David's relatives. What if they were as ambitious for David as Kish and Abner had been for Saul? David's relatives—Joab, Abishai, and Asahel—were known to be cunning warriors. And they would urge David to follow the ways of the surrounding nations.

"And may you treat me with the faithful love of the Lord as long as I live. But if I die, treat my family with this faithful love, even when the Lord destroys all your enemies from the face of the earth."

"I will never break my covenant with you, Jonathan. I am your friend until my last breath!"

"And I yours." Jonathan felt something else, something far bigger than he could understand, at play here. Only one thing did he hold tight. His father might suffer from fits of rage, but he was not David's enemy. However, there might be several enemies in the ranks of his father's advisors. Snakes coiled and ready to strike. "May the Lord destroy all your enemies, no matter who they are."

Jonathan tried to think of where the safest place would be for David to hide until he could set his mind at ease about Saul. "As you said, tomorrow we celebrate the new moon festival. You will be missed when your place at the table is empty." Jonathan would make certain the seating arrangements were unchanged. David was irreplaceable. "The day after tomorrow, toward evening, go to the place where you hid before, and wait there by the stone pile. I will come out and shoot three arrows to the side of the stone pile as though I were shooting at a target. Then I will send a boy to bring the arrows back. If you hear me tell him, 'They're on this side,' then you will know, as surely as the Lord lives, that all is well, and there is no trouble. But if I tell him, 'Go farther—the arrows are still ahead of you,' then it will mean that you must leave immediately, for the Lord is sending you away."

David thanked him. They embraced and turned their separate ways.

Michal's words came back to Jonathan, strident with warning. Could he be mistaken about his friend? No. He couldn't be wrong about David. He knew him as well as he knew himself. But he could not forget about Samuel's prophecy. God had torn the kingdom from Saul and given it to another. And not long after that proclamation, Samuel had gone to Bethlehem. Saul had sent men to question him, and Samuel had said he had gone to sacrifice. But why there? And now, with this trouble between his father and David, his friend had run to Samuel.

Is David the one, Lord? Or am I to be king after my father? If Samuel had anointed David in Bethlehem, it would explain his father's wild behavior. But Samuel had said he had gone to sacrifice. Would a prophet lie?

The tribe of Judah might still covet the crown.

Jonathan turned back. "David!" When his friend turned, he called out to him. "And may the Lord make us keep our promises to each other, for He has witnessed them." As long as they were true friends, all might be well, no matter what happened.

"Forever!" David raised his hand.

Jonathan smiled and waved. David's word was enough. It was his bond.

+ + +

When the new moon festival came, Jonathan sat in his usual place opposite his father. Saul held a spear in his hand. Abner sat beside the king and they whispered together several times. Both commanded a full view of the entire room and entrance, and their relatives sat in the best positions to guard Saul.

The king looked at David's empty seat. Irritation flickered, but he said nothing about his absence. Jonathan relaxed and ate. David's worries were unnecessary. Jonathan could hardly wait to tell him. Still, he should wait until tomorrow and see if the king said anything about David on the second day.

And the king did ask. "Why hasn't the son of Jesse been here for the meal either yesterday or today?" Something in his father's face made the sweat break out on the back of Jonathan's neck when his father raised the question.

No. David cannot be right. Michal exaggerated. Father would not plot murder. He could not!

The room fell silent. Jonathan looked around at his relatives. "David earnestly asked me if he could go to Bethlehem." He looked into his father's eyes. *Don't let it be true!* "He said, 'Please let me go, for we are having a family sacrifice. My brother demanded that I be there. So please let me get away to see my brothers.' That's why he isn't here at the king's table."

Saul's eyes went black with malevolence. "You stupid son of a whore!"

Shocked, Jonathan stared speechless. And then a rush of anger spilled into his blood. His mother, a whore?

"Do you think I don't know that you want him to be king in your place, shaming yourself and your mother?" Face florid, hands clenched white, Saul glared, a muscle twitching near his right eye.

It's true! Everything David said is true! God, help us all!

"As long as that son of Jesse is alive, you'll never be king."

"It is not *my* kingship that worries you."

"Now go and get him so I can kill him!"

Jonathan came to his feet. "But why should he be put to death? What has he done?"

Screaming in rage, Saul hurled the spear at Jonathan with all his might.

Jonathan barely avoided being pinned to the wall. Men scrambled. Servants fled. Relatives shouted. Stunned and furious, Jonathan rushed to the doorway. "Your struggle is not with David or me, Father. It is with the Lord our God!" He strode from the room, grinding his teeth in anger.

Storming into his house, he ordered the servants out, closed all the doors, and gave vent to his wrath. Holding his head, he screamed in frustration. *Am I becoming like my father? Lord, don't let me become a captive of fear!* He longed to leave Gibeah. He wanted to get as far away from Saul as he could. How could he have been so wrong? Was it possible to spend so much time with a man and not know what went on in his mind?

What do I do now? What is right?

He moved near the lamp and took the Law from beneath his tunic.

God, help me. What am I to do?

"Be holy as I am holy. . . ."

How, Lord? How could he get past words like *honor your father . . . ?*

How do I honor a man who plots murder, who grasps hold of power like a child holds on to a toy, who ignores the needs of his people to satisfy his own lusts for power and possessions. What happened to the father I knew, the man who didn't want to be king?

"Show me the path, Lord! Help me!" His hands trembled as he read, for words he had loved to read now cut deep and made his soul bleed.

"Honor your father. . . ."

If he sided with David, he dishonored his father. If he sided with his father, he would sin against God. Honor. Truth.

I love them both!

His soul was in anguish.

You anointed my father king over Israel. But if You have chosen David now . . . which one do I serve, Lord?

Serve Me.

Tears dripped onto the parchment. He carefully dried them so they would not smudge the Word of the Lord. He rolled the scroll up, tucked it into its casing, and slipped it back inside his tunic. Gathering his bow and arrows, he opened the door.

Ebenezer waited just outside. "I will go with you."

"No." Jonathan strode out the door. As he walked through Gibeah, young boys ran alongside him. He chose one young boy from among them to accompany him. "The rest of you, go back inside the gates." He looked up at the watchman above him. The man gave a solemn nod.

They went out into the fields. "Start running, so you can find the arrows as I shoot them."

"Yes, my lord." The boy pranced with eagerness and then ran like a gazelle.

"The arrow is still ahead of you!" Jonathan called out. Had David heard him? Jonathan glanced back. What if his father had sent men to watch? They might capture David, and then his father would have innocent blood on his hands. "Hurry, hurry, don't wait."

The boy ran faster, gathering up the arrows and racing back.

Emotion filled Jonathan as he saw David's head rise a little from the rocks where he hid. Would David trust him? Why should he trust anyone in Saul's house? Jonathan slipped the arrows back into the quiver and handed it to the boy. He handed over his bow as well. "Go. Carry them back to town." David could see now that he had no weapons. Jonathan walked slowly toward the stone pile.

David came out and dropped to his knees, bowing down three times with his face to the ground.

Jonathan's throat closed. "Get up, David. I am not the king." Jonathan embraced him. They kissed as brothers. Jonathan wept. How long before they saw one another again? before they could sit by lamplight and read the Law together?

"I know the truth now, David. God will help us both. It is not right that this has happened to you, but the Lord will bring good from it. I am convinced of that."

David cried. "I can't go to my wife. I can't go home or Saul might think everyone in my family is his enemy. I can't go to Samuel without risking his life. Where am I to go, Jonathan?"

Tears ran down Jonathan's cheeks. "I don't know, David. All I know is this: The Lord will not abandon you. Trust in the Lord!"

David sobbed.

Jonathan looked back toward Gibeah. There was no time. His father's men might come at any minute.

What did the future hold?

Jonathan gripped David's arms and gave him a gentle shake. "Go in peace, for we have sworn loyalty to each other in the Lord's name. The Lord is the witness of a bond between us and our children forever."

David looked bereft. His mouth worked, but no words came.

Jonathan fought against the shame that filled him. How could his father hate David? How could he not see the goodness in him, the desire to serve the Lord with gladness and fight beside his king? Did any man in Israel love the Lord as David did? Sorrow filled him. *"Go!"* He gave him a shove. "Go quickly, my friend, and may God go with you!"

Still weeping, David ran.

Throat tight, tears streaming, Jonathan looked up. He raised his hands in the air. No words came. He didn't know what to pray. He just stood, feet spread, in the middle of the fields of the Lord, and silently surrendered to whatever God would do.

FIVE

Saul had Jonathan brought to him, the prince fully expecting to be executed for treason. Refusing to bow his head, he stood before his father and waited.

What could he say? The king would not listen to the truth. *My life is in your hands, Lord. Do what You will.*

"I know of your covenant with David! You incited him to lie in wait for me!"

"Everyone knows of my friendship with David. They also know he has never lain in wait for you, nor have I betrayed you. He is your strongest ally, and your son by marriage."

"You are my son! You owe me loyalty!"

"And you have it! Who among your sycophants will tell you the truth, whether you want to hear it or not?" Jonathan was so angry he trembled.

Saul's eyes flickered. He turned away. He paced and then sat. "I was not myself when I threw the spear. Surely, you must know I would not kill you."

Jonathan didn't know whether to believe him or not. "It would appear I don't know anything anymore." Least of all the heart of his father.

✦   ✦   ✦

Saul kept Jonathan close, including him in council meetings and when he listened to the people's cases beneath the tamarisk tree. Reports began to come in: David's parents now lived in Moab under the protection of its king. David had gone to Gath. At the news, Jonathan's heart leapt. Could David fool King Achish into believing he had turned his back on Israel?

"Do you see how David betrays me? He runs to our enemy!"

Abner smiled grimly. "King Achish will execute him. Goliath was not just Philistia's champion, but Gath's favorite son."

Saul waved a parchment and threw it down. "He pretends he is mad. They won't touch him for fear he is possessed by one of their gods."

Jonathan lowered his head so that neither his father nor Abner would see how excited he was. If David was hiding in Gath as the reports said, he was there for a reason other than to wait out Saul's wrath.

He would find out how to forge iron weapons!

+ + +

Months passed and all was quiet. Jonathan attended his father and offered sound advice when asked. Saul loosened his hold and gave Jonathan more freedom. Jonathan continued to study the Law, while keeping abreast of what was happening through Ebenezer, now a trusted officer in the court.

One day Ebenezer came to Jonathan. "Your father is in a rage, my lord. David is no longer in Gath. One of your father's men saw David with Ahimelech, the leading priest in Nob. The king prepares to leave within the hour with a contingent of warriors."

Knowing anything he might say could fan his father's anger, Jonathan ran to Abner. "You must dissuade the king from this venture. Nothing good can come of it!"

Abner strapped on his sword. "Your friend may not be as loyal as you believe. Every man has his ambitions. Did you hear of Doeg's report?"

"Will you trust Doeg? an Edomite? You know what they are like. The man is a troublemaker who would say anything to find favor with the king."

"The king will be waiting."

"David will never raise his hand against the king!"

"How can you be so sure?"

"Because I know him! And so does the nation!"

"Your father is the king!"

"No one knows that better than David, or has shown the king more honor and loyalty. I didn't go down into that valley to fight Goliath. Nor did you. And yet David went to Gath. Why, do you suppose? To learn how to make iron weapons!"

Abner looked uncertain. "If that's so, why didn't he come to Saul?"

"And be speared before he could open his mouth?"

"I must go."

"You would do King Saul and our people more good if you told him the truth rather than follow like a sheep!"

Abner turned, his face livid. "Perhaps you should rethink your alliances, Jonathan. If Saul falls, so will you! David may be your friend, but there are those in Judah who would gladly see you dead if it placed David on the throne!" He headed out the door.

"Abner!" Jonathan went to him. "I know of your loyalty and fierce heart. But remember, whatever you do, God is watching. And God will judge your actions. Remember that when you are in Nob."

+   +   +

Each time a messenger entered the city, Jonathan dreaded the news. He prayed that David had escaped; he didn't want to hear of his friend's death. He prayed that his father would repent and turn back from Nob, not wanting to hear that his father had insulted Ahimelech or any other priest in Nob. The people seemed to feel the tension, for squabbles broke out and Jonathan found himself acting as mediator.

Jonathan did not wish to share his concerns with Ebenezer or any other officer, but his mother became his willing confidante.

"There is nothing you can do but wait, my son. David is just one man with a few followers. He can move faster than your father and his train of warriors. David will stay out of reach of the king."

"I can only hope so."

"Your father won't give up easily. Samuel's prophecy has given him cause to fear and become suspicious of any man who rises in power. David rose to the heights with one stone, and continued to add to his popularity with every victory."

"God gave him that success, Mother."

"Yes, and that adds to your father's frustration. I don't need to remind you that your future is also in the balance, Jonathan."

"My future is in God's hands, Mother. He is sovereign."

She searched his face. "You must rule in the king's absence, Jonathan. Whether Saul realizes it or not, he has left us vulnerable to our enemies."

No one knew that better than Jonathan. "Gibeah is well protected." And he had already sent word to the outposts to keep close watch on any movement of the Philistines.

"You cannot leave things to the officers your father left behind. Who are they? What are they? You are his eldest son. The people respect you. You have fought bravely, and God has been with you. You are honest and courageous and bold."

"You make me blush with your flattery."

"I do not speak merely with the pride of a mother. You have nobility of heart, my son." She put her hand on his arm. "If anything happens to your father, you will rule, whether you wish it or not." Her eyes glowed. "And then Israel will know what it is to have a truly great king!"

"Mother, we had the greatest king in all the earth. The Lord God of Israel was our king. And He has rejected Saul. Do not put your hope in me, Mother. There will be no dynasty."

She shook her head. "Jonathan, Jonathan." Her eyes grew moist. "The Lord rejected your father. He did not reject *you*."

✦   ✦   ✦

A messenger arrived sweat-streaked and ashen. "I come from Nob." He trembled. "Ahimelech is dead! He is dead and every member of his family, and every priest in Nob."

Jonathan leapt to his feet. "The Philistines attacked?"

"No, my lord." He bowed his face to the ground and would not raise his head.

"The king ordered Ahimelech and his whole family killed. And then all the priests of the Lord."

"No!" Jonathan shook violently. "It can't be. *No!* Saul couldn't. Abner wouldn't! No one would dare commit such a sin against God!"

"Abner and his men didn't, my lord. They refused to obey the king's command, but Doeg went ahead with it. He killed eighty-five men, still wearing their priestly garments! And then he put the sword to the priests' families— even the women, children, and babies in Nob. Even the infants, the cattle, the donkeys and sheep. He murdered everything in Nob that breathed!"

Jonathan cried out and tore his robe. He fell to his knees and pounded his thighs. Wrath and despair filled him. Doeg, that evildoer, disgraced God's people! Who but an Edomite would dare raise a sword against priests and their families? Who would give in to a king's mad order and carry out such evil?

His father would live to regret this. It would haunt him more than the loss of the crown and dynasty. It would plague him until he breathed his last.

In an agony of shame at what his father had commanded, Jonathan raised his arms. "May the face of the Lord turn against Doeg! May You cut off the memory of him from the earth! May his children be fatherless and his wife a widow! May his descendants be cut off, their names blotted out from the next generation!"

Even as the curses tore from his throat, Jonathan wondered how he could still love and serve the king who had ordered such an atrocity. *How can I honor this man? I am ashamed of the blood that runs in my veins!*

The Law broke his heart and burned his soul. It did not say the father had to be worthy to be honored.

"*God!!*"

What hope of mercy now? What hope of forgiveness for a king who murders priests? What hope for his people?

✦   ✦   ✦

King Saul returned to Gibeah under the cover of night and went out the next morning as usual to hold court.

Abner looked years older. "The people fear Saul now. They fear him more than they love David."

"It is the Lord they should fear." Jonathan turned away. He could not bear to look at his father. Not yet. He went into seclusion. He read the Law until he could not keep his eyes open and slept with the scroll in his hand.

Spies reported that David had gone to a great and defensible cave in Adullam. David's brothers and his father's entire household went down to him there. Others joined him when they heard what Saul had done to the priests of Nob and their families. Some debtors and malcontents, men of violence, and raiders joined David. Even one whole tribe, the Gadites, defected to David.

Jonathan prayed unceasingly that David would hold firm to his faith in God and do what was right in all circumstances, no matter what Saul attempted to do or what others might advise.

Keep David strong in the power of Your strength, Lord, or how will he keep those men from becoming worse than the Philistines? God, use this time to train David in faith. Give him wisdom and courage to endure! No matter what my father does, keep David faithful and within the bounds of Your perfect Law! Lord, may he never sin against You!

Saul raged. "My enemies increase with every day that passes!"

When a few Benjaminites deserted to David, Saul grew more afraid than ever. He summoned Jonathan every morning and kept him close. Was his own tribe about to turn against him? "You won't desert me, will you? You're my son, heir to my throne. You and Abner are the only ones I can trust!"

Jonathan pitied him.

Malkishua and Abinadab, now warriors themselves, stayed close to the king. Though they were his brothers, Jonathan felt no true closeness with them, not as he had with David. They saw God as their enemy and feared His judgment. He encouraged them to study the Law, but they "had no time for such pursuits." They were eager to bring glory to Saul and themselves in battle, failing, as their father had, to grasp the truth: Victory came from the Lord!

And Jonathan's mother lay dying, shame corroding her life. She no longer desired to live and locked herself away from everyone except Jonathan. "I'm glad he has Rizpah. For if he called for me, I would send word I never want to see his face again!" Jonathan saw her every day that he was home. Then he was sent out to destroy Philistine raiders. When he returned, his mother was dead. Whether she died by her own hand, he never heard. Nor did he ask.

Saul mourned. "Your mother wanted you to marry, Jonathan. And so you must."

Jonathan did not want the king choosing his bride. He would not take an idol worshiper to wife, nor anyone outside the tribe of Benjamin. She must be a virgin and a woman of faith. He knew whom his mother had chosen, one who met his criteria. Rachel was of the tribe of Benjamin and a woman of excellence. She was not fascinated by idols and divination, by jewels and entertainments like Michal and so many others. "I will marry Rachel, Father."

"Rachel? Who is Rachel?"

"Mother's nurse for the past two years." Clearly, the king had not bothered to visit his queen. "She is a relative, on Mother's side."

"Your mother comes from a long line of farmers."

"As were we, before you became king. And happier then than now."

Saul's eyes narrowed. "We can find a much more suitable match for you than a poor farmer's daughter. After all, you are the crown prince. One day, you will be king."

Jonathan was weary of his father's insistence that his marriage be used to forge a military alliance. He would marry in accordance with the Law and to please the Lord, not his father.

"The Law is clear, Father, and I would not risk incurring more of God's wrath upon our house by marrying someone outside the tribe of Benjamin."

Saul frowned. "I suppose you are right." He smiled. "Her father will be pleased with the match. The bride-price can be dispensed with easily enough. A year's exemption from taxes should suffice."

"I hope you will be more generous than that, my lord."

"Two years, then. That is more than generous."

"How many years exemption did you give Rizpah's family?" Jonathan had difficulty keeping his voice even.

Saul glared at him, his face reddened. "Do you dare to criticize me?"

The richer his father became, the more tightly he held the purse. While the people sacrificed to pay taxes in order to keep Saul's army equipped and paid, the king gave up none of his pleasures. Instead, he increased and spread gifts and allowances among his advisors and counselors and higher officials. Did he hope to buy loyalty? *Human lusts are never satisfied!*

Furious, Jonathan did not retreat from his father's glare. "Surely King Saul can be as generous to the family of the future princess of the realm as he was to the family of his concubine."

His father's chin jutted. "Fine. Have your way! A royal price for a humble bride."

Tense with anger, Jonathan bowed low. "Thank you, my lord. May your generosity be rewarded a hundredfold." He could not keep the sarcasm from his voice.

"I still have three other sons who need wives. I doubt they will be as difficult to please as you are."

"No doubt." And more laws would be broken, adding to the sins already blackening Saul's reign.

+   +   +

Veiled and seated on a platform, Rachel was carried to Jonathan through the throng of well-wishers. Careless of custom, he lifted her down and took her hand. It was cool and trembled in his. "You don't need to be afraid of me," he whispered in her ear as those around them laughed and shouted blessings.

Wed, he lifted the veil and stared into wide, innocent eyes, bright with tears of happiness.

When they were alone, Jonathan found himself more afraid of her than of any man he had ever faced in battle. He almost laughed. How was it possible that he could scale a cliff and defeat an army of Philistines, and yet stand trembling before this lovely, fragile girl? It took all his courage to bend and kiss her. When she stepped easily into his embrace, her body pressed to his, he felt exalted. The sweet taste of her lifted him into the heavens.

The wedding celebration lasted a week. The people danced and sang. Jonathan wished his mother had lived to see the fulfillment of her hopes.

Ebenezer acted as Jonathan's best friend and made certain there was plenty of food and wine for everyone. But he was not David. David had been Jonathan's equal. David would have written a song for the wedding and sung it himself.

How Jonathan missed his friend! With hundreds of people celebrating his marriage, with a beautiful young wife at his side, Jonathan had never felt more lonely.

+   +   +

God had commanded that a new husband have no work for a year so he could make his bride happy, but Jonathan and Rachel were not to have that pleasure.

David was in Keilah, fighting the Philistines who had been looting the threshing floors, and Saul saw an opportunity he could not resist.

"God has handed him over to me! David has imprisoned himself by entering a town with walls and gates!" Saul called up his forces for battle and left Jonathan to guard and administer the affairs of the kingdom in his absence.

After all this time Jonathan no longer wasted breath trying to dissuade his father from chasing David. God would protect David. Jonathan poured himself into holding the tribes together and strengthening them against the Philistines. Every morning, he rose before dawn to pray and read the Law. Only after that did he go out to administer justice to the people. He entrusted little to his father's advisors, who changed their minds with every argument. Decisions must reflect the Law he still kept tucked against his heart. Judgments must be made in reverent fear of the Lord.

A steady stream of messengers kept Jonathan apprised of what happened elsewhere. David had escaped from Keilah and was now in hiding. Jonathan gave thanksgiving offerings.

What the king had ordered in Nob haunted Jonathan.

"Keep my father from shedding more innocent blood, Lord. Guard David. Let his love and righteousness grow so that all men may see his good works and glorify You!"

Ruling for an absent king was exhausting work. Jonathan loved Rachel, but he had little time with her. His passion was for the Lord and Israel.

Standing up or sitting down, walking or practicing with his bow, or even stretched out upon his bed, Jonathan spoke to the Lord, his mind filled with hope and the possibilities if men would but turn their hearts fully to God. *Lord, You made me. You created me for such a time as this. Help me to honor my father and serve Your people. I am Your servant! Give me the sense to follow Your commands and teach the people to do likewise!*

How he longed to talk with David! He imagined the campaigns they could plan against the Philistines! If only things had turned out differently. Often, he remembered how it was to talk to David about the Lord, about battles they had fought together, about the future of Israel, twelve tribes united under one king. How many years had it been since he'd last seen his friend?

Ebenezer announced another messenger. "I don't know him, my lord. And he is a Hittite."

"I'll hear what he has to say."

Ebenezer returned with a stranger. The man bowed, but it was little more than a mockery of respect. "I am Uriah, and I have been sent with an important message for the prince." He had the rough look of a brigand, still dusty from hard travel. He hadn't bothered to wash or change his clothes before delivering his message.

"And what is your message?"

"I have brought you a gift." He took something from his pouch.

Jonathan recognized the stripes of Judah on the cloth that wrapped the gift. "Leave us!" he told his guards.

"My lord . . . ," Ebenezer protested, keeping his gaze fixed upon the sneering Hittite.

Jonathan forced a laugh. "He is but one man, and I am well armed. Do as I say."

Ebenezer left the chamber.

Jonathan crossed the room and took the small parcel. He unwrapped it and found a scroll. He read quickly, a smile blooming. A psalm of praise and hope. His eyes grew moist. "I will read it again to my wife. She will be pleased." His heart was so full, he might even sing. No, that would be a mistake. He laughed again, his heart lightened. He rolled the scroll and tucked it beneath his breastplate. "Please tell my friend that I am greatly honored and humbled by his gift."

The Hittite stood silent, studying him.

"You must eat and rest before you return. I will see that you have safe quarters. You are under my protection until you leave. Do you understand?"

Uriah bowed formally this time.

Jonathan wanted news. "How does our friend fare?"

"How would any man fare in his circumstances? He is innocent of any wrong and yet pursued by a king and an army determined to kill him."

Jonathan felt the sharp stab of guilt over his father's actions. "I pray my friend has trustworthy men around him."

"More each day, and any one of them willing to die to protect his life."

"Good."

Uriah's eyes flickered with surprise.

Jonathan met his gaze squarely. "May the Lord continue to protect him."

Uriah bowed his head. "And you, my lord prince."

"You did not answer my question."

The Hittite looked at him. "Nor will I."

"Where is he?"

"Well hidden from the hands that would take his life."

There was no reason for Uriah to trust the son of Saul, who pursued David out of jealousy. Nor would it matter to the Hittite that Jonathan had done all he could to dissuade his father from his mad pursuit. Even if he could explain, it would take too long. "I long to see him."

"He would be the better for a visit from a trusted friend."

Jonathan smiled, his mind set. "Then I will come."

"What?"

"I will go back to his camp with you."

"That would be unwise. You would be in greater danger than he is." He shook his head. "Nor can I guarantee your safety in getting there."

"Nevertheless, I will go with you." Jonathan gave the man instructions to camp in the field beside the stone pile. He gave him two shekels. "Buy what you need in the marketplace and make sure those at the gate see you leave."

After the Hittite left, Jonathan summoned Ebenezer and told him he must be "away on the king's business."

"I would go with you."

"I know you would, but you won't." Jonathan clapped a hand on Ebenezer's shoulder. "You're needed here."

"May the Lord be with you."

"And with you."

Uriah was waiting at the stone pile astride a Philistine stallion. Jonathan was impressed. "That is a fine mount you have."

Uriah grinned. He reined the horse around and came alongside Jonathan's mount. "We have taken a number of horses from the Philistines. Perhaps my master will give you one."

And how would Jonathan explain such a gift to his father, the king?

"You are alone with one of David's servants. Are you not afraid?"

Jonathan looked into the Hittite's eyes. "I travel under the protection of our mutual friend. David did not send you to assassinate me."

"He didn't tell me to bring you back either."

"That might be. But I don't believe the Lord God, who led me to rout a Philistine army at Micmash, would let me fall to one lone Hittite!" He rested one hand on the hilt of his sword. "Your manner tells me David needs encouragement."

Uriah laughed coldly. "You might say that."

"Then let's go!"

They skirted Bethlehem on the way south. Better to avoid people wherever possible so that no one would report to the king. They rode through the mountains down into the wilderness. David and his men were in Ziph.

An alarm was shouted long before they reached the camp. Men came out, armed and ready to fight, and then stood about glaring up at Jonathan as he rode into their midst. He recognized some of his kin—disgruntled, disillusioned, and defiant men who had defected from the villages of Benjamin.

"Uriah has taken Saul's son hostage!"

Men cheered, brandishing weapons. Their faces were hard, wary.

"He is no hostage!" Uriah shouted, drawing his sword. "He is David's guest. Back away!"

Joab, David's nephew and older than he by some years, stood before the rest. He flipped a Philistine knife up and down in his hand. "Greetings, Jonathan, son of King Saul." He did not address him as "my lord, the prince."

His tone set Jonathan on edge. Swinging his leg over the horse, Jonathan slid to the ground. He would not turn his back on Joab. "I come under the protection of my friend, David."

"Did he ask to speak with you?"

"Jonathan!"

Jonathan stepped past Joab and smiled in greeting.

Face strained, David strode toward him. "Get back! Stand away from him!" Men moved at David's command. He glowered at Joab. "The prince is my guest! See that the men are more suitably occupied."

"Yes, my lord." Joab bowed. His dark eyes glanced at Jonathan before he turned and shouted for the others to go about their business.

David turned on Uriah. "I told you to deliver a wedding gift to Prince Jonathan, not take him captive!"

"I came of my own accord, David. If Uriah had not agreed to bring me,

I would have followed him." He extended his hand to Uriah. "May the Lord bless you for your kindness to me."

"And you as well, my lord." The Hittite left them alone.

David looked sick with apprehension. "You should not have come here." He glanced around pointedly. "Are you eager to die?"

"Is that any way to greet a friend?"

They embraced and slapped one another on the back. Jonathan laughed. "It has been too long, my friend." So many years had passed since last they spoke. "You have an army now."

"Your father will one day catch up with me. Sooner or later, he will hunt me down and trap me in some dank cave. He has three thousand men, the best warriors in all Israel. And I have only six hundred."

"I brought you something." Jonathan reached inside his breastplate.

"My sling!" David took it. He looked up. "But I gave it to you as a gift."

"Yes, and I'm giving it back to you. Do you remember the last time you used that?"

"The day I killed Goliath."

"You were not afraid that day, and your courage rallied every Israelite who witnessed what you did. The Lord gave us victory."

"I was a boy, then, racing into battle with the belief that the Lord was with me."

"And so He was."

"The Lord has forsaken me."

Jonathan understood now why he had felt impelled to see David. "Ah, my friend, the Lord has not abandoned you. And it is better to be a poor but wise youth than an old and foolish king who refuses all advice." He smiled sadly. "Such a youth could come from the sheep pastures and succeed. He might even become king, though he was born to poverty. Everyone is eager to help such a youth, even to help him take the throne."

David stared at him. "Surely you know better. I don't want the throne!"

"Neither did my father. Once. Long ago. Now, he hangs on to it with every fiber of his strength and wields fear like a whip over God's people."

"Why are you saying these things to me?"

Jonathan wanted to say more, but he didn't want to speak before David's men and plant thoughts of rebellion. It was one thing to run *from* a king, another to run *after* him. "Can we leave your camp and walk a while? Alone?"

David gave orders to his guards. They didn't look pleased as they walked way, but they kept their distance.

"What am I to do, Jonathan? You know I've never done anything against the king." Tears flowed. "I have served him with everything I had. And yet he hates me! He hunts me like an animal! Everywhere I go, someone betrays me and sends word to Saul. They seek a reward for my life. And I must live with men who live by violence, men I barely trust."

Jonathan was reminded of his father as he listened to David's outburst. Tempestuous. Filled with fear. *Steady him, Lord.* "Don't be afraid, David. Trust in the Lord and the power of His strength to protect you. My father will never find you!"

"How can you be so sure?"

It was time to speak what he knew in his heart. "Did Samuel not anoint you king years ago in Bethlehem?"

Color surged into David's cheeks. "How did you know?"

"It was obvious that you were God's servant the first time I heard you sing in my father's house. And when you went down to face Goliath, and all the times you fought against the enemies of the Lord. When we sat and studied the Law together, I knew you were a man after God's own heart. You *are* going to be the king of Israel, and I will be next to you, as my father, Saul, is well aware. The Lord is our rock. He is your deliverer." He gave a soft laugh. "What a pity I cannot play the harp and sing songs that will fill you with hope."

Jonathan spread his hands. "I have spent hours—days—thinking about what you're going through, consumed with guilt because it is my father who causes you trouble. And I must believe that the battles you're facing now aren't coming to you apart from God."

"Then where is He?"

"The Lord watches over you, David. He sees your coming out and going in. He is training you for a higher purpose. My father, even now, is being given opportunities to repent, and it grieves me beyond words to watch his heart grow harder with every test he faces." His voice broke.

David put his hand upon his arm.

Jonathan swallowed hard. "May your heart soften like rich, plowed earth in which God will plant His seeds of truth and wisdom." He spoke with conviction. "God has not forsaken you, David, nor will He. Not as long as you hold fast to Him and you walk—or run—in His ways."

David relaxed. His muscles loosened, and he smiled faintly. "I have missed you, Jonathan. I have missed your counsel."

Jonathan's throat closed.

David looked out over his camp. "You see the sort of men I command. Fugitives. Malcontents. Men bent on violence. I hate living like this!"

"If you could rule such men and turn their hearts toward God, what a king you would be!"

David kept his face turned away. "They urge me to fight back, to kill your father and destroy the house of Saul."

It was the custom of the nations around them.

Jonathan spoke carefully. "God anointed my father king, but He anointed you as well. What does the Law say?"

David grew pensive. He closed his eyes. " 'You must not murder.' "

"So what does that leave you?"

"I must wait."

"And teach your men to wait upon the Lord as well." He went to David and stood with him, looking out over the wilderness. "No one can truly lead men until he learns to follow God."

David smiled ruefully. "I never thought it would be this difficult."

Jonathan put his hand on David's shoulder and squeezed. "Do what you know is right, what we talked about all those evenings we read the Law together so many years ago. Do not repay evil for evil. Don't retaliate when my father and those who follow him tell lies about you. Do good for the people. That is what God wants you to do, no matter what your circumstances."

"You see the way I live. From hand to mouth. Running, always running."

Jonathan wept. "I can only tell you what I know. The eyes of the Lord watch over those who do right, and His ears are open to your prayers. The Lord turns His face from evil. I have watched how God has turned from my father because Saul rejected Him. The Law tells me to honor my father. It does not say honor him only if he is honorable." His sorrow sometimes pulled him down into despair.

"I walk a narrow path, David, between a king whose heart grows harder with every year that passes and a friend who will be king. But I will keep to it in obedience to the Lord. A man who lives by his own light and warms himself by his own fire one day will lie down in eternal torment. Such is the life my father leads, David, seeing enemies where there are none, hungry and thirsty for the Word of God and not even knowing it. His every act of disobedience widens the gap between himself and the One who can give him peace: the Lord!"

Jonathan raised his hands in anguish. "Lord, I do not want to follow my father. I long to follow after You, to be where You are. Don't You jealously long for Your people to be faithful? Surely You offer us the strength we need to keep faith. Give us strength!"

David looked at him, eyes awash. "I had not thought how this must be for you."

Jonathan's shoulders relaxed. His mouth tipped. "You've had other things on your mind. Surviving, for one."

"But what about you, Jonathan? You are the prince of Israel, heir to your father's throne."

"Don't make the same mistake my father has. It's not my father's throne. It's God's throne to give to whomever He chooses. And the Lord sent Samuel to anoint *you* the next king of Israel." He wanted David to understand.

"I love my father, David, but I'm not proud of him. When I heard what he ordered at Nob, I was ashamed of the blood that runs in my veins."

David spoke in a quick rush of words. "It was my fault that happened, Jonathan. I saw Doeg. If I'd killed that Edomite, none of those priests would have died. Their wives and children would still live." He nodded toward the camp. "Ahimelech's son, Abiathar, is with us and under our protection."

"My father gave the order. What Saul does in the name of his kingship makes my bones ache with shame." He lowered his head and fought his emotions. "I pray unceasingly that my father will repent. We would both know if that happened. He would remove the crown from his head and place it on yours."

How different Israel would be if his father returned to the Lord.

If only, Lord. If only . . .

"You came a long way to see me, my friend." David spoke quietly, his voice hoarse with emotion. "Come. Eat. Rest."

"I came to encourage you."

"We will encourage one another." David slapped him on the back as they headed back to camp. "We will sing songs of deliverance to our God. We will praise the Lord together." He grinned. "We will make joyful noise before the Lord."

Jonathan laughed. Here was the David he remembered and loved so dearly, the friend who was closer than a brother.

They did celebrate far into the night.

And David's men watched in wonder.

+   +   +

When Jonathan awakened, he saw David stretched out across the entrance to the tent. He sat up and David awakened, reaching for the sword at his side. "We're safe, David. All is well." And then it occurred to Jonathan what David had been doing. "Am I a lamb that you must sleep at the gate of the sheepfold?"

"My men—"

"You don't have to explain." He gave David a nod and grinned. "I am honored to have the commander of such an army as my personal bodyguard."

David called for his servant to bring food. They breakfasted together.

"You eat well."

David shrugged. "Some of the people are good to us."

"Be careful whom you trust. Even though you delivered Keilah from raiders, they were only too eager to turn you over to Saul."

David nodded, pensive. "How is Michal?"

Jonathan felt the heat mount in his cheeks. Michal was like those of Keilah. Fickle and shallow, she had nothing good to say about David.

Jonathan shook his head. "She is well and lives alone." He didn't want to speak against his sister.

David looked grim. "This is no place for a woman like Michal. We're always on the run."

"One day you will come home, David."

"For now, I must live in the wilderness."

"Remember our history. The wilderness is a sacred place to our people. God called us into the wilderness. It was in the wilderness God met with our forefathers and traveled with them. It was in the wilderness God performed His great miracles."

"It is a barren, difficult place where every day is a challenge to the body and soul."

"The wilderness refined the faith of our forefathers and prepared them to enter the Promised Land. It is in the wilderness that you will learn God is sovereign. The Lord will meet your needs. He will train you as He trained Joshua and Caleb. God prepared them for battle and gave them victory. Surely, God's voice is heard more easily here in the quiet than in the cacophony of a king's court."

David grinned. "And yet you would make a king of me."

"Only great men like Moses have the wisdom to follow on the heels of God." Jonathan rose. "It is time for me to return to Gibeah."

David helped him with his breastplate.

Jonathan strapped on his sword. Grief welled up in him as he looked at David's face. "The king has left me in command of the kingdom while he—" He could not speak. How many years might pass before he saw his friend again?

"Stay with me, Jonathan!"

"I can't. But I will never raise my hand against you. I will do all I can to guard the kingdom and teach the people to revere the prophets and obey the Law." He embraced David. "I must go."

They went out together and Jonathan faced David's men. He saw death in their faces, an eagerness to conquer. Jonathan turned to David and they clasped hands. "If anything happens to me, David, protect my wife and children."

"You have a child?"

"Not yet, but God willing, I hope to have as many as the arrows in my quiver."

"May the Lord so bless you. You have my word, Jonathan. I will protect your wife and children."

Jonathan bowed at the waist as he would to the king.

Uriah stood holding the reins of the horse. Jonathan took them and mounted. "I know the way back."

"May the Lord your God watch over and protect you."

Jonathan looked at David, raised his hand in fellowship, and then rode away alone.

+   +   +

King Saul returned to Gibeah, morbid and glum. Jonathan relinquished his duties beneath the tamarisk tree and turned his attention to strengthening the tribes.

Months passed.

Ziphites came. David was hiding among them in the strongholds of Horesh. They would hand David over to Saul if the king came down to capture him.

"I have also received reports, Father. David has protected their flocks and herds. What reason have they to betray David? Do not trust these men. They are too eager to take you away from Gibeah." His arguments merely delayed Saul's departure and planted more seeds of suspicion.

"The Lord bless you," Saul told the Ziphite messengers. "At last someone is concerned about me! Go and check again to be sure of where he is staying and who has seen him there, for I know that he is very crafty. Discover his hiding places, and come back when you are sure. Then I'll go with you. And if he is in the area at all, I'll track him down, even if I have to search every hiding place in Judah!"

Jonathan sent Ebenezer to warn David against the Ziphites.

But before the week was over, Saul summoned his warriors and headed south into Judah's territory.

+   +   +

Jonathan awakened in the middle of the night. His body streamed sweat, his heart pounded. He had dreamed that his father was riding along one side of a mountain with his warriors while David and his men were on the other side running for their lives. The king had them trapped and outnumbered.

Someone pounded on his door.

Rachel awakened beside him. "What is it?"

Jonathan threw his clothes on. "I'll send your maid. Bar the door until I return." He ran out the door, shouting to the servants.

Ebenezer had come for him. "The Philistines are heading this way, my lord."

"Send word to King Saul! Tell him, 'Come quickly! The Philistines are attacking!' " Jonathan strapped on his sword as he ran.

Perhaps it was a blessing in disguise.

The wandering king would have to come home. For now. But Jonathan knew that as soon as the immediate crisis subsided, his father would once again resume his mad quest to kill David.

SIX

As Jonathan had feared, King Saul continued after David even as the Philistine threat grew. "He's gone to En-gedi. I have him now! I'll get him this time!"

Year after year, the chase went on, Saul never tiring of the hunt.

"Let him go, Father! We must keep our eyes upon the Philistines! Would you have them overrun the land and put the yoke of slavery around our necks? Israel needs you here!"

"What good if I am no longer king?"

Saul took his contingent of three thousand and went after David once again, hunting him and the growing numbers following him near the rocks of the wild goats.

Left to defend the kingdom, Jonathan sent for representatives from the tribes to gather and discuss defense tactics. He worked night and day, hearing reports, sending out warriors to strengthen defenses, and soothing the people's fears.

When Saul again returned home, unsuccessful, he compounded his sins by arranging a marriage between Michal and Palti, the son of Laish.

"You cannot do this, Father! You'll make her an adulteress!"

"Palti is besotted with your sister. I can use that to my advantage. If Michal were not agreeable to the match, I might hesitate."

Jonathan knew he argued in vain, and sent a message to Samuel, pleading that the seer come and speak to the king. When Samuel did not answer, Jonathan went to his sister, but she was far from mourning the arrangement. As far as she was concerned, David had deserted her.

"Why shouldn't I have some happiness? David is such a coward! All he does is run and hide in caves like a wild animal."

"Would you prefer he defended himself and killed our father?"

"Why should I spend the rest of my life without a husband, locked away in my chambers?"

"You *have* a husband! David is your husband!"

"Then where is he? Does he send me love songs? Does he long for me as I longed for him for years? He doesn't care about me. He never did. He thought our marriage would put him a step closer to the throne." She lifted her chin. "Besides, Father wants me to marry Palti and I'm going to obey. And Palti is far more handsome than David."

"Is that all you care about, Michal? What the man looks like?"

Her eyes darkened. "Palti loves me! Have you seen how he looks at me? We will have many fine sons. Beautiful, strong sons. I will help build up Saul's house!"

"Be careful how you talk, little sister. One day, David *will* be king."

"You speak treason against the king, our father!"

"Father knows. Samuel told him that God had chosen another. It's why Saul hates David so much, why he pursues him relentlessly. But God will prevail—"

"God! God! All you ever think about is God."

"David will reign, Michal. If you wait, you will be his queen. If you go through with this marriage, what do you suppose David will do with you when he returns?"

The fire went out of her eyes. She turned away and lifted her shoulders. "David will take me back." She faced him again. "I will tell him King Saul *commanded* me to marry, and I had no choice in the matter. It's true, after all."

"It won't matter. According to the Law, you will be defiled. David will never sleep with you again."

"He will!"

"No, he won't."

She burst into tempestuous tears. "It's not my fault what plans are made for me."

She sickened him. "You go into this marriage as a willing participant!"

"You care more about that wretched shepherd than you do about your own sister!"

"You, my sister, are no better than a harlot who gives herself to the highest bidder and prostitutes herself before idols!"

Stunned, she stared at him, fear filling her eyes. "I loved David. You know I loved him." Angry color surged into her cheeks. "And what good did it do me? Do I have sons? It's so easy for you to condemn me. You have a wife. Soon you will have a son!"

Her mouth twisted as she spat bitter venom. "She'll probably have a dozen sons and daughters for you, perfect as you are. God's delight! Firstborn son and the delight of the king! And what hope have I ever to have a son of my own? Tell me that, brother. If David won't defend himself against father, then he's destined to run and keep running for however many years father lives. And Father is a strong man, isn't he? I'll be an old woman by the time David returns, if he returns. Too old to have children! *I hate him!* I hate the life I live because of him! *I wish Father would kill him and we'd all be done with it!"*

"May the Lord reveal the truth about you!" Jonathan left, vowing never to look upon his sister's face again.

+ + +

Saul returned once again and retreated into his house. Only Jonathan and the king's most trusted personal servants were allowed close. Saul paid little attention to matters of state. He sat brooding, chin in hand, face sallow, dejected as Jonathan went over the reports that came in from the tribes. Only maps of the regions interested him, especially those showing areas in which David lived.

Frustrated, Jonathan summoned Abner. "What happened at the rocks of the wild goats to put the king in such a foul mood?"

A muscle twitched in the commander's jaw. "We almost captured David. We were so close. We just didn't realize how close."

"What do you mean?"

Abner looked embarrassed. "The king needed to relieve himself. He went into a cave while guards stood outside, keeping watch. When the king returned, we were ready to set off again and then David appeared."

"Where?"

"At the entrance to the cave. He and his men had been inside with the king." His eyes darkened. "How they must have laughed."

"What did David do?"

"He called down to us. He said his men had encouraged him to kill Saul."

"Joab and his brothers, no doubt." Jonathan could imagine those men urging David to take advantage of the moment, murder the king and take the crown for himself.

"What did David say?"

Abner's jaw clenched. "He said a lot of things." The commander glowered, lips pressed tight.

"Tell me everything, Abner."

"He said he'd spared the king because Saul is God's anointed. But he had cut away a piece of your father's robe to prove how close he had been. Of course, he claimed he was innocent of any wrong. And then he cried out for the Lord to judge between him and your father, and prayed that God would take revenge for all the wrongs he claims the king has done to him." Abner sneered. "Oh, of course, David swore his hand would not touch the king. He said, 'From evil people come evil deeds.' He dared speak as though your father were the interloper. That man has done more damage to your father than any Philistine ever hoped to do!"

"And what damage would that be, Abner, when Saul broke faith with David?"

"Your loyalty must be with your father."

"It is! Am I not here running the kingdom while he runs after David? Have I not proven my loyalty year after year?"

"David humiliated Saul before his men. Do you not call that damage? You could have spared your father long ago. You had opportunity after opportunity to destroy his enemy."

"David is not the king's enemy!"

Abner leaned close, furious. "Saul wept aloud! And then he confessed loud enough for all of us to hear! He said that miserable Judean shepherd is a better man than he. Saul said he had treated David badly and David had returned nothing but good."

Tears sprang to Jonathan's eyes, tears of joy, but Abner didn't understand. He and David's relative Joab had much in common. "The Lord delivered King Saul into David's hands, and David honored him."

"Honor?" Abner's eyes darkened. "What honor did he show when he cut into the royal vestments? Where is the honor when men hide in the darkness to snigger at the king who seeks privacy for his most personal needs?!"

"Where is the honor in hunting down a man who has done nothing but serve king and people?" Abner drew back at Jonathan's words, eyes fierce. Jonathan held his stare. "No answer to that, Abner? Then how about this? Did you send warriors into the cave *before* my father went in?"

Abner flushed deep red.

"Perhaps it is your own failure to do your duty that angers you most. You failed to protect the king."

Abner's eyes grew colder. "It might interest you to hear that King Saul said the Lord would reward *David* for his treatment. King Saul said *David* would surely be king and that the kingdom of Israel would flourish under *his* rule. You were not mentioned, my prince. Although King Saul did beg David not to murder all his descendants and wipe his family from the face of the earth."

Jonathan smiled. "David follows the Law of the Lord our God. He does not follow the customs of the nations around us."

"Then why are they now his allies?"

+ + +

Samuel died. King Saul and all Israel assembled to mourn for him. King Saul spoke to the throng of people. The king spoke glowing words of praise for the seer, and led the procession to the prophet's resting place.

Jonathan had insisted that raisin cakes be given to the people before they returned home. Some had come great distances to pay Samuel respect. Saul had groaned loudly, claiming such gifts would impoverish him, but Jonathan persisted. "A generous king is loved by his people. The people will pay their taxes more willingly when they know the king has an open hand in their regard."

The king sat on a dais beneath an elaborate canopy and watched the crowds. He was looking for one man: David. He had stationed men throughout in case David appeared. Abner made certain if David did come, there would be no escape.

Thousands filed past the stacks of cakes, receiving their allotment. Jonathan spoke blessings and words of encouragement to those who came through his line.

A man dressed in rags and bent with years hobbled forward. His head covered, his beard dusty, he leaned heavily on a crooked cane. His head bobbed in repeated bows as he mumbled.

Jonathan stepped closer and supported the man's arm as he gave him a raisin cake.

"My lord the prince is most kind to his people," the man murmured.

"It is the kindness of God who gives us the wheat and the grapes to make these cakes. Praise His name."

The man took the proffered raisin cake, shoved it into his pouch, and grasped Jonathan's hand. His grip was not that of an old man. "May the Lord bless you for your generosity, my son." David lifted his head just enough that their gazes met.

Jonathan held firmly to David's hand. "And may the Lord God of Abraham, Isaac, and Jacob protect you in your travels."

+   +   +

The Philistines raided the land once again, and Saul and Jonathan led warriors to fight.

When the Ziphites reported that David was hiding on the hill of Hakilah that faced Jeshimon, Saul turned aside, took Abner and his three thousand chosen warriors of Benjamin, and went after him, leaving Jonathan to drive the Philistines back. Ebenezer, now one of Jonathan's most trusted commanders, remained to protect Gibeah.

When Jonathan returned home, he learned that Rachel had given birth to their first child. But infection had set in, and Rachel was dying. "Nothing can be done, my lord," he was told.

Jonathan went to her.

"Your son." Rachel gazed at the baby in the crook of her arm. "So beautiful. Like his father." Her breath was faint. She looked at the nurse standing close by, who, weeping, leaned down and took the infant.

Jonathan's throat closed. He was filled with regrets. He loved his wife, but Israel had always been his passion. Not once had Rachel complained. Now, she wore the pallor of approaching death. He struggled with guilt. "He is perfect, Rachel. A gift from the Lord." His voice caught in his throat. He took his wife's hand and kissed the palm. "Thank you."

"Jonathan. Do not look so sad, my love." She could barely whisper. "The people need you." He leaned down so that her lips were against his ear. "Our son must have a proper name."

His eyes filled. "Try to rest."

"No time," she whispered. "Merib-baal is a good name."

One who contends against idols. Jonathan couldn't speak. He held her hand tighter.

Her fingers moved weakly. "Or Mephibosheth."

One who would destroy the shame of idol worship in Israel. Jonathan could only nod. *Let it be so, Lord. May my son rise up to praise Your Name.* He kissed Rachel's hand again and held it cradled tenderly between his own. She sighed softly, the light fading from her eyes. He closed them with shaking fingers and wept.

He did not leave her chambers until morning light. He washed, prayed, gave offerings as the Law prescribed, and then returned to the increasingly difficult duties of a prince guarding the realm for an absent king.

+ + +

Jonathan kept his son close as he grew. He read the Law aloud to Merib-baal even as a babe still in the arms of a nurse. When Jonathan held court beneath the tamarisk tree, he held Merib-baal in his lap as he heard cases and made judgments in accordance with God's law. When the child grew restless, Jonathan gave the boy over to his nurse.

When Merib-baal began to walk, he toddled among the elders and counselors. Jonathan wanted Merib-baal accustomed to the counsel of men. His son must have no fear when voices were raised in disagreement. For one day, God willing, his son would have a place among the council and would fight for the abolition of all idols from Israel.

Jonathan made a miniature bow and arrows for his son and patiently taught him how to shoot into a basket.

Merib-baal wanted to go everywhere Jonathan did, and was often seen out in the field, watching and playing as his father practiced with his bow.

"You cannot go with me to war, my son." Perhaps, one day, when his son was grown, he would have to go, but Jonathan prayed continually that Israel would conquer their enemies and end the wars. He prayed that his son's generation could sit without fear beneath their olive trees and watch their crops grow. But the day when King Saul rested peacefully with his forefathers—and Jonathan stood beside the next king, David—was a dream yet to come.

Jonathan continued his work to unite the tribes against their common enemy, the Philistines. He urged his younger brothers to follow God rather than men. He pressed his father to repent and trust in the God who had called him to be king over Israel.

And often he despaired, for his efforts changed little. Least of all the heart of a jealous king, or of the king's youngest sons.

+ + +

Yet again, Saul heard reports of David's hiding place, and prepared to go after his sworn enemy.

"David spares your life time and again!" Jonathan reminded him, knowing it was futile.

"Only to humiliate me!"

"He has sworn he will not raise a hand against you."

"Should I believe such a vow when he gathers an army around him? He will never raise his hand against me because I will kill him first!"

"How many years will it take before you realize David will never fight against you?"

Deaf to all reason, Saul stormed out.

Abner looked grim. Was he growing weary of this chase? "If anything happens to your father, I will make sure the crown is placed upon your head and no other."

"The crown will go to the man God chooses."

"And why wouldn't God choose you? The people love you. You look like a king. You tend the people like a king. It would be to everyone's advantage if you *were* king."

Jonathan went cold. *God, spare us from ambitious men!* He gripped the neck of Abner's breastplate and yanked the commander forward. Nose to nose, he spoke in a low voice. "If my father falls, Abner, you had better fall with him!"

+ + +

The outposts Jonathan had established sent out warriors to keep watch over the Philistines. Jonathan pored over maps, afraid of what the future held.

Reports came more frequently. "King Saul returns from the wilderness of Ziph."

Relieved, Jonathan went out to greet his father at the gate. Saul came toward Gibeah, head down, shoulders slumped, riding well in front of his officers.

"May the Lord bless your homecoming, my lord." Jonathan bowed low.

As he raised his head, he saw a look on his father's face that gave him hope that the long years of chasing David were at an end.

Saul dismounted and embraced him. "I trust no one but you, my son!" He cast a quick glance at Abner and turned to the elders who had come to welcome him home.

Jonathan followed the king to his palace.

As soon as he was out of sight of the welcoming crowds, King Saul kicked over urns and shouted at the servants to get out of his sight. Even Rizpah, the king's mistress, fled. Saul flung himself onto his throne and buried his head in his hands. "I can trust no one." He groaned as though in terrible pain.

"What happened in the wilderness, Father?"

Moaning, he gripped his head. "David! *I hate the very name!*" He surged to his feet. "I awoke one night with him shouting down at me. I thought I was dreaming, but there he was, standing on the hill across from our camp. David said Abner deserved to die for not protecting me. Abner and all his men deserved to die." Saul paced.

Jonathan offered him a goblet of wine to calm him, but the king threw it across the room.

" 'Look around!' David said. 'Where are the king's spear and the jug of water that were beside his head?' He held up my water jug and spear!" Saul trembled as he looked at Jonathan. "Tell me! How is it possible for a man to walk through three thousand men and reach me? Is he a sorcerer? Is he a ghost? Or do my own warriors hope he will kill me?"

"Father—"

Exasperated, Saul raised his hands in the air. "I cried out to him, 'Is that you, my son David?' " His eyes grew wild. "I called him *my son*. And he demanded to know why I'm pursuing him. He demanded to know what he had done, what crime he was guilty of. He accused my servants of inciting me against him! And he cursed them! He claims they've driven him from his home and the inheritance God promised him. He said they hoped he would serve other gods. He cried out that I must not allow him to die on foreign soil, far from the presence of the Lord."

Saul's face twisted in an agony of frustration as he continued. "He said I had come out to look for a flea as I would hunt a partridge in the mountains!" He sank onto his throne and sobbed. "If he were a flea, I would have crushed him long ago!"

Jonathan pitied his father. Pride goeth before a fall.

Saul pounded his knees. "I said I would not harm him. I said I had been a fool and very, very wrong." His eyes were black holes of despair. "And he would not come to me! *He would not come!* He threw *my* spear so that it was between us and ordered one of *my* men to get it. Do you see how he taunts me? And then he said the Lord gives His own reward for doing good and for being loyal. He boasted that the Lord had placed me in his power and he had refused to kill me."

Saul held his head, eyes shut, as though he wanted to crush the words echoing in his mind. "David said, 'Now may the Lord value my life, even as I have valued yours today. May He rescue me from all my troubles.'"

"David will never raise his hand against you, Father."

Saul rose. "He won't have to when the kingdom goes after him. All my men watched. I could do nothing but bless my enemy." His mouth twisted as he spat out bitter words. "'You will do many heroic deeds, and you will surely succeed.' I said that to him and then he turned his back on me and went away. *He turned his back on me!*" He pounded his chest. "I am king! No matter what Samuel said, I hold the power! I—" The madness suddenly went out of his eyes and he looked frightened. "How did David come so close? He must have stood over me, my own spear in his hand."

"And yet, did not kill you."

Saul didn't seem to hear. "Abner was right beside me. My men were all around me. Sleeping! Or were they? Maybe they watched and hoped David would kill me."

"It is the Lord who allowed David to come close to you. The Lord has given you another opportunity to repent."

Saul's head came up. "Repent?" Saul shook his head. "I've done nothing wrong. God chose me to be king! Is it not right that a king should protect his kingdom?" He clenched his hands. "Why won't you go out with me against my enemy David? He would come to you, Jonathan, and I could kill him. And then this rebellion would all be over! You're my son, heir to my throne! Why won't you fight to hold on to what belongs to us?"

Long ago, Samuel had told Jonathan to speak the truth, even when the king wouldn't want to hear it. "I will fight beside you against any enemy of Israel. But David is not one of them."

"David is my worst enemy!" Saul's face contorted in rage. "David must die!"

Years of frustration and crushed hope ripped away the walls of restraint. Furious, Jonathan cried out. "Lies and deceit! All of it! *You are your own worst enemy! Pride rules your heart and we all suffer for it!*"

Eyes wide, Saul sank back into his throne. "Is it not enough that God hates me? Now my own son—my favorite, my heir—hates me, too?" When not shouting like a madman, Saul whined like a child.

"I don't hate you. God knows! I honor you. You're my father. But I have watched the Lord give you chance after chance, and you continue to reject Him!"

Saul put his fists over his eyes. "The Lord has clothed me in disgrace!" His mouth trembled.

An inexplicable compassion filled Jonathan. Words of the Law filled his mind and heart: *The Lord is slow to anger and rich in unfailing love, forgiving every kind of sin and rebellion.* "The Lord forgives those who turn back to Him." The promise of a dynasty was gone, but surely peace with God was worth more than any crown upon a man's head! "Return to the Lord, Father, for if you don't, the Lord will not allow your sin to go unpunished. The Lord will punish the children for the sins of their parents to the third and fourth generation. Your rebellion against God will cause Merib-baal and all his cousins to suffer!"

"I'm tired." Saul let out a heavy breath. "I'm so tired of chasing after David . . ."

"Then *stop!*"

Saul looked up at him, his eyes glistening. "You will make a fine king one day. Far better than I."

"I do not wish to rule, Father—only to serve." Jonathan went down on one knee before his father. "When a man loves the Lord God of Israel with all his heart, mind, soul, and strength, perhaps then he may ask for the desire of his heart."

Saul's expression softened. "What do you desire, my son?"

"I want to destroy the Philistines. I want to drive God's enemies from our land. I want to unite our people beneath one king, the king God has anointed. I want our people to be at peace with God!"

"You want God back on the throne."

"Yes!" With all his heart, Jonathan wished it could be so.

+ + +

David escaped to Philistia with his army and lived in Gath under the protection of King Achish. David had two wives with him. One had brought him an alliance with Jezreel, and the other, the great wealth of Nabal of Carmel.

Jonathan grieved at the reports he heard. Had David forgotten the Law? The Law said a king was not to have multiple wives! Women would divide his heart. Had the years of fleeing Saul made David value military alliances over obeying the Lord their God?

"So much for your friend's loyalty. He beds down with our enemies," Saul said.

"And may return with information we sorely need."

Saul shook his head, refusing to believe any good of David. "If he learns the secret to forging iron, he will use it to make weapons against us."

Abner looked at Jonathan grimly. "Achish has given David Ziklag."

Saul raged. "He is out of my reach living in Philistine territory."

Anger welled in Jonathan. "It will please you both to remember that Goliath was from Gath. David will be no more welcome in Gath than he is in Judah."

"I had forgotten." Saul laughed. "Goliath's relatives will serve me well if they kill him."

Jonathan knew better. Not even Goliath's relatives would last long against David and his mighty men. The Lord protected them.

+ + +

Over the ensuing months, Jonathan heard rumors. David went out on raids and returned with sheep and cattle, donkeys and camels. But none of the villages that had been raided in Israel had seen David.

Jonathan remembered how he and David had plotted raids upon the Geshurites, Girzites, and Amalekites, enemies of Israel from ancient times. The Amalekites had been the worst of all, murdering the weak and weary stragglers who could not keep up with the slaves fleeing Egypt.

Jonathan suspected where David gained his wealth. But the raids added to the danger David was in. Being familiar with the Hebrew songs honoring David for killing his tens of thousands, the Philistine commanders would have no reason to trust David! And knowing that David ran from Saul, they'd wonder what better way to prove himself and win back Saul's favor than by betraying his hosts, the Philistines.

Jonathan laughed at David's boldness, as David grew rich from raiding Philistine villages while living under the protection of the king! Surely the Lord laughed as well. David would have time now to learn the secrets of forging iron.

Not a doubt regarding his friend entered Jonathan's mind. One day, David would return to Israel, and he would bring with him the resources and knowledge gained from the Philistines.

The only question was whether the Lord would allow David to return in time to save Saul from his own miscalculations.

+ + +

Heading for Aphek, the Philistines gathered their forces, and Jonathan feared they brought God's judgment with them.

Jonathan lifted Merib-baal onto his shoulders and went out into the fields. "Run, Abba! Run!" Merib-baal spread his arms like an eagle and squealed with laughter as Jonathan ran.

Reaching the stone pile, Jonathan lifted his son down and set him upon his feet. "I must go away again, my son."

"Me go, too."

"No."

"Don't go." Merib-baal wrapped his arms around Jonathan's neck and clung.

Jonathan held him tight and then pried his son's arms loose and held them at his side. "Stand still. You must listen now, Merib-baal. This is important. Look at me!" The boy raised his tear-streaked face. "Remember what I've taught you. Always worship the Lord our God with all your heart, mind, soul, and strength."

Jonathan touched his son's chest and forehead, and ran his hands down his son's arms. He struggled against the emotions filling him. Was his son too young yet to understand? *Lord, make him understand. Open his heart to my words.*

Digging his fingers into the earth, Jonathan took Merib-baal's hand. He poured soil into it. "This is land the Lord our God gave to us. It is our inheritance. We are God's people. Your abba must go away and fight to make sure no one takes it from us. Do you understand?"

"I don't want you to go." Merib-baal had his mother's eyes. Doe eyes filled with innocence and sorrow.

Oh, God, protect my son! The boy's weeping pierced Jonathan's heart. Jonathan knew there was always a chance he might not return. He had never talked of David with his son before, but perhaps he was old enough now. He had to be old enough. He held Merib-baal away. "Do you know who David is?"

"Enemy."

"No. No, Merib-baal. You must listen to me. David is my friend. He is your friend, too." Jonathan cupped his son's face. "Remember this, Merib-baal. One day you will meet David. When you do, I want you to bow down to him. Bow down with your face to the ground the way men do before Grandfather. God has chosen David to be the next king over Israel. David will be your king. Do whatever David asks of you. Be his friend as your abba has been his friend. Don't make him sad."

Merib-baal nodded.

Lifting his son, Jonathan swung him back onto his shoulders and headed back to Gibeah.

The child's nurse waited at the city gate and followed them to the house.

Jonathan put his son down, hugged and kissed him. He buried his face in the side of his son's neck, inhaling his scent.

Merib-baal's arms tightened around his neck. "I love you, Abba."

Jonathan's heart lurched. "I love you, too, my son." He combed his fingers through the thick curly locks of soft hair. "Practice with your bow. Listen to the reading of God's law every day." Jonathan had made arrangements for it to be read in his absence. "Go now and play while I speak with your nurse." He straightened, watching his son scamper off.

"If you should hear that the Philistines have defeated us, hide my son quickly. Do you understand?" The Philistines would sweep across the land, hunting down all of Saul's relatives and putting them to the sword if they could.

"Yes, my lord."

He saw the nurse understood. "Do as I've instructed. Do not wait for the counsel of others. Get Merib-baal away from Gibeah. Keep him safe until David becomes king. Then take my son to him."

"But, my lord—"

"You need not fear David." Jonathan prepared to leave. "He and I made a covenant of friendship. David will keep his oath."

+ + +

Jonathan saw terror in his father's eyes when the king heard that a great multitude of Philistine warriors was headed for Shunem, and David was sighted among their numbers, marching at the rear with King Achish.

Saul turned to Jonathan. "Your friend fights for our enemies now."

"Never." Jonathan remained convinced. "When the battle begins, King Achish will be the first to fall, and David will attack the Philistines from the rear."

Abner looked grim. "If that happens, we may have a chance."

Without David's help, there was no hope. The Philistines vastly outnumbered the Israelites. Deserters had bled Saul's army, and swollen the ranks of David's. Even the tribe of Manasseh and some from Benjamin had joined David. He led a great army now, like the army of God.

"We will camp at Gilboa."

+ + +

When Jonathan stood on the hill above the Philistines' camp at Shunem, he drew his breath. His heart sank. There were so many warriors, as many as the grains of sand on the seashore.

Beside him, Saul stared, appalled. "We are undone." He backed away. "I must . . . pray. I must inquire of the Lord." When Jonathan turned to follow, Saul shook his head. "Go and see to our men, Jonathan. Encourage them. Abner will assist you."

It was nightfall before Jonathan returned from his mission, and his father was nowhere to be found. Jonathan went to the king's priests. "Where is Saul?"

"He left with two of his attendants."

It was close to dawn when the king returned to his tent, disguised as a commoner. Jonathan thought he was an intruder and drew his sword, but the king threw off his disguise and sank to his bed, his attendants melting away into the darkness.

"What does all this mean?" Jonathan grew alarmed. "Where have you been?"

Saul buried his head in his hands. "Endor."

"Endor! Why would you go there?"

"To learn what will happen in the battle."

Jonathan felt a wave of fear sweep over him. "What have you done?"

Saul lifted his head, wild-eyed. "Inquired of a sorceress."

"No." Jonathan shut his eyes. *"No!"*

"I had to speak to Samuel. I had to raise him from the dead. And only she had the power to do it!"

"You know it is forbidden!" Jonathan covered his head in shame. "As God required! You expelled the mediums and spiritualists from Israel."

"She conjured the prophet from his grave!" Saul cried out.

"And did you get your answer? You have killed us all!" Jonathan wanted to grab his father and shake him. "Even now you rebel against the Lord. You bring God's wrath upon us!"

"I had to know what would happen tomorrow. Samuel was angry. He wanted to know why I bothered him now that the Lord has turned against me and become my enemy. All I wanted was some hope, Jonathan! Is there anything wrong with that?"

Everything in the way he sought it. "And did Samuel offer you any?" Jonathan knew better.

"He said the Lord has done what he predicted and torn the kingdom from me, giving it to one of my rivals—to *David*!" Saul rocked back and forth, his face ashen. "All because I didn't obey the Lord and carry out God's anger against the Amalekites. The Lord will hand us over to the Philistines. I will die tomorrow. I will die and so will—" he groaned, pressing the heels of his hands into his eyes—"my sons! *My sons*!"

After the first sharp, hot stab of fear, calmness came over Jonathan. *So be it, Lord. Your will be done.* His father had waged war against God, and his entire family would bear the consequences.

Jonathan felt a stillness inside himself. Perhaps he had known all along in the deepest recesses of his heart that he too had to die, before David could become king. For if he survived his father, there would always be those in Benjamin, like Abner, who would want him to fight to keep the crown. Even if he swore allegiance to David, the struggle would go on and on.

Saul wailed. "What have I done? *What have I done?*" He fell to the ground and wept bitterly. "My sons will die and the blame must be laid upon my head. If I could live my life over, I would—"

"Get up, Father." The time for self-recrimination was over. Dawn approached. The enemy would not wait. "I will help you put on your armor. We will go out and face the Philistines together. And may God yet show mercy upon us."

God promised to show mercy to a thousand generations to those who loved the Lord. *God, dare I hope You will bless my son? Please, protect him. Keep him out of the clutches of evil men.*

"You will go with me?" Saul's eyes were wide with fear. "Even after what I've done?"

"I will not abandon you. Have I not always honored you as a son should honor his father?"

"And I have brought you to this." Tears glistened in Saul's eyes.

Jonathan gave him a hand up. "I will be where I belong, fighting at your side!"

He lifted his father's armor and helped him strap on the breastplate. When the king was ready, they went out together. Abner and the other commanders waited, faces grim.

Jonathan saw his brothers among them, fine men of valor. His throat tightened at the knowledge that they would die today. All of them, except the youngest who was safe in Gibeah. But safe for how long?

The king's armor bearer came forward and bowed low. "I was not summoned."

"My son Jonathan assisted me. Take your place beside me." The young man took up two shields and stood ready.

The battle lines were drawn. A great horde of Philistines filled the horizon, and their battle cry rose.

Jonathan turned, clinging to one last hope. "Abner! What word of David?"

"He is no longer with the Philistines."

Jonathan met his father's gaze and saw a waking world in Saul's eyes. Was he remembering the horde of Philistines they faced so many years ago and the boy who had rallied Israel's courage with a sling and a stone? How different today would be with David on their side!

Saul gave a single nod.

Jonathan drew his sword and started his run into the valley of death.

The shofars were blown.

Men shouted war cries.

The earth shook as thousands poured down the hillsides. The enemy came on like avengers lusting for blood.

Jonathan fired arrows until he had none left.

The sound of battle became deafening. Screams of pain. The crash of swords, iron shattering bronze. Wheels rolling. Horses galloping. The hiss of a thousand arrows.

Malkishua was the first of Saul's sons to fall, four arrows in his chest.

Then Abinadab gave a cry of pain, struck in the thigh. An arrow through his right eye sent him backward into the dust.

Dying men shrieked in terror and were silenced by a sword. Jonathan shouted orders to retreat. The Israelites fled before the Philistines, many falling with arrows in their backs.

Philistines surged up Mount Gilboa. *"Kill the king! Kill Saul!"*

Saul shouted, "Guard me! Keep them back!"

Jonathan swung to the right and to the left. He parried and thrust, blocked and made an upward cut. But there were too many. Too many!

His father ran up the hill. Jonathan followed. Arrows rained down around him. Suddenly Jonathan felt a hard blow in his side. Then another in his left shoulder.

"Jonathan!" Saul shouted.

Jonathan tried to raise his sword, but his strength was gone. At first, he felt no pain, and then pain so terrible he couldn't move. Two more arrows struck him in the chest. His knees buckled.

"My son!" Saul screamed. "My son!" A sound of rage and despair.

Swaying, Jonathan dug the point of his sword into the earth, but he could not hold himself up. When another arrow hit him, he fell heavily, driving the arrows in deeper. He rasped for breath and tasted blood. He felt the earth and grass against his cheek. He couldn't lift his head. Darkness closed in around him.

Body tensing, Jonathan fought against death, his fingers digging into the soil.

David! *David!*

Lord, be with my friend when he receives the crown. Give him wisdom to rule Your people Israel!

Battle sounds muted.

Everything within him fixed upon a single spot of light in the darkness. Surrendering, Jonathan sighed, blood bubbling in his throat. Then he felt lifted and drawn back like an arrow fitted into a bronze bow.

Back . . .

> *Back . . .*
>
> *Back . . .*

And then release!

Pain vanished. Grief fell away. He burst into freedom. In the twinkling of an eye, he moved into glorious colors and sounds, past myriads of singing angels, straight and true to the mark set in heaven.

And then Jonathan stood there, astonished and overwhelmed with joy, as he was embraced by the True Prince, who ushered him into the presence of God.

EPILOGUE

❖❖❖❖❖❖

After the battle, the Philistines returned to Mount Gilboa and stripped the dead. When they found the bodies of Saul and his three sons, they cut off the king's head, removed his armor, and sent out messengers across the land to boast of victory. They displayed King Saul's armor in the temple of the Ashtoreths. His body and those of his sons hung as trophies on the walls of Beth-shan.

When the people of Jabesh-gilead heard what the Philistines had done to Saul, they remembered how he had saved them from King Nahash and the Ammonites years before. Their valiant men traveled by night and took Saul and his sons down, carrying the bodies back to Jabesh, where they placed them on funeral pyres.

One item was removed from Jonathan's body before the fires were lit. Their remains were buried under a tamarisk tree at Jabesh, and the people fasted seven days to honor the dead.

Some were afraid of what David might do when he learned they had thus honored the former king. After all, Saul had been his enemy. Would David remember Jonathan as a friend and have mercy upon them?

They called for a volunteer to speak on their behalf.

"Take this to David. Perhaps he will remember his covenant of friendship with the king's son." The head of the elders' council gave the young man a small bundle wrapped in white linen. "All Israel knows that Prince Jonathan and David were best friends. May David honor the fallen prince and forgive any trespasses he sees against us. Go quickly! And may God be with you!"

The messenger headed south, traveling again through dangerous Philistine territory until he found David and his army in Ziklag.

Grim news had traveled quickly. An Amalekite had arrived the day before, boasting that he had taken the crown from Saul's head. David had had him executed.

Now, David mourned and ordered his followers to do the same.

Upon arriving at David's camp, the messenger insisted that he must speak with the king personally. The fate of Jabesh-gilead rested in David's hands.

A guard ushered the young man into David's presence.

The king of Judah raised his head. "I am told you are from Jabesh-gilead."

"I bring you news, my lord."

David's eyes darkened. "Better news than what I heard yesterday, I hope."

The young messenger bowed his head. "King Saul and his sons no longer hang on the walls of Beth-shan, my lord. Our warriors retrieved the bodies, and we have given them an honorable burial for rescuing our city from the Ammonites. I bring you this." He held out the parcel. "It belonged to your friend Prince Jonathan. No other should have it."

One of the guards took the small package and brought it to David.

David untied the leather cords and unrolled the cloth. His face contorted with grief, and tears streamed down his cheeks. "The Law." He held the scroll Jonathan had written and carried with him through the years. Worn from daily reading, stained with Jonathan's blood, it revealed to all the man he had been.

King Saul had pursued David across the land, driving him from place to place, but not once had Jonathan raised a hand against David! Instead, he had remained behind, holding the tribes together so they might stand firm against their common enemy: the Philistines. In obedience to the Law, Jonathan had honored his father and died beside him on Mount Gilboa.

David rolled the scroll carefully and placed it back in its torn leather casing. He drew the loop over his head and tucked the scroll inside his tunic against his heart. "Never did a man have a truer friend!"

That night, David wrote a song to honor Jonathan and King Saul.

> *Your pride and joy, O Israel, lies dead on the hills!*
> *Oh, how the mighty heroes have fallen! . . .*
> *How beloved and gracious were Saul and Jonathan!*
> *They were together in life and in death.*
> *They were swifter than eagles,*
> *stronger than lions. . . .*
> *Oh, how the mighty heroes have fallen in battle!*
> *Jonathan lies dead on the hills.*
> *How I weep for you, my brother Jonathan!*

David ordered all the men of Judah to learn the "Song of the Bow." It was sung for years to come.

David kept his promise to Jonathan. Although nearly all of Saul's grandsons were executed, one survived: Jonathan's only son, Merib-baal, also known as Mephibosheth. Crippled when his nurse fell upon him during the flight from Gibeah, he was kept hidden until David found him and took him into his household, where he lived out his life as an honored guest of the king.

An even greater promise was kept, too—one from the Lord God of Israel, who said in the Law that He would lavish love for generations to come upon those who loved Him: From Mephibosheth came many descendants, and like Jonathan, they became mighty warriors, renowned as experts with the bow.

SEEK AND FIND

❖❖❖❖❖❖❖

Dear Reader,

You have just finished reading the poignant story of Jonathan, prince of Israel, by Francine Rivers. As always, it is Francine's desire for you the reader to delve into God's Word for yourself and discover the real story of Jonathan.

Jonathan's legacy was faithfulness. He was obedient to God at all costs, a loyal servant and regent of Israel. He was a trustworthy friend, an honorable son, and a protective father. He willingly accepted the course God charted for him and embraced his faith with all his might.

May God bless you as you discover the course He has laid out for you. May you willingly embrace it and find your legacy in Him.

Peggy Lynch

FAITHFUL TO GOD

SEEK GOD'S WORD FOR TRUTH

Read the following passage:

"But when you were afraid of Nahash, the king of Ammon, you came to me and said that you wanted a king to reign over you, even though the LORD your God was already your king. All right, here is the king you have chosen. You asked for him, and the LORD has granted your request.

Now if you fear and worship the LORD and listen to his voice, and if you do not rebel against the LORD's commands, then both you and your king will show that you recognize the LORD as your God. But if you rebel against the LORD's commands and refuse to listen to him, then his hand will be as heavy upon you as it was upon your ancestors.

"As for me, I will certainly not sin against the LORD by ending my prayers for you. And I will continue to teach you what is good and right. But be sure to fear the LORD and faithfully serve him. Think of all the wonderful things he has done for you. But if you continue to sin, you and your king will be swept away."

Saul was thirty years old when he became king, and he reigned for forty-two years. Saul selected 3,000 special troops from the army of Israel and sent the rest of the men home. He took 2,000 of the chosen men with him to Micmash and the hill country of Bethel. The other 1,000 went with Saul's son Jonathan to Gibeah in the land of Benjamin.

Soon after this, Jonathan attacked and defeated the garrison of Philistines at Geba. The news spread quickly among the Philistines. So Saul blew the ram's horn throughout the land, saying, "Hebrews, hear this! Rise up in revolt!" All Israel heard the news that Saul had destroyed the Philistine garrison at Geba and that the Philistines now hated the Israelites more than ever. So the entire Israelite army was summoned to join Saul at Gilgal.

The Philistines mustered a mighty army of 3,000 chariots, 6,000 charioteers, and as many warriors as the grains of sand on the seashore! They camped at Micmash east of Beth-aven. The men of Israel saw what a tight spot they were in; and because they were hard-pressed by the enemy, they tried to hide in caves, thickets, rocks, holes, and cisterns. Some of them crossed the Jordan River and escaped into the land of Gad and Gilead.

Meanwhile, Saul stayed at Gilgal, and his men were trembling with fear. Saul waited there seven days for Samuel, as Samuel had instructed him earlier, but Samuel still didn't come. Saul realized that his troops were rapidly slipping away. So he demanded, "Bring me the burnt offering and the peace offerings!" And Saul sacrificed the burnt offering himself.

Just as Saul was finishing with the burnt offering, Samuel arrived. Saul went out to meet and welcome him, but Samuel said, "What is this you have done?"

Saul replied, "I saw my men scattering from me, and you didn't arrive when you said you would, and the Philistines are at Micmash ready for battle. So I said, 'The Philistines are ready to march against us at Gilgal, and I haven't even asked for the LORD's help!' So I felt compelled to offer the burnt offering myself before you came."

"How foolish!" Samuel exclaimed. "You have not kept the command the

LORD your God gave you. Had you kept it, the LORD would have established your kingdom over Israel forever. But now your kingdom must end, for the LORD has sought out a man after his own heart. The LORD has already appointed him to be the leader of his people, because you have not kept the LORD's command."   1 SAMUEL 12:12-15, 23-25; 13:1-14

+ List the warnings Samuel proclaimed at Saul's coronation.

+ Who else besides Saul would have heard these admonitions?

+ What actions did Saul take?

+ What did Samuel tell him? List the specifics.

+ How would this affect Saul's son Jonathan?

+ What effect might information like this have had on Jonathan's attitude toward God? toward his father?

FIND GOD'S WAYS FOR YOU

Think of someone you admired who made poor choices that affected you and your future. What was the outcome?

+ What was (or is) your attitude toward this person? toward God?

Those who listen to instruction will prosper; those who trust the LORD will be joyful.   PROVERBS 16:20

+ What advice is offered in this verse?

STOP AND PONDER

Be careful how you live. Don't live like fools, but like those who are wise. Make the most of every opportunity in these evil days. Don't act thoughtlessly, but understand what the LORD wants you to do. Don't be drunk with wine, because that will ruin your life. Instead, be filled with the Holy Spirit.

EPHESIANS 5:15-18

FAITHFUL SERVANT

SEEK GOD'S WORD FOR TRUTH

Read the following passage:

One day Jonathan said to his armor bearer, "Come on, let's go over to where the Philistines have their outpost." But Jonathan did not tell his father what he was doing.

Meanwhile, Saul and his 600 men were camped on the outskirts of Gibeah, around the pomegranate tree at Migron. Among Saul's men was Ahijah the priest, who was wearing the ephod, the priestly vest. Ahijah was the son of Ichabod's brother Ahitub, son of Phinehas, son of Eli, the priest of the LORD who had served at Shiloh.

No one realized that Jonathan had left the Israelite camp. To reach the Philistine outpost, Jonathan had to go down between two rocky cliffs that were called Bozez and Seneh. The cliff on the north was in front of Micmash, and the one on the south was in front of Geba. "Let's go across to the outpost of those pagans," Jonathan said to his armor bearer. "Perhaps the LORD will help us, for nothing can hinder the LORD. He can win a battle whether he has many warriors or only a few!"

"Do what you think is best," the armor bearer replied. "I'm with you completely, whatever you decide."

"All right then," Jonathan told him. "We will cross over and let them see us. If they say to us, 'Stay where you are or we'll kill you,' then we will stop and not go up to them. But if they say, 'Come on up and fight,' then we will go up. That will be the LORD's sign that he will help us defeat them."

When the Philistines saw them coming, they shouted, "Look! The Hebrews are crawling out of their holes!" Then the men from the outpost shouted to Jonathan, "Come on up here, and we'll teach you a lesson!"

"Come on, climb right behind me," Jonathan said to his armor bearer, "for the LORD will help us defeat them!"

So they climbed up using both hands and feet, and the Philistines fell before Jonathan, and his armor bearer killed those who came behind them. They killed some twenty men in all, and their bodies were scattered over about half an acre.

Suddenly, panic broke out in the Philistine army, both in the camp and in the field, including even the outposts and raiding parties. And just then an earthquake struck, and everyone was terrified.

Saul's lookouts in Gibeah of Benjamin saw a strange sight—the vast army of Philistines began to melt away in every direction. "Call the roll and find out who's missing," Saul ordered. And when they checked, they found that Jonathan and his armor bearer were gone.

Then Saul shouted to Ahijah, "Bring the ephod here!" For at that time Ahijah was wearing the ephod in front of the Israelites. But while Saul was talking to the priest, the confusion in the Philistine camp grew louder and louder. So Saul said to the priest, "Never mind; let's get going!"

Then Saul and all his men rushed out to the battle and found the Philistines killing each other. There was terrible confusion everywhere. Even the Hebrews who had previously gone over to the Philistine army revolted and joined in with Saul, Jonathan, and the rest of the Israelites. Likewise, the men of Israel who were hiding in the hill country of Ephraim joined the chase when they saw the Philistines running away. So the LORD saved Israel that day, and the battle continued to rage even beyond Beth-aven. 1 SAMUEL 14:1-23

✦ Describe what you learn about Jonathan from this passage.

✦ Who or what was the source of Jonathan's daring feat?

+ How did God honor Jonathan's faith?

+ Where were Saul and the rest of the army? What were they doing?

+ What was Saul's reaction to the event? What did he do?

+ What did God do for all of Israel that day?

FIND GOD'S WAYS FOR YOU

Describe a time when you plunged ahead in your job, community, family, or other circle of influence to do something others thought was not possible. What was the outcome? Who or what motivated you?

+ Do you consider yourself a faithful servant? Why or why not?

> The name of the LORD is a strong fortress; the godly run to him and are safe.
>
> PROVERBS 18:10

+ What does God offer those who run to Him?

STOP AND PONDER

> Jesus told them, "I tell you the truth, if you have faith and don't doubt, you can do things like this and much more. You can even say to this mountain, 'May you be lifted up and thrown into the sea,' and it will happen. You can pray for anything, and if you have faith, you will receive it."   MATTHEW 21:21-22

FAITHFUL FRIEND

SEEK GOD'S WORD FOR TRUTH

Read the following passage:

> As Saul watched David go out to fight the Philistine, he asked Abner, the commander of his army, "Abner, whose son is this young man?"
>
> "I really don't know," Abner declared.
>
> "Well, find out who he is!" the king told him.
>
> As soon as David returned from killing Goliath, Abner brought him to Saul with the Philistine's head still in his hand. "Tell me about your father, young man," Saul said.
>
> And David replied, "His name is Jesse, and we live in Bethlehem."
>
> After David had finished talking with Saul, he met Jonathan, the king's son. There was an immediate bond of love between them, and they became the best of friends. From that day on Saul kept David with him and wouldn't

let him return home. And Jonathan made a solemn pact with David, because he loved him as he loved himself. Jonathan sealed the pact by taking off his robe and giving it to David, together with his tunic, sword, bow, and belt.

Whatever Saul asked David to do, David did it successfully. So Saul made him a commander over the men of war, an appointment that was welcomed by the people and Saul's officers alike.

When the victorious Israelite army was returning home after David had killed the Philistine, women from all the towns of Israel came out to meet King Saul. They sang and danced for joy with tambourines and cymbals. This was their song:

"Saul has killed his thousands,
and David his ten thousands!"

This made Saul very angry. "What's this?" he said. "They credit David with ten thousands and me with only thousands. Next they'll be making him their king!" So from that time on Saul kept a jealous eye on David.

Saul now urged his servants and his son Jonathan to assassinate David. But Jonathan, because of his close friendship with David, told him what his father was planning. "Tomorrow morning," he warned him, "you must find a hiding place out in the fields. I'll ask my father to go out there with me, and I'll talk to him about you. Then I'll tell you everything I can find out."

The next morning Jonathan spoke with his father about David, saying many good things about him. "The king must not sin against his servant David," Jonathan said. "He's never done anything to harm you. He has always helped you in any way he could. Have you forgotten about the time he risked his life to kill the Philistine giant and how the LORD brought a great victory to all Israel as a result? You were certainly happy about it then. Why should you murder an innocent man like David? There is no reason for it at all!"

So Saul listened to Jonathan and vowed, "As surely as the LORD lives, David will not be killed."

Afterward Jonathan called David and told him what had happened. Then he brought David to Saul, and David served in the court as before.

1 SAMUEL 17:55–18:9; 19:1-7

+ What were the circumstances surrounding Jonathan's introduction to David?

+ What was Jonathan's response to David?

+ How did Saul react to David?

+ Discuss Jonathan's boldness in opposing his father on behalf of his friend.

+ List the considerations Jonathan laid out for his father regarding David. How effective was his approach?

FIND GOD'S WAYS FOR YOU

+ Share about a time when you experienced immediate friendship. Are you still close to that person?

✦ Has one of your friendships ever created conflict with your family? If so, what steps did you take to resolve the conflict? What was the outcome?

> There are "friends" who destroy each other, but a real friend sticks closer than a brother.   PROVERBS 18:24

✦ How would you define friends in this verse?

STOP AND PONDER

> Two people are better off than one, for they can help each other succeed.
> If one person falls, the other can reach out and help. But someone who falls
> alone is in real trouble. Likewise, two people lying close together can keep
> each other warm. But how can one be warm alone? A person standing alone
> can be attacked and defeated, but two can stand back-to-back and conquer.
> Three are even better, for a triple-braided cord is not easily broken.
>   ECCLESIASTES 4:9-12

FAITHFUL LEADER

SEEK GOD'S WORD FOR TRUTH

Reread the following passage that was covered in the last study:

> Saul now urged his servants and his son Jonathan to assassinate David.
> But Jonathan, because of his close friendship with David, told him what
> his father was planning. "Tomorrow morning," he warned him, "you
> must find a hiding place out in the fields. I'll ask my father to go out there
> with me, and I'll talk to him about you. Then I'll tell you everything I can
> find out."
>
> The next morning Jonathan spoke with his father about David, saying
> many good things about him. "The king must not sin against his servant
> David," Jonathan said. "He's never done anything to harm you. He has
> always helped you in any way he could. Have you forgotten about the time
> he risked his life to kill the Philistine giant and how the LORD brought a
> great victory to all Israel as a result? You were certainly happy about it then.
> Why should you murder an innocent man like David? There is no reason for
> it at all!"
>
> So Saul listened to Jonathan and vowed, "As surely as the LORD lives, David
> will not be killed."
>
> Afterward Jonathan called David and told him what had happened. Then
> he brought David to Saul, and David served in the court as before.
>   1 SAMUEL 19:1-7

✦ In this passage, what leadership skills and attributes does Jonathan exhibit?

Read the following passage:

Now the men of Israel were pressed to exhaustion that day, because Saul had placed them under an oath, saying, "Let a curse fall on anyone who eats before evening—before I have full revenge on my enemies." So no one ate anything all day, even though they had all found honeycomb on the ground in the forest. They didn't dare touch the honey because they all feared the oath they had taken.

But Jonathan had not heard his father's command, and he dipped the end of his stick into a piece of honeycomb and ate the honey. After he had eaten it, he felt refreshed. But one of the men saw him and said, "Your father made the army take a strict oath that anyone who eats food today will be cursed. That is why everyone is weary and faint."

"My father has made trouble for us all!" Jonathan exclaimed. "A command like that only hurts us. See how refreshed I am now that I have eaten this little bit of honey. If the men had been allowed to eat freely from the food they found among our enemies, think how many more Philistines we could have killed!"

Then Saul said, "Let's chase the Philistines all night and plunder them until sunrise. Let's destroy every last one of them."

His men replied, "We'll do whatever you think is best."

But the priest said, "Let's ask God first."

So Saul asked God, "Should we go after the Philistines? Will you help us defeat them?" But God made no reply that day.

Then Saul said to the leaders, "Something's wrong! I want all my army commanders to come here. We must find out what sin was committed today. I vow by the name of the Lord who rescued Israel that the sinner will surely die, even if it is my own son Jonathan!" But no one would tell him what the trouble was.

Then Saul said, "Jonathan and I will stand over here, and all of you stand over there."

And the people responded to Saul, "Whatever you think is best."

Then Saul prayed, "O LORD, God of Israel, please show us who is guilty and who is innocent." Then they cast sacred lots, and Jonathan and Saul were chosen as the guilty ones, and the people were declared innocent.

Then Saul said, "Now cast lots again and choose between me and Jonathan." And Jonathan was shown to be the guilty one.

"Tell me what you have done," Saul demanded of Jonathan.

"I tasted a little honey," Jonathan admitted. "It was only a little bit on the end of my stick. Does that deserve death?"

"Yes, Jonathan," Saul said, "you must die! May God strike me and even kill me if you do not die for this."

But the people broke in and said to Saul, "Jonathan has won this great victory for Israel. Should he die? Far from it! As surely as the LORD lives, not one hair on his head will be touched, for God helped him do a great deed today." So the people rescued Jonathan, and he was not put to death.

Then Saul called back the army from chasing the Philistines, and the Philistines returned home.   1 SAMUEL 14:24-30, 36-46

+ What do we learn about Jonathan's leadership abilities from this passage?

+ Contrast Jonathan's relationship with the people to his father's.

+ Compare Jonathan and Saul regarding wisdom and logic.

+ Of what value was Jonathan to his father?

+ How did the people value Jonathan? How did they show it?

FIND GOD'S WAYS FOR YOU

+ How do your peers perceive you? What about those in authority over you?

+ What leadership skills do you have? Have you made them available to God?

> Search me, O God, and know my heart; test me and know my anxious thoughts. Point out anything in me that offends you, and lead me along the path of everlasting life.   PSALM 139:23-24

+ How do you think God will measure your abilities?

STOP AND PONDER

> A person who is put in charge as a manager must be faithful. As for me [the apostle Paul], it matters very little how I might be evaluated by you or by any human authority. I don't even trust my own judgment on this point. My conscience is clear, but that doesn't prove I'm right. It is the LORD himself who will examine me and decide.   1 CORINTHIANS 4:2-4

FAITHFUL SON

SEEK GOD'S WORD FOR TRUTH

Read the following passage:

> David now fled from Naioth in Ramah and found Jonathan. "What have I done?" he exclaimed. "What is my crime? How have I offended your father that he is so determined to kill me?"
>
> "That's not true!" Jonathan protested. "You're not going to die. He always tells me everything he's going to do, even the little things. I know my father wouldn't hide something like this from me. It just isn't so!"
>
> Then David took an oath before Jonathan and said, "Your father knows perfectly well about our friendship, so he has said to himself, 'I won't tell

Jonathan—why should I hurt him?' But I swear to you that I am only a step away from death! I swear it by the LORD and by your own soul!"

"Tell me what I can do to help you," Jonathan exclaimed.

David replied, "Tomorrow we celebrate the new moon festival. I've always eaten with the king on this occasion, but tomorrow I'll hide in the field and stay there until the evening of the third day. If your father asks where I am, tell him I asked permission to go home to Bethlehem for an annual family sacrifice. If he says, 'Fine!' you will know all is well. But if he is angry and loses his temper, you will know he is determined to kill me. Show me this loyalty as my sworn friend—for we made a solemn pact before the LORD—or kill me yourself if I have sinned against your father. But please don't betray me to him!"

"Never!" Jonathan exclaimed. "You know that if I had the slightest notion my father was planning to kill you, I would tell you at once."

Then David asked, "How will I know whether or not your father is angry?"

"Come out to the field with me," Jonathan replied. And they went out there together. Then Jonathan told David, "I promise by the LORD, the God of Israel, that by this time tomorrow, or the next day at the latest, I will talk to my father and let you know at once how he feels about you. If he speaks favorably about you, I will let you know. But if he is angry and wants you killed, may the LORD strike me and even kill me if I don't warn you so you can escape and live. May the LORD be with you as he used to be with my father. And may you treat me with the faithful love of the Lord as long as I live. But if I die, treat my family with this faithful love, even when the LORD destroys all your enemies from the face of the earth."

So Jonathan made a solemn pact with David, saying, "May the LORD destroy all your enemies!" And Jonathan made David reaffirm his vow of friendship again, for Jonathan loved David as he loved himself.

Then Jonathan said, "Tomorrow we celebrate the new moon festival. You will be missed when your place at the table is empty. The day after tomorrow, toward evening, go to the place where you hid before, and wait there by the stone pile. I will come out and shoot three arrows to the side of the stone pile as though I were shooting at a target. Then I will send a boy to bring the arrows back. If you hear me tell him, 'They're on this side,' then you will know, as surely as the LORD lives, that all is well, and there is no trouble. But if I tell him, 'Go farther—the arrows are still ahead of you,' then it will mean that you must leave immediately, for the LORD is sending you away. And may the LORD make us keep our promises to each other, for he has witnessed them."

So David hid himself in the field, and when the new moon festival began, the king sat down to eat. He sat at his usual place against the wall, with Jonathan sitting opposite him and Abner beside him. But David's place was empty. Saul didn't say anything about it that day, for he said to himself, "Something must have made David ceremonially unclean." But when David's place was empty again the next day, Saul asked Jonathan, "Why hasn't the son of Jesse been here for the meal either yesterday or today?"

Jonathan replied, "David earnestly asked me if he could go to Bethlehem. He said, 'Please let me go, for we are having a family sacrifice. My brother demanded that I be there. So please let me get away to see my brothers.' That's why he isn't here at the king's table."

Saul boiled with rage at Jonathan. "You stupid son of a whore!" he swore at him. "Do you think I don't know that you want him to be king in your place, shaming yourself and your mother? As long as that son of Jesse is alive, you'll never be king. Now go and get him so I can kill him!"

"But why should he be put to death?" Jonathan asked his father. "What has he done?"

Then Saul hurled his spear at Jonathan, intending to kill him. So at last Jonathan realized that his father was really determined to kill David.

Jonathan left the table in fierce anger and refused to eat on that second day of the festival, for he was crushed by his father's shameful behavior toward David.

The next morning, as agreed, Jonathan went out into the field and took a young boy with him to gather his arrows. "Start running," he told the boy, "so you can find the arrows as I shoot them." So the boy ran, and Jonathan shot an arrow beyond him. When the boy had almost reached the arrow, Jonathan shouted, "The arrow is still ahead of you. Hurry, hurry, don't wait." So the boy quickly gathered up the arrows and ran back to his master. He, of course, suspected nothing; only Jonathan and David understood the signal. Then Jonathan gave his bow and arrows to the boy and told him to take them back to town.

As soon as the boy was gone, David came out from where he had been hiding near the stone pile. Then David bowed three times to Jonathan with his face to the ground. Both of them were in tears as they embraced each other and said good-bye, especially David.

At last Jonathan said to David, "Go in peace, for we have sworn loyalty to each other in the LORD's name. The LORD is the witness of a bond between us and our children forever."

Then David left, and Jonathan returned to the town.   1 SAMUEL 20:1-42

+ What is Jonathan's first response to David's accusations regarding his father?

+ What does Jonathan's oath imply?

+ Jonathan took his usual approach with his father regarding David. What happened this time?

+ Do you think Jonathan believed his father was capable of murdering David? Why or why not?

+ What convinced Jonathan?

+ Upon hearing the outcome of Jonathan's confrontation with his father, David fled. What did Jonathan do?

FIND GOD'S WAYS FOR YOU

Do you believe the best about your parents? Why or why not?

+ Have you ever gone against your parents' wishes? If so, what happened? If not, why not?

My child, listen when your father corrects you. Don't neglect your mother's instruction. What you learn from them will crown you with grace and be a chain of honor around your neck. PROVERBS 1:8-9

+ What does God promise to those who obey their parents' teaching?

STOP AND PONDER

Dear children, remain in fellowship with Christ so that when he returns, you will be full of courage and not shrink back from him in shame. Since we know that Christ is righteous, we also know that all who do what is right are God's children. 1 JOHN 2:28-29

FAITHFUL FATHER

SEEK GOD'S WORD FOR TRUTH

Review 1 Samuel 20:1-42 (printed at the beginning of the previous chapter).
+ What arrangements did Jonathan make for his family?

+ Who was he trusting to see that the arrangements were carried out?

Read the following passages:

Now the Philistines attacked Israel, and the men of Israel fled before them. Many were slaughtered on the slopes of Mount Gilboa. The Philistines closed in on Saul and his sons, and they killed three of his sons—Jonathan, Abinadab, and Malkishua. The fighting grew very fierce around Saul, and the Philistine archers caught up with him and wounded him severely.

Saul groaned to his armor bearer, "Take your sword and kill me before these pagan Philistines come to run me through and taunt and torture me."

But his armor bearer was afraid and would not do it. So Saul took his own sword and fell on it. When his armor bearer realized that Saul was dead, he fell on his own sword and died beside the king. So Saul, his three sons, his armor bearer, and his troops all died together that same day.

When the Israelites on the other side of the Jezreel Valley and beyond the Jordan saw that the Israelite army had fled and that Saul and his sons were dead, they abandoned their towns and fled. So the Philistines moved in and occupied their towns. 1 SAMUEL 31:1-7

Then David composed a funeral song for Saul and Jonathan, and he commanded that it be taught to the people of Judah. It is known as the Song of the Bow, and it is recorded in *The Book of Jashar*.

"Your pride and joy, O Israel, lies dead on the hills!
  Oh, how the mighty heroes have fallen!
  Don't announce the news in Gath,

don't proclaim it in the streets of Ashkelon,
or the daughters of the Philistines will rejoice
and the pagans will laugh in triumph.
O mountains of Gilboa,
let there be no dew or rain upon you,
nor fruitful fields producing offerings of grain.
For there the shield of the mighty heroes was defiled;
the shield of Saul will no longer be anointed with oil.
The bow of Jonathan was powerful,
and the sword of Saul did its mighty work.
They shed the blood of their enemies
and pierced the bodies of mighty heroes.
How beloved and gracious were Saul and Jonathan!
They were together in life and in death.
They were swifter than eagles,
stronger than lions.
O women of Israel, weep for Saul,
for he dressed you in luxurious scarlet clothing,
in garments decorated with gold.
Oh, how the mighty heroes have fallen in battle!
Jonathan lies dead on the hills.
How I weep for you, my brother Jonathan!
Oh, how much I loved you!
And your love for me was deep,
deeper than the love of women!
Oh, how the mighty heroes have fallen!
Stripped of their weapons, they lie dead."   2 SAMUEL 1:17-27

+ How—and with whom—did Jonathan die?

+ What did the people of Israel do after Saul and Jonathan were killed?

+ How did David honor his covenant with Jonathan?

Discuss David's tribute to Jonathan.

FIND GOD'S WAYS FOR YOU

+ What arrangements have you made for those you love after you die?

+ What kind of legacy will you leave?

A good reputation is more valuable than costly perfume. And the day you die
is better than the day you are born.   ECCLESIASTES 7:1

+ What do you think your dearest friends will say about you when you
are gone?

STOP AND PONDER

Because we are united with Christ, we have received an inheritance from God, for he chose us in advance, and he makes everything work out according to his plan. When you believed in Christ, he identified you as his own by giving you the Holy Spirit, whom he promised long ago. The Spirit is God's guarantee that he will give us the inheritance he promised and that he has purchased us to be his own people.   EPHESIANS 1:11, 13-14

THE LEGACY

Jonathan was a prince, a fine son, a loving friend, a caring father. And as a leader, he was a selfless servant. His life whispers of another Prince—a fine Son, a loving Friend, a caring Leader, and a selfless Servant: Jesus.

Let Jesus' words penetrate your heart and provide your legacy:

I have loved you even as the Father has loved me. Remain in my love. When you obey my commandments, you remain in my love, just as I obey my Father's commandments and remain in his love. I have told you these things so that you will be filled with my joy. Yes, your joy will overflow! This is my commandment: Love each other in the same way I have loved you. There is no greater love than to lay down one's life for one's friends. You are my friends if you do what I command. I no longer call you slaves, because a master doesn't confide in his slaves. Now you are my friends, since I have told you everything the Father told me. You didn't choose me. I chose you. I appointed you to go and produce lasting fruit, so that the Father will give you whatever you ask for, using my name. This is my command: Love each other.   JOHN 15:9-17

BOOK FOUR

THE PROPHET

ONE

❖❖❖❖❖❖❖

They were coming.

They moved swiftly, keeping low to the ground, silent streaks of black in the fading light. Amos didn't have to see them or hear them to know the enemy was closing in. He felt it, through instinct honed by years of living in the wilderness. Three sheep were missing—the same stubborn dam who so frequently troubled him, and her twin lambs. He must act quickly.

Calling to his flock, he watched them race toward him. They sensed his urgency and followed him into the fold. He closed the gate behind them and secured it. Assured of their safety, he was free now to go after the lost ones.

He ran, and the stones in his pouch rattled. He took one out and fitted it to his sling.

A lamb bleated, and he raced toward the frightened sound. The foolish dam remained intent upon having her own way. Rather than stay in the green pastures to which he led her, she continued to choose brambles and brush.

Amos saw the wolves. He raised his arm, the sling emitting a high-pitched whir before he released the stone. With a yelp of pain, the pack leader went down heavily, but quickly regained his feet.

Amos came on. Snarling, the wolf advanced in a low crouch, hackles raised. The others circled, teeth bared, determined. The dam did not move, frozen in fear, while her helpless lambs bleated in confusion and fear. When one ran, a wolf leapt at it. Before it could sink its jaws into the young throat, Amos sent another stone flying. It struck hard and true. The wolf dropped, a stone embedded in its skull.

Most of the others fled, but the alpha remained to challenge. Amos hurled his club, and struck it hard in the hip. With another cry of pain, the wolf limped into the brush and disappeared.

The lamb lay still. Amos lifted it tenderly, examining it. No wounds, but it was limp in his arms. Shock and fear had killed it.

He sighed heavily. How many times had this dam led others into danger? How many times had he rescued her, only to have to hunt her down again?

He cared deeply for all his sheep, even this dam who habitually caused trouble. But he could not allow her to go on leading others into the jaws of predators.

The other twin bleated pitifully. The dam paid little attention. Safe now, she moved stiff-necked, ruminating as she gazed once at Amos before heading toward the brush. Shaking his head, Amos placed the dead lamb on the ground, unsheathed his knife, and went after her.

When the deed was done, Amos felt only sorrow. If only she had stayed close to him, he would not have found it necessary to end her life for the sake of the others.

He carried the surviving twin back to the fold.

✦   ✦   ✦

Another dam accepted the lamb. Having finished nursing, the lamb cavorted with others. He was old enough to nibble tender shoots of grass. Amos leaned on his staff and watched the lambs play. He laughed at their antics. All seemed well.

A bleat of distress drew his attention. One of the rams had cast himself in a low spot. He lay in a hollow, feet in the air.

"Easy there, old man." Twice, the ram kicked Amos. Taking strong hold, Amos heaved him over and lifted him.

The ram couldn't walk.

"Hold on." Amos held him firm between his knees. He massaged the animal until the circulation returned to its legs. "Go ahead." He gave the ram a push.

The ram stumbled once and then walked stiff-legged, head up, ignoring Amos.

"Next time, find a flat place to rest."

Amos turned from the ram and made a quick count of the flock. His mouth tightened.

The lamb was missing again.

Amos called to his sheep and led them to the shade of the sycamore trees. They would settle quickly there in the heat of the afternoon. He scanned the area, hoping the lamb would come scampering back.

A buzzard made a wide circle overhead. It wouldn't be long until another joined it. There was no time to waste. Leaving the ninety-nine others, Amos headed west. Staff in hand, he wove his way among the rocks and brambles, searching, hoping he would find the lamb before a predator did. The wolf pack had kept its distance, but there were lions in these hills.

Coming to a rise, Amos spotted the lamb standing near some bushes. As he approached, he saw its wool had snagged in a thornbush. One hard tug, and the lamb could have freed itself, but it was not in his nature to do so. Instead, the animal would stand still until rescue came—or a predator, eager to make a meal of him.

Amos stood grimly, considering what to do. Less than a week ago, he had been forced to kill the lamb's mother. He had known for months he might have to dispatch her, but held off doing so because she was perfectly proportioned with well-set, alert eyes and was one of the strongest sheep in his flock. But her stubborn habits had endangered the entire flock. Half a dozen times he had rescued her and her offspring. He had hoped to give the lambs more time to be fully weaned and on their own. Now, it seemed he had waited too long, for the lamb had learned his mother's bad habits.

"It's this or death, little one." Amos took a stone from his pouch, weighing it in his hand. Too heavy and it would kill the lamb; too light and it would not serve to discipline him. Amos swung his sling and released the stone, striking the lamb in a front leg, just above the knee. With a startled bleat of pain, the lamb went down.

Tears burning, Amos went to the wounded lamb and knelt. "I am here, little one. I would rather wound you myself than see you come to greater harm." He knew after a gentle examination that the leg was broken, but not shattered. It would heal. "You belong with the flock, not out here on your own where death will find you." He worked quickly, binding the leg and tugging the lamb free of the brambles. "I know I hurt you, but better you suffer an injury that will heal than become dinner for a prowling lion." He ran his hand gently over the lamb's head. "You will learn to stay close to me where you're safe." He cupped the lamb's head and breathed into its face. "No struggling or you will cause yourself more pain." He gently lifted the lamb onto his shoulders and carried him back to the flock.

The goats grazed in the hot sun, but the sheep still rested in the shade, ruminating. Amos sat on a flat rock that gave him a full view of the pasture. Lifting the lamb from his shoulders, he held it close. "You will learn to trust me and not think you can find better forage on your own. I will lead you to green pastures and still waters." He took a few grains of wheat from the scrip he wore at his waist and shared his food with the lamb. "Sometimes I must wound in order to protect." He smiled as the lamb ate from his hand. "You will get used to my voice and come when I call." He rubbed the notch in the lamb's ear. "You bear my mark, little one. You are mine. Let me take care of you."

Amos looked out over the others. They were content. There was still plenty of grass. One more night here, he decided. Tomorrow he would move the flock to new pastures. Too long in one pasture, and the sheep grew restless and would not lie down. They would begin to compete for space. Too many days in one field and the flies and gnats would begin to pester. Conditions must be just right for his sheep to be at peace.

Later in the afternoon, the sheep rose from their rest and grazed again. Two dams pushed at each other. Amos carried the lamb with him as he separated them with his staff. "There's forage enough for both of you." He stood between them until they settled. His presence soothed them, and they lowered their heads to graze.

From Jerusalem to the high country, Amos knew every pasture as well as he knew his family's inheritance in Tekoa. He worked part of each year in the sycamore groves near Jericho in order to pay for grazing rights. Incising sycamore figs to force ripening was tedious work, but he wanted only the best pasturage for his flock. During the winter months when the sheep were sheltered in Tekoa, he went out to clear reeds, deepen or enlarge water holes, and repair old or build new sheepfolds.

A dam jumped, startled by a rabbit that leapt from a patch of grass and bounded off. She started to run, but Amos caught her with the crook of his staff before she could spread panic.

He spoke softly and put his hand on her to soothe her. "I am with you. No need to fear." He carried the lamb with him wherever he went and placed it on the ground where it could sleep on its side in the shade. He fed it wheat and barley and the best grass.

The old ram was cast again. He left the lamb near the quietest dam and went to attend to the old codger. The animal had found another hollow in which to rest. As the ram slept, his body had rolled onto its side. Bleating angrily, the ram kicked as Amos approached, and succeeded only in rolling onto his back, legs in the air.

Amos shook his head and laughed. "A pity you don't learn, old man."

Belly exposed, the ram was helpless. Amos bent to the task of righting the animal and setting it back on its feet. He held it firmly between his knees until he was certain the ram had feeling in his legs.

"You always find the low spots, don't you?" He massaged the legs and gave the ram a push. "Back you go. Find a flat spot in the shade this time."

The ram walked away with wounded dignity, stiff-legged, head in the air. He soon found a good patch of grass.

Retrieving the lamb, Amos carried it around on his shoulders. He felt great peace out here in the open, away from Jerusalem, away from the marketplace and corrupt priests. But he missed his family. Sometimes he could almost hear his father's voice: *We tend the Temple flocks, my son. It is a great honor to work for the priests.*

As a youngster, how Amos had reveled in that! Until he learned the truth about his family's relationship with the priest Heled. He sighed. Nearly twenty years had passed, but his disillusionment was as fresh as ever.

When Amos was a child, it had been a common occurrence for Joram, a servant of Heled, to come to Amos's family's home and take several blemished lambs, leaving perfect ones to replace them. When Amos asked his father where the blemished lambs were taken, he said, "To Jerusalem."

"But why does he bring us the same number of lambs he takes away?" Amos had wondered. He could make no sense of it, and his father's answers never satisfied him.

Then, during a visit to Jerusalem for a festival one year, the year he was eleven, he had watched everything that went on around the stalls his older brothers managed, and what he saw greatly disturbed him.

"Father, aren't these the lambs Joram took a week ago?"

"Yes."

"But doesn't God require lambs without blemish for sacrifice? That one has a damaged hoof, and the other over there has a spot inside its ear. I can show you."

"Be quiet, Amos!"

Confused, Amos held his tongue. He watched a priest examine a lamb. Amos went closer and saw for himself the animal was perfect, but the priest shook his head and pointed to the stalls. Frowning, the man carried the lamb he had brought for sacrifice to Amos's brother. Bani put it in a pen and then caught the lamb with the blemish inside its ear and handed it over. The man argued, but Bani waved him off. When the man returned to the priest, the new lamb was accepted, but not before the man paid a fine for the exchange.

"Did you see that, Father? The priest—"

"Stop staring! Do you want to cause trouble?"

"But the lamb that man originally brought is better than the one Bani gave him. God will not be pleased."

"Heled rejected the man's sacrifice. That's all you need to know."

"But why? What was wrong with it?"

His father gripped Amos's shoulders and stared into his face. "Never question what the priests decide! Never! Do you understand?"

Amos winced at the pain. He did not understand, but he knew better than to ask more questions now. His father let go of him. As he straightened, Amos saw Heled scowling at him. He motioned to Amos's father.

"I must speak with Heled. Wait here."

Amos watched them. Heled did all the talking, and his father kept his eyes downcast and nodded and nodded.

Ahiam grabbed Amos and spun him around. "Father told you not to stare, didn't he? Go get feed for the lambs."

Amos ran to do his brother's bidding.

When he came back, his father took him aside. "Remember, priests are servants of the Lord, Amos. They see imperfection where we do not and their decisions are law. If you question their judgment, they will say you question God Himself. They would bar you from the synagogue and Temple. And then what would happen? No one would have anything to do with you. You would become an outcast with no way to make a living. You would have to sell yourself into slavery."

Amos hung his head and blinked back tears.

His father squeezed his shoulder. "I know you don't understand what's happening here." He sighed. "Sometimes I wish I didn't. But you must trust me, Amos. Say nothing about the lambs, good or bad. And don't watch what Heled does. It bothers him. The priests are very powerful and must be treated with great respect. We are only hirelings paid to tend the Temple flocks. That's all. Perhaps someday we will have sheep of our own and be free again. . . ."

After that day, Amos had begun to observe everything that went on around the folds of Tekoa, in Jerusalem, and around the Temple.

Discolorations on a lamb would disappear under the care of his brothers.

"We're miracle workers!" Ahiam laughed, but when Amos surreptitiously examined one, he found the wool stiff with white stuff that rubbed off on his fingers.

"Father will have your hide," Amos told Bani.

Ahiam overheard and knocked him on his backside. "Father knows, you little runt."

The next time Joram came, Amos realized the priest's servant deliberately chose weaker lambs. As soon as Amos found his father alone, he reported what he had observed.

His father gazed out over the fields. "One lamb is much like any other."

"But that's not true, Father. You've told me yourself how every lamb is different, and—"

"We'll talk about it later, Amos. We have too much work to do right now."

But *later* never came, and every time Amos went with his father to Jerusalem, he was afraid God would do something horrible when one of those blemished lambs was offered as a sacrifice.

"What's wrong with your brother?" Heled scowled as he spoke to Ahiam.

"Nothing. Nothing is wrong with him. He's just quiet, that's all."

"Quiet . . . and all eyes and ears."

Ahiam slapped Amos hard on the back. When he gripped Amos, his fingers dug in deep and shook him as he grinned down, eyes black. "He's not used to city life yet."

"Get him used to it!" Heled walked away and then called back over his shoulder. "Or keep him away from Jerusalem altogether."

Ahiam glowered at him. "Make yourself useful. Add feed to the bins if you have to hang around here. Do something other than *watch*."

Amos worked in silence, head down, afraid. He kept to himself and kept busy for the rest of the day. He said so little, his family grew concerned when they gathered for the Passover meal.

"What's wrong, little brother? Aren't you feeling well?"

"He's upset about the lambs," Ahiam said grimly. "You'd better tell him, Father."

"Not yet."

"Why not? He's old enough to understand." Ahiam's expression was grim. "I think he's figured out most of it on his own."

"Later."

Amos wasn't hungry. He felt like an outcast, and fought tears. But he had to know, and so he asked again. "Why does Joram take the weak lambs and leave the good ones?"

His father bowed his head.

Chin jutting, Ahiam answered. "Why slaughter a perfect lamb when one bearing a spot will do just as well?"

Ahiam's wife, Levona, hung her head as she turned the spitted lamb over the fire. "What a waste to kill a prized ram that could reproduce itself ten times over!"

For a moment, the only sound in the room was the pop and hiss of fat as it dripped into the burning coals.

No one would meet Amos's eyes. "Is our lamb perfect?"

"Of course, it's perfect!" Bani burst out. "Do you think we'd offer anything less?"

"But what about those others? the weak ones from our flock?" Amos turned to his father, then to Bani and Ahiam. "The Law says only perfect lambs are acceptable as Temple sacrifices. But Joram brought the weak ones from Tekoa, and they are the ones you exchanged today." Amos's heart beat heavily as the tension built.

Levona kept her eyes on the roasting lamb. Mishala, Bani's wife, placed the bitter herbs on the table. Bani looked at their father, expression pained.

Ahiam banged his fists on the table, making everyone jump. "Tell him, Father, or I will!"

"Who decides if the Law has been fulfilled, Amos?"

"God."

"And who speaks for God?"

"The priests."

"Yes!" Ahiam glared. "The priests! The priests decide which lamb is fit and which isn't."

His father sighed. "You saw who sent those people to our pens, Amos."

"The priests. But is this the way it's supposed to be?"

"It is the way it is." His father sounded worn down, defeated.

Fear filled Amos. "What will the Lord do? Is He satisfied?"

Ahiam poured wine. "What sign do we see that the Lord is not pleased with what is given to Him? The priests get richer each year. We are close to paying off all our family debts. The nation prospers. The Lord must be satisfied."

Bani grimaced as he ate the bitter herbs. "You have been taught as we all have, Amos—riches are the reward of righteousness."

God said He would bless those who obeyed His commands, making sure those who loved Him would have lives of abundance. Amos's father had taught him that meant a fine home, flocks and herds, orchards of fruit trees, olive trees, a vineyard, and lots of children. The priests had all of these things and more, and his father and brothers were working hard toward the same end. Should he question things he didn't understand?

Confused, disheartened, he fought against the thoughts that raced through his mind.

When his father stood, Amos did also. Tunics girded, sandals on their feet, they ate the Passover meal standing in memory of God's deliverance of the Hebrews from Egypt.

Where is God now? Amos wondered.

"Eat, Amos."

"I'm not hungry."

His father dipped unleavened bread into the salt water that represented the tears the Hebrews shed while slaves in Egypt. Everyone ate in silence. When the meal was over, Amos's father, Ahiam, and Bani sat while Levona and Mishala cleared the table and the children went into another room to play.

Ahiam glared at nothing, a muscle twitching in his cheek. Bani sat with head down.

Amos's father cleared his throat and turned to Amos. "It is time you understand what we do. You must know the whole story to understand."

Amos's heart began to beat loudly.

"Your great-grandfather fell into debt. It was a time of war, and the priests levied higher fines on guilt and sin offerings to raise money for the army. Grandfather paid what he could, but each year, the interest increased and debt grew rather than diminished. When he died, my father continued to pay on the debt. By then, we owed so much that there was no hope of ever paying it off. When my father died, the debt fell to me. Heled came to me in Tekoa and offered me a way to pay off our family disgrace. Because I did not want it to fall upon your brothers or you or any of your children, I agreed."

Ahiam's eyes darkened. "If Father had not agreed, we would all be slaves. Do you understand now, little brother?"

"There is no reason to take your anger out on him, Ahiam." His father put a hand on Amos's shoulder. "Heled hired us to tend the flocks of lambs that were brought as gifts for God."

Amos's stomach churned. "So the priests take the perfect lambs intended for God and give them to us to tend, and they give the weaker ones to people to sacrifice at the Temple."

His father's hand fell away. No one spoke.

"Yes," Ahiam said finally. "Yes, that's exactly what we do. Because we have no choice."

It was all becoming clear to Amos. He shuddered as he thought aloud. "So the priests keep the perfect lambs. They will produce valuable wool year after year. Then they force the people to buy imperfect lambs to sacrifice, so they make money that way too." He looked up at his father. "And on top of all that, they make the people pay a fine for the exchange!" Why weren't his father and brothers as outraged as he was?

Bani leaned his arms on the table and clasped his hands. "We have our inheritance back, Amos, the land that God gave our fathers who came across the Jordan River."

"The debt is almost clear," his father added quietly. "By the time you are sixteen, it will be paid off."

Ahiam stood and turned his back.

Bani glanced up at Ahiam and then spoke softly. "They are priests, Amos. We dare not question them. Do you understand?"

"We serve the Lord!" Ahiam said loudly. "We tend the Temple flocks. There is honor in that."

Honor? Amos hung his head. *We're stealing from God.* Tears burned his eyes.

Their father rose and left the room.

Bani sighed. "Father had no choice. None of us have a choice."

"We're not the only ones," Ahiam said. He met Amos's eyes, face hard. "It's been done for as long as I can remember."

"Do all the priests do the same thing?"

"Not all," Bani said.

Ahiam snorted. "But you don't hear them saying anything against those who do. God gave the tribe of Judah the scepter, but he gave the Levites the priesthood. And that's where the real power is. They can interpret the Law any way they want. They even add to it on a daily basis. They use it to squeeze the people for as much as they want. Better we stand with them than against them."

"When you're a little older, you'll be free of all this, Amos." Their father had come back into the room. "By the time you're a man, we will be done with it."

"We live better now than we did before our agreement with Heled," Ahiam said, but his eyes were dark with bitterness.

Anger grew inside Amos. "It's not right what the priests did to you, Father. It's not right!"

"No, it isn't. But we adjust to the way things are, my son. And they have been this way for a long, long time."

Shaken, Amos was left to wonder whether God was truly holy. Was He truly just? If so, why did He allow these things to go on in His own Temple? Why would a righteous, holy God reward corrupt, scheming men who misused His Name?

The revelations of that night had sowed seeds of anger that sent shoots of bitterness into Amos's heart. From that day on, Amos hated the required visits to Jerusalem. He paid no more attention to the priests and what they said, focusing instead on visiting his brothers, their wives and children. He gave the offerings required by Law only because they were necessary for business. Amos always chose the best lamb and sought out a priest who examined the animal properly. He did it to save the fine, rather than to please God.

In his mind, it was a small rebellion, a way of getting back at Heled without risking retaliation against his father.

These days, he didn't think about God anymore. With all he had seen around the Temple pens, he believed God had forgotten about them, and all the rituals were to profit men rather than to honor a silent monarch who reigned so far up in the heavens. Did God see? Did God hear? Did He care what went on in His own Temple?

✦   ✦   ✦

Amos's father had not lived long enough to see the family debt paid off. Long after he was buried, Bani and Ahiam continued to work for the priests at the stalls in Jerusalem. Years of habit, convenience, and prosperity choked honesty. Amos remained among the shepherds of Tekoa, tending his flock of goats and sheep.

He felt at peace in the hills and dales of Judah, alone with his sheep. Each year, he had grown less able to tolerate the busy streets of Jerusalem—the chattering crowds, shouting street vendors, and arguing scribes. Relieved when his obligations were completed, he would eagerly depart the confines of those great walls, returning to the open fields where the sun blazed and the wind blew, where he could breathe fresh air again.

Life was not easy, but it was simple without the intrigues, coercion, or pressures he knew his brothers lived with on a daily basis. They had spent so many years in the stalls, tending corralled animals and dealing with Heled and others like him, that they knew no other way to live. They had become merchants, accustomed to trade, and did not see the result of their labors in the same way Amos did. They did not stand in the Temple, full of questions, angry and anguished.

Amos hated seeing humble men with barely enough to live on cheated by priests who grew richer each year. Men came to pray and instead found themselves preyed upon. Maybe God didn't know what went on in His Temple. Maybe He didn't care.

"You hardly speak, little brother. You have lived too long with your sheep. You've forgotten how to be among men."

"I have nothing to say." *Nothing anyone would want to hear.*

Amos had earned enough from his flock to plant a few olive trees and a vineyard. In time he had hired servants. They received a share of the crops as payment for overseeing the vineyard, the olive trees, and the small fields of wheat and barley.

Amos did not have a wife, nor any desire to find one. He was too busy working near Jericho for grazing rights, tending his growing flock, and pruning and incising the fruit of his sycamore trees. He kept what he needed and sold the rest as cattle fodder. At least, he was free now. Free of Heled's hold, free to make his own choices. He knew better, though, than to show disrespect—lest a fine be created to enslave him again.

As his flock had grown, Amos asked Bani and Ahiam to send their sons to help. "Within a few years, each will have a small flock of his own. What they do with it will be up to them." But it was an opportunity to break free.

Bani sent Ithai, and Ahiam sent Elkanan, and Amos taught them all he knew about tending a flock. When he felt they were ready to be sent out alone, he gave them each a ram and ten ewes with which to start.

"Whatever increase comes shall be yours." Maybe they would take to the life as he did and not follow in the ways of their fathers.

He knew little of what happened in the kingdom while he tended his flock, but when he made his pilgrimages to Jerusalem, his brothers told him what they had heard during the months he had been in distant pastures.

Judah was prospering under King Uzziah's rule, though relations with the ten tribes of Israel were still hostile. The tribes that had broken away from Solomon's foolish son continued to worship the golden calves in Bethel and Dan. Jeroboam II now ruled, and Samaria had become a great city a mere two-day journey from Jerusalem. King Jeroboam had taken back lost lands and cities from Lebo-hamath to the Dead Sea, expanding Israel's boundaries to those from the time of King David and King Solomon. In a bold move to gain more power, he captured Gilead, Lo-debar, and Karnaim, all important fortress cities along the King's Highway, thus controlling the major trade route from the Tigris-Euphrates river valley to the Gulf of Aqaba and Egypt.

Trade now flourished with the safe passage of caravans from Gabal and Syria to the north and Egypt and Arabia to the south.

From boyhood, Amos had witnessed King Uzziah's work going on throughout Judah. The king mended Judah's defenses, reorganized and better equipped his army, built towers in Jerusalem at the Corner Gate and the Valley Gate, and fortified the buttresses. He had also built towers in the wilderness to keep watch over the Philistines and Edomites. Work crews made cisterns so that there would be water wherever the army moved. When Uzziah went to war against the Philistines, he triumphed and tore down the walls of Gath, Jabneh, and Ashdod. Slaves now bent to the task of rebuilding fortress cities that would guard the trade route called the Way of the Sea.

Amos's home, Tekoa, was only seven miles from Jerusalem, but far enough away for him to turn his mind to his own endeavors. Amos saw the changes in Jerusalem and in the countryside as he moved his flock from one pasture to another, but he spent little time contemplating the ways of kings and nations. What use in leaning on his own understanding when he had none? Why trouble his mind with matters over which he had no control? Could he change anything that happened in Judah, let alone Assyria or Egypt or Israel, for that matter? No! While his brothers praised Uzziah or fretted over the threat of enemies, Amos concentrated on his sheep. He brought tithes and offerings to the priests, visited briefly with his brothers and their families, and then returned to Tekoa, then out into the pasture-lands with his flock. He felt at home there.

Out in the open with his sheep, he felt free, even though he knew that freedom could be easily stripped from him. Out in the open Amos could believe in God. In Jerusalem, seeing and hearing the priests living any way they chose while claiming to represent God, Amos grew disheartened. Why study the Law when the priests could add to it any day they pleased? And then there were the traditions to add an even greater burden! He preferred a few select psalms written by David, a king who had grown up as a shepherd. David had understood the pleasures of walking over the land, tending his sheep, sleeping under stars scattered across the night sky.

Sometimes, when the sheep were restless or disturbed, Amos would play his zamoora, the reed flute he'd made, or sing psalms to comfort them.

Each time he ventured inside the walls of Jerusalem, he tucked away his uneasy faith, lest a priestly heel crush it. Private, protected, precious, he kept it hidden.

And it grew in ways he did not expect.

+　+　+

"Come, sheep!" Amos called as he headed for the fold he had made last year. The sheep came in a rush, clustering and following close behind him. He opened the gate and used his rod to separate the goats into another area, then checked each sheep carefully for injury or hint of illness.

He stretched out across the entrance while the sheep slept safely in the fold. Amos would awaken at the slightest change. He knew the sound of every insect species and listened for predators. When a wolf howled from a distant hilltop, he sat up. A lamb bleated. "Be still. I am here."

Rising, he kept his eyes on the wolves running in the moonlight. When they ventured closer, he used his sling to send a well-aimed stone flying at the leader. The wolf retreated with a yelp. The pack followed, disappearing over the hill. The sheep rose and moved around, nervous, trembling.

Entering the fold, Amos lifted his wounded lamb to protect it from further injury. He held it close in his arms, stroking its head and kneading its soft ears as he spoke softly to the others. "Rest now, sheep. You've nothing to fear. I will never leave you."

He stood for a long time in their midst, waiting for them to settle and sleep like the lamb in his arms. His presence calmed them. One by one, they lay down again. He set the lamb down and went back to the narrow gate, making himself a barrier against anything that might threaten his flock. Amos closed his eyes then and slept, staff and club close at hand.

Rising with the dawn, Amos opened the gate. As each lamb passed under his rod, he stopped it and examined it. Parting the wool, he checked the skin for scabbing and ran his hands over the animal to feel for any signs of trouble. He rubbed a mixture of oil, sulfur, and tar around the eyes and nose to keep the flies away. One limped, and Amos removed a rock embedded in its hoof. Straightening, he tapped the animal with his staff and watched it bound out into the field. One tried to sneak past him. He hooked the crook of his staff around its neck and turned it back. "One day you'll learn to stand and wait."

When the last sheep was examined and tended, he lifted the wounded lamb to his shoulders, closed the gate, and went out with his flock. He led them to new green pastures. Amused, Amos watched them kick up their hooves and spread out to graze. The sheep loved finding thick tufts of grass. The lambs frolicked while the dams and rams grazed.

Leaning on his staff, Amos kept watch, finding pleasure in the contentment of his flock.

✦   ✦   ✦

Spring came, bringing with it swarms of nasal gnats hatching in vast numbers near the streams and water holes. Amos rubbed oil over the sheep's faces to repel the insects. But even with that remedy, the sheep shook their heads and stamped their feet, bothered by the constant buzzing. When one bolted, others followed. Amos usually managed to stop them before they tangled themselves in the brush.

He led his flock to the more arid pastures near Tekoa, knowing the best place, for he had spent a long, cold winter month clearing rocks, tearing out brush and roots so that more grass could grow. Rich grazing away from the torment of flies renewed the strength of the tired sheep, and there were trees enough to provide shade from the heat of the day.

The lamb's leg had healed. After so many weeks of being carried and tended, the animal had bonded to Amos. It grazed close to him and followed wherever he went. When he sat, the lamb rested in his shadow and ruminated.

The water holes dried in the heat of summer, but the sheep had enough water by grazing at dawn hours when the grass was drenched with dew. The ewes produced plenty of milk to fatten the lambs.

Amos led the flock into Tekoa for shearing. The heavy wool had become so thick, the weight of it could make an animal unable to get up from the soft ground they so often sought out for rest. Cast sheep were easy prey. Though the sheep hated being sheared, they bounded away with renewed vigor when the work was done. Amos handed over the thick bundles of lanolin-scented wool to workers who would remove the burrs and debris, wash the wool, and prepare it for sale.

Amos let the sheep into the fields he had planted with grains and legumes. The animals feasted for a week, and then he led them out again to cooler pastures higher in the mountains. He knew every gully, ravine, and cave between Tekoa and the mountain meadows where he kept the flock for the rest of summer. When he found lion spoor, he put himself between the flock and the brush where the beast might hide.

Girding his loins so he could move more quickly, Amos filled his pouch with stones. A lion was the most cunning of animals—patient, watchful, seizing the perfect opportunity for a kill. Staff in hand, Amos kept close watch on the brush where one might be lying in wait. Sheep had no defense. They could not run like a gazelle, nor had they teeth or claws to fight back. Attacked, they often became so frightened and confused they scattered or, worse, stood still. He had seen sheep freeze at the roar of a lion, but run in terror when startled by a rabbit.

Listening to every bird sound, watching every movement of grass, Amos stood guard over his flock. If one of his sheep strayed even a short distance, he called. If it didn't turn back, he used the crook of his staff or threw his club.

Quail burst into the air on the opposite side of the flock. A spine-tingling roar brought Amos around.

Half the sheep scattered; the rest stood, feet planted, too terrified to move as a lioness burst from the high grass and headed straight for one of the lambs.

Amos used sling and stone to stop her. The rock struck the lioness, and she went down heavily amid bleating, scattering sheep. Dazed only, she sprang to her feet. Amos ran at her, club in hand. Crouching, she roared in fierce frustration. When she charged him, he clubbed her. She raked her claws across his right arm as she fell. He drew his knife and ran at her, but she gained her feet, scrambled back, and clawed at him. When he did not back off, she roared in defiance and disappeared into the brush.

Panting, heart pounding, Amos sheathed his knife and retrieved his club before he checked his wounds. He stanched the blood flow quickly while keeping his eye on the bushes. The lioness would return at any opportunity. "Come, sheep!"

The flock raced to him. Rams, ewes, and lambs clustered close as he led them to safety. He kept looking for signs of the lioness. If he had one of his nephews with him, he would have tracked and killed her. But alone, he would not leave his flock unprotected with a lion so close.

The sheep quickly forgot the danger and spread out to graze. Amos tended his wounds while keeping watch, walking around them to keep them close together. The lamb followed at his heels. A domineering ewe butted another away from the best grass, and stood her ground, defending her spot. When a lamb came too close, the ewe lowered her head and charged.

Amos tapped her with his staff. "There's grass enough for all."

Looking disgruntled, she ruminated for a few minutes, but lowered her head again when the lamb came close. Amos tapped her harder. Startled, she bleated, moved to one side, and lowered her head again. This time, Amos thrashed her. When the discipline was done, the ewe walked away with stiff-legged pride to another patch of grass. Shaking his head, Amos kept an eye on her.

Bumping and shoving tended to cause the others to grow nervous and then irritable. When discontent set in, appetites waned, and the entire flock suffered. A bullying ewe could cause more trouble to a flock than a lion.

+ + +

As the end of summer approached, Amos led his sheep to the most distant pastures in the lowlands. He had paid for grazing rights with long hard hours, days, and weeks of incising the sycamore fruit. Now his animals benefited from his labors, growing fat and content.

Nights became cold. Nasal flies and insects disappeared. Leaves turned crimson and gold. Amos built fires to keep warm at night.

The rams came into rut. Necks swelling, they strutted like proud monarchs among a harem. To prevent them from injuring one another, Amos rubbed their heads with thick grease before releasing them into the pasture. They ran, banged heads, and glanced off each other. Often they stumbled and landed in a heap. Confused, dazed, they would rise, looking almost embarrassed as they stood. All those rams could think about were the ewes! And it wasn't long before they charged again. Stubborn, they tried to lock horns, and Amos had to get between them with his club.

The days grew colder, nights longer. Amos led the flock back toward Tekoa where the sheep would spend the winter in corrals. Though he moved the flock each day, he gave them time to lie down in green pastures and rest. He led them through the valleys, keeping them away from the shadows where predators lay in wait. He anointed each sheep's head with oil and treated every wound, most having been inflicted upon one another.

The first sight of Tekoa always filled Amos with mixed emotions. It was refreshing to come home after long months of solitude. His time of living off the land came to an end, and he looked forward to enjoying his sisters-in-law's hot meals. But in Tekoa, he would have to tend to business, meet with other herders, deal with the market in Jerusalem as well as the corrupt priests who controlled it, and face his brothers, who complained and fretted and yet never changed their ways. He would rather spend his days tending sheep and his nights beneath the star-studded canopy of the heavens than live in the confines of a house. But even a house was preferable to the chaos and cacophony of the crowded markets near the Temple.

Amos comforted himself by making plans.

As soon as the animals were wintered and tended by trustworthy servants, and the business dealings and religious obligations over, he would go back out and survey the route for next year. He would spend a month plowing and planting the pasture near Tekoa, then move on to work in the sycamore groves in Jericho. He would pull poisonous plants, remove debris from water holes, repair folds, and hunt down and kill that troublesome lioness.

Come spring, the route would be ready for his flock.

✦ ✦ ✦

"Ithai and Elkanan left eight days ago," Eliakim told Amos. "Their lambs have already been taken to Jerusalem."

Amos trusted Eliakim, his servant, over his own family members.

"Who bought them?"

"Joram. He said he would return tomorrow in the hope you would be here."

Amos despised Joram. He was as corrupt as his master, Heled. "Did he cheat us again?"

"No."

Though Eliakim said nothing more, Amos knew he had stood by as an advisor and probably saved Amos's young nephews their profits. Had they bothered to reward Eliakim? Amos would see to it that his servant never lacked for anything. "Where are Ithai and Elkanan now?"

"They returned to Jerusalem, saying they would be back after the new moon festival."

"Was Joram pleased when he left?"

"Pleased enough."

That meant trouble had been averted. This time.

Separating the best lambs as they entered the sheepfold, Amos cut out those that had the slightest blemish. He would keep them in other pens until later.

Joram arrived two days later, eager to conduct more business. "What do you have for me?"

Amos showed him.

"These are better than the ones I've brought you."

"These are the best I have." Amos named his price.

Joram's brows rose. "We exchange lambs. We don't pay for them."

"I know. But I made it clear to you things would change when our debts were paid in full."

"Your nephews are less exacting."

"You're not dealing with my nephews."

Joram scowled at him and walked to the pen that held the blemished lambs. "What about these?" He pointed. "I'll take that one, and the other over there."

Both had blemishes that could easily be covered. "I've already sold them," Amos lied.

Joram turned, eyes dark. "Heled will not be pleased about this, Amos."

Amos tried not to show how much that news pleased him.

"You know we have had a congenial arrangement for years."

Congenial?

Joram raised his brows. "It has benefited all of us, has it not?"

To say it hadn't would be to declare war on the priests who had used his father and brothers for years. Amos knew he must tread carefully or risk having sin and guilt offerings levied against him for any infraction that wretched priest could find—or invent. Even with family debts cleared, the priest thought he owned them.

Deciding not to press his luck, Amos forced a cool smile and spoke cautiously. "The arrangement stands, Joram. You can have the lambs I showed you." If Joram refused, Amos would be free to offer his lambs to other priests in Jerusalem, priests who examined animals as though the eye of God were upon them.

"I didn't come to trade perfect lambs for other perfect lambs."

"It does seem a waste of time."

Joram's chin jutted out. "So you think you are more righteous than Heled?"

"Me? Only God is higher than Heled. I merely wish to offer you what the Lord requires for sacrifice: unblemished lambs. Why should you complain?"

"And you are an expert on the Law? You? A shepherd?" He sneered.

Heart drumming, Amos stood still, hoping his anger did not show. *Do You see, God? Do You even care about Your people?*

Dark eyes narrowed at Amos's silence. "Heled has given you every advantage, Amos, and you abuse his kindness. If not for his generosity, your family would still be in debt."

Amos understood the threat, and spoke through clenched teeth. "We paid our debt in full, at a rate higher than the Law demands."

Joram's lips whitened. "You could find yourself in debt again. Easily."

Fear coursed through Amos's body. Joram stalked him like a lion, and all Amos could do was stand defenseless. One word of indignation or rebellion and Joram would pounce, setting the teeth of his threat into motion. He could pull Amos down. The priests had done it before. They could do it again.

Amos raged inwardly while showing nothing on the outside. *So this is the way it is. The way it will always be. Freedom earned can be ripped away. This is how You would have it! Power in the hands of a few who do what they want when they want. And poor men who want to do what is right suffer. The guild of priests decides what's right and wrong. These purveyors of Your Law! They can twist it and use it any way they want. They ignore what they don't like and add what will give them profits. And they keep adding and adding until the weight of their regulations crushes us! And we are told You are a just God.*

Joram smiled, smug. "I will overlook your small show of defiance, Amos. You have served us well—and profited from our relationship, I might remind you. Bring whatever you have to offer us. The other lambs will be ready for you, and the usual stipend for your labors." He slapped Amos on the shoulder.

The wound the lion had inflicted had not yet fully healed and Amos winced. The sharp pain made something snap inside him. "I have nothing for you, Joram." The lambs might not be blemished, but he would be marked by sin for being a party to stealing from men like himself who had worked hard and done what they thought right only to suffer for it.

Joram grew frustrated. "We need to add to the Temple pens! I've brought you perfect lambs."

An indictment of himself and the priest he served. Not that Joram cared. Not that he need care. He was safe, in favor, a Levite born to be a priest, or to serve one. He could play the game any way he chose for the rest of his life and never worry about where he would find his next meal or if he would have to sell himself into slavery to pay an unfair debt levied by a lying priest.

"Go ahead." Amos gestured grandly toward the walled fields surrounding his few acres of land. There were other sheep owners in Tekoa. Perhaps one of them would enjoy the arrangement Joram would offer. Let them add their sheep to the Temple flocks. "Talk to the owners over there and there and there." Thousands of sheep grazed in the pastures of Tekoa. Most belonged to the priests and the king. "These sheep belong to me, Joram. I have built this flock from the portion I earned. And I've already made plans for them."

"What's wrong with you, Amos? After all these years . . ."

Because he didn't know, he lied. "I guess I feel the eyes of the Lord upon me."

Joram's face went deep red. "Oh, you think you're that important. Well, someone's eye is on you. Mine!" Cursing him, Joram turned on his sandaled heel and strode away.

Amos sat and buried his head in his hands. *Will You allow them to strip me of all I've worked for, Lord? Is that Your justice and mercy?*

✦ ✦ ✦

The next morning, Amos headed for Jerusalem. He carried extra provisions for the poor, and one perfect lamb on his shoulders while driving six goats along the road ahead of him. Beggars sat before the gate, calling out for alms. Some were tricksters who had found an easy way to make a living, but others, in truth, were in dire need.

A crippled man hobbled toward him. "Good Amos. Have you anything for a poor old man?"

"A blessing upon you, Phineas. How is your wife? your daughters?" Amos gave him a pouch of grain and sycamore figs.

"Well. A blessing upon you for asking, Amos. Has it been a good year for you?"

Phineas had once been a shepherd. A boar had wrecked one leg and almost taken his life. Now, he was relegated to begging to survive. "I had to put down a dam. She kept leading others astray."

"I had a few of those in my time."

Amos had placed a few shekels in the bag as well, knowing Phineas would find them later and squeeze them for all the good they could provide. "May the Lord bless and multiply this gift, and make it last a month."

"And a greater blessing upon you, my friend. May the Lord our God smile upon you for your kindness."

Amos had seen no evidence that God smiled on anyone but the priests who stole from poor men like this one. He gave other gifts to the poor he recognized, then entered the city.

The goats brought a good price in the market. From there, he took the lamb to the Temple, where he sought out a priest who didn't know him. The lamb was deemed acceptable. *One honest priest,* Amos thought cynically. His obligations complete, he went to see his brothers.

As Amos left the Temple, he put a shekel in the plate of a blind man.

The man felt the coin eagerly and grinned. "Thank you for your kindness."

"Consider yourself blessed that you do not have to witness what goes on inside this place," Amos said as he walked away.

+   +   +

"We've been waiting for you." Bani glared, face flushed with anger. "You were supposed to bring us more lambs!"

Clearly, Joram had assumed he would think things over and capitulate. "I don't have any lambs to bring."

"What do you mean, you have no lambs?" Ahiam stared.

"I'm building my flock. The wool will—"

"Wool?" Bani came to the fence. "Why did you do that? There's more money in—"

"Have you seen the crowds?" Ahiam glared. "There's money to be made. And we need more lambs!"

"Crowds need to eat. I sold a half-dozen goats in the market."

Ahiam grabbed Amos's robe. "Joram said you insulted him. I didn't believe him. Now, I'm wondering!"

"Don't wonder." Amos tried to jerk free. "I offered him the best of the flock, and he refused."

Ahiam let go of him. "What's the matter with you, Amos? What's happened?"

"We removed the yoke, Ahiam, but you and Bani have become accustomed to it!" He stormed away.

Though his brothers called out to him, he didn't turn back. He wanted to get away from the stalls, away from the Temple, and out of the city. He gave offerings because it was expected, because his father had done it before him, and his father before that back to the time of Moses.

But what did it all mean?

He had heard the stories from the time he was a boy, but now he found himself wondering if God really existed. Maybe the priests taught their lessons merely to exert control over the people.

"God is righteous!"

"God is just!"

"God is holy!"

Amos wanted to shout, *Then why don't I see it in Your Temple? Why is there so little evidence of righteousness, justice, holiness among the priests who serve in Your name?*

"Look around you, Amos!" his brothers would say. "See how God blesses Judah. See how He blesses us."

Amos sneered as he strode through the city streets, heading for the

Sheep Gate. What about the nations around Judah? What about Israel? They bowed down to idols and prospered even more, no longer bothering to come to Jerusalem to worship. Jeroboam's golden calf still stood in Bethel and another in Dan, and what had God done about that? Nothing! The apostates grew richer and more powerful each year.

Amos could make no sense of it.

Lying beneath a canopy of stars, it was not difficult to believe God existed. But here, in Jerusalem—God's holy city—the animal pens, the courts, the Temple were all putrid with the stench of sin. The priests levied fines for infractions written the day before. They laid down law after law until not even a camel could carry all their scrolls!

If You are sovereign, why doesn't justice reign? Why are the humble crushed by the proud, the poor impoverished by the rich? Why are those who hold the power never held accountable for anything? Why don't You keep Your word?

Tears almost blinding him, Amos pressed his way through the crowd. "Let me through! Let me out!" All he wanted was to escape, to get away from this place that filled him with such confusion and anguish. Only seven miles to walk and he would be in Tekoa.

Dusk gave way to night, but the moon lighted his way. When he reached town, he didn't go to his house, but to the walled pasture.

Eliakim stood guard. He turned to Amos in surprise. "I didn't expect you back for a few days."

"I finished my business there." He wished he never had to go back, but the Law required . . .

Amos heard a familiar bleat. He put his hand on Eliakim's shoulder. "The Lord bless you, Eliakim."

"And you, my lord."

Opening the gate, Amos entered the fold. The lamb he had wounded came to him. Hunkering down, he smiled and rubbed its face. "Rest now. I'm here."

Weary, he stretched out on the ground outside the latched gate. He put his hands behind his head and looked up at the stars. He would leave in the morning and head back out to go over his route. He needed to dig another water hole and stack more rocks for the fold on the mountain. After that, he would work in the sycamore groves to expand his grazing rights near Jericho.

The next morning, he refilled his leather scrip with grain, raisins, and almonds and set out.

And then God spoke to him, shattering all the plans Amos had made.

TWO

Amos had never heard the Voice before, but the marrow of his bones and the blood that ran in his veins recognized it. His body shook as God whispered:

I am.

The air he inhaled tingled in his lungs, as though he had been dead and now suddenly came to life. Throwing himself on his face, Amos covered his head with his hands.

Elohim. El Elyon. El Roi.

Power and majesty. Above all gods. King of all creation.

A quickening lit Amos's soul. He was in God's presence, surrounded by Him, immersed in His Spirit, imbued by Him. Even as Amos tried to flatten himself on the earth, he was fully exposed. God knew everything about him, from first thought to final terror.

Adoni. Qedosh Yisrael. El Olam.

Head over all. Holy One of Israel. Everlasting God.

Amos cried out in fear and pleaded for his life, his voice muffled against the grass-covered earth. He had fled Jerusalem in anger and despair, doubting God even existed, let alone saw or cared what happened in His Holy City. He had even cast blame upon the Lord for the sins men committed against one another. And now this! Surely God would kill him.

Yahweh Tsidkenu. Yahweh Shammah. Attiq Yomin.

Righteous God. Present always. Ancient of Days, Ruler of all, Judge of the nations.

"No more. I am a dead man."

You live.

Amos wept, the dry heart within him fluttering and drowning in the flood of revelation.

See. Hear.

Amos felt lifted by unseen hands. He saw the Temple on Mount Zion. There was a sound like a lion's roar, but it wasn't like any lion Amos had ever heard as he guarded his sheep in the wilderness. This roar was filled with wrath. The sound grew louder, making the hair rise on the back of his neck and his blood go cold. Even the land felt the sound, for the ground rippled and rose and fell like a blanket shaken clean. Though people screamed and ran, they could not escape judgment.

Thunder crashed from Jerusalem, and came down like a wave filling the fields, valleys, plains. The sky turned bronze. The lush pastures of Mount Carmel withered and died. Streams dried. Water holes evaporated, their basins cracking, leaving nothing but dust. Sheep, cattle, goats lay dead, carrion birds picking at their drying carcasses. Confused, trembling with fear, Amos found himself in the midst of it; the unrelenting sun beat down on his head. Wilting to the ground, he panted like a deer thirsting for water.

And the Word came to him, blessings and curses written down generations ago, long forgotten. His mind drank in living water.

Opening his eyes, Amos found himself on his knees. Raising his head, he looked around. Everything was as it had been; the rich pasture, the water hole, his pack just where he had dropped it. Bowing his head to the ground, he sobbed in relief.

Had it been a dream? A thought turned sour in his mind? The Voice! He had not imagined the Voice. Or had he?

Weak-kneed, Amos rose and went to the stream. Hunkering down, he cupped his hands and splashed water over his face. Maybe he had a fever.

I have given you a vision of what is to come.

"But why? Why me? What good would showing a poor shepherd do? Is it in my power to change anything? No!"

Amos rubbed his eyes, wishing he could rub away the images that still flickered in his mind. He heard the echo of the lion's roar and the screams in his head. Sinking back on his heels, he waited until his heart slowed its wild beat and his breathing calmed. On shaking legs, he went back to the water hole. Work would make him feel better. Work would fill his mind. He spent the last hours of daylight cutting and pulling reeds that might spread and choke the water hole. His sheep must have good water to drink. Cool, still waters were best, for the ripples of a stream frightened them.

The more determined he was not to think about the vision, the more his mind turned back to it. Again and again, over and over, it held his mind captive.

When the sun cast spears of color in the west, he set up his camp and sat in the doorway of his small tent. He had not eaten since early morning. Though he had little appetite, he forced himself to eat a small barley cake, a few dates, and sycamore figs.

A wolf howled.

Brush rustled close by.

Wind whispered softly. Night fell away in a blaze of light. And Amos knew. . . . "No, Lord, please . . ." He groaned as he felt hands lifting him again. Weariness fell away and his entire being awakened, absorbing everything around him.

Remember Gilead.

Horror filled him. "No, Lord. Please. I know what happened there. . . ."

He stood in the midst of people running. They screamed and scattered as the Aramean army advanced. Warriors swung their swords, making no distinction between men, women, and children. They came like sledges, scraping over the wounded, crushing them beneath their feet. The ground drank Israel's blood.

Amos covered his face. "Stop them! Lord, stop them!" He could hear screams of terror, cries of pain, and moans of the dying. Sobbing, Amos covered his ears. A man raised his hand in a plea for mercy just as a soldier lopped his arm off, then hacked him down with glee. Amos longed to grab a sword and fight back, but he could not move. He could only see, hear, smell. . . .

Carnage, everywhere, carnage.

Ben-hadad of Damascus, King of Aram, shouted commands. "Kill the vermin! Kill them all!"

Warriors beat down the people of Gilead like stalks of wheat—cut, threshed, and blown to the wind.

When the attack ended, brutal laughter echoed across the devastated land. Ben-hadad rode over the body of a child, his fist raised in triumph, as though defying the God of heaven and earth.

Bodies bloated in the sun. Flies buzzed. Maggots squirmed. The smell of death filled Amos's nostrils. "My people. My people . . ."

Sobbing, he dropped to his knees and wretched violently. When the wave of sickness passed, he raised his head slowly, exhausted.

All was peaceful. Above him stars shone brightly against the canopy of night.

Anger swelled. "Why didn't You save them? They were Your people!" He raised his arms and cried out. "Why do You show me these things?"

The people of Damascus have sinned again and again, and I will not let them go unpunished!

Relief flooded him, and then exultation. The Lord would avenge those who had been butchered in Gilead. Amos jumped up and spread his arms wide. "Yes, Lord, yes! Let them feel the edge of the sword." He cried out as he saw a consuming fire come down from heaven, blackening the walls of a huge fortress, devouring the mighty gates of a great city. "Yes! Lay waste to them as they did in Gilead." He cheered, ecstatic. "Terrify *them*! Shatter *them* like earthenware."

Men battled in a great valley. Blades crashed, horns sounded, chariot wheels broke, spilling warriors into the fray. Horses reared and screamed, trampling their masters as the king who had threshed Gilead fell by the sword. The Aramean king lay dying, eyes staring up at heaven as he uttered a last curse against God.

Screams of pain rent the air as conquerors drove hooks through the noses of the survivors, looped ropes through the rings, tying the captives together. Amos watched the Arameans be led away like cattle, a long line of them being dragged away to Kir. "Yes, Lord! So be it. Let them reap what they have sown."

Did you enjoy this vision, My child?

"Yes, Lord, yes!" How long had he and others longed to do unto them as they had done unto the people of Gilead?

His mind and heart drank in the vision of vengeance without thought of where it might lead, or if it was pleasing to God. Nor did he think at all about the stillness that surrounded him after he made his confession. He thought about the last vision. And thought about it. Savoring it.

Let it be soon, Lord. Let it be soon.

+   +   +

Amos awakened to rain pattering softly. He lay faceup like the dead king, staring into the darkness. The cool drops soothed his burning face. The rain stopped. Amos spread his fingers against the ground and found it dry. Groaning, he sat up and felt his face. It was dry and hot.

A fever. Nothing more.

Pushing himself up, he held his head. His stomach ached with emptiness. How long had he been unconscious? How long since he had eaten? He saw his scrip where he had dropped it. Taking it up, he pinched off a piece of barley bread. After a mouthful, he retied the scrip to his sash. Parched, he went down on his hands and knees and drank like a sheep from the stream.

He wanted to get away from this place of dreams.

Grabbing his pack, his staff, and his club, he took the route toward Jericho. He would look over the pastures between here and the sycamore groves, and make certain there were no poisonous plants or . . .

His mind wandered.

He had heard stories of Jonah, who had not been able to run from God. There were stories of how the prophet had boarded a ship to Tarshish only to be tossed overboard during a storm, then swallowed by a huge fish, and finally vomited onto the beach. "Go to Nineveh," God had told Jonah. It didn't matter how far Jonah ran or how deep in the hull of a ship he might hide, God knew where he was and what He wanted him to do. Relentless. God is relentless. Bani said Jonah still lived outside the walled city, waiting for destruction to come.

Amos shook his head. Why did he think about that now? Rumors, probably. A story his brother had heard from traveling merchants. Nothing more.

Please let it be nothing more.

Reaching the next pasture, Amos surveyed the grasses. Walking the field, he pulled up poisonous weeds and bundled them. Stacking the bundles on rocky soil, he set them on fire. As he watched the smoke rise, he heard a whisper:

I will remove the evil from the land.

Amos pressed his hands over his ears. "It's just the wind. The wind in the grass." After a long moment, he drew his hands away tentatively and heard nothing but the crackling fire.

When the flames died down and only embers remained, Amos scooped dirt over them so that no sparks could float into the good grass that remained. He moved on the next morning.

Even as he tried to concentrate on work, the weeds, and water holes, his thoughts kept circling back to the Voice that came from without and within. Part of him waited for the Lord to speak again. Dreading it. Longing for it. He prayed he would hear it again and yet feared he would. When God spoke to a man, it was to send the poor fool on a mission or a long journey or to his death! His heart warred within him. Amos worked harder, faster. He forgot to eat until his stomach was gripped with pain.

He moved on again. When he reached the next pasture, he sat beneath a terebinth tree and did nothing. The sky grew dark before he got up and entered the sheepfold he had built two years before. A snake slithered hissing from the wall, startling him. Angry, he used his staff to break into its hiding place, loop it with the crook, and drop it to the ground where he killed it with his club. Even with its head crushed, the body writhed.

Moments later came the words:

I am the Lord your God.

Clutching his head, he wailed. "Why do You speak to me, Lord? I am a sinful man! I give You offerings to avoid trouble, not to praise Your Name.

I despise Your priests. I can't wait to get out of Your Holy City. I can't stand being around Your people. I . . . I . . ."

Words of confession spilled from his lips. Doubt had consumed him since he was a boy, doubts that had grown into contempt for God's servants. Hadn't he thirsted for revenge after seeing his father weep over debts owed and the only manner in which he could repay them? The priests served God, didn't they? If they represented God, then God must be to blame.

"All my life, I've been made part of schemes and thievery. When I wanted to do right, I caused trouble for my brothers and their families." He saw a bigger truth now. It came to him like a lamp in a dark cave, showing the secret sins he failed to see in himself. "The trouble I caused had nothing to do with me striving for righteousness. It came from hate! I wanted to cut the bonds that held my family captive to the priests, not because they were wrong but because my pride rebelled. I have hated them. And I have hated You because of what they do in Your Name."

Sobbing, he confessed every sin he remembered and knew there were a thousand more he wouldn't even know.

"I am a sinful man, Lord. A sinful man deserving of death." Eyes tightly closed, he bowed his head to the ground.

Do not fear. I knew you before I formed you in your mother's womb. You are Mine.

Amos waited. His muscles slowly relaxed. His stomach stopped churning. He waited a long time before he raised his head enough to see around him, and even longer yet before he dared stand. He closed his eyes in gratitude. "Holy is the Lord, and abounding in mercy."

When he lay down again, he slept the rest of the night without dreams.

✦   ✦   ✦

Amos did not hear the Voice again until he was working in the sycamore groves. Others worked around him, talking, laughing, but not hearing. Grasping a fig, he made a small cut. He felt the air grow warm around him. Everything went still. Sounds faded.

The people of Gaza have sinned again and again, and I will not let them go unpunished!

Amos saw the Philistines leading whole villages of Israelites away from their burning homes. Using whips, they forced the people to march to Edom, where they sold them as slaves.

Indignation choked him. "Our brothers make profit on our misery!" Edomites were descendants of Jacob's brother, Esau. "Should one brother purchase another as a slave, Lord?" He hated the Edomites as much as he hated the Philistines, and so was vaguely disappointed when he saw fire descended only on the walls of Gaza and not Edom as well. An invading army from the north slaughtered everyone in Gaza and then marched on to Ashkelon. Ekron was the last to fall and lay ruined like Gath.

The last few survivors of the nation that had often oppressed Israel fell, dissolved into dust, and blew away in the wind, leaving only an echo of Philistia's grandeur.

"So be it, Lord!" Amos rejoiced. "So be it."

"*Amos!*"

He blinked, swayed slightly on the ladder, and grasped hold of a sycamore branch to keep from falling. "What?"

"What? *What*, you say? What's the matter with you, my friend?" Jashobeam, the owner of the grove, stood staring up at him, arms akimbo.

"Nothing."

"Nothing? You've been shouting."

Other workers stared at him.

"I was having a vision."

"Oh, a vision." Jashobeam threw back his head and laughed loudly. He waved his hands as he called out to the others. "Amos was having a vision!"

Some laughed. Some leaned out from beneath branches to grin at him.

Jashobeam put his hands on his hips and looked up at him. "Perhaps you need to come down and rest in the shade awhile. Too much heat, I would say. Go have a long cool drink of water with a little wine."

Face burning, Amos ducked his head. "I'm fine." Clenching his teeth, he grasped another sycamore fig and made the small slice.

"A vision." Jashobeam shook his head. "If you have another, try not to shout about it. You distract my workers." Jashobeam walked away.

+ + +

Amos was on his way home to Tekoa when the Lord spoke to him again.

The people of Tyre have sinned again and again, and I will not let them go unpunished!

Dropping to his knees, Amos threw himself onto his face.

Israelites stood in the court of the Phoenician king. The heads of state signed documents, swearing a treaty of brotherhood and friendship between Phoenicia and Israel. But then Phoenicians raided, and took whole villages captive to Edom, selling them as slaves.

Amos slammed his fists on the ground. "They tricked us. They broke their word!"

God's wrath descended in a spear of flame that set the great city of Tyre on fire. The mighty fortresses crumbled in the inferno.

There was no respite for Amos this time as a fourth vision came. Edomites with raised swords chased down their Israelite brothers. Every face was like Esau's, filled with bitterness and hatred against his brother Jacob, with generation after generation of them raised on the story of how the younger brother had bought the elder's birthright with a bowl of lentil soup and stripped Esau of his blessing. They sought every opportunity to inflict pain and suffering on Jacob's descendants. They savored revenge like a sweet dessert, not knowing it would turn their souls sour with poison.

Wailing to heaven, Amos gripped his head. "Stop, Lord. I don't want to see any more."

The Edomites caught up with and cut down the fleeing Israelite men. With cries of jubilance and triumph, they stabbed and slashed them, giving free rein to years of pent-up jealousy and rage.

So I will send down fire on Teman, and the fortresses of Bozrah will be destroyed.

Amos watched punishment come upon Esau's sons. The horror of it made him collapse. He spread his arms, clutching the grass, his cheek pressed against soft earth.

+   +   +

He wandered for days, unsure what to do. "Why do You show me these things, Lord? What am I to do with this knowledge? Tell me!"

The Lord did not answer.

Distraught, burdened by the images of destruction, Amos headed again for Tekoa. He climbed the mountain road from Jericho and took shelter for the night in a small cave. He could look out over the Sea of Salt. To the north were the mountains of Ammon. To the south was Moab.

The people of Ammon have sinned again and again, and I will not let them go unpunished!

Terror gripped Amos as he dwelt within the vision. All his senses awakened. He smelled the smoke of Gilead, the burning flesh. He tasted ash in his mouth. Ammonite warriors attacked Gilead. Lungs straining, he ran with the fleeing Israelites. Gilead burned, but even this destruction did not satisfy the Ammonites, who sought to wipe out the race by knocking pregnant women to the ground. As the women screamed for mercy, the warriors ripped their clothing and cut their bellies open with their swords to kill their unborn children.

Amos screamed. "Why do You stand idly by? Why are You silent? Don't You see Your enemies killing Your people?" Tears poured down his cheeks as he raged. "Do to them what You did to Egypt and the Midianites. Crush their pride. Destroy them!"

See what I will do.

Fire descended on Rabbah, blazing through the fortresses until they crumbled. Battle cries rose like a whirlwind in a mighty storm and the Ammonites fell, thousands of them, until only a remnant remained. When the battle ended, the king and his princes were fitted in yokes and led away to slavery.

"Yes, Lord!" Amos raised his hands. "Let all the nations see You are supreme over all the earth!"

Another vision came in the wake of Ammon's destruction.

Moabites opened the graves of Edom's kings and piled up the bones to burn. When the fires grew cold, workers scraped and swept the lime ashes into vats, where they pounded what remained to dust that they used to make plaster. Amos watched in horror and disgust as the Moabites coated their houses with the bones of Edom's kings.

"Not even in death are their victims shown mercy!" Amos shouted.

Before his eyes, an army attacked Moab. Foreign warriors shouted. Rams' horns blew. Flames reached into the sky as Kerioth burned while the people of Moab fell in the noise of battle. Neither their king nor their princes survived the slaughter. Those who had taken the bones of the dead from tombs would never rest in one.

The enemies of Israel would fall. Those who thought they held power would become powerless. God would avenge those who had been skinned alive, those who had been executed, their heads stacked as trophies before the Aramean city gates. No more would Philistia profit on slave trade. No more would Phoenicia break treaties of peace and take whole villages captive into slavery. No more would Edom grow rich on revenge. All of them would die, having drunk the poison of lust and hatred, from Damascus to Ammon and Moab, begun by Lot's incestuous daughters. All of them would be crushed like scorpions beneath the heel of God's anger.

A deep satisfaction had filled Amos at the thought of their destruction. Exhausted, Amos curled on his side in the shallow cave, comforted. *When, Lord? When will it happen?*

Soon, he hoped. He would relish the sight of it.

✦   ✦   ✦

Amos arose in the morning and offered a prayer of thanksgiving. It was the first he had said—and meant—in years. "Give thanks to the Lord Almighty, for the Lord is compassionate and gracious, slow to anger, abounding in love."

Caravans wound their way up the Benjamin Mountains. Men pulled at roped donkeys laden with packs. As Amos walked up the mountain road, uneasiness filled him. When he reached the Mount of Olives, he stopped and stared, troubled in his soul. He thought again of the corruption he saw every time he went to Jerusalem. Priests like Heled profited off stealing from God. Had Amos not cut his share and built his flock from those same lambs? He shuddered at his guilt. What choice had those priests given his father? Frustrated by helplessness, he tried to make excuses. None sufficed. Words spoken long ago, when he was a child attending classes, came back to him. Burning words that rent his conscience:

"Hear, O Israel. You must love the Lord your God with all your heart, all your soul, and all your strength."

Love had not motivated his rebellion against Heled, nor had righteousness or any desire to worship the Lord. He had not loved God. He had blamed the Lord for the trouble men caused and the contract under which his family lived. Each time he went to the Temple, he did so grudgingly and offered only what was required to keep in good standing with the authorities.

Uzziah might be king, but all too often it was the priests who ruled the lives of common people like himself and his brothers.

The Lord is God!

But even now, as he stood looking up at King David's Zion, Amos knew idols still pocked Judah's landscape, and pagan altars still remained despite King Uzziah's attempt to destroy the foreign gods that had dwelt in the hearts of King Solomon's wives and concubines. How could a wise man be so foolish as to build pagan temples and altars? Amos saw the remnants of those gods as he moved his flocks. Sometimes he had been tempted to follow the processions up those hills so that he could spread himself beneath the leafy branches and enjoy the sensual pleasures offered there. It had not been fear of the Lord that kept him away, but fear of leaving his flock untended.

You must not have any other god but Me. You must not make for yourself an idol of any kind.

Sin was everywhere. It was in the nations surrounding Judah and Israel. It was in Israel and Judah.

It was in *him*.

Not once have I sought out one of the few priests known to serve in fear of the Lord! I have held my anger close, embracing it, fanning my hatred against all Your priests. I have rebelled against You.

You must not misuse the name of the Lord your God.

Amos cringed. Yes, Heled and others like him were guilty, but Amos's family had entered into a contract that dishonored God as well. How many times had they used God's name to seal a bargain?

"Stand aside!" Someone shoved him from behind.

Amos moved out of the way, seeing everything differently.

Remember to observe the Sabbath day by keeping it holy.

Did the gates of Jerusalem not stand open for trade every day of the week? The markets of the great city never rested. Amos watched the beehive of activity as merchants bore their wares into Jerusalem past elders holding court in the gate.

Other commandments came in a rush:

Honor your father and mother. You must not murder. You must not commit adultery. You must not steal. You must not testify falsely against your neighbor. You must not covet your neighbor's house. You must not covet your neighbor's wife, male or female servant, ox or donkey, or anything else that belongs to your neighbor.

Amos closed his eyes. Though he had never broken these commandments in deed, he knew he had broken every one of them in thought.

He had loved his father, but had been bitterly disappointed in him. Not once after he had learned the truth had he believed anything his father said.

And how many times had he lusted for revenge against Heled? He had even thought of ways to kill him, savoring the thought in his mind. If he could have found a way to kill the priest and escape, he might have done it!

From the time he was born until two years ago, he had been a thief, a party to the priests who testified falsely against those who brought perfect offerings to the Lord, only to have them rejected.

As for the sin of coveting, had he not coveted the priests' power, freedom, and wealth? He had not so much wanted it for himself as he had wanted to see it ripped from the hands that had grasped it and held on at such cost to the people.

Amos saw what God wanted him to see and stood mortified by the sins of the people, sins he himself had committed on a daily basis.

And when God spoke, His next words were no surprise.

The people of Judah have sinned again and again, and I will not let them go unpunished! They have rejected the instruction of the Lord, refusing to obey His decrees. They have been led astray by the same lies that deceived their ancestors.

The hair on the back of Amos's neck prickled. He dropped to his knees and covered his face. He rocked forward, covering his head with his hands. "No, Lord, please, don't show me." He drew his knees up under him. "Have mercy on us."

But the images came upon him relentlessly, melting his heart and filling him with a sorrow and compassion he had never felt before when looking upon his own people. The compassion he'd felt until now only for his defenseless sheep. He wept.

"You there. You're blocking us." Hauled up, he was pitched aside and fell heavily. "Stay off the road!"

Heavy wheels crunched the rocks. Oxen blew out their breath. The voices of a thousand people mingled as Amos sat in the dust, his head in his hands.

"To what end, Lord? To what end will You destroy the people You chose?"

From the ruins I will rebuild it and restore its former glory, so that the rest of humanity, including the Gentiles—all those I have called to be Mine—might seek Me.

✦   ✦   ✦

"What are you doing back so soon?" Bani rose from his money table. When he came close, he frowned. "What's happened? Is Ithai well?"

"I have not seen Ithai or Elkanan in months. Remember, they had finished their business with Joram before I returned with my flock. They came here to Jerusalem before I did."

Ahiam closed the gate of a stall, a lamb in his arms. "The boys went home to Tekoa not long after the new moon festival."

Amos looked at his two brothers. "The Lord spoke to me. I have seen visions."

Ahiam laughed. "Go sleep off the wine over there." He walked away with the lamb.

"You've probably had a fever." Bani searched Amos's face. "You do look ill."

"I have seen the destruction of Jerusalem."

"You're mad. With Uzziah on the throne?" Bani shook his head. "Jerusalem is secure, and our borders are protected."

"But I'm telling you the truth! I saw—"

"Fever-induced dreams, Amos." Bani gripped his arm. "That's all. Besides, why would God speak to you, a shepherd? You're not a member of the priests' guild. You're not a Levite. When God speaks, He talks to one of the trained prophets or priests. Go over there. Sit. You look tired." He led Amos to the bench beneath the canopy where their tables were set up for business.

Amos saw the open box with its neat rows of coins and shuddered.

Bani slapped him on the back. "Have some wine, little brother. Eat something. Forget about whatever you thought you saw. You'll feel better." Bani poured him a cup of wine and offered him bread and dates. "You spend too much time alone with that flock of yours, little brother. You always have."

The hum of conversations merged with the bleating sheep until the sounds seemed the same. Amos clutched his head. *Am I going mad that men are beginning to sound like sheep, or sheep are beginning to sound like men?*

Ahiam returned. "Heled is not pleased to see you, Amos. Joram gave him a bad report when he returned from Tekoa, and Heled hasn't forgotten."

Amos raised his head. "If you don't end your dealings with that thief of a priest, you and your family will suffer for it."

Ahiam's face hardened. "Live your life, Amos, and leave mine in peace." He gave a hard laugh. "If we took your advice, we'd all be living in the hills, half starved and seeing visions."

"Leave him alone, Ahiam."

"He makes trouble for us. Even when he can keep his mouth shut, he allows his contempt to show. Look at him!" Ahiam leaned toward Amos. "You look like a beggar."

"He's given both our sons a start on flocks of their own."

"A lot of good it will do them if he keeps on as he has. Everything we've *all* worked for, for over two generations, will be gone!" He glared at Amos. "It happened before. Remember what Father told you. It can happen again. Don't think it can't." He jerked his head. "You forget who holds the power around here."

Amos rose, shaking with rage. "God holds the power!"

Chin jutting, Ahiam came close enough to stand nose to nose with Amos. "And *He* gave it to *them* to use as *they* will."

Amos stood his ground. "The people of Judah have sinned—"

"All of a sudden, you're the judge?" Ahiam gave him a hard shove. "Go home. Prophesy to your sheep."

"Listen to me," Amos cried out in desperation.

"If you made any sense, I might." Ahiam glanced back over his shoulder. "Send him home." He nodded to Bani. "We've got a business to run here." Turning his back on them, he walked toward a customer looking over the lambs. Smiling, he spread his arms in greeting.

Bani drew Amos aside and spoke quietly. "Go back to my house. A few nights' rest in a good bed and some of my wife's cooking and you'll be yourself again."

Amos knew he would never be the same again. Everywhere he looked, he saw things differently than he had before the Voice had spoken to him.

Dream or no dream, his life had changed forever.

+   +   +

Amos left the Temple Mount and its stalls of sacrificial animals, passing tables where money changers stacked shekels and half shekels. He went down to the market square where bellowing camels with tasseled harnesses stood laden with huge packs of merchandise. The animals were lined up behind owners who displayed their wares on woven rugs. The scents of dung and spices mingled while vendors shouted their wares, competing with one another as possible customers wandered the bazaar. Shekels clinked and money boxes slammed shut. Donkeys burdened with bundles were pulled along by hard-faced men, cursing and making threats if others did not make room.

Bludgeoned by sound, Amos sought quieter streets. He wandered along narrow alleys lined with booths. Vendors haggled with customers over prices while competitors called enticements to steal patrons away.

"Good shepherd!" one called to Amos. "Come, come! You need a new pair of sandals. Those look worn through. I will give you a good price."

"I will give you a better price."

"He's a thief. Don't listen to him. I have better—"

"Here! Come look at what I have to offer."

The narrow street widened, and Amos stopped to watch stonemasons working on a new house, a foreman shouting instructions to his crew. A few doors down, a carpenter worked on a cart. Wheels of all sizes lined the wall of his shop. Another man planed a table while his wife showed a bench to a woman with three children.

On another street, metalworkers pounded ingots into utensils while coppersmiths pounded trays. A goldsmith displayed earrings, bracelets, necklaces, and cylinders ready for engraving into family seals. Weavers sold cloths and rugs on another street, while the next was lined with bakers. Amos's stomach clenched with hunger, but he didn't stop. He had no money with which to buy. Distracted, he took dried grain from his scrip to ease the ache in his belly.

He wandered into the valley of cheese makers and back up to the cano-pied stalls with baskets of barley and wheat, jars of oil and jugs of wine, bins of olives and baskets of early figs. Combs of golden honey dripped into bowls, while nearby another merchant called out balm for sale.

Rug merchants and basket weavers called out to him as he passed. A tentmaker haggled with a customer.

Jerusalem was, indeed, a city of wealth and commerce. The people seemed to want for nothing. What they lacked had little to do with the body and everything to do with the heart and soul. All their strength was spent on what they could hold in their hands.

Pausing, Amos listened to a young man play a lyre for a customer while his father attached strings to a kinnor. The customer pointed to a beautifully carved ten-string nebel displayed alongside a row of bone pipes. The boy picked it up and began to play it. At a signal, the boy handed the instrument to his father. He allowed the customer to hold it, pluck the strings, and stroke the carved wood. Amos picked up some reed pipes and admired them. The lust to own would seal the bargain. He put them down quickly and walked away.

Amos went through a gate and down a pathway. Weary, he sat in the shade of a mustard plant and leaned against a wall. Hyssop grew from between the stones. Across from him was the Mount of Olives. It was quiet here, quiet enough to think, though pondering what he had just seen was the last thing he wanted to do. He pressed the heels of his hands against his eyes.

"I see sin, Lord." Enticing, tempting, seeming to delight and bring satisfaction. "I see it. I see!"

Pride promised pleasure and security, but would bring despair and death instead.

✦   ✦   ✦

Amos walked home in the moonlight. He went to the fold and entered by the narrow gate, walking quietly among the animals, checking each one. When the sun rose, he would let them out into the south pasture. Soon, it would be time to lead them away from Tekoa. One of the lambs heard his voice and came to him quickly, pressing against his leg. Amos hunkered down. "Yes, I'm home, little one." He rubbed the lamb's face.

Go prophesy to My people Israel.

Confused, Amos stood. "Israel?" He spread his hands, looking up at the sky.

"The northern kingdom, Lord? Samaria?"

Go to Bethel.

Why would God send him to speak to the ten tribes who had broken away from Solomon's son Rehoboam? Hadn't they followed after Jeroboam the son of Nebat, foreman of Solomon's workforce? Why not call one from among the ten rebellious tribes to prophesy to their breakaway nation?

"I told my brothers I had seen visions, Lord. They didn't believe me! They thought I was drunk or suffered delirium."

The lamb bleated. The flock sensed his turbulent emotions and moved, restless, nervous.

"Shhhhh. It's all right, sheep." Amos lifted the lamb. He moved slowly among his animals, speaking softly, soothing their fears. He set the lamb down and moved to the gate. Drawing his reed pipe from his belt, he played whatever sweet melody came to mind. The sheep settled again.

Amos looked up at the stars. Before the visions began, he had believed that God didn't notice him or what he did or thought. Now, he realized God saw and knew everything. Still, Amos didn't understand why God would call a poor shepherd—a simple, ordinary man—to speak the Word of the Lord.

My love is unfailing and everlasting. I will be with you wherever you go.

You love me, and yet You send me north with a message of destruction. Even as he wanted to question, Amos knew why. God had filled him with understanding, and was sending him to call His lambs back from destruction.

Had God ever given a prophet a message the people wanted to hear? a message they welcomed and celebrated? Perhaps Israel would listen this time. Even to a shepherd. Why wouldn't they, when the visions God had given him showed the destruction of enemies that surrounded them? They would celebrate just as he had, before he understood that the sins of Judah were not hidden from God's clear and holy gaze. Wealthy, powerful Israel would gloat even more over the judgment upon the nations, and probably gloat over the destruction of their Judean brothers as well, for then, Samaria would become the city on the mountain.

Or would it?

Solomon's foreman had crowned himself King Jeroboam the First, with dreams of a dynasty to follow. To carry that out, he had abolished the Levitical priesthood and established his own. He had turned the people away from Jerusalem by setting up golden calves for them to worship in Bethel and Dan!

They do all these things, Lord, and yet, Judah *is to be destroyed? How can I say these things? How can I leave my own people and go to them? Judah! What of Judah?*

You will be My prophet in Israel. My Spirit will come upon you, and you will speak the Word of the Lord.

Amos felt the weight of his calling, and went down on his hands and knees to plead with God. "I'm not a city dweller, Lord. You know that. I'm a shepherd. A man of flocks and fields. I hate going to Jerusalem and now you want me to go to Bethel, a place even more corrupt? I've done everything I could to stay away from cities. I can't bear being around so many people. And the noise, the confusion is unbearable to me. I'm just a shepherd."

I am your Shepherd, Amos. Will you obey Me?

Though the words came softly and full of tenderness, Amos knew the course of his life lay in the answer. "I am not worthy."

I have called you by name. You are mine.

"But, Lord, You need someone who will make them listen. You need a powerful speaker. You need someone who knows the Law. You need someone who will know how to persuade them to do what You want." He bowed his head, ashamed. "You need someone who loves them, Lord. And I don't care what happens to them!"

I don't need anyone, My child. I want you. Go to Bethel, Amos. My grace is all you need. I will tell you when to speak and what to say.

Grieving, Amos hung his head. "What about my sheep, Lord? How can I entrust them to hirelings?" He looked up, gulping sobs. "My sheep." Tears ran down his cheeks. "No one loves them as I do."

A quiet breeze blew softly through the winter grass, and God whispered:

Feed My sheep.

+ + +

Amos slept fitfully at the gate of the sheepfold, wakening before dawn. He sat on the wall and gazed at his animals. He knew the traits and personalities of every one of them. He had saved one from a ledge, another from the attack of a lion, another from floodwaters of a wadi. Some stayed close, never venturing far from the flock, while others were prone to wander. Some learned quickly, while others seem destined to get themselves into trouble with every new pasture. His heart ached because he loved them.

"Feed My sheep," the Lord had said last night as dusk came upon the land.

"Forgive me, Lord, but I care more for these animals than I have ever cared for people. Men take care of themselves. They do what they want. Sheep are helpless without a shepherd."

Even as he said the words aloud, he wondered if they were true. He saw things differently this morning. Maybe it was the visions of destruction that haunted his thoughts.

"Feed My sheep."

Were men like sheep? He had always thought of them as wolves or lions or bears . . . especially priests who could make life miserable if they so chose, and even tear it apart. But what of the common people, men and women like him who wanted to do what was right, but often ended up doing what was expedient? He had been taught never to argue with a priest, but his heart had often raged within him.

He turned toward the north, thinking of Bethel. This city of the northern kingdom was not that far away—only eleven miles—but it seemed a distant country. His journeys had kept him in the pastures of Judah and Benjamin's territory, always circling him back home to Tekoa. Bethel was the last place he wanted to go. But he would have no peace until he obeyed the Lord.

In the cool of the morning, Amos spotted Elkanan and Ithai as they led their flocks out to pasture. Amos remained on the wall of his fold, watching his nephews with the flocks he had started for them. What he saw pleased him. Stepping down, Amos opened the gate and led his sheep out. Elkanan and Ithai saw him and raised their hands in greeting. Amos headed toward them.

Elkanan greeted him warmly. "Uncle!"

As soon as Elkanan withdrew, Ithai embraced him as well. "You spend less time in Jerusalem each year." Ithai laughed.

Jerusalem. Sorrow gripped Amos as the vision came flooding back. *Jerusalem!* How long had he despaired at what he saw there. Never had he felt such a wave of sorrow as he did now with dark wrenching memories of the future.

He stayed with his nephews for the rest of the day, listening to their stories of predators thwarted, sick lambs tended, wandering sheep found, sheepfolds expanded to accommodate more animals. Amos understood. Rather than go out alone with their flocks, they had stayed together, sharing the burden of tending the sheep.

His moment came to speak. "I have been called away."

Elkanan glanced at him. "Away? When? Where?"

"Before sunrise tomorrow." He leaned heavily on his staff and swallowed the lump in his throat. "Add my flock to yours and tend them as I would."

Elkanan looked at the sheep and then at Amos. "Should we stay here in Tekoa until you return, Uncle?"

"No. Take them to fresh pastures. The pastures of Jericho are open to you. If Jashobeam questions you, tell him these are my sheep. I paid for grazing rights by working in his sycamore groves. If I have not returned by the time you come back here to winter the flocks, take only the *best* lambs to Jerusalem."

His pulse raced suddenly, as he remembered the Lord roaring like a lion inside his head. "Whatever you do, do it as the Lord would have you do it. Do what is right, no matter what others do. Run from evil."

Elkanan stared. "What's happened, Uncle?"

"The Lord has shown me what will happen to us if we don't repent and turn back to Him."

A flood of questions came from his nephews. Amos found solace that they did not suggest he rest. They did not tell him to eat something so that he would feel like himself again. "Sin brings death, my sons. Do what is right. Convince your fathers of this. God sees what men do. He knows their hearts. Do what is right and live."

"We will tell them, Uncle."

They seemed troubled. Even if they could be convinced, would Ahiam and Bani listen? Amos doubted it. Bani might consider turning away from the business practices that had made him prosper, but not for long. Ahiam would wear him down and turn him back to worshiping profits. Amos remembered how his father's conscience had suffered. But Ahiam and Bani had lived most of their lives in the shadow of the Temple among corrupt priests that saw nothing wrong with what they did. Now, they equated their increasing wealth to God's blessing on what they did.

"Uncle? Why are you crying?"

Amos struggled against the emotions overwhelming him, and tried to keep his voice steady. "I must go to Bethel." He headed across the field.

"Bethel! But, Uncle . . . how long will you be gone?"

"I don't know." *A few weeks, Lord? A month? A year?*

Silence.

Maybe it was better not to know.

THREE

Amos camped in the hills near Bethel. He could see lamplight on the wall and knew soldiers were stationed in the watchtowers.

Bethel! After stealing Esau's birthright, Jacob had fled and stopped to rest here, using a stone for a pillow. In his vision, he saw a ladder to heaven with angels going up and down, and God had made a covenant with him. No wonder Jeroboam I had claimed this city to start his new religion. Even having been delivered from Egypt, the Israelites had quickly returned to the pagan worship of their oppressors while Moses was on top of Mount Sinai receiving the Law of God. Jeroboam had seduced the ten northern tribes with the same god—a golden calf. And the people wanted convenience. Why walk eleven miles to Jerusalem to worship the true God three times a year, when there was another god right here in Bethel? Jeroboam had known the people well. He gave them what they wanted: empty idols made by human hands and the illusion of control over their own lives.

Jeroboam, a goat leading the sheep to slaughter. He knew what places meant the most to the people and claimed them. Another golden calf resided in Gilgal where the Israelites had crossed the Jordan River after forty years of wandering in the wilderness. Gilgal, the place where the people of Israel had reconsecrated themselves to God and celebrated the first Passover in Canaan; the place where they had eaten the first fruit of the land after forty years of manna. And now it, too, stood defiled by pagan worship. Even Beersheba, where God first made promises of blessing to Abraham, then Isaac, and finally Jacob, was now a major place of worship for Jeroboam's unholy religion.

Amos slept uneasily and awakened in darkness. He rose and went down the hill to the road and followed it up to the gates of Bethel where he waited until morning. Merchants arrived with their goods, ignoring the beggars who approached them. Some of the poor had little more than a tunic to keep them warm. When the gates were opened, Amos tensely moved among the crowds making their way to the center of the city where Jeroboam's temple stood, housing the golden calf.

The mount was an anthill of activity with pilgrims carrying their offerings up and into the temple. Neophyte priests dressed in fine linen ephods stood greeting them as they entered. Not one Levite stood among them, for Jeroboam I had abolished the rightful priesthood and established his own. All a man needed to become a priest was one young bull and seven rams! And who with the means would not pay it when all the benefits of priesthood could so enrich a man and his family? Power, wealth, and prestige came with the post, and the ability to strip the people of whatever they decided was a "proper offering" to stay in the good graces of Jeroboam's false and capricious gods.

Having driven even the faithful Levites from the northern cities, no one remained to teach people the truth.

"Alms for the blind . . . ," a man whined at the bottom of the steps, a small woven basket in his hand. He held it out at the sound of people passing. "Alms for the blind. Have pity on me."

Amos paused to look into his face. The man's eyes were opaque, his face brown and lined from years in the sun. He was clothed in rags, and his gnarled hands revealed that blindness was not his only infirmity. Amos had brought only a few shekels with him. He took one from his pouch and leaned down. "May the Lord have compassion on you." Amos placed the coin in the basket.

The man's fingers fumbled over the coin as he declared his thanks.

As Amos went up the steps, he watched priests take gifts of money and tuck them into their personal purses. One put his hand out as Amos came level with him. Amos looked at him in contempt.

The priest stiffened. "Those who do not give to god cannot expect blessing."

"I will not receive a blessing from your god." Amos started to walk by.

"Indeed not if you are so ungracious and ungrateful. You will have a curse on your head. . . ."

Pausing, Amos turned and gazed deeply into the man's eyes. "Woe to you, false priest. You already live under a curse of your own making." Turning his back on him, Amos walked into the temple.

He moved with the others, watchful, taking in everything. Were men so eager to be fleeced? Amos went as far as the inner corridor and stood aside. Leaning on his staff, he watched and listened to men and women murmuring incoherently as they moved forward, intent upon seeing the golden calf in which they placed their hope. Some carried small woven prayer rugs that they unrolled and knelt upon in comfort. They raised their hands and bowed in adoration before the horned altar. They sang songs of praise.

Priests waved incense burners. The streaks of cloying gray smoke made a cloud over the worshipers held there by a fog of lies.

And there stood their god in all its glory. Did these people really believe that bloodless empty statue could answer prayers?

So it seemed.

These Israelite brothers no longer knew the difference between righteousness and blasphemy. How was it possible to put such ardent faith in that great hunk of hollow gold, molded and shaped by a man? That calf couldn't help itself, let alone do anything for them! Men without God put their trust in a spider's web, not even knowing they had been captured and bound. Everything these people counted upon to keep them safe would fall, pulling them down with it.

Musicians strummed lyres and kinnors. Priests chanted.

A woman rushed tearfully to her husband, displaying a talisman sold to her by a priest. "He says we will have a child. . . ."

A man, sallow and gaunt, had paid for a spell to be cast so that he would be healed of his troubles.

Amos followed a father and son out of the temple. "I've already put in my request, Son. You will be well pleased with the one I have chosen. Since it is your birthday, you will go first, and I will wait my turn."

When they went into another building next door, Amos followed. As he entered the door, he heard laughter. Men and women lounged in a room off to his right. Someone strummed a lyre.

A girl dressed in finery, her dark eyes made up with Egyptian kohl, rose to greet him. Her smile did not reach her eyes. "Come with me." Bells tinkled as she walked.

Amos didn't move. "What is this place?"

She turned and stared at him. "The temple brothel." When her expression became curious, it was the first sign of life in her face. "Do you prefer boys?"

"Boys?"

She shrugged. "Some do."

Amos left the house quickly. He crossed the courtyard and stood in the shadows of a temple wall. A vision came back: the screams of the dying, the smoke, bodies sprawled in the streets. Leaning heavily on his staff, he bowed his head. *Now, Lord? Do I speak now?*

God did not answer.

Amos sat on the temple steps and waited. All around him, people hurried to sin, laughing as they went. The wealthy pushed past the impoverished. If they paused at all, it was to mock rather than show pity.

How had Israel sunk to this? Did it go back to the days of Solomon when that great king of supposed wisdom had allowed his wives and concubines to turn his heart from God? The Lord had used the foreman of Solomon's workforce to break the kingdom in two. The king's spies had told him a prophet foretold Jeroboam as ruler over ten of the twelve tribes. Rather than heed God's warning and repent, Solomon attempted to kill Jeroboam.

Escaping to Egypt, Jeroboam waited until the king's death and then returned to make his move for power. He asked Rehoboam, Solomon's son, now king, to lighten the workload upon the people.

God knew the pride of men, but still gave them opportunity to repent. Wise counselors surrounded Rehoboam and gave him sound advice. Rehoboam refused to listen, preferring instead the witless counsel of spoiled, arrogant young men who told him he would be greater even than the great King Solomon.

King Solomon had loved women more than God. His desire to please them led the people astray, for one wife wanted an altar for the pagan god Chemosh, another bowed down to the detestable idol of Moab, and others worshiped Molech, the idol of Ammon, on the mountain east of Jerusalem. Solomon was even led to worship Ashtoreth, the goddess of the Sidonians, and Milcom of the Ammonites.

How could a man reputed to be the wisest on earth have been so foolish?

King Rehoboam attempted to show his authority by sending a servant to call the people back to work. When the servant was stoned to death, Rehoboam fled to Jerusalem. He rallied the tribes of Judah and Benjamin and called up warriors to go to war, but the Lord sent word through His prophet to stop what he was doing. "Do not go to war against your brothers!" This time, Rehoboam listened and repented. Any man who fought against God was destined to lose, and he wanted to retain the power he had. He stayed in Jerusalem and ruled over Judah and Benjamin, expecting the other ten tribes to return. After all, the Lord required them to come three times a year to Jerusalem to worship, and the Levites would draw them back to God—and to the rightful king.

Jeroboam knew the risks. He had no trust in God even though the Lord had given him the ten tribes. He made his own plans and gave the Israelites the god their ancestors had worshiped in Egypt—a golden calf. Hadn't the tribes wanted to return to Egypt? Hadn't they always been tempted to follow the ways of the other nations? Even Aaron, brother of the great law-giver Moses, had made a golden calf. Jeroboam gave them two and placed them in cities where God had spoken to the patriarchs—Bethel and Dan.

"Here are your gods, Israel!"

The people rejoiced and flocked to worship the golden calves.

Jeroboam's religion grew so rapidly and prospered so greatly he set up golden calves and goats in Gilgal and Beersheba. He built palaces on "watch mountain," Samaria, his capital. Shrines sprung up like poisonous plants throughout the territories. He silenced all protests by abolishing the

Levitical priesthood established by God. The new priesthood did as the king wanted, raking in proceeds from the royal sanctuaries.

Jeroboam's cunning plan worked. Men wanted ease, after all, not hard work. Ah, yes, why not worship idols? A man would have immediate pleasure with temple prostitutes. Sin would be approved. No one need consider what is right or wrong. Live for yourselves. Go ahead: lie, cheat, steal— everyone is doing it—as long as you give the king his share of the offerings! Why serve a holy God who demanded you follow the Law, when other gods would allow you to wallow in self-gratification? People rejected truth and gulped down lies, turning their backs on the loving, merciful God who provided their every need. Instead, they followed a king who ruled over them as he pleased.

Shall I speak here, Lord? Shall I speak now against all I see?

Still, God did not answer.

Frustration filled Amos. His anger grew the longer he waited. Sin stood upon the altar, and the people praised it! Bethel, once a holy place, now a city of blasphemy! He could not bear to listen to the priests calling the people into that foul temple for worship. Turning away, he pushed through the crowd. "Let me through!" he cried out, eager to make his way off the temple mount and down the thronged street.

Only after he left the city behind did he feel he could breathe again.

He gave a cry of pent-up emotion and went out into the hills. Jerusalem was bad enough, but now he saw this place! He spread his arms and roared, "Israel! Israel!" The ten tribes wallowed in sin and did not even recognize it. He paced and circled, muttering to himself. Finally, he sank down and tried to plead. "Lord . . . Lord . . ."

A glorious sunset crossed the western sky. The tinkle of bells made him raise his head. A shepherd led his sheep across a field toward home.

Amos held his head in his hands. "Send me home, Lord. Let me prophesy to Your people in Judah and Benjamin. Please, Lord."

No answer came.

Amos wept.

✦   ✦   ✦

Amos wandered the city of Bethel each day, waiting for the Lord to tell him to speak. On the temple mount, he smelled the stench of incense the priests offered, heard their chants and songs. Along streets and in markets, the wealthy used their power to take whatever they wanted from lesser people, parading their finery and privilege before those they cheated.

Sometimes he'd stand in the shadows of a gate and listen to the elders turn laws to their own favor and strip the poor of what little they had. One judge took the robe from a poor man and handed it over to a merchant for a jug of wine. Another took an unfortunate's sandals as pledge for a debt, and had not even a grimace of guilt as the man hobbled away to work in a rock quarry.

Shaking with rage, Amos turned away and headed up the hill. He heard shouts of greeting and looked back. A delegation approached.

Holy fire poured into Amos's veins as God spoke to him. He strode down the hill and extended his staff, pointing at them as the Lord spoke through him. "This is what the Lord says: 'The people of Damascus have sinned again and again, and I will not let them go unpunished!' "

Amos's voice rose above the din of the crowd, echoing in the narrow street. " 'They beat down My people in Gilead as grain is threshed with iron sledges. So I will send down fire on King Hazael's palace, and the fortresses of King Ben-hadad will be destroyed. I will break down the gates of Damascus and slaughter the people in the valley of Aven. I will destroy the ruler in Beth-eden, and the people of Aram will go as captives to Kir,' says the Lord."

"Who is this beggar who speaks insults?" Faces red with consternation, the Assyrians protested loudly. "Is this the way Ben-hadad's servants are greeted when they come in peace?"

Amos came on. "You speak of peace, but war is in your hearts."

"Be careful what you say. You may find your head on a pole!"

"Go back to Damascus!"

The people moved away from Amos, staring, as he cried out, "Go and tell your king what the Lord God has said! Get out of here!"

People whispered and then began talking. Some called out. Soon, the street was full as people surrounded Amos. Heart pounding, he shouted and raised his staff again. The people let him pass as he strode down the street. He was eager to get away from this place, away from them.

They called out questions. He didn't answer.

"Who is he?"

"I don't know."

"He looks like a shepherd."

"But did you hear him speak!"

"Just a madman talking."

"I've never heard a man speak with such authority. Have you?"

The Lord's judgment excited them. Hadn't he felt the same? *"Let it come, Lord! Let it come."*

People shouted from all directions.

"Did you hear what the prophet said?"

"Damascus in ruins!"

"That's a sight I'd like to see."

When it had to do with judgment upon their enemies, why wouldn't they celebrate? Why not cheer and shout? The Lord had given them words to savor, visions to delight. They listened to His Words.

Would they keep listening?

Amos ducked down a side street.

"Where is he going?"

"Prophet! Wait! Give us another prophecy."

Amos remembered other visions the Lord had shown him and ran. Now was not the time. He must wait upon the Lord. He must wait! Some gave chase. Turning down another street and then another, Amos left them behind. Out of breath, his body shook violently. Emotions warred within him—wrath that made him grind his teeth and groan, anguish that brought a torrent of tears. "Lord, *Lord*!"

The wave of emotion crested and ebbed, leaving him drained. He sank against the wall, squatting on his heels. His staff clattered to the packed ground. Still panting, he rested his arms on his raised knees and bowed his head.

A door opened, and a woman stood staring at him. When he met her gaze, she stepped inside and closed the door.

Children played in the street.

A bird chirped from a sprig of hyssop growing from a high wall.

A man and woman argued across the way.

Tensing at the sound of running feet, Amos stood. Shouts and curses. Excited laughter. Youths ran past. One spilled a few coins. Their sandals echoed as an angry man came tearing around the corner, pausing long enough to snatch up the dropped coins and take after them again.

A lattice window opened above him. Amos looked up as a woman leaned out. Dressed in an expensive Babylonian robe, she sipped from a silver goblet. "What are you doing down there?" Not waiting for an answer, she disappeared and a servant appeared at the window and dumped a bowlful of something. Amos barely managed to evade being covered by household slops. The wealthy woman leaned out again and laughed at him.

Amos found his way to the main gate. A man recognized him and whispered to the elders. He did not stay long enough for anyone to detain him.

+   +   +

Amos found a small cave in the hills where he could spend the night. The next morning, he waited and prayed until God impelled him to return to Bethel where, as soon as he entered the gate, he heard the buzz of whispers.

"He's back! The prophet is back."

A young man pressed through the crowd and ran up the street. No one tried to stop Amos or ask questions when he passed through the gate and entered into the city. People followed him to the temple mount and then stood watching, talking behind their hands to one another, eyes eager. He sat on the lowest step of the temple and waited. Someone put a plate down in front of him, and people began putting coins into it. Angry, he kicked it away. With a collective gasp, they drew back and stared. Some quickly retrieved the coins they had offered.

"The priests are coming. . . ."

"The priests . . ."

The young man who had run from the gate came down the steps with two priests. Amos did not stand for them. They murmured to one another and then stood between him and the people.

The taller priest spoke quietly. "You stirred the people yesterday with your prophecy against Damascus."

Some people edged closer, faces rapt and eager.

Amos looked from them to the priests. He rested his staff across his knees. "These people are easily stirred."

"We would like to talk with you, Prophet, hear what you have to say." The tall priest glanced pointedly toward the men and women closing in. "Perhaps you prefer somewhere more private."

"Ask what you will here and now, though I probably will not be able to answer."

"What is your name?"

"Amos." He had never given much thought to his name, but now he wondered if God had caused his parents to give it to him: "burden bearer." His heart was truly burdened with the task God had given him, burdened even more by the visions he carried in his mind.

"And your village?"

"Tekoa."

People whispered, murmured.

"You are Judean."

"Yes, and God has called me here to speak His Word."

"What else would God have you say to us?"

"I speak in His time, not mine."

"Your prophecy against Damascus is well received. We all gave thanks to God yesterday. We would have invited you to speak again, but you disappeared. Where did you go?"

"Out into the hills."

"You should have shelter."

"The Lord is my shelter."

"Come, Prophet. Join us inside the temple. We have room for you here. We will worship together."

Heat filled Amos's face. He had no intention of being drawn inside that vile place. "I will come and sit here and wait upon the Lord."

Dark eyes glinted, smooth words were murmured. "As you wish." They bowed in respect and went back up the steps. The man who had reported

Amos's arrival remained outside. He insinuated himself among the watchers. Two temple guards came down and took positions. Amos smiled faintly.

The morning passed slowly. People drifted away. When Amos was thirsty, he lifted his skin of water to his lips. When he was hungry, he took grain and raisins from his scrip.

The guards sought shade. Others came to take their place.

Amos left as the sun was setting, but he returned the next day and the next, and the next after that. His tongue felt like a weight in his mouth. Day after day, he watched the people of Bethel live their lives, cheat one another, seek the solace of prostitutes, and give their offerings to idols. He waited and prayed. And people forgot about him.

When he came one morning, Philistines stood in the gate. Backs straight, heads high, they spoke to the elders who deferred to them nervously.

Fire flooded Amos's blood, and the quickening of the Holy Spirit took hold.

"This is what the Lord says." He strode toward them. "The people of Gaza have sinned again and again, and I will not let them go unpunished! They sent whole villages into exile, selling them as slaves to Edom. So I will send down fire on the walls of Gaza, and all its fortresses will be destroyed."

Fury spread across the faces of the Philistines. Two drew swords.

Amos blocked one with his club and used his staff to yank the other man around and pitch him to the ground. Swords clattered on the stones. When the fallen warrior tried to rise, Amos slammed his heel on his back. He sent the other crashing against a wall.

"*This is what the Lord says!*" His voice thundered in the gate. "I will slaughter the people of Ashdod and destroy the king of Ashkelon. Then I will turn to attack Ekron, and the few Philistines still left will be killed." He lifted his foot and stepped back so the fallen man could scramble to his feet. "Go back!" He drove them from the gate. "Go and take the Word of the Lord with you to your king."

Pandemonium reigned. A crowd surrounded Amos. People pressed in upon him from all sides. Strangely, he felt no fear, no desire to run away again. Even as he was swept along like a leaf on a stream, he felt calm. The temple of Bethel loomed before him, a gathering of priests waiting. Guards poured down the steps and took Amos into custody while the priests calmed the crowd.

One priest came close and put his hand upon Amos's arm. "You bring us good news."

Amos withdrew his arm. "I speak the Word of the Lord."

The priest's eyes grew cold, calculating, searching. "As do we."

Another beckoned. "You must have lodgings within the city."

Amos held his staff in front of him. "I have lived my life in the fields of the Lord."

"A man of your importance should live in comfort."

Someone tugged Amos's sleeve. "I can give you lodgings."

"No! Come with me."

"I have a summer house you can stay in!"

Surprised by such offers, Amos turned to the people. "The Lord has provided me with a place to live." He headed down the steps.

"Prophet!" one of the priests called out. "Will you give us no answer?"

Amos regarded the group in their finery. "God will answer you." Turning, he headed across the courtyard. People clustered around him, asking questions, praising him, pleading for another prophecy. They crowded so close to him, he could scarcely move.

"Let him pass!" a priest shouted.

The people retreated enough so he could proceed toward the street leading to the main gate. Guards appeared, and the people quieted. Amos breathed in relief when he left the confines of Bethel. Glancing back, he saw a group of men following him and tried to send them away.

"We just want to talk with you!"

Flustered, needing solitude, Amos headed for the hills. He walked in a seemingly aimless pattern, knowing the city dwellers would grow tired and give up. When the sun began to set, Amos went to the small cave in a hillside where he had left his supplies, and settled down for the night.

Voices whispered outside.

"Why does he live in a cave when he could have a room near the temple?"

"I don't know."

Amos pulled his robe up over his head.

Foxes had holes, but it seemed a prophet of the Lord would have no place private to lay his head.

✦ ✦ ✦

When Amos arose, he found gifts at the mouth of his cave. The first day, there was a small basket of fruit. The second, he found a pouch of roasted grain and a woven coat. He awakened to clinking the third day and came outside to find a bowl and offering of coins. Amos took the tunic and coins with him to Bethel. A man in a worn tunic shivered, waiting for the gate to open. Amos tapped him on the shoulder. When the man turned, Amos held out the coat. "This will keep you warm."

The man's eyes narrowed. "Do you mock me? I can't afford such a coat."

"I'm giving it to you."

The man stared at him in surprise and then looked at the coat with longing. Still, he did not raise his hand to take it.

"What's your name?"

"Issachar."

"Why will you not accept the coat, Issachar? You have need of it."

Issachar became angry. "As soon as I show my face inside the gate, I'll be accused of stealing it. I've lost everything. I'd like to keep from having my hand cut off."

"I'll make it clear you came by it honestly."

"And who are you to speak for me? A stranger. I'll still lose it."

"Why?"

"There are those who would take it from me as payment for a debt."

"Only for a day and then, by law, they must return it."

Issachar gave a snort of disdain. "No such law prevails here."

"How much do you owe?"

Issachar told him, and the amount was far less than the offering that had been left in the basket outside Amos's cave. "Take it." Amos stood beside him. "We will settle your debt when the gate opens."

As he walked the streets, he gave a coin to a man without sandals, and another to an aging Nazirite. While buying what he needed in the marketplace, he saw a widow with four children begging for bread. He gave her the rest of what he had and told her to thank God for the provisions.

Each day, he found more gifts left outside his cave dwelling.

The people showed generosity to him, a stranger, and remained blind to the poor of their city. They liked what he had said. They wanted more favorable prophecies and thought these bribes would keep them coming. It did not occur to them that the Word of the Lord was not for hire.

Amos marveled at how God used their attempts to control prophecy to provide for him and even bless a few of the forgotten and impoverished in Bethel.

Still, Amos knew the time was coming when these gift givers and flatterers would turn against him.

"When will you speak again, Prophet?" an official called out as he entered Bethel one day.

"When God gives me the words."

After a while, no one paid attention to him when he entered Bethel. Even the beggars left him alone, quickly aware that the gifts had stopped and they would receive nothing from his hand. Amos wandered and observed, waiting upon the Lord in the midst of the crowd, thankful he was no longer the center of attention.

He knew it was the calm before the storm.

He spent long hours walking the hills, squatting on his heels or sitting on a boulder to watch the shepherds with their flocks. He was more at home alone than among the well-dressed, well-fed, prosperous crowds.

One day, he walked long enough and far enough that he could see Tekoa. His heart squeezed tight with pain. Leaning on his staff, he pleaded. "Why must I wait, Lord? Why can I not speak all the visions at once and have done with them?" He felt the answer in his soul and bowed his head.

Oh, that he should care so little about people whom God loved so much.

The sun set. Darkness came. Amos looked up and imagined the hand of God flinging stars like shining dust across the heavens. No. He was wrong to think such pagan thoughts, for God had only to utter a word and it was done. Only man had He shaped with His hands, using dust He created to form His most precious and amazing creation. Only man was molded and loved into being, the breath of life in his lungs given by God.

The canopy of night soothed Amos. He felt God's presence over him. Surely his ancestors had felt the same as they wandered in the wilderness with the cloud by day and pillar of fire by night. God might be silent, but He was near—oh, so near—only a breath away. Burdened with the task God had given him, Amos also felt cherished. Wayward, stubborn, contentious as he was, God loved him.

Did He not also love the people of Bethel and Dan, Gilgal, and Beersheba? Wayward, stubborn, sinful though they were?

"Feed My sheep," God had said.

"Help me see them through Your eyes, Lord. Let me feel what You feel toward Your people so that I might better serve You."

And suddenly he did. Anguish, rage, passion. A father grieving over a wayward son, crying out to him to *come back to me where you are safe, come back.* . . . Judgment thrown down as a hedge to keep that son from plunging over a precipice straight into the arms of death.

Do you not see? Do you not know? I am your salvation.

Amos dropped to one knee, clutching his staff, swaying with the force of emotions. He moaned. "Lord, Lord . . ."

God had called him to be a prophet, and with each day, he surrendered more. For in those moments when the Spirit of the Lord came upon him, he was *alive*. It was only later when the Lord departed from him that Amos felt the loneliness of his soul. No longer was it enough to know God existed: God heard, saw, and knew him. Amos ached to have God remain indwelled, transforming his mind and heart. He wanted the intimacy to last.

He thought of Elijah taken up to heaven in the flaming chariot, never tasting death, standing now in the presence of the Lord; of Elisha, parting the Jordan River, raising a dead boy. And of Jonah running and hiding, only to be found and made more useful despite his disobedience. Who could doubt the word of a man half digested and vomited on the beach by a fish? Even the hated Assyrians in Nineveh had listened and repented!

For a while anyway.

Amos closed his eyes. "These are Your people, Lord, Your wandering children. You are my Shepherd. Lead me, Lord, so that I might lead them away from death. Help me."

He would speak the Word of the Lord. But would they come to God's call upon their hearts and minds?

He already feared he knew the answer. Had not the Lord already shown him what would happen?

How soon men forget the Word of the Lord.

And choose to perish in the midst of God's patience.

+   +   +

Amos watched a caravan make its way up the hill toward Bethel. His vision blurred, and he saw siege machines, warriors attacking, smoke and fire. He heard screams of terror and pain.

Surging to his feet, he cried out in a loud voice and strode through the orchard. He came out onto the road and raised his staff. "This is what the Lord says: 'The people of Tyre have sinned again and again, and I will not let them go unpunished!'"

Camel jockeys shouted profanities at him.

"They broke their treaty of brotherhood with Israel, selling whole villages as slaves to Edom. So I will send down fire on the walls of Tyre, and all its fortresses will be destroyed."

Animals bayed and paced. Attendants ran back and forth, trying to keep them in line.

Amos ran and placed himself between the caravan and the city. He pointed his staff toward Edom.

"This is what the Lord says: 'The people of Edom have sinned again and again, and I will not let them go unpunished!'"

Visitors backed away from him as he cried out.

"They chased down their relatives, the Israelites, with swords, showing them no mercy. In their rage, they slashed them continually and were unrelenting in their anger."

People lined the walls of Bethel.

"The prophet! The prophet of the Lord speaks!"

"From your mouth to God's ears!"

"This is what the Lord says." Amos pointed his staff toward Ammon. "The people of Ammon have sinned again and again, and I will not let them go unpunished! When they attacked Gilead to extend their borders, they ripped open pregnant women with their swords. So I will send down fire on the walls of Rabbah, and all its fortresses will be destroyed. The battle will come upon them with shouts, like a whirlwind in a mighty storm. And their king and his princes will go into exile together!"

Amos's lungs filled. His heart rose. He entered the gates, his voice like thunder echoing down the streets.

"This is what the Lord says: 'The people of Moab have sinned again and

again, and I will not let them go unpunished! They desecrated the bones of
Edom's king, burning them to ashes. So I will send down fire on the land
of Moab, and all the fortresses in Kerioth will be destroyed. The people will
fall in the noise of battle, as the warriors shout and the ram's horn sounds.
And I will destroy their king and slaughter all their princes.'"

"The Lord defends Israel!" men shouted.

"Israel is great!"

Blood on fire with the Spirit of the Lord, Amos came outside the gates once
again and cried out against Judah. "This is what the Lord says." Tears filled his
eyes and sorrow, his voice. "The people of Judah have sinned again and again,
and I will not let them go unpunished! They have rejected the instruction of
the Lord, refusing to obey His decrees. They have been led astray by the same
lies that deceived their ancestors. So I will send down fire on Judah, and all
the fortresses of Jerusalem will be destroyed." His voice broke.

The Spirit of the Lord lifted. Amos's blood cooled. He heard people
cheering, shouting from the top of the wall. "Bring on the Day of the Lord!"
People rushed from Bethel and clustered around him, their voices like chattering birds. "Let it come! Let it come!"

Only a few appeared to be troubled that the Lord's judgment had fallen
so close to home.

Is it time, Lord? I have given every prophecy but one. Is it time, Lord?

Wait.

The crowd parted as several priests came toward him. The eldest spoke
with cool respect. "Your prophecies please the people." Tightly spoken
words, eyes ablaze with jealousy.

"I speak the Word of the Lord."

"So we have been told. And it is true you speak with great power, Amos
of Tekoa."

People talked among themselves. "He prophesies against his own
country. . . ."

Amos turned away.

The priest quickly caught up with him. "Come." A command.

Amos ignored it.

The priest spoke with less force. "We will reward you for your words."

Amos pressed his way through the throng of people and kept walking.

"Where is he going?"

The priest's voice rose above the din. "We want to hear more of what
you have to say to us."

Angry, Amos faced him. "You hear, but you do not understand."

People whispered. "What don't we understand?"

"Shhh. Let him speak."

"Stop shoving!"

"What does he say?"

"Let the Day of the Lord come," the priest called out. "It's what we wait for. We are ready for it!"

Others called out in agreement.

Amos looked up at the wall lined with people. "The Day of the Lord will not be as you imagine."

The people fell silent.

Unable to say more, Amos walked away.

Ducking into the orchard where he had sat all morning, he ran.

+   +   +

Sitting in his cave, Amos pressed the heels of his hands against his eyes. *Judah!* His throat tightened. *Judah!*

"Prophet?" Someone stood outside, a dark silhouette against the setting sun. "May I speak with you?"

"Go away!"

"Please." A young voice, broken, questing. "I have to know. Is this judgment upon Judah certain, or will God show mercy upon us?"

Us?

Shuddering, vision blurred by tears, Amos rose. When the young man bowed before him, he shouted, "Get off your knees! Am I God that you would bow down to me?"

The young man scrambled to his feet and flinched as though expecting a blow. "You are the Lord's messenger!"

Shoulders sagging, Amos let out a long sigh, sat, and rested his staff across his knees. "Unwilling messenger." He scowled at the intruder. "What do you want?"

"Judah *will* be destroyed, or *may* be destroyed?"

Amos struggled with emotion. "If the people repent, perhaps the Lord will show mercy on us." Amos held out little hope of that happening. Only an invading army seemed to turn men's hearts back to God.

"I have family in Judah. Uncles, aunts, cousins."

"I have brothers." He saw something in the young man's face that made him soften. "Why are you here? What do you want of me?"

"You are the Lord's prophet. I want to know. Will not the Lord hear your prayers?"

"The Lord hears, but so far the Lord had said no to everything I've asked of Him. Better if you tell your uncles, aunts, and cousins to *repent*. Tell them to return to the Lord. Prod them. Plead with them. Pray they will listen!"

The young man looked toward Bethel. "The people of Bethel hang on your every word. They love what you have to say."

Amos leaned back, depressed. "Yes. They do, don't they?" Because every word that had come from his mouth thus far had proclaimed destruction on their enemies—or competitors.

"Is there no hope for Judah?"

"I told you. *Repent!* And why are you here in Bethel if you are a Judean?"

"I'm a Levite."

"All faithful Levites returned to Judah long ago."

The young man held his gaze. "Some felt impelled to return here."

"Impelled by God, or self-interest?"

Troubled, the young man bowed his head and didn't answer.

"Afraid to answer?"

The lad's eyes were awash with tears. "In truth, I don't know." He stood and walked away, shoulders slumped.

Amos went into his cave, sank down, and put his head in his hands.

+ + +

The Lord told Amos to return to Bethel and repeat the prophecies about the surrounding nations. Amos went, calling out as he entered the city. Crowds gathered eagerly to hear him. The young Levite stood in their midst. Unlike those around him who cheered, he listened intently, troubled rather than jubilant. He didn't approach Amos again.

Gifts continued to pile up outside the entrance of Amos's cave. He thanked God for the provisions and gave away everything but the little food he needed.

Each day, Amos preached on the steps of Bethel's temple. "Those who oppress the poor insult their Maker, but helping the poor honors Him."

The people listened, but did not apply the words to their own lives. Even the priests thought he spoke only of the surrounding nations and Judah to the south.

"Fools make fun of guilt, but the godly acknowledge it and seek reconciliation with God! Godliness makes a nation great, but sin is a disgrace to any people."

The people clapped at his preaching, nodding and smiling to one another. Was there any nation as religious as Israel? Fervent in worship, they flocked to the temples and shrines, singing and dancing. They poured out offerings. Puffed up with pride and prosperity, they grew smug and self-righteous. *Look at us! Look at the evidence of our righteousness!*

They had gold in abundance and an army ready to defend them. King Jeroboam II lived in splendor in the capital of Samaria, having succeeded in pushing back the borders to what they had been during the reign of the great King Solomon. Such blessing had to be a sign of God's approval.

Amos knew better. He preached on the sins of the nations, but no one saw any similarity to the way they thought and lived. They continued to look at the nations around them, rather than into their own hearts.

The trap was set . . . and would soon be sprung.

+   +   +

One afternoon Amos again found the young Levite waiting outside his cave, along with several others. He stood as Amos approached. "May I speak with you?" He spoke more softly. "In private?"

Amos sent the others away. Leaning on his staff, he looked at the young man. "You have not returned to Jerusalem."

"I spent a week with my relatives in Jerusalem. I told them everything you said."

"Good." Amos went inside. "Did they believe you?"

The young man followed him. "No."

"But you do."

"Yes."

Amos felt a softening toward this young man. He sat on his pallet and waited for the visitor to speak.

"Why do you live in such a mean place?"

"I would rather live in a cave, than trapped in the city."

The young man sat tensely. "I came back to explain why we're here and not in Jerusalem."

"Confess your reasons to God."

"God knows, and I want you to understand. There was not land or work enough for everyone in Jerusalem when my grandfather returned. I mean no disrespect, but the families who had lived and served in that district were not willing to step back and make room for others to serve."

Amos thought of Heled and Joram. The young man's words held the ring of truth. Like sheep, even the Levites had their butting order, and those long established in Jerusalem might have looked upon the influx of Levites with jaundiced eyes. He could not imagine Heled or others like him willingly giving up any of the benefits of their position, even to a brother in need.

"And I will confess—" the young man bowed his head—"Bethel has always been my home." He met Amos's eyes again. "My ancestors were born here."

"So you believe you belong here?"

"Perhaps God has kept me here for a reason."

"Do you follow after their ways?"

"Neither my father nor I nor any member of our family has bowed down to the golden calf, nor used the temple prostitutes."

"But you live comfortably in hypocrisy."

The young man's face reddened. "Would you have us live as they do?"

"Do they know you don't?"

"My father and I grieve over what you said about Judah."

"Grieving isn't enough to change God's mind." He leaned forward. "When our ancestors rebelled against the Lord in the desert, God was ready to wipe them out and make a dynasty of Moses' family. Moses pleaded for our salvation, and God changed His mind, withholding His wrath."

"Then you must pray for Judah!"

Amos nodded. "I have prayed, and will continue to do so, but I am *not* Moses."

"How many prayers will it take? My grandfather and father have prayed for years. I have prayed since I was a boy for Israel to return to God and for the tribes to reunite." The young man's eyes filled with tears. "Why is Jerusalem to be judged when Samaria and Bethel and Beersheba wallow in sin? You live here. You must see it even more clearly than I do. But it's different in Judea. King Uzziah worships the Lord our God and follows the Law. And Judah is to be consumed by fire?"

Lord, he speaks as I did. What is it in us that rejoices at the judgment upon others, while pleading that our sins be overlooked? "You will not be satisfied until everyone is dead. Better judgment should fall here on Israel than Judah. Is that it?"

"No. I did not mean that. I don't want that anyone should die."

"Then you are a better man than I. When the Lord first gave me these visions, I felt the same exhilaration I see in these people. *Destroy Assyria! Yes, Lord.* I see the gloating faces, hear the cruel laughter. *Send fire on the fortresses of Philistia and Phoenicia. Yes, yes! Consume Edom with fire. Crush the Ammonites. Wipe out the Moabites!* He gave a mirthless laugh. "But Judah? *My* home? *My* family? We're better than the rest, aren't we?" He shook his head. "We haven't the excuse of ignorance. We know when we turn our backs on God. We make the choice to go our own way. Isn't that worse than what others do? They don't even know better."

"But Jerusalem. The Temple. God resides there!"

Amos shook his head. "No temple is large enough to contain the Lord our God."

"Perhaps I have seen more of Jerusalem and the Temple Mount than you have. Sin may not be as rampant there yet as it is here, but the Temple of the Lord stands there—if there is any place on earth that should stand firm upon the Law, shouldn't it be there?"

Amos sighed, weary, heartsick. A year ago, he wouldn't have cared about what happened to these people. And then he had prayed and God had answered. Now he cared so much that his heart broke every time he thought of Jerusalem, every time he entered the gates of Bethel, every time he looked into the faces of the people who could not stand before the judgment of a righteous God, least of all he. God was holding the nations accountable for what they'd done against His people, but the Lord would also hold His people accountable for the way they live before the nations. God chose them to be His people. He called them out of Egypt to be unique, an example to all the nations. And look how they lived, chasing after worthless idols. Thankless, faithless children. Lost sheep.

"Today, in Bethel, men heard the Word of the Lord against Judah and were silent. Judgment hit close to home this time again, but do they even wonder?"

The young man paled. "Wonder what?"

"If it applies to them. The Lord sees what men do. He hears what they say and how they live. The Lord knows we are like sheep, prone to wander. We cast ourselves into sin and can't get out. We look for better pastures among the religions of the nations around us and feed on poison. We drink from other men's wells and are infected with parasites. And still, the Lord sends prophets to call the people back to Him. But do they listen?"

"I'm listening."

"Yes." Amos's muscles relaxed. Why would God send him to Bethel if there was no hope?

"King David said God is faithful. His faithful love endures forever."

Amos had never given much thought to the word the shepherd-king had used. "His love *endures.*"

God put up with their rebellious nature, suffered their rejection, and witnessed their desertion. God grieves over their lack of love. He sent prophet after prophet to call them back to Himself *before* He had to use His rod and staff of discipline. Even then, when discipline had to come, the Lord extended His mighty hand to deliver them again.

But then the cycle would repeat: faith for a generation, then complacency, soon followed by adultery as the people chased after false gods. Man decided how and what he wanted to worship and substituted idols for the living God. Sin took root and spread tendrils of arrogance and pride into every area of life. Eyes became blind to God's presence, ears deaf to His Word. And the curses came again, often not even recognized for what they were—a call to return to the Lord.

"His faithful love endures forever."

There were far worse things than discipline. *A father who does not discipline his son hates him.* The same held true of a nation.

If the northern tribes refused to listen again, God would let them go their own way. They would continue to follow after Jeroboam, the son of Nebat.

FOUR

"What are you doing here?" Ahiam glared. "Get away from our stalls! Go back to Israel."

Amos stood shocked at his brother's greeting. "I've just come from offering my sacrifices to the Lord."

"Offer them in Bethel, you betrayer."

Heat surged into Amos's face. "I betray no one!"

When his brother took a swing at him, Amos blocked it with his staff, resulting in Ahiam's yelp of pain as he hit the ground. He scrambled up, ready to attack Amos again, but Bani put himself between them.

"People have heard what you've been saying in Bethel, Brother. They are not happy."

"Don't call him 'brother'!" Ahiam raged. "He makes nothing but trouble for us. He always has!"

"What trouble have I made?" Amos ground out and then sneered. "Is business down?"

"You! A prophet!" Ahiam laughed derisively. "You look like a beggar in your shepherd's rags."

"Better a poor man than a dishonest one."

With a roar, Ahiam came at him again. Amos hooked his shepherd's staff around Ahiam's leg and flipped him onto his back. Bani tried to intercede, but Amos shoved him back. "I told you both before I left that the Lord had given me visions of the nations." When Ahiam tried to rise, Amos held the end of the staff over him. "You wouldn't even listen to me!"

Ahiam slapped the shepherd's staff away and rose, face flushed.

Amos stepped forward. "God sent me to Bethel, Ahiam, and the prophecies are not mine, but the Lord's."

"You speak against Judah!" Ahiam spat on the ground. "That's what I think of you."

Amos went cold and then hot. "It is not me you spit upon, Brother."

"Enough!" Bani shouted at them.

Startled, the sheep leapt and moved restlessly in the stalls. Amos went over and spoke softly to the animals. Ahiam raised his hands in frustration.

Bani turned to Amos. "Tell us what's happened."

"I tried to tell you. When God called me to prophesy, I resisted." He looked between them. "You needn't tell me I'm unworthy. I know better than you both that I am not a learned man. What I know of God, I learned in the pastures and from the stars. God forgive me, I still resist Him." His mouth worked. "But I *must* speak what the Lord tells me."

Ahiam brushed himself off. "And we're supposed to believe He speaks destruction upon *us*?" He pointed north. "We, who are more faithful than that nation you now call your own?"

"I am Judean."

"Then *why*?"

"Because God wants it so. The northern tribes are still our brothers, though they wander like lost sheep with wolves for shepherds. We were once one flock! *Twelve* sons of Jacob, *twelve* tribes that God made into a nation. Have we all forgotten that?"

"Jeroboam claimed God gave him the ten northern tribes, and look what that usurper did with them!"

"And God sends me to remind them they yet belong to the Lord. Why else would He send me to prophesy other than to confront their sin and call them back to Him?"

"It's not *their* sin you've confronted, is it? You cry down destruction on *us*! I'll bet they loved that message. I'll bet they paid you well."

Amos shook his head. "Who are we to be so self-righteous? We all sin against the Lord. Our family's wealth has grown out of it. And it will all turn to dust in our mouths if we don't repent."

"Don't preach at me." Ahiam flipped his hand, dismissing Amos's words. "We've known you since you were a baby messing yourself."

"A prophet is never heard in his own home or by his own family."

"You're misguided. You've been too long in the sun. You're beginning to bleat like your sheep."

"Careful what you say, Brother."

Something in Amos's voice silenced his brothers.

Bani spread his hands. "Forgive us if we have misunderstood. Tell us of the visions, Amos. Tell us everything."

"Yes." Ahiam's mouth twisted sardonically. "Tell us everything that we might be as wise as you."

Ignoring his older brother's sarcasm, Amos told them everything except the final vision he had yet to speak in Bethel.

Ahiam snorted. "Words to feed their pride. That's what you're giving them."

Sorrow filled Amos. "Pride goes before destruction, and haughtiness before a fall." He looked up at the Temple, then to the stalls of animals gained by deceit. He turned his gaze from the priests collecting fines to Bani and then to Ahiam. Grief overtook him, and fear for those he loved and could not convince. "Nothing is done in secret. The Lord sees what you do. He hears the words of your mouth. He knows what you hold most dear."

Ahiam frowned, but said nothing. Amos felt a moment of hope when he saw fear flicker in his brothers' eyes.

Fear of the Lord is the foundation of wisdom.

+ + +

"Make your offerings quickly," Bani said. "And give them to Elkanan or Benaniah. If Heled sees you, he will try to bar you from the Temple."

"Has he caused you trouble?"

"He is the one who told us of your prophecies against Judah."

"Is he unwilling to confess his sins before the Lord and repent?"

"It is no laughing matter, Amos!"

"Do you see me laughing?" He grasped Bani's arm. "Take the Lord's word to heart, Brother, before time runs out. I spoke the truth. Judah is judged! Repentance may bring mercy for a time, but you know as well as I how quickly men return to sin to make their own way in the world." Ahiam had given himself over to profits.

"And what would I do?"

"Be a shepherd again."

"Mishala would not be happy as a shepherd's wife, Amos."

"She would prefer it to being a widow. Without you, how will she live? How will she provide food for your children?" Many widows were forced to turn to prostitution for food money.

Amos gave his offerings and worshiped before the Lord. He spent the entire day inside the Temple, watching and listening. Not all the priests were like Heled, but the few who were had done great damage to the many who came with sincere hearts to worship the Lord.

I must keep my mind and heart fixed upon You, Lord, and not upon those who would lead me astray. How long had he allowed bitterness against Heled to rule his thinking?

He spent the night at his home in Tekoa. Eliakim gave him good reports about Ithai and Elkanan. They had faithfully obeyed Amos's instructions, and they had not traded spring lambs with Joram.

Amos walked with Eliakim to the boundary of his family's ancestral land. "If God allowed, I would stay."

Eliakim turned to him. "Will you return soon?"

"I will return to Jerusalem as often as the Law requires."

"I meant come home to stay. Here, in Tekoa."

"I know what you meant, Eliakim, but I don't know. I can only hope—" his throat tightened—"one day, perhaps, my friend. Look after everything as though I were here with you."

Eliakim bowed low. "May the Lord protect you."

"The eyes of the Lord are upon all the people, Eliakim. All His people." Judah and Israel might be God's chosen people, but the Lord rules the nations as well. Empires rise and fall at His command. Amos put his hand on Eliakim's shoulder. "God will strongly support the one whose heart is completely His." He looked back toward Jerusalem and thought of Bani and Ahiam. "Terrible days are coming."

He walked away, shoulders slumped with the burden of the message he carried to Israel, the same message only a few in Judah had heeded.

✦ ✦ ✦

The waiting was over.

Amos knew it the moment he entered the gates of Bethel. The Spirit of the Lord came upon him, and he saw everything differently. The beautiful woven veil of wealth had been lifted to reveal the corruption and foulness hidden beneath. Everywhere he looked, he saw sin.

His anger mingled with sorrow. He saw his own sin, too—his pride, his aloofness. He had withheld his love. Now, he walked among the people of Israel as he had his sheep, seeing both vulnerable lambs and dangerous predators.

The wealthy fed off the poor, stripping them of robes and sandals as collateral for loans that could never be repaid, while their wives lounged on Egyptian pillows in their second-story summer houses decorated with inlaid ivory furniture. Men hired to build in the city were cast out, their wages withheld by the wealthy to buy drink and delicacies.

The few men who dedicated themselves to the Lord as Nazirites were persecuted. Ordered to show their fealty to King Jeroboam, they drank wine before the elders who knowingly forced them to break their vows to God.

Everyone ran to do evil on that mountain with its golden calf. Incense smoke curled up from roofs. Mediums who claimed they could interpret dreams sat before the temple, grabbing their share of the offerings brought to the royal sanctuary. Idol makers thrived. These people were passionate for divination, and poured themselves out to wanton living and idol worship.

And yet God loved these lost people of Israel the way Amos loved and cared for his sheep. The truth shamed him and warmed his heart at the same time. And just as Amos sometimes found it necessary to wound a straying sheep in order to save it, so God must now discipline His straying people. If only they would listen, hear, before it was too late.

With new resolve, Amos strode up the street toward the temple of Bethel. "Come! Listen to the message that the Lord has spoken!"

"The prophet!"

"The prophet has returned!"

"Speak to us, Prophet!"

"Bring on the Day of the Lord!"

"We have been waiting for it to happen!"

"The nations will bow down before *us*!"

The excitement grew as Amos mounted the temple steps. He stopped halfway up and faced the people who stood eager to hear his words, certain he would proclaim continued prosperity and blessing. They nudged one another, gleeful, proud, stuffed with self-assurance. The square filled with excited people, all come to hear how God's wrath would be poured out on others. It was sin God hated, and here before him were a thousand sinners who believed they stood on firm foundations. They knew nothing.

Feed My sheep. . . .

Amos raised his staff. "This is what the Lord says: 'The people of Israel have sinned again and again, and I will not let them go unpunished!'"

"What is he saying about Israel?"

People murmured. People shifted. Some drew back slightly and began talking among themselves.

Amos pointed toward the priests gathered at the entrance of the temple. "They sell honorable people for silver and poor people for a pair of sandals. They trample helpless people in the dust and shove the oppressed out of the way."

A rumble began as people talked—confused, disappointed, angry.

Amos pointed toward the side streets and the temple brothels. "Both father and son sleep with the same woman, corrupting My holy name. At their religious festivals, they lounge in clothing their debtors put up as security. In the house of their god, they drink wine bought with unjust fines."

Faces flushed. Eyes narrowed. Mouths curled.

Amos threw his arms wide and cried out, "But as My people watched, I destroyed the Amorites, though they were as tall as cedars and as strong as oaks. I destroyed the fruit on their branches and dug out their roots. It was I who rescued you from Egypt and led you through the desert for forty years, so you could possess the land of the Amorites. I chose some of your sons to be prophets and others to be Nazirites."

Amos looked into dark, pitiless eyes. "'Can you deny this, My people of Israel?' asks the Lord."

He pointed to one, then another, and another. Faces hardening, they stared back.

He raised his staff again. "So I will make you groan like a wagon loaded down with sheaves of grain." Amos continued pointing as he came down the steps. " 'Your fastest runners will not get away. The strongest among you will become weak. Even mighty warriors will be unable to save themselves. The archers will not stand their ground. The swiftest runners won't be fast enough to escape. Even those riding horses won't be able to save themselves. On that day the most courageous of your fighting men will drop their weapons and run for their lives!' says the Lord."

People cried out from every side, some in fear, others in rage.

"Lies! He speaks lies."

"There must be some mistake!"

"He's demon-possessed!"

"We are the chosen people! Look at how God has blessed us!"

"He's mad!"

They had cheered and celebrated judgment on other nations for brutality, slave trade, broken treaties, and desecration of the dead, but cried out in anger when confronted with their own sins.

How many months had he sat here on these steps and seen what they deemed sacred? An unholy mix of perversion and greed! They bowed down to their fleshly desires and exploited the poor without a twinge of conscience. They mocked the righteous, continuing to follow the Law while revering a band of robber priests who fleeced them of their money and, in return, gave back false hopes and promises of safety from a hollow idol that couldn't even protect itself.

"Listen to this message that the Lord has spoken. . . ."

"You prophesied against the nations. How can you now prophesy against us?"

"We have given you gifts and treated you kindly!"

"We believed you!"

"Listen to this message that the Lord has spoken. . . ." Amos cried out again.

"This is the thanks we get for taking care of a foreigner!"

"But the Lord sent him!"

"He *says* the Lord sent him. I'm not so sure."

Amos raised his hands. "Listen to this message that the Lord has spoken against you, O people of Israel and Judah: 'From among all the families on the earth, I have been intimate with you alone. That is why I must punish you for all your sins.' "

"No!" men shouted.

"Not us!" women wailed.

Children cried in confusion.

Temple guards surrounded Amos. "Come with us!"

When he tried to get through them, his staff was wrestled from him and he was taken by force.

"This way, Prophet." They hauled him up the steps and inside the temple.

"Let go of me!"

"Do you think you can start a riot on the temple steps and not answer for it?" The captain ordered him taken to Amaziah, the high priest. The guards hit and punched Amos until he sagged, then half dragged him through a shadowed corridor to a chamber. "Keep him here." The captain entered a room and spoke in hushed tones to several priests.

Amos wiped blood from his mouth.

After what seemed hours, a plainly gowned priest came out. "I am Paarai ben Zelek, son and servant of the most high priest, Amaziah. You will come in now. Do not speak unless you are spoken to, Prophet. Do you understand?"

Amos's heart raged within him. But the Lord held his tongue.

Several priests stood talking to the high priest, who gazed out a window that overlooked the square. He took a long drink from a goblet, handed it to a servant, said something under his breath to the others, and turned. His head lifted as he studied Amos coldly. "I am Amaziah, high priest of the temple of Bethel."

"And I am Amos, servant of the Lord our God."

Amaziah gestured for Amos to come forward. Amos stood still, his gaze unfaltering.

The priest's eyes darkened. "We thought it best to bring you here. For your own protection, of course."

"If you wish to protect the people, you will let them listen to the message that the Lord has spoken!"

A muscle tensed in Amaziah's cheek, but he spoke calmly, even pleasantly. "You have thrilled our hearts with your prophecies over the past eighteen months." His eyes narrowed. "Why do you change your message now?"

"The message is not changed. Judgment is coming upon the nations, Judah and Israel included. Unless we humble our hearts and turn to the Lord, we have no hope."

The high priest spread his hands, the rich fabric of his robes flowing like dark wings around him. "This is the holy city." He raised his hands. "And this is the holy temple. You have lived here long enough to know our people are devoted to God—more devoted to God than anyone in Judah."

Amos went hot with fury. "Does that golden calf you worship have ears that can hear your prayers? Does it feel anything? Can it walk on its golden legs? Or utter one word from its golden throat?"

"Silence him!" Paarai commanded.

A guard hit him hard across the face.

Amaziah smiled faintly, eyes like obsidian. "You must not blaspheme the Lord."

"It is *you* who blaspheme the Lord."

The guards pummeled him until he lay half conscious on the floor. One kicked him hard in the side.

"Enough," Amaziah said and waved them away. "Lift him up."

A guard grabbed Amos and hauled him to his feet. Gritting his teeth, he kept from groaning aloud.

Amaziah reached for a golden pitcher. "A goblet of wine, perhaps. It is the finest in all Israel." When Amos didn't answer, he raised his brows. "No? A pity." He set the urn down. Crossing his arms, he tucked his hands into the heavy sleeves of his elaborately embroidered robe. "Why have you come to Bethel?"

"The Lord sent me to speak His Word to the people."

"And they have listened to you in growing numbers since you first entered our gates eighteen months ago. They have listened to your prophecies and brought offerings because of them."

Heat flooded Amos at the thought of those offerings being given to that hollow calf.

"The people have loved you." Amaziah smiled as he gently mocked. "Until today. Today, you spoke most unwisely, Amos."

"I spoke the truth."

"Truth as you see it, perhaps."

"I speak the words God gives me."

"Leave me alone with him."

"My lord?" The others protested.

Amaziah smiled and waved them away. "Paarai will remain with me."

Amos wondered what subterfuge the high priest intended to try. *Lord, give me wisdom*. The attending priests entered a side room, and the guards remained outside the door.

"You are not the only man to see visions, my young friend. I have had many visions over my years in the priesthood and received abundance because of them. And I tell you God's blessing is upon Israel. It is evident for all who have eyes to see. Look around you! We have wealth. We live in a time of great prosperity. We serve King Jeroboam, and he is as great as his grandfather, who was greater than Solomon's son Rehoboam."

Amaziah shook his head. "And yet you would tell our people we face destruction? We are strong enough now that no enemy dares come against us." He clicked his tongue. "You should go back to your sheep. The people will not listen to you now. You have overstayed your welcome." He shook his head in condescension. "We have nothing to fear from you."

"From me, no. But you should fear the Lord."

"Fear the one we love? Even after all these months of sitting on the temple mount and wandering our streets, you have learned so little about our people. You are blind and deaf. Have you missed the crowds who flock to the temple to give offerings to our god? Have you been deaf to their songs of praise? Have you failed to see the wealth of the temple itself? Our people are far more devout in worship and happy in life than those in Judah."

"I see those who prey on the poor, your rich women who eat like cows. They fatten themselves for the slaughter!"

"Father, do not allow him to speak—"

"Be quiet!" Amaziah's lips whitened. He spoke to his son as he glared at Amos. "A few stubborn fools still return to Jerusalem to worship, but they will not go back to the old ways. Nor do they need to. They have all they want right here."

Amos glared back. "Not for long." *Let these wicked 'priests' be disgraced, Lord. Silence their lying lips. Don't let them live long lives of leisure.*

Amaziah smiled coldly. "If you have such a calling to become a priest, why don't you bring us what is required and become one? We would welcome you to our society." He looked at Paarai. "Wouldn't we?"

Paarai hesitated and then agreed.

Amos narrowed his eyes. "Only a Levite can be a priest of the Lord."

"But apparently anyone can be a prophet." Amaziah smirked as he took in Amos's old clothes, his sandaled feet. "Here, in Bethel, you can be a priest *and* a prophet. That is the way it's done."

Paarai smiled.

Amos looked between them. "Once, we were one nation under God."

"You live in the past, Amos. It is unwise."

"Are you threatening to kill me?"

"If I wanted to see you dead, I would have left you to the mob." Amaziah clucked his tongue. "You disappointed them today."

"I told them the truth."

The high priest's eyes flashed. "Where is your evidence? Where is the lightning and thunder? Nor have your other prophecies proven true. Had even one come about, your name would be great in Israel, and your place among the prophets assured. But all is as it has been. Nothing has changed. We merely grow stronger while you crow like a rooster."

Paarai chuckled. "Careful you do not cause so much disruption you end up in a stew."

Amos saw them clearly. Evil men who had no fear of God to restrain them. In their blind conceit, they couldn't see how vile they really were. Everything they had said thus far was crooked and deceitful. "Everything will happen just as the Lord has said, and it will happen in His time, not yours."

"We await the Day of the Lord as eagerly as you do." Amaziah's voice took on lofty tones. "For in that day, all our enemies will be put under our heel!"

"So speaks the Lord." Paarai's eyes glowed.

The Spirit of the Lord took hold of Amos and spoke through him. "What sorrow awaits you who say, 'If only the Day of the Lord were here!' You have no idea what you are wishing for. That day will bring darkness, not light."

Amaziah's eyes went black. "You do not listen well, do you? Some men must learn the hard way." He raised his voice. "Guards, take him! Give him twenty lashes and send him on his way." He pointed at Amos. "Your false prophecies will gain you nothing. The people will never listen to you!"

"Repent! For judgment is at hand."

Paarai smirked as the guards entered and took hold of Amos. "Get him out of here."

+   +   +

It was night when Amos was thrown out of the temple. He fell down the steps, banging his shins, his shoulder, his head. As he lay at the bottom, he heard a voice from above him.

"Don't forget this!"

His staff clattered down the steps. He reached for it, using it to brace himself as he slowly stood. On fire with pain, shoulder and head aching, Amos managed to stumble from the square.

"There he is. . . ."

Fearful of another beating, Amos hurried down a narrow street. A wave of dizziness came over him and he fell against a wall. He clutched his staff, his only defense. But someone grasped it and held it still.

"Let me help you, Amos." The voice was familiar. Amos looked up. Though his vision was blurred, he recognized the young Levite who had come to ask him questions about Judah.

"You . . ."

"This is the man I've told you about, Father." He slipped his arm around Amos. "When the guards took you inside the temple, I went for my father. We've been waiting. . . ."

Amos groaned in pain.

The older man took charge. "We will take him home with us and see to his wounds."

The two men lifted him to his feet and supported him on each side. "Easy."

"Our house is not far from here, Amos."

They half carried him down a street, around a corner, and through a doorway. Amos lifted his head enough to see the dimly lit room. A woman asked whom they had brought.

"The man I told you about, Mother. The prophet of the Lord our God."

"Oh! What have they done to him?"

"We'll explain later, Jerusha." The father sent her for water as they helped Amos to a pallet.

Amos fought the waves of nausea.

"Rest, now. You are safe here." The older man squeezed his shoulder. "You are fortunate your skull didn't crack like a melon on those steps."

"I have a hard head."

The elder man smiled grimly. "A prophet of the Lord needs one. I am Beeri. Jerusha is my wife."

She knelt and began to gently wash his bruised and bleeding face. "Our son, Hosea, has told us much about you."

Amos took the damp cloth from Jerusha's hand. "I will see to my own wounds."

She blushed. "I did not wish to offend. . . . "

"You didn't. I must go. I do not want to bring trouble on you." When he tried to get up, he gasped in pain.

All three protested. "There is nowhere for you to go, Amos. The gates are closed for the night. You can't sleep out in the cold. Stay with us. Please!"

Amos sank back with a grimace.

Hosea hunkered down before him. "His eyes are swelling shut, Father."

"We have balm that will help heal his wounds." Jerusha crossed the room and took something from a cupboard.

Darkness closed in, and Amos felt gentle hands lower him.

When next he opened his eyes, moonlight streamed through a high window. He saw Hosea sleeping on a nearby pallet. A small clay lamp cast a soft glow, by which he could see a table, two small benches, some storage urns, bowls, a water jug, a cabinet built into the wall. Every bone and muscle in his body ached when he pushed himself up.

Hosea also sat up. "You're awake!"

"Barely."

"How do you feel?"

"As though someone whipped me and threw me down some stone steps."

"You've lain like death for three days."

So long! He remembered none of it. "May the Lord bless you for your kindness." Had he made it outside the city, he might have been lying in a field somewhere, unconscious and prey to scavengers.

"How is your head?"

Amos felt the bandages. He had a slight headache, but the dizziness was gone. "I'll live." His stomach growled loudly.

"It will be morning soon." Hosea grinned. "My mother will make bread."

Amos smiled.

"It is good to have you as our guest, Amos." He grimaced. "Despite the circumstances, of course."

Amos rubbed his head. A bump still protruded, but it was not as tender as the day he had received it. He still had trouble seeing, and realized after a slight exploration that his eyelids were swollen almost shut.

"I can't serve you bread, but there is some wine."

"A little wine and I'd probably sleep for another two days. Water, please." Amos found his staff beside the pallet and struggled to rise.

Hosea helped him. "Please. Don't go. Everyone shouted so loudly in the square I could not hear what you had to say. I want to know what you prophesied about Israel."

"It is the Lord's Word and not mine that stands against Israel for all its many sins."

"You said God will punish Damascus, Gaza, Tyre, Edom, Ammon, Moab, and Judah. And now God will bring judgment on Israel as well. The entire world is condemned. Not one nation will remain standing after God's judgment."

Amos sank wearily onto the bench and leaned his forearms on the table. "Judah will be the last to fall."

"Is there hope if Judah repents?"

"There is always hope when a nation repents." But they seldom did. It took famine, drought, or flood to bring a nation to its knees before God. It took war!

Hosea poured water and handed the cup to Amos. "But Judah will still fall in the end?"

Amos drank deeply and held out the cup for more. "Men fell long ago and still refuse the hand of God to help them rise again." He drained the cup again.

"What then will be left, Amos?"

"God's promise, my young friend. You reminded me that His faithful love endures forever. So it does. His mercy is poured out upon those who love Him. The eyes of the Lord search the whole earth in order to strengthen those whose hearts are fully committed to Him. Destruction will come as surely as the sun rises in the morning, but a remnant will remain. Men like you who love the Lord and want to follow Him. The rest will be like chaff in the wind, here one day and gone the next."

"I should feel more hope than I do. I feel I must do something to help you."

"*Listen*. And encourage others to do likewise. And then do what the Lord commands."

The sun rose and with it Beeri and Jerusha. She prepared the morning meal. They prayed and broke bread together.

"Why don't you stay here in Bethel, Amos?" Hosea looked at his father. "Wouldn't it be far better for him to live here with us?"

Beeri nodded.

Amos fought the temptation. "More convenient, perhaps, but dangerous for you. I have a place to live."

"At least stay a few more days." Jerusha offered him more bread. "Until you've recovered from your fall."

Amos thanked them.

After another day, Amos longed to stay. He enjoyed the conversations with Beeri and Hosea that lasted far into the night, always centering on the Lord and His commandments.

Beeri worked as a scribe, and Hosea studied the scrolls his father kept in the cabinet. Jerusha used what little money they had wisely. Beeri read from the Scriptures locked in the cabinet each evening. Much he knew by memory, and Hosea along with him. "They were taken away once," Beeri told him, "but I had another copy hidden."

Beeri questioned Amos only once. "How is it a prophet of God does not know the Scriptures?"

"I've spent my life in the pastureland with my sheep. Other than a few years when I was a boy, I've had little opportunity to sit before a rabbi and learn the Law. What I know is given to me by God."

Beeri was quick to apologize. "I did not mean to question your calling, Amos."

"I take no offense, but I will say that had I had the opportunity, I doubt I could do as you have done. Some men have minds that can take in knowledge, like you and Hosea. What I know is the land, the night skies, my sheep."

Beeri nodded. "That is a great deal in itself, my friend."

"The Lord is our shepherd," Hosea said. "Surely the Lord sent you here to show us the way home."

"I've usually had to deal with a few wayward sheep." Amos shook his head. "But never an entire flock such as Israel so determined to find trouble."

After six days Amos knew he must leave. Here, in this quiet, devout household, he slept comfortably, ate well, and enjoyed warm fellowship. But, in this small dwelling tucked away in the labyrinth of Bethel, among these hospitable people, he could not hear the Lord's voice as he could when he stood beneath the stars in an open field.

"I must go."

"Back to Jerusalem?" Hosea leaned forward, eager. "Say the word and I will go with you!"

"No. I must go out into the hills and return to my place of rest."

"But it's only a cave."

"I've slept at the entrance of many caves, Hosea. It is a sheepfold and reminds me of the simpler life I had before the Lord called me to come to Bethel."

Jerusha looked downcast, Beeri confused. "Surely this is more comfortable than a cave."

"Yes, it is." But distracted by the pleasure of their company, he could not clear his mind long enough to hear the quiet Voice that directed his footsteps and his words.

Neither Hosea nor his father tried to convince him otherwise. Jerusha filled his scrip with roasted grain and raisins, almonds and barley bread.

Just before dusk, Hosea walked with him to the city gate. When he started to follow Amos outside, Amos turned.

"Go back, Hosea. Convince your father to move to Judah. Go to Tekoa and speak with my servant, Eliakim. Tell him I sent you. He will help you find a priest in Jerusalem to help you get settled. I know it will be difficult to start over there, but you have no future here."

Hosea nodded. "I will tell my father everything you have said."

"May the Lord bless you and protect you. May the Lord smile on you and be gracious to you. . . ." He could not finish.

Hosea clasped his hand. "May the Lord show you His favor and give you His peace."

Amos walked away, shoulders bent and aching. *Spare them, Lord. Pluck them out of the destruction to come. Especially young Hosea, who has such a hunger and thirst for You.*

+ + +

The first night proved the most difficult, for after days with kind friends, loneliness set in and with it a longing to go home to Tekoa and his sheep. The Lord spoke to him in his dreams. When Amos awakened with the dawn, he rose with renewed strength.

Return to Bethel and speak to My people again.

He knew what he must do. If it meant another lashing, another beating, or even death, Amos would do what the Lord called him to do.

Still bruised and sore, he limped down the hill and stood at the gates, waiting for them to open. When they did, he went forward, staff in hand.

The guard looked far from pleased. "You!"

Without a word, Amos walked past him and up the street. He stood in the temple square. "The idols you've made will disgrace you. They are frauds. They can do nothing for you. The Lord your God is the Creator of everything that exists, and you are His special possession. Come back to

Him. Turn away from godless living and sinful pleasures. We should live in this world with self-control, right conduct, and devotion to God!"

The few who paused to listen quickly changed their minds and passed him by. Guards stood at the temple doorway, sniggering.

After a week, the temple guards locked him in stocks.

+   +   +

Issachar came in the night and spoke from behind a pillar. "You should say the things you first said, Amos. Then you wouldn't be locked up in the stocks. You wouldn't be a joke to everyone who passes by."

Amos lifted his head. Had Issachar come only to taunt? "I speak the Word of the Lord." Exhausted, every muscle aching, hungry, thirsty, he fought the depression filling him. "You would do well to heed it."

After a nervous glance around, Issachar came out and stood before him. "You've only to look around Bethel to see how God has blessed us!" He spoke low, half pleading, half frustrated.

Amos felt Issachar's tension. He watched him look around and edge back toward the deeper shadows. "Fear God, not men."

Issachar leaned close, angry. "I'm here for your own good. Stop speaking against Israel. You insult us!"

"God gives you an opportunity to repent."

"*Raca!* Fool. You're going to get yourself killed if you keep on this way." He disappeared into the night without offering so much as a piece of dried bread or a sip of water.

"This is your hour, Issachar. The hour of darkness." Amos wept softly.

+   +   +

Though he became a joke in Bethel, he did not stop speaking the Word of the Lord after he was released from the stocks.

Every morning, he came into city. Every day, he spoke.

No one listened. No one left gifts at the entrance of his cave anymore. His only regret over that was not having anything to offer the poor he saw each time he entered the city, the men whose robes and sandals had been stripped from them as collateral for debts they would never be able to pay. Amos writhed inwardly over the mercilessness of the rich. He could only offer encouragement to the poor whose outer garments had not been returned when the night chill set in. "The Lord hears your prayers." Even they would not listen to him.

He saw the widow in the marketplace again. She saw him as well and turned her back to him, ordering her hungry children to do the same.

No one listened to him anymore. Those who had so relished the first prophecies turned deaf ears to anything said against Israel.

Lord, when they see me on the street, they turn the other way. I am ignored as if I were dead!

For six months, he stood waiting at the gates in the morning and departed just before they were shut at night. Day after day, Amos preached the Word of the Lord and day after day, he suffered mockery and disdain. The neophyte priests gloated while Amaziah watched balefully from a high temple window.

Even as he cried out the truth, people walked up the steps and into the temple of Bethel, day by day sealing their fate with their indifference toward the Lord. Life and death were before them.

And they continued to embrace death with foolish abandon.

+ + +

"Listen to the message that the Lord has spoken!"

"He's back again," people muttered.

"Who is he?" visitors to the city asked.

"Just a self-proclaimed prophet. He never says anything good."

"He just harps on and on about our sins."

"Don't pay any attention. He's mad."

Someone bumped Amos. "Go back to your sheep!"

Another bumped, harder this time, almost knocking him from his feet. "We're not a bunch of sheep you can herd."

Another shoved him. No one made an effort to stop them.

Amos raised his staff. "Listen, O Israel. You have sinned against the Lord your God!"

The youths backed off, laughing and cursing him.

"Why don't you shut up!" someone shouted. "We spend more time worshiping the Lord than you do! All you do is talk and talk."

Others took up the cry. "He talks and talks."

Others laughed. "And nothing happens."

Amos looked at his tormentors. "Can two people walk together without agreeing on the direction? Does a lion ever roar in a thicket without first finding a victim? Does a young lion growl in its den without first catching its prey? Does a bird ever get caught in a trap that has no bait? Does a trap spring shut when there's nothing to catch? When the ram's horn blows a warning, shouldn't the people be alarmed?"

"And I suppose you're the trumpet?"

Men and women laughed. "Listen to him trumpet doom!"

Amos kept on. "Does disaster come to a city unless the Lord has planned it?"

"What disaster, Prophet? Where?"

"Just ignore him. He doesn't know what he's talking about."

People walked away.

Amos raised his voice. "Indeed, the Sovereign Lord never does anything until He reveals His plans to His servants the prophets. The lion has roared—"

"Sounds more like a mewing kitten to me!"

More laughter.

"So who isn't frightened? The Sovereign Lord has spoken—so who can refuse to proclaim His message?"

"Go back to your cave in the hills!"

"No wonder he speaks of lions and birds. He lives like an animal."

Amos paced on the temple steps. "Announce this to the leaders of Philistia and to the great ones of Egypt: 'Take your seats now on the hills around Samaria, and witness the chaos and oppression in Israel.'"

"You said Philistia was to be destroyed! Have you changed your mind?"

"False prophet!"

"He makes no sense."

"'Therefore,' says the Sovereign Lord, 'an enemy is coming! He will surround them and shatter their defenses!'" Amos shouted, his throat raw from speaking. "Then he will plunder all their fortresses." Filled with the Spirit of the Lord, Amos strode up a few steps, standing below the entrance to the temple of Bethel. "This is what the Lord says: 'A shepherd who tries to rescue a sheep from a lion's mouth will recover only two legs or a piece of an ear.' So it will be when the Israelites in Samaria are rescued—" Amos's voice caught—"with only a broken bed and a tattered pillow."

Tears ran down his cheeks. "'Now listen to this, and announce it throughout all Israel,' says the Lord, the Lord God of Heaven's Armies. 'On the very day I punish Israel for its sins, I will destroy the pagan altars at Bethel. The horns of the altar will be cut off and fall to the ground.'"

The ground beneath Amos trembled.

"Did you feel that?" someone spoke in alarm.

Amos's lungs filled. Fire and strength poured through his body. "And I will destroy the beautiful homes of the wealthy—their winter mansions and their summer houses, too—all their palaces filled with ivory—" Amos roared like a lion—"*says the Lord!*"

Another tremor, longer this time.

People looked at one another. "What's happening?"

The ground rolled; the earth quaked.

Some cried out. Others screamed.

A low rumble sounded from the depths of the earth. The giant stones of the temple grated against each other. People poured outside, shrieking with terror. They covered their heads. A section of the portico fell with a mighty crash, shattering stone in all directions. People fled down the steps. Some tripped and fell, tumbling, taking others down with them. A dozen disappeared beneath the falling wall of a temple brothel. Broken lamps spread ignited oil that fed on the expensive Babylonian draperies, and smoke billowed from summer houses.

People knocked one another down in their panic. A woman in her finery lay trampled at the base of the temple steps.

Bumped and jostled by the fleeing crowd, Amos fought to maintain his balance.

Oh, God, don't let it be too late. Have mercy upon them! Have mercy. . . .

Amos saw a mother and child trampled on the street. By the time he reached them, they were dead.

Surrounded by screams of terror, Amos braced himself and raised his staff. "Repent before it's too late!" Dust billowed around him. *"Repent!"*

The din of chaos and terror swallowed his voice.

FIVE

Even when the earthquake ended, dust continued to billow from collapsing buildings and portions of the city wall. The screaming subsided, and people moved around in shock, climbing over the debris-filled streets as they called for loved ones. Many were trapped inside buildings.

Every few hours, the earth trembled again, with less violence than before. But with each aftershock, the people's fear rose. Some panicked and fled the city, leaving the helpless to cry pitifully for help. Others worked frantically to uncover family members. Many died, crushed beneath their ashlar houses.

Amos stayed to help. "There's another over here!" He lifted stones carefully so that he wouldn't cause others to fall inward on the moaning person beneath the pile.

"Amos . . ." A soft groan came from beneath the rubble, a bloody hand extended.

Amos worked quickly, carefully, and uncovered Issachar.

"Amos . . ." He grasped Amos's hand tightly. His mouth moved, but no words came. His eyes pleaded as he coughed. Blood trickled from the corner of his mouth. His hand gripped tighter, eyes filled with fear. He choked.

Amos stayed with him until his struggle ended. Then he rose to help others. "Here! There's another here!"

People scrambled over fallen stones. Some came to help. Others used the confusion to steal whatever they could grab.

"Stop, thief! Stop him! He's stealing from my shop!"

A young man raced down the street, leaping over rubble as a goldsmith cried for help. Amos ignored the thief as he lifted another stone. A naked prostitute stared up at him with dead eyes. The man who had shared her bed had been crushed beneath a wall.

"Help me. . . ." A weak voice came from farther back, inside the tumbled structure.

A hand protruded from a narrow hole, fingers moving as though to seek the light. "Help me, please." A woman's broken voice.

Amos took her hand. "I'm here." Her fingers tightened as she sobbed. After removing several stones and fallen timbers, he reached her. He grabbed a Babylonian drapery to cover her. She cried out in pain as he lifted her and carried her over the rubble. Placing her gently on the stones of the courtyard, he left her among other wounded.

A priest appeared at the top of the temple steps, his vestments dust covered. He scrambled over the fallen stones and made his way down the steps. When he reached the bottom, he looked at Amos, face ashen with shock. "Did you do this to us, Prophet?"

"Am I God that I can make the world tremble?"

"The horns of the altar are broken! And the golden calf . . ."

Amos felt exultant. "What? You mean it couldn't run away and save itself?"

"Blasphemy!"

"Look around you, Priest. Look and be warned! If you set up that golden calf again, worse will befall the people. You will be the goat that leads them to slaughter!"

Another aftershock rattled the doors of the temple, and the priest's eyes went wide with fear. Dodging falling stones, he stumbled away, joining another holy man who had managed to run from the temple with the first wave of terrified worshipers, and now sat bereft and confused. Watching Amos, they leaned close and talked.

Amaziah came out of the temple. Clearly shaken, he stared at Amos.

"Come and help your people!" Amos shouted, but the old man ducked inside again.

Night began to fall. Dozens of people still needed help. Amos worked through the night, resting when he could not go on. When he could do no more, he made his way to the city gate that stood open, damaged.

Guards shouted orders. "Heave! Again! Heave!" Rock tumbled.

Bodies had been laid out in a line outside the walls, awaiting burial.

This is not the vision I saw, Lord. This was not devastation. This was only a sound shaking, a warning to listen.

He overheard two merchants. "Jerusalem is worse off than we are."

Jerusalem! Horrified, Amos ran down the road. Had Bani and Ahiam survived? What of their wives and children?

Stumbling, he stopped to pull the hem of his long robe up between his knees and tuck it securely into his belt. His fear had overtaken his reason. He couldn't run all the way to Jerusalem. Setting off again at a brisk walk, he tried to restrain his panic.

Nearly three hours later, he reached the top of a hill and leaned on his staff to catch his breath, seeing Jerusalem in the distance. Solomon's Temple caught the sunlight and shone brilliant white and gold. Amos gave a cry of relief.

Tents dotted the hillsides, sheltering the hundreds who had left the city until the aftershocks subsided. Everywhere was the din of human voices as people searched for friends and family members. Donkeys brayed. Camels bellowed.

Merchants lined the road to Jerusalem with their booths.

"Tents of the finest goatskin!"

"Water jars!"

"Oil lamps!"

"Blankets."

Supplies had been brought from other towns and were being dispensed by soldiers keeping order.

The Sheep Gate stood open and still intact. Amos pressed his way through the throng and headed toward the Temple Mount. If he didn't find Bani and Ahiam near their stalls, he would go to their homes.

He spotted his brothers repairing a pen while young boys kept the nervous sheep contained. "Bani! Ahiam!" He ran and embraced each of them. "You are alive!" He drew back and looked them over. "You are not hurt?"

"You're shaking, little brother." Bani took Amos by the arm and made him sit. Dipping a gourd cup into a barrel of water, he held it out.

"I came as soon as I heard. . . ." Amos drank deeply. "Bethel was struck also. The damage is horrendous." He wiped droplets of water from his beard.

Ahiam looked up at the Temple. "God did this because King Uzziah sinned."

Amos raised his head. "Sinned? How?"

"Three days ago, he went into the Temple with a censor in his hand and lit the incense."

It was a great sin, indeed, to usurp the privileges ordained by God to the priesthood. Had Uzziah attempted to take over the Temple and do things his own way just as Jeroboam, the son of Nebat, had done?

Bani handed Amos another cup of water. "The priests were in an uproar trying to stop him."

Ahiam pointed. "I was over there when the king came up the hill. I knew something was happening, so I followed the entourage inside. Several of the priests met the king and argued with him."

"I heard the uproar from here. It sounded like a riot. I went running to see what was going on."

"Even the high priest couldn't dissuade Uzziah," Ahiam said. "The king intended to make a fragrant offering to the Lord, and no one was going to stop him."

"The minute he lit—"

"Let *me* tell him!" Ahiam gave Bani a shove. "I was there, not you."

"So tell him!"

Amos grew impatient. "One of you tell me; it matters not which."

Ahiam waved his hand. "The moment King Uzziah lit the incense, he was covered with leprosy. I've never heard a man scream like that. The judgment of the Lord was on him and he knew it! The priests rushed him out of the Temple."

"And then the earthquake started."

"Only minor damage to the Temple," Ahiam said, "though I thought it would come down on our heads."

"Some areas of the city were hit hard. Hundreds are homeless."

"Your homes?"

"Both need repair, but at least we still have roofs over our heads. And our wives and children are safe."

"Where is King Uzziah now?"

"No one knows for sure. In seclusion. Somewhere outside the city, safe and guarded. His son, Jotham, brought guilt offerings yesterday and today."

"And the priests have been in constant prayer since it happened."

Ahiam straightened and went back to work fitting two rails together. "Our situation has changed over the past few days."

Somewhat rested, Amos stood and gave him a hand. "How do you mean?"

Bani answered. "Heled was killed. Squashed like a bug under a fallen building." He gave a short, mirthless laugh. "At a money changer's office."

Amos saw that fear of the Lord had taken root in Ahiam's eyes. For Amos, it was a spark of hope in a sea of darkness. *Let it grow, Lord. Let it flourish into awe and worship so that my brothers might not sin against You again.* "God sees what men do. He knows their hearts."

"So you have said. Perhaps you should tell me again what you saw. I failed to listen last time you were here."

Amos did tell him. All day, they talked. When he went to Bani's house, the family gathered. They listened, quiet and intent, grim-faced and with a fear that went deeper than what had been aroused by the earthquake.

Amos awakened in the predawn hours. The clay lamp cast a soft glow. Ahiam sat silent, staring at him.

Sitting up slowly, Amos looked back at him, and frowned. "What's wrong?"

"Stay here, Amos. Stay in Jerusalem. Speak to our people about what the Lord has told you."

Amos shook his head. God had already sent a prophet to Jerusalem. "Listen to Isaiah. I must go where God called me to go."

Ahiam lowered his eyes. "If all you say is true . . ."

"If?"

Ahiam lifted his head. "A prophet is seldom recognized by his own family, Amos. You know how I've doubted you." He grimaced. "Because you're my brother. My *younger* brother. I've known you since you were a baby. You've always been hotheaded and opinionated. And now you—" he struggled for words—"you speak with authority. I believe you, Amos, but God help my unbelief."

"Nothing I've said has not been said before by God Himself. He made it known to us from the beginning. We've simply forgotten." Amos shook his head. "No. Not forgotten. We *rejected* His Word. He told us of the blessings He would pour upon us if we followed Him. He also warned us of the cursings if we turned our backs on Him. It's all there in the Scriptures." Beeri had read them aloud to him. "Though the priests may speak little of it these days."

"Even where there was obedience, Amos, there was hardship."

"Of course. Life is hard. Knowing God makes a vast difference in how we live. Don't you long to see that cloud overhead again? that pillar of fire that kept the darkness back?" How Amos longed for those days when there was physical evidence of God's presence. But even then, men refused to believe. "When I have heard God's voice speak to me, I have felt *alive*, Ahiam. Even when I have not rejoiced at the message I must carry, I rejoice that He still speaks to men, even simple shepherds like me."

"If you asked God, would He listen to your prayer? Would He let you stay here among your brethren?"

"I did ask, Ahiam. I spent months out in the pastureland arguing and pleading with the Lord to take this burden from me." He shook his head. "I must go back to Israel."

"But you've told them what will come! You've done what God sent you to do."

"They've yet to hear."

"You told them! If they refuse to listen, then their blood is on their own heads. I've heard about the way you were treated. They welcomed the judgments upon the nations around them. They even rejoiced when they heard Judah would be overrun by enemies. Has anything changed?"

Amos shrugged. He had been popular for a while. He had drawn crowds until he told them what the Lord said about Israel. The priests had always watched him with jaundiced eyes, coveting the crowds who gathered to hear him speak. As long as the prophecies focused on the sins of the surrounding nations, they could say little against him without the people wondering why. But as soon as the Lord focused His judgment upon Israel, all restraints were removed. It had been easy to drive the frightened, angry flock back into the stall of the golden calf and serve them up to idol worship.

"They didn't listen, did they?" Ahiam challenged. "Not any more than I did."

"No. They didn't. Perhaps the earthquake will open their eyes and ears as it has yours. Now is the time to speak. Now, before it's too late."

"For how long, Amos?"

"How long does it take to decide to turn back from destruction, Ahiam? One word from the Lord may be enough now to make them repent and trust in God again."

"One decision isn't enough, Amos. Don't you understand? They will hear you for a day, a week, maybe a month or two. But they must decide each day what they will do. Each and every day, from now on."

"What hope can they find in the protection of golden idols and pagan worship? It's all smoke, Ahiam, sweet-smelling and deadly."

"They may not find truth, Amos, but they find pleasure. God has allotted seventy years to men—maybe more, maybe less. That's not long on this earth. And you said yourself, life is difficult. They have shaken off the burden of the Law. They won't easily shoulder it again." He rose. "They will turn on you, Amos. They will tear you to pieces like a pack of wolves."

"Yes. Or they may repent."

"Israel, Judah. We share the same blood. I believe you now, Amos, and yet, I don't believe you. I want to believe God is the one who rules, but forty-five years in the shadow of the Temple has shown me how men work—men like Heled."

"Heled is dead. You're free."

"Free of him. Free to wonder who will try to enslave me now." Ahiam looked away, the muscle working in his jaw. "I can only hope to align myself with priests who fear the Lord." He turned back to Amos. "As you did, Brother. As you taught Ithai and Elkanan. But there are precious few you can trust these days."

"More today than yesterday!" The earthquake would shake men's souls.

"Perhaps." Ahiam gave him a tight smile. "Time will tell, won't it?"

Amos put on his outer robe. "I must go."

Ahiam grasped his arm. "Don't. Stay here." Tears filled his eyes. "Help us rebuild."

A surge of emotion swept through Amos. If he stayed, he would be disobeying God. The priests of Israel would not easily release their hold on the lost sheep they had rustled from God and now held captive with lies. Amos's eyes grew hot and moist, for he knew Ahiam did not understand the spiritual battle that raged in Amos. He missed his family. He loved Judah. But Amos felt the stirring within his soul. The call to go back to Bethel. If he didn't . . .

"The safest place I can be is in the will of God, Ahiam."

"They will kill you."

"I can't think about that. I must speak. I am compelled to do so. The Word burns in my soul like a consuming fire." God cared passionately about His people. God fathered and mothered mankind, and yet His children wandered away in the wilderness. "I must call out to them, Ahiam." God had sent him to call Israel home to Him, to warn them of punishment if they refused. For to keep going the way they were meant eternal death, separation from God for all time.

Amos took up his belt, wound it around his waist, and tied it securely. "Do not make me question what God calls me to do." He put on his sandals.

Ahiam followed him out the door. "You're my brother, Amos. We've had our differences, but . . . I love you."

An admission choked out and all the more precious. Amos embraced him tightly. "Better if you love God." He took his staff and left.

+ + +

A cry went up from the watchtower as Amos came up the road to Bethel. "The prophet! The prophet returns!"

He stopped when a dozen well-armed warriors poured out the gate. Heart in his throat, he clutched his staff. Did they intend to arrest him? Would they drag him into their temple this time, place him on trial, and execute him?

The warriors took their places in two perfect lines on either side of the road, backs rigid, eyes straight ahead. The elders waited before the gate. Amos drew air into his lungs, straightened, and walked forward. He stopped, face-to-face with the judges and elders. A crowd gathered on the wall and behind the open gates.

"You have returned to us."

He could not tell if they were pleased or dismayed, but the fear in their eyes was evident. "Yes. I have returned." These people burdened his heart and mind.

"Do you have more to tell us?"

"I will speak only what the Lord gives me to speak."

They all began talking at once. They praised and pleaded, cajoled and flattered. Foolishly, they thought a prophet held the power to bring about natural disasters.

He raised his hands. "Quiet! Listen to me. It is the Lord you should fear. Not I. I bring you His Word, but power rests in *His* hands!"

"But will you be our advocate?" One of the judges came forward. "Will you plead for us before God?"

He had not been called by God to be their advocate, but to warn them to repent, to tell them of what lay ahead if they did not. Though they slay him, he must speak the truth. Life and death lay before them; they must choose. "The eyes of the Lord watch over those who do right, and He hears their prayers."

"Will God leave us alone? Or does He intend to bring further disaster on us?"

Amos looked around at the faces pressed close and waiting for his answer. "The Lord has told you what He will do if you don't repent. He turns His face against those who do evil, and He will erase the memory of them from the earth."

A nervous twitter ran through the crowd. An elder spoke. "When you first came to us, all your prophecies were against our enemies. Why do you now turn against us? Why do you call down destruction upon a city devoted to worship?"

Angry, Amos stepped toward the accuser. "I have spoken openly for two years, and you have not heard a word of what I've said!" He thrust out his staff, pointing up the street. "If that golden calf you love had any power at all, would it have been toppled from its altar?" People moved back from him as he searched their faces. "The Sovereign Lord never does anything until He reveals His plans to His servants the prophets. I have told you the Word of the Lord. *If* you listen, *if* you learn, *if* you turn your hearts and minds fully to the Lord your God, perhaps He will change His mind and withhold judgment."

"Then teach us," someone called from the back. "I will listen."

"So will I!"

"As will I!"

So many spoke in quick agreement. Was their acquiescence a sign of repentance? Or were they merely attempting to mollify a prophet they mistakenly believed had the power to turn away God's wrath?

"I will tell you what the Lord says: My people have forgotten how to do right. Their fortresses are filled with wealth taken by theft and violence." He saw the subtle change of expression in some of their faces: a stubborn tilt of chin, glittering eyes. The hint of rebellion stood all around him. He did not retreat. "You may fool me with your words. But do not think you can fool God. He sees your hearts and knows your inner thoughts. And He will judge you accordingly."

"Stop your shoving!" someone grumbled.

A man in front of Amos lurched aside as someone behind him shoved forward. A diminutive man with a scruffy beard stepped up, ignoring the muttered curses directed at him. "It would be my honor if you would come with me, Prophet! I have a booth. You can share it with me."

"Get out of here, you little weasel, before we skin you and hang you up on a wall."

The little weasel did not retreat at rough handling. He fought the hands trying to pull him back and kicked one man in the shins while shouting at Amos. "What better place to present your case than in the marketplace? Everyone comes there!" Six to one was no match and he disappeared in the throng, trailed by threats of what might happen to a man who dared insult a prophet who could bring on an earthquake.

The elders wanted Amos to talk only to them, but God's message was for everyone.

Amos looked over the crowd toward the little man. "What's your name?"

"Naharai ben Shagee," the man called from the back of the crowd.

The elders cast dark glances, but it did no good. Naharai's head appeared for an instant at the back; first to the left and then to the right as he jumped up and down in an attempt to see over others' heads.

"Pay him no attention."

"He's no one important."

Amos headed into the crowd. Men moved away from him, afraid, and then closed in behind, squabbling quietly about Naharai's interruption. "Please, stay and talk with us."

Amos found Naharai. "About that booth."

Naharai grinned broadly. "It's right in the middle of the market. A good spot. I will show you." He cast a triumphant look at the men standing in the gate before leading Amos away. "I saw you in the marketplace a few times. You never bought anything."

"What do you sell?" Amos walked alongside him.

"Sandals." He looked down. "You look as though you need a new pair."

Amos cast him a baleful look. "Is it the Word of the Lord you hunger for, or my money?"

"Both!"

Surprised, Amos laughed. *Here, Lord, is an honest man!*

+   +   +

One year passed into another, and then into another. The terror that came with the earthquake waned and people returned to their old ways. And still Amos kept on, teaching and preaching the Word of the Lord, praying constantly that the people would listen and repent.

Every day, Amos taught from the scrolls Beeri had copied and given to him before leaving Bethel. He pored over them, prayed over them, and discussed the Law with anyone who came to him. The Israelites argued over every word of it, turning it this way and that, trying to get out from under the Law. They had wax in their ears and scales over their eyes. Or was it merely their lust for sin that made them deaf and blind to the clarity of God's message?

"Of all the nations and families on the earth," Amos told his small gathering, "He chose us to be His people. The nations have witnessed what the Lord has done for us from the time He sent plagues upon Egypt and delivered us from slavery, then brought us into this land. More recently, the nations have seen how we have forgotten Him."

"You there, Naharai!" A merchant stood over Naharai, hands on hips.

"You invited him here, and look how he draws my customers away with all his prattle about law and judgment."

"If your goods were worth anything, customers couldn't be so easily drawn away!"

"Rodent!" He reached for Naharai.

Naharai evaded him easily, and shouted, "Ribai is a cheat! He mixes sand in with his grain."

Some altercation occurred every day, not always at Naharai's booth, but somewhere in the chaos of the marketplace. Yesterday, it had been two women arguing over the price of melons and cucumbers. Today it was the merchant who often sold moldy grain to those who had the least money. Those who walked and talked in awe of their gods on the temple mount preyed on one another here, and Ribai was one of the worst.

Amos rose when Ribai caught hold of Naharai. He used the crook of his staff to prevent a fist from landing.

The merchant swung around, face flushed. "Stay out of it, Prophet."

"Those who shut their eyes to the cries of the poor will be ignored by the Lord in their own time of need. To cheat the poor is to spit in the face of God."

"Mind your own business." Ribai stormed back to his stall, shouting at his son to watch out for thieves.

"The Lord hears their prayers." Amos returned to his place and sat. Only a few had come today to hear him read the Law. The young man who sat waiting only did so until Naharai could repair his sandals. And a mother had come with two boys, but left them behind so that she could barter for trinkets.

Now, another, dressed in fine linen and veils, approached. She stood listening as Amos read aloud. A servant held a shade over her while another peeled a pomegranate. When the slave girl stopped for a moment to listen intently to him, her mistress pinched her for neglecting her duties and threatened her with more abuse if she did not peel the pomegranate more quickly. Spotting a friend, the woman called her over.

Amos knew them. He had seen them often and been told by Naharai not to offend them. Wives and daughters of priests. They strolled through the market, demanding samples of whatever caught their fancy. And no one dared refuse. Like fat cows, they grazed continually. No one dared deny them.

The two whispered while Amos tried to teach. They laughed low and sneered. Another woman joined them, bejeweled with necklaces and earrings and tinkling bracelets.

Amos looked up at them. "The life of every living thing is in God's hands, and the breath of all humanity. Remember the Word of the Lord, the Law written down by Moses. If we sin, the Lord will scatter us among the nations. But if we return to Him and obey His commandments, even if we are exiled to the ends of the earth, the Lord will bring us back to the place He has chosen for His Name to be honored."

Naharai called the young man. He rose quickly, paid for his repaired sandals, and departed, leaving only the two boys who argued and shoved at one another.

Amos ignored them, continuing to address his words to the smug, indolent women who had come out of boredom and only wanted to mock. "You cannot live as you please, breaking God's commandments at every turn, and still expect to receive His blessings."

"In case you hadn't noticed, we already live under God's blessing," one woman said with a derisive laugh.

"God is warning you now. Don't count on your possessions to protect you in the coming day. Return to the Lord and the power of His strength."

"Listen to this fool. . . ."

"You should not take whatever you want from the poor, but show compassion and mercy upon them." What would it take to make these people listen? Another earthquake? Would they try God's patience until the promised disasters came upon them?

The woman used her maid's shawl to wipe pomegranate juice from her hands. "You should have a cup of wine, Prophet. Perhaps then you would not be so filled with gloom." She tossed the shawl heedlessly aside.

"Always the same speech." Her friend shrugged. "He never speaks of anything pleasurable."

"A visit to the temple brothel would put him in better spirits."

The women laughed together.

The first woman waved her hand airily at the two boys. "Don't listen to him, my fine young fellows. What he wants to do is take all the pleasure from our lives and make us reunite with Judah. We don't need Judah."

Fire spread through Amos's blood. "You fat cows! Keep fattening yourselves for the slaughter."

Red-faced, the woman shoved her maid aside and stepped forward. "What did you call me?"

"You heard me." Amos rose, his eyes fixing upon the three women. "You're fed on the finest grains, tended with the greatest care, and for what? One day you will lose everything you value, including your life!"

"You don't know who I am!"

"I know who you are. And I know your kind." He had had sheep like them, butting the younger ones, bullying. Greedy, possessive, danger to the flock. If not dealt with, they led others astray.

Naharai shook his head at Amos and mouthed, *Don't say any more.*

But Amos had to continue. If he did not speak the truth to these women, their blood would be on his conscience. These women walked about on the temple mount, heads held high because their husbands served as priests or officials. He saw them here often, extorting whatever they wanted at the expense of those far less fortunate than they. "You are women who oppress the poor and crush the needy, and who are always calling to your husbands, 'Bring us another drink!' "

"A wiser man would keep his mouth shut!"

One of them sang a mocking tune, one that had grown common over the past months.

The Word of the Lord came in a hot rush from Amos's lips. "The Sovereign Lord has sworn this by His holiness!" He pointed at the women mocking him. " 'The time will come when you will be led away with hooks in your noses. Every last one of you will be dragged away like a fish on a hook! You will be led out through the ruins of the wall; you will be thrown from your fortresses,' says the Lord. 'And I will destroy the beautiful homes of the wealthy—their winter mansions and their summer houses, too—all their palaces filled with ivory.' "

Face flushed red in anger, the first woman cried out. "I worship God! I'm at the temple every morning, and I bring generous offerings."

"Stolen offerings to a false god!"

Others in the marketplace paused to stare. Naharai ducked back into his booth and hid in the back.

Amos came toward the women. "Go ahead and offer your sacrifices to the idols. See if they can help when your enemies breach the walls. Keep on disobeying. Your sins are mounting up."

She sputtered while her friends closed in.

"Come away."

"Don't listen to him."

"He's mad. Just ignore him."

"A curse on you, Prophet!"

As they walked away, Amos shouted, "Prepare to meet your God!"

"He's not my god!" she shrieked back at him.

The others put their arms around her and drew her away.

Amos shook his head. "Fools are wise in their own eyes, but the Lord prevails." He took his place again and looked at the two boys, now silent, big-eyed, watching him. Only three others remained.

"You'll be sorry, Amos."

"More sorry if I had held my tongue."

One of the men did not understand. "Why has the Lord not spoken to us before now?"

Stifling his impatience, Amos leaned forward. "He has spoken to the ten tribes many times. He sent famine to every town and kept the rain from falling to make us turn back. He struck farms and vineyards with blight and mildew. He even sent plagues like the ones He sent against Egypt. Our young men died in wars, and some cities were destroyed. The Lord told us these things would happen if we turned our backs on Him. The Lord is the one who shaped the mountains. He stirs the winds and reveals every thought of man. He turns the light of dawn into darkness."

"But what God asks of us is too complicated!"

"The command God gave us through Moses is not too difficult for you to understand, and it is not beyond your reach. It is not kept in heaven, so distant that you must ask, 'Who will go up to heaven and bring it down so we can hear it and obey?' It is not kept beyond the sea, so far away that you must ask, 'Who will cross the sea to bring it to us so we can hear it and obey?' No, the message is very close at hand; it is on your lips and in your heart so that you can obey it. God gave us a choice between life and death, between prosperity and disaster. But you have allowed your hearts to be drawn away from Him to worship other gods.

"Listen! He is the Lord our God. You must not have any other god but Him. You must not make for yourself an idol of any kind. You must not misuse the name of the Lord your God. Remember to observe the Sabbath day by keeping it holy. Honor your father and mother. You must not murder. You must not commit adultery. You must not steal. You must not testify falsely against your neighbor. You must not covet anything that belongs to your neighbor."

"Why can't we worship the Lord and other gods, too?"

"Because the Lord God is One! There is no other god."

One of the men rose. "I don't believe that. I won't believe it." He walked away.

Amos spoke intently to the few who remained. "Return to the Lord and live. Don't go to worship the idols of Bethel, Gilgal, or Beersheba. For the people of Gilgal will be dragged off into exile as well, and the people of Bethel will come to nothing!"

"Life doesn't have to be so hard. Look around you, Amos. We have wealth on every side. The famines are over. We have food enough to grow fat like the cows of Bashan." The man stood. "No one will slaughter us, because King Jeroboam has assembled and equipped an army so that we can stand against anyone."

Nothing Amos said seemed to sink in. He might as well have been pouring water into sand. These people had lost the knowledge of their foundation. Ignorance would bring them to destruction. But they did not have hearts soft enough to be molded by God's Word. They were hard and proud, putting their confidence in the wealth and power of their king and country.

Another man stood. "Even if I believed—which I can't because of all

I see around me—I would be one of few who followed your teachings." He shook his head. "But we're free here. We are not bound by your laws. Life is to be lived. It is to be enjoyed."

Free to sin, he meant. Angry, frustrated, anguished, Amos cried out. "You cannot stand against God. He takes away the understanding of kings, and He leaves them wandering in a wasteland without a path."

The man's face grew rigid with defiance. "You said all blessings come from the Lord, but the truth is God didn't give us any of what we have! Jeroboam, the son of Nebat, gave Israel freedom and prosperity. He removed Solomon's yoke from our necks!"

"And put on the yoke of sin, which will lead you to death."

Angry, the young man lashed out. "We are stronger than you think! You are a blind prophet, so you can't see that. And why shouldn't we be proud? The dynasty of Jeroboam has grown more powerful each year. We hold our land. Our borders are expanding. Samaria is a greater capital city than Jerusalem!"

"Israel will answer to God."

"So you keep saying. Year after year, you say the same thing and nothing happens! It is you who must learn, Prophet. You have nothing to offer our people. You're a fool, Amos. You speak from madness, not wisdom."

"Only by the power of God can we push back our enemies; only in His name can we trample our foes."

"Then how did all this come to be after we broke away from the rulers in Jerusalem!"

"God is patient. He—"

"Patient? Your god is *weak*. I prefer bowing down to a god with power!"

"The one who toppled during the earthquake? The one who broke the horns off his own altar as he fell? That's the god you think has power?"

The young man's eyes flickered, and then darkened. "A curse on your prophecies. A curse on you!" Turning his back, he walked away.

Others who had watched and listened, clapped and cheered. Again, Amos heard taunting.

Lord, You have shot an arrow into my heart. All day long these people sing their mocking songs.

Amos struggled with anger and grief. Words rose in his throat, but they were not from God, and he swallowed them, clenching his teeth to keep from sinning. "The Lord does not enjoy hurting people or causing them sorrow. Repent! Accept His discipline when it comes. Return to the Lord. Hear, O Israel! The Lord is One. Love the Lord your God with all your heart, all your soul, and all your strength. . . ."

The people turned away.

Amos's eyes grew hot with tears. "If we will humble ourselves and pray and seek God's face and turn from our wicked ways, the Lord will hear from heaven and will forgive our sins and restore our land. If we do not repent and return to Him, the Lord has said Philistia and Egypt will sit around the hills of Samaria and witness what punishment He will bring upon us for our sins."

No one listened.

✦ ✦ ✦

Naharai drew the flap down on his booth and came to sit with Amos. "This was a very bad day." He rubbed his hands.

Amos read the signs. "What troubles you, Naharai?" He knew already, but hoped having to voice it would cause Naharai to think longer.

"You used to draw crowds. Everyone wanted to hear what you had to say."

Because the earthquake had aroused the fear of the Lord in them. Within a year, though, it had lessened. Now, it was all but forgotten.

Naharai rubbed his palms over his tunic-covered knees and left damp spots. "The people don't want to listen to you anymore, Amos." He shook his head. "Three years ago—even a year—and I would not worry, but times have changed. Despite what you claim, no one believes God had anything to do with the earthquake. It just . . . happened."

Amos said nothing, but his heart broke. Even Naharai was deaf to the Word of the Lord. "Even after all this time, and hearing everything I have said, you fail to believe that God will bring judgment upon Israel."

"Why would anyone want to believe such a thing, Amos? Even if they did believe it, wouldn't that be all the more reason to eat, drink, and be merry? If death is coming and there is no way to stop it, then we must take all the pleasure we can now."

"Repentance—"

Naharai waved his hands impatiently. "Yes, yes, you've said that word a thousand times. It rubs men raw."

"Not raw enough."

"You should respect me more."

"What are you talking about?" Amos stared at Naharai in confusion.

"I tried to warn you not to insult those women today, but you ignored me." He pointed to himself. "Me! The one who gave you the use of this booth."

Amos had never been fooled by Naharai's generosity. The merchant's motives had always been selfish. "You made this booth so that I would draw a crowd and you could sell your sandals."

Naharai's eyes flashed. "Even so, you should thank me. Instead, you cause trouble. Did you have a single thought for me or my business when you insulted those women? Fat cows, you called them!"

"And so they are."

"No! Say no more! Not another word! You've said too much already. You never think of the consequences, do you? You just keep pointing your finger, making accusations, and pretending you know everything that will happen." He stood. "You are bad for business, and I want you to go away. *Now!*"

Amos stared at him. He had hoped to reach these people, and had not reached even one. Naharai had boasted once that he did not bow down to a golden calf. True enough. He had never given up bowing down to profits.

Weary, Amos took his staff. He looked long at Naharai. "I had hoped . . ." Tears welled in his eyes. Shaking his head, he walked away.

Naharai called after him. "I like you, Amos." His tone filled with uneasiness. "I mean no disrespect to you or your God, but a man has to make a living."

"You have chosen, Naharai."

One day, sooner than he thought, death would be at his door.

✦   ✦   ✦

As Amos walked through the streets of Bethel, he looked into the faces of the people. Despite their sins, he had come to love them. They were like a flock of sheep, dumb and prone to wander, ignorant of the dangers that lurked everywhere, oblivious to the enemy Satan who longed to devour them. They followed their desires, foraging in foreign religions that fanned their pride and base passions. They thought they could live without God's rules and made up rules of their own. They couldn't seem to understand that every man cannot live for himself without bringing chaos. The very things they longed for were within reach if only they would return to God.

The love God offered each of them would fulfill the longing of their souls, while the love offered in the temple of Bethel would leave them empty and diseased. The freedom God offered would build them up and give them purpose while the freedom offered by idols would captivate and enslave them. They wanted fair treatment and would have it if they obeyed the law of God. Instead, they bowed down to man-made rules that gave corrupt men power to grind the poor beneath their heels and grow rich upon others' labors.

Their hearts were like stone, impenetrable. They wore the armor of pride.

Anguish filled Amos. He had seen their end. Crying out, he wept and tore his robe. "Come, let us tell of the Lord's greatness; let us exalt His name together. I prayed to the Lord, and He answered me. He freed me from all my fears. Those who look to Him for help will be radiant with joy; no shadow of shame will darken their faces. The Lord will set us free from fear!"

His words fell on deaf ears, for they had lost their fear of the Lord. Earthquakes came and shook their confidence. But when the rubble was cleared away, the warning was forgotten and they returned to their old ways.

"Listen, you people of Israel!" Amos cried in anguish. "Listen to this funeral song I am singing!" His voice rose in a sad lament to the virgin

Israel's fall from grace, never to rise again. He sang of her lying abandoned on the ground with no one to help her up.

People came out of their houses, peered down from their windows, paused in their work to listen, for his voice was like that of the Lord, beautiful and terrible at the same time. His song echoed in the gates and then drifted on the wind as he left the city and walked slowly, shoulders slumped, to his cave.

And the people talked among themselves.

"I hope he never comes back."

"I wish he would go away."

"Someone should go out there and shut him up for good."

"He never has anything good to say to us."

"Doom and gloom. That's all he's about."

"All he ever does is tell us what he thinks we're doing wrong."

Amos sat inside his cave, head in his hands, shoulders shaking with sobs. "Oh, Lord, oh, Lord. Turn their hearts to soft clay. Please, Lord . . . "

But he already knew the answer. The people had turned away. Their hearts were hardened.

And God was storing up wrath for the day to come.

SIX

❧❧❧❧❧❧❧

Amos walked the hills. He looked out over the land. Bethel stood proud in the distance.

Why are Your people so stubborn, Lord?

Why do they turn privilege into perversion? They don't even know right from wrong anymore. Their homes are filled with possessions they've stolen from others. Looters! That's what they are. Thieves and brigands. Godless women. Hypocrites. They laugh at me when I warn them of what will happen to them. They refuse to believe Your Word. You, the Living God who created heaven and earth. How can they be so foolish as to think their idols can save them?

Amos rubbed his face in disappointment. He had failed. Nothing he had said had made any difference in the way they lived.

Maybe if he had been a more learned man, or more eloquent or forceful or persuasive in his speech, they might have listened.

How long, O Lord, You have weighed me down with love for these people. How long must I stay and see how they turn their backs on You? I am crushed by their sins, burdened by their complaints, awash with tears over their rebellion! When will You let me go home?

God had given them opportunity after opportunity to turn away from their false gods and pagan worship. *Repentance* was a foul word in their mouths. "Repent of what?" they said, convinced their wealth would save them. They called for the Day of the Lord to come and had no idea that when it came it would sweep over them and blow them away like chaff before the wind.

They're like children, Amos thought, *holding Your hand while plotting mischief. They think You'll do nothing to them because You chose them out of all the people of the earth as Your possession. But will a father ignore the disrespect of his children? Will he allow his children to spit in his face? If a human father will not allow it, why should they think the Lord God will?*

Shoulders heaving, he sobbed. He had told them the truth and been reviled. And they went on trampling the poor among them. Their leaders continued to extort bribes and repress justice. Many grew lazy and complacent, lounging in luxury, indulging themselves on choice meat, and singing songs about nothing. "Let's eat, drink, and be merry," they said to one another, thinking God would not hold them accountable because they were sons of Jacob. To them, Jehovah was just another god among their pantheon, and the least favorite because the Lord God of Israel called for holy living and self-sacrifice for the sake of others. And because of their rejection, their hearts grew harder, their ears deafer. They didn't know truth from lies.

"I've told them, Lord. I've told them and told them."

Those who tried to live righteous lives before God suffered. Beeri, Jerusha, and Hosea had gone back to Jerusalem. Amos hoped they had found others who loved the Lord as they did, who clung to the Torah for wisdom and guidance, who lived to please not men, but God.

Grief and anger filled Amos. He felt torn between loving and hating the people of Bethel.

It is not you they have rejected, Amos. They have rejected Me.

"But, Lord, they don't understand that they are going to get what they deserve! They will get exactly what they're asking for: the Day of the Lord. It will come upon them sooner than they think."

Rather than be victors over their enemies, they would be broken and deserted. The ten tribes would fall, never to rise again. Nine out of ten of their soldiers would die in battle, the rest enslaved. Weeping would be heard everywhere, and still things would go from bad to worse. The Day of the Lord would be a day without a single ray of hope. All their worship would end. Their songs would be silenced. Those who survived the battles would be led away as slaves, their pride and the glory that was Israel obliterated, all their wealth in the hands of their enemies.

Amos knelt, head to the ground. "What do I do, Lord? What do I say to them to turn them away from destruction?"

Stand firm! Continue to tell them the truth!

Colors changed around him. He felt God's presence enveloping him, comforting while showing him the future. He saw locusts come up out of the ground, vast numbers of them, like an army of millions upon millions, marching, spreading across the land, taking flight. Everything in their path disappeared. The land became a black sea of moving insects gorging on crops, trees, brush, even people.

"O Sovereign Lord!" Amos cried out, hands raised. "Please forgive us or we will not survive, for Israel is so small."

The vision disappeared.

I will not do it.

Even as Amos thanked God for not obliterating the land and people, another vision filled his mind. Scorching heat bubbled in the bottom of the ocean, sending clouds of steam into the air. Fire raged from the mountainous depths of the sea, rising, rising, a cauldron of bubbles and steam, spreading and devouring the entire land.

"God, no!" Amos cried out in fear. "O Sovereign Lord, please stop or we will not survive, for Israel is so small."

The Lord spoke in a still, quiet voice:

I will not do that, either.

The fire disappeared and the land was as it had been.

Amos's heart pounded, for the Lord was not finished showing His great power over all creation. Discipline would come. It must come to turn His people back. Amos prayed for mercy upon them. "Leave a remnant, Lord. Please, leave someone alive to praise Your Name."

Amos, what do you see?

Amos opened his eyes. "A plumb line." The Law was the weight on the end of it.

**I will test My people with this plumb line. I will no longer
ignore all their sins. The pagan shrines of your ancestors
will be ruined, and the temples of Israel will be destroyed;
I will bring the dynasty of King Jeroboam to a sudden end.
Go and tell them!**

Ten tribes had aligned themselves with the pagan gods of Canaan, Moab, Ammon, and the rest. Not one in all Israel would stand straight and true beside the law Moses had brought down from Mount Sinai, the law God had written in His own hand.

How could they not see that God pursued them with relentless love? How could they not respond?

Burdened by sorrow, Amos headed back to Bethel.

The people had refused to heed the Lord's warning. They had planted the wind; now, they would harvest the whirlwind of a righteous, holy God.

✦ ✦ ✦

Amos knew as he approached the temple that his time was short. Already, men ran up the steps to report his presence.

"Listen to the Word of the Lord!" he shouted. "Recite My law no longer, and don't pretend that you obey Me. You refuse My discipline and treat My laws like trash!" He listed all their sins, despite catcalls, mock bows, shouted curses, and insults. "Your mouths are filled with wickedness, and your tongues full of lies. While you did all this, I remained silent, and you thought I didn't care! But now I will rebuke you!"

"He's speaking against the king!"

A commotion started above and behind him. The temple guards ran down the steps and surrounded him. "You are ordered to be silent!"

"Repent!"

"Shut up!" Two guards with swords took hold of him.

Amos struggled. "Repent, all of you who ignore the Lord, or He will tear you apart, and no one will help you!"

The guards grappled with him. When he tried to use his staff, two guards wrenched it from his hand.

"Silence him!"

The guards struck him with his own staff. Stunned by the blows, Amos sagged. Guards grabbed him, hauling him up and half carried, half dragged him up the steps. The air chilled inside the temple. He was brought into a large chamber and dropped on the stone floor. He groaned and tried to get up. A guard kicked him. The others joined in. Pain shot through him. He could hardly breathe.

"Enough!"

"What do you want done with him, my lord?"

My lord. Wrath filled Amos, and he struggled to his feet and faced Amaziah. "There is no other Lord but Jehovah."

The high priest's eyes blackened with hatred. "For ten years I've suffered your presence in my city, but no more. Finally, you have gone too far. No one is permitted to prophesy against the king!"

"It was the Lord who gave ten tribes to Jeroboam, and what did Jeroboam do to show his gratitude?" Amos sneered. "He set up golden calves and led the people away from the God who blessed him. *Jeroboam's dynasty will come to an end!*" Struck again, Amos fell. He raised his head with an effort. "The Lord has spoken."

"The king will hear your words, Amos. Then you will die."

"Tell him!" Amos struggled with all his strength, but could not gain freedom. "Tell him what the Lord says. If he has any sense, he will repent and lead his people back to God."

"Lock him away!"

✦   ✦   ✦

Heaved into darkness, the door closed and barred behind him, Amos lay facedown on the cold earth. The stench of the fetid palace underworld made his head swim and his stomach heave. A rat scrambled up his leg. He drew back and hit it away. Squeaking, it scurried away to wait for a more opportune time.

Fear gripped Amos by the throat. Never had he been in such darkness. Always there had been the stars overhead. But this blackness had teeth that sank into his soul. He fought to keep from screaming and felt the walls for a way out. There was none.

"God, help me." Even his whisper echoed softly.

Sinking down, he pressed his back against the wall. He strained to see even a small flicker of light—somewhere, anywhere. Nothing. Only by closing his eyes could he imagine it. A man used to open spaces and the sheepfold, Amos fought against panic with prayer.

"Lord, You are my deliverer. Blow them away like chaff in the wind— a wind sent by the angel of the Lord. Make their path dark and slippery, with the angel of the Lord pursuing them. Although I did them no wrong, they laid a trap for me. Although I did them no wrong, they dug a pit for me. So let sudden ruin overtake them. Let them be caught in their own snares!"

Time passed slowly, but Amos kept his thoughts fixed upon the Lord. He shouted God's Word into the darkness. *"Return to the Lord!* Giving thanks is a sacrifice that truly honors Him. If you keep to His path, He will reveal to you the salvation of God!" Anger filled him. "The wicked plots against the righteous and gnashes his teeth at him. The Lord laughs at him, for He sees his day is coming!"

A guard raged, "Will you never learn to hold your tongue, Prophet? When the order comes, it will please me to cut it out!"

He was given only enough food and water to keep him alive. Standing in the darkness of his prison, he wailed over the fate of the people. "This is what the Lord says: 'From among all the families on the earth, I chose you alone. That is why I must punish you for all your sins. Listen, all the earth! I will bring disaster upon My people. It is the fruit of their own sin because they refuse to listen to Me!'"

"Shut up!"

"You boast that you are more powerful than any other nation! You think you can dodge the grave. You say the Assyrians can never touch you, for you've made strong towers. Hear, O Israel! You live in a refuge made of lies and deception!"

More guards entered. The torchlight was so bright it blinded him. They cursed him, punched him, and kicked him until he lost consciousness.

When he awakened in darkness, he crawled into a corner and prayed. "Lord, deliver me. . ."

+   +   +

The door opened to a shout of, "Get up!" When he couldn't, two guards grabbed hold of him and pulled him up, uncaring of his pain. "You stink, Prophet."

He was brought upstairs and outside.

The sunlight hurt his eyes and blinded him. *Is this the way it is for these people, Lord? They close their eyes to the light of truth because it is too painful to accept? It will mean they have to change their ways!*

How long had he been imprisoned? A week? A month? He filled his lungs with clean air.

Amos found himself standing before Paarai, Amaziah's son. Attired in the garb of a priest—jeweled with insignias of his office—he held his head high. Lip curled, he surveyed Amos with cold eyes. "The king has been informed of the plots you've tried to hatch against him."

"Lies! I have hatched no plots."

A guard struck him. He was dragged up again before the high priest's son.

"We have witnesses. Right here in Bethel, on the doorstep of King Jeroboam's royal sanctuary, you spoke of a plot to end his life and destroy his dynasty. You said he would soon be killed, and the people of Israel sent away into exile."

You said . . . you said . . . Amos understood. "Jeroboam's dynasty shall end. Yes. Not my words, but the Lord's."

Eyes hot, face flushed, Paarai shouted at him. "Hear the word of my father, Amaziah, high priest of Bethel and servant of Baal! Get out of here, you prophet! Go on back to the land of Judah, and earn your living by prophesying there! Don't bother us with your prophecies here in Bethel. This is the king's sanctuary and the national place of worship!"

Amos knew Amaziah was somewhere close, listening. "I'm not a professional prophet, not like you and your father and others like you who speak whatever is pleasing to the ear of the one who pays you! I was never trained to be a prophet. I'm just a shepherd, and I take care of sycamore-fig trees. But the Lord called me away from my flock and told me, 'Go and prophesy to My people in Israel!'"

Amaziah entered the room. Face mottled, he spat out words of hatred. "Get him out of my sight! He is banished from Bethel. See that no one allows him in the gate again!"

"What's the matter, Amaziah? Did Jeroboam defeat your plan to kill me? Is there a residue of fear of the Lord left in Israel? Pray it is so!"

"Let the people see him banished, Father."

"So be it!" Amaziah agreed.

The Spirit of the Lord came upon Amos in power, and he cried out in a loud voice. "Now then, listen to this message from the Lord, Amaziah. You say, 'Don't prophesy against Israel. Stop preaching against My people.' But this is what the Lord says: 'Your wife will become a prostitute in this city, and your sons and daughters will be killed. Your land will be divided up, and you yourself will die in a foreign land. And the people of Israel will certainly become captives in exile, far from their homeland.'"

Gagging him, the guards took him outside, whipped him, and tied him in an oxcart. They paraded him through the streets of Bethel. People shouted insults and curses.

"What of your prophecies now, Prophet?"

Some laughed.

"Out of our way!" the temple guard shouted.

"Get him out of here!"

Some threw refuse.

"Send him home to Judah!"

The oxcart took him into the shadow of the gate and then out into the sunlight where the guards released him.

Half-starved, beaten, Amos could barely stand. He pointed to those shouting down at him from the walls. "You will become captives in exile, far from your homeland."

No one heard him.

No one cared enough to listen.

+ + +

Amos dreamed that night, a waking dream as he walked beneath the stars.

What do you see, Amos?

"A basket full of ripe fruit." Fruit ready to be eaten.

The ten tribes were ripe for punishment. The singing in the temples of Israel would turn to wailing. Dead bodies would be scattered everywhere. The survivors would be taken out of the city in silence. The ten wayward tribes would be led away into slavery. Even the land would suffer because of them.

Israel first.

Then Judah.

Wailing, Amos sank to his knees and threw dust in the air. He raged against the people's sins and grieved through the night. In the morning, he got up from the dust and walked back to Bethel.

"You can't come in, Prophet. You heard the orders yesterday."

"These walls will not protect you from the judgment of God!"

"Go away! Don't make trouble for me."

"Listen to the message that the Lord has spoken!" Amos shouted up at the people on the wall. "Listen to this, you who rob the poor and trample down the needy! You can't wait for the Sabbath day to be over and the religious festivals to end so you can get back to cheating the helpless."

All day, Amos walked along the walls of Bethel. "The Day of the Lord will come unexpectedly, like a thief in the night! 'In that day,' says the Sovereign Lord, 'I will make the sun go down at noon and darken the earth while it is still day. I will turn your celebrations into times of mourning and your singing into weeping. You will wear funeral clothes and shave your heads to show your sorrow—as if your only son had died. How very bitter that day will be!'"

Throat raw, Amos stared up at the walls. Tears ran down his cheeks at the thought of the destruction to come.

The Spirit of the Lord renewed his strength and gave power to his voice as he warned them of the worst curse that could come upon man. "'The time is surely coming,' says the Sovereign Lord, 'when I will send a famine on the land—not a famine of bread or water but of hearing the Words of the Lord.'" Sobbing, Amos tore his robes. "People will stagger from sea to sea and wander from border to border searching for the Word of the Lord, but they will not find it. Beautiful girls and strong young men will grow faint in that day, thirsting for the Lord's Word."

He pointed to the people lining the walls on either side of the main gates. "And those who swear by the shameful idols of Samaria—who take oaths in the name of the god of Dan and make vows in the name of the god of Beersheeba—they will all fall down, never to rise again."

A rock struck him in the forehead and he fell. Blood poured down his face. He wiped it away and pushed himself up. Another stone and another. Pain licked through his shoulder and side.

Amos backed away from the walls. "'Are you Israelites more important to Me than the Ethiopians?' asks the Lord. 'I brought Israel out of Egypt, but I also brought the Philistines from Crete and led the Arameans out of Kir. I, the Sovereign Lord, am watching this sinful nation of Israel. I will destroy it from the face of the earth!'"

Amaziah stood in the shadows shouting, "We will not listen to you any longer! Close the gate!"

The merchants protested; he could hear them arguing. No one cared about hearing the Word of the Lord—they only fought to reopen the gates so that commerce could continue!

Amos turned away, head throbbing, and staggered down the hill. Coming at last to a quiet orchard, he collapsed.

✦   ✦   ✦

Awakening in the middle of the night, Amos managed to make his way to the sheepfold cave where he had lived for ten years. Hungry and thirsty, he fell on the hard-packed earth and curled up like a babe in the womb. Would he die here like an animal in its hole?

"Lord, why have You abandoned me? I tried to feed Your sheep. They would not partake." Broken in spirit, he sobbed. Throat raw and lips cracked and bleeding, he whispered, "You are God and there is no other. Blessed be the Name of the Lord."

He dreamed that angels came and gave him bread and water while God whispered to him like a father to a troubled child.

Be still, and know that I AM God.

The pain went away and Amos's body relaxed beneath the ministering hands. "Abba . . . Abba . . . they wouldn't listen." He heard weeping.

Release came, and another task with freedom.

Tomorrow, he would go home to Tekoa, and write all the visions the Lord had given him. He would make a copy for Israel and another for Judah. The indictment would be on scrolls so that when the Lord fulfilled His Word, the people would know He had warned them before sending His judgment.

+   +   +

The eleven miles to Tekoa felt like one hundred, but the sight of the fields and flocks of sheep filled Amos with joy. He spotted Elkanan and Ithai in the pastures, but could not raise his arm or call out to them.

Elkanan studied him.

Ithai approached, staff and club in hand. "You there! Who are you and what do you want?"

Had he changed so much in appearance? Swaying, Amos dropped to his knees.

Ithai hurried toward him. When Amos lifted his head, Ithai's eyes went wide. "Uncle!" Dropping his club, he put his arm around him. "Let me help you." He shouted, "Elkanan! It's Uncle Amos! Call for help!"

"I will be all right. I just need to rest here awhile." When Amos looked out at the sheep, his throat closed, hot and thick. Why couldn't Israel be drawn together and led back to the Lord? Why couldn't they graze on the Scriptures rather than eat the poisonous teachings of men like Jeroboam, Amaziah . . . Heled?

"Amos is back!"

"Hush." Amos shook his head. "Don't frighten the sheep." His voice broke. *If only God's sheep were frightened of what was to come. If only they could be called back. . . .*

Others came to help. Eliakim reached for him, tears running freely as he looped his arm gently around Amos and helped him walk.

Amos smiled. "My friend, I need you to purchase reed pens, a full ink-horn, a small knife, and a roll of papyrus right away."

"I will, Amos."

+ + +

Amos slept for three days.

Finally he rose, stiff and aching, and set to work on the scroll. The Word of the Lord flowed from him, the Spirit of the Lord helping him to remember every word God had spoken. When his emotions rose too high, he left the work briefly and paced so that his tears would not stain the document.

Eliakim set down a tray with a jug of wine, some bread, and a bowl of thick lentil stew. "You must eat."

Amos did so. Replete, he returned to his work.

Eliakim came to get the tray and bowl. "Will the Lord send you back to Israel?"

"I don't know." He was not the same man who had left Tekoa years ago. "I will go wherever God sends me." His heart still ached for the Israelites.

"Much has changed in Jerusalem since the earthquake. Uzziah lives in solitude. Jotham carries out his commands."

"Did the king repent?"

"Yes."

"And the people?" He thought of his brothers, their wives and young ones. "Have they returned to the Lord?"

"Many have."

His servant's hesitance grieved Amos. "My brothers . . ."

Eliakim shrugged. "It appears so."

Out of obligation or thanksgiving? Amos had not the heart to ask. He prayed that his brothers bowed down willingly to the Lord and could rejoice in their salvation.

He worked day by day, carefully writing the first scroll. There must be no mistakes. When he finished writing the visions, the Lord spoke to him again, and the Word He gave filled Amos with hope for those who trusted in the Lord.

He finished writing, left the table, and went outside. Raising his arms in praise to the God who had called him away from the fields and flocks, he thought of the future and hope God offered His people.

"In that day I will restore the fallen house of David. I will repair its damaged walls. From the ruins I will rebuild it and restore its former glory. I will bring My exiled people of Israel back from distant lands, and they will rebuild their ruined cities and live in them again. They will plant vineyards and gardens; they will eat their crops and drink their wine. I will firmly plant them there in their own land."

All would not be lost. God always left a remnant.

Amos went back to his writing table, and over the next weeks made two perfect copies of the scroll. The first he sent by messenger to King Jeroboam in Samaria, the second to King Uzziah in Jerusalem, and the third he placed in Eliakim's trustworthy hands. "Keep this safe lest the others be destroyed." Some men would do anything to pretend God did not speak or warn of what was to come.

His work done, Amos went out to examine the flocks. He saw the increase that had come from Elkanan's and Ithai's care over the last ten years and was pleased.

+   +   +

Much had changed during his absence, and dismayed, Amos had to accept that his sheep no longer recognized his voice. The lamb he had tended had grown old. The animals moved at the sound of Elkanan's and Ithai's voices, but they did not come when Amos called. Like the Israelites, they had forgotten their master's voice. They no longer knew or trusted him. Working with his nephews, Amos allowed the animals time to become familiar with his voice.

When they finally answered to his voice, he took a portion of the flock to another pasture. He walked among them and talked softly to them. Some inclined their ears, others did not. At night, with the howl of wolves, he played his reed pipe or sang to them. The sound of his presence helped the sheep rest while keeping predators away.

Even after weeks away from Bethel, he often thought of the people there and what the future held for them. *Should I go back, Lord? Should I try again? How like wayward sheep they are! They don't know Your voice or see Your presence all around them.*

The ten tribes did not know God was close, ever watchful, trying to protect them from harm. They rejected the gift of salvation. They refused to be led to safety, rejecting an abundance of love, joy, peace, patience, kindness, goodness, faithfulness, gentleness, and self-control. Against such things there is no law. Did they even guess at the sorrow they caused God by their adultery with other gods, gods empty and false, mere reflections of their own inner depravity? Their false gods would lead them to slavery and death.

Amos prayed unceasingly. Every thought that came into his mind he captured and turned to the Lord. He wanted to be cleansed of all the iniquity he had seen in Bethel, the sins that had spread through the ten tribes like a plague. Death would come when they least expected it, like a thief in the night.

He grieved over Judah, too, for he had returned to Jerusalem and seen his brothers. And he knew their repentance did not run deep. Amos prayed for Isaiah's words to echo through the land and turn the people away from sin.

Make them listen, Lord!

He brought his flock back to the fold in Tekoa.

Eliakim came out to help him. "King Jeroboam is dead."

Amos heard the news in silence. Dread filled him. *So it begins.*

Eliakim told him the rest. "His son Zechariah is to rule."

The last sheep entered the fold. Amos closed the gate securely and bowed his head in grief. "Not for long."

◆   ◆   ◆

The next morning, Amos led his sheep out the gate and into the east pasture. Leaning on his staff, he watched the rams and ewes rush to fresh grasses while the lambs cavorted playfully. He smiled. This was the life he knew best, the life he loved. He knew sheep, but he could never fathom men. He thought of Bethel and Israel and prayed for the people who had persecuted him.

How little pleasure You get from Your flock, Lord. You cry out for Your lost children to come home, only to have them run in the opposite direction.

Often Amos's sheep wandered. Did that mean he loved them less? Did it mean he would turn his back on them if there was any chance to save them?

I am but a man, thought Amos, *and I love them until my heart feels as though it will break. How much greater is Your love. It runs deeper, is more pure, is holy. Your love runs like living water unseen, beyond comprehension, beneath the surface of what we see and hear. Faith stretches toward it and drinks and drinks so that we might grow strong and upright, a tree of life to all of us.*

"Amos!"

Startled, Amos straightened and glanced up. The sheep moved, frightened by the stranger among them. Amos called them back and moved between the flock and the man approaching. Grinning, he spread his arms. "Hosea!"

They embraced. Hosea drew back. "I went to Tekoa. Your servant said you would be here."

"You came five miles to see me?"

"I would have walked farther."

Touched, Amos leaned on his staff and smiled faintly. "You look well and prosperous."

Hosea bowed his head. "The Lord has blessed our family. My father is performing priestly duties and receives his portion."

"Ah, yes. And all it took was an earthquake to make men turn their eyes back to the law of God." He saw this was no idle visit. "What brings you to me?"

"God has called me back to Israel, Amos."

"Now?"

"Yes."

Amos sighed heavily. "I hope you will find listening ears and open hearts, my young friend."

Hosea bowed his head. "God has told me to marry a prostitute."

Amos stared at him. "Are you certain God is the one speaking to you?"

Hosea lifted his eyes. "When you were called, was there any doubt in your mind that it was God who spoke to you?"

"No. I knew His voice instantly though I had never heard it before. Everything within me recognized Him." Amos gave a faint smile. "I did not welcome Him. I begged Him to leave me alone. I feared the task. I told Him I would not be up to it." He looked north. "And I wasn't." The grief welled again, deep as an ocean. "They refused to listen."

"You spoke the truth, Amos. You warned them of the destruction coming, and now, God is sending me back to live a life filled with pain." Hosea's shoulders sagged. "My father thinks I yearn for Israel's ways. He thinks I want to return to Bethel so I can revel in the pleasure of women! He refuses to speak to me, Amos. I have never lain with a woman. Never! I have waited in hope of finding a God-fearing Hebrew girl who would be the mother of my children." His eyes filled. "And now God tells me to go and marry a prostitute. How can I love such a woman? How can she love me?"

"What else did God say to you?"

He swallowed hard and looked away. He remained silent so long, Amos thought he would not answer. "Israel is like an unfaithful wife. But God is ever faithful. As I must be."

Is this the way of it, Lord? Hosea will be the faithful husband to the adulterous wife, the husband who cherishes his bride, only to see her run to other men. What suffering this young man will experience! And all to show God's anguish. Hosea will show them how You suffer when Your people embrace other gods.

Will the people even know what they see, Lord? Will they understand the depth of Your passion for them? Fear did not turn them back to You. Will love do what fear could not?

You extend Your hand yet again, Lord.

For just a moment, Amos felt God's anguish over His chosen people.

"I don't want to go back to Bethel, Amos. I want to stay in Jerusalem and immerse myself in the study of the Law."

"And you think you will be safe from harm there?" Amos shook his head.

Hosea struggled as he had. Wasn't every day a struggle to obey God rather than do as he pleased? "The only safe place is in God's will, my friend." He put his hand on Hosea's shoulder. "And the Lord is with you. That is worth everything. Perhaps we are all called to be like Job and be able to speak his words from our hearts: 'God might kill me, but I have no other hope.' " *But doesn't the Lord suffer all the more? He loves us like a father loves a child, only more so.*

They walked together. Amos told him the way of a shepherd and pointed out the different sheep and their personalities. Hosea laughed and shook his head. And it occurred to Amos as he was instructing Hosea that all of creation taught about the character of God. Everything has a lesson. But how many took the time to look and listen? How many understood that to seek after God brought wonder and joy to a life and made all the other things pass away?

I have loved the shepherd's life, Lord. I have loved being alone in the pasturelands, drinking in Your creation, watching over Your sheep. Unlike life in Bethel amid the mess and chaos of humanity, life is simple here. People are complex and yet simple. They want their own way! They fashion idols they think allow them to descend into dark passions and self-centered existence. They use the creative abilities You gave them to make new gods that can neither punish nor rescue them. For a while, I saw them as sheep. But they are even more foolish and bent on destruction than these animals. Is this love I feel for them even a spark of what You have felt from the beginning? You are the shepherd on high, calling out to us, "Come home! Come back to Me! Return to the fold where you will be safe and loved!" You sing songs of deliverance every day through the wind, the birds, the night sounds.

If only we would listen.

"We must go wherever God sends us, Hosea." If God called him back to Israel, Amos would not argue this time. He would go without hesitation. He would speak again though it would mean beatings, imprisonment, even death. How had God brought him to this point of surrender, stubborn, wayward man that he had been? Israel had not turned back from rebellion, but the Lord had done a mighty work in him.

Hosea walked, head down. "What the Lord has told me to do is against everything in me."

"And in the midst of it, the Lord will be with you. You will learn to pour compassion on the one who hates you."

Hosea's eyes glistened with tears. "And will I destroy the one I love in the end as God says He will destroy us?"

Amos paused and leaned heavily on his staff. He was a simple man, not a philosopher; a shepherd, not a priest with years of study behind his opinions. "I don't know the answers, Hosea. But in the years I spent in Bethel, I knew it was not God's hatred of men that sent me there, but His great love. It is sin He hates because sin kills. Sin separates us from God, and He wants us close. In His fold." He looked out over his flock. "Sometimes it is the simple act of grazing that gets a sheep into trouble. Nibble a little here, a little there, a little more over in another area, and pretty soon, they are far from the shepherd. And then a lion comes. Or wolves. How many times over the centuries has God rescued us from our own stupidity?" He shook his head. "Too many times to count."

Will we never learn, Lord? Will our hearts never change? Would You have to make us into new creatures for us to follow You?

He went after a sheep who headed for some brush. Hosea watched. When the sheep was safely back among the others, Amos returned to him.

"A shepherd sometimes has to discipline a wayward sheep. Some are bent upon going their own way. They will go into gullies and into brambles, and lead others to death right along with them. I've had to kill a few sheep to keep the rest safe."

"As God will a few of us."

"More than a few, my friend."

"How can God love us so much and yet unleash cruel, despotic enemies upon us?"

"I've asked the same question, Hosea, and I have no answers. But I know this. The fault of much of what is coming upon us is due to our own choices. We worshiped out of habit. We gave because it was required in order to do business. In our ignorance, we equated corrupt priests with God. Or I did. We are destroyed by our own ignorance, and yet how few have the desire to learn the truth that will save them." Amos sighed. "But I talk about things I don't know or understand. If I could explain everything, would God be God? I never stood before the people of Bethel and spoke my own ideas. I spoke only the words God gave me. Anything else would have been sin. I hated the people in the beginning. In truth, I preferred the company of sheep to men. The sights, the sounds, the smells of Bethel's populace assaulted me from every side. It took a few years for God to pry open my eyes so that I could see them as lost sheep."

He shook his head. "Some things will be beyond our understanding. Even the animals know their owner and appreciate his care, but not God's people. No matter what He does for them, they still refuse to understand. Does a sheep tell the shepherd what to do? Why should man feel he can tell God what to do? But the impossibility of it all doesn't stop our people from trying. God won't let man have his way, so he carves an idol of wood or stone, props it up, and bows down to it. And his god has all the power of a scarecrow guarding a field of melons. I wanted my way for a long time, Hosea, but God had His way with me in the end." His eyes filled with tears. "And I thank God for it! I thank God every day!"

"But God is sending us with such different messages."

"Is He? Are they really that different? Surely salvation is near to those who honor Him. God's unfailing love and truth are one, and a life lived in striving for righteousness brings peace."

"Not always."

Amos knew Hosea meant to remind him of the ways in which he had suffered during his ten years in Bethel. "Is it peace with men that matters most, my friend? Or peace with God? I told the people the consequences of sin. Perhaps it is your work to show God's grace and mercy if they repent."

"I don't think I can do what He asks."

"You can't. Neither could I. I am a shepherd. I tend sheep and prune sycamore figs. Who would think me equipped or even worthy to preach God's Word in Bethel? Yet God made it so. I could say or do nothing until the Spirit of the Lord came upon me, and then anything was possible. God will make it possible for you to do the task He's given you. Your work is to trust Him."

"Will you go back to Bethel with me?"

Amos saw the hope—and fear—in Hosea's eyes. He shook his head. "No. This is where God wants me. For now." Hosea would have to rely on the Lord to complete his mission. And the Lord would be there with him at all times.

Hosea smiled ruefully. "I didn't think you would agree, Amos, but I had to ask. No man wants to be alone."

"You won't be."

Hosea understood and nodded. "I will remember you. Your courage. Your obedience. I will remember what you said and heed well the warning."

"And I will pray for you and continue to pray for all those you are sent to serve."

They embraced.

You call Your prophets to a hard life of pain and suffering, Lord.

The Spirit moved within him, and Amos knew God suffered far more than any man could imagine. The One who created man, the One who molded and loved him into existence was treated like a cast-off lover. *You suffer more, Father, for Your love is greater.*

Amos's throat tightened. He bowed his head. *Oh, may the words of my heart be pleasing to You, Lord, for You are my Shepherd.*

When he raised his head, Amos looked north and saw Hosea standing on the top of the hill. They raised hands to one another, and then Hosea disappeared over the horizon.

Israel refused to heed the warnings. Would they also scorn love?

Tears ran down Amos's cheeks, for he knew the answer.

✦   ✦   ✦

Amos brought the flocks back to Tekoa and wintered them in the protected pastures and shelters of home. Leaving his trusted servants in charge, he went up to Jerusalem to worship in the Temple and visit his brothers.

Bani told him the news. "King Zechariah has been assassinated in Samaria."

Ahiam poured feed into a manger. "He was struck down in his capital right in front of the people. And his assassin, Shallum, is now king of Israel."

The Word of the Lord given to Jehu all those years ago had been fulfilled, and Jeroboam's dynasty had not lasted past the fourth generation. In fact, Zechariah had lasted only six months, and no other member of the family of Jeroboam remained alive to retake power from the crowned usurper.

Within a month, Amos heard from a merchant passing through Tekoa on his way to Jerusalem that Shallum had been executed and still another king was on the throne of Israel.

"Menahem refused to bow down to an assassin. So he came up to Samaria from Tirzah, killed Shallum, and crowned himself king of Israel."

And so a terrorist always claims a noble excuse for murder.

Having turned away from the loving-kindness of God, the people now lived under the shadow of a murderer.

And worse would come.

✦ ✦ ✦

With each day that passed, Amos's sense of foreboding grew. He had killed a lion four days ago, and heard wolves last night, but there was something else, something even more ominous in the air. He kept the sheep close, his gaze moving to any disturbance.

A man came over the hill.

Amos raised his hand to shade his eyes. It was not Elkanan or Ithai or Eliakim. The man kept walking toward Amos with purposeful strides. When Amos recognized him, he knew why he had come.

"Paarai."

"Greetings, Prophet."

Strange that fear should leave him now. Amos inclined his head, his mouth curving in a bleak smile. "How does your father fare these days?"

"My father is the one who sent me." Paarai drew a sword.

Amos had faced far worse than this arrogant young braggart. He could easily have defended himself with his club. But he did nothing. "What do you think you will accomplish by murdering me?"

"Your prophecies die with you! Our family will remain in power. And you will be food for the buzzards!"

Amos grasped the one last opportunity given him to speak the truth. "You're wrong." Amos dropped his staff and club and spread his arms. "Kill me if you think you must, but know this. Men plan, but God prevails. The Word of the Lord will stand. And everything will happen just as God had me say it!"

Paarai cried out in rage and thrust his sword into Amos's stomach. He leaned forward, using both hands to push the blade all the way through and then let go and stepped back. Amos couldn't breathe through the pain. Looking down, he grasped the bloody hilt and sank to his knees.

"Who holds the power now?" Paarai ground out. Uttering a guttural cry of rage, he put his heel to Amos's chest and shoved him back. The blade thrust upward, slicing Amos's hands. He lay on his back, writhing in pain. "This is what you get for making a better man than you suffer! My father will be able to sleep now! He will be able to eat! He will no longer fear your words ringing in his ears!"

Standing over him, Paarai pulled the sword out slowly. Amos cried out in agony, and saw that Paarai relished it.

He knelt at Amos's side. Leaning over, he gave a feral grin, eyes black with triumph. "I'm going to leave you here now to suffer. Pray you die before a lion comes. Or the wolves. It gives me pleasure to think of your flesh being torn by hungry animals!" He stood, spit on him, and cursed him by the gods of Bethel. After kicking dust into Amos's face, he walked away. Paarai scooped up a handful of rocks, flung them at Amos's sheep, and laughed as they ran in panic.

Amos tried to rise and couldn't. When he turned his head, he saw the sheep scattering. Tears filled his eyes. He cried in pain and despair as the sun set and his lifeblood soaked into the ground. He heard the wolves and saw them gathering on the hillside. The sheep moved restlessly, no shepherd to guide or protect them.

Like Israel.

And the nations will gather around the hills of Samaria. . . .

Amos wept. *By Your mercy, I will not live to see it happen.*

Had his father once said to him that the righteous often pass away before their time because the Lord protects those He loves from the evil that is to come?

A wolf came close, crouching low, growling. Amos was helpless to protect himself. His strength was gone. The wolf came a foot closer and then bolted away, frightened by something unseen.

A gentle breeze stirred the grass. It would be night soon. Darkness was closing in. Amos felt himself lifted by strong arms. He looked into a face he had never seen before and yet his soul recognized. "Oh!" Joy filled him and he kept his eyes fixed upon the One he loved.

"Do not fear." Tears fell upon Amos's face. "All that has been said will come to pass. And then I will restore the fallen house of David. I will rebuild its ruins and restore it so that the rest of humanity might seek Me, including the Gentiles—all those I have called to be Mine."

The hope of salvation filled Amos, but he had not the strength left even to smile.

The Lord kissed his forehead. "Rest, Amos. Rest, My good and faithful servant."

Amos closed his eyes as the Good Shepherd carried him home.

EPILOGUE

Not long after Amos died, his prophecies began to come true.

The town of Tappuah and all the surrounding countryside as far as Tirzah rebelled against Menahem. In retribution, Menahem sacked the city, killing men, women, and children, and even going so far as to follow the brutal Assyrian custom of ripping open the bellies of pregnant women and thus annihilating the next generation.

King Menahem reigned for ten years, and then the Assyrian king, Tiglath-pileser, invaded Israel and forced Menahem to pay thirty-seven tons of silver. He extorted the money from the rich of Israel. Upon Menahem's death, his son Pekahiah ascended the throne, only to be assassinated two years later by Pekah, the commander of his army. Pekah then declared himself king of Israel.

Twenty years passed as the people fell deeper into pagan worship. Hosea the prophet obeyed God's command to marry a prostitute. Time after time, Hosea took his wife back, but the people around him failed to understand the living parable of God's love for wayward Israel.

King Tiglath-pileser attacked again and captured the major cities and primary regions, taking the people captive to Assyria. Among them were Amaziah and his son, their wives left behind to fend for themselves as prostitutes.

Pekah was soon deposed by Hoshea who reigned in Samaria for nine years before King Shalmaneser of Assyria defeated him and plundered the country. When King Hoshea attempted to enlist the help of King So of Egypt, the King of Assyria returned, besieged Samaria, and razed it.

Just as Amos and other prophets warned, Israel was devoured by war. Assyrian wolves preyed upon the sheep of Israel. Those who survived were led away to foreign lands, leaving enemies to enjoy the bounty of the land God had given them. Dispersed, the ten tribes disappeared.

Judah repented under the reigns of King Hezekiah and King Josiah, but all too soon the southern kingdom also turned away from the Lord.

One hundred and sixty-four years after Amos's death, Babylon invaded and conquered Judea. As the people were led away to slavery, Babylonians stripped Solomon's Temple and tore it down stone by stone.

Only then did the people repent and cry out to the Lord, and God heard their prayers.

Seventy years later, the Lord fulfilled His promise to bring them home.

For from Judah would come the Messiah. And on His shoulders would rest the government that would never end, and He would be called Wonderful Counselor, Mighty God, Everlasting Father, Prince of Peace. Jesus, the Christ, God the Son, would be the Good Shepherd who would save His people and lead them into the folds of the Lord God Almighty.

SEEK AND FIND

Dear Reader,

You have just finished reading the story of Amos the prophet, as told by Francine Rivers. As always, it is Francine's desire for you the reader to delve into God's Word for yourself to find out the real story—to discover what God has to say to us today and to find applications that will change our lives to suit His purposes for eternity.

Amos was a humble shepherd and gardener. His heart for God helped him to weather the times he lived in and to face rejection. Amos did not shrink from the task to which God called him. Rather, he stepped forward and embraced his calling. Amos's obedience to God's call on his life is extraordinary. It foreshadows another prophet—the ultimate Prophet, Jesus of Nazareth.

May God bless you and help you to discover his call on your life. May you discover a heart of obedience beating within you.

Peggy Lynch

THE CALL

SEEK GOD'S WORD FOR TRUTH

Read the following passage:

> This message was given to Amos, a shepherd from the town of Tekoa in Judah. He received this message in visions two years before the earthquake, when Uzziah was king of Judah and Jeroboam II, the son of Jehoash, was king of Israel. . . .
>
> Then Amaziah, the priest of Bethel, sent a message to Jeroboam, king of Israel: "Amos is hatching a plot against you right here on your very doorstep! What he is saying is intolerable. He is saying, 'Jeroboam will soon be killed, and the people of Israel will be sent away into exile.'"
>
> Then Amaziah sent orders to Amos: "Get out of here, you prophet! Go on back to the land of Judah, and earn your living by prophesying there! Don't bother us with your prophecies here in Bethel. This is the king's sanctuary and the national place of worship!"
>
> But Amos replied, "I'm not a professional prophet, and I was never trained to be one. I'm just a shepherd, and I take care of sycamore-fig trees. But the LORD called me away from my flock and told me, 'Go and prophesy to my people in Israel.'"
>
> AMOS 1:1; 7:10-15

+ Who was Amos and where was he from? What was his profession and sideline?

+ When and how was Amos called to be a prophet? What kind of prophet was he? What kind of training did he have?

+ How was Amos received by the religious leaders, and why? How was he received by the political leaders?

+ How did Amos respond to the religious and political leaders? How did he respond to God?

FIND GOD'S WAYS FOR YOU

+ Who are you and what kind of training do you have?

> God knew his people in advance, and he chose them to become like his Son, so that his Son would be the firstborn among many brothers and sisters. And having chosen them, he called them to come to him. And having called them, he gave them right standing with himself. And having given them right standing, he gave them his glory.
>
> ROMANS 8:29-30

+ According to these verses, to what has God called you and why?

+ What is your response to God? Explain.

STOP AND PONDER

Remember, dear brothers and sisters, that few of you were wise in the world's eyes or powerful or wealthy when God called you. Instead, God chose things the world considers foolish in order to shame those who think they are wise. And he chose things that are powerless to shame those who are powerful. . . . As a result, no one can ever boast in the presence of God.

1 CORINTHIANS 1:26-29

MESSAGE FOR OTHERS

SEEK GOD'S WORD FOR TRUTH

Read the following passage:

This is what the LORD says:

"The people of Damascus have sinned again and again,
    and I will not let them go unpunished!
They beat down my people in Gilead
    as grain is threshed with iron sledges.
So I will send down fire on King Hazael's palace,
    and the fortresses of King Ben-hadad will be destroyed.
I will break down the gates of Damascus. . . .
I will destroy the ruler in Beth-eden,
    and the people of Aram will go as captives to Kir,"
    says the LORD.

This is what the LORD says:

"The people of Gaza have sinned again and again,
    and I will not let them go unpunished!
They sent whole villages into exile,
    selling them as slaves to Edom.
So I will send down fire on the walls of Gaza,
    and all its fortresses will be destroyed.
I will slaughter the people of Ashdod. . . .
Then I will turn to attack Ekron,
    and the few Philistines still left will be killed,"
    says the Sovereign LORD.

This is what the LORD says:

"The people of Tyre have sinned again and again,
    and I will not let them go unpunished!
They broke their treaty of brotherhood with Israel,
    selling whole villages as slaves to Edom.
So I will send down fire on the walls of Tyre,
    and all its fortresses will be destroyed."

This is what the LORD says:

"The people of Edom have sinned again and again,
and I will not let them go unpunished!
They chased down their relatives, the Israelites, with swords,
showing them no mercy.
In their rage, they slashed them continually
and were unrelenting in their anger.
So I will send down fire on Teman,
and the fortresses of Bozrah will be destroyed."

This is what the LORD says:

"The people of Ammon have sinned again and again,
and I will not let them go unpunished!
When they attacked Gilead to extend their borders,
they ripped open pregnant women with their swords.
So I will send down fire on the walls of Rabbah,
and all its fortresses will be destroyed . . . ,"
says the LORD.

This is what the LORD says:

"The people of Moab have sinned again and again,
and I will not let them go unpunished!
They desecrated the bones of Edom's king,
burning them to ashes.
So I will send down fire on the land of Moab,
and all the fortresses in Kerioth will be destroyed . . . ,"
says the LORD.   AMOS 1:3–2:3

+ Name the six neighboring people/cities/nations on which Amos
  pronounced God's judgment.

+ What did these neighbors have in common? Why was God angry
  with each of them?

+ What judgment was decreed?

+ What can we learn about God from this passage?

+ What is implied about Amos? Explain.

FIND GOD'S WAYS FOR YOU

+ What similarities do you see, if any, between the behavior listed in this
  passage and what is going on in the world today?

I am warning you ahead of time, dear friends. Be on guard so that you will
not be carried away by the errors of these wicked people and lose your own

secure footing. Rather, you must grow in the grace and knowledge of our Lord and Savior Jesus Christ.   2 PETER 3:17-18

+ What warnings are we given in the above passage, and why?

+ What are we to do to remain secure? Are you doing it?

STOP AND PONDER

The day of the Lord will come as unexpectedly as a thief. Then the heavens will pass away with a terrible noise, and the very elements themselves will disappear in fire, and the earth and everything on it will be found to deserve judgment.   2 PETER 3:10

MESSAGE FOR KINSMEN

SEEK GOD'S WORD FOR TRUTH

Read the following passage:

This is what the LORD says:

"The people of Judah have sinned again and again,
and I will not let them go unpunished!
They have rejected the instruction of the LORD,
refusing to obey his decrees.
They have been led astray by the same lies
that deceived their ancestors.
So I will send down fire on Judah,
and all the fortresses . . . will be destroyed."

This is what the LORD says:

"The people of Israel have sinned again and again,
and I will not let them go unpunished!
They sell honorable people for silver
and poor people for a pair of sandals.
They trample helpless people in the dust
and shove the oppressed out of the way.
Both father and son sleep with the same woman,
corrupting my holy name. . . .

"So I will make you groan
like a wagon loaded down with sheaves of grain.
Your fastest runners will not get away. . . .
The archers will not stand their ground. . . .
On that day the most courageous of your fighting men

will drop their weapons and run for their lives,"
    says the LORD. . . .

"My people have forgotten how to do right,"
    says the LORD. . . .

"Come back to the LORD and live!
Otherwise, he will roar through Israel like a fire,
    devouring you completely. . . .
You twist justice, making it a bitter pill for the oppressed.
    You treat the righteous like dirt. . . .

"How you hate honest judges!
    How you despise people who tell the truth! . . .

"Do what is good and run from evil
    so that you may live!
Then the LORD God of Heaven's Armies will be your helper,
    just as you have claimed.
Hate evil and love what is good;
    turn your courts into true halls of justice.
Perhaps even yet the LORD God of Heaven's Armies
    will have mercy on the remnant of his people. . . .

"I hate all your show and pretense—
    the hypocrisy of your religious festivals and solemn
    assemblies. . . .

"Away with your noisy hymns of praise! . . .
Instead, I want to see a mighty flood of justice,
    an endless river of righteous living. . . ."

What sorrow awaits you who lounge in luxury . . .
    and you who feel secure . . . !
You are famous and popular . . .
    and people go to you for help. . . .
    How terrible for you. . . .

The Sovereign LORD has sworn by his own name, and this is what he, the
LORD God of Heaven's Armies, says:

"I despise the arrogance of Israel,
    and I hate their fortresses.
I will give this city
    and everything in it to their enemies."

AMOS 2:4-7, 13-16; 3:10; 5:6-7, 10, 14-15, 21, 23-24; 6:1, 4, 8

✦ Why was God angry with Judah? with Israel?

✦ How were the complaints against them similar to those against the
surrounding people? How were they different?

✦ What warnings were given? What judgments were promised?

+ What can we further learn about God from this passage?

+ What is implied about Amos? Explain.

FIND GOD'S WAY FOR YOU

What similarities do you see, if any, between the behavior listed in the following passage and what is going on in our nation? our churches? our homes?

> Get rid of all evil behavior. Be done with all deceit, hypocrisy, jealousy, and all unkind speech. Like newborn babies, you must crave pure spiritual milk so that you will grow into a full experience of salvation . . . now that you have had a taste of the Lord's kindness.   I PETER 2:1-3

+ What are we told to get rid of?

+ What are we told to do?

+ What do you need to get rid of?

STOP AND PONDER

> Dear friends, I warn you as "temporary residents and foreigners" to keep away from worldly desires that wage war against your very souls. Be careful to live properly among your unbelieving neighbors. Then even if they accuse you of doing wrong, they will see your honorable behavior, and they will give honor to God when he judges the world.   I PETER 2:11-12

A PROPHET'S PLEA

SEEK GOD'S WORD FOR TRUTH

Read the following passage:

> The Sovereign LORD showed me a vision. I saw him preparing to send a vast swarm of locusts over the land. . . . In my vision the locusts ate every green plant in sight. Then I said, "O Sovereign LORD, please forgive us or we will not survive, for Israel is so small."
>
> So the LORD relented from this plan. "I will not do it," he said.
>
> Then the Sovereign LORD showed me another vision. I saw him preparing to punish his people with a great fire. The fire had burned up the depths of the sea and was devouring the entire land. Then I said, "O Sovereign LORD, please stop or we will not survive, for Israel is so small."

Then the LORD relented from this plan, too. "I will not do that either," said the Sovereign LORD.

Then he showed me another vision. I saw the Lord standing beside a wall that had been built using a plumb line. He was using a plumb line to see if it was still straight. And the LORD said to me, "Amos, what do you see?"

I answered, "A plumb line."

And the Lord replied, "I will test my people with this plumb line. I will no longer ignore all their sins. The pagan shrines of your ancestors will be ruined, and the temples of Israel will be destroyed; I will bring the dynasty of King Jeroboam to a sudden end."

AMOS 7:1-9

✦ In what ways were the first two visions similar? How were they different?

✦ How did Amos respond to what the Lord had planned in these two visions? What did he ask? What was God's response?

✦ How was the third vision different, and what was Amos's response? What significance do you see, if any, to the third vision and this response?

✦ What can we learn about God from these visions?

✦ What is implied about Amos? Explain.

FIND GOD'S WAYS FOR YOU

Try to recall a time when you pleaded with God on behalf of someone else.

Are any of you sick? You should call for the elders of the church to come and pray over you, anointing you with oil in the name of the Lord. Such a prayer offered in faith will heal the sick, and the Lord will make you well. And if you have committed any sins, you will be forgiven. Confess your sins to each other and pray for each other so that you may be healed. The earnest prayer of a righteous person has great power and produces wonderful results.

JAMES 5:14-16

✦ What instructions are given in this passage? What conditions are specified?

✦ What results are we to expect? Why?

STOP AND PONDER

The Holy Spirit helps us in our weakness. For example, we don't know what God wants us to pray for. But the Holy Spirit prays for us with groanings that cannot be expressed in words. And the Father who knows all hearts knows what the Spirit is saying, for the Spirit pleads for us believers in harmony with God's own will.

ROMANS 8:26-27

MESSAGE OF RESTORATION

SEEK GOD'S WORD FOR TRUTH

Read the following passage:

> "I, the Sovereign LORD,
>   am watching this sinful nation of Israel.
> I will destroy it
>   from the face of the earth.
> But I will never completely destroy the family of Israel,"
>   says the LORD.
> "For I will give the command
>   and will shake Israel along with the other nations
> as grain is shaken in a sieve,
>   yet not one true kernel will be lost. . . .
>
> "In that day I will restore the fallen house of David.
>   I will repair its damaged walls.
> From the ruins I will rebuild it
>   and restore its former glory.
> And Israel will possess what is left of Edom
>   and all the nations I have called to be mine."
> The LORD has spoken,
>   and he will do these things.
>
> "The time will come," says the LORD,
> "when the grain and grapes will grow faster
>   than they can be harvested.
> Then the terraced vineyards on the hills of Israel
>   will drip with sweet wine!
> I will bring my exiled people of Israel
>   back from distant lands,
> and they will rebuild their ruined cities
>   and live in them again.
> They will plant vineyards and gardens;
>   they will eat their crops and drink their wine.
> I will firmly plant them there
>   in their own land.
> They will never again be uprooted
>   from the land I have given them,"
>   says the LORD your God.   AMOS 9:8-9, 11-15

✦ Along with God's judgment to uproot and sift Israel, what did God promise never to do?

✦ Whose kingdom was to be restored? In what ways?

✦ What further promise did God make to His exiled people?

✦ What phrases are used that offered Israel hope?

+ What permanency did God promise Israel?

+ What can we learn about God from these promises?

SEEK GOD'S WAYS FOR YOU

+ Which of the promises of restoration listed in Amos 9 took place for Israel? Explain.

> Humble yourselves under the mighty power of God, and at the right time he will lift you up in honor. . . . In his kindness God called you to share in his eternal glory by means of Christ Jesus. So after you have suffered a little while, he will restore, support, and strengthen you, and he will place you on a firm foundation.   1 PETER 5:6, 10

+ What has God promised those whom He has called? What is our part?

+ In what ways has God restored, supported, or strengthened you?

STOP AND PONDER

> Oh, how great are God's riches and wisdom and knowledge! How impossible it is for us to understand his decisions and his ways!   ROMANS 11:33

THE PROPHET'S PROMISE

AMOS AS PROPHET

> The LORD sent prophets to bring them back to him. The prophets warned them, but still the people would not listen.   2 CHRONICLES 24:19

+ According to this verse, why did God send prophets to his people?

> Jesus told them, "A prophet is honored everywhere except in his own hometown and among his own family."   MATTHEW 13:57

+ How were prophets generally treated?

> Above all, you must realize that no prophecy in Scripture ever came from the prophet's own understanding, or from human initiative. No, those prophets were moved by the Holy Spirit, and they spoke from God.
>   2 PETER 1:20-21

+ Who is the source of true prophecy?

AMOS AS SHEPHERD

Amos was a shepherd by profession. Read what Jesus said about shepherds in the following passage:

The one who enters through the gate is the shepherd of the sheep. . . . The sheep recognize his voice and come to him. He calls his own sheep by name and leads them out. . . .

The good shepherd sacrifices his life for the sheep. A hired hand will run when he sees a wolf coming. He will abandon the sheep because they don't belong to him and he isn't their shepherd. . . . I am the good shepherd; I know my own sheep, and they know me.   JOHN 10:2-3, 11-12, 14

✦ How might Amos's experience as a shepherd have prepared him to be one of God's prophets? How would his shepherding knowledge have helped him respond to God's call?

AMOS AS GARDENER

In addition to his work as a shepherd, Amos also tended fig trees. Read what Jesus said about gardeners in the following passage:

[The gardener] cuts off every branch . . . that doesn't produce fruit, and he prunes the branches that do bear fruit so they will produce even more. . . . A branch cannot produce fruit if it is severed from the vine.   JOHN 15:2, 4

✦ How might caring for trees have helped Amos understand the need for God's judgment?

✦ How would it have prepared him to obey God regardless of what others thought?

AMOS AND JESUS

Amos was an obedient man. His shepherding prepared him to prod people in a caring way. His gardening skills allowed him to see that people, like plants, need to have the wild, unproductive growth removed in order to produce fruit. His obedience—along with his training—foreshadows another prophet, Jesus. Jesus said, "I am the good shepherd" (John 10:14) and "I am the true grapevine, and my Father is the gardener" (John 15:1).

✦ In Revelation we find Jesus' prophetic warning and promise to the churches:

Look, I am coming soon! Blessed are those who obey the words of prophecy written in this book. . . . Look, I am coming soon, bringing my reward with me to repay all people according to their deeds. . . . I, Jesus, have sent my angel to give you this message for the churches. I am both the source of David and the heir to his throne. I am the bright morning star. . . . Yes, I am coming soon!   REVELATION 22:7, 12, 16, 20

May Jesus be heard in our world, our nation, our churches, our homes. May we each hear and heed His call before He comes!

BOOK FIVE

THE SCRIBE

PROLOGUE

Silas walked to the house where Peter and his wife were hidden, aggrieved by the weight of the news he bore.

Tapping three times, lightly, he entered the room where they had often met with brothers and sisters in Christ or prayed long hours when alone. He found Peter and his wife in prayer now. Peter's wife raised her head, and her smile vanished.

Silas helped her up. "We must go," he said softly, and turned to assist Peter. "Paul has been captured. Soliders are searching the city for you. You must leave tonight."

As they headed out, Silas explained further. "Apelles is with me. He will show you the way."

"What about you?" Peter spoke with grave concern. "You must come with us, Silas. You've served as Paul's secretary as well as mine. They will be looking for you too."

"I'll follow shortly. I was working on a scroll when Apelles brought me the news. I must return and make certain the ink is dry before I pack it with the others."

Peter nodded gravely, and Silas ducked into the house where he had been staying. All the papyrus scrolls, except the one on which he had been working, were already rolled and stored carefully in leather cases. Silas had known the day would come when he would have to grab the pack and run. Lifting the weights that held open the newest scroll, he rolled the papyrus, and tucked it carefully into its case. As he slung the pack over his shoulder, he felt the full weight of responsibility to safeguard the letters.

As he stepped out into the street again, he saw Peter and his wife and Apelles waiting. Silas ran to them. "Why are you still here?"

Apelles looked frantic. "They wouldn't go farther without you!"

Torn between gratitude for his friends' loyalty and fear for their safety, Silas urged them on. "We must hurry!"

Apelles was clearly relieved to be moving again. He gave further instructions in an urgent whisper. "We have a carriage waiting outside the city gates. We thought it best to wait until nightfall, when the ban on wagons lifted. It will be easier to slip out now."

Peter was well-known in Rome, and would be easily recognized. They would have a better chance of escape in the confusing influx of goods into the city and the cover of darkness beyond the walls.

Peter walked with difficulty, his arm protectively around his wife. "When did the guard come for Paul?"

"They took him to the dungeon this morning." Apelles raised his hand as they came to the end of the street. He peered around the corner and then beckoned them on. The young man made an effort to appear calm, but Silas felt his fear. His own heart beat with foreboding. If captured, Peter would be imprisoned and executed, most likely in some foul spectacle designed by Nero to entertain the Roman mob.

"Silas!" Peter's wife whispered urgently.

Silas glanced back and saw Peter struggling for breath. He caught up to Apelles and grasped his shoulder. "More slowly, my friend, or we'll lose the one we're trying to save."

Peter drew his wife closer and whispered something to her. She held tightly to him and wept into his shoulder. Peter smiled at Silas. "Right now would be a good time for God to give me wings like an eagle."

Apelles led them more slowly through the dark alleys and narrow streets. Rats fed on refuse as they passed by. The sounds of wagon wheels grew louder. While the city slept, a tide of humanity poured through the gates, bringing with it goods for the insatiable Roman markets. Some drove overladen wagons; others pushed carts. Still others carried heavy packs on their bent backs.

So close to freedom, Silas thought, seeing the open gates just ahead. Could they get through without being recognized?

Apelles drew them close. "Wait here while I make certain it's safe." He disappeared among the wagons and carts.

Silas's heart pounded harder. Sweat trickled down his back. Every minute they stood on the public street added to Peter's danger. He spotted Apelles, his face pale and strained with fear as he struggled through the crowd.

The young man pointed. "That side. Go now! Quickly!"

Silas led the way. His heart lurched when one of the Roman guards turned and looked at him. A Christian brother. Thank God! The Roman nodded once and turned away.

"Now!" Silas made a path for Peter and his wife to pass through the flow. People bumped into them. Someone cursed. A wagon wheel almost crushed Silas's foot.

Once outside the gates and away from the walls, he let Peter set the pace.

An hour down the road, two more friends ran to meet them. "We've been waiting for hours! We thought you'd been arrested!"

Silas took one of them aside. "Peter and his wife are exhausted. Have the coach meet us on the road."

One remained to escort them while the other ran ahead.

When the coach arrived, Silas helped Peter and his wife up and then climbed in with them. Shoulders aching, he shrugged off the heavy pack and leaned back, bracing himself as they set off. The sound of galloping horses soothed his frayed nerves. Peter and his wife were safe—for the moment. The Romans would search the city first, leaving them time to reach Ostia, where the three of them would board the first ship leaving port. Only God knew where they would go next.

Peter looked troubled. His wife took his hand. "What is it, Peter?"

"I don't feel right."

Silas leaned forward, concerned. "Are you ill?" Had the rush through the night been too much for the venerable apostle?

"No, but I must stop."

His wife voiced an objection before Silas could do so. "But, my husband . . ."

Peter looked at Silas.

"As you say." Silas leaned out to signal the coachman.

Peter's wife grabbed him. "Don't, Silas! Please! If they capture Peter, you know what they'll do."

Peter drew her back and put his arm around her. "God has not given us a spirit of fear, my dear, and that's what has sent us racing into darkness."

Silas struck the side of the coach. Leaning out, he called up to the driver to stop. The coach jerked and bounced as it drew to the side of the road. While his wife wept, Peter climbed down. Silas followed. The horses snorted and moved restlessly. Silas shrugged at the driver's questioning look and watched Peter walk off the road.

Peter's wife stepped down. "Go with him, Silas. Reason with him! Please. The church needs him."

Silas walked to the edge of the field and watched over his friend. Why did Peter tarry here?

The old apostle stood in the middle of a moonlit field, praying. Or so Silas thought until Peter paused and tipped his head slightly. How many times over the years had Silas seen Peter do that when someone spoke to him? Silas went closer, and for the barest second something shimmered faintly in the moonlight. Every nerve in his body tingled, aware. Peter was not alone. The Lord was with him.

Peter bowed his head and spoke. Silas heard the words as clearly as if he stood beside the old fisherman. "Yes, Lord."

When Peter turned, Silas went out to him, trembling. "What are we to do?"

"I must go back to Rome."

Silas saw all the plans that had been made to protect Peter crumble. "If you do, you'll die there." *Lord, surely not this man.*

"Yes. I will die in Rome. As will Paul."

Tears welled in Silas's eyes. *Both of them, Lord?* "We need your voice, Peter."

"My voice?" He shook his head.

Silas knew better than to attempt to dissuade Peter from doing whatever the Lord willed. "As God wills, Peter. We will return to Rome together."

"No. *I* will return. You will remain behind."

Silas felt the blood leave his face. "I will not run for my life when my closest friends face death!" His voice broke.

Peter put a hand on his arm. "Is your life your own, Silas? We belong to the Lord. God has called *me* back to Rome. He will tell *you* what to do when the time comes."

"I can't let you go back alone!"

"I am not alone. The Lord is with me. Whatever happens, my friend, we are one in Christ Jesus. God causes everything to work together for the good of those who love God and are called according to His purpose."

"And if they crucify you?"

Peter shook his head. "I am not worthy to die in the same way the Lord did."

"They will do everything they can to break you, Peter. You know they will!"

"I know, Silas. Jesus told me years ago how I would die. You must pray for me, my friend. Pray I stand firm to the end." When Silas opened his mouth to argue further, Peter raised his hand. "No more, Silas. It is not for us to question the Lord's plan, my friend, but to follow it. I *must* go where God leads."

"I will not abandon you, Peter." Silas fought to keep his voice firm. "Before God, I swear it."

"I swore the same thing once." Peter's eyes shone with tears. "I didn't keep my vow."

Peter ordered the driver to turn the coach around. His wife insisted upon going back with him. "Wherever you go, I will go." Peter helped her into the coach and stepped up to sit beside her.

Determined not to be left behind, Silas climbed up. Peter shoved the pack of scrolls into his arms. The unbalanced weight made Silas step down. Scroll cases tumbled. As Silas scrambled for them, Peter closed and locked the coach door. He hit the side of the coach. The driver tapped the horses' flanks.

"Wait!"

Peter looked out at him. "May the Lord bless you and protect you. May the Lord show you his favor and give you his peace."

Silas frantically retrieved scrolls, shoving them into the pack. *"Wait!"*

Slinging the pack over his shoulder, Silas ran to catch up. As he reached for the back of the coach, the driver gave a harsh cry and cracked his whip. The horses broke into a full gallop, leaving Silas choking in the dust.

ONE

※✦✦✦✦✦※

Silas sat at his writing table. His mind screamed *why?* as his dreams collapsed in grief and defeat. Clenching his hands, he tried to still the shaking. He dared not mix the ink or attempt to write now, for he would only ruin a section of new papyrus. He breathed in slowly, but could not calm his raging emotions.

"Lord, why does it always come to this?" Resting his elbows on the table, he covered his face with his hands. He could not blot out the horrific images.

Peter's wife screaming.

Peter calling out to her in anguish from where he was bound. *"Remember the Lord! Remember the Lord!"*

The Roman throng mocking the big fisherman from Galilee.

Silas groaned. *Oh, Lord. Even had I been blind, I would have heard the wrath of Satan against mankind in that arena, the lustful rejoicing at bloodshed. He murders men, and they help him do it!*

Silas felt pierced anew by the memory of seeing Christ crucified. At the time, Silas had questioned whether Jesus was the Messiah, but nonetheless he had been appalled by the cruelty of the Jews celebrating the death of a fellow Jew, that they could hate one of their own so much they would stand and mock him as he hung on the cross, beaten past recognition. They had stood sneering, calling out in contempt, "He saved others, but He can't save himself!"

Now, Silas tried to see past this world into the next, as Stephen had when members of the high council had stoned him outside the gates of Jerusalem. But all Silas saw was the darkness of men, the triumph of evil. *I am tired, Lord. I am sick of this life. All Your apostles, save John, are martyred. Is anyone else left who saw Your face?*

Lord, please take me home, I beg of You. Don't leave me here among these wretched people. I want to come home to You.

His eyes grew hot as he put shaking hands over his ears. "Forgive me,

Lord. Forgive me. I'm afraid. I admit it. I'm terrified. Not of death, but of *dying.*" Even now, Silas could hear the echoes on Vatican Hill, where Nero's circus stood.

When his wife lay dead, Peter had bowed his head and wept.

The crowd had cheered when a cross was brought forth. "Yes! Crucify him! *Crucify him!*"

Peter's voice boomed above the noise. *"I am not worthy to die as my Lord did! I am not worthy!"*

"Coward!" Romans screamed. "He pleads for his life!"

Romans—so quick to worship courage—failed to recognize it in the man before them. They shrieked curses and cried out for further torture.

"Impale him!"

"Burn him alive!"

"Feed him to the lions!"

The big fisherman had left the shores of Galilee to throw the net of God's love to save masses drowning in sin. But the people swam in Satan's current. Peter had not asked for an *easier* death, only one *different* from the one his precious Lord had suffered.

Peter had never forgotten, had often recounted his failure to Silas. "The Lord said I would deny Him three times before the rooster crowed, and that's exactly what I did."

When the Romans nailed Peter to the cross, Silas had bowed his head. He couldn't watch.

Did I betray him the way he betrayed You, Lord? Did I fail him in his hour of need? When he looked again, he saw the centurion leaning down over Peter, listening. The Roman straightened, then stood for a moment before summoning two others. They levered up the cross and added ropes. Peter's body writhed in agony, but he made no sound.

The crew of soldiers strained at the task of turning the cross upside down.

The mob went quiet, and in that single moment Peter called out, his deep voice carrying up through the rows of spectators. "Forgive them, Father; they don't know what they are doing."

The Master's words.

Tears had welled in Silas's eyes.

It had taken all his will to stand in the arch in the upper corridor and keep his eyes fixed upon Peter in his suffering. "Pray when I face my death, Silas," Peter had requested weeks before his capture. "Pray that I will remain faithful to the end."

And so Silas had prayed, fiercely, determined, in anguish, in fear. *Lord, if it ever comes to this for me, let me in faith endure to the end as Peter did. Do not let me recant what I know! You are the way, the truth, and the life. Lord, give my friend comfort in his agony. Lord, give Your beloved servant Peter strength to cling tightly to his faith in You. Lord, let him see You as Stephen did! Fill him with the joy of homecoming. Speak to him now, Lord. Please say those words we all long to hear: "Well done, my good and faithful servant."*

He was, Lord. Your servant Peter was faithful.

God, I beg of You, let this be the last execution I witness!

Last night Silas had awakened, certain he heard Paul's voice dictating another letter. Relieved, joyous, he had jumped up. "Paul!" The dream was so vivid it took a moment for the truth to strike him. When it did, it felt like a physical blow. *Paul's dead.*

Silas put his hands flat on the writing table. "You are the resurrection and the life." He must remind himself. "The resurrection." What were the words John had said when they last met in Ephesus? "Anyone who believes in Jesus will have . . ." *No. That isn't right.* "Anyone who believes in God's Son *has* eternal life." Paul's words echoed in his mind. "While we were utterly helpless, Christ died for us sinners." John's conviction cried out to him. "Love each other . . ."

A shout from outside made Silas stiffen. Were they coming for him now? Would he face another imprisonment, another flogging, more torture? *If I try to escape suffering by telling them I'm a Roman citizen, will that make me a coward? It's true, but I despise everything about this empire. I hate that even in the smallest way I'm part of it. Lord, I was strong once. I was. Not anymore . . .*

Paul's voice echoed again. "When I am weak, then I am strong. . . ."

Silas gripped his head. "You, my friend, not I . . ."

He could not think clearly here in the confines of Rome with the cacophony of voices, trampling feet, vendors' cries. The mob, the ever insatiable mob on his heels. *I have to get out of here! I have to get away from this place!*

He scrambled to gather his writing materials and few possessions. The scrolls! He must safeguard the scrolls!

Heart pounding, Silas left the small, stifling room.

The proprietor spotted him the moment he came out the door, as though the man had been watching for him. "You there!" He crossed the narrow street. "You're leaving?"

"My business here is finished."

"You don't look well. Perhaps you should stay a few more days."

Silas glanced at him. The man cared nothing about his health. Money was all the man wanted—more money.

The noise of humanity seemed to grow louder around Silas. Wolf faces everywhere. Romulus and Remus's offspring filled the street. Silas looked at the people milling about, talking, shouting, laughing, arguing. The poor lived here—huddled, hungry masses that needed so much more than food.

They reeked of discontent, cursing one another over the least provocation. These were the people Rome appeased with blood sport. It kept their minds from dwelling on the lack of grain.

Silas looked into the proprietor's eyes. Paul would have spoken the words of life to him. Peter would have spoken of Jesus.

"What?" The proprietor frowned.

Let him die, Silas thought. *Why should I cast pearls before this pig?* "Perhaps I've got the fever," he said. "It swept through the village where I stayed a few weeks ago." True enough. Better than saying, "I went to the games three days ago, and watched two of my closest friends executed. All I want now is to get as far away from this wretched city as I can. And if the whole population of Rome is sucked down to hell, I will stand and shout praises to God for their destruction!"

As Silas expected, the proprietor drew back in alarm. "Fever? Yes, you must go."

"Yes, I must." Silas smiled tightly. "Plagues spread quickly in narrow streets, don't they?" *Especially the plague of sin.* "I paid for a week, didn't I?"

The man blanched. "I don't remember."

"I didn't think you would." Silas shouldered his pack and walked away.

✦   ✦   ✦

After several days of walking, Silas reached Puteoli. He did not have the stamina he once had, nor the heart.

He made his way to the harbor and wandered in the marketplace. *Where do I go from here, Lord?* Semaphores flashed, signaling the arrival of grain ships, probably from Egypt. Workers hurried past him, hastening to unload sacks of grain, carry them to the *mensores* for weighing. Other vessels anchored farther out, *lenuncularii* operating tenders between ship and shore. Merchandise came from all over the empire to satisfy the Roman markets: corn, cattle, wine, and wool from Sicily; horses from Spain; slaves from Britannia and Germania; marble from Greece; multicolored rugs from Asshur. The port was a good place to lose himself and still find what he most needed.

The scents made Silas's head swim: salt-sea air, animal dung, spices, wine, and human sweat. Seagulls screeched overhead as fish were piled on a cart. Criers shouted goods for sale. Sheep bleated from holding pens. Wild dogs from Britannia snarled from crates. Foreign slaves stood naked on platforms, sweating in the sun as they were auctioned. One fought against his bonds while a woman and child were pulled away. Though he shouted in a strange language, his anguish was well understood. The woman's weeping turned to hysterical screams as her child was wrenched from her. She tried to reach him, but was dragged in another direction. The child wailed in terror, arms outstretched toward his mother.

Throat tight, Silas turned away. He couldn't escape injustice and misery. It was all around him, threatening to suffocate him. The seed of sin planted centuries ago in the Garden of Eden had taken root and spread its shoots of wickedness everywhere. And all feasted on this poisonous fruit that would bring them nothing but death.

It was late afternoon when he saw a familiar symbol carved into a post of a booth filled with barrels of olives and baskets of pomegranates, dates, figs, and nuts. His stomach growled. His mouth watered. He hadn't eaten anything since leaving The Three Taverns two days ago.

He listened to the proprietor bargain with a woman. "You know these are the best dates in all the empire."

"And you know I cannot pay such a high price."

Neither shouted nor grew vitriolic, a common occurrence in marketplaces. She made an offer; he countered. She shook her head and made another offer. He laughed and made yet another. When they reached agreement, the proprietor grabbed a handful of dried dates and put them on his scale. He wrapped them in a cloth the woman handed him and received payment. As she walked away, he turned his attention to Silas. "Olives? Dates?"

Silas shook his head. He had spent his last coin on bread. He looked at the symbol carved into the pole. Had this grinning pirate put it there? Before he could find a way to ask, the man cocked his head and frowned. "I know you. Don't I?"

"We've never met."

"You look familiar."

Silas's heart pounded. He thought of turning away, but where would he go? "I am a friend of Theophilus."

The man's eyes cleared. "Ah!" He grinned. "How is he these days?"

"Not well." Silas took a step back, thinking he might have made a mistake in saying anything to this man.

The merchant glanced one way and then the other and beckoned Silas closer. "Silas. Is that not your name?"

Silas blanched.

"Do not look distressed, my friend," the man said quickly. He dropped his voice. "I heard you preach once, in Corinth. Years ago—five, maybe six. You look tired. Are you hungry?"

Silas couldn't answer.

The man grabbed some dates and figs and pressed them into Silas's hand. "Go to the end of the street; turn left. Follow that street to the end. It will wind like a serpent before you reach your destination. Pass two fountains. Take the first street on the right just after. Knock on the door of the third house. Ask for Epanetus."

Could he remember all that, or would he find himself wandering Puteoli all night? "Whom shall I say sent me?"

"My apologies. In my excitement at meeting you, I forgot to introduce myself." He laughed. "I'm Urbanus." He leaned forward and said gruffly, "You are an answer to many prayers."

Silas felt the weight of the man's expectations. "Peter is dead."

Urbanus gave a solemn nod. "We heard."

So soon? "How?"

"Bad news travels fast. Our brother Patrobas arrived day before yesterday. He could not find you in the catacombs."

Patrobas. Silas knew him well. "I feared someone might follow and others be taken."

"We feared you had been arrested." Urbanus grasped Silas's arms. "God has answered our prayers. You are well. We did not expect the added blessing of your presence here."

Blessing? This man remembered his face from one encounter. What if others, enemies, also recognized him as Peter's scribe? His presence might endanger these brothers and sisters.

Lord, will all we've worked for be destroyed in a bloodbath?

Urbanus leaned closer. "Do not look so troubled, my friend. Puteoli is a busy city. Everyone has an eye to business and little else. People come; people go." He repeated the directions, slowly this time. "I would show you the way myself, but I cannot entrust my booth to others. They're all thieves . . . just as I once was." He laughed again and slapped Silas on the shoulder. "Go. I will see you later." He called to a group of women passing by. "Come! See what good olives I have! The best in the empire!"

Urbanus did not lie. Two dates and a fig took the sharp edge of hunger away, and they did taste better than anything Silas had eaten in Rome. He kept the rest in the pouch tied to his belt.

The day was hot, and Silas felt sweat trickle down his back as he walked. Merchants' booths gave way to streets lined with tenements. Shoulders aching, he shifted his pack. Over the years, he had carried far heavier loads than this, but the weight of the scrolls seemed to increase with every step.

A servant opened the door when he knocked. The Ethiopian's inscrutable gaze took Silas in from dusty head to sandaled feet.

"I am looking for the house of Epanetus."

"This is the house of Epanetus. Who may I tell my master is come?"

"A friend of Theophilus."

The servant opened the door wider. "I am Macombo. Come. Enter in." He closed the door firmly behind Silas. "Wait here." He strode away.

It was the house of a rich man. Pillared corridors and frescoed walls. An open court with a white marble statue of a woman pouring water from an urn. The sound of the water made Silas realize his thirst. He swallowed hard and longed to shrug the pack from his shoulders and sit.

Footsteps approached—the hurried slap of sandals. A tall, broad-shouldered man strode across the courtyard. His short-cropped hair was gray, his features strongly carved. "I am Epanetus."

"Urbanus sent me."

"Which Urbanus would that be?"

Caution was to be expected. "From the agora." Silas opened his pouch and took out a handful of plump dates.

Epanetus laughed. "Ah, yes. 'The best dates and figs in all the empire.'" He extended his hands. "You are welcome here."

Silas received the greeting, knowing his own response was somewhat less enthusiastic.

"Come." Epanetus gave a quiet order to Macombo and then led Silas across the court, through an archway, and into another area of the house. Several people sat in a large room. Silas recognized one of them.

Patrobas came swiftly to his feet. "Silas!" Grinning broadly, he came to embrace him. "We feared you were lost to us." He drew back and kept one hand firmly on Silas's arm as he addressed the others. "God has answered our prayers."

They surrounded him. The heartfelt greetings broke down Silas's last defenses. Shoulders sagging, he bowed his head and wept.

No one spoke for a moment, and then they all spoke at once.

"Pour him a little wine."

"You're exhausted."

"Sit. Have something to eat."

"Macombo, set the tray here."

Patrobas frowned and guided Silas. "Rest here."

When someone took hold of his pack, Silas instinctively gripped it tighter. "No!"

"You are safe here," Epanetus said. "Consider my home yours."

Silas felt ashamed. "I must safeguard these scrolls."

"Put the pack here beside you," Patrobas said. "No one will touch it unless you give permission."

Exhausted, Silas sat. He saw nothing but love and compassion in the faces surrounding him. A woman looked up at him, eyes welling with tears. Her concern pierced him. "Letters." He managed to shrug the pack from his shoulders and set it down beside him. "Copies of those Paul sent to the Corinthians. And Peter's." His voice broke. Covering his face, he tried to regain control and couldn't. His shoulders shook with his sobs.

Someone squeezed his shoulder. They wept with him, their love leaving no room for embarrassment.

"Our friend is with the Lord." Patrobas's voice was thick with grief.

"Yes. No one can harm him or his wife now."

"They stand in the Lord's presence as we speak."

As I long to be, Silas wanted to cry out. *Oh, to see Jesus' face again!* To have an end of trials, an end to fear, an end to the attack of doubt when he least expected it. *I am losing the battle inside myself, Lord.*

"We must hold firm to that which we know is true."

Paul's words, spoken so long ago. They had been sitting in a dungeon, darkness surrounding them, their bodies laced with pain from a brutal whipping. "Hold fast," he had said.

"I'm trying," Silas moaned.

"What is he saying?"

Silas mumbled into his hands. "Jesus died for our sins and was raised from the grave on the third day. . . ." But all he could see was the Lord on the cross, Paul beheaded, Peter crucified. He pressed the heels of his hands into his eyes.

"He's ill."

"Shhhh . . ."

"Silas." A firm hand this time, a Roman hand. A tray laden with food was set before him. Epanetus and Patrobas encouraged him to eat. Silas took bread in trembling hands and tore it. *This is My body. . . .* He held the two halves, shaking. "Do I dare eat of it?"

Whispers of concern.

Epanetus poured wine into a cup and held it out to him. "Drink." Silas stared at the red fluid. *This is My blood. . . .* He remembered Jesus on the cross, blood and water pouring from the spear wound in His side. He remembered Peter hanging upside down.

Pain gripped his chest. His heart raced faster and faster. The room grew dark.

"Silas!"

He heard the roaring of the Roman mob. Hands grabbed hold of him. *So be it, Lord. If I die, there will be an end of suffering. And rest. Please, Lord. Let me rest.*

"Silas . . ." A woman's voice this time. Close. He felt her breath on his face. "Don't leave us. . . ."

Voices above and around him, and then no sound at all.

✦   ✦   ✦

Silas roused, confused. A clay lamp burned on a stand. Someone came close. A cool hand rested on his brow. Silas groaned and closed his eyes. His throat squeezed tight and hot.

A strong arm slid beneath him and raised him. "Drink." Macombo held a cup to Silas's lips.

Something warm and sweetened with honey.

"A little more. It will help you sleep."

Silas remembered and struggled to rise. "Where are they? Where . . . ? The letters!"

"Here." Macombo lifted the pack.

Silas took it and clutched it close, sighing as he lay back on the bed.

"No one will take anything from you, Silas."

Voices came and went, along with dreams. Paul spoke to him across a campfire. Luke dressed his wounds. They sang as they followed the Roman road. He awakened to footsteps and fell asleep again. Paul paced, agitated, and Silas shook his head. "If you will but rest, my friend, and pray, the words will come."

Voices again, familiar now. Macombo and Epanetus.

"To whom does he speak?"

"I don't know."

"Silas . . ."

He opened his eyes. A woman stood with the sunlight at her back. When she came close, he frowned. "I don't know you."

"I'm Diana. You've been sleeping a long time."

"Diana . . ." He tried to remember. He had seen her face, but where?

She put her hand on his shoulder. "I'll just sit with you awhile."

"How is he?" Epanetus spoke from somewhere close.

"He has no fever."

"Pain?"

"His dreams trouble him."

Time passed; how much, Silas didn't know or care. He awakened again to voices in the corridor outside the room.

"It's not just exhaustion that makes him sleep so long. It's grief."

"Give him time. He will find his strength in the Lord."

Murmuring and then Macombo's voice. "He seems little interested in food or drink."

"I heard him speak in Corinth," said Urbanus, the pirate merchant who sold the best dates in the empire. "He was magnificent. Think of the honor the Lord has bestowed on us by sending him here. Silas saw Jesus in the flesh."

"And saw Him crucified." Patrobas spoke with quiet firmness.

"And risen! We've only heard about the Lord. We never saw Him face-to-face. We never ate with Him or walked with Him. . . ."

Silas put his arm over his eyes.

"Let him rest a little longer before you try to wake him. It's only been three days, and he's endured more than any of us. . . ."

Three days! No matter how much Silas might long to escape the sorrow of this world, he could not will himself to heaven. He reached down. The pack of precious scrolls lay beside him. His body ached as he sat up. He rubbed his face. His joints and muscles screamed as he stood. He rolled his shoulders and stretched slowly. Raising his hands in habitual praise, he prayed. "This is a day that You have made, Lord, and I will rejoice in it." He might not feel like it, but he would do so in obedience. Grudging obedience.

Dogged, determined, he picked up the pack and followed the sound of retreating voices. He stood in the archway of a large room. Men and women of all ages sat together, enjoying a meal. Silas stayed in the shadowed corridor, studying them. He saw meat on a fine pottery platter, and fruit being passed in a simple, woven basket. Everyone had brought something to share.

A love feast.

Silas remembered the gatherings in Jerusalem, the first year after Jesus ascended, the excitement, the joy, the openhanded charity between brothers and sisters.

Jerusalem! How he longed to go home to those halcyon days.

But even if he could go back to Judea, he knew nothing would be the same. Persecution had driven the followers of Jesus to other cities and provinces, leaving behind Jewish factions that constantly warred with one another. One day, Rome would make peace for them, with the army, the way Rome always made peace. If only they would listen!

Jesus had warned of Jerusalem's destruction. John had told Luke what Jesus said, and Luke had written it all down in the history he was collecting. The good doctor had been hard at work on it during the years Silas had known him, when they both traveled with Paul. A kind man, educated, inquisitive. A gifted physician. Paul would have died several times if not for Luke's ministrations. *And I along with him.*

Had Luke escaped from Rome? Had he gone back to Corinth or Ephesus?

Timothy's most recent letter said John was living in Ephesus. Mary, Jesus' mother, lived with him. Her sons, James and Jude, who became believers when they saw the risen Christ, had joined the apostles on the council in Jerusalem.

"Silas!"

Startled from his reverie, Silas saw Epanetus cross the room. "Come. Join us." Patrobas rose, as did several others.

Epanetus led Silas to a place of honor. Diana rose and prepared a plate of food for him. She smiled into his eyes when he thanked her. A young man sitting beside her whispered in her ear. "Not now, Curiatus," she replied.

Everyone talked at once, until Epanetus laughed and raised his hands. "Quiet, everyone! Give Silas time to eat before we attack him with questions."

They talked among themselves again, but Silas felt their glances. He gave silent thanks to God for what was placed before him. Pork, and judging by the quality, from a pig fattened in oak forests. A Roman delicacy, and unclean by Mosaic law. He took some fruit instead. Even now, after years of being freed from the Mosaic law, he had difficulty eating pork.

Others arrived—a family with several children, a young couple, two older men . . . The room filled. And each wanted to meet him, to clasp his hand.

Silas felt alone in the midst of them, trapped inside himself, captive to thoughts that buzzed like angry bees. He longed for solitude, and knew how ungrateful it would be to rise and leave them now. And where could he go other than that silent room with its rich surroundings that reminded him of things he had worked so hard to forget?

Everyone had finished eating, and he lost his appetite. He saw their expectation, felt their hunger to hear him speak.

The boy spoke first. "You knew the Lord Jesus, didn't you?" He ignored his mother's hand on his arm. "Would you tell us about Him?"

And then the others began. "Tell us everything, Silas."

"What was He like?"

"How did He look?"

"What did you feel when you were in His presence?"

"And the apostles? You knew them all, didn't you? What were they like?" The boy again, all eyes and pleading. "Will you teach us as you've taught others?"

Hadn't he preached hundreds of times in dozens of towns from Jerusalem to Antioch to Thessalonica? Hadn't he told the story of Jesus crucified and risen to small crowds and large, some praising God, others mocking and hostile? Hadn't he worked with Timothy in teaching the Corinthians? He had traveled thousands of miles alongside Paul, establishing churches in city after city.

Yet, here among these friendly, hospitable brothers and sisters, he could think of nothing to say.

Silas looked from one face to another, trying to sort his thoughts, trying to think where to start, when all he could see in his mind's eye was Peter hanging upside down, his blood forming a growing pool beneath him.

Everyone was looking at him, waiting, eager.

"I fear . . ." His voice broke. He felt as though someone had clamped strong hands around his throat. He swallowed convulsively and waited until the sensation passed. "I fear I endanger you." He spoke the truth, but doubted it commended him. "Paul is beheaded; Peter crucified. The apostles are scattered, most martyred. No one can replace these great witnesses of God. No one can speak the message of Christ as effectively as they have."

"You spoke effectively in Corinth," Urbanus said. "Your every word pierced my heart."

"The Holy Spirit pierces you, not I. And that was a long time ago, when I was younger and stronger than I am today." Stronger in body; stronger in faith. His eyes blurred with tears. "A few days ago in Rome, I watched a dear friend die a horrible death because he carried the testimony of God. I don't think I can go on. . . ."

"You were Peter's secretary," Patrobas said.

Leading words. They wanted to draw him out into the open.

"Yes, and my presence brings danger to all of you."

"A danger we welcome, Silas." The others murmured agreement with Epanetus's firm declaration.

"Please. Teach us." The boy spoke again.

He was not much younger than Timothy had been the first time Silas met him. Diana looked at him with her beautiful dark eyes, so full of compassion. His heart squeezed at the sight. What could he say to make them understand what he didn't understand himself? *Oh, Lord, I can't talk about crucifixion. I can't talk about the cross . . . not Yours or Peter's.*

He shook his head, eyes downcast. "I regret, I cannot think clearly enough to teach." He fumbled with the pack beside him. "But I've brought letters." Exact copies he had made from originals. He looked at Epanetus, desperate, appealing to him as host. "Perhaps someone here can read the letters."

"Yes. Of course." Smiling, Epanetus rose.

Silas took one out and, with shaking hand, presented it to the Roman.

Epanetus read one of Paul's letters to the Corinthians. When he finished, he held the scroll for a moment before carefully rolling it and giving it back to Silas. "We have yearned for such meat as this."

Silas carefully tucked the scroll away.

"Can we read another?" Curiatus had moved closer.

"Pick one."

Patrobas read one of Peter's letters. Silas had made many copies of it and sent them to many of the churches he had helped Paul start.

"Peter makes it clear you were a great help to him, Silas."

Silas was touched by Diana's praise, and wary because of his feelings. "The words are Peter's."

"Beautifully written in Greek," Patrobas pointed out. "Hardly Peter's native language."

What could he say without sounding boastful? Yes, he had helped Peter refine his thoughts and put them into proper Greek. Peter had been a fisherman, working to put food on his family's table. While Peter had toiled over his nets, Silas had sat in comfort, yoked to an exacting rabbi who demanded every word of the Torah be memorized. God had chosen Peter as one of His twelve companions. And Peter had chosen Silas to be his secretary. By God's grace and mercy, Silas had accompanied Peter and his wife on their journey to Rome. He would be forever humbled and thankful for the years he spent with them.

Though Aramaic was the common language of Judea, Silas could speak and write Hebrew and Greek as well as Latin. He spoke Egyptian enough to get by in conversation. Every day, he thanked God that he had been allowed to use what gifts he had to serve the Lord's servants.

"What was it like to walk with Jesus?"

The boy again. Insatiable youth. So much like Timothy. "I did not travel with Him, nor was I among those He chose."

"But you knew Him."

"I knew *of* Him. Twice, I met Him and spoke with Him. I know Him now as Savior and Lord, just as you do. He abides in me, and I in Him through the Holy Spirit." He put his hand against his chest. *Lord, Lord, would I have the faith of Peter to endure if I were nailed to a cross?*

"Are you all right, Silas? Are you in pain again?"

He shook his head. He was in no physical danger. Not here. Not now.

"How many of the twelve disciples did you know?"

"What were they like?"

So many questions—the same ones he'd answered countless times before in casual gatherings from Antioch to Rome.

"He knew them all," Patrobas said into the silence. "He sat on the Jerusalem council."

Silas forced his mind to focus. "They were strangers to me during the years Jesus preached." Jesus' closest companions were not people with whom Silas would have wanted contact. Fishermen, a zealot, a tax collector. He would have avoided their company, for any commerce with them would have damaged his reputation. It was only later that they became his beloved brothers. "I heard Jesus speak once near the shores of Galilee and several times at the Temple."

Curiatus leaned forward, resting his elbows on his knees and his chin in his hands. "What was it like to be in His presence?"

"The first time I met Him, I thought He was a young rabbi wise beyond His years. But when He spoke and I looked into His eyes, I was afraid." He shook his head, thinking back. "Not afraid. Terrified."

"But He was kind and merciful. So we've been told."

"So He is."

"What did He look like?"

"I heard He glowed like gold and fire poured from His lips."

"On a mountain once, Peter, James, and John saw Him transfigured, but Jesus left His glory behind and came to us as a man. I saw Him several times. There was nothing in Jesus' physical appearance to attract people to Him. But when He spoke, He did so with the full authority of God." Silas's thoughts drifted to those days before He knew the Lord personally, days filled with rumors, whispered questions, while the priests gathered in tight circles, grumbling in Temple corridors. It had been their behavior most of all that sent Silas to Galilee to see for himself who this Jesus was. He had sensed their fear and later witnessed their ferocious jealousy.

Epanetus put his hand on Silas's shoulder. "Enough, my friends. Silas is tired. And it is late."

As the others rose, the boy pressed between two men and came to him. "Can I talk with you? Just for a little while."

Diana reached for him, cheeks flushed, eyes full of apology. "You heard Epanetus, my son. Come. The meeting is over for the evening. Give the man rest." She drew her son away.

"Could we come back tomorrow?"

"Later. Perhaps. After work . . ."

Curiatus glanced back. "You won't leave, will you? You have words of truth to speak."

"Curiatus!"

"He wrote all those scrolls, Mother. He could write all he's seen and heard. . . ."

Diana put her arm around her son and spoke softly, but with more firmness this time, as she led him from the room.

Epanetus saw everyone safely away. When he returned, he smiled. "Curiatus is right. It would be a good thing if you would write a record."

Silas had spent most of his life writing letters, putting down onto scrolls the encouragement and instructions of men inspired by God. The council in Jerusalem, James, Paul, Peter. "For the most part, I helped others sort and express their thoughts."

"Would it not help you to sort your thoughts and feelings if you did? You suffer, Silas. We all can see that. You loved Peter and his wife. You loved Paul. It is never easy to lose a friend. And you've lost many."

"My faith is weak."

"Perhaps that is the best of all reasons for you to dwell on the past." Epanetus spoke more seriously. "You have lived your life in service to others. Your ink-stained fingers are proof of it."

The darkest part of night had come, a darkness that crushed Silas's spirit. He looked down at his hands. They indicted him.

"Curiatus is named aptly." Epanetus spoke gently. "But perhaps God brought you to us and put the idea in the boy's head. Is that not possible?"

Silas closed his eyes. *Can I dwell on the past without being undone by it? I regret, Lord; I regret the wasted years. Is that a sin, too?*

Epanetus spread his hands. "Precious few are left who were in Judea when Jesus walked this earth."

"That's all too painfully true." Silas heard his bitterness.

Epanetus sat, hands clasped, expression intense. "I will not share my story until I know you better, but know this: you are not alone in your struggle with faith. Whatever sorrow you carry other than the death of your friends is not hidden from the Lord. You know and I know Jesus died for all our sins and rose from the dead. Through faith in Him we have the promise of everlasting life. We will live forever in the presence of the Lord. But like the boy, I crave to know more about Jesus. So much of what we hear drifts away. Those scrolls, for example. Patrobas and I read two tonight. But if you leave tomorrow, how much will we all remember by next week or next month? And what of our children?"

"Another has already set about the task of writing the history: Luke, the physician."

"I have heard of him. That's wonderful news, Silas, but where is he now? He left Rome after Paul was beheaded, didn't he? How long before we receive a copy of what he has written?"

"He was not the only one. Many have undertaken the task of compiling an account of things that happened and what's been accomplished."

"That may be so, Silas, but we have received nothing in the way of letters, other than the one written by Paul. You are here with us! We want to know what you learned from Peter and Paul. We want to see these men of faith as you did. They endured to the end. As you endure now. Share your life with us."

"What you ask is a monumental task!" *And I'm so weary, Lord. Let someone else do what he asks.*

"The task is not beyond your abilities, Silas." Epanetus gripped his arm. "Whatever you need, you have only to ask. Scrolls, ink, a safe place to write without interruption. God has blessed me with abundance so that I might bless others. Give me the blessing and honor to serve you." The Roman stood. "May you be at peace with whatever God asks of you."

"Epanetus!" Silas called out before he left him alone in the room. "It is not easy to look back."

"I know." The Roman stood in the doorway, mouth tipped. "But sometimes we must look back before we can move forward."

TWO

✦❖✦❖✦❖✦

Silas, *a disciple of Jesus Christ, eyewitness to the Crucifixion, servant of the risen Lord and Savior, Jesus Christ, to the family of Theophilus. Grace to you and peace from God our Father and the Lord Jesus Christ.*

The first time I heard the name of Jesus was in the Temple in Jerusalem. Rumors of false prophets and self-proclaimed messiahs were common in those days, and priests were often called upon to investigate. A few years earlier, Theudas had claimed to be the anointed one of God. He gained four hundred disciples before he was slain by the Romans. The rest dispersed. Then, during the census, Judas of Galilee rose up. Soon, he too was dead and his followers scattered. My father had warned me against men who grew like weeds among wheat. "Trust in the law of Moses, my son. It is a lamp to guide your feet and a light for your path."

John the Baptist began gathering crowds at the Jordan River, baptizing for the repentance of sins. A delegation of priests went out to question him. Upon their return, I overheard angry words in the hallowed corridors.

"He's a false prophet who comes out of the wilderness and lives off locusts and honey."

"The man is mad!"

"The man wears a garment of camel's hair and a leather belt!"

"He dared call us a brood of snakes."

"Mad or not, he has the people listening to him. And he cried out against us, asking who'd warned us against God's coming wrath. We must do something about him!"

Something was done, but not by the priests and religious leaders. John confronted King Herod for his adulterous relationship with Herodias, his brother Philip's wife. Arrested, he was held in the palace dungeon. Herodias held a celebration for the king's birthday and used her daughter to entice Herod into making a foolish promise: if she would dance for his guests, he would give her whatever she wanted. The trap closed. The girl demanded John the Baptist's head on a platter, and happily gave the gruesome gift to her scheming mother.

Those who thought John the Baptist was the Messiah grieved over his death and lost hope. Others said he pointed the way to Jesus, and went after the rabbi from Nazareth. Some, like me, waited cautiously to see what happened. All Jews lived in hope of the Messiah's coming. We longed to see the chains of Rome broken, and our oppressors driven from the land God had given our ancestors. We wanted our nation to be great again, as it had been during the time of King David and King Solomon, his son.

Some buried their hope in the shallow grave of a false messiah only to have it arise again when a new one appeared on the horizon. Hope can be a terrible taskmaster!

There were many rabbis in Judea, each with disciples yoked to his teachings. Some met in the corridors of the Temple, others in distant synagogues. Some traveled from town to town, gathering disciples as they went. It was not uncommon to see a group of young men following in their rabbi's footsteps, hanging on his every word.

I thought none so wise as my father, who had told me to memorize the Law and live by it. I thought the Law would save me. I thought by following the commandments, and giving sacrifices, I could garner God's favor. Hence, I was often in the Temple, bringing my tithes and offerings. The Law was my delight, and my bane. I prayed and fasted. I obeyed the commandments. And still I felt I existed on the edge of a great precipice. One slip, and I would fall into sin and be lost forever. I longed for assurance.

Or thought I did.

The stories about Jesus persisted and grew in magnitude.

"Jesus gave sight to a blind man!"

"Jesus made a paralyzed man walk in Capernaum."

"He cast out demons!"

Some even claimed He raised a widow's son from the dead.

The leading priests who had gone out to investigate John the Baptist met in chambers with the high priest, Caiaphas. My father, who had been a longtime friend of Annas's family, told me later how incensed they became when it was asked if Jesus might be the Messiah.

"The Messiah will be a son of David born in Bethlehem, not some lowly carpenter from Nazareth who eats with tax collectors and prostitutes!"

Neither they, nor I, knew at the time that Jesus had in fact been born in Bethlehem of a virgin betrothed to Joseph. Both Mary and Joseph were of the tribe of Judah and descendants of the great King David. Further evidence came when Isaiah's prophesy was fulfilled, for Mary had conceived by the Holy Spirit. These facts became known to me later and merely affirmed all I had, by then, come to believe about Jesus. To my knowledge, nothing ever changed the minds of Annas, Caiaphas, and other priests who clutched so tightly to the power they imagined they held in the palms of their hands. Annas is dead now. And Caiaphas too is long gone.

What kept me away from Jesus for so long was the company He kept. I had never heard of any rabbi eating with sinners, let alone inviting them to be His friends. I pursued discipleship with a well-respected rabbi and was not received by him until I proved myself worthy to be his student. Jesus went out and chose His disciples from among common men. I had spent my life in caution, avoiding all those things the Torah declared unclean. I did not converse with women, and I never allowed a Gentile into my house. I knew my rabbi would not hear the name of Jesus. The Nazarene was a renegade. Jesus healed lepers. Jesus taught the women who traveled with Him. He gathered the poor, the downtrodden, the defiled on hillsides and fed them. He even preached to hated Samaritans!

Who was this man? And what good did He think He was doing by shattering the traditions accumulated over the centuries?

I longed to discuss all these matters with my father, but could not. He was too ill and died in the heat of summer. I sought out one of his most respected friends, a member of the high council, Nicodemus. "Is the Nazarene a prophet or a dangerous revolutionary?"

"He speaks with great compassion and knows the Law."

I was astounded. "You have met the man?"

"Once. Briefly." He changed the subject and would not be drawn back to it.

I wondered how many others among the leading priests and scribes had gone out to hear Jesus preach. Every time Jesus' name was mentioned, I listened. I learned He spoke in many synagogues and taught about the Kingdom of God. The desire to leave my careful life grew in me. I wanted to see Jesus. I wanted to hear Him preach. I wanted to know if He was the one who could answer all my questions.

Most of all, like many others, I wanted to see Him perform a miracle. Perhaps then I would know whether to take this particular prophet seriously or not.

So I went to Galilee.

✦   ✦   ✦

The crowd in Capernaum felt bigger than any I had seen at the Temple, except during the Passover celebration, when Jews came from Mesopotamia, Cappadocia, Pontus, Asia, Phrygia, Pamphylia, Egypt, and even Rome. The people I found in Capernaum that day frightened me, for they were wretched. A blind man in rags, destitute widows, mothers holding crying children, cripples, people dragging stretchers on which lay sick relatives or friends, lepers and outcasts, all calling out and trying to push forward and get closer to Jesus. Of course, I had seen many poor and sick begging on the Temple steps, and often gave them money. But never had I seen so many! They filled the streets and spilled down to the shoreline of the Sea of Galilee.

"Jesus!" Someone shouted. "Jesus is coming!"

Everyone began to call out to Him at once. The sound of anguished, pleading, hopeful voices was deafening.

"My father is sick. . . ."

"My brother is dying. . . ."

"I'm blind. Heal me!"

"Help me, Jesus!"

"My sister is demon-possessed!"

"Jesus!"

"Jesus!"

I stretched up, but could not see over the people. My heart raced with excitement as I caught their fever of hope. Hauling myself onto the wall, I stood precariously balanced, desperate to see this man so many called a prophet, and some said was the Messiah.

And there He was, moving through the people. My heart sank.

Jesus was not like any rabbi I had ever seen. This was no gray-haired scholar with flowing white robes and scowling face. He was young—no more than a few years older than I. He wore simple, homespun garments, and had the broad shoulders, strong arms, and dark skin of a common laborer. Nothing in His appearance commended Him. Jesus looked at those around Him. He even touched some. One grasped Jesus' hand, kissing it and weeping. Jesus moved on through the crowd as people cried out in joy. "A miracle!"

Where? I wondered. *Where is the miracle?*

People tried to reach over others. "Touch me, Jesus! Touch me!" His friends moved closer to Him, trying to keep the people back. The eldest—Peter—shouted for them to make room. Jesus stepped into one of the boats. Disappointment filled me. Had I come so far to have only a glimpse of Him?

Jesus sat in the bow as His disciples rowed. They had not gone far when they dropped anchor. Jesus spoke from there, and the crowd grew quiet. They sat and listened as His calm voice carried across the water.

I cannot tell you all that Jesus said that day, or His exact words, but His teaching caused great turmoil within me. He said the heart of the Law was mercy; I had always thought it was judgment. He spoke of loving our enemies, but I could not believe He meant the Romans who had brought idols into the land. He said not to worry about the future, for each day had trouble enough. I worried all the time about keeping the Law. I worried that I would not live up to my father's expectations. I worried from morning to night about a hundred inconsequential things. Jesus warned us against false prophets, while the scribes and Pharisees looked upon Him as one.

Jesus' voice was deep and flowed like many waters. My heart trembled at the sound of it. Even now after so many years, I wait to hear His voice again.

When He finished speaking, the people rose and cried out, not for more of His wisdom, but demanding miracles. They wanted healing! They wanted bread! They wanted an end to Roman domination!

"Be our king!"

Peter raised the sail. Andrew drew up the anchor. People waded into the water, but the wind had already moved the boat well away from shore.

I wanted to cry out, too; not for bread, of which I had plenty, nor for healing, of which I had no need, but for His interpretation of the Law. His words had filled me with more questions than those that had brought me to Galilee. From boyhood, I had listened to scribes and religious leaders. Never had a man spoken with authority like the carpenter from Nazareth.

When people ran along the shore, I gathered my robes, shed my dignity, and ran with them. The boat turned and sailed toward the distant shore. Others kept running, intending to reach the other side of the lake before He did.

Weary, out of breath, I sat, arms resting on my raised knees, and watched Jesus sail away, taking my hope with Him.

✦   ✦   ✦

Jesus traveled from town to town. He spoke in the synagogues. He spoke to growing crowds on hillsides. He taught through stories the common people understood better than I, stories about soil, seeds, wheat and weeds, hidden treasure in a field, fishing nets, things unfamiliar to someone who had grown up in Jerusalem. People argued over Him constantly. Some said He was from heaven; others refused to believe He was even a prophet. Scribes and Pharisees demanded a miraculous sign, and Jesus refused.

"Only an evil and adulterous generation would demand a miraculous sign; but the only sign I will give them is the sign of the prophet Jonah."

But what did that mean?

Many disciples left Jesus, some out of disappointment, others because they could not understand or believe.

I left out of fear of what the religious leaders might do if they saw me among Jesus' followers. I had my reputation to protect.

"Did you find the Messiah?" My rabbi mocked me.

"No," I said, and soon after left him.

Jesus came to Jerusalem and taught in the Temple, much to the ire of the scribes and Pharisees. They questioned Him, and he confounded them with His answers. They set traps; He sprang them. They asked trick questions about the Law, and He exposed their deceit, challenged their knowledge of the Torah, and said they did not serve God, but their father, the devil.

The city was alive with excitement. Everyone was talking about Jesus.

And then, He was gone again, out in the countryside and villages among the people. He went as far as Caesarea Philippi with its idols and the Gates of Hell, where Gentiles believed demons passed in and out of the world. He traveled through the Ten Towns and stayed in Samaria. And though I did not follow Him, I pondered His words. "The Kingdom of Heaven is like a merchant on the lookout for choice pearls. When he discovered a pearl of great value, he sold everything he owned, and bought it!" What was this pearl? What did I have to sell to buy it?

As the Law required, He returned to Jerusalem three times each year, for the Festival of Unleavened Bread, the Festival of Harvest, and the Festival of Shelters. And each time Jesus came with His offerings to God, the priests grew more hostile, more determined to turn the people against Him. They even became allies with those they despised, the Herodians, who asked questions that could have caused Him to come into conflict with Roman law.

"Tell us—is it right to pay taxes to Caesar or not?"

In response, Jesus asked for a coin. When given a denarius, He asked the Herodian scribes whose picture and title were on it. Caesar's, of course. "Give to Caesar what belongs to Caesar, and give to God what belongs to God."

Sadducees questioned Him on the resurrection of the dead, and Jesus said they were mistaken in their understanding of Scripture. "God said to Moses, 'I *am* the God of Abraham, the God of Isaac, and the God of Jacob.' So He is the God of the living, not the dead."

His words astonished me. All Jews knew the bones of the patriarchs lay in the cave of Machpelah near Hebron. And yet, they lived? What He said confused me more than enlightened me. The harder I tried to understand what I had learned, the more confused I became.

The multitudes grumbled. Some said He was a good man; others said He led the people astray. The priests wanted Him seized, but no one dared lay hands on Him. He and His disciples camped on the Mount of Olives, but I didn't go there, afraid of what others would say if I was seen. So I waited, knowing Jesus would come early to the Temple.

I was there when some scribes and Pharisees dragged a half-clad woman before Him. "Teacher," they said, though I knew the title rankled them, "this woman was caught in adultery, in the very act. The law of Moses says to stone her. What do you say?" The trembling woman covered herself as best she could. She tucked her legs beneath her and covered her head with her arms. Men stared, whispering, for she was beautiful. Some sniggered.

I moved behind a column and watched, sickened. I had seen her that morning with one of the scribes.

Jesus stooped and wrote on the ground. Did He write that the Law also prescribed the man who shared her bed be stoned with her? I could not see. When Jesus straightened, I held my breath, for the Law was clear. The woman must die. If He told them to let her go, He would break the Mosaic law, and they would have cause to accuse Him. If He said to stone her, He usurped the power of Rome, for only the governor could order execution.

"Let the one who has never sinned throw the first stone." He stooped and wrote again.

No one dared lift a stone, for only God is sinless. I stayed behind a pillar to see what Jesus would do. Next He looked at the woman. "Where are your accusers? Didn't even one of them condemn you?"

"No, Lord." Tears streaked down her face.

"Neither do I. Go your way. From now on, sin no more."

Though I was touched by His mercy, I wondered. What of the Law?

I did not follow Him then, though I drank in His words. Even when many of the leading priests called Him a false prophet, despising and rejecting Him, He drew me with His teaching.

"A Nazarene carpenter as the Messiah of God! It is blasphemy even to suggest it!"

None of us—not even his closest friends—guessed what Jesus had meant when He said, "When you have lifted up the Son of Man, then you will understand that I Am He."

✦   ✦   ✦

Near the end of the week, with trepidation, yet full of hope, I went to Jesus. I had met Peter and Andrew and Matthew. I knew John, and he encouraged me: "Speak to the Master." I dared not share my deepest hope with John: to become a disciple, to be worthy enough to travel with Him.

Surely, all my training, all my hard work and self-sacrifice, had prepared me to be counted among His disciples. I thought I could help Him. I had connections, after all. I wanted Jesus to know how hard I had worked all my life to keep the Law. When He knew these things, I expected Him to give me the assurance I wanted. I had much to offer Him. He would welcome me. Or so I thought.

I was a fool!

I will never forget Jesus' eyes as He answered my questions.

I had sought His approval; He exposed my pride and self-deceit. I had hoped to become one of His disciples; He told me what I must give up to become complete. He gave me all the proof I needed to confirm He was the

Messiah. He saw into the heart of me, the hidden secrets even I had not suspected were there.

And then Jesus said what I had longed to hear. "Come, follow Me."

I could not answer.

Jesus waited, His eyes filled with love.

He waited.

God waited and I said nothing!

Oh, I believed in Him. I did not understand all He said, but I knew Jesus was the Messiah.

And still, I walked away. I went back to all I knew, back to the life that left me empty.

✦   ✦   ✦

Months passed. How I suffered, my mind tortured by thoughts of Sheol! When I went up the steps of the Temple, I put coins in the hands of beggars, and cringed inwardly. I knew the truth. I gave not for their sake, but my own. A blessing—that's what I was after! Another mark in my favor, a deed to bring me closer to the assurance of hope and better things to come. For me.

What I had viewed as blessing and God's favor had turned out to be a curse testing my soul. And I had failed, for I had no conviction to give up what gave me honor and position and pleasure. Again and again, I failed. Day after day, week after week, month after month.

I wished I had never heard the name of Jesus! Rather than ease the restlessness of my soul, His words scourged my conscience and tore at my heart. He turned the foundations of my life into rubble.

Passover approached. Jews poured into Jerusalem. I heard Jesus had ridden the colt of a donkey up the road lined by people waving palm fronds and singing, "Praise God for the Son of David! Blessings on the one who comes in the name of the Lord! Praise God in highest heaven!"

Jesus, the Messiah, had come.

I didn't go out to see Him.

When He entered the Temple, He took a whip and drove out the money changers and merchants who filled the court that should have been left open for Gentiles seeking God. He cried out against those who had made His Father's house of prayer into a robbers' den. People scattered before His wrath.

I wasn't there. I heard about it later.

He taught in the Temple every day. His parables exposed the hypocrisy of the religious leaders, fanning their hatred while they pretended not to understand. They twisted His words, trying to use them against Him. They oppressed those who loved Him, even threatening a poor cripple with expulsion from the Temple because he carried his mat after Jesus healed him on the Sabbath.

"Woe to you, scribes and Pharisees, hypocrites!"

I trembled when I heard Him. I hid at His approach.

"Everything you do is for show! On your arms you wear extra wide prayer boxes with Scripture verses inside, and you wear robes with extra long tassels. And you love to sit at the head of the table at banquets and in the seats of honor in the synagogues! *Woe to you!*" His voice thundered and echoed as He strode the corridors of the Temple. "You shamelessly cheat widows out of their property and then pretend to be pious by making long prayers in public."

Scribes shouted against Him, but they could not drown out the truth that poured from His mouth. He indicted the priests, who were to be shepherds of God's people and behaved, instead, like a pack of wolves devouring the flock.

"You take a convert and make him twice the child of hell you yourselves are! Blind guides! Fools! You are careful to tithe even the tiniest income from your herb gardens, but you ignore the more important aspects of the law—justice, mercy, and faith."

The walls of the Temple reverberated at the sound of His voice. The voices of those He confronted sounded as nothing before His wrath. I shook with fear.

"You will never see me again until you say, 'Blessings on the one who comes in the name of the Lord!'"

He left the Temple. Like sheep after the shepherd, His disciples followed. Some looked back in fear, others with excited pride. Voices rose in anger. The scribes and Pharisees, the priests, everyone seemed to be shouting at once. Would the anger inside this place overflow to the streets beyond? Faces twisted in rage. Mouths opened in curses upon the Nazarene. Some tore their clothing.

I fled.

I remember little of what I felt that day other than I had to get away from the wrath inside the Temple. Jesus walked away with His disciples. Part of me wanted to follow; the practical side of me held back. I told myself I had no choice. What Jesus asked of me would dishonor my father. I knew He had not asked the same of others. Why did He demand so much of me?

His words were like a two-edged sword, slicing through the lies I believed about myself. I was not the man of God I thought I was.

And then Jesus turned and looked at me. For the barest moment, I saw the invitation. Did I want to go back inside the Temple to my prayers and quiet contemplation, ignoring all that went on around me? Or did I want to follow a man who looked into me and saw the hidden secrets of my heart? One way required nothing; the other, everything.

I shook my head. He waited. I backed away. I saw the sorrow come into His eyes before He walked away.

I feel that sorrow now. I understand it more today than ever before.

The next time I saw Jesus, He hung on a cross between two thieves at Golgotha. A sign written in Hebrew, Latin, and Greek, hung above his head: "Jesus the Nazarene, the King of the Jews."

I cannot explain what I felt when I saw Jesus outside the city gate, nailed on a Roman cross. Men I knew hurled insults at Him. Even in His hour of suffering and death, they had no pity. I felt anger, disappointment, relief, shame. I justified myself. It seemed I had not turned my back on God after all. I had rejected a false prophet. Hadn't I?

What does that say of me? I thought myself a righteous young man striving always to please and serve God. Jesus exposed me as a fraud. The shame comes back to me now, years later. Such was my arrogance! Such was my willful blindness to the truth! I was equally ashamed of the religious leaders. Men I respected, even revered, stood below the cross, smirking, casting insults, mocking Jesus as He died. They felt no pity, showed no mercy. Not even the wailing of Jesus' mother or the weeping women with her could rouse their compassion.

The rabbi I had followed for so long was among them. They reminded me of vultures tearing at a dying animal.

Would I become like them?

And where were Jesus' disciples? Where were the men who had lived with Him for the past three years, who had left their homes and livelihoods to follow Him? Where were those who had stood along the road waving palm fronds and singing praises as Jesus entered Jerusalem? Had it been less than a week ago?

I remember thinking, *Was it this poor carpenter's fault that we expected so much of Him?* When given the choice between an insurrectionist like Barabbas and a man who spoke of peace with God, the people clamored for the freedom of the one who killed Romans.

Nicodemus stood in the gate, tears streaming down his face, into his beard. Arms crossed, hands shoved deeply into his sleeves, he rocked back and forth, praying. I approached my father's old friend, alarmed to see him in such distress. "May I help you?"

"Be thankful your father did not live to see this day, Silas. They would not listen! They set out to do what they would do. An illegal trial by night, false accusations, false witnesses; they've condemned an innocent man. God, forgive us."

"You are an honest man, Nicodemus." I thought to absolve him. "It is Rome who crucifies Jesus."

"We all crucify Him, Silas." Nicodemus looked up at Jesus. "The Scriptures are being fulfilled even as we stand here watching Jesus die."

I left him to his grief. His words frightened me.

I celebrated Passover as the Law required, but felt no joy in reliving the deliverance of Israel from Egyptian bondage. Jesus' words kept coming back to me. "God blesses those who are poor and realize their need for Him, for the Kingdom of Heaven is theirs."

God had made death pass over His people in Israel. If Jesus was the Messiah, as I had once thought and Nicodemus still believed, what vengeance would God take against us? What hope had we of God's intervention?

I dreamed of Jesus that night. I saw His eyes again, looking at me, waiting as He had that day when He left the Temple. When I awakened, the city was dark and silent. My heart beat heavily. I felt something in the air.

"I am the way and the truth and the life," Jesus had said. The proclamation of God or words of a madman? I didn't know anymore.

The way was lost, the truth silenced, the hope of the life Jesus offered as dead as He was.

It seemed the end of everything.

✦ ✦ ✦

"You have been hard at work for a long time, Silas." Epanetus stood in the doorway. "When we asked you to write your story, we did not intend you to become a slave to it."

Silas put the reed into the pen case and blew on the last few letters he had written. "I've been lost in the past."

"Has it been a comforting journey?"

"Not entirely." He rolled the scroll carefully. His muscles were stiff, his back aching. As he rose, he stretched. "I was deaf and blind."

"And Jesus gave you ears to hear and the eyes to see. Come, my friend. Walk with me in the garden."

The warmth of the sun melted the tension in Silas's shoulders. He filled his lungs with the sea air. Birds flitted about the garden, *ta-ta-whirring* from hidden perches. He felt safe here, as though a thousand miles from Rome, the arena, the maddened, screaming mob, but still not far enough away to escape from the memories of what happened there.

"Where are you in your story?"

"Jesus' death."

"I would give all I own to see His face, even for a moment."

Silas winced inwardly, thinking of the years he'd wasted when he could have been with Jesus.

"What is it you remember most about Jesus?"

"His eyes. When He looked at me, I knew He saw everything."

Epanetus waited for him to say more, but Silas had no intention of satisfying the Roman's curiosity about what *everything* he meant.

"Do you long for Jerusalem, Silas?"

That was an easy enough question to answer. "Sometimes. Not the way it is now. The way it once was." Was that even true? Did he long for the days before Christ came? No. He longed for the *new* Jerusalem, the one Jesus would bring at the end of the ages.

"Do you still have family there?"

"No blood relations, but there may be Christian brothers and sisters still there." Perhaps a few remained firmly rooted, like hyssop in the stone walls of the city. He hoped so, for he prayed continually that his people would repent and embrace their Messiah. "I don't know if anyone remains or not. I only hope. It's been years since I stepped foot in Judea." *May the Lord always call someone to preach there, to keep the gate open for His people to enter into the fold.*

"Perhaps you will go back."

Silas smiled bleakly. "I would prefer God called me to the heavenly Jerusalem."

"He will. Someday. We all pray that your time will not be soon."

Some prayers Silas wished were left unsaid. "Had I remained in Rome, I might be there now." Perhaps he should have stayed.

"God willed you here, Silas."

"The scrolls are precious. They must be safeguarded." He paused before a fountain, soothed by the sound of water. "I should be making copies of the scrolls, not writing about my trials."

"We need the testimony of men like you, who walked with Jesus, who heard His teaching, who saw the miracles."

"I didn't. I told you. My faith came late."

"But you were there."

"In Judea. In Jerusalem. Once in Galilee. In the Temple."

"Write what you remember."

"I remember sorrow. I remember the joy of seeing Christ risen. I remember my shame and guilt being washed away. I remember receiving the Holy Spirit. I remember men who served Christ and died for it. So many I've lost count. My closest friends are with the Lord, and I feel . . ." He clenched and unclenched his hands.

"Envy?"

He let out a sharp breath. "You see too clearly, Epanetus." Silas wished he could, for he felt lost in the mire of his own emotions. "I am so filled with *feelings*, and I fear none reflect the Spirit of God."

"You are a man, not God."

"A ready excuse I can't accept. Peter hung upside down upon a cross, dying in agony, and still he prayed for those who nailed him there! He prayed for every person in that arena. He prayed the same words our Lord did: 'Father, forgive them.' Forgive the whole wretched mass of mankind. And what did I pray? For judgment! For their annihilation! I would have rejoiced to see every Roman burned by God's fire, and Rome itself made ash!"

He felt Epanetus's silence and thought he understood it. "Do you still want me under your roof?"

"Roman blood runs in my veins. Do you pray now that God will judge me?"

Silas shut his eyes. "I don't know."

"An honest answer, and I won't put you out for it. Silas, I knew the same kind of bitterness when several of my friends were murdered by zealots in Jerusalem. I hated every Jew in sight and took vengeance whenever allowed. I don't know how many of your people I killed or arrested. And then I met a boy. About Curiatus's age. And he had more wisdom than any man I'd ever known." He laughed softly. "He said he knew the God of all creation, and that same God wanted to know me, too. It was the first time I had heard of Jesus. The miracle was I listened."

"You were wiser than I."

"You came to faith eventually. That is what matters."

"When were you in Judea?"

His eyes flickered. "Years ago. What a country! Intrigue and savagery are not limited to Rome, my friend. Men are the same everywhere."

"Some men never change. After all these years, I find my faith as frail as it was in the first weeks after Jesus ascended."

"You suffer because you love Him, Silas. You love His people. Love brings suffering. God will help you find your way."

Macombo came out to them. "The brothers and sisters are beginning to arrive."

Silas joined them in prayer and singing praises to Jesus. He closed his eyes and covered his face as Patrobas read Peter's letter. No one asked him to say anything. Even Curiatus remained silent, though he sat close to Silas. Diana was there also. Silas thought of Peter and his wife. They had teased each other with the familiarity of long years together rich in love.

Diana smiled at him, and his heart quickened.

He had felt euphoria before. And every time it had had to do with Jesus.

He looked at Epanetus talking with Macombo, Urbanus laughing with Patrobas. These people reminded him piercingly of those who had met in the upper room in Jerusalem so many years ago—men, women, slave, free, rich, poor. Jesus brought them all together and made them one family. One in Christ, one body, one Spirit.

The darkness he had felt pressing in around him rolled back a little and gave him a glimpse of the confidence he had lost. Not confidence in himself, but in the One who saved him.

———————————————————   ✦ ✦ ✦   ———————————————————

I laugh now as I think of it. How can I express the joy I felt on the day I saw Jesus alive again? He looked at me with love, not condemnation! A friend of mine knew where the disciples had hidden, and we went to tell them the good news. We were both shaking with exhaustion and excitement by the time we knocked on the door of the upper room.

We heard voices inside, frightened, arguing. Peter, firmly commanding, "Let them in."

My friend whispered loudly, "Let us in!"

"Who is with you?"

"Silas! A friend of mine. We have news of Jesus!"

Peter opened the door. I could see he did not remember me, and I was glad of it. My friend blurted out, "Jesus lives!"

"He was just here."

My heart raced as we entered. I looked around the room. I wanted Jesus to know I'd changed my mind. I would do whatever He asked of me now. "Where is He?"

"We don't know. He was here for a while, and then He was gone."

"We were all sitting here and suddenly, there He was."

"It was no ghost," I said. "It was Jesus. We must go to the Temple."

Matthew laughed. "So we can be arrested?"

"I'll go." I was brave in that brief moment.

Peter put his hand on my arm. "Caiaphas and the others will silence you."

"Stay with us," John said.

"We'll leave soon. Come with us to Galilee."

For months, I had wished to be a part of this group of chosen men, but I could not in good conscience leave Jerusalem. "I can't!" How could I go knowing that Jesus was alive? "Others must hear the good news. I must tell Nicodemus."

I knew where to find my father's old friend. Nicodemus saw me coming, and met me in the portico. A finger to his lips, he drew me aside. "I can see by your face the news you bring. Rumors abound."

"It's no rumor, Nicodemus."

"Jesus' body is missing. That does not mean He's come back to life."

I leaned close. "I've seen Him with my own eyes, Nicodemus. He's alive!"

His eyes glowed, but he looked around cautiously. "Unless Jesus walks into the Temple and declares Himself, nothing will change."

"How can you say that? Nothing will ever be the same again."

His fingers dug into my arm as he guided me to the Temple steps. He spoke low, head down. "Caiaphas and several others met with the Roman guards left in charge of the tomb. They have paid them a large bribe to say Jesus' disciples came during the night while they were sleeping, and stole His body."

"The moment Pontius Pilate hears of this, they will be executed for negligence of duty."

"Lower your voice, my son. The priests will stand up for the guards who have agreed to be part of this plan. Go back to Jesus' disciples. Tell them what Caiaphas and the others have done. They intend to spread this rumor quickly and as far as possible in order to discredit any claims that Jesus lives. Go! Hurry! They must convince Jesus to come to the Temple and declare Himself."

I told Peter what Nicodemus had said, but he shook his head. "None of you must make the same mistake I did. I tried to tell Jesus what to do once. He called me Satan and told me to get away from Him."

"But surely it would make all things clear to Caiaphas and members of the high council if He did go to the Temple."

Simon the Zealot stood. "I heard Jesus say that even if a man returned from the dead, those men would not believe. If Jesus stood before them and showed them His nail-scarred hands and feet, they would still deny He is the Christ, the Son of the living God!"

Seven of Jesus' disciples left for Galilee.

Peter told me later that Jesus had built a fire, cooked fish, and met with the seven disciples on the shores of the Sea of Galilee. He appeared to a crowd of five hundred—I among them—and then to His brother James. For forty days, Jesus walked the earth and spoke with us. I have not the words to tell you the many things I saw Him do, the words He said. He blessed us, and then He returned to the home from which He came: heaven.

I saw the Lord taken up in a cloud. The disciples and all the rest of us would still be on that mount had not two angels appeared. "Someday He will return from heaven in the same way you saw Him go!"

Oh, how I long for that day to come.

All of them are gone now, those friends I held so dear. Of the 120 who met in the upper room to praise God and pray, the 120 who first received the Holy Spirit who lit our faith on fire, and sent us out to proclaim Him, only two remain: John, the last of the Twelve, whose faith flashes like a beacon from Patmos, and me, the most unworthy.

Every day, I look up and hope I'll see Jesus coming through the clouds.

Every day, I pray *someday* will be today.

THREE

After Jesus ascended to His Father, those of us who followed Jesus remained in Jerusalem. The Twelve—except for Judas the betrayer, who killed himself—stayed in the upper room, along with others who had come from the district of Galilee, including my friend Cleopas. Mary, Jesus' mother, and His brothers, James, Joseph, Jude, and Simon were there, along with the Lord's sisters and their families, and Mary's sister as well. Nicodemus and Joseph of Arimathea came and went. We prayed for them constantly, for Caiaphas had learned they had taken down Jesus' body, anointed it, and placed it in Joseph's tomb, and he now threatened them with expulsion from the Temple. Mary Magdalene, Joanna, Mary the mother of James the younger, and Salome were also there with us, along with Matthias and Barsabbas, who had followed Jesus from the day John baptized Him in the Jordan River. The Lord chose Matthias to replace Judas as one of the Twelve.

Fifty days after Jesus had been crucified, forty-seven after He arose, seven days after He ascended to His Father in heaven, on the day of Pentecost, when Jews from all over the empire gathered in Jerusalem, there came upon that house a violent, rushing wind such as I had never heard before or since. It filled the place, and then tongues of fire appeared on each of us. The Holy Spirit filled me, and I felt compelled along with the others to run outside. The fear of men that had haunted us was gone! We rushed headlong into the crowd, crying out the Good News!

A miracle took place inside us. We spoke languages we had not known. Peter spoke before the crowd with eloquence and a knowledge of Scripture that astounded the scribes. Where did a common fisherman come by such wisdom? We know it came from Jesus, poured into him through the Holy Spirit!

I had a gift for languages, but on that day, I spoke to Parthians, Medes, Elamites, and Mesopotamians, all in languages unknown to me until then. That day of miracles, Christ spoke to all men through us. The Lord declared Himself to men and women from Cappadocia, Pontus, Asia, and Phyrgia.

The Good News was preached to families from Pamphylia, Egypt, Cyrene, and as far away as Libya and Rome itself! Even Cretans and Arabs heard Jesus was the Savior, Lord of all!

Of course, some did not understand. They scoffed, hearing only babbling and gibberish. Their minds were closed and dark, their hearts hardened to the truth. But thousands heard, and three thousand men accepted Jesus as Savior and Lord. In one day, our little band of 120 believers grew to over three thousand! I've wondered since: was it one language we all spoke? the language all men knew before the Tower of Babel? the language all believers will one day speak in heaven? I know not.

When Pentecost ended, though we did not want to depart from one another, most went home, carrying with them the knowledge that Jesus Christ is the resurrection and the life, Lord of all creation. Later, when I began my travels with Peter and Paul, we found those whose faith had taken root on Pentecost, and begun to grow in a hundred different places.

Those of us who lived in Judea remained in Jerusalem. We were one family, meeting together to hear the apostles teach all Jesus had taught them. We shared meals together, prayed together. No one suffered from need, for we all shared everything we had.

The Lord continued to manifest His power through Peter, who healed a lame man.

Peter, who had once denied Christ three times and hidden with the other disciples out of fear for their lives, now preached boldly in the Temple, along with young John.

The Sadducees and priests, led by Caiaphas and Annas, denied the Resurrection, and put forth lies they had paid the Roman guards to tell. But where was Jesus' body? Where was the proof? In heaven!

The message spread, maddening the high council. The Holy Spirit moved like wildfire through the streets of Jerusalem. Two thousand more soon accepted Christ Jesus as the way, the truth, and the life.

Persecution and suffering came swiftly as Caiaphas and others of like mind tried to put out the fire of faith. Nicodemus and Joseph of Arimathea were expelled from the high council and shunned by religious leaders. Peter and John were arrested. Gamaliel, a righteous man devoted to God, spoke wisely, suggesting the council wait and see if the movement would die on its own. "If this is from God, you will only find yourselves fighting against God." The high council ordered Peter and John flogged before being freed.

We all hoped Gamaliel's advice would sway the leaders. We prayed they would turn to Christ for salvation and join us in worshiping the Messiah we had been praying for centuries would come.

It was not to be. They hardened their hearts against the proof, more afraid of losing their power and prestige than of spending eternity in Sheol, away from the mercy of God.

In truth, I have learned over the years that most men refuse the free gift of salvation through Christ, and continue to believe they can save themselves by their good deeds and adherence to laws and man-made traditions. It is a miracle of God that any are saved at all.

We met every day in the Temple. Smaller groups met in houses throughout the city. Those of us who had the means took in those who lost their homes and livelihoods. God provided. We kept right on teaching and preaching, despite threats and beatings.

All my doubts had been swept away when I saw the risen Jesus; my fears, on Pentecost. I testified out of the joy of my salvation. Every breath was a thanksgiving offering to the Lord who saved me. God had sent His Son, appointed heir of all things, through whom He made the world. Jesus radiates God's own glory, and expresses the very character of God. He sustains everything by the mighty power of His command, proven by His death on the cross and His resurrection. He purified us from sins, and now sits at the right hand of God Almighty. He is King of kings, Lord of lords!

I could not speak enough of Him. I could not spend enough time in the company of those who loved Him as I did. I could not wait to tell the lost sheep: "He is the Christ of God, the Savior of the world, the Shepherd who will lead you home."

+   +   +

Perhaps it was due to my ability to write that I was made a member of the first council, for I was certainly not worthy to be counted among them.

"I was his brother and I didn't know Him," James told me when I tried to decline. "I stayed away when He was crucified because I was ashamed of Him. And yet, He came to me and spoke with me after He arose." James became one of the leaders, along with Peter, who had become an immovable rock of faith.

With each week that passed, more came to believe, and the number of gatherings swelled. As our numbers increased, so too did our troubles. The devil is cunning; rousing anger was one of his many weapons. Arguments broke out between Jews who had lived in Judea all their lives and those who came from Greece. The Twelve spent most of their time serving Communion and settling disputes with little time left over to teach what Jesus had taught them. They grew exhausted. Tempers flared, even among the Twelve.

"Jesus sought solitude to pray!" Matthew said. "He needed time to be alone with His Father! Yet I have not a moment to myself!"

Philip groaned. "The only time we're alone is in the middle of the night."

John leaned back. "And by then, I'm too tired to think, let alone pray."

"The Lord always found time." Peter paced. "We must find time as well."

"These people have so many needs!"

James, Jude, and I had discussed the problem at length and prayed about it. We sought to encourage and help if we could, but a solution eluded us.

Then someone said, "How long can we shoulder the whole load ourselves without complete collapse? Even Moses had seventy helpers."

It caused me to think. "A landowner has foremen who hire workers to plow, sow seed, and harvest crops."

"Yes, and an army has a commander who gives orders to his centurions who lead soldiers into battle."

The Twelve huddled together in prayer, and then called all the disciples together. Seven men were to be chosen from among us to serve tables. From that day forward, to the benefit of all, the Twelve devoted themselves to prayer and teaching the Word.

Our meetings were peaceful and joy filled.

But outside, in the city streets, persecution grew worse. The religious leaders said we were a cult drawing the people away from worshiping the Lord in His holy Temple. We met daily in the corridors, and were sometimes driven out. When we preached in the streets, they arrested us. Stephen, one of the seven chosen to serve the church, performed signs and wonders that brought many to believe in Christ. Members of the Synagogue of Freed Slaves argued with him. Failing in that, they lied, and told members of the high council that Stephen spoke blasphemy. Arrested, Stephen was taken before the high council. His words so infuriated the members, they drove him out of the city and stoned him to death.

Grief did not stop the spread of the Good News. Though the apostles remained, persecution drove many believers from Jerusalem, scattering them throughout Judea and Samaria. Like seeds blown by the wind, their witness for Christ was planted everywhere they settled.

The council tried to stifle the message, but the Holy Spirit blazed within us. We went daily to the Temple, to the neighborhood synagogues, and from house to house, teaching and preaching Jesus as the Christ. Philip went to Samaria. When we heard how many came to faith in Christ there, Peter and John went down to help.

I felt no call from God to leave Jerusalem, not even when I was dragged out of my bed in the dead of night and beaten so severely it took months to heal.

"You blaspheme against God by calling Jesus of Nazareth the Messiah!" Six Pharisees smashed every urn, tore down curtains, cut open cushions and poured oil on the Persian carpets while I was accused, beaten, and kicked.

"We should burn this place down so they can't meet here again!"

"If you set fire to this house, it may spread to the street and beyond."

"If you preach one more word about that false messiah, blasphemer, I'll kill you."

I wanted to have the faith of Stephen and ask God's forgiveness for them, but had not the breath to speak. All I could do was look up into my attacker's face.

I had seen him in the Temple among Gamaliel's students. We all learned to dread the name Saul of Tarsus.

✦   ✦   ✦

Over the next months, while I convalesced, serving with reed pen and ink, I heard of Saul's conversion. I gave little credence to the rumors; for I had seen his face so filled with hatred he seemed grotesque. I had felt his heel in my side.

"I heard he met Jesus on the road to Damascus."

I thought immediately of my own experience, but brushed the thought aside. Others said Saul was blind. Some said he still lived in Damascus with a man who accepted Christ as Messiah during Pentecost.

We knew Saul had gone north to Damascus with letters from the high council giving him permission to find all who belonged to the Way, and bring captives bound for judgment back to Jerusalem. Nicodemus and Joseph of Arimathea told us Saul had been with the men who killed Stephen. I wrote letters to warn them of danger and trusted in God to protect His own.

We heard the great persecutor had been baptized. A report came that Saul was declaring Jesus the Christ in the synagogues of Damascus. Another reported Saul the Pharisee had gone away to Arabia. Why, no one could say.

Men live in hope of their enemies repenting, and Saul of Tarsus had proven what an enemy he was.

I doubted all the reports about Saul's transformation. I hoped never to see his face again.

Joseph, a Levite of Cypriot birth, told me, "Saul is in Jerusalem!" We all called Joseph "Barnabas" because he constantly encouraged everyone in their faith, even those who whined incessantly about their circumstances. "He would like to speak with us."

Ah, Barnabas, the one to always think the best of a man. Even a man like Saul of Tarsus! I remembered being angry at him for the first time. I had not forgotten the night that Pharisee entered my house, nor the weeks of pain I'd suffered until my broken ribs healed. "I don't trust him."

"The Pharisees despise him, Silas. He's in hiding. Did you know priests went up to Damascus to find him, and when they did, he was preaching in a synagogue and declaring Jesus is the Christ? They argued, but he confounded them with proof from the Scriptures. He knows the Torah and Prophets better than anyone."

I grew more stubborn. "The best way to find and kill all of us is to pretend to be one of us, Joseph."

Barnabas studied my face with eyes too much like Jesus'. "Do you hold a grudge against him for what he did to you?"

His words cut deeply, and I answered through gritted teeth. "I have no right to judge any man. None of us do." And then the knife. "But we must be discerning, Joseph. We must see what fruit a tree bears."

Barnabas wasn't fooled. "And how can we see unless we look?"

"You've met him."

"Yes. I've met him. I like him."

"You like everyone. If you met King Herod, you'd like him."

"You're afraid of Saul."

"Yes, I'm afraid of the man. Anyone in their right mind would be afraid of him!"

"I assure you I am in my right mind, Silas, and we must meet with Saul. He is a believer. More zealous than anyone I know."

"Indeed, he's zealous. I saw how zealous. Were you in Damascus?"

"No."

"I'm not as quick as you to believe reports from men I don't know. What if it's all an elaborate plot to hunt down and kill Peter and the rest?"

"Jesus said not to fear death, Silas. Perfect love expels all fear."

Gentle words gently spoken, but a spear to my heart. "Then we know, don't we? My love is not perfect."

His eyes filled with compassion. "Is it fear, Silas, or hatred at the heart of your suspicions?"

Confronted, I confessed. "Both."

"Pray for him, then. You cannot hate a man when you pray for him."

"It depends on the prayer."

He laughed and slapped me on the back.

The council met. Barnabas defended Saul vehemently. His words challenged our faith in God. We should fear no man, only God. And God had received Saul already. Proof was in his changed character, the power of his preaching—both evidence of the Holy Spirit.

Of course, Barnabas turned to me. "What do you think, Silas? Should we trust him?"

Another test of my faith. I wanted to say I was too biased to give an opinion. A coward's way out. Jesus knew the truth, and the Holy Spirit dwelling within me would give me no peace until I repented of my bitterness. "I trust you, Barnabas. If you say Saul of Tarsus believes Jesus is the Christ, then he does."

When the man I hoped never to see again stood before the members of the council, I wondered if he had changed. He no longer dressed in the finery of a Pharisee, but the eyes were the same, dark and bright, and his face full of tension. He looked around the room, straight into the eyes of each man who received him. When his gaze fixed upon me, he frowned. He was trying to remember where he had seen me before. I knew the moment he remembered.

Saul blushed. I stood stunned when his eyes filled with tears. But he surprised me even more. "I beg your forgiveness," he said in a pained voice. I never expected him to speak of that night, certainly not here among these men.

It was the look of shame in his eyes that convicted me most. "I should have forgiven you a long time ago." I rose and stepped toward him. "You are welcome here, Saul of Tarsus."

+   +   +

Saul did not remain long in Jerusalem. His zeal got him into trouble with the Greek-speaking Jews who could not defeat him in debate. Barnabas was afraid for him. "They've already tried to kill you more than once! They'll succeed if we stay here."

"If I die, it's God's will." He had changed in faith, but not personality.

"God's will or your own stubbornness?" I asked.

Barnabas spoke up again. "We are not to test the Lord."

Saul's face stiffened. "You misunderstand me."

"Oh?" I met his glare. "Then what do you call it when you put your head into the lion's mouth?" We always seem blind to our own weaknesses, and quick to point out those of others.

We sent him down to Caesarea and put him on a ship back to Tarsus.

The apostles came and went, preaching in other regions. Jesus' brothers and I, along with Prochorus, Nicanor, Timon, Parmenas, and Nicolas, remained in Jerusalem, attending the flock Caiaphas, Annas, and the others were so intent upon destroying. It was a daily struggle, encouraging the discouraged, teaching those new to the faith, and providing for those who were driven from their homes. By the grace of God, no one went hungry and all had a place to live.

Sometimes I long for the months following Pentecost, when Christians met openly in the Temple and in homes throughout the city. We ate together, sang together, and listened eagerly to the apostles' teaching. Joy filled our hearts to overflowing. Our love for one another was evident to everyone. Even those who did not embrace Jesus as Savior and Lord thought well of us! Not Caiaphas, of course. Not the religious leaders who saw Jesus as a threat to their hold on the people.

I did not run from suffering, nor did I run to it. I had seen Jesus on the cross. I saw Him alive several days later. I had no doubt that He was the Son of God, the Messiah, Savior and Lord. If only all Israel would receive Him!

✦ ✦ ✦

Even after several years, even after Philip told an Ethiopian eunuch about Jesus, we did not fully understand that Jesus meant His message for every man and woman, Jew and Gentile. When Peter baptized six Romans in Caesarea, some of us took issue. How could a pantheistic Roman be acceptable to God? Jesus was our Messiah, the One *Israel* had expected for centuries. Jesus was the Jewish Messiah.

What arrogance!

Cleopas reminded me I was a Roman. Offended, I told him it was only because my father had purchased citizenship.

"You were still born a Roman, Silas. And what about Rahab? She wasn't a Hebrew."

"She became one."

And there was the line of my reasoning, for a while at least. Some said these men Peter brought back with him would have to be circumcised before they could become Christians.

Simon the Zealot took one look at Cornelius, a Roman centurion, and flushed to the roots of his black hair. "The Law forbids us to associate with foreigners, Peter, and yet you entered the house of an uncircumcised Roman and ate with him and his family." He pointed. "Surely *this* is not the Lord's will at work here!" He glared at Cornelius who looked back at him with calm humility, his sword still in its scabbard.

Peter stood firm. "Three times the Lord told me, 'Do not call something unclean if God has made it clean.'"

Everyone spoke at once.

"How can these people become one body with us?"

"They know nothing of the Law, nothing of our history."

"Ask the Roman if he knows what *Messiah* means!"

"Anointed One of God," Cornelius said.

Two Jews had come from Caesarea with Cornelius and his family. "This man is highly respected by the Jews in Caesarea. He is devout and fears God, he and all his household. He prays continually and gives generously to the poor."

"I assure you they understand as well as any of us here." Peter told how an angel had come to Cornelius and told him to send for Peter, who was staying in Joppa. "At the same time the angel spoke to Cornelius, the Lord showed me a vision. *Three* times the Lord spoke to me so that I would not go on thinking a man is unclean because of what he eats or whether he has been circumcised. God is not partial. The Scriptures confirm this. Here is the great mystery that has been hidden from us for centuries. The Lord told Abraham he would be a blessing to *many nations*. And this is what the Lord meant. Salvation through Jesus Christ is for all men, everywhere—for Jew *and* Gentile."

Cleopas looked at me and raised his brows. I knew the Scriptures, and felt the conviction of the Holy Spirit.

Peter spread his hands. "Why should we doubt this? Jesus went to the Samaritans, didn't He? He went to the Ten Towns. He granted the request of a Phoenician woman. Why should it surprise us that the Lord has sent the Holy Spirit to a Roman centurion who has prayed and lived to please God?"

The net of grace was cast wider than we imagined.

Peter left Jerusalem and traveled throughout Judea and Galilee and Samaria. The Lord worked mightily through him wherever he went. He healed a paralytic in Lydda, and raised a woman from the dead in Joppa.

Some Christians moved to Phoenicia, Cyprus, and Antioch to get away from the persecution. Soon believers from Cyprus and Cyrene arrived in Antioch and began preaching to Gentiles. We sent Barnabas to investigate. Rather than return, he sent letters instead. "I have witnessed the grace of God here." He stayed to encourage new believers. "Great numbers are coming to Christ. They need sound teaching. I am going to Tarsus to find Saul."

These were hard years of deprivation due to drought. Crops failed from lack of rain. Wheat became expensive. It became increasingly difficult to provide for those who remained in Jerusalem. We managed and asked nothing from nonbelievers, but prayed for God's wisdom in making the best use of our resources.

Barnabas and Saul arrived with a box full of coins from Gentile believers. "Agabus prophesied a famine will come over and affect the entire world."

A Gentile prophesying? We marveled.

"The Christians in Antioch send this money to help their brothers and sisters in Judea."

All of us, Jew and Gentile, were bound together by a love beyond our understanding.

The famine did come, during the reign of Claudius.

✦   ✦   ✦

Persecution worsened.

King Herod Agrippa arrested several of the apostles. To please the Jews, he ordered James, the brother of John, put to death by sword. When Peter was arrested, we scrambled for information in hope of rescuing him, but learned he had been delivered to four squads of guards and was chained in the lower part of the dungeon beneath the king's palace.

We met in secret at Mary's house, wild with worry. Her son, John Mark, had also gone to Antioch with Barnabas and Saul. We discussed all kinds of plans, outrageous and hopeless. With so many guards, we knew no one could ever make their way into the prison, free Peter, and get him out alive. Peter was in God's hands, and we could do nothing but pray. This we did, hour after hour, on our knees. We pleaded with God for Peter's life. He was like a father to us all.

The city filled with visitors for Passover. King Herod promised to bring forth Jesus' greatest disciple, "the big fisherman," Peter. We knew if God did not intervene, Peter would be crucified just as Jesus had been.

We prayed that if Peter was crucified, God would raise him like Jesus. Who then could deny Jesus as Messiah, Lord and Savior of the world?

I confess I had no hope of ever seeing him again.

Someone knocked at the door. Whoever it was knew our code. We sent a servant girl to open the gate, but she ran back. "It's Peter."

"You're out of your mind, Rhoda."

"I know his voice."

"How can he be at the gate when he's chained in the dungeon?"

The knock came again, more firmly this time. Cleopas and I went. And there he was, big and bold as ever! Laughing, we opened the door and would have shouted to the others had he not had the presence of mind to quiet us. "They will be looking for me."

What a story he told us! "I was struck awake while sleeping between two guards. And there stood an angel of the Lord, right in my cell. It was all alight. The chains fell off my hands and the door opened. And I just sat there." He laughed. "He had to tell me to get up! 'Quick!' he told me. 'Put on your coat and follow me.' I did. Not one guard saw us as we passed by. Not one! He took me to the gate." He spread his arms wide. "And it opened by itself! We went along a street and then the angel vanished. I thought I was dreaming!" He laughed again.

We all laughed. "If you're dreaming, so are we!"

"We must tell the others you're safe, Peter."

"Later," I said. "First we must get him out of Jerusalem before Herod sends soldiers to find him."

Herod did search for him, but when Peter could not be found, he had the two guards crucified in Peter's place on charges of dereliction of duty, and left their bodies to rot on Golgotha.

✦   ✦   ✦

John Mark returned to Jerusalem, and Mary came to speak to me. Her husband and my father had known each other. "He's ashamed, Silas. He feels like a coward. He won't tell me what happened in Perga. Maybe he'll talk to you."

When I came to the house, he couldn't look me in the eyes. "My mother asked you to come, didn't she?"

"She thought it might be easier for you to talk to me."

He held his head. "I thought I could do it, and I couldn't. I'm as much a coward now as I was the night they arrested Jesus." He looked up at me. "I ran away that night. Did you know? A man grabbed hold of me, and I fought so hard my tunic was torn off. And I ran. I kept on running." He buried his head in his hands. "I guess I'm still running."

"Everyone deserted Him, Mark. I rejected Him, remember? It wasn't until I saw Jesus alive again that I acknowledged Him."

"You don't understand! It was my opportunity to prove my love for Jesus, and I failed. Paul wanted to keep going. I told Barnabas I'd had enough. Paul scared me to death. I wanted to come home. Not much of a man, am I?"

"Who's Paul?"

"Saul of Tarsus. He's using his Greek name so they will listen to him." He stood up and paced. "He's not afraid of anyone! When we were in Paphos, the governor, Sergius Paulus, had a magician, a Jew named Elymas. He had the governor's ear and caused us all kinds of trouble. I thought we'd be arrested and thrown in prison. I wanted to leave, but Paul wouldn't hear of it. He said we had to go back. He wouldn't listen to reason."

"What happened?"

"He called Elymas a fraud! He was, of course, but to say it there in the governor's court? And he didn't stop there. He said Elymas was full of deceit and the son of the devil. And there was Elymas, calling down curses on us, and Sergius Paulus's face was turning redder and redder." He paced back and forth. "He signaled the guards, and I thought, *This is it. This is where I die.* And there's Paul, pointing at Elymas and telling him the hand of the Lord was upon him and he'd be blind. And suddenly he was. The guards backed away from us. Elymas flailed around, crying for help." John Mark paused. "The governor went so white I thought he'd die. But then he listened to Paul. He was too afraid not to listen."

John Mark flung his arms high in frustration. "He even ordered a banquet, and Paul and Barnabas spent the whole night talking to him about Jesus and how he could be saved from his sins. But all I wanted to do was get out of there and come home!"

"Did Sergius Paulus believe?"

John Mark shrugged. "I don't know. He was amazed. Whether that means he believed, only the Lord knows." He snorted. "Maybe he thought Paul was a better magician than Elymas."

"How did you get home?"

He sat and hunched his shoulders again. "We put out to sea from Paphos. When we arrived in Perga, I asked Barnabas for enough money to get home. He tried to talk me out of leaving. . . ."

"And Paul?"

"He just looked at me." John Mark's eyes filled with tears. "He thinks I have no faith."

"Did he say that?"

"He didn't have to say it, Silas!" Folding his arms on his knees, he bowed his head. "I have faith!" His shoulders shook. "I do!" He looked up, angry in his own defense. "Just not the kind to do what he's doing. I can't debate in the synagogues or talk to crowds of people I've never met. Paul speaks fluent Greek like you do, but I stumble around when people start asking questions. I can't think fast enough to recite the prophesies in Hebrew let alone another language!" He looked miserable. "Then later, I think of all the things I could have said, things I should have said. But it's too late."

"There are other ways to serve the Lord, Mark."

"Tell me one thing I can do, one thing that will make a difference to anyone!"

"You spent three years following Jesus and the disciples. You were at the garden of Gethsemane the night Jesus was arrested. Write what you saw and heard." I put my hand on his shoulder. "You can sit and think about all that, then write it down. Tell everyone what Jesus did for the people, the miracles you saw happen."

"You're the writer."

"You were there. I wasn't. Your eyewitness account will encourage others to believe the truth—that Jesus is the Lord. He is God with us."

John Mark grew wistful. "Jesus said He came not to be served, but to serve others and to give His life as a ransom for many."

The young man's countenance transformed when he spoke of Jesus. He relaxed into the firsthand knowledge he had of the Lord. No one would ever doubt John Mark's love for Jesus, nor the peace given to him through his relationship with Him.

"Write what you know so that others can come to know Him also."

"I can do that, Silas, but I want to do the other, too. I don't want to run and hide anymore. I want to tell people about Jesus, people who never even imagined such a God as He is. I just don't feel . . . prepared."

I knew one day Mark would stand steady before crowds and speak boldly of Jesus as Lord and Savior of all. And I told him so. God would use his eager servant's heart. He had spent his life in synagogues and at the feet of rabbis, as I had. But his training had not extended into the marketplaces or gone so far as Caesarea and beyond.

"If you want to go out among the Gentiles to preach, Mark, you must do more than speak their language. You must learn to *think* in Greek. It must become as natural to you as Aramaic and Hebrew."

"Can you help me?"

"From this day forward, we will speak Greek to one another."

And so we did, though his mother grimaced every time she heard her son speak the language of uncircumcised, pagan Gentiles.

"I know; I know," she said after questioning my wisdom on the matter. "If they understand who Jesus is and accept Him as Savior and Lord, then they will no longer be *goyim*; they will be Christians." Sometimes the old prejudices rose to challenge our faith in Jesus' teaching.

John Mark joined us. "In the eyes of Caiaphas and the rest, Mother, we are as *goyim* as the Greeks and Romans."

"You were listening at the door."

"Your voice carries. The old has passed away, Mother. Christians have no barriers of race, culture, or class between them."

"I know this in my head, but sometimes my heart is slow to follow." She reached up and put her hands on his shoulders. He leaned down to receive her kiss. "Go with my blessing." She waved her hand at both of us.

+   +   +

Paul and Barnabas wrote letters from Antioch of Pisidia, where they preached in the synagogues. Some Jews listened and believed; many did not. A few incited the influential religious women and city leaders, and caused a riot. Paul and Barnabas were driven from the town.

"Everywhere we go, certain Jews follow, determined to stop us from preaching Christ as Messiah in the synagogues. . . ."

Even when they went on to Iconium and preached to Gentiles, these enemies came to poison minds against the message. As always, Paul dug in his heels. "We will stay here as long as God allows and preach Christ crucified, buried, and arisen."

They stayed a long time in Iconium, until Jews and Gentiles banded together in a plot to stone Paul. They escaped to Lystra and then to Derbe. Despite the risks, they continued to preach. They healed a man born a cripple in Lystra, and the Greeks thought they were gods. Paul and Barnabas tried to restrain the crowd from worshiping them, and Jews from Antioch used the opportunity to turn the mob against them.

"Paul was stoned by the mob," Barnabas wrote. "The Jews from Antioch dragged his body outside the city gate and dumped him there. We all went out and gathered around him and prayed. When the Lord raised him, our fear and despair lifted. Neither Jew nor Gentile dared touch Paul when we went back into the city. The Lord is glorified! Friends ministered to Paul's wounds, and then we traveled to Derbe and preached there before returning to Lystra to strengthen believers, appoint elders, and encourage our brothers and sisters to hold firmly to their faith when persecution comes. . . ."

Another letter arrived from Pamphylia. They preached in Perga and Attalia. Others wrote as well. "Paul and Barnabas returned by ship to Antioch of Syria. . . ."

The reports encouraged us in Jerusalem.

But troubles arose. False teaching crept in when disciples moved on. Returning to Antioch, Paul and Barnabas discovered trouble that threatened the faith of Gentiles and Jews alike. They came to Jerusalem to discuss the question already causing dissension between Jewish and Gentile brothers.

"Some Jewish Christians are teaching circumcision is required of Gentiles for salvation."

Every member of the church council in Jerusalem had been born a Jew and followed the Law all his life. All had been circumcised eight days after birth. All had lived under the sacrificial system established by God. Even in the light of Christ crucified and risen, it was difficult to shed the laws by which we had been reared.

"It is a sign of the covenant!"

"The old covenant!" Paul argued. "We are saved by grace. If we demand these Gentiles be circumcised, we're turning back to the Law which we've never been able to keep. Christ freed us from the weight of it!"

None of us on the council could boast Paul's heritage. Born a Jew, son of the tribe of Benjamin, a Pharisee and celebrated student of Gamaliel, he had lived in strictest obedience to the law of our fathers, his zeal proven in his brutal persecution of us before Jesus confronted him on the road to Damascus. Yet, here Paul stood, debating fiercely *against* placing the yoke of the Law upon Gentile Christians!

"It is false teaching, my brothers! The Holy Spirit has already manifested Himself in the faith of these Gentiles. Don't forget Cornelius!" Everyone looked at Peter, who was nodding thoughtfully.

Paul and Barnabas reported signs and wonders that had occurred among the Greeks in Lystra, Derbe, and Iconium.

"Surely these events are proof enough of God's acceptance of them as His children." Paul grew passionate. "God accepts them. How can we even consider going back to the Law from which Christ freed us? This cannot be!"

We asked Paul and Barnabas to withdraw so that we could pray on the matter and discuss it further. His eyes blazed, but he said no more. He told me later he wanted to argue the case further, but knew the Lord was training him in patience. How I laughed over that.

It was not an easy matter for us to decide. We were all Jews with the law of Moses ingrained in our minds from childhood. But Peter spoke for all of us when he said, "We are all saved the same way, by the undeserved grace of the Lord Jesus." Still there were other concerns to address, reasons why some direction must be given these new Gentile Christians so that they wouldn't be easily enticed back into the licentious worship of their culture. I had traveled more widely than most of those on the council and could speak of the issues with personal knowledge. I had seen pagan practices, and so had my father, who had traveled to Asia, Thrace, Macedonia, and Achaia and told me what he saw. We could not just say we are all saved by grace, and not say more!

James spoke for compromise.

While the council discussed the issues, I acted as secretary and made a list of the most important points on which we agreed. We needed to reassure the Gentile Christians of salvation through the grace of our Lord Jesus and encourage them to abstain from eating food offered to idols, engaging in sexual immorality, eating meat from strangled animals, and consuming blood—all things they may have practiced while worshiping false gods. They all agreed that James and I should draft the letter.

"Someone must carry it north to Antioch so that none there can say that Paul or Barnabas have written it."

James was needed in Jerusalem. Judas (also called Barsabbas) volunteered, and then suggested me as his companion.

Peter agreed. "Since the letter will be written by your hand, Silas, you should go and testify to it. Then there will be no question of its origin."

Oh, how my heart beat with excitement. And dread. It had been over ten years since I had ventured outside the boundaries of Judea.

It was time I did.

+ + +

As I prepared for the journey with Judas, Paul, and Barnabas, John Mark came to see me. His Greek was greatly improved, as was his confidence, and he believed strongly that the Lord was calling him back to Syria and Pamphylia. He asked me to speak to Paul on his behalf, which I agreed to do.

I did not expect so firm a refusal from a man who argued so passionately for grace!

"Let him stay in Jerusalem and serve! He was called once before and turned his back on the Lord."

"Called, Paul, but not fully prepared."

"We haven't time to coddle him, Silas."

"He doesn't ask it of you."

"And how long would it be before he missed his mother again?"

His sarcasm grated. "He had reasons other than missing his family, Paul."

"None that convince me he is trustworthy."

I left the matter then, determined to take it up again the next day when he'd had time to think more on the matter. Barnabas tried to warn me.

"It is a sin to hold a grudge, Barnabas." We are so swift to see the faults in others, failing to see the same fault in ourselves.

"It's his determination to spread the message of Christ that presses him on like no other man I know. Paul cannot understand other men who are not so driven as he."

Ignoring his wise advice, I tried again. I thought to go to the heart of the matter.

"You spoke eloquently of grace, Paul. Can you offer none to John Mark?"

"I forgave him."

His tone rankled. "How kind of you."

How easily we forget that harsh words serve only to fan anger into flame.

Paul looked at me, eyes dark, cheeks flushed. "He deserted us in Perga! I can forgive him, but I cannot afford to forget his cowardice."

"John Mark is no coward!"

"I would have more respect for him if he spoke for himself!"

All I had done was make matters worse.

✦ ✦ ✦

Immediately upon our arrival in Antioch of Syria, I read the letter to the congregation. The Gentile Christians were relieved by the instructions of the Jerusalem council, while some Jewish Christians protested. When the seed of pride takes root, it is hard to dig out. Judas and I stayed to teach Christ's message of grace to all who had faith in His crucifixion, burial, and resurrection. A few Jews left, rather than hear more. We continued to encourage those who had not been deceived by men's pride in their own good works. We hoped to strengthen their faith so that they could stand firmly against the persecution we knew would come.

Often, I heard Paul preach. He was a great orator who presented the message with proof from Scripture. He could switch from Greek to Aramaic with ease. He never surrendered when debated, but used his considerable intellect to win converts—or rouse an angry mob! No question confounded him.

I began to understand John Mark's difficulty. A man with Paul's dramatic conversion experience, intellectual powers, and education could make the most earnest Christian feel ill equipped to serve beside him. If not for the advantages given me in my youth, I too might have been intimidated. I was not afraid of Paul, but his impassioned character and his confidence that he was always right annoyed me on numerous occasions. That he *was* right gained my respect if not affection. Brotherly affection developed through longer acquaintance.

A letter came from Jerusalem.

Paul watched me read the scroll. "What's wrong?"

"Nothing is wrong." I rolled it again, wondering why I felt such deep disappointment to be called home. "Judas and I are called back to Jerusalem."

"Once matters are settled there, come back to Antioch."

His command surprised me. We had said little to each other since our argument over John Mark. While we respected each other, shared faith in Jesus, there remained a barrier between us that neither of us had made great efforts to tear down.

"You are a fine teacher, Silas."

I raised my brows at the compliment and inclined my head. "As are you, Paul." I did not flatter him. "I've never heard a man argue the case for Christ so thoroughly. If faith came through reason, the whole world would accept Jesus as Lord."

"We must do as Jesus commanded! We must go out into all the nations and make disciples!"

"And so you and Barnabas shall." I smiled faintly. "And others." I meant John Mark.

"You are well equipped to do the work, Silas. The council has twelve members, and they can draw from others who knew Jesus personally and walked with Him during those three years He preached. Let the council cast lots for another to replace you."

A man likes to think himself indispensable. "I would not presume—"

"Is it presumption to ask God's will in the matter? I could see it in your face when you read that letter you're holding. You prefer teaching to administration."

"I know more of administration than I do of teaching."

"When we delight in the Lord, He gives us the desire of our hearts. The Scriptures tell us that. And your desire is to go out into the world and preach. Can you deny that?"

"We each have our place in the body of Christ, Paul. I must serve where I'm needed."

He started to say more and then pressed his lips together. With a shake of his head, he spread his hands and walked away.

Judas and I returned to Jerusalem and the council. I spoke with John Mark and saw his disappointment. "I will go to Antioch and speak to Paul myself. Perhaps after we talk, he will see I've lost my timidity."

I thought that a wise idea. The young man was Barnabas's cousin, and Barnabas would encourage Paul to give him a second chance. As for my desire to return to Antioch, I left it to the Lord. I knew there were others who could travel with Paul, men wiser than I in how to deal with his strong personality. But I wanted to go. He challenged my faith. One could not be complacent in his company.

Not long after John Mark left Jerusalem, a letter came from Antioch addressed to Peter and James.

"Silas, Paul asks that you be released from the council so that you can travel with him throughout Syria and Cilicia. He wants to visit the churches he started and see how they're doing."

The request surprised me. "What of Barnabas? Has he fallen ill?"

"He and John Mark have gone to Cyprus."

I could imagine what had happened between Paul and Barnabas. Paul had not relented, and Barnabas could not crush the spirit of his cousin. Nor should he.

Peter looked at me. "Did Paul speak with you about this while you were in Antioch?"

"Yes." I could feel the others staring. "I told Paul I would serve wherever I'm needed."

James studied my face. "You have been praying about this for some time, haven't you?"

"Unceasingly."

The council members discussed the matter. Some did not want me to leave Jerusalem. My administrative abilities had been of use in the church. But I knew Paul was right. Others could take my place—men of strong character and faith who stood firm despite persecution.

"You've traveled far more than any man here, Silas. You would be a good companion to Paul. Do you feel the Lord calling you to this work?"

"Yes." I had asked the Lord to give me clear opportunity if that was His will, and Paul's letter and the council's response eliminated my doubts.

Other questions would have to wait until I met Paul in Antioch.

We prayed and cast lots. Barsabbas was chosen to take my place. He was an honest, hardworking man who had proven his love of Jesus and the church on many occasions.

I left the next morning for Antioch.

✦   ✦   ✦

Paul's greeting was cool. "You sent him, didn't you?"

I didn't have to ask whom he meant. His face said it all. Would his anger run so deep we would be unable to work together?

"John Mark told me he intended to speak to you. He thought once you talked with him, you would see he is no longer as timid as he was. I take it things did not go well between you."

"Well enough for others, but I didn't want him on this trip."

By *others*, he meant Barnabas.

"Why not?"

"I have no way of knowing how long we will be gone, Silas. A year at the least, probably longer. I'm not convinced of his dedication."

"And Barnabas disagreed."

"It was the first time I've seen him angry. He insisted Mark go with us. I refused to take the risk."

I smiled faintly. "How do you know I'll have the courage to stay the course?"

A muscle worked near his right eye. "The night I broke down your door, had you beaten, and smashed everything we could lay hands on, you didn't curse me—not once—nor did you cry out against what I was doing." He met my gaze. "I intended to kill you, but your manner stayed my hand."

"*God* stayed your hand."

"I wish He had stayed my hand on other occasions."

I knew he meant his part in the stoning of Stephen. "Our past is the burden we left at the cross." I told him what I had done so there would be no secrets between us.

"At least . . . you never committed murder."

I could not help but smile. "I can see clearly you're an ambitious man, Paul, but let's not compete over who is the greater sinner!"

He looked surprised and then paled. "No! We all have sinned and fallen short of God's glorious standard. This is the truth men need to know so that they will understand their need of our Savior, Jesus Christ."

His anguished declaration told me that the training of a Pharisee continued to test his faith. He had great regret. But didn't we all feel remorse over things of the past—our blindness, the wasted days and years we did not live for Christ? We must remind one another: by grace we are saved, not by works. "There is no condemnation for those who belong to Christ Jesus." Paul would need to be reminded of his own words—often. "God saved us by His grace when we believed. And we can't take credit for this; it is a gift from God." God had chosen this man to bear testimony, and his violent, self-righteous past was proof of God's ability to change a man into a new creation and set him upon a new course.

His eyes grew bright with tears. "We've been washed in His blood."

"And clothed in His righteousness."

"Amen!" We said in unison. We laughed with the joy of free men joined in common purpose.

Paul grasped my arms. "We will do well together, my friend."

Yes, we would, though neither of us knew yet how difficult our days together would be.

FOUR

❖❖❖❖❖❖❖

Before we began our travels, Paul and I discussed our strategy. "The Greeks know nothing of the Scriptures," he said, "so we must speak to them in ways they will understand."

My father had said the same thing in several ways. "My father insisted I have training in logic and Greek poetry." I had to know how to think like the Greeks in order to best them in trade.

We would not burden the fledgling congregations with our support. I had some resources on which we could depend, but Paul insisted he would work for a living.

"Doing what?"

"I come from a family of tentmakers. What can you do?"

"I can translate and write letters."

We decided to stay to the major trade routes and centers so the message would have the best chance of being carried more quickly through the empire. We would start with the synagogues. There we expected to be welcomed as travelers and given lodgings as well as the opportunity to preach. We agreed to maintain contact with the Jerusalem council through letters and messengers.

"Even if the Jews welcome the Good News, we must not neglect preaching to the Gentiles in the agoras."

The marketplace was the center of all social, political, and administrative functions in every city from Jerusalem to Rome, and as such would afford us greater opportunity to meet men and women unfamiliar with the news we carried.

Once we made our plans, we set out, visiting the churches in Syria as we headed north. It was hard going. I was not used to traveling on foot. Every muscle in my body ached, each day adding to my discomfort, but Paul was driven, and so drove me as well. I did not protest, for we both thought time short and that Jesus would return soon. I knew I was not so old that my body would not become accustomed to the hardship of travel. We carried in our hearts the most important message in the world: the way of salvation for mankind. Discomfort would not delay us.

Though robbers did.

We were set upon by six men as we traveled north through the Taurus Mountains. When they surrounded us, I wondered if Paul and I would ever make it to Issus or Tarsus. One robber held a knife to my throat while another searched me. Two others dug around in Paul's clothing to find something of value. I should not have been surprised that he carried nothing. He had said from the first day that he would trust in God to provide for us. I was not so mature in my faith, though I had been a believer longer than Paul. I had a pouch of coins tucked into my sash, which a brigand found almost immediately. Other than my coat, a sash my father gave me, the inkhorn and pen case containing reeds, and a small knife for erasures and cutting papyrus, I had nothing of value.

"Look at this!" The robber held up my money pouch and shook it. He tossed it to the leader, who opened it and spilled the denarii into the palm of his hand. He grinned, for it was not a small amount, but enough to carry us for many weeks.

Another searched Paul. "Nothing!" He thrust Paul away in disgust.

"I may not have money," Paul said boldly, "but I have something of far greater value!"

"And what would that be?"

"The way to your salvation!"

They hooted in laughter. One of them stepped forward and put his blade against Paul's throat. "And what about yours, you fool?"

Paul's face flushed. "Even thieves and robbers are welcome at the Lord's table, *if* they repent."

I could see how little they welcomed that declaration, and I prayed our journey would not end with our throats slit on a dusty mountain road. If that was to be our end, I decided not to go silently to the grave. "Jesus died for all our sins—yours as well as mine."

"Who's Jesus?"

I told them everything in short order, while praying that my words would fall like seeds onto good soil. Perhaps their hard lives had plowed the ground and made it ready for sowing. "I saw Him crucified, and met Him four days later. He spoke to me. He broke bread with me. I saw His nail-scarred hands."

"He confronted me on the road to Damascus months later," Paul said, undaunted by the knife at his throat. He gripped the man's wrist and looked at him. "If you leave me dead on this road, know that I forgive you." He spoke with such sincerity, the man could only stare. Paul let go of him. "I beseech the Lord not to hold your sins against you."

"Let him go!" The leader growled.

The robber withdrew, confused.

"Here!" The leader flung the pouch of coins. I caught it against my chest.

"What are you doing?" The others protested. "We need that money!"

"Would you have their god on our heels? Others will come along this road."

Did I trust in God's provision or not? "Keep it!" I tossed the pouch back. "Consider it a gift from the Lord we serve. Better to accept it than rob others and bring further sin upon yourselves."

"You should be careful what you say." A robber held up his knife.

"The Lord sees what you do." Paul stepped forward, and looked up at the man on horseback. "These men follow in your steps."

He shifted uneasily upon his horse and held my money pouch like a poisonous snake.

"The next band will be sorely disappointed in how little these men have to offer."

I felt encouraged by the robber's sudden concern for our well-being. Fear of the Lord is the foundation of true knowledge. However, his next words filled me with misgivings. "Bring them along!"

They took us into the mountains. Their camp reminded me of En-gedi, where David had hidden in the wilderness from King Saul and his army. Plenty of water, cliff walls for protection, a few women and children to greet them. I was exhausted. Paul talked all night and baptized two of the robbers on the third day of our captivity.

They accompanied us as far as the mountain pass called the Cilician Gates.

"Jubal said to give this to you." The man tossed me the pouch of coins.

God had brought us safely through the mountains. The Cilician plain spread out before us, lush green from the waters of the Cyndnus.

✦ ✦ ✦

We stayed with Paul's family in Tarsus and preached in the synagogues. Paul had come here after meeting the Lord on the Damascus road and spent time in seclusion before he began preaching the message of Christ. The seeds he had planted had taken root and flourished. The Jews received us with joy.

We moved on to Derbe, a city in Lycaonia, named after the junipers that grew in the area. Again, we preached in the synagogues, and met Gaius, who became a good friend and, later, a traveling companion to Paul. Gaius knew the Scriptures well and embraced the Good News before anyone else.

Lystra filled me with dread. The last time Paul had preached in the Roman colony near the unsettled southern mountains, he had been stoned.

"God raised me," Paul said. "I walked back into the city on my own two legs. Friends washed my wounds and helped me escape with Barnabas." He laughed. "I guess they feared if I remained, my enemies would kill me *again*."

I didn't think it amusing. But I was curious. How many men have died and lived again to tell of it? I asked him what he remembered, if anything.

"I can't say what I saw. Whether my soul left my body or was still in my body, I don't know. Only God knows what really happened, but I was caught up somehow to the third heaven."

"Did you see Jesus?"

"I saw the heavenly realm and earth and all beneath it."

In awe, I pressed. "Did the Lord speak to you?"

"He said what He said to me before. I cannot describe what I saw, Silas, but I was in a state of misery when I came back. That I remember quite well." He smiled wistfully. "The only one who could understand what I felt is Lazarus." He put his hand on my arm, his expression intense. "It is better that we don't speak of the experience, Silas. Those in Lystra know something of it, but I dare not add more."

"Why not?" It seemed to me his experience confirmed our lives continued after our bodies rested.

"People are likely to become more interested in heavenly realms and angels than in making a decision about where they stand with Jesus Christ *in this life*."

As I have said, Paul had more wisdom than I.

I wanted to ask more, to press him for everything he remembered, but I respected his decision. And I did not want to make assumptions about his course of action regarding Lystra. "Those who sought your death would be confounded if they were to face you now." Whether we passed through Lystra or remained to preach was for him to decide. I knew God would make His will known to Paul. The man never ceased to pray for His guidance.

"They *will* be confounded. Whether they listen and believe this time remains to be seen."

Lystra is a Latin-speaking Roman colony in the consolidated province of Galatia. Remote and filled with superstition, it proved hard ground for the seed we bore. But our time there yielded a few tender shoots. And we met one who was to grow tall and strong in faith; a young man named Timothy. His mother, Eunice, and grandmother, Lois, believed in God. His father, however, was a Greek pagan who remained devoted to idol worship.

Eunice came to me and asked to speak with me alone. "I'm afraid to speak to Paul," she confessed. "He is so fierce."

"What troubles you?"

"My son is loved by many, Silas, but as you have probably guessed, he is not a true Jew." She lowered her eyes. "I took him to the rabbi when he was eight days old, but he would not circumcise him because of his mixed blood. And he's never been allowed to enter the synagogue." She worried her shawl. "I was young and headstrong. I married Julius against my father's wishes. I have many regrets, Silas." She lifted her head, eyes moist. "But having Timothy is not one of them. He has been the greatest blessing of my life and my mother's."

"He is a fine boy."

"We saw Paul when he came before. When he was stoned . . ." She clasped her hands tensely. "My son could talk of nothing else after Paul left. He said if Paul ever came back he would follow him anywhere. And now Paul is here again, and Timothy has such hope." Her eyes welled. "Paul is a Pharisee, a student of the great Gamaliel. What will he say when Timothy approaches him? I cannot bear to see my boy crushed again, Silas. I cannot."

I put my hand on her shoulder. "He won't be."

Paul, who had no wife or children of his own, loved this young man like a son. "His mother and grandmother have taught him well. He has a quick mind and an open heart to the Lord. See how he drinks in the Word of God, Silas. He will be of great use to God."

I agreed, but was concerned. "In time, Paul, but he's only thirteen and reserved by nature." I feared that Timothy might prove to be like John Mark, too young to be taken from his family.

"He thinks before he speaks."

"He's somewhat timid in a crowd."

"What better way for him to outgrow those tendencies than to join us in carrying the message to other cities? He will learn to be bold among strangers."

A pity Paul had not encouraged John Mark in this way, but I did not mention this. Both young men had similar traits, though Paul seemed determined not to notice. "Timothy might grow even more timid if persecuted." What Eunice had told me was also heavily on my mind, but I did not know how much to divulge to Paul without causing her embarrassment.

Paul gave me a level look. "He is younger than John Mark, but stronger in faith."

That sarcasm again. I felt the heat rush into my face, and held my tongue with difficulty. Any time anyone argued with Paul, he engaged his considerable talents at debate. In this case, it would serve no other purpose than to pour salt on old wounds. Both of us would suffer in an argument over John Mark.

A few hours later, Paul said, "Perhaps I am unfair."

Perhaps? "John Mark made good use of his time in Jerusalem."

Paul said nothing for a while, but I could see our difference of opinion plagued him. "Persecution will come whether Timothy stays here or goes with us," he said finally. "He might be safer with us than left behind. Besides, we already have leaders in place here, Silas. Timothy can be of much more use elsewhere."

I knew I must voice my other concerns. "As fine a young man as he is, Paul, he will cause us nothing but trouble. You were a Pharisee. You know as well as I do that no Jew will listen to him. No matter how fine his reputation here, everywhere else he will be seen as a Gentile because of his father. Timothy is uncircumcised and, therefore, unclean in their eyes. We both agreed we must meet people and speak to them in ways they will understand. How can he go with us? He won't be allowed in the synagogues! You know as well as I if we try to take him inside with us, there'll be a riot. The Good News won't be heard at all with Timothy as our traveling companion. Let him cut his teeth teaching Gentiles here."

Paul chewed on his lip, eyes narrowed in thought. "I think we should lay the matter before Timothy and see what he says about it."

Timothy presented the solution. "Circumcise me. Then no one can protest my presence in the synagogue."

The boy's courage and willingness to eliminate any obstacles served to gain my full support in taking him with us. Paul made all the arrangements, and a week later, when Timothy's fever abated and he was well enough to travel, we gathered the church elders from Lystra and Iconium. We all laid hands on Timothy and prayed the Holy Spirit would give him the gift of prophecy and leadership. His mother and grandmother both wept.

I could see how difficult this parting was for the two women. Together, they had raised Timothy to please God, and now they presented him to God as their thanksgiving offering to Jesus Christ. Timothy had been their comfort and joy. Their love of the Lord and the Torah had prepared the way for them all to believe the Good News.

"God will send you where He wills, my son."

Timothy stood tall. "Tell Father I will continue to pray for him." His voice choked with emotion.

"As will we." Eunice laid her hand against his cheek. "Perhaps his love for you will open his heart one day."

We all hoped. And prayed.

+ + +

The three of us traveled from town to town. We spent long hours around campfires talking about Jesus. I told Timothy all I knew, amazed that the memories of Jesus' teachings were so clear—proof that the Holy Spirit refreshed my mind. Paul and I preached whenever and wherever allowed. Timothy did as well, though he would sometimes be so tense and nervous, he would vomit before we approached the synagogue. I saw him sick many times while we worked together in Corinth, and later heard from Paul that even after years in ministry, Timothy still suffered greatly from a nervous stomach. Much of this I'm sure was due to his love for his flock in Ephesus. Timothy always agonized over the people in his care, even those who were wolves among the sheep.

But I digress.

In the beginning, we had Timothy stand with us, a silent encourager, speaking only when questioned directly. When he did speak, he revealed the remarkable wisdom God had given him. He was especially useful in reaching the younger people. While children were sometimes frightened by Paul's passion and put off by my grave dignity, they flocked to Timothy. The boys thought him brave and adventurous; the girls thought him handsome. I laughed when I saw how they surrounded him, first out of curiosity, later out of fond regard.

Paul worried. "It is no laughing matter, Silas. With such admiration comes temptation and sin." He spent a great deal of time instructing Timothy on how to stay pure and avoid temptation.

"Think of the younger ones as your sisters."

"And the older ones?"

"Older ones?" Paul blanched. He looked at me.

I nodded. I had seen more than one young woman approach Timothy with the clear intent of seducing him. "Never be alone with a woman, Timothy. Young or old. Woman is temptation for a man. Treat the older ones with the respect you would show your mother and grandmother."

Paul continued to stare at me. "Was there more you wanted to say?"

"No."

He took me aside later. "I never thought to ask if you had difficulty with women."

I laughed. "All men have difficulty with women, Paul. In some manner or form. But be assured. I take my own advice."

"It is a pity he's so good-looking."

The boy's beauty was a gift from God. As far as I know, Timothy heeded our instructions. I have never heard a word of doubt regarding his integrity.

+ + +

Silas put his reed pen in its case and sat thinking of Diana. Every time she looked at him, he felt a catch in his breath and a tightening in his stomach. Was this what it was like to fall in love with someone? How could he love her after such short acquaintance? And the boy, Curiatus . . . He felt drawn to him as Paul had felt drawn to Timothy. The woman and boy made Silas wonder what it might have been like to marry and have children of his own, a son to bring up for the Lord.

Many of the disciples had wives and children. Peter's sons remained in Galilee. His daughter had married, had children, and gone with her husband to another province.

Paul had been adamant about remaining unmarried, and encouraged others to follow his example. "We should remain as we were when God first called us. I had no wife when Jesus chose me to be His instrument, and will never take one. Nor should you, Silas. Our loyalties must not be divided."

Silas had not agreed with him. "Peter's wife has never been a distraction to his love of Christ or his dedication to serving the Master. She shares his faith. She walks the roads with him. She is a great comfort to him when he's weary. And Priscilla and Aquila—look at all they have accomplished. They are yoked together with Christ."

"Peter was married when he met Jesus! So were Priscilla and Aquila."

"God had said, 'It is not good for man to be alone.' "

Aggravated, Paul had glared at him. "Is there a woman you want to make your wife? Is that the point of this argument?"

Silas wanted to pound his fists in frustration. "No."

"Then why are we having this discussion?"

"Not all men are called to be celibate, Paul." Silas spoke quietly, but with firmness. "You don't hear yourself, but sometimes you speak as though celibacy is a new law within the church."

Paul opened his mouth to retort. Uttering an exasperated snort, he surged to his feet and left the fire. He stood out in the darkness looking up at the stars. After a long while, he came back. "Who are we talking about?"

Silas named two couples who had approached him on the subject.

"They're young. Their feelings will change."

"If pounded into submission?"

Paul's eyes went dark again. Silas cocked his head and looked at him gravely.

"Time is short, Silas, and we should not waste any of it pleasing another person."

"I'll tell Timothy that, the next time he strives to live up to your expectations."

"The Scriptures say a man should remain at home for a year and give his wife pleasure! I say what time we have must be dedicated to spreading the news of Jesus Christ."

"Yes. *You* say."

"We carry the message of life! What is more important than that?"

"Nothing. But it does not have to be carried alone."

"We're not alone. We travel in pairs."

"And some of the pairs could be husband and wife."

Paul's eyes blazed. "The Lord could return tomorrow, Silas. Should we devote ourselves to anything or anyone that does not further the message of Christ?"

"If we don't love others, Paul, what good is all our fine preaching?"

"You're talking about *lust*, not love!"

"Is this discussion about winning a debate, Paul, or about the very real struggles of people within the body of Christ? Some will be called to marry and have children. Will you tell them they are not allowed to do so because *you* are called to celibacy and dedication to evangelism?"

"There is no time for marriage!"

"So, now you know when Jesus will return. Is that what you're saying? Even Jesus said He didn't know! Only the Father knows!"

Silas took a deep breath, realizing his voice had risen in anger. Anger would accomplish nothing. Oh, but Paul could be so adamant, so fiercely stubborn.

"You were called of God to travel and preach, Paul. I've been called, of late, to accompany you. Each of us is called to different tasks and places within society. You have preached so yourself."

"All to build the body—"

"Yes. To build! And if everyone *refuses* to marry or have children, even if God leads them to do so, what happens to our numbers within a generation?"

Paul drew back and frowned.

Silas spread his hands. "God made marriage, Paul. The Lord sanctifies the relationship." He shrugged. "Perhaps the question is not whether men and women should marry, but how they should behave when they do. What is a Christian marriage to look like to the world around us? *Love each other*. What does that mean in terms other than the physical? Peter and his wife have been an inspiration to many. . . ."

Over the months, they had discussed marriage and prayed for God's guidance in what to teach about it. Everywhere they went, they had seen the way unrestrained sexual passion could destroy lives. Such passions were the foundation of idol worship.

Silas took up the reed pen again and ran it between his fingers. When his father died, he'd had no time to consider marriage. The young woman who might have become his wife was given to another with his blessing. The loss had not touched his heart. He had barely known her.

He wanted to know Diana and, because of these feelings, did his best to avoid her.

But she was always at meetings, sitting nearby, attentive. It took determined efforts on his part to keep his gaze from drifting back to her. And her smile . . .

He could not allow himself to think of her. It led him to thoughts of what might have been and could never be.

Mixing another supply of ink, Silas set his own scroll aside and worked until late copying Peter's letters. Only then did he allow himself to linger on his past again.

+ + +

Paul and I planned to go to Asia, but were prevented when Roman foot soldiers stopped us on the road and enlisted us to carry their gear. They demanded only the distance Roman law allowed. We saw this as an opportunity to tell them about Jesus and traveled with them all the way to the border of Mysia. We prayed about whether God wanted us to cross the mountains into Asia, but the Holy Spirit sent us north instead, and then east along the border of Bithynia and on to Troas.

We knew the Lord had led us there. Troas is a strategic meeting point of sea routes on the northwestern coast of Asia, southwest of the old city of Troy. Its position close to the mouth of the Hellespont has made the Roman colony grow. The citizens have made harbor basins, which provide shelter from the northerlies for ships. Troas is the main port for crossing to Neapolis in Macedonia and reaching the land route to Rome. The Good News could spread easily in all directions from Troas.

We met Luke, the physician, in Troas. Paul needed salve for an infection, and Luke was recommended to us. What a great friend he became, not just to Paul and Timothy and me, but to other brothers and sisters. He left his practice to join us in our travels. As soon as he accepted Christ, the Holy Spirit filled him with purpose, that of gathering facts and information about Jesus' birth, teaching, miracles, death, burial, and resurrection. When he was not attending someone as a physician, he could be found hard at work compiling his reports.

When we were in Ephesus, Luke spoke for long hours with Mary, the mother of Jesus, and John the apostle, with whom she lived. He met Lazarus and his sisters before they sailed to Tarsus. In Jerusalem, he spoke to James and several disciples. If he ever completes this history, the church can know it is a trustworthy account.

While we were in Troas, Paul had a vision. "A man of Macedonia keeps calling out to me, 'Come over here and help us!'"

The four of us sailed to Samothrace and reached Neapolis the next day. We only stayed long enough to eat and rest before we headed for Philippi.

We were all excited about what the Lord would do, for Philippi, a prosperous Roman colony, was on the Egnatian Way, the military road that joined Rome and the East. It was along this great highway that information traveled from one end of the empire to the other. From Troas, the message would travel by sea; from Philippi, by land.

We spent several days looking for a synagogue.

Paul grew dismayed. "We must be the only Jews in the entire city." All it required to establish a synagogue was ten men who were heads of households.

On the Sabbath, we went outside the city in search of a place of prayer under the open sky and near a river. We found a suitable place where the road crossed the Gangites River. Several women were already gathered there, praying. While Luke, Timothy, and I hesitated, Paul walked down the bank.

"Come on." He motioned to us to follow.

One of the servant girls looked at Timothy and whispered to her friend, who giggled.

A woman in a fine tunic with purple trim took charge. Shushing the girls, she stood and gave Paul an imperious look. "We are Jews seeking a quiet place to worship God."

I took those words as a plea for us to leave. Paul was not so easily shaken.

"We are Jews also," Paul told her. "And these two are devout men of God." He introduced each of us. "We bring you Good News."

The woman frowned. "What do you mean by 'Good News'?"

"We are followers of the Lord's Messiah, Jesus. He was crucified, buried, and raised from the dead after three days. This man——" he pointed to me—— "saw Jesus numerous times and saw Him ascend into heaven."

"Please." She gestured, seating herself on an expensive Babylonian blanket. "Join us." Timothy and Luke held back. "All of you." She smiled. "I am Lydia from Thyatira. I'm a merchant in Philippi. I sell purple fabrics. And these are my servants—good young ladies, all of them." She gave a pointed look at one who had sidled closer to Timothy and patted the place beside her. The girl obeyed. "Tell us more about this Jesus," Lydia said.

We did, with great pleasure. She listened intently and believed every word. So did those with her. "Is there any reason we cannot be baptized here?" Lydia wanted to know. "Today?"

Paul laughed. "None!"

The younger ones laughed joyfully and splashed one another in their exuberance, while Lydia stood on the bank, dripping with dignity. "Please, come to my house. I have plenty of room, and you may stay for as long as you like."

Paul shook his head. "We are thankful for your generous invitation, Lydia, but we wouldn't want to make things difficult for you."

"I have a *large* house, Paul."

"Even in Macedonia, I'm certain neighbors might wonder what four strange men are doing in your house."

She dismissed his argument with a wave of her hand. "If you agree that I am a true believer in the Lord, come and stay at my home. My neighbors know me, and I will make certain they soon know you. You can tell them all you have told me."

Lydia's house was indeed large, and she treated us as honored guests. Within a few days, we had started a small church in her house. We often went back to the river to baptize new believers and preach to those who stopped to watch.

And then the trouble began, as it so often did when many came to Christ.

A slave girl began to follow us from the city one day. She shouted at everyone. "These men are servants of the Most High God, and they have come to tell you how to be saved."

Paul stopped and faced her.

Lydia shook her head. "Leave her alone, Paul. You will only bring trouble on all of us if you argue with her. She's a famous fortune-teller. Her owners are among the leaders of the city, and they make great sums of money off her prophecies."

I glanced back at the girl. "She's speaking the truth right now."

"Not out of love," Paul said.

She went as far as the city gate. Her face looked grotesque, and her body twitched as she pointed at us. "Those men are servants of the Most High God. . . ."

A few who had started to follow us were afraid to pass by her.

The next day, she followed us again. This time she came out through the city gates, and stood on the road above the riverbank. Paul tried to preach, but she kept shouting. No one could concentrate on anything Paul or Timothy or I said. Everyone kept looking up at that poor, wretched, demon-possessed girl.

When she followed us yet again, we tried to approach and speak with her. She fled into the house of one of her owners. "You have to pay to see her," the guard told Paul.

"I didn't come to hear her prophesy, but to speak with her."

"No one talks to her unless they pay the master first."

We discussed the situation. "All we can do is ignore her," I said, "and hope she will tire of this."

"And in the meantime, our brothers and sisters learn nothing."

"Continue to meet in my house."

"There are already too many, Lydia. Many more can gather at the river."

"If you confront her, you will only bring trouble down on us."

Every day for days on end, the slave girl followed us, shouting. I saw anguish as well as anger in her face and was reminded of Mary Magdalene, from whom Jesus had cast out seven demons that had tormented her. I prayed, but the girl continued to follow.

Though I pitied the girl, Paul grew increasingly frustrated.

"Nothing can be accomplished with all her shouting and screaming. The demon distracts us from teaching and others from hearing the Word of God!"

When she ran up close behind us and screamed in rage, Paul turned on her.

"*Silence, demon!*" He pointed at her. *"I command you in the name of Jesus Christ to come out of her and never enter her again!"*

The girl stood for a moment, eyes wide, and then gave a long sigh. I caught her before she fell. People ran to see what had happened, clustering close.

"Is she dead?"

"He's killed her."

"She's alive," Luke said. "Give her room to breathe!"

She roused, her face smooth in wonder. "It's gone." A child's voice, perplexed, hopeful.

"Yes." I set her upon her feet. "The demon is gone."

Her eyes filled with fear. "It'll come back."

Paul put his hand on her shoulder. "No. If you accept Jesus as Lord, He will fill you with the Holy Spirit, and no demon will ever possess you again."

"Who is Jesus?"

"Let me through!" A man shouted at the back of the crowd. "Get out of my way!" He pushed toward us. One look into her face and he grew alarmed. "What have you done?" He grasped the girl by the arm and held her close at his side. "What did you do to her?"

Everyone spoke at once.

"They cast out a demon!"

"This man told her to be silent."

"He called the demon out of her."

The man thrust the girl toward Paul. "Call it back into her!"

"Jesus . . ." The girl covered her face and sobbed. "Jesus."

"Shut up, girl. Now is not the time." He glared at Paul. "You'd better do what I say."

"Never."

"You've ruined her, and you'll pay for it!"

Others arrived claiming to own her and joined in haranguing Paul.

"You will make her as she was, or we'll sue you."

"Our livelihood depends on her."

Men grabbed hold of us, shouting. Punched and shoved, I lost my footing. Dragged up, I spotted Paul, mouth bleeding. Timothy and Luke shouted in our defense, but were pushed aside. "Get out of here! We have no quarrel with you!"

The girl's owners hauled us none too gently to the marketplace. "These men have destroyed our property!"

The officials tried to calm the men, but they grew more vitriolic. "Call the chief magistrate. He knows of our girl. She's prophesied for him several times, to his benefit. Tell him she can no longer prophesy because of what these Jews have done! He'll judge in our favor!"

When the chief magistrate came out, the men shouted even louder against us, adding false accusations. "The whole city is in an uproar because of these Jews! You know what trouble they are, and here they come to our city now teaching customs that are illegal for us Romans to practice!"

"That's not true!" Paul called out.

I fought the hands that held me. "Allow us to declare our case!" A man struck me in the side of the head.

The man who had come for the girl shouted, "It is forbidden, for Romans are not allowed to engage in any religion not sanctioned by the emperor!"

"Emperor Claudius has expelled all Jews from Rome because of the trouble they cause. . . ."

"They speak against our gods!"

Their hatred of us grew to encompass all Jews.

Paul shouted. "We speak only of the Lord Jesus Christ, Savior—"

"They are causing chaos!"

The chief magistrates ordered us beaten.

I called out. "The Lord has sent us to tell you the Good News. . . ."

None listened.

"Show them what happens to Jews who cause trouble!"

Hands dug into me. Pulled, yanked, shoved, my robe torn from my back, I found myself stretched out and tied to a post. The first lash of the rod sent a shock of pain through my body, and I cried out.

I could hear Paul. "The Lord has sent us to tell you the Good News. Jesus is Lord! He offers salvation. . . ." Blows rained upon him.

The second and third blows drove the breath from my body. I clawed at the post, twisting against the ropes that held me, but there was no escaping the pain. Paul and I hung side by side, bodies jerking with each blow. I opened my mouth wide to gasp for breath and thought of Jesus hanging on the cross. "Father, forgive them," Jesus had said. "They don't know what they are doing."

I closed my eyes tightly, gritted my teeth, and prayed for the flogging to end.

I don't know how many blows we took before the magistrate ordered us cut down and thrown into prison. Paul was unconscious. I feared they had killed him. I longed for death. Every movement sent spears of agony.

They dragged us to the jailer. "Guard them securely! If they escape, your life is forfeit!"

He ordered us carried down to the inner dungeon. They dumped us on cold stone inside a cell and fastened our feet in stocks. I gagged at the foul smell of human excrement, urine, fear-inspired sweat, and death. I tried to rise, but collapsed again. My back throbbed and burned. Weak, I couldn't move, and I lay in a pool of my own blood.

Paul lay close by, unmoving. "Paul!" He stirred. Weeping, I thanked God. I reached out and gripped his wrist gently. "It's over."

Moaning, he rolled his head toward me. "I had you beaten once. This may be a hint of atonement."

"Perhaps, if I hadn't received the same treatment." I gave him a pained grin. "And as I remember, you kicked me three times. No one used a wooden rod on me."

"I won't argue with you."

I gave a soft laugh and winced. "My consolation."

Gritting my teeth, I sucked in my breath and managed to sit up. Chains jingled as Paul slowly did the same. We leaned forward, resting our arms on our raised knees, waiting until the pain in our backs subsided enough so that we could breathe normally.

"By God's grace, we share in Christ's suffering." Paul raised his head. "We have company."

Looking out through the bars of our cell, I saw other men in the dungeon with us—silent, dark-eyed men without hope, waiting for an end to their ordeal.

Paul smiled at me. "Even in a dungeon, God gives us opportunities."

And so he preached. "By God's great mercy, He washed away our sins, giving us a new birth and new life through the Holy Spirit, which He generously poured out upon us through Christ Jesus, our Savior."

I considered it a privilege to suffer for the name of Jesus Christ, to share in some way the sufferings my Lord endured for me. I counted it an honor to suffer with Paul.

We sang songs of deliverance in that dark place, and laughed as we did, for the sound filled that great, yawning hole where human misery dwelt. We rejoiced in our salvation, our rescue from sin and death, our assurance in the promises of God and heaven. Our voices rose and swelled, flowing along stone corridors to the guards. They did not order us to be silent. We had a congregation in that prison. Chained, yes, but undistracted by a girl's raving. Rapt and eager, they listened to the only hope in a living hell on earth.

One confessed to committing murder. Paul said he had also, and told how God had forgiven, reclaimed, and set him on a new path.

Another declared his innocence. Once I had thought myself innocent and above reproach. I told him all men are sinners in need of grace.

An earthquake came around midnight and shook the foundations of the prison house. Stone grated against stone, and dust billowed around us. Men screamed in fear. The prison doors burst open. The chains around our ankles fell off as though unlocked by invisible hands.

"What's happening?" Men cried out, confused, afraid to hope.

"It is the Lord's doing!" Paul answered. "Stay as you are. Only trust in Him!"

Running steps approached, and I caught sight of the jailer. He looked around frantically, saw opened cells in horror, and drew his sword. When he removed his breastplate, we knew what he meant to do. Death by his own sword would be preferable to crucifixion for dereliction of duty. He thought we had all escaped!

"Stop!" Paul shouted. "Don't kill yourself! Do no harm to yourself! No one has left! We are all here!"

Lowering his sword, the jailer shouted for torches. Guards ran toward our cell, filling it with torchlight. The jailer fell on his knees before us.

"Get up!" Paul told him. "We're not gods that you should worship us. We came with a message of salvation."

A prisoner called out. "They speak of a god who died and rose again."

"And still lives," another joined in.

"Come out of here!" The jailer beckoned, shaking, his eyes wide with fear. "Come out!"

He led us out of the prison and took us to his house in the compound. He called for water, salve, and bandages. A woman hovered, several children clutching at her. She kept her arm around them as she spoke to the jailer. "I feared for you, my husband. The gods are angry. They shook the foundations of our house!"

"It's all right now, Lavinia. Hush! These men serve a god of great power."

"He is the only God!" Paul said. "There is no other."

The jailer stared at us. "Sirs, what must I do to be saved?"

"Believe in the Lord Jesus Christ," Paul told him, "and you will be saved."

I smiled at the woman and children. "Along with everyone in your household."

"The earthquake that brought your freedom is proof of His great power." The jailer took the basin of water from a servant and washed our wounds himself. "Tell me about this God who can open prison doors and remove chains."

The jailer—whose name, we learned, was Demetrius—and his family believed everything we told them. We baptized them. Not even a dungeon could shut out the light of Jesus Christ!

Food was prepared, and we broke bread together.

"How can I return you to the prison when you've brought us life? I will send word to your friends. I'll get you out of the city. They can meet you with supplies. . . ."

For a moment, I was tempted. Thankfully, Paul declined. "We will not flee. We obey the law. God can rescue us from the false accusations that put us in prison."

Guards took us back to our cell.

A few hours later, Demetrius returned. "I sent word to the magistrates and told them what happened last night, of the earthquake. They felt it, too. When I told them about the cell doors opening and your shackles falling away, they said to let you go. You are free to leave Philippi."

"Free to leave?" I said. "Or ordered to leave?"

"They want you out of the city."

Disappointment filled me. We had accomplished so much. But there was still so much to do. The Lord had saved this man and his household, and now, unknown to him, Satan was using him to silence us.

Paul put his hands on his knees. "We're not leaving!"

"You have no choice!" Guards waited outside to escort us out of the city.

"They have publicly beaten us without a trial and put us in prison—and we are Roman citizens. So now they want us to leave secretly? Certainly not! Let them come themselves to release us!"

Demetrius blanched. "You're Romans? You should have said something!"

I smiled wryly. "They never gave us the chance."

Demetrius sent the message. He returned with the officials. The man who had ordered us flogged stood pale-faced with fear of retribution. "I beg your forgiveness. Had we known you were Roman citizens, we would never have allowed anyone to lay hands on you let alone seen you beaten in the marketplace!"

"Please believe us!"

"You judged us without trial, based on false accusations," Paul said. "And now you banish us from Philippi."

"No, no, you misunderstand us!" The chief magistrate spread his hands. "Crispus, Pontus, and the others swayed me with their accusations. They are still furious over their slave girl. And they have cause. The girl is worthless now."

What would happen to the poor girl? I wondered. "If she's worthless, tell her owners to sell her to Lydia, the merchant who sells purple cloth." She would free the girl.

"There will be trouble if you remain in Philippi," said another.

They insisted. "We cannot promise your safety if you remain here."

"We accept your apology," Paul told them.

"And you will leave." Clearly, they wanted us gone as soon as possible.

Paul nodded. I wanted to argue, but he gave a look that silenced me. "As soon as we meet with others of our faith."

We went to Lydia's house, where we found Luke and Timothy. They had been praying all night. "God has answered your prayers," I said, laughing despite the discomfort of my wounds.

Luke checked the dressing. "More needs to be done." When he added salt to prevent infection, I passed out.

Paul roused before I did and asked that the believers gather. When they all arrived, we gave them what instructions we could in the little time we had. "Be strong in the Lord and in His mighty power," Paul said.

I promised we would write to them.

Paul and I, with Luke and Timothy, left Philippi late that afternoon.

Of all the churches I helped plant over the years, the Philippian believers suffered the greatest hardships. Some lost their lives; many, their homes and businesses. Yet, they remained steadfast. Though impoverished by persecution, God made them rich in faith and love.

May the grace of our Lord Jesus Christ continue to sustain them until the day Jesus returns.

FIVE

✦✦✦✦✦✦

We traveled through Amphipolis and Apollonia and on to Thessalonica. We found a synagogue and stayed with Jason, a Jew who had accepted Christ in Jerusalem years before during Pentecost. We did not want to be a burden to him. Paul found work as a tentmaker; I wrote letters and documents. Every Sabbath, we went to the synagogue and reasoned with the Jews. We showed them proofs through the Scriptures that Jesus is the Messiah of God, the Christ whom God sent to fulfill the Law and ransom us from sin and death, but few believed.

The greatest number of new believers came from among the God-fearing Greeks who followed the teachings of the Torah. They embraced Christ with zeal and spread word through the city about Jesús. Many Jews became incensed as the number of believers grew. Finding troublemakers in the agora, they formed a mob and descended upon Jason's house, expecting to find Paul and me there. Paul worked just outside the city, and I was off somewhere helping an official write a letter. So they grabbed Jason along with a few others and dragged these poor men before the city authorities.

It happened just as it had in Philippi!

They accused Jason and the other believers they'd seized of causing chaos, when it was they who stirred the city into confusion. They claimed we taught Jesus was a king like Caesar and that we encouraged the people to rebel against Rome!

I found friends of my father and arranged for bond to be paid. Jason and the others were set free. But the trouble was far from over.

Jason insisted Paul and I leave the city. "The Jews are intent upon killing Paul. They despise you, too, Silas, but see you as a Greek. They see Paul as a traitor to his race and a priest of apostasy. Every word he speaks is blasphemy to their ears, and they will stop at nothing to kill him if he remains here. You must go. *Now!*"

"I'll go with you," Timothy said, packed and ready.

"You will stay here with Luke." Paul remained adamant despite Timothy's plea. "We will meet later." I knew Paul feared for the boy and did not want to put him in danger, and he entrusted him to Luke.

We left under cover of darkness and headed for Berea. We went straight to the synagogue there. I expected more trouble, but we found the Berean Jews open-minded and open of heart. They listened and then examined the Scriptures to see if what we said was true. The body of Christ grew rapidly in Berea as Jews and prominent Greeks, both men and women, embraced Christ.

Luke and Timothy arrived, eager to help. On their heels came some of the Thessalonican Jewish leaders, who had taken such offense to our teaching. They intended to destroy the church. "You must head south," the Berean believers told us.

Paul did not want to leave. "We cannot abandon these lambs, Silas."

I feared for his life. Luke and Timothy joined in my efforts to persuade him, but Paul protested. "It is stubbornness and pride that brings these Thessalonicans after me again. I will not give in to them."

"Is that not pride speaking, Paul?" Harsh words, I knew, but sometimes that was the only way to get through to Paul. "Do not give sin an opportunity. If we leave, they will disperse, thinking this flock cannot survive without a shepherd."

"Will they?"

"The seed has taken root in them, Paul. They know the truth and the truth has set them free. The Holy Spirit and the Scriptures will guide them. We must go for their sake as well as yours."

The more difficult parting took place at the coast. We had only enough money for two passages to Athens. "You've been ill. Luke must go with you."

"You know the respect and love I have for Luke, Silas, but I chose *you*."

"The wound on your back continues to fester. You need a physician more than a coworker."

"I'll be fine!"

"Yes, you will, with the proper care God wants you to have."

"But—"

I lost patience. "Don't argue! Why must you always argue, even with those who believe as you do! Now, bridle your tongue, and get on that boat!"

He laughed. I was immediately ashamed at my loss of temper. "There are other lost sheep, Paul. Think of them. And don't forget God called you to be His chosen instrument to bear His name before the Gentiles and kings and people of Israel. You cannot remain here and let them kill you. Kings, Paul! That's what the Lord told Ananias! Perhaps one day you'll speak before Caesar, and God willing, the emperor will listen. You must go now. God wants it so!"

He wept.

I embraced him. "You are by far the more persuasive preacher among us." I did not speak from flattery. When I drew back, I gripped his arms. "Your life must not end here."

"What of you and Timothy?"

"We'll go back to Berea and live quietly. We will teach and encourage our brothers and sisters and join you later."

Paul embraced Timothy. The boy wept.

"Come, Paul!" Luke said. "We must go!"

I held firm to Timothy's shoulder as the two men boarded the ship. "God will watch over him, Timothy. We'll stay until they leave the harbor. Just in case our good friend decides to jump ship."

Timothy gave a broken laugh. "He might. He worries about me."

"You must learn to stand without him, Timothy. He is called to spread the Good News. Others are called to remain behind and teach."

He looked up at me. "Not yet."

"Soon." God had told me so.

Life would never be easy for Paul.

Nor for anyone who traveled with him.

+   +   +

While we waited for word from Paul and Luke, Timothy and I found work to support ourselves and met with believers each evening. I taught; Timothy encouraged.

We received frequent letters from Paul and Luke about their progress in Athens. Our friend had not gone into hiding.

"I spoke in the synagogues, but the Athenian Jews have hearts of stone. I now preach in the public square, where people are more willing to listen."

But Athens grieved his spirit.

"I cannot turn right or left without coming face-to-face with an idol that promotes debauchery and licentious behavior. The people flock to these gods."

He met a few Epicurean and Stoic philosophers in the marketplace.

"Athenians crave new ideas, and the message of Christ intrigues them. They invited me to speak on the Areopagus before the council. I went, praying the Lord would give me the words to reach the hearts of these people. God answered my prayer when I saw an altar with the inscription, 'To an Unknown God.' Jesus is the Unknown God. All but a few thought me a babbler proclaiming a strange deity. They laughed when I told them of Jesus' resurrection. Yet, a few are saved. You will meet Dionysius when you come. He is a member of the council. Another believer is Damaris, a woman of good reputation. We hold meetings in Dionysius's house daily. He lives near the Areopagus."

The next letter came from Luke.

"We have moved south to Corinth."

He did not say why, but I imagine Paul was driven out of town again, either by the Jews or members of the council.

"We met two Jews expelled from Italy by Emperor Claudius's edict. Priscilla and Aquila are tentmakers and have invited Paul to join in their business. I am staying with them as well. Paul is exhausted, but I cannot stop him from working. When he isn't sewing hides together, he is in the synagogue debating with the Jews and Greeks. He needs help. I am a doctor, not an orator. Come as soon as you can. We have great need of both you and Timothy."

I had earned barely enough for my passage, but when the Bereans heard of Paul's need, they raised funds to pay for Timothy's passage. Timothy wrote a beautiful statement of faith to encourage them. "If we die with Him, we will also live with Him. If we endure hardship, we will reign with Him. If we deny Him, He will deny us. If we are unfaithful, He remains faithful, for He cannot deny who He is." I made a copy to give to Paul.

Later, Paul used these same words to encourage Timothy when he was shepherd to the flock in Ephesus, a place of such evil practices we all thought it the throne of Satan himself.

Timothy's words encourage me now.

We all must face persecution because of the evil that grips this world. Yet, Jesus Christ is Lord! I know this: our future is secure! I know this, too: Christ reigns in our hearts, minds, souls. Our lives are living testimonies of the truth of Jesus Christ, crucified, buried, and raised.

One day, Jesus will return, and the days of tribulation will be over.

Come, Lord Jesus. Come soon.

+ + +

"Can you not rest awhile, Silas?"

His heart leaped at the sound of Diana's voice. He turned and saw her in the doorway. "What are you doing here?"

"Epanetus sent me." She looked embarrassed. "I don't know why he thought I might be able to get you to leave this room."

"Is Curiatus with you?"

"He's in the garden."

Silas put the reed pen in its case and rose.

"Are you in pain?" She came a step closer.

He held up his hand. "No. I get stiff from sitting so long."

"Sitting too long isn't good for anyone, Silas."

The caring in her voice made his heart drum. He sought a way to build walls. "I'm old."

"You are no older than my husband would have been had he lived."

He looked at her then. There had been no wistfulness in her voice, no sorrow. "How long ago did he die?"

"Five years."

They looked at each other for a long moment, silent. She gave a soft gasp. He felt the heat climb into his face. "I'm sorry," he said roughly.

She held his gaze.

He swallowed hard and avoided her gaze. "We should join the others."

‡ ‡ ‡

It was an easy voyage to Athens, though I, not being much of a sailor, spent most of it with my head over the gunwales.

We met Priscilla and Aquila and liked them immediately. They had accepted Christ within hours of meeting Paul in the synagogue. "Paul is very persuasive." They proved good friends to their mentor.

Luke returned to writing his history and giving care to those in need, especially Paul, who suffered chronic pain. The beatings had taken a toll on his body, and his vision was impaired. He could no longer write, except in large letters. "I need a secretary now more than ever," he told me. I was honored to serve in that capacity.

Timothy quickly found work in Corinth, as did I. We made enough to support ourselves and Paul. This proved a great blessing, for Paul was able to dedicate himself to preaching. We assisted him by instructing those who accepted Christ.

Letters arrived from Thessalonica, filled with attacks against Paul's integrity and the message we preached. Several beloved brothers had been killed for their faith in Christ, and their friends and relatives now questioned Paul's teachings. They had expected the Lord to come before anyone died. A few took advantage of the confusion, and proclaimed Paul a liar who preached only for profit.

I had never seen Paul so hurt by accusations. How he grieved! I was more angry than Paul. Who taught with more risk to their lives than Paul? No one!

Tears streamed down his cheeks. "Such is the work of Satan!"

I felt defeated. All our work! All our prayers! The converts forgot all the sound teaching and listened to lies!

"We must go back and confront these false teachers before they turn our brothers and sisters away from Christ!"

I felt like flotsam, moving back and forth on the tide. If Paul wanted to go, I would go. If Paul wanted to stay, I would stay. I had come on this journey to stand beside him no matter the risk. If left to myself, I might have gotten on the first ship sailing for Caesarea!

We made it as far as Athens and had to wait. Paul fell ill again. I cared for him as best I could, but he needed a doctor. "I'm sending for Luke."

"No!" Paul lay pale, but vehement as ever in his opinions. "I will be all right in a few days. Luke is needed where he is. God can heal me, if He wills. And if not, then this is a burden I must carry."

As soon as Paul was well enough, we set out again, only to be attacked near the port and stripped of our passage money. Damaris helped us, but one thing after another happened to keep us from going north. "Perhaps it is the Lord keeping us here, Paul," I pointed out.

Paul, still not fully well, grew impatient. "It is Satan who delays us! We can't wait any longer! Someone must go to Thessalonica and tell our brothers and sisters the truth before their faith is murdered by lies."

Timothy said he would go. We laid hands on him, blessed him, and sent him off, eager to defend Paul and explain more fully Jesus' promise to return. I admit I feared the young man's natural reserve might keep him from being effective. Paul worried he might be killed. We both prayed unceasingly.

It was not an easy time for us.

Paul's health grew worse, and he fell into a deep depression. "I'm afraid all we've worked so hard to accomplish is lost."

We could do nothing but pray and trust in the Lord. The waiting proved a greater test of our faith than floggings and imprisonment!

But God was faithful!

Timothy returned zealous and with good reports. Rejoicing, we three returned to Corinth, renewed in faith and strength. Our good spirits dampened again though when, after a few weeks, the Corinthian Jews refused to believe a word Paul or I said. No matter how much proof we showed from the Scriptures, they hardened their hearts against Jesus. The last time Paul entered the synagogue, the gathering storm burst forth and some who despised Paul insulted and blasphemed Jesus to his face.

"Your blood is upon your own heads!" Paul cried out and left the synagogue. He stood outside, shaking his robes in protest. "I shake the dust of this place from me!" He raised his arm. "You and you and you." He pointed to specific men. "I am innocent. Let your blood be on your own heads, for you have rejected the Lord God. From now on, I will go preach to the Gentiles!"

The neighborhood remained in an uproar that day and for days following.

Paul might say he consigned them to God's wrath, but in truth the man refused to give up hope. I laugh now, for he moved in with Titius Justus, a Gentile believer. Titius lived right next door to the synagogue!

Not a day went by that the Jews did not see Paul receiving visitors. Crispus, one of their leaders, came to reason with Paul. Away from the sway and jealousy of the others, he received Christ. Soon, Crispus brought his entire family to hear about Jesus. Our enemies ground their teeth and muttered at those who came. Jews and Gentiles under one roof, breaking bread together? The Christ of God for all men? The hard-hearted refused to believe.

Paul received constant threats, and, as his friends, so did Timothy and I and others. But the attacks were far worse upon him. He became afraid. I am convinced that his fear rose from exhaustion. He worked constantly, from before dawn to long after dark. Even a man of his amazing stamina needs to rest. I certainly did. But Paul felt compelled to preach, compelled to answer every question with proof, compelled to pour himself out like a liquid offering. When he was not preaching, he studied the scrolls we carried, preparing for the next battle. He dictated letters far into the night.

A tired man is more easily shaken.

"I'm afraid," he confessed to me one night. "It's one thing for people to attack me, but my friends . . ." His eyes filled with tears. "I'm afraid of what my enemies will do next, Silas, who they might harm because of what I say." I knew he feared for Timothy, and not without cause. But Timothy was as on fire for Christ as he. The young man had given his life as a living sacrifice for the Lord.

"You must do whatever the Lord tells you to do, Paul. If the Lord says speak, you already know you have Timothy's blessing. And mine as well."

Titius Justus wondered if Paul should press on. "He has good reason to be afraid, Silas." Titius told me Paul received threats every time he left the house. The day before, the Judaizers had cornered Paul in the marketplace, and said they would kill him if he continued. When I confronted Paul about this, he said it was true.

"Perhaps we should move on again. We have planted the seeds. God will water and make them grow."

Paul smiled bleakly. "It will be the same anywhere I go, Silas. You know that as well as I."

Trouble followed Paul in the same way trouble had followed Jesus.

How many times had I seen the Good News greeted with anger and scorn? Most people don't want to hear the truth, let alone embrace it. To accept Christ's gift means admitting that everything on which we based our lives before has gained us nothing. It means surrendering to a power greater than ourselves. Few want to surrender to anything but their lusts. We cling to our vanity and go on striving to find our own way when there is only one way.

I praised God every time I saw truth dawn in someone's eyes, the veil of Satan's lies dissolved, a heart of stone beating with new life. The new believer stood on a mountaintop looking out at the vast hope laid wide open before them, an eternal, lifelong journey with the Lord. They became a living, breathing temple in which God dwelled. The rebirth was a miracle as great as Jesus' feeding thousands on a few loaves of bread and fish, because it was evidence He lived; His promises continued to be fulfilled daily.

But fear sets in so easily.

We decided to be cautious. We thought it wise, but, in truth, Paul was silenced, and so was I. We had forgotten we must step out in faith, not sit and wait for it to grow in shadows.

By the grace of God, Jesus spoke to Paul in a vision. "Don't be afraid! Speak out!" Jesus said many people in the city already belonged to Him. All we had to do was go out and find them!

We obeyed. With such great encouragement, how could we not?

We set out, faith renewed, zeal restored.

For eighteen months.

And then a new governor came to Achaia, and everything changed again.

Soon after Gallio took office, the Jews rose up against Paul, took him to the judgment seat and accused him of teaching men to worship God in ways contrary to Roman law. But Gallio was not like Pontius Pilate, easily swayed by a mob. Paul did not even say a word in his own defense before Gallio ended the session.

"Since this is merely a question of words and names and your Jewish law, take care of it yourselves. I refuse to judge such matters." With a jerk of his head, guards moved and drove the Jews away from the judgment seat.

Greeks grabbed hold of Sosthenes, the leader of the synagogue, and began beating him. Gallio continued to conduct business and ignore the fracas. A Gentile punched Sosthenes, knocked him down, and kicked him right there before the judgment seat.

Paul tried to push through. "Stop!" Unwittingly, he used Aramaic.

I cried out in Greek and then Latin. They withdrew, leaving Sosthenes half conscious and bleeding on the stone pavement. The rabbi's friends were nowhere to be seen. He shrank back from us in fear, though we only wanted to help him.

"Let us help you!"

"Why do you do this for me?" Sosthenes rasped. "You, of all people . . ."

"Because Jesus would do it," Paul said, straining to help lift him.

Sosthenes stumbled, but we kept him from falling. He wept all the way to Priscilla and Aquila's. Luke dressed his wounds. We sent word to the synagogue, but none came for him. They would not enter the house of a Gentile.

When Sosthenes became feverish, we took turns caring for him. We told him about Jesus. "He made the blind see, and the deaf hear. He raised a widow's son and called a friend from the tomb in which he had lain for four days."

I told him of Jesus' trial before Pontius Pilate, of how He died on the cross on Passover, and three days later, arose. I told him of my life in Jerusalem and Caesarea and how it changed on the road to Emmaus. Paul told him of seeing Jesus on the road to Damascus.

Sosthenes tried not to listen at first. He wept and covered his ears. But gradually he did listen. "It was not your words that convinced me," he told us. "It was your love. I was your enemy, Paul, and you and Silas lifted me up."

We baptized him.

He returned to the synagogue, determined to sway the others. He could not.

"It is not by your word or mine that men are saved," Paul told him when he came to Titius's home, "but by the power of the Holy Spirit."

"They are my friends," Sosthenes wept. "My family."

"Continue to love them. And keep praying."

+ + +

A few months later, Paul decided to go to Cenchrea and fulfill a vow of thanksgiving to the Lord. "Jesus has protected me here in Corinth." The vow required he cut off his hair and shave.

I helped him prepare. "How long will you remain in solitude?"

"Thirty days."

"Will you return here, or do you want us to join you there?"

"You and Timothy must remain here. There is still much work to do. When the time of the vow is complete, Aquila and Priscilla will join me, and we'll sail to Syria."

I was stunned. And hurt. "Are you telling me you no longer need my services?"

He grimaced as though in pain. "Don't look at me like that, Silas. I must go where the Lord leads, even if it means I must leave beloved friends behind."

Paul left the next day. The parting was especially difficult for Timothy, whom Paul commanded to remain with me in Corinth.

The church met in Chloe's home. And what a church it was, made up of reformed thieves, drunkards, idol worshipers, and adulterers. They flocked to Christ, who cleansed them of sin and made them like newborn babies. They rejected their previous practices of promiscuity, homosexuality, and debauchery and dedicated themselves to Christ, living holy lives pleasing to God. They became miracles, living testimony to the power of God to change men and women from the inside out.

Apollos, a Jew from Alexandria, arrived with a letter from Priscilla and

Aquila. They commended him to us and asked that we welcome him. We did so, and he proved to be as great an orator as Paul, refuting the Jews with Scripture.

The church of Corinth was firmly established and continued to grow.

When Paul wrote that he intended to visit the churches we had planted in Phrygia and Galatia, I thought it time to rejoin him. Stephanas, Fortunatus, and Achaicus proved themselves as able leaders, along with Sosthenes. We sent word of our plans, but when we reached Ephesus, it was Aquila and Priscilla, and not Paul, who greeted us. "He's gone on to Jerusalem for Passover."

The news alarmed me.

"I should've come sooner and dissuaded him! The high council will look for any opportunity to kill him!"

Timothy was grievously disappointed. "Why didn't he wait?"

"We all tried to dissuade him, Silas, but you know how Paul is when he's determined to do something. There's no stopping him."

When they told me Paul had left his books and papers behind, I knew my friend was well aware of what awaited him in Jerusalem. "Paul would rather run toward death than leave the Jews in darkness."

I thought of going after him, but after much prayer, knew God wanted me in Ephesus.

Timothy was not yet ready to stand alone.

✦   ✦   ✦

"Landing place" is an apt name for Ephesus. It is the intersection of the coastal road running north to Troas and the western route to Colosse, Laodicea, and beyond. Ships from all over the Roman Empire sailed in and out of its port. With its magnificent road lined with marble columns, its theater, baths, library, agora, and paved streets, Ephesus rivals the grandeur of Rome and its infamous debauchery. The city is temple-warden to the three emperors, each honored by an enormous temple. However, it is the Temple of Artemis that dominates. Four times larger than the Parthenon in Athens, it draws thousands of devotees each year, eager to partake of the most depraved worship man creates. Add to this ships that arrive daily, unloading cages of wild animals from Africa and gladiators for the games.

Ephesus was a great trial to me. Everywhere I looked I saw astounding beauty and knew it housed horrendous sin. I longed for the religiosity of Jerusalem, the struggle of men to follow moral laws, the solitude of scholarly pursuits.

Priscilla and Aquila, already established as tentmakers, gathered believers in their home. They nurtured and taught new believers. Timothy and I preached in the agora. When Apollos returned, he preached with the logic of a Roman and the poetry of a Greek. Crowds gathered to hear him speak, and many came to faith in the Lord through his teaching.

Timothy grew as a teacher. Some questioned him because of his youth, but he was mature in the Lord and ready for leadership. Gaius was a great help to him. Erastus, also, proved helpful. He had been an *aedile* in Corinth, and used his administrative gifts to help the church in Corinth. No one lacked provisions.

We were a motley group, much like our sisters and brothers in Corinth. Repentant idolators, fornicators, adulterers, homosexuals, swindlers, and drunkards—all now living lives above reproach, helping one another and others. I quickly saw more miracles in Ephesus than I had in Israel during those three years that Jesus ministered. The Lord was alive, and His Spirit moved mightily in the midst of beautiful, wretched Ephesus.

When I received a letter from the council asking me to return to Jerusalem, I knew it was time for me to step down and place Timothy in leadership.

Though confident in the Lord, Timothy had little confidence in himself. "I am not ready, Silas."

But the Ephesians were not easily led, and there were always wolves intent upon attacking the flock. "You are ready, Timothy. You have the heart and the knowledge. We are each called to a different task. I must go. You must stay."

"But am I capable?"

I gave him what advice I could. "God has equipped you for the work. Remember: we can ask God for wisdom, and He will give it without rebuking us for the asking. But be sure when you ask Him that your faith is in the Lord alone. Don't waver, Timothy. And don't try to work things out on your own. Trust Jesus to show you the right path. Then take it! When He gives you the words to speak, speak them. Do those things and God will do His work here in Ephesus."

He had good friends to stand with him—Aquila and Priscilla, Apollos, Gaius—all devoted servants of the Lord. I left with saddened heart, but fully confident that the Lord would use Timothy mightily to strengthen the Ephesian church.

It has been years now since I have seen Timothy, though we have exchanged letters. His heart is no less humble, though the Lord has strengthened him over the years, and sent others to encourage him, including John, the apostle, and with him, Jesus' mother, Mary.

Mary has gone to be with the Lord now, but John remains.

✦   ✦   ✦

Time has a way of turning in upon itself as you grow older. I cannot remember when some things happened, or how, or in what sequence events occurred.

Paul's time to depart this world had not yet come. After a brief stay in

Jerusalem, he returned to Antioch, where he reported on his journey. Then he returned to Ephesus. I was gone by then, home in Jerusalem. But when I heard, I knew Timothy would be much relieved to have his mentor back at his side, and would be all the more strengthened by Paul's instruction and example.

Luke remained Paul's companion and wrote to me often. God gave Paul miraculous power, which turned many from worshiping false gods. Those who made idols caused a riot. Fearing Paul would be murdered, the church sent him to Philippi. Timothy went with him, but returned soon after.

Others traveled with Paul after that. Some fell away in exhaustion. Others could not get along with him. Paul kept going. He was the most dedicated man I knew. He told me once, "Faith is a race, and we must run it with all our strength." I imagine him now wearing the laurel wreath.

I miss him.

Had I remained with him, my suffering might be over now. But the path the Lord has laid out before me is longer and winds more than I ever imagined it would.

I, like so many others, thought Jesus would return in a few days or weeks. Then we thought our Lord would return in a few months, then a few years. He said He would wait until all the world had the opportunity to hear of Him. And the world is larger than we ever imagined.

Paul planned to go to Gaul and never made it.

But again I digress. A tired man's musings. I waste this scroll.

＋ ＋ ＋

Silas wanted to quit the task Epanetus had given him. His neck, back, and shoulders ached. His fingers felt stiff. But it wasn't the physical pain of so many hours laboring at the table. It was remembering the years and miles, the friends saved and lost.

Macombo brought a tray. "Have you finished?"

"No."

"You have lived a rich life."

Silas covered his face with his hands.

That night, he slept deeply and dreamed of Jesus. The Lord filled His nail-scarred hands with grain and cast it in all directions. Seeds took root—tiny shoots rising in deserts, on mountaintops, in small villages and great cities. Some drifted on the sea toward distant lands.

Jesus placed a scroll in Silas's hand and smiled.

＋ ＋ ＋

Paul felt drawn back to Jerusalem. Like me, it was his home, the center of all we had known and held dear. The Temple was still the house of God. I could not go up the steps and stand in the corridors and not think of Jesus or hear His voice echoing in my mind. My heart ached every time I stepped foot in that place meant to be holy and now so defiled by corruption.

We received word Paul had arrived in Caesarea. He stayed with Philip the Evangelist and his four daughters, all unmarried and with the gift of prophecy. They, like others—myself included—had chosen not to marry, but to await the return of the Lord. Agabus went to see Paul. He'd had a dream that Paul would be imprisoned if he came to Jerusalem.

Paul refused to go into hiding.

When Paul and Luke reached Jerusalem, Mnason welcomed them to his home. I would have enjoyed offering them hospitality, but my circumstances had changed over the years, and I no longer owned a house in Jerusalem or Caesarea. I did not see Paul or Luke until they came to the council, but when I did, it was clear nothing had changed between us.

"Silas!" Paul embraced me. I wept with joy. I had such mixed feelings about him being in Jerusalem. While I longed for our deep conversations, I feared he would be hunted down and killed. The Pharisees had never forgiven him for abandoning their cause. James and all the council members greeted him warmly. We all shared the same concerns about his welfare.

Paul gave a good account of his journeys, often calling upon me to add anything he might have forgotten regarding the cities we had visited together. He had forgotten little.

Of course, Paul longed to go to the Temple. James and I had discussed this possibility with the others and thought trouble might be averted if Paul took with him four men who had completed vows. By joining them in the purification ceremony and paying for their hair to be shaved, perhaps the Jews would see he had not rejected the Law.

Men plan, but God prevails.

Paul went to the Temple. He spent seven days worshiping there, rejoicing in the Lord. And then some Jews from Asia saw him, and spoke out against him. "Everywhere this man goes, he brings trouble upon us!"

I sought to defend him. "You bring trouble upon yourself by rousing mobs and causing riots!"

When anger meets anger, nothing good comes of it.

Accusations filled the air. Some claimed Paul had brought Greeks into the Temple to defile the holy place. Trophimus the Ephesian had been seen near the Temple, and they assumed Paul had brought him inside. The Jewish leaders grabbed Paul and dragged him from the Temple. They threw him outside and slammed the doors. Others began beating him. I cried out for them to stop and found myself in the midst of the fray.

Never had the sight of Roman soldiers and centurions so pleased me as that day! We would have died without their intervention. They surrounded

Paul, and used their shields to keep the Jews back. The commander drew his sword and pounded it on his shield. "Quiet! All of you!" He shouted in heavily accented Aramaic, and then commanded his soldiers in Greek. "Put that man in chains until I find out what's going on this time!"

Paul swayed under the weight of iron while the commander tried to gather the facts. "Who is this man you're trying to kill? What has he done?"

"He stirs up dissension!"

"He's desecrated the Temple of our God!"

"He's Saul of Tarsus, and unjustly accused. . . ." We tried to come to his defense. Someone punched me in the side of the head. By the grace of God, I overcame the temptation to swing back.

"He's the ringleader of a cult that defies Rome!"

Everyone shouted, each with a different answer, none near the truth.

Two soldiers hauled Paul up the steps of the barracks while others faced the crowd, shields locked in a wall of protection. Somehow Paul convinced the commander to let him speak to the crowd.

When Paul called out in Hebrew, the Jews fell silent. "I am a Jew, born in Tarsus, a city in Cilicia, and I was brought up and educated here in Jerusalem under Gamaliel. As his student, I was carefully trained in our Jewish laws and customs. I became very zealous to honor God in everything I did, just like all of you today. And I persecuted the followers of the Way." He confessed the bloodguilt of holding the coats while others stoned Stephen, and going after others in his zeal against Christians, even traveling to Damascus to transport Christians from there to Jerusalem for punishment.

"As I was on the road, approaching Damascus about noon, a very bright light from heaven suddenly shone down around me. I fell to the ground and heard a voice saying to me, 'Saul, Saul, why are you persecuting me?'"

They listened intently until he told them how God called on him to take the message of Christ to the Gentiles. Wrath came upon them like a fire.

Men ripped off their cloaks in protest and threw dust into the air.

"Away with such a fellow!"

"Kill him!"

"He isn't fit to live!"

Friends grabbed me and pulled me against a wall and we watched the mob surge up the steps, trying to reach Paul. The commander shouted. Soldiers locked shields. Men fell back, tumbling into others. Some fell, trampled by those still pressing from behind. The shouting became deafening. Faces reddened and twisted with rage.

The commander had Paul hauled inside the barracks and the doors barred.

I ran for Luke. By the time we returned to the Roman barracks, the mob had been dispersed. I demanded to see the commander and told him Paul was a Roman citizen. He had us escorted to Paul.

He sat against the wall, badly bruised, his mouth split and bleeding. "At least I escaped a scourging."

Luke saw to his wounds. I put my hand gently on his shoulders, and saw even that touch caused him pain. "Everyone is praying." I had brought bread, almonds, raisin cakes, and watered wine.

Tears ran down his face. His shoulders slumped. "If only they would listen."

Luke spoke gently. "They did, for a while."

"The Lord gives them opportunity day after day, Paul. We will keep on praying and speak when we can. There are still many in Jerusalem who follow Christ, and the city has not been left to Ananias and his mob."

Luke shook his head. "The swelling will go down soon, Paul. But the blows may have worsened your eyesight."

The guard said we had to leave.

Paul sighed. "Perhaps these Roman guards will listen."

That made me smile.

The commander took Paul to the high council, and we heard Paul divided them by proclaiming he was on trial for believing in resurrection. The debate between Pharisees and Sadducees became so heated and disorderly, that the Roman soldiers took Paul under guard and returned him to the fortress.

I knew it would not end there. The city was in turmoil over Paul. Rumors flew about plots against his life. I prayed unceasingly.

The Lord reminded me that my friend was destined to go to Rome.

When I went to tell him, the Roman guard said, "He is not here."

"Where have they taken him?"

He refused to answer.

I went to Paul's sister. She had seen him. So had her son. "I heard some men talking in the Temple," the boy told me. "They'd joined others in a plot to kill my uncle. They said they would fast from food and drink until he's dead. There are forty of them, Silas! I went and told Paul, and he told me to tell the officer in charge."

We made inquiries and soon learned two hundred soldiers under the command of two centurions had left Jerusalem the night before. "I have a friend among the soldiers," one of the brethren said. "And he told me seventy horsemen and two hundred spearmen went with them."

"And Paul?"

"He couldn't say for sure, only that they had a prisoner in chains and were taking him to Caesarea to the Roman governor."

I laughed. "Even the Roman army bends to the Lord's will and protects God's chosen servant!"

Luke left immediately for Caesarea, but one crisis after another kept me in Jerusalem.

"The high priest has gone to Caesarea," James told me. "And he's taken Tertullus with him."

"Tertullus might be famous for arguing Jewish and Roman law, but all the forces Satan can muster will not prevail against the Lord's plans for Paul."

+ + +

Luke wrote to me, and I kept the council apprised of Paul's well-being and state of mind. By the time I was able to make the journey to see him, Ananias, the Jewish leaders, and Tertullus had long since failed in their attempts to sway Governor Felix into handing Paul over to them. In truth, I think Felix enjoyed aggravating them. He was a freed slave from Emperor Claudius's household, and ambitious. He married Drusilla, the great-granddaughter of the infamous King Herod the Great, thinking the alliance would commend him favorably to the Jews. It did not. The Herodians are hated for their Idumean blood. His marriage merely mixed it more.

Paul looked well, but I knew imprisonment chafed him. He could only preach to few.

"Ah, Silas, you are a friend who knows me." Paul grasped my arms in greeting, much pleased at the writing supplies I had brought him. "I have a dozen letters to answer and had no means to do so."

"Has there been any indication yet what the governor plans to do with you?"

"Nothing. He calls for me and I tell him about Jesus. I live in hope he will listen."

I stayed a few weeks and wrote letters he dictated, then returned to Jerusalem. I went back to Caesarea after Passover and found Paul frustrated.

"The governor finds me entertaining!" He paced, wretched with impatience. "He hopes in vain for a bribe. Had I money to offer, I would not!"

Governor Felix's heart proved to be hard.

"Why does God leave me here?"

"To refine you, perhaps, for a time when you will meet and speak to another far greater: Caesar."

He prayed all the time, not for himself, but for the churches he had planted. He is the only man I have ever known who could remember names, hundreds of them, and the circumstances of each person's salvation. His love grew and could not be bound within those stone walls. Prayer gave his love wings. He wrote countless letters, some to me, though they are gone now, passed on to others or burned by enemies. Those in my possession will survive. I have made copies to leave behind. Paul spoke words from the Lord, instructions and counsel to the congregations struggling against Satan, who will never cease to prowl. We must trust in the Lord, His Word, and the power of His strength to overcome, to endure to the end.

I thought some change would come when Rome recalled Felix. Judea made a man's career, or destroyed him. When later I came to Rome, I heard Felix had been banished in disgrace, and saw it an apt end for a man who left Paul in prison for no other reason than to please his enemies. Perhaps in exile, Felix's heart will soften.

Porcius Festus became governor. He came up to Jerusalem and was greeted by the chief priests and leading men of Jerusalem. They had not forgotten Paul, and asked the governor to have him brought to the city and put on trial. Festus did not give in to their demands. He courted Jewish favor to keep the peace, but did not relinquish any of his power. He said if the Jews had charges against Paul, they must come to Caesarea and make them before the Roman tribunal.

Before Festus left Jerusalem, the Lord gave me a vision of what was to come, and I went immediately to Caesarea.

"Under no circumstances must you agree to return to Jerusalem for trial, Paul."

"I will go where I am led."

"If you return to Jerusalem, it is not God leading you, but Satan! Listen to me! Their purpose is not to put you on trial, but to kill you on the way. You will be silenced."

"Christ will never be silenced."

"If you will not take into account my vision, remember what the Lord told you years ago. You will speak before kings! Stand firm, my friend, and the Lord will keep you to the course. You will testify before Caesar!"

When Festus ordered him to stand before the Jews and answer their charges, Paul called upon his right under Roman law to be heard. When Festus asked if he would be willing to return to Jerusalem, Paul refused. "I appeal to Caesar!"

Festus and his advisers quickly agreed, no doubt grateful to pass along responsibility for so troublesome a prisoner. Festus may have thought sending Paul away would assure some peace in Jerusalem.

King Agrippa and Bernice, his sister, came to Caesarea to pay their respects to the new Roman governor. Festus honored them with an elaborate ceremony and brought Paul out to speak before the king.

One of our Roman brethren told me, "He challenged Agrippa as a man might challenge a friend. Paul asked if he believed in the Jewish prophets. I know nothing of these things, but the king was disturbed by the questions Paul raised. He left the room. Festus and Bernice went with him. I was told Paul might have been set free if he hadn't appealed to Caesar."

Soon after, I received a letter from Luke.

"The governor has given orders for Paul to be taken under guard to Rome. Can you accompany us?"

I longed to go with them and prayed fervently that God would allow me to do so. I spoke with the others on the council and we all prayed about it. None had peace about letting me go, though they sent me to Caesarea to bless Paul and bring him provisions.

He wept when he saw me. He must have seen in my face that I could not go. "I knew it was too much to ask, but I hoped . . ."

"I'm needed here, for now, at least. When do you leave?"

"Within the week." He grasped my arms. "We worked well together, my friend. Think of all those thousands from Antioch to Athens and back again." He sighed. "I wish you were coming with me. I could have used your help."

I tried to soften his disappointment and my own. "You've written a few good letters without me."

He laughed.

What little time we had together, we used to write letters.

I saw him off. It was a difficult parting. We thought we would never see each other again.

But as I have learned over the years, God always seems to have other plans.

SIX

✦✦✦✦✦✦✦

Someone cleared his throat. Silas turned.

Epanetus crossed his arms and leaned against the doorframe. "I have never seen a man so dedicated to a task." He searched Silas's face. "I did not intend to add to your grief."

"I have more good memories than bad, Epanetus." Silas smiled wistfully. "When Paul sailed from Caesarea, I never thought to see him again."

"You've lost many friends."

Silas rose from the writing table. "As have we all." He stretched. "Thankfully, they are not lost to us forever."

The Roman smiled. "The Lord is renewing your faith."

"Even a dog gets tired of licking its wounds."

"Patrobas said word has spread that you're here. Many have asked to come. Do you feel up to teaching?"

Teaching was second nature to Silas, but he feared that the larger gathering might endanger this small congregation. He voiced his concerns. "Perhaps I should move soon."

"I've lived with danger all my life, Silas, but never with a greater purpose than now. But I leave it to you." He chuckled. "Curiatus is especially eager to speak with you. The boy has come every day that you've been here. He knocked at my door again this morning."

"He reminds me of Timothy." Silas thought of Diana and wondered what life would have been like to have a wife and children and why this longing came now when it was past hope.

"What do you say?"

"Say about what?"

"I wonder at your reverie, Silas." Epanetus seemed amused. "Shall I send word to Diana that she may bring Curiatus?"

Silas turned away and fiddled with the reed pens. "Just send for the boy."

Curiatus came, and Silas spent an hour answering his questions before the others arrived for the meeting.

People sat close together to make space for everyone. Silas looked into their eager faces—strangers most of them, yet all bound together by love of Jesus.

"I heard the Lord speak in Galilee," he said. "He stood on a boat a little way from shore while thousands sat on the hillside listening. His voice carried to where I stood on the edge of the crowd, above them." He smiled wryly. "I did not understand all of what He said, but what I did disturbed me greatly. His words went into me like a sword, cutting through all the notions I had about who I was and what I was meant to do with my life. To follow Him, I would have to change everything. That frightened me. So I left."

Resting his forearms on his knees, Silas leaned forward and clasped his hands in front of him. He could not see their faces through his tears. "I look back and see how many opportunities the Lord gave me, how often I knew His words were directed at the sin that held me captive, how long it took before I let Him remove all the traps that kept me caged." He covered his face. "Oh, what fools we can be, holding tight to the things of this world and believing they are our salvation."

"But you let go, Silas. You gave your life to Christ. You wouldn't be here with us now if you hadn't."

Curiatus with his compassionate heart. Timothy all over again. Silas lowered his hands. "I can't tell you I haven't struggled or thought of what my life might have been." He looked at Diana. "Or what I gave up."

Her expression softened. "We all struggle, Silas." Her mouth curved so gently. "Each day has its trials to face."

"Yes." He sighed. "Each day is a struggle to hold tight to faith." Especially when one saw men and women executed for following Jesus' teaching to love God, love one another, and treat everyone with compassion, mercy, and truth, even when it would not be returned in kind. "Jesus told us not to worry about tomorrow, for tomorrow will bring its own worries. Today's trouble is enough for today, as we all well know. Jesus tells us to seek the Kingdom of God above all else, and live righteously, and He will give you everything you need. I saw Jesus. I heard Him speak. But you, here with me now . . . Your work will always be to have faith in what you have not seen with your own eyes, to trust in the testimony of men like Peter and Paul and John Mark."

"And you," Diana said. "We trust in your word, Silas."

His throat tightened. He could not hold her gaze.

"The world is Satan's battlefield, but if we live in Christ, we live victorious through His death and resurrection. To believe is the hardest work of all when the world stands shoulder to shoulder against you."

"I've heard Christians say there never was a resurrection."

Silas glanced up sharply and saw Urbanus standing back. "I assure you Jesus lives."

"And what of the reports that Jesus' body was hidden so that the disciples might make false claims about his resurrection?"

"It is not a new claim, Urbanus." Silas shook his head. "Those rumors have circulated for years. The Jewish leaders paid the guards at the tomb to spread them. I might've believed them had I not seen Jesus for myself. But I and the disciples were only some of the many who saw Jesus. He spoke to hundreds of His followers. He spent forty days with us *after* He arose from the tomb, teaching us and preparing us to go out and make the truth known: that we all can be reconciled to God through Him. Later, He appeared to Paul." He spread his hands and shrugged. "The world will always lie about Jesus."

"And hate those who follow Him," Epanetus said.

"If only He had stayed with us, the world would know."

Silas smiled. "Someday, at the name of Jesus every knee will bow and every tongue confess that Jesus Christ is Lord."

Curiatus looked back at the others. "Miracles are proof."

Diana put her hand on her son's knee. "Miracles don't sway people. Remember Silas telling us about the ten lepers Jesus healed? Only one went back to thank Him."

Epanetus agreed. "It wouldn't matter if five hundred witnesses of Christ's resurrection testified in a court of law. The fact is, my friends, some will refuse to believe, and no amount of evidence will ever sway them."

Silas felt their dejection. He had felt little hope when he came here. Yet, the weeks and work of remembering had helped renew him enough to give them some encouragement.

"The proof is in this room." He looked around slowly at each of them. "When Christ comes in, we change." He smiled, his heart lifting as he thought of others he had known. "I've seen thieves become honorable and generous. I've known temple prostitutes who married and now live as faithful husbands and wives. I've seen homosexuals become chaste servants of God."

"Even so, Silas," Patrobas said bleakly, "don't you long for heaven? Don't you long for an end to the suffering? for the fear to be over?"

Silas let out his breath softly. He stared down at his clasped hands before speaking. "Every day over the past months, I've asked the Lord why I'm left behind when all but a handful of friends have gone on to be with Him." He looked into the faces of those listening. "I'm not alone in those feelings. Life is a struggle. Even in the best of times, it's a battle to live for Jesus in this fallen world." Hadn't he felt the emptiness and vanity of life when he had everything a man could want? "It would be a relief for anyone to accept Christ one day and be caught up into heaven with Him the next."

There was a soft twittering of laughter.

Oh, Lord, I have lived like a man without strength for too long. Help me speak what I know is true, and heal my angry, doubting heart.

He brought them back to earth. "But what of the lost?" He smiled sadly. "Remember. Jesus called us the salt of the earth. Our presence preserves life and gives others time to know the truth. The Lord will come when God decides. For now, we hold fast to faith. We cling to Jesus' promises in the midst of tribulation."

Sometimes the tribulation came from within the body of Christ. He and Paul and Peter had written countless letters to the churches, warning them against false teaching, encouraging believers to turn back and follow Jesus' example. *Love others! Live for what is right! Live pure and blameless lives! Be faithful!*

Tribulation came from losing sight of Jesus and looking at the troubled, fallen world. Peter walked on water until he took his eyes off Jesus.

Everyone in the room sat silent, the only sound the water splashing from the fountain.

"I came to you broken in spirit and struggling in faith. The world is a sea of despair, and I was drowning in it. I have said words to you that I'd forgotten." He looked up at Epanetus standing in the corner. "Thank you for making me remember."

When I returned to Jerusalem, the council gave me a letter from Peter, who had gone north to Antioch to encourage the church there. I struggled to read Peter's writing. He had taken his wife and several traveling companions. Now, we learned he had sent four of those companions north—two to preach in Cappadocia, while two others traveled farther to reach Parnassus in Galatia. Peter intended to visit the churches in Pamphylia and Phrygia, travel on to Ephesus, then sail to Rome. Several men from Antioch had offered to go with him, but Peter said they were needed in Syria. I felt a fillip at those words.

"I leave on the new moon and pray the Lord will provide me with a companion who can write in Hebrew, Greek, and Latin. Jesus called me a fisher of men, but never a man of letters."

I could almost see Peter's self-deprecating smile, and chuckled. "He needs a secretary."

"Yes. He does."

James's tone made me look up. He smiled at me. "Paul and Peter in Rome. Think of it, Silas."

I caught his excitement. "The Lord aims at the very heart of the empire."

"Who will we send?" another asked.

"Someone must go and help Peter."

From the moment I read the first few lines, I had known what the Lord wanted of me. Smiling, I rolled the scroll and held it like a baton. "Send me."

And so they did.

I took John Mark with me.

+   +   +

I sold the last of my reserves, accepted the help of others within the body of Christ, and headed north. We all knew Peter could be impetuous. He might not wait. When I arrived and was brought to him, I saw I had barely reached Antioch in time. "Oh, ye of little patience," I said, grinning.

Peter had finished packing. He turned to me with a laugh. "Silas! I dared not hope!"

We embraced. Though much older than I, he still was the stronger. A look of relief came into his wife's face. "God is kind to send you with my husband."

I kissed her cheek. "I am the more blessed."

Peter slapped me hard on the back.

I laughed. It was good to see him. Of all the disciples, Peter remained my favorite. The first time he told me he had denied Jesus three times before the Lord was crucified, I knew we had much in common.

"We leave for Tarsus in the morning," Peter told me.

"Will you allow Silas so little time to rest, Peter?"

"We have little time, beloved. Besides, I grow older by the day."

Old, perhaps, but robust. He was twenty-five years older than I, and I was hard-pressed to keep up with him. There were days when I longed for sunset so that he would stop and I could rest!

His wife managed without apparent difficulty. "The Lord has given me fifty years to learn to keep pace with him, Silas." She even managed to prepare meals when we camped!

I never tired of listening to Peter talk about Jesus. Who could speak with more authority than one who had been among the first to be called? Jesus had lived in Peter's house in Capernaum. Peter had seen his mother-in-law healed of a debilitating fever. He had seen Jesus turn water into wine at a wedding in Cana. Peter had been on the mountain when Moses and Elijah appeared and spoke to Jesus. Peter had seen Jesus as He truly was: God the Son, the Light of the world. God had revealed Jesus as Messiah to this humble, oft-stubborn, hot-tempered fisherman. Peter had been in the garden of Gethsemane, where Jesus prayed in preparation for His crucifixion. While others fled into the night, Peter had followed after Jesus and the mob that arrested Him, staying close enough to see Him interrogated. Peter had listened to Mary Magdalene, and entered the empty tomb. And he had been in the upper room with the disciples when Jesus came and proved death had no power over Him.

Before the Lord ascended, He commissioned Peter to "feed My sheep." And while doing so, Peter never lost sight of his weakness. He always spoke freely of his failings.

"Jesus asked me to pray, and I fell asleep during His hours of greatest need. When Jesus was arrested, I tried to kill Malchus," a fellow brother now, and one of those who had traveled north with Peter. I had heard them joke about Peter's bad aim.

"I denied even knowing Jesus, not once, but three times." Tears often streamed down his cheeks when he spoke. "Jesus called me *Petros*, 'the rock,' and my faith was sand. And still He loved me, as He loves you. He forgave me, as He has forgiven you. He restored me, and will restore you. Jesus asked me three times if I loved Him, once for each time I denied Him. Jesus knows us better than we know ourselves. . . ."

I wondered at times why there were no riots in the cities we visited, few attempts to murder Peter. He spoke the same message Paul did and with the power of the Holy Spirit. Yet, the Jews paid no attention to him. I can only surmise the Jewish leaders thought a fisherman beneath contempt. Paul was a scholar; Peter was not. Paul had been one of their own, even one elevated in stature by his intellect and training under Gamaliel, the grandson of Hillel, to whom only the best and brightest could apply. Peter had been trained by Jesus, the One who opened the gate to all willing to come into His fold.

Thousands came to know Jesus through Peter's testimony. I saw the light come into the eyes of so many.

As we traveled the same route Paul and I had taken, I saw and was able to introduce dear friends. Aquila and Priscilla opened their home to us in Ephesus. Timothy and I spent precious hours together. He missed Paul, but had become an able leader. He loved Paul like a father, and grieved deeply over his imprisonment. "I fear he will die in Rome."

And so he would. I knew at the time, but did not tell Timothy lest his confidence be crushed. He still worried he was not up to the task Paul had given him.

"Paul would not have sent you back to Ephesus to deal with difficulties among these believers if he had not had confidence in your faith and ability to teach. Hold fast to what you know, Timothy. Do you remember what Paul taught you?"

"He taught me many things."

"And what did he say about Scripture?"

"It is inspired by God and is useful to teach us what is true and to make us realize what is wrong in our lives. It corrects us when we are wrong and teaches us to do what is right."

"And through the Scriptures, God prepares and equips His people to do every good work."

"Yes," Peter said, "but remember, too, my friends, it is not you who saves. It is the Lord who captures the heart. Unless the Lord calls someone, they will not come."

"I am learning that every day," Timothy said bleakly. "My words often fail to convince—"

"Your work is to believe, my son." Peter spoke firmly. "And testify to the truth of Christ. Jesus is the only begotten Son of God, crucified for our sins, buried three days, and raised. You teach that, and the Holy Spirit will do the rest."

Peter spoke in simple words, and God used them to crack open the hardest hearts.

Yet, still, I have learned that it is not in the nature of some men to allow God to do the work. People—even those with the best of intentions—try to save others by their own strength, thinking their words can persuade and change hearts. They often find themselves disciplined by God. I pray Timothy never went down that path.

We sailed from Ephesus. Peter stood at the helm, savoring his time on the sea, while I groaned for the feel of land beneath my feet. We arrived safely in Greece and met with Apollos.

Men were often in awe of Peter, and he knew how to put them quickly at ease. He revealed his frailties and failures. "We are all ordinary men who serve an extraordinary God."

Priscilla and Aquila had sent their greetings to Apollos.

"I am indebted to Priscilla and Aquila," Apollos said. "They had courage enough to take me aside and correct my teaching. I knew nothing of the Holy Spirit."

I laughed. "Priscilla is like a mother hen."

Apollos grinned. "Indeed, she is. She took me under her wing rather firmly."

Corinth was beset with problems.

"So many turn back to their old habits." Apollos sought Peter's advice. "The people can't seem to break away from sin."

"Without God, it is impossible. Even those who have accepted Christ and received the Holy Spirit contend with the sin nature. I battle natural inclinations every day." Peter slapped Apollos on the shoulder. "The problem, my young friend, is not how to break the chains—God has already done that—but the willingness to enslave ourselves to Jesus, who sets us free."

"A great paradox."

"Our faith is full of paradoxes. It takes the mind of Christ to understand."

Peter laughed. "That's why the Lord had to give us the Holy Spirit. So we could understand."

While the Lord promised peace of mind and heart to believers, the Christian life is a constant battleground, for the world is set against God. We also struggle with the power of sin. We fight against sinful desires. We war against our selfishness. Even when we do good, pride tries to steal glory from God. One paradox after another. The only way to win is to lay down our arms. The only way to live is to die, to give up our life to Christ. Jesus is the only victor, and only by surrendering completely to Him do we share that victory.

Peter said it more simply. "Trust in the Lord and the power of His strength. . . ."

The church leaders gathered daily, plying him with questions, and the once hotheaded, impetuous fisherman spoke with the patience of the Master.

The oft-asked question: "How do we avoid persecution?"

Peter said, "Jesus did not avoid crucifixion. He gave up His life for our sake, and calls us to do the same for others." He never wasted words. "Trials will show that your faith is genuine. Be glad when persecuted. Instead of asking to avoid it, ask for the strength to endure."

Believers walked with us over the Corinthian isthmus. Peter used every moment to teach. "We are one body, together in Christ. Nothing can separate us. Think clearly in the midst of tribulation. Exercise control. The Lord has given us the ability to restrain ourselves. Don't complain. Live as God's obedient children. Don't slip back into your old ways. Remember, the heavenly Father to whom you pray does not have favorites. He will judge or reward you according to what you do. Believe in Him and behave in a way pleasing to the Lord."

Before we boarded the ship, he gathered them close. "Hold fast to your faith, children. Live your life in reverent fear of the Lord, who loves you and sent His Son to die for your sins. Rid yourselves of evil and show sincere love for each other. Pray. . . ."

I longed to unfurl a scroll and write his words down, but had not the opportunity then. But I remember now. He dictated short, beautiful letters, copies of which I keep with me. The words they contain are my shield of hope against arrows of doubt. I tell you, whenever Peter spoke, his words came like pearls from God's treasure box.

"If we die with Him . . ." he said.

They responded as we had taught them. "We will also live with Him."

"If we endure hardship . . ."

"We will reign with Him."

"If we are unfaithful . . ."

"He remains faithful, for He cannot deny who He is."

Peter embraced and kissed them one by one as he had kissed his own children good-bye, trusting God to protect and guide them in the difficult days ahead.

I often think of Apollos, Aquila and Priscilla, and so many others I met along the road.

And I pray for them, knowing, if they live, they still pray for me.

✦   ✦   ✦

We had hoped to board a ship destined for Rome, but ended up sailing to Tarentum instead. Perhaps I became used to sailing, for the journey across the Savonic Gulf did not leave me a huddled mass beside a putrid basin in the belly of the ship, or hanging over the stern. I even joined Peter at the bow, though I had cause to think better of it later. When the ship dipped, a wave splashed up over me and had not Peter grasped hold of my belt, I would have slid down the deck and underfoot of working sailors. His laughter boomed. How I loved that man! He was so unlike the scholarly men I had known, and yet, like a father.

I have not been on the sea since that voyage, but when I stand by the window here in Puteoli, and smell the salt sea air, I think of Peter and his wife. Not as they died, but as they lived, and live still in the presence of the Lord. All pain and suffering is over.

For them.

Before we reached land, Peter had become acquainted with every sailor aboard our ship. He knew wind and sails, and they knew he was one of them—a man of the sea. When his Galilean accent proved too difficult for some, I translated. He told them sea stories: the Flood and Noah's ark! Moses parting the Red Sea! Jonah swallowed by a huge fish! the stormy Sea of Tiberias and God the Son, Jesus, who walked on water! Jesus, crucified, buried, raised, offered life eternal to anyone who believed.

As we neared Tarentum, Juno, the first mate, came to Peter. "I have decided to give up the sea for the Lord. As soon as we reach port, I will ask Asyncritis to release me and go to Rome with you."

Peter put his arm around him and faced him out to sea. "I told you of the fierce gale when we were on the Sea of Galilee and how Jesus slept? how we awakened Him, and He commanded the wind and sea to hush and be still?"

"Yes."

Peter put his hands on the rail. "We crossed to the country of the Gerasenes. No sooner had we come out of the boat than we saw a wild man running out from among the tombs. He came toward us. He had been chained and shackled there numerous times, but nothing could hold him. I was much younger then, and far stronger than I am now, but I feared the man would do harm to Jesus. He screamed curses at us and frothed at the mouth. When he picked up stones, I thought he meant to hurl them at us. Instead, he gashed himself until his arms and legs streamed blood. Jesus said, 'Come out of the man, you evil spirit.' Just a few words, quietly spoken as the man ran toward us. I thought the demoniac meant to attack Jesus, and I got in his way." He gave a self-deprecating laugh. "I often put myself in front of Jesus. You see, I still didn't understand who He was."

Peter gripped Juno's arm. "Jesus took hold of me and stepped past. He went out to meet the demoniac." His voice roughened. "The man fell to his knees and bowed down, crying out, 'I beg you, don't torture me!' His name was Legion. That's how many demons lived in him!" He let go of Juno. "They spoke. We were all terrified of him. Voice after voice came from that wretched man, pleading with Jesus not to send them to some distant place. The demons knew who Jesus was and from where He had come. Jesus cast them out after they asked permission to enter a herd of pigs feeding on mountain grasses."

He leaned his hip against the rail and looked at Juno. "The herdsmen saw everything just as we did and ran away. They brought the townspeople back. We had bathed the man, by then, and baptized him. Nathanael had given him a tunic and belt, John a robe. When the townspeople all saw him in his right mind, they were even more afraid. They begged Jesus to leave the Ten Towns and go away."

"Fools, all of them!"

"Do not be so quick to judge, Juno. Some are not ready to accept Jesus the first time they meet Him."

I knew the truth of that only too well.

"Did Jesus say or do anything to change their mind?"

Peter smiled. "No. He got into the boat."

"And set sail?"

"Yes."

The sudden flap of a sail made Juno glance up sharply. He barked an order; several sailors moved quickly to do his bidding. He returned his attention to Peter. "Jesus took the man with Him."

"No. He didn't. The man begged to come with us. Jesus told him to go home and tell everyone what great things the Lord had done for him. 'Tell them how merciful God has been.'"

Juno scowled. "You said Jesus called men to follow Him."

"Yes, Juno, but sometimes following means staying where you are." Peter put his hand on Juno's arm and smiled. "Remain as first mate on this fine ship. Serve your captain as you would serve the Lord. Wherever you are bound, God goes with you. What you carry now within you is precious cargo, cargo more precious than all the gold in the empire. *The Good News of*

Jesus Christ. Carry it to distant shores. Spread the Word among all those you meet. Remember what Jesus said to the demoniac: 'Tell them everything the Lord has done for you and how merciful he has been.'"

"I understand," Juno said grimly, "but I would rather go with you and Silas."

"Ah, yes, and I would rather be with the Lord." He spread his arms. "But here we are—you, me, my wife, Silas—all of us servants of the Lord who saved us and called us to Himself. We do His will, not our own."

We stayed in Tarentum a few weeks, during which Peter met often with Juno. Two other sailors came with him. Peter blessed Juno before we left. "The Lord is your captain."

We followed the road over the mountains. While resting in Pompeii, we spoke to people in the agora. Then we headed north for Rome.

Word spread of Peter's arrival, and Jewish believers came to see him. Some of them had been in Jerusalem during Pentecost when the Holy Spirit had come, and were among the three thousand saved.

There was no word of Paul.

Rome is both magnificent and depraved, a towering achievement of man's efforts and limitless vanities. We found our way around the city easily and learned many things from the Jews who had returned from exile after Emperor Claudius's death. Some said Agrippina poisoned her husband soon after he adopted her son Nero. Britannicus, natural son of Claudius and his heir, died mysteriously during a dinner party, leaving Agrippina to rule. She did so, later declaring Nero emperor of Rome. Many knew she held the reins of power. Roman coins bore her likeness facing Nero, signifying their equality.

Letters arrived from Puteoli. Paul had arrived in Italy under Roman guard, after he and Luke had spent three months on the island of Malta, where they had been shipwrecked. "He will stay at the Forum on the Appian Way and then at The Three Taverns. . . ."

John Mark and I hastened to meet them, and I was filled with joy at the sight of them. Laughing, Paul embraced me. "I did not think I would see you again! And here you are in Rome ahead of us. And John Mark!" He embraced the young man, their misunderstanding long since put to rest.

"I understand you had quite a voyage." John Mark grinned.

"A long, dark, wet voyage, but filled with opportunity!" He introduced us to Julius, the Roman officer in charge of him, and then greeted the others who had come with me. Luke and I talked. His first concern was Paul's health.

"Julius said Paul can have his own lodgings while he awaits trial. Can you arrange for this, Silas?"

"Yes. Peter knows several people who can secure lodgings for you both." I smiled. "So, Paul made a believer of his guard!"

"Julius has not said so directly, but he has the greatest respect for Paul, and God has used him mightily in protecting our friend from harm. When the ship wrecked within sight of shore, the other soldiers wanted to execute all the prisoners so their lives wouldn't be forfeit if any escaped. But for Paul's sake, Julius ordered them all spared."

Luke explained how Paul had warned the ship's captain from the onset of the voyage that they would be shipwrecked and all cargo lost. "No one would listen. We ran before a northeastern storm for days. We couldn't see the stars, so there was no way to know where we were going."

They had lightened the ship by casting the cargo overboard, and then some of the gear as well.

"Some feared we would end up shipwrecked on the African coast. In truth, Silas, I thought we would die. Only Paul had hope. God had told him he would stand trial before Caesar, not that any man aboard believed him. The ship hung up between two rocks. We could see a beach. Those who could swim to shore did so. The rest of us clung to whatever floated. I drank my share of seawater. So did Paul."

"How were you received on Malta?"

"Very well. It was cold and raining. The people built a fire on the shore. A poisonous snake bit Paul, and he shook it off into the fire." He chuckled. "The people thought he must be a murderer and justice would prevail. They sat around watching and waiting for Paul to die. When he didn't, they thought he was a god and took us to Publius, who honored us even more when Paul healed his father. The man was dying of dysentery. Malta brought their sick to Paul, and he healed them." He shook his head. "I've often wondered why he cannot heal himself of his impaired vision and the infection that plagues him."

"He told me once those things keep him dependent upon God's strength."

I sent word ahead to Rome. Paul wanted to meet with Peter and then as many Jewish leaders as would come.

Within days of his arrival, the Jewish leaders filled Paul's rented house to hear what he had to say.

"I am bound with this chain because I believe that the hope of Israel—the Messiah—has already come."

They shook their heads. "We have had no letters from Judea or reports against you from anyone who has come here. The only thing we know about this movement is that it is denounced everywhere."

What they said was true. We had been denounced by many whose hearts had become so hard that no seed of truth could be planted. Jews as well as Gentiles. We prayed constantly that we would have time to spread the Good News in Rome, for all roads led to the great city. Those same roads would carry Christians to every province in the world.

Another meeting was set. Many more came to hear Paul. He preached from morning through the day and into evening, offering proof from the five books of Moses and the Prophets.

When he finished, the Jewish leaders rose. "We will discuss the matter among ourselves."

I despaired at those lukewarm words. I knew those who believed at that moment had not the strength of faith to come back and hear more. The others stood stiff-necked with pride, rejecting the idea that the Messiah would choose to die rather than call upon angelic forces to purge Israel of its Roman oppressors. They wanted nothing less than that their Messiah restore their kingdom as it had been under Solomon's reign. They wanted King David, the warrior, not King Jesus, Prince of Peace.

Paul rose, too, face flushed, eyes blazing.

"The Holy Spirit was right when he said to your ancestors, 'The hearts of these people are hardened, and their ears cannot hear, and they have closed their eyes. . . .'"

They bristled.

He calmed, but still spoke bold truth with no hint of compromise. "I want you to know that this salvation from God has also been offered to the Gentiles, and *they will accept it.*"

They left. From the beginning, the Scriptures proclaimed Jesus Lord over *all* the earth. All those who turned to Him would be accepted. God told our father Abraham that he would be a blessing to others, that all the families of the earth would be blessed through him. The Messiah would come through the Jews.

If only they would receive Him . . .

I often weep for my people. I pray they will turn their hearts back to God. And I will continue to pray for that as long as I have breath.

Of course, Paul continued to receive and teach in the house we rented for him. He welcomed all who came to visit, spoke the truth and won many to Christ, including Julius, who was eventually reassigned to another post, we knew not where. We prayed for him daily, that the Lord would protect him. A fire started, and a large section of Rome burned. Roman guards came with orders to move Paul to the emperor's dungeon. We knew the end was near.

Nero reigned like a petulant child, ordering the death of anyone he suspected of plotting against him. He had his own mother, Agrippina, executed; though I saw this as a just ending for a woman as wicked as King Ahab's wife, Jezebel, who led so many astray by idol worship. She made her murdered husband, Claudius, into a god, and herself his high priestess, though the cult fast became a joke in Rome once she was dead.

Seneca and Burrus are dead, and with them any hope of justice. Nero now listens to the counsel of Tigellinus, who has revived the treason law.

Many Roman nobles have been executed on suspicion of conspiracy against the emperor. No one is safe. Even Octavia, Nero's cast-aside wife of noble blood, has been executed, while his new empress, Poppaea, fans his growing vanity.

The proverb holds true: "When evil sits upon the throne, good people hide."

Only Christians have the assurance of heaven.

The emperor cast blame on the Christians for the fire because Paul and Peter prophesied the judgment will come with fire in the end. Some say Nero ordered it himself, to clear the way for his plans to rebuild Rome and call it Neropolis. Only God knows who did it and why, but we suffer for it. We are hunted down. We are bound to arena columns, doused with pitch, and set on fire to serve as torches for Nero's games.

We suffer the loss of those we love.

Paul is beheaded. I have the coat he sent to me, a cherished gift from the Jerusalem council.

Peter and his wife are crucified.

Hundreds are in hiding, meeting in caves and holding fast to their faith in darkness.

Luke left Rome.

This world is not my home. Each day I live in it, I struggle. I remind myself that the battle is won, the victory is secure, and my life safe in the hands of Jesus, who will bring me home to heaven. And still, every day is a struggle to hold fast to that which I know to be true.

Oh, how I long for the day when Christ will call me home and this war within me will be over!

But I know this now in this quiet room in Puteoli: the Lord has left me here for a purpose. I must go on. I must run the race Paul spoke of so often. My friend reached the finish line and wears the laurel wreath. I imagine him now, sitting in the stadium of heaven, cheering me on.

For Peter, life was a voyage, the Holy Spirit propelling him across the sea. The Lord has brought him and his wife to safe harbor.

Those I loved most dearly are not lost, only beyond my sight.

I cannot give up!

I cannot fail!

I must go on!

SEVEN

Silas put his reed pen aside and carefully cut the papyrus scroll so that none was wasted. He rolled the unused portion and tucked it into his pack. He blew on the last few letters he had written. They dried quickly. Removing the weights, he let his memories roll closed. With a deep sigh of satisfaction, he rested his elbows on the table and rubbed his face. The task Epanetus and the others had given him was finished.

Copies of Peter's letters had been sent to faithful friends in the five provinces of Asia, one to each elder trained by Paul. He had also made copies of Paul's letter to Roman Christians, giving one to Patrobas. "Take this north to John Mark. If he has left Rome, give the letter to Ampliatus. He will guard it with his life."

He made another copy for Epanetus. It would help him teach those under his care.

He had made copies of the letter Paul had asked him to write to all Hebrew Christians everywhere. He had fasted and prayed before writing it. The Lord revealed to him how the commandments, the rituals, and the prophets presented God's promises and showed the path to forgiveness and salvation through Jesus Christ, the long-awaited Messiah. He knew well the struggle of the old faith and the new life in Christ, for he had lived it. He poured his heart into the letter, wanting all Jews to know Jesus was superior to angels, leaders, and priests. The old covenant was fulfilled in Christ, and the new had given them freedom in Christ. The sanctuary was no longer the Temple in Jerusalem, for the Lord now dwelled within the heart of everyone who accepted Him as Savior and Lord. Christ, the perfect sacrifice, had set them free. The letter commanded brothers and sisters to hold fast to their new faith, encourage one another, and look forward to Christ's return. And it gave them instructions on how to live godly lives.

Paul had read the letter and given him a satisfied smile. "Well written, my friend!"

High praise, indeed, from a man Silas greatly admired. But he could take no credit. "The Lord gave me the words."

"Of that, Silas, I have no doubt."

How Silas missed talking to Paul about the Word of the Lord. He missed Paul's passion, his dedication, his perseverance. He had been honored to watch Paul grow more humble over time, and had seen him near the end so filled with love and compassion that it spilled from him as it had from Christ. Paul's touch healed many; his words rang with truth. God, in His infinite wisdom, had chosen an enemy and made him into a most intimate friend.

Silas laid out the scrolls before him. His life's work. He would not part with any of them, but would continue to guard the original letters Paul had dictated, and those he had helped Peter write, along with the one he had written but left unsigned. He weighed Paul's letter to the Romans in one hand while holding several smaller scrolls in the other, smiling at the difference. Paul, the scholar, could not say anything in less than a few hours, while Peter, the fisherman, could speak the wisdom of the ages in a few minutes. Both had confounded the greatest minds in the empire, for the wisdom of this world is foolishness to God.

Anguish and joy welled up in him. Clutching the scrolls against his chest, Silas bowed his head, tears of gratitude flowing down his cheeks. "Oh, Lord, that You would allow me such privilege . . .".

How few had been given the opportunity to travel with one, let alone two great men of God. The Lord had placed Silas at Paul's side when he had gone out to spread the Good News to the Greeks, and then, beside Peter when he made the long journey to Rome. He had served as secretary to each. He had walked thousands of miles with Paul, and sailed with Peter. He had seen both men perform miracles. He had helped them establish churches. They had been his friends.

". . . that You would use me, the least deserving . . ."

I chose you. I formed your inner parts and knit you together in your mother's womb. You are Mine.

"May it always be so, Lord. Search me and know my heart. Test me and know my anxious thoughts. Point out anything in me that offends You, and lead me along the path of everlasting life."

He carefully arranged the scrolls so that none would be damaged when carried. He left one on the table. He would read it tonight when everyone met.

He felt a great burden lift from him. He had been cloistered far too long. It was time to go for a walk outside the walls of Epanetus's fortress home.

Macombo stood in the courtyard, holding a pitcher.

"Tell Epanetus the task is finished."

Macombo straightened from watering a plant. "You look better than I've seen you."

"Yes." Faith restored, he felt healed of affliction. "I'm going outside to see Puteoli. It's about time, isn't it?" He laughed. "I'll be back before the meeting."

Silas wandered the streets all afternoon. He talked with strangers and lingered at the port. The sea air brought a flood of memories.

"Silas?"

His heart took a fillip at the familiar voice. He turned, pulse racing. "Diana." She had a basket of fish on her hip. He looked for Curiatus. "Your son is not with you?" He never saw them apart.

"He's working. Over there. He's a diver." She pointed. "You can see him on the dock between those two ships."

Men shouted and Curiatus dove into the water. He came up next to a box floating near a ship and began securing a rope around it.

"He's a strong swimmer."

She had moved closer to him and looked up at him. "I've never seen you down here."

He felt lost in her gaze. "I haven't been outside the house since I arrived on Epanetus's doorstep." Embarrassed, he gave a soft laugh and looked away. Had he been staring? "I've been wandering since early this afternoon." He was an old fool. But he couldn't seem to help himself.

Her face lit up. "You've finished, haven't you?"

He nodded because he couldn't trust his voice. It would soon be time to leave. He'd never see her again. Why should that hurt so much? He hardly knew her. He had not allowed himself to get too close to anyone in Puteoli, least of all this beautiful widow.

"There's so much I want to know about you, Silas." She blushed and gave an embarrassed laugh. "I mean, we all want to hear your story." She turned as Curiatus shouted for the box to be raised. "My son has pressed you since first you arrived."

"He helped renew my faith, Diana." He should not have said her name.

"We all saw how you were suffering when you came to us."

"We all suffer."

"Some more than others. I never met Paul or Peter. I've never met anyone who walked with Jesus. Only you."

Silas winced inwardly. The old regret rose. "I didn't walk with Him. Not the way you mean. Only once and for a few miles along the road, after He arose." He could not look at her for fear of the disappointment he might see in her beautiful, dark eyes. "I must go back." He smiled over her head. "I wouldn't want Epanetus to think I've run away again."

Macombo answered the door at the first knock. "Thank God! Come. Epanetus is pacing."

"There you are!" The Roman strode through the courtyard. "You've been gone long enough to reach Pompeii!" He said nothing about Diana.

"I left the scrolls."

"And finished the one everyone has been waiting to hear. I saw it." Epanetus's concern seemed unusually grave.

"What's happened?"

"Things have changed." Nero had widened the search for Christians. Some of the most honorable senators were dead now for no other reason than they were born of noble blood, executed by Tigellinus, the Sicilian upstart exiled by Emperor Caligula. "Tigellinus feeds Nero's vanity as well as his fears. If anyone falls asleep during one of Nero's performances, his life is forfeit! We can be thankful for one thing: an emperor who takes no time to rule his kingdom will not rule long."

Andronicus, Junia, Rufus, and his dear mother, who had all been so kind to Paul, had been martyred. "They are with the Lord now," Silas said.

"I would like to see the death of those who killed them!" Epanetus said fiercely.

Silas realized with some surprise that he felt no such hatred. "I do not wish death on any man unsaved."

Epanetus turned. "Even Nero?"

"Even him."

Epanetus considered him for a moment. "Julius told me Paul had great respect and affection for you. Paul told him you were a man of great intellect and compassion, a friend to him in all circumstances."

Silas felt the prick of tears at such words. "How did you come to know Paul's guard?"

"We served together in Judea before I fled."

"Fled?"

"Let's just say I made it out of Judea by the skin of my teeth and still keep an eye over my shoulder." He glanced around. "This house doesn't belong to me."

Silas resisted the desire to know more. "Where is Julius now?"

"I don't know. I haven't heard from him in weeks. Patrobas couldn't find him."

Silas feared he knew what that meant. "Are you in danger?"

"Not from Rome. Not yet, at least." The Roman relaxed somewhat, and beckoned. "Come. Have something to eat before the others arrive. You'll never have a chance otherwise."

"I must thank you for all you've done for me," Silas said, following him.

Epanetus snorted. "I feared I chained you to your desk."

"The task steadied me. When I came to your doorstep . . ." He shook his head. "I had little hope."

"I've known men whose minds broke with less provocation than you have had, my friend. All you needed was rest and time to remember."

✦   ✦   ✦

Silas read the scroll that evening, from beginning to end. When he rolled it closed, he knew there were many things he had left unsaid, things more important for them to know than about his life.

Had he made himself look good by writing only the best about himself? He knew he had. Diana sat close at his feet, Curiatus beside her. Those in Jerusalem had known everything about him. These two who had come to mean so much knew nothing.

"You said nothing of your family, Silas."

"No, I didn't. Perhaps it's time I do." He had not included the shameful truth of the kind of man he had been when first he met Jesus. His heart quaked as he looked into Diana's eyes. "There are things I must tell you." He pulled his eyes away from her, addressing everyone. "Things I have neglected to say. I've tried to forget, or atone for, perhaps. . . ." He stumbled over words. "I . . ." He kept his eyes averted from her face and from Curiatus.

"My mother died when I was very young, my father when I was twenty-two. I was an only son, and inherited all the accumulated wealth of my father and his father and his father before him. From the time I could walk, I was treated as a prince, and given every advantage money could buy: education, every comfort, position. We had houses in Jerusalem and in Caesarea. With all due respect, Epanetus, I grew up in a grander house than this, with servants to answer every whim."

He had not felt so nervous even when speaking before the Lyconians.

"Whenever my father traveled, which was often, he took me with him. I had an aptitude for languages and business, and he encouraged me, giving me responsibility at a young age." He wrung the scroll in his hands. "I was taught that we were better than others, and believed it because of the way we were treated wherever we went. Our wealth was evidence of God's favor, and everyone acknowledged it. Even Jesus' disciples thought wealth meant God's favor until Jesus told them otherwise. It is no guarantee."

He looked around the room. *Lord, forgive me. I allowed them to hold me in high esteem.*

Diana took the scroll from him. "I'll hold this while you speak, lest you ruin it."

He swallowed hard. "I had heard about Jesus and the miracles He did, and believed Him to be a prophet of God. I wanted to meet Him. So I donned my finest robes, mounted my best mule, called for my bodyguard and servants to see to my safety and comfort, and went out to meet Him."

He had never felt such silence.

"I wondered at His disciples, for they were the sort of men my father had taught me to avoid. Laborers, uneducated, or at least not educated to the extent I had been." People like these looking at him now. "One was reputed to be a tax collector. I stayed on the outer edge of the crowd because I did not want to brush my robe against any of them; I thought they would make me unclean."

He shook his head, tears filling his eyes. "Such was my pride when I went out to meet the Lord." A moment passed before he could speak. "I was too far away to hear everything Jesus said, and listened hardly at all. I was too busy thinking about what *I* would say and how to say it when I got close enough to Him to speak."

Silas closed his eyes. "He saw me coming toward Him and said something to the others. They made room for me to approach. I paid no attention to them. I'd been treated with that kind of respect all my life. People always made room for me."

His voice roughened. "I went up to Jesus. I called Him 'Teacher.' To honor Him, you see. Maybe even to flatter Him. And then I asked . . ." He had to swallow before he could speak. "I asked, 'What good deed must I do to have eternal life?'"

He felt a gentle touch on his foot. Diana looked up at him, her eyes filled with tears.

"Such was my pride, you see. I had given money to the poor every time I entered the Temple. I had always tithed as the Law required. One day, I would rise as a ruler among God's people. Because of wealth . . . I thought I was so *good* Jesus would have to say, 'Nothing more is required of you, Silas. The Lord is well pleased with you.' Words of praise! That's what I had heard all my life. That's what I expected, fool that I was. I wanted God's assurance before witnesses that I had a right to live forever."

He let out his breath slowly. "Jesus looked at me with such love. 'If you want to receive eternal life,' He said, 'keep the commandments.'

"'Which ones?' I asked Him, thinking one was more important than another, and Jesus listed them. 'You must not murder. You must not commit adultery. You must not steal. You must not testify falsely. Honor your father and mother. Love your neighbor as yourself.'

"I had kept all those commandments. I even thought I had kept the last one by giving a few coins to the hungry widows and orphans who sat on the steps of the Temple, the poor and destitute I graced with a paltry gift in the streets! I was so sure of myself that I said I had obeyed all the commandments and then asked what else I must do. I wanted to hear Him say, 'Nothing more.' But Jesus didn't say that."

He looked at Epanetus. "Jesus looked into my eyes and said, 'If you want to be perfect, go and sell all your possessions and give the money to the poor, and you will have treasure in heaven. *Then* come, follow Me.'

"I felt as though the breath had been punched from me. All the assurance

I had lived with all my life fell away. If obedience to the Law wasn't enough, if wealth was not a sign of salvation, I was undone. I had no hope! 'Then come,' Jesus had said. If I was willing to give up everything my father and his father and his father before him had gained, and give up all the increase I had worked to achieve, *then* I could become His disciple."

Silas gave a bleak laugh. "It was the first time my money and position had closed rather than opened a door. I went away, confused and miserable because I knew I couldn't give up anything."

"But you went back!"

"No, Curiatus. I didn't."

"But you must have!"

"I never approached Him again. Not directly. When Jesus looked at me that day, I knew He saw *inside* my heart. I was laid bare before Him. Nothing was hidden. Even the things I didn't know about myself were clear to Him. I thought it had to do with money, but He had many wealthy friends. He raised one from the grave! I didn't understand why He said all that to me, and not to others. It was a long time before I fully understood my sin.

"Money was my god. Worshiping the Lord had become mere ritual in order to retain it. 'Let go of it,' Jesus had said, 'and then you can come to Me.' And I was unwilling. I clung to what I had inherited. I continued to build upon it."

Oh, how Silas regretted the time he had wasted!

"I wanted to be able to worship God without giving up anything. So I did what I had always done. I worked. I went to the Temple. I gave my tithes and offerings. I gave generously to the poor. I read the Law and the Prophets." He clenched his fists. "And I found no peace in any of it, because I now knew that all my money would *never* be enough to save me. Jesus' words made me hunger and thirst for righteousness. I wanted to please God. I couldn't stay away from Jesus, but I couldn't face Him either."

He smiled ruefully. "Whenever Jesus came near Jerusalem or into the city, I went to hear Him. I would lose myself in the crowd or stand behind men taller and broader. I stood in shadows, thinking I was hidden from Him."

"And found you couldn't hide from God," Epanetus said.

Silas nodded. "Sometimes I talked with the disciples—never the twelve closest to him, for fear they might recognize me, but others, like Cleopas. We became good friends."

He closed his eyes. "And then Jesus was crucified."

No one moved. Silas sighed and looked around the room. The memories flooded him. "Some of my father's friends were among those who held an illegal trial in the middle of the night and condemned Him. They could not execute Jesus, so they enlisted the help of our enemies, the Romans, in order to carry out their plans. I understood them. I knew why they did it.

Wealth and power! They loved the same things I did. That's what the trial was all about. Jesus was turning the world upside down. They thought when He died everything would go back to the way it was. Caiaphas and Annas, along with many of the priests and scribes, thought they could still hold everything in the palms of their hands."

He looked at his palms, and thought of Jesus' nail-scarred hands. "In truth, they held no real power at all."

"Were you at the Crucifixion?"

"Yes, Curiatus. I was there, though I wish I could have stayed away. When Cleopas and I saw that Jesus was dead, I remember being thankful it hadn't taken Him days to die."

Silas shook his head. "The disciples had all scattered the night Jesus was arrested at Gethsemane. Cleopas didn't know what to do. I let him stay with me. He went out a few days later to find the others and then came back. Jesus' body had been removed to a tomb, but now He was missing. One of the women claimed she had seen Him alive and standing in the garden outside the tomb. But this was the same woman who had had seven demons cast out of her, and I thought she had gone mad again.

"Cleopas and I were both eager to be away from the city, away from the Temple. He feared capture. I did not want to see the smug satisfaction of the scribes and priests, the Pharisees who had plotted and schemed and broken the Law to murder Jesus. Nor did I want to be around to see how the religious leaders might hunt down the disciples one by one and do to them what they had done to Jesus." His mouth tipped. "I even left my fine mule behind, and we set off for Emmaus."

Silas clasped his hands, but could not still the trembling inside. "As we walked along, we talked about Jesus. He had been a prophet; of that I had no doubt. But we were both left with so many questions.

"'I thought Jesus was the one,' Cleopas kept insisting. 'I thought He was the Messiah.' I had thought so, too, but I truly believed that had He been the Messiah, they couldn't have killed Him. God wouldn't have allowed it.

"'But the signs and wonders!' Cleopas said. 'He healed the sick! He made the blind see and the deaf hear! He raised the dead! He fed thousands of people with nothing more than a loaf of bread and a few fish! How could He do all those things if He was not anointed by God?'

"I had no answers, only questions, like he did. Cleopas was grieving. So was I. A man we didn't recognize came and joined us. 'What are you discussing so intently as you walk along?' He wanted to know. Cleopas told Him He must be the only person in Jerusalem who hadn't heard about all the things that had happened over the last few days. 'What things?' He said. Cleopas told Him, not patiently, about Jesus. We said He was a man we believed to be a prophet who did powerful miracles. He was a great teacher we thought was the Messiah, and our leading priests and religious leaders had handed him over to be condemned to death and crucified by the Romans."

Silas rubbed his hands together and wove his fingers tightly. "And then Cleopas told Him about the women who had gone to the tomb and found it empty, and Mary Magdalene, who claimed she saw Jesus alive. I'll never forget the man's words. He spoke to us as though we were frightened children, as indeed we were.

"The man sighed and called us foolish. 'You find it so hard to believe all that the prophets wrote in the Scriptures. Wasn't it clearly predicted that the Messiah would have to suffer all these things before entering His glory?' He reminded us of prophecies we had not wanted to remember. The Messiah would be despised and rejected, a man of sorrows, acquainted with deepest grief. His people would turn their backs on Him. He would be struck, spat upon by His enemies, mocked, blasphemed, and crucified with criminals. Others would throw dice for his clothing.

"The stranger spoke the words of Isaiah I had heard, but never before understood: 'He was pierced for our rebellion, crushed for our sins. He was beaten so we could be whole. He was whipped so we could be healed. All of us, like sheep, have strayed away. We have left God's paths to follow our own. Yet the Lord laid on Him the sins of us all.'"

Silas felt the tears gather again. "I trembled as the stranger spoke, the prayer shawl over His head. I knew the truth of every word He said. My heart burned with the certainty of it. The day was late when we reached Emmaus, and we asked the man to stay. When He hesitated, Cleopas and I pleaded.

"He came in with us. We sat at the table together. The stranger broke bread and held it out to each of us. It was then I saw the palms of His hands and the scars on His wrists." Silas blinked back tears. "I looked at Him then. He drew the mantle back, and we both saw His face. For the first time since that day when He told me to go and give everything I owned to the poor, I looked into His eyes . . . and then He was gone."

"Gone? How?"

"He vanished."

Everyone whispered.

"What did you see in Jesus' eyes, Silas?" Diana spoke gently.

He looked at her. "Love. Hope. The realization of every promise I'd ever read in Scripture. I saw an opportunity to change my mind and follow Christ. I saw my only hope of salvation."

"What about all your money, the houses, the property?" Urbanus asked.

"I invested it. I sold off property as needs arose in the church. Food, a safe place to live, passage on a ship, provisions for a journey—whatever was needed. I sold off the last of my family holdings when Peter asked me to come with him to Rome."

Epanetus smiled. "You gave up all of your wealth to spread the message of Christ!"

"I gained far more than I gave up. I've been welcomed to hundreds of houses, and had a home in every city I've lived in." He looked around the room, into each pair of eyes. "And brothers and sisters, fathers and mothers, even children beyond counting." He opened his hands, palms up. "And along with all those blessings, I gained the desire of my heart: the assurance of eternal life in God's presence." He laughed softly and shook his head. "I haven't a single shekel or denarius left to my name, but I am richer now by far than I was when all Judea gave deference to me as a rich young ruler."

✦   ✦   ✦

The hour was late when the gathering dispersed. Small groups left at intervals and went out different doors so they could melt back into the city without rousing suspicion. Diana and Curiatus had been among the first to go. A few lingered.

"What you've written will be read for generations to come, Silas."

Silas could only hope the copies of Paul's and Peter's letters would be protected. "The letters will guide you. . . ."

"No. I meant *your* story."

The woman turned away before Silas could say anything. He stood, a sick feeling in the pit of his stomach, as the last few disappeared into the night.

One man's view of what had happened was not a complete record of important events! All he had done was immerse himself in his memories, write his own views of what had happened. He had allowed himself to dwell on his feelings.

Silas had never walked with Jesus during those years when He preached from Galilee to Jerusalem, or traveled with Him to Samaria or Phoenicia. Silas was not an eyewitness to the miracles. He had not sat at Jesus' feet. When Jesus had told him what he must do, he had refused!

I came late to faith, Lord. I was slow to hear, slow to see, and oh, so slow to obey!

Silas took the scroll and went into his room. *Of what value is this scroll if it leads any of Your children astray?* He added a piece of wood to the fire Macombo had built on the brazier. *Let this be my offering to You, Lord. My life. All of it. Everything I've ever done or will do. Let the smoke rising be a sweet incense to you. Set my heart aflame again, Lord. Don't let me waste my life in reverie!*

"What are you doing!" Epanetus strode across the room.

When he reached to pull the scroll out of the fire, Silas grasped his wrist. *"Leave it!"*

"You spent weeks writing the history, and now you burn it? Why?"

"They will make too much of it. And I don't want to leave anything behind that might confuse the children."

"It was all true, wasn't it? Every word you wrote!"

"Yes, as far as *I* saw it. But we serve a greater truth than my experiences or thoughts or feelings, Epanetus. The other scrolls—the ones I've copied for you—hold that truth. Paul and Peter spoke the words of Christ, and those words will remain." He released Epanetus. The scroll burned quickly now. "What I wrote there served its purpose. It's time to let it go."

Epanetus glared at him. "Are you not Jesus' disciple, too? Why shouldn't you write what you know so that it can be a record for those to come?"

"Because I was not an eyewitness to the most important events of Jesus' life. I didn't walk with Him, live with Him, eat with Him, hear every word He spoke from morning to night. I wasn't there when He walked on water, or raised a widow's son to life. Peter was."

"Paul wasn't!"

"No, but Paul was Jesus' chosen instrument to take His message to the Gentiles and to kings as well as the people of Israel. And the Lord confirmed that calling when He spoke to Ananias, and when He revealed it to me."

"Jesus called you, too, Silas. You are also a prophet of God!"

"He called me to give up that which I held dearer than God, to give it back to the One who gave it in the first place. The Lord spoke to me so that I might encourage Paul and Peter in the work He had given them. Jesus called you, too. He called Urbanus, Patrobas, Diana, Curiatus. He will call thousands of others. But what I wrote was not inspired by the Holy Spirit, my friend. It was nothing more than rambling recollections from a man in need of renewed strength. You and I and all the rest will not write anything that will stand the test of time as will words inspired by the Holy Spirit. God will use men like Paul for that, and Peter, and others."

Epanetus's face was still flushed. "The church needs its history, and you've just burned it!"

Silas gave a soft laugh. "Epanetus, my friend, I'm just a secretary. I write the words of others, and, at times, help them improve what they must say. I helped Paul because his vision was impaired. I helped Peter because he could not write Greek or Latin." He shook his head. "Only once did I write a letter, and only because I was commanded to do so. And the Holy Spirit gave me the words. Paul confirmed them."

"Believers want to hear everything that happened from the time of Jesus' birth to His ascension."

"And God will call someone to write it! But I am not a historian, Epanetus."

God knew who it would be. The Jerusalem council had discussed the matter often. Perhaps it would be Luke, the physician. He had spoken to those who knew Jesus, and he had been constantly writing notes. He had spent days with Mary, the mother of Jesus, while in Ephesus, and with John, the one Jesus treated like His younger brother. Luke had lived and traveled with Paul far longer than Silas had, and he was a learned man, dedicated to truth. Or perhaps John Mark would finish what he had set out to do the first time he had returned to Jerusalem.

Silas nodded confidently. "God will call the right man to record the facts."

Epanetus watched the scroll blacken and shrink. "All your work in ashes."

Not all. There were the letters of Paul and Peter. "It is better to burn the whole of my life than allow one word, one sentence, to mislead those who are like infants in Christ. Read the letters I'm leaving with you, Epanetus. Christ is in them. He breathed every word into Paul's ear and Peter's."

"I have no choice now."

"No. Thank God." Silas felt impelled to warn him. "You must be careful what you accept as the Word of the Lord, Epanetus. There are many who would create their own version of what happened. Just as I did with that scroll. You must measure whatever you receive against the letters I'm leaving with you. Stories can become legends, and legends myths. Do not be fooled! Jesus Christ is God the Son. He is the way, the truth, and the life. Do not depart from Him."

Epanetus frowned. "You're leaving."

"It's time."

"Where will you go?"

"North, perhaps."

"To Rome? You'll be dead in a week!"

"I don't know where God will send me, Epanetus. He hasn't told me yet. Only that I must go." He gave a soft laugh. "When a man spends so much time looking back, it's difficult to know what lies ahead."

It was late, and both were tired. They said good night to each other, heading to their chambers.

Epanetus stopped in the corridor. "Someone asked me if you ever married. If you had children. In Jerusalem, perhaps."

"I never had time."

"Were you ever so inclined?"

"Did I ever love anyone, you mean? No. Were plans ever made for me to have a wife? Yes. My father had a wife in mind for me, a girl half my age and of good family. Her father was almost as rich as mine. My father's death ended any thought of marriage in my mind. I was too busy holding the inheritance he and my ancestors had accumulated. Besides, she was very young." He smiled and shrugged. "She married and had children. She and her husband became Christians during Pentecost."

They had lost everything when the persecution began, and he had bought a house for them in Antioch. There had been times when he had wondered what his life might have been had he married her.

"You look wistful."

Silas looked up at him. "Perhaps. A little. We all thought Jesus would return in a few weeks or months. A year or two at the most."

"You miss not having a family."

"Sometimes. But I could not have done what I did if I'd had a wife and children. And I wouldn't have missed the years I spent traveling with Paul and working with Timothy."

"You traveled with Peter. He had a wife."

"We come as we're called, Epanetus. Peter had a family when Jesus called him as a disciple. I admit when I traveled with Peter and his wife, I often yearned for what they had. It was not in God's plan for me."

"There's still time."

Silas thought of Diana and heat flooded his face. He shook his head.

Epanetus gave him an enigmatic smile. "A man is never too old to marry, Silas."

"Because he *can* doesn't mean he *should*."

Epanetus nodded thoughtfully. "She would have to be a special woman, I would imagine."

"I can think of several who would make *you* a suitable wife."

Epanetus laughed. He slapped Silas on the back. "Good night, Silas."

✦   ✦   ✦

Silas awakened to Curiatus's voice in the corridor. "But I have to see him!"

"He's still asleep." Macombo spoke in a hushed voice.

"The sun is barely up." Epanetus spoke from farther away. "Why are you here so early?"

"Silas is leaving."

"How do you know that?"

"Mother told me. She said she dreamed he was on a ship and he was sailing away."

Silas heard the anguish in the boy's voice and rose from his bed. "I'm here, Curiatus. I haven't gone anywhere." *Yet.* "It was just a dream." And it had touched some chord inside him and made him tremble.

The boy came to him. "When are you going?"

He looked at Epanetus and Macombo, and down into Curiatus's distressed eyes. "Soon."

"How soon?"

"In three days," Epanetus said and looked sternly at Silas. "No sooner than that."

"I'm going with you."

Epanetus stepped forward. "Is that the way you ask—?"

Silas raised his hand. "I don't know where I'm going, Curiatus."

"You'll go where God sends you, and I want to go along! Please, Silas, take me with you! Teach me as you and Paul taught Timothy! Circumcise me if you have to! I want to serve the Lord!"

Silas felt his throat tighten. The thought of going out alone was what had held him back so long, but should he take this boy with him? "Timothy was older than you when he left his mother and grandmother."

"A year makes no difference."

"A year made a great deal of difference to John Mark."

"I'm old enough to know when God is calling me!"

Silas smiled ruefully. "And how can one argue with that?" Could he take the word of a passionate boy?

Curiatus looked crestfallen. "You don't believe me."

David had been anointed as king when he was just a boy. Silas put his hand on the boy's shoulder. "I need to pray about it, Curiatus. I can't say one way or the other until I know what God wants."

"He's told you to go."

"Yes, but not where."

"He sent disciples out two by two. You went with Paul. You went with Peter. Let me go with you!"

"And what about your mother, Curiatus. Who will take care of her?"

"Timothy had a mother. She let him go!"

There was no use arguing with the boy. "If God has called you to come with me, Curiatus, He will confirm it by telling me." What would Diana say about giving up her son when she might never see him again?

Curiatus stepped closer. "I know God will tell you. I know He will."

"Can we go back to bed now?" Epanetus spoke drily. "At least until the sun comes up?"

+ + +

Silas fasted all day, but had no answer. He fasted a second day and prayed.

Epanetus found him sitting in the back of the garden. "Curiatus came again. Do you have an answer for him yet?"

"God's been silent on the matter."

"Maybe that means you can decide either way, though there seems no doubt in Curiatus's mind what God wants him to do."

"John Mark went out too soon."

"Timothy was younger and never looked back."

"I thought everything was settled."

"Ah yes; just pick up your pack of scrolls and walk away."

Silas cast him a dark look. Why did the Roman take such perverse plea-sure in taunting him?

Epanetus grinned. "I suppose the decision is even harder when you can't have one without the other."

Silas glared at him, heart pounding. "That's the answer, then." He felt a check in his spirit, but ignored it. "If the boy isn't ready to leave his mother, I dare not take him with me."

Epanetus groaned in annoyance. "That's not what I said. And even if it was, there is a solution! You could—"

Silas stood abruptly. "I don't know where God will lead me, or whether I will ever come back this way again." He stepped past Epanetus and headed for the house. "When I leave, I will go alone." Why did he feel no relief in saying it?

"You're running scared again!" Epanetus called after him.

Silas kept walking.

Epanetus shouted this time. "Take Diana with you!"

Heat poured into Silas's face. He turned. "Lower your voice."

"Ah, that imperious tone. I've heard it often from Roman nobles. I wanted you to hear!"

"I can't take a woman! Her reputation would be ruined and my testi-mony meaningless!"

Epanetus snorted. "I'm not suggesting you make her your concubine. *Marry her!*"

Silas thought of Peter bound and helpless, crying out to his wife as Nero's soldiers tortured her, *"Remember the Lord! Remember the Lord!"*

Silas's throat tightened in anguish. "God forgive you for suggesting it!" His voice broke.

Epanetus's face filled with compassion. "Silas, I've seen the way you look at her, and the way she looks—"

"I'd rather kill myself now than see a woman I love tortured and mar-tyred in front of me."

"I see," he said slowly. "But I ask you: all the while you've fasted and prayed, were you asking God what He wants you to do next, or pleading with Him to agree with what you've already decided?"

✦   ✦   ✦

When Silas told Curiatus of his decision, the boy wept. "I'm sorry." Silas could barely get the words out for the dryness of his throat. "Maybe in a few years . . ."

"You'll leave Italy and never return."

"It's best if I go alone."

"No, it isn't."

"You're not a man, Curiatus."

"I'm as much a man as Timothy was when you took him with you."

"That was different."

"How was it different?"

Silas begged God for a way to explain, but no words came. Curiatus waited, eyes pleading. Silas spread his hands, unable to say anything more.

The boy searched his face. "You just don't want me to go with you. That's it, isn't it?"

Silas couldn't look into his eyes anymore. Curiatus stood up slowly and walked away, shoulders hunched.

Silas covered his face.

Epanetus's voice rumbled low, indistinct words, but the tone was clear. He comforted the boy. Silas expected his host to come into the *triclinium* and admonish him. Instead, he was left alone.

Silas read to the gathering that evening—Peter's letters to the five provinces. Diana and Curiatus didn't come. Silas was almost thankful. He said his good-byes to the people and tried not to think about the boy and his mother. He was given a love offering to carry him on his way. His brothers and sisters wept as they laid hands on him and prayed God would bless and protect him wherever he went. He wept, too, but for reasons he did not want to think about too deeply.

"We will pray for you every day, Silas."

He knew they would keep their promise.

Early the next morning, he rose with the certainty of how he would travel, if not where. He dreamed the Lord beckoned him to a ship. He donned the new tunic Epanetus had given him. He wound the sash and tucked the pouch of denarii into it. He pinned the silver ring and knotted the leather straps that held the case containing his reed pens and knife for making corrections and cutting papyrus. Then he tied on the inkhorn. He took the coat Paul had given him and put it on, then shouldered the pack of scrolls.

Epanetus waited for him in the courtyard. "Do you have all you need for your journey?"

"Yes. Thank you. I've traveled with far less. You and the others have been more than generous."

"It has been an honor having you here, Silas."

He clasped Epanetus's arm. "An honor to me as well."

"Are you taking the road north to Rome or going down to the sea?"

"The sea."

Epanetus smiled strangely. "In that case, I'll walk with you."

They left the house and headed down the winding streets. The agora bustled with people. Urbanus gave a nod as they passed. When they came to the port, Silas looked from young man to young man.

"Are you looking for someone?" Epanetus said.

"Curiatus. I had hoped to say good-bye."

"They're over there."

Silas turned, and his heart leaped into his throat. Diana and Curiatus walked toward him, each carrying a bundle. He greeted them. "I'm glad to see you. I missed you last night."

Diana set her bundle down. "We had to make arrangements."

Arrangements?

Curiatus looked at the docks. "So which ship are we taking?"

Silas stared. "What?"

Laughing, Epanetus grasped the boy by the shoulder. "Come with me, my boy. We'll see which ship has room for extra passengers."

Silas looked from them to Diana. "He can't go with me."

"We must."

We?

She looked up at him gravely. "Silas, we prayed all night that the Lord would make it clear to us what we should do. Everyone in the church has been praying for us. You know the heart of my son. So we laid out the situation before the Lord. If you took the road north, you were to go alone. If you came to the port, we were to leave with you." She smiled, eyes glowing. "And here you are."

He struggled not to cry. "I can't take you with me, Diana. I can't."

"Because you fear harm would come to me. I know. Epanetus told me."

"You don't know."

"My body may be broken, my life taken, but I will never be harmed, Silas. Nor will Curiatus. Besides, don't the Scriptures say three together are stronger than one alone? The Lord will not give us more than we can bear, and we have heaven to receive us. And He will be with us wherever we go."

"Think how it will look to others, Diana, a man traveling with a woman. You know what people will think. How can I teach holy living if we appear to be . . ." He glanced away. "You know what I mean."

She nodded. "Living in sin?"

"Yes. So, it's settled."

Her eyes grew soft. "Yes. Of course it is. We must marry."

He blushed. "You should stay here and marry a younger man."

"Why would I want to do that when it's you I love?" She stepped close, reached up, and cupped his face. "Silas, I knew when I first saw you that I wanted to be your wife. And when Curiatus became so determined to have you take him with you, it merely served to confirm what I've come to believe: God directed your steps. The Lord brought you here, not just to rest, but to find the family He prepared for you." Her eyes glistened. "We've been waiting such a long time."

His heart pounded. "I couldn't bear to see you hurt."

"If you leave us behind, you will break our hearts."

"That's unfair!"

"Is it? It was the Lord who said a man is not meant to be alone. All these years, you've dedicated your life to helping others—Paul, Peter, Timothy, John Mark, the churches you've served. And now, God offers you a family of your own, something I know you've missed, something I know you want." She looked up, her heart in her eyes. "It is the Lord who pours down blessings upon those who love Him, Silas. You have taught that. You know it's true."

And like grace, this was a free gift he had only to receive.

"Diana . . ." He leaned down and kissed her. Her arms came around him, sliding up his back. He stepped closer and took her firmly in his arms. She fit him perfectly.

"And the Lord gave sight to the blind!" Epanetus said.

Silas drew back, but he couldn't take his eyes from Diana's face flushed with pleasure, her eyes bright with joy. He had never seen anyone more beautiful. He took her hand and smiled at Epanetus. "Indeed, He did." *And I thank You for it, Lord.*

Epanetus stood arms akimbo. "As you told me, Silas—'You can make many plans, but the Lord's purpose will prevail.'" He winked at Diana.

The joyful sound of her laughter made Silas catch his breath. Gratitude rose up inside him like a spring of living water. She loved him! She really loved him! *I never thought to have this blessing, Lord. Never, in all my life.*

Curiatus shouted from down the quay and ran toward them. Out of breath, he reached them. He looked at Silas's hand clasping his mother's, and his face lit up. He pointed back. "There's room on that ship."

Epanetus clapped the boy on the back. "There'll be another ship, another day. First we have a wedding to arrange."

✦ ✦ ✦

The wind filled the sails, and the boat surged through the Mediterranean waters. As the bow dipped, a wave splashed up, a salty mist spraying the deck, a welcome coolness in the heat of the afternoon sun.

Silas talked to several crew members and then came to Diana. He leaned on the rail beside her. She smiled at him. "Where's Curiatus?"

"Helping one of the sailors move some cargo."

She looked out again, her expression rapt with pleasure. "I've never seen such blues and greens." She had the wonder of a child. She leaned against his shoulder. "I've never been more happy, Silas. Wherever it is we're going, I know God is the wind in the sails."

"We sail to Corsica," he said. "And then on from there to Iberia."

She glanced up at him in surprise. "Iberia?"

He saw no fear in her eyes. "Yes."

Paul had begun making plans soon after he arrived in Rome. "Peter is here," Paul had said, restless in confinement, "and so are you. We will have a church established in Rome and the work will go on. If Caesar hears my case and dismisses the charges against me, I will go to Spain. I must go, Silas! No one has gone there yet. We must reach everyone."

We.

Even under house arrest, Paul had continued the work God had given him. He had continued to dream and plan.

"We have brothers and sisters of strong faith to carry on here, Silas! But there are others who have yet to hear the Good News of Jesus Christ. Someday I will go, God willing, and if not I, the Lord will send someone else who can preach and teach. . . ."

Silas clasped his hands loosely on the rail. The sky was an expanse of blue and white.

Up there perhaps was a crowd of witnesses watching him, praying for him, cheering him on. Paul, Peter, all the friends he had known and loved.

And Jesus watched, too. *Go and make disciples of all the nations, baptizing them in the name of the Father and the Son and the Holy Spirit.*

Epanetus and the others would pray. "Yes, Lord." Spain first, and then on from there, God willing. He and Diana would keep on going as long as body and breath allowed.

Curiatus shouted, and Silas looked up. The boy climbed the mast.

Diana laughed. "He's seeing what's ahead."

When body and breath failed Silas, another would be ready to carry on. The Word of Truth would be spoken. The Light would continue to shine. And God would lead His flock through the gates of heaven.

SEEK AND FIND

❈❈❈❈

Dear Reader,

You have just finished reading the story of Silas, scribe to the early church and traveling companion of Paul and Peter, as told by Francine Rivers. As always, it is Francine's desire for you, the reader, to delve into God's Word for yourself to find out the real story—to discover what God has to say to us today and to find applications that will change our lives to suit His purposes for eternity.

Though we are told little in Scripture about Silas's personal life, we do find evidence of a very committed man. He was a prominent church leader and a gifted prophet who chose to set aside what the world would view as a very promising career. He willingly became a scribe, or secretary, recording the letters of the apostles Paul and Peter.

It is interesting to note that while three of the Gospels record the story of the rich young ruler, only the Gospel of Luke refers to him as a rich *religious* leader. The account of the two followers of Jesus on the road to Emmaus is also found only in the Gospel of Luke. Silas was a religious leader and a travel companion of Luke. So the conjectures in this story—equating Silas with both the rich young ruler and the companion of Cleopas on the road to Emmaus—certainly aren't impossible.

Whatever the specifics of his life, we do know that Silas shed his earthly trappings of position and power in order to walk with the Lord. His life echoes that of another writer, the Author and Finisher of our faith, the Living Word, Jesus. May God bless you and help you to discover His call on your life. May you discover a heart of obedience beating within you.

Peggy Lynch

CHOSEN

SEEK GOD'S WORD FOR TRUTH

Read the following passage:

> When they arrived in Jerusalem, Barnabas and Paul were welcomed by the
> whole church, including the apostles and elders. They reported everything
> God had done through them. But then some of the believers who belonged
> to the sect of the Pharisees stood up and insisted, "The Gentile converts must
> be circumcised and required to follow the law of Moses."
>
> So the apostles and elders met together to resolve this issue. Peter stood
> and addressed them as follows: "God knows people's hearts, and he confirmed
> that he accepts Gentiles. He made no distinction between us and them, for he
> cleansed their hearts through faith. We believe that we are all saved the same
> way, by the undeserved grace of the Lord Jesus."
>
> James stood and said, "My judgment is that we should not make it difficult
> for the Gentiles who are turning to God. Instead, we should write and tell them
> to abstain from eating food offered to idols, from sexual immorality, from eating
> the meat of strangled animals, and from consuming blood."
>
> Then the apostles and elders together with the whole church in Jerusalem
> chose delegates, and they sent them to Antioch of Syria with Paul and Barnabas
> to report on this decision. The men chosen were two of the church leaders—
> Judas (also called Barsabbas) and Silas.
>
> The messengers went at once to Antioch, where they called a general meeting
> of the believers and delivered the letter. And there was great joy throughout the
> church that day as they read this encouraging message.
>
> Then Judas and Silas, both being prophets, spoke at length to the believers,
> encouraging and strengthening their faith.
>
> After some time Paul said to Barnabas, "Let's go back and visit each city
> where we previously preached the word of the Lord, to see how the new
> believers are doing." Barnabas agreed and wanted to take along John Mark.
> But Paul disagreed strongly, since John Mark had deserted them in Pamphylia
> and had not continued with them in their work. Their disagreement was so
> sharp that they separated. Barnabas took John Mark with him and sailed for
> Cyprus. Paul chose Silas, and as he left, the believers entrusted him to the
> Lord's gracious care.   ACTS 15:4-9, 11, 13, 19-20, 22, 30-32, 36-40

+ What was the concern of the early church leaders that led to this general
  meeting?

+ Which noteworthy leaders were present?

+ Who was chosen to accompany Paul and Barnabas to deliver the letter?
  How were these two men specifically gifted?

+ What was their mission? How were they received?

+ What events took place to part Barnabas and Paul?

+ Whom did Paul choose as a travel companion, and where did they go?

FIND GOD'S WAYS FOR YOU

✦ Have you ever tried to impose restrictions on others? What happened?

✦ Share a time when someone imposed restrictions on you. How did that work out?

✦ Whom do you need to encourage and lift up? What stops you from doing so?

STOP AND PONDER

Let us hold tightly without wavering to the hope we affirm, for God can be trusted to keep his promise. Let us think of ways to motivate one another to acts of love and good works. Encourage one another, especially now that the day of his return is drawing near.   HEBREWS 10:23-25

CONVICTED

SEEK GOD'S WORD FOR TRUTH

In this story, the teachings of Christ disturbed Silas. Read the following words of Jesus, and see how they might be difficult for a prominent leader to hear and accept:

Love your enemies! Pray for those who persecute you! If you love only those who love you, what reward is there for that? Even corrupt tax collectors do that much. If you are kind only to your friends, how are you different from anyone else? You are to be perfect, even as your Father in heaven is perfect.   MATTHEW 5:44, 46-48

✦ What does Jesus expect? Why?

If any of you wants to be my follower, you must turn from your selfish ways, take up your cross, and follow me. What do you benefit if you gain the whole world but lose your own soul? Is anything worth more than your soul?   MATTHEW 16:24, 26

✦ How might Jesus' expectations have bothered Silas?

If you love your father or mother more than you love me, you are not worthy of being mine; or if you love your son or daughter more than me, you are not worthy of being mine. If you cling to your life, you will lose it; but if you give up your life for me, you will find it.   MATTHEW 10:37, 39

✦ Why would Silas have struggled with these words of Jesus?

Don't do your good deeds publicly, to be admired by others, for you will lose the reward from your Father in heaven. Give your gifts in private, and your Father, who sees everything, will reward you.

When you pray, don't be like the hypocrites who love to pray publicly on street corners and in the synagogues where everyone can see them. But when you pray, go away by yourself, shut the door behind you, and pray to your Father in private.

When you pray, don't babble on and on. Your Father knows exactly what you need even before you ask him!   MATTHEW 6:1, 4-8

✛ What instructions does Jesus give here? What warnings?

✛ Who would Silas think Jesus was talking about? Why might he be bothered?

Don't store up treasures here on earth. Wherever your treasure is, there the desires of your heart will also be. No one can serve two masters. For you will hate one and love the other; you will be devoted to one and despise the other. You cannot serve both God and money.   MATTHEW 6:19, 21, 24

✛ Again, what does Jesus expect and why?

✛ How might these words have disturbed Silas before he chose to follow Christ?

FIND GOD'S WAYS FOR YOU

✛ Which of these teachings seem difficult for today's culture? Which seem unfair?

✛ What seems to be the recurring theme?

✛ Which teaching is difficult for you personally? Why?

STOP AND PONDER

Don't let your hearts be troubled. Trust in God, and trust also in me.   JOHN 14:1

COMPELLED

SEEK GOD'S WORD FOR TRUTH

Read the following passage:

On the day of Pentecost all the believers were meeting together in one place. Suddenly, there was a sound from heaven like the roaring of a mighty windstorm, and it filled the house where they were sitting. Then, what looked like flames or tongues of fire appeared and settled on each of them. And everyone present was filled with the Holy Spirit and began speaking in other languages, as the Holy Spirit gave them this ability.

At that time there were devout Jews from every nation living in Jerusalem. When they heard the loud noise, everyone came running, and they were bewildered to hear their own languages being spoken by the believers.

They were completely amazed. "How can this be?" they exclaimed. "These people are all from Galilee, and yet we hear them speaking in our own native languages about the wonderful things God has done!" They stood there amazed and perplexed. "What can this mean?"

But others in the crowd ridiculed them, saying, "They're just drunk, that's all!"

Then Peter stepped forward with the eleven other apostles and shouted to the crowd, "Listen carefully, all of you, fellow Jews and residents of Jerusalem! Make no mistake about this. What you see was predicted long ago by the prophet Joel:

> 'In the last days,' God says,
> 'I will pour out my Spirit upon all people.
> Your sons and daughters will prophesy.
> Your young men will see visions,
> and your old men will dream dreams.
> In those days I will pour out my Spirit
> even on my servants—men and women alike—
> and they will prophesy.
> And I will cause wonders in the heavens above
> and signs on the earth below
> before that great and glorious day of the LORD arrives.
> But everyone who calls on the name of the LORD will be saved.'

"People of Israel, listen! God publicly endorsed Jesus the Nazarene by doing powerful miracles, wonders, and signs through him, as you well know. But God knew what would happen, and his prearranged plan was carried out when Jesus was betrayed. With the help of lawless Gentiles, you nailed him to a cross and killed him. But God released him from the horrors of death and raised him back to life, for death could not keep him in its grip. And we are all witnesses of this."

Peter's words pierced their hearts, and they said to him and to the other apostles, "Brothers, what should we do?"

Peter replied, "Each of you must repent of your sins and turn to God, and be baptized in the name of Jesus Christ for the forgiveness of your sins. Then you will receive the gift of the Holy Spirit. This promise is to you, and to your children, and even to the Gentiles—all who have been called by the Lord our God."

Those who believed what Peter said were baptized and added to the church that day—about 3,000 in all.

All the believers devoted themselves to the apostles' teaching, and to fellowship, and to sharing in meals (including the Lord's Supper), and to prayer.   ACTS 2:1-8, 11-14, 16-24, 32,37-39, 41-42

✦ Discuss the prayer meeting described in this passage. Who was meeting together and why? Describe what took place.

✦ How did the people respond?

✦ What did Peter do?

✦ What are some key points from Peter's message that day?

✦ What were the results of Peter's message? Why do you think this happened?

FIND GOD'S WAYS FOR YOU

✦ Where do you spend your time and with whom? Why?

✦ What influence do you have on other people? What influence do they have on you?

✦ What lasting effect will your life have? What lasting effect do you *want* it to have?

STOP AND PONDER

Don't copy the behavior and customs of this world, but let God transform you into a new person by changing the way you think. Then you will learn to know God's will for you, which is good and pleasing and perfect.

ROMANS 12:2

CONFIRMED

SEEK GOD'S WORD FOR TRUTH

Read the following passage:

Paul went first to Derbe and then to Lystra, where there was a young disciple named Timothy. His mother was a Jewish believer, but his father was a Greek. Timothy was well thought of by the believers in Lystra and Iconium, so Paul wanted him to join them on their journey.

Next Paul and Silas traveled through the area of Phrygia and Galatia, because the Holy Spirit had prevented them from preaching the word in the province of Asia at that time.

That night Paul had a vision: A man from Macedonia in northern Greece was standing there, pleading with him, "Come over to Macedonia and help us!"

We boarded a boat at Troas and sailed straight across to the island of Samothrace, and the next day we landed at Neapolis. From there we reached

Philippi, a major city of that district of Macedonia and a Roman colony. And we stayed there several days.

On the Sabbath we went a little way outside the city to a riverbank, where we thought people would be meeting for prayer, and we sat down to speak with some women who had gathered there. One of them was Lydia from Thyatira, a merchant of expensive purple cloth, who worshiped God. As she listened to us, the Lord opened her heart, and she accepted what Paul was saying. She was baptized along with other members of her household, and she asked us to be her guests. "If you agree that I am a true believer in the Lord," she said, "come and stay at my home." And she urged us until we agreed.

One day as we were going down to the place of prayer, we met a demon-possessed slave girl. She was a fortune-teller who earned a lot of money for her masters. She followed Paul and the rest of us, shouting, "These men are servants of the Most High God, and they have come to tell you how to be saved."

This went on day after day until Paul got so exasperated that he turned and said to the demon within her, "I command you in the name of Jesus Christ to come out of her." And instantly it left her.

Her masters' hopes of wealth were now shattered, so they grabbed Paul and Silas and dragged them before the authorities at the marketplace. "The whole city is in an uproar because of these Jews!" they shouted to the city officials. "They are teaching customs that are illegal for us Romans to practice."

A mob quickly formed against Paul and Silas, and the city officials ordered them stripped and beaten with wooden rods. They were severely beaten, and then they were thrown into prison. The jailer was ordered to make sure they didn't escape. So the jailer put them into the inner dungeon and clamped their feet in the stocks.

Around midnight Paul and Silas were praying and singing hymns to God, and the other prisoners were listening. Suddenly, there was a massive earthquake, and the prison was shaken to its foundations. All the doors immediately flew open, and the chains of every prisoner fell off! The jailer woke up to see the prison doors wide open. He assumed the prisoners had escaped, so he drew his sword to kill himself. But Paul shouted to him, "Stop! Don't kill yourself! We are all here!"

The jailer called for lights and ran to the dungeon and fell down trembling before Paul and Silas. Then he brought them out and asked, "Sirs, what must I do to be saved?"

They replied, "Believe in the Lord Jesus and you will be saved, along with everyone in your household." And they shared the word of the Lord with him and with all who lived in his household. Even at that hour of the night, the jailer cared for them and washed their wounds. Then he and everyone in his household were immediately baptized. He brought them into his house and set a meal before them, and he and his entire household rejoiced because they all believed in God.   Acts 16:1-2, 6, 9, 11-34

+ While in Lystra, Paul and Silas met Timothy. Discuss that encounter and the results.

+ Why did they travel to Phrygia and Galatia? Why did they avoid Asia?

+ Describe the encounters in Philippi.

+ What led to Paul and Silas's imprisonment? How did they demonstrate their peace?

+ Discuss the earthquake and how the two missionaries responded.

+ What were the results of their disciplined response in the midst of mayhem?

FIND GOD'S WAYS FOR YOU

+ How do you handle the unexpected?

+ Describe a time God kept you safe.

+ What "chains" are keeping you imprisoned?

STOP AND PONDER

"For I know the plans I have for you," says the LORD. "They are plans for good and not for disaster, to give you a future and a hope."   JEREMIAH 29:11

CONFLICTED

SEEK GOD'S WORD FOR TRUTH

Silas traveled with both Paul and Peter. In this story, he wrestled with the issue of celibacy versus marriage in relation to serving God. The following passages may shed some light on why this may have been a struggle for Silas.

The apostle Paul wrote:

Now regarding the questions you asked in your letter. Yes, it is good to live a celibate life. But because there is so much sexual immorality, each man should have his own wife, and each woman should have her own husband.

I say to those who aren't married and to widows—it's better to stay unmarried, just as I am. But if they can't control themselves, they should go ahead and marry. It's better to marry than to burn with lust.

Each of you should continue to live in whatever situation the Lord has placed you, and remain as you were when God first called you.

But let me say this, dear brothers and sisters: The time that remains is very short. So from now on, those with wives should not focus only on their marriage. Those who weep or who rejoice or who buy things should not be absorbed by their weeping or their joy or their possessions.

An unmarried man can spend his time doing the Lord's work and thinking how to please him. But a married man has to think about his earthly responsibilities and how to please his wife. His interests are divided. In the same way, a woman who is no longer married or has never been married can be devoted to the Lord and holy in body and in spirit. But a married woman has to think about her earthly responsibilities and how to please her husband. I am saying this for your benefit, not to place restrictions on you. I want you to do whatever will help you serve the Lord best, with as few distractions as possible.   I CORINTHIANS 7:1-2, 8-9, 17, 29-30, 32-35

✦ What did Paul have to say about marriage? about celibacy?

✦ What reasons did Paul give for not being concerned with marriage at that time?

✦ How might these instructions have perplexed Silas? What "stamp of approval," if any, did Paul offer?

The apostle Peter wrote:

In the same way, you wives must accept the authority of your husbands. Then, even if some refuse to obey the Good News, your godly lives will speak to them without any words. They will be won over by observing your pure and reverent lives.

Don't be concerned about the outward beauty of fancy hairstyles, expensive jewelry, or beautiful clothes. You should clothe yourselves instead with the beauty that comes from within, the unfading beauty of a gentle and quiet spirit, which is so precious to God.

In the same way, you husbands must give honor to your wives. Treat your wife with understanding as you live together. She may be weaker than you are, but she is your equal partner in God's gift of new life. Treat her as you should so your prayers will not be hindered.

I have written and sent this short letter to you with the help of Silas, whom I commend to you as a faithful brother. My purpose in writing is to encourage you and assure you that what you are experiencing is truly part of God's grace for you. Stand firm in this grace.   I PETER 3:1-4, 7; 5:12

✦ Discuss Peter's view of a godly wife.

✦ How did Peter view a wife's role? How does a husband's treatment of his wife affect him?

✦ What did Peter think of Silas? What encouragement did he offer?

FIND GOD'S WAYS FOR YOU

✦ How do you view your place in life? What roles do you have in various relationships or organizations?

+ How is God speaking to you about your personal relationships? Be specific.

+ Do you use your position/role to promote or hinder others? to restrict or to encourage those around you?

STOP AND PONDER

Finally, all of you should be of one mind. Sympathize with each other. Love each other as brothers and sisters. Be tenderhearted, and keep a humble attitude.

1 PETER 3:8

CONFESSED

SEEK GOD'S WORD FOR TRUTH

Read the following passage:

Once a religious leader asked Jesus this question: "Good Teacher, what should I do to inherit eternal life?"

"Why do you call me good?" Jesus asked him. "Only God is truly good. But to answer your question, you know the commandments: 'You must not commit adultery. You must not murder. You must not steal. You must not testify falsely. Honor your father and mother.'"

The man replied, "I've obeyed all these commandments since I was young."

When Jesus heard his answer, he said, "There is still one thing you haven't done. Sell all your possessions and give the money to the poor, and you will have treasure in heaven. Then come, follow me."

But when the man heard this he became very sad, for he was very rich.

When Jesus saw this, he said, "How hard it is for the rich to enter the Kingdom of God! In fact, it is easier for a camel to go through the eye of a needle than for a rich person to enter the Kingdom of God!"

Those who heard this said, "Then who in the world can be saved?"

He replied, "What is impossible for people is possible with God."

Peter said, "We've left our homes to follow you."

"Yes," Jesus replied, "and I assure you that everyone who has given up house or wife or brothers or parents or children, for the sake of the Kingdom of God, will be repaid many times over in this life, and will have eternal life in the world to come."

LUKE 18:18-30

+ What was the first issue that Jesus pointed out to the young man? Why?

+ What was the second issue that Jesus wanted the young man to see? How did he respond?

+ What lesson was Jesus teaching His disciples? How did they respond?

+ What do you think Jesus meant when He said, "What is impossible for people is possible with God"?

+ How did Jesus answer Peter? What was in it for Peter and the other disciples?

+ What is the relative importance of things and people in God's economy?

FIND GOD'S WAYS FOR YOU

+ What "trappings" in your life need to go?

+ How will you respond to Jesus? When?

STOP AND PONDER

Now may the God of peace make you holy in every way, and may your whole spirit and soul and body be kept blameless until our Lord Jesus Christ comes again. God will make this happen, for he who calls you is faithful.

1 THESSALONIANS 5:23-24

COMMITTED

While many of the details in this story have been fictionalized, we know that the historical Silas was a wealthy, educated, and gifted individual. He was a respected church leader and prophet. He deliberately chose to be committed to Christ—to leave behind his material possessions to become a colaborer and correspondent with Peter and Paul. Silas embraced the role of scribe, writing the words of others to promote the Kingdom of God. He chose to serve rather than to be served. He accepted God's call on his life and furthered the claims of Jesus. And in so doing, he gained an incorruptible inheritance.

Jesus was God's only Son. He left His heavenly throne, His royal priesthood and kingly comforts, to come to earth. He too chose to be committed—committed to God's eternal plan for mankind's salvation. Jesus is also a type of scribe. He writes His words on our hearts; He is the Living Word.

In the beginning the Word already existed. The Word was with God, and the Word was God. He existed in the beginning with God. God created everything through him, and nothing was created except through him. The Word gave life to everything that was created, and his life brought light to everyone. The light shines in the darkness, and the darkness can never extinguish it.   JOHN 1:1-5

+ Beloved, may you deliberately choose to commit yourself to Jesus and walk in His light.

ABOUT THE AUTHOR

New York Times best-selling author Francine Rivers began her literary career at the University of Nevada, Reno, where she graduated with a bachelor of arts degree in English and journalism. From 1976 to 1985, she had a successful writing career in the general market, and her books were highly acclaimed by readers and reviewers. Although raised in a religious home, Francine did not truly encounter Christ until later in life, when she was already a wife, a mother of three, and an established romance novelist.

Shortly after becoming a born-again Christian in 1986, Francine wrote *Redeeming Love* as her statement of faith. First published by Bantam Books, and then rereleased by Multnomah Publishers in the mid-1990s, this retelling of the biblical story of Gomer and Hosea, set during the time of the California Gold Rush, is now considered by many to be a classic work of Christian fiction. *Redeeming Love* continues to be one of the Christian Booksellers Association's top-selling titles, and it has held a spot on the Christian best-seller list for nearly a decade.

Since *Redeeming Love*, Francine has published numerous novels with Christian themes—all best sellers—and she has continued to win both industry acclaim and reader loyalty around the globe. Her Christian novels have been awarded or nominated for numerous honors, including the RITA Award, the Christy Award, the ECPA Gold Medallion, and the Holt Medallion in Honor of Outstanding Literary Talent. In 1997, after winning her third RITA Award for inspirational fiction, Francine was inducted into the Romance Writers of America's Hall of Fame. Francine's novels have been translated into more than twenty different languages, and she enjoys best-seller status in many foreign countries, including Germany, the Netherlands, and South Africa.

Francine and her husband, Rick, live in northern California and enjoy time spent with their three grown children and taking every opportunity to spoil their grandchildren. Francine uses her writing to draw closer to the Lord, and she desires that through her work she might worship and praise Jesus for all He has done and is doing in her life.

Visit her Web site at www.francinerivers.com.

BOOKS BY BELOVED AUTHOR
FRANCINE RIVERS

The Mark of the Lion series
(available individually or as a boxed set)
A Voice in the Wind
An Echo in the Darkness
As Sure as the Dawn

A Lineage of Grace series
(available individually or in an anthology)
Unveiled
Unashamed
Unshaken
Unspoken
Unafraid

Sons of Encouragement series
(available individually or in an anthology)
The Priest
The Warrior
The Prince
The Prophet
The Scribe

Marta's Legacy series
Her Mother's Hope
Her Daughter's Dream

Children's Titles
The Shoe Box
Bible Stories for Growing Kids
(coauthored with Shannon
Rivers Coibion)

Stand-alone Titles
Redeeming Love
The Atonement Child
The Scarlet Thread
The Last Sin Eater
Leota's Garden
And the Shofar Blew
The Shoe Box (a Christmas novella)

www.francinerivers.com

have you visited
tyndalefiction.com
lately?

Only there can you find:

→ books hot off the press

→ first chapter excerpts

→ inside scoops on your
favorite authors

→ author interviews

→ contests

→ fun facts

→ and much more!

*Sign up for your **free** newsletter!*

Visit us today at: **tyndalefiction.com**

Tyndale fiction does more than entertain.

→ *It touches the heart.*
→ *It stirs the soul.*
→ *It changes lives.*

That's why Tyndale is so committed to being first in fiction!

TYNDALE
FICTION

CP0021